Critical acclaim for C. J. Hop

"A brilliant (and hilarious) criti.
the meaninglessness of the popu
- **Toronto Globe & Mail**

"A blistering revelation ... Hopkins' ⸱wes a huge debt to the absurdists and so manages to blast be⸱ ⸱ ⸱u the merely political or allegorical to the existential." - **Time Out New York**

"Sharp, brilliant, intense, fast-moving, made for the moment we live in ... a portrait of a culture caught in a strange and painful paradox between progressive and reactionary attitudes." - **The Scotsman**

"A feral ferris-wheel of comedy, confusion, contradiction, obfuscation and bent-out-of-shape straight talking that leaps out of the room at you and harnesses you to its mischievous mindset." - **Metro**

"America's relationship with consumerism and the media is unerringly skewered." - **The Times**

"Sharp-toothed satire ... a dystopia in which the desire for consumer goods and high ratings trumps all principles." - **Village Voice**

"Hilariously at odds with the mainstream, and much bigger and deeper than the sum of its apparent parts." - **The Herald**

"Perfectly skewers all the little lies and double-thinks which comfort us, not to mention the absurdities of this kind of television, that it is impossible to resist." - **STV**

"Stimulating and thought-provoking ... a welcome addition to the canon of all things absurd and beautiful." - **The List**

"A gripping satire, which spills into sinister weirdness." - **Die Tageszeitung**

ZONE 23

C. J. HOPKINS

SNOGGSWORTHY, SWAINE & CORMORANT

Snoggsworthy, Swaine & Cormorant Paperbacks
a division of Consent Factory Publishing

This Snoggsworthy, Swaine & Cormorant trade edition May 2017.

SNOGGSWORTHY, SWAINE & CORMORANT is a trademark of Consent Factory Publishing.

Snoggsworthy, Swaine & Cormorant is an imprint of Consent Factory Publishing, a wholly-owned subsidiary of Amalgamated Content, Inc., distributors of high quality literary content throughout the developed and developing worlds. For more information about Consent Factory Publishing, visit the Consent Factory's website: consentfactory.org.

The characters and events in this book are fictitious. Any similarity to actual persons, corporations, or their subsidiaries, agents, or assigns, is not intended by the author, and is either a coincidence or the work of devious supernatural forces which neither the author nor the publisher would ever claim to understand or speak for.

Cover design by Anthony Freda and Dan Zollinger.

Printed in the United States of America

ISBN 978-3-00-055526-8 (pb)

For Billie and her cowboy ...

ZONE 23

1.

The Normals

For the Normals, the vast majority of consumers living and working in Northeast Region 709 of the United Territories, a globalized
monetary and fiscal alliance of the nominally sovereign, democratic
nations that were huddled together side by side on the habitable
upper third of the planet, 17 April, 2610, or 02 Iyyar, 6370, or 01
Shawwal, 2049, or Day 600 in the Year of the Lemur (or any of a
host of alternative dates, depending on their proprietary calendars),
was just another perfect, peaceful day in the Age of the Renaissance
of Freedom and Prosperity.

Or at least it started out that way.

At approximately 0530 that morning, having finished their normal morning ablutions (i.e., waterless showering, laser body shaving,
anal bleaching, and other ablutions), and having broken the seals on
the recyclable containers of their anti-oxidant, soy-milk smoothies
and lowfat, totally gluten-free breakfasts, Normals and their families
were gathered together in their temperature-regulated, self-cleaning kitchens, heads slightly bowed in an attitude of prayer, scanning,
each on their All-in-One Viewers, their personally programmed
proprietary streams of individualized Morning Content, a lively mix
of information, entertainment and social networking customized to
reflect their interests and individual purchasing patterns ... everything was just as normal as could be.

The forecast that morning was particularly pleasant ... clear and
sunny throughout the Region. Winds were out of the west and light.
The projected high was 46 Celsius. Heat advisories remained in effect
for Communities south of the 45th parallel. Consumers were advised to refrain from any non-essential outdoor activity. Everything
else was looking rosy. SatCom signal strength was excellent. Check-

in times at the local airports were averaging under fourteen hours, down from their previous eighteen hours, down from their previous twenty-two hours. The odds of a devastating Terrorist attack with an improvised low-yield nuclear weapon, or some horrible chemical or bio-agent that would kill you the second it touched your skin, were low to acceptable.

Life was good.

Business was good. Extremely good. Little green upward-pointing arrows were dancing across the bottom of their screens. They were chasing a parade of little three-letter acronyms ... CRS ... BBB ...HCM ... FFC ... each of which stood for some corporate entity, all of whose shares were trading heavily. Normal consumers could track this trading in Real-Time right on the screens of their Viewers, or they could download individualized streams of market data from selected Regions. Or they could visit these Regions on their Real-Life maps, search nearby for business establishments, zoom right into their virtual interiors, and virtually experience their virtual environments. Or they could search for Entertainment Content in which these business establishments were featured, or the names of which were casually mentioned ... household names like Chloe's, Chaney's, VR Universe, and Big-Buy Basement, where every GMAX Model 30, whatever that was, was drastically reduced. Or they could comparison shop at CRS, Big-Buy Basement's fiercest competitor, which would match or beat Big-Buy's best price on any prescription medication. Cylozilatrin Z, for example, a popular Amyloidosis preventative, or Buxafenanadrine, or something like that, which reduced the adverse effects of ... something. And that wasn't all, oh no, far from it, because the Normals were free to share this offer (the conditions of which were subject to change) with their Big-Buy Family, Friends & Contacts, some of whom were just bound to be fans of Brandon Westwood, the Content designer, who had just won a Golden Penguin in Gothåb, where currently it was 18 Celsius and partly cloudy with scattered light showers, and to which last-minute round-trip tickets were being offered at the following portals ...

Which millions of Normals were actually doing, or were seriously considering contemplating doing (i.e., sharing this offer with their Friends & Contacts, or checking on last-minute flights to Gothåb, or searching to find out where that was, assuming it was somewhere that actually existed), when suddenly the peace of their perfect morning, or the fugue state they were gradually entering, was shattered by an all caps BREAKING NEWS message.

The news was bad. Extremely bad. Jimmy "Jimbo" Cartwright, III, founder and CEO of Finkles, had lost his battle with intestinal cancer, and died at the age of one hundred and thirty. The actual message read as follows:

CANCER SCOURGE CLAIMS FINKLES JIMBO!

Now this kind of thing didn't happen all that often. In the Age of the Renaissance of Freedom and Prosperity, given the rather staggering cost of intra-provider coordination (and the corresponding loss of advertising revenues), these multi-platform BREAKING NEWS messages were normally reserved for horrible accidents, or catastrophic hemispheric weather events, or the thwarting of devastating Terrorist attacks by the various corporate Security Services. The death of a single individual, even an extremely important individual, like a CEO, or COO, or the head of some Info-Entertainment conglomerate, newsworthy though it may have been, hardly warranted interruption of the constant flow of Info-streams upon which the global economy depended and to which most of the Normals' eyes were glued at every waking moment.

But then Jimmy "Jimbo" Cartwright, III, was not just any important individual. No, "Jimbo" was a larger-than-life individual, an embodiment of the spirit of the age, a living symbol of all that was good and right in the world in the 27th Century. In addition to his bold and steadfast leadership of Finkles and the Finkles Family of Companies, and his tireless philanthropic activities, and generally serving as a living beacon of dauntless entrepreneurial vehemence, interdependent market fervor, and freedom, and, well, an inspiration to all, he was one of the shrewdest large investors in the annals of public and private equity, whose every random homespun utterance was parsed for meaning like Delphic prophecy. A quadrillionaire by the age of forty, with luxury condos and country estates in the most exclusive Communities in the North, where he hosted extravagant

V.I.P. galas for A-List celebrities and the super-abundant (a limited selection of photos of which were sold to consumers and traded
avidly), and being just unimaginably wealthy, and this quasi-Arthu-
rian father-type figure whose face you saw like twelve times a hour
beaming secret enlightened wisdom down at you out of some virtual
screen, the news of his tragic and untimely death was a crushing
emotional blow to the Normals, many of whom felt like they were
facing the loss of a much loved member of their personal families.

People broke down and wept in their smoothies. They choked on
their anti-oxidant breakfast bars. Those with irritable bowel syndrome (more than you would probably like to imagine) shuffled, or
kind of crabwalked their way, to the nearest available waterless toilet.
Families joined hands at breakfast tables and recited prayers and
affirmations. Networks interrupted programming. Servers flooded
with Fleeps and Tweaks. Luminaries were reached for comment.

All this went on for several minutes.

Once the initial shock had worn off, and the heartbreaking news
of the death of "Jimbo" had been moved down to the headline
creeper that scrolled across the bottom of everyone's screen, and the
various medications they were taking, the doses of which they had
immediately increased, had upped their serotonin levels, and bound
to their benzodiazepine receptors, flooding their brains with a mild
but measurable sense of inner peace and well-being, the Normals
went back to consuming their breakfasts and scanning their individualized streams ... sad, yes, definitely sad, deeply sad (very, very sad),
but not in any debilitating, or excessive, or self-indulgent way that
might have negatively affected their performances at work (which
they knew were being continually monitored) or caused anyone to
feel uncomfortable, because deep down, in addition to the meds they
were on, they just knew in their hearts (and they reminded themselves on a daily basis with their affirmations), that the sadness they
were feeling was just a feeling ... a feeling that would eventually pass,
and that all they had to do was detach from the feeling, and try
not to label or to judge the feeling, or the painful event that had
triggered the feeling ... because everything, even painful events, like
the tragic and untimely passing of "Jimbo," or even just frightening
and horrible facts, like the scourge of aggressive intestinal cancer, or

colon cancer, or prostate cancer, or malignant melanoma, or fronto-temporal dementia, or the more or less constantly imminent threat of a sudden and devastating Terrorist attack, or catastrophic weather event, or some other type of horrible accident, or even the knowledge that they, the Normals, represented the last generations of the subspecies Homo sapiens sapiens, which due to a flaw in its genetic sequence was gradually being phased out of existence ... all of it, everything under the sun, no matter how frightening, or depressing, or horrible, or incomprehensible, or completely nonsensical, was part of some perfect, ineluctable, convoluted cosmic plan, or story, or evolutionary process, or had something to do with the concept of progress ... and anyway they were due at work, and the BREAKING NEWS message was gone from their Viewers, which were streaming and fleeping and tweaking again and ...

Taylor

Meanwhile, while the Normals were viewing their individualized streams of Content and enjoying their lowfat, gluten-free breakfasts in their comfortably air-conditioned, self-cleaning kitchens, Taylor Byrd was lying on his back on a sweat-soaked, sweat-stinking futon mattress, staring at a fuzzy little dot on the ceiling, which, the odds were, was some kind of mutant cockroach. This dot was more or less right in the center of an insanely intricate mandala-like pattern of moldy, quasi-concentric rings, or semi-orbiculate moldy shapes, the detailed dendrochronology of which was not, at the moment, of interest to Taylor. The dot, however, was of interest. It was more or less directly above his head, possibly preparing to drop down onto his face and crawl up his nose or something. This kind of thing happened on a regular basis. For reasons no one entirely understood, mutant insects, and particularly cockroaches, liked nothing better than to crawl up the noses, and into the mouths and ear canals, of unsuspecting sleeping persons, or to suddenly fly directly at them flapping their filthy little cockroach wings. Fortunately, there were ways to avoid this, most of which Taylor was familiar with. The thing to do was, get out of bed, or at least sit up, or just move, basically, extricating his face from the possible mutant cockroach's downward trajectory. Taylor, however, was unable to do this (i.e., get out of bed, or sit up, or move), as his brain had been disconnected from his body. He lay there in the suffocating heat and humidity, staring upward, apparently paralyzed, trying to remember when it was, and where he was, and how he had gotten there.

Out the window of Taylor's room (so, OK, good, that's where he was) a Public Viewer was playing some sort of sickeningly sappy funereal music, which at this time of morning, or night, or dark, or whatever time it was exactly, was not what it was usually doing. So, OK, something odd was happening, apparently something historic, and sad. Taylor had no idea what it was, as due to the inscrutable vicissitudes of Fate, or the Will of the One Who Was Many, or something, he was one of an unfortunate minority of persons who were not in possession of an All-in-One Viewer, or a Multi-Max Viewer, or Mondo Viewer, or any other type of interactive device providing a stream of individualized anything. And thus, he had not heard the news of the tragic and untimely passing of "Jimbo" ... nor would he have given a rat's ass if he had. It wasn't just that he appeared to be paralyzed, and so trapped there beneath what was very possibly an orifice violating mutant cockroach, or even the fact that he had just been awoken by the sound, first, of glass shattering, second, Rusty Braynard screaming, third, Alice Williams screaming, and, finally, whatever the fuck they were doing hopping and kind of conga line dancing around the room in circles like idiots ... well, all right, that was definitely part of it, but the other and more significant part of it was that the tragic and untimely death of "Jimbo," the prescription sale at CRS, the drastic reductions at Big-Buy Basement, the markets, the shares, the temperature in Gothåb ... all these bits of information around which the lives of the Normals revolved, and upon which, of course, their livelihoods depended, none of that shit meant shit to Taylor.

Taylor Byrd was an A.S.P. 3 ... a Class 3 Anti-Social Person. "[A] person," according to the DSM, "constitutionally predisposed to pervasive violation of the rights of others and disregard for social norms." He stood just under two meters tall, was heavily, if disproportionally muscled, prodigiously scarred about the chest and forearms, extensively, and rather poorly tattooed, and just overall looked like a dangerous character. Which, no doubt about it, he definitely was. By any definition of the word, he was. However, the only definition that counted was the one in the DSM XXXIII, which listed a number of hallmark symptoms commonly exhibited by Anti-Social Persons, more or less all of which Taylor exhibited.

Taylor, for example, was "prone to irritability." He often "failed to plan ahead." He "lied repeatedly," and failed to maintain "a consistent pattern of work behavior." He frequently appeared to "lack remorse," or "rationalize having mistreated others," or "otherwise demonstrate an incapacity to process guilt and learn from experience, particularly experience involving punishment." On top of which, he drank, smoked, urinated openly in public spaces, abused an assortment of illicit substances, frequently used offensive language, was uncooperative, sexually promiscuous, disrespectful, and just generally unpleasant. All of which was noted in his file:

asmedbase.ute/ASP3/BYRD/Taylor.0820.2565.709.Z23.

Now, whereas, in less enlightened epochs, a person such as Taylor Byrd would have been deemed an incorrigible criminal and locked away in a deep dark hole, probably for the remainder of his natural life, in the Age of the Renaissance of Freedom and Prosperity, the *Diagnostic and Statistical Manual of Mental Disorders* (or "DSM") had rendered the whole of Criminal Law and every edifice stemming therefrom as obsolete as the manual typewriter. According to the DSM, Anti-Social Persons like Taylor were neither evil nor maladjusted, but suffered an incurable medical condition, and could no more control their aggressive behavior than one could control one's sexual preferences, or the color of one's eyes or hair ... OK, granted, you could always dye your hair, or have your irises surgically altered, which people did, quite often, actually, just like the vast majority of people (i.e., people over the age of thirty, the so-called "Variant-Positive Normals") took some form of medication to curb their latent Anti-Social tendencies, all of which, for most people, worked like a charm.

Unfortunately, there were these other people, people like Taylor Byrd, for example, who were non-responsive to pharmatherapy and thus, sadly, were more or less doomed to a life of squalor and social deviance. The DSM was quite clear on this point. As difficult as it was to accept, Anti-Social Persons like Taylor were beyond the reach of modern medicine, so, regrettably, there was nothing to do but quarantine them, humanely, of course, for the good and safety of all concerned.

Of course, as far as Taylor was concerned, you could wipe your ass with the DSM, which was basically a load of pseudoscience the

Normals had invented to brainwash people, segregate anyone who wouldn't "cooperate," and blame it on their "defective" genes. And, all right, if you ever actually read the language in the DSM, Axis II, Cluster B, and thought about it for half a minute, you had to admit he had a point. For instance, you probably couldn't help but question the etiological value of phrases like "disregard for social norms" or "lack of respect for legitimate authority," which did maybe seem kind of vague and relative, and possibly not even all that medical.

On the other hand, there was no denying that Taylor Byrd, throughout his life (although mostly in his younger days, so back in the officially 2590s), had evinced quite a lot of aggressive behavior, and had pervasively violated the rights of others, particularly others who had gotten in his face, some of whose rights he'd pervasively violated in extremely repulsive and egregious ways, like with the jagged ends of broken bottles, and knives, and sticks, and bricks, and so on, which luckily had never been linked to Taylor, or he wouldn't have been lying in his bed that morning. Which isn't to say his file was clean. No, Taylor, who was forty-five at this time, had a lengthy and meticulously detailed record of violations of the rights of others, each of which were documented incidents, about which there was nothing pseudo. It was just that none of these documented incidents (the ones in Taylor's medbase file, as opposed to the ones he'd gotten away with) had involved the use of deadly violence ... but all of that was about to change.

Taylor, right that very moment, so approximately 0530 o'clock, lying there, possibly fatally hungover, contemplating that spot on the ceiling (which was definitely some form of mutant insect, like a cockroach, but with all these centipede legs), was soon to be wanted for detention and questioning in connection with a recent series of incidents ... incidents involving the egregious violation of the rights of certain individuals, corporations, and their subsidiaries and assigns, whose rights one didn't egregiously violate, or not and get away with it anyway, chief among them being none other than the Hadley Corporation of Menomonie, Wisconsin.

The Hadley Corporation of Menomonie, Wisconsin, despite the folksy-sounding name, was one of the largest, most diversified, powerful, profitable, structurally impenetrable, forward-looking corporate entities in the corporate history of corporate entities. It was one of a handful of other such entities, like Oodleeoo, Inc., the Eschaton Group, SeCom, and the Finkles Family of Companies, that dominated the totally open and unrestricted market economy that served the evolving needs of consumers throughout the entire United Territories ... or whatever it was it said on their website.

In other words, nobody knew what it was. No one had the slightest idea. To the Normals who nominally worked for the company (i.e. for some division or subsidiary of the company, none of which bore the Hadley name, except for the various Security divisions), the Hadley Corporation of Menomonie, Wisconsin was like corporate Valhalla, or Oz, or somewhere ... somewhere where important decisions were made by extremely senior executives, whose names they were not privy to, but whose fingers were on the pulse of everything, anticipating needs, driving trends, setting paces, examples, records, breaking ground with their cutting edges, and tirelessly generating wealth for everyone. To everybody else it was just this vast, and powerful, and completely inscrutable conglomerate, whose name you saw everywhere you went, along with the company's official slogan:

HERE FOR YOU ALWAYS ... NOW MORE THAN EVER!

Among its numerous other activities, the Hadley Corporation of Menomonie, Wisconsin, operating through its wholly-owned subsidiary, IntraZone Waste & Security Services, Inc., which was technically not a subdivision or in any other way organogramically related to Hadley Global Security, Inc., administrated the specially-designated Post-Emergency Quarantine Zones (commonly known as "A.S.P. Zones"), where afflicted people like Taylor lived. These A.S.P. Zones were not like prisons, or concentration camps, or things like that. They were "Special Residential Areas," where Anti-Social Persons could live, segregated according to class, in three concentric, alpha-coded sectors, surrounded by enormous Security Walls. These Zones were big, seriously big, many of them having once been cities, or the central districts of former cities, which over the course of hundreds of years, due primarily to urban sprawl and economic decentralization, had fallen into disrepair. Which, of course, had made it relatively easy for market leading Security firms (or the Security divisions of massive conglomerates, like the Hadley Corporation of Menomonie, Wisconsin), when the time to quarantine finally came, to erect their originally modular aluminum and later reinforced concrete walls around these former districts and cities, the majority of which were already encircled by a ring or loop of highway or train tracks. The walls themselves were nothing fancy, a series of dull gray concrete slabs, ten meters high, three meters wide, the inaccessible tops of which, presumably out of an abundance of caution, were dressed with concertina wire.

Although each Zone had its unique character, the basic layout was always the same; three concentric alpha-coded sectors, one for each of the A.S.P. classes. The outermost sector, Sector A, was reserved for Class 1 Anti-Social Persons, most of whom were totally harmless and could, with proper clearance, of course, leave the Zone to work outside at menial jobs in the Residential Communities, mostly as janitors and manual laborers, some of them even as household servants. Sector B was for A.S.P. 2s, and was usually the largest sector in the Zones, the 2s being only potentially dangerous, so manageable, as long as you watched them closely. A.S.P. 2s were not allowed out, but they were permitted to work In-Zone, alongside the vast majority of 1s, who didn't have Out-of-Zone travel privileges. They worked at the corporate assembly plants, processing plants, tool & die shops, garment factories, textile factories, precision metals and plating factories, stripping engines, building motherboards, ducts, housings, timers, collars, display screens, cells, screws, you name it … anything not Security-Sensitive. They also worked the In-Zone stores, manned the stalls at the open-air markets, ran the makeshift storefront taverns, made deliveries, and picked up garbage. A.S.P. 2s who demonstrated "an appropriate, respectful and cooperative attitude" could, theoretically at least, earn an upgrade to A.S.P. 1 and relocate to Sector A, where the housing was better and the markets were located, and maybe even wangle a Travel-to-Work pass. In practice, however, this hardly ever happened. Intra-Zone Waste & Security Services upgraded maybe ten 2s a year, usually around the Christmas Holidays, the majority of whom were severely disabled. The innermost sector, Sector C, was strictly reserved for A.S.P. 3s,

who typically had a history of violence, or disruptive or defiant behavior, were disinclined to any type of work, and responded poorly,
or not at all, to any form of incentivization. The 3s were not prohibited from working, as in there wasn't an actual ordinance against it,
or from otherwise one day resolving to demonstrate an "appropriate,
respectful and cooperative attitude," but there wouldn't have been
much point in it, really, as the A.S.P. Human Resources professionals
at the In-Zone factories, plants, and stores regarded them, essentially, as feral animals who you didn't want to look directly in the eye but
didn't want to turn your back on either.

Taylor lived on Mulberry Street, Sector C, Zone 23, Northeast
Region 709. Mulberry Street was deep in the heart of an area called
the English Quarter. There wasn't anything English about it. It was
just this grid of grimy little streets lined with eight hundred year-old
tenements. Anti-Social Persons lived there, three, four, and five to
a room, crowded into any apartment where the plumbing still kind
of halfway worked and wasn't totally infested with rats and swarms
of giant flying cockroaches. Tangible amenities were neo-Medieval.
People didn't tend to bathe all that much. Ancylostomiasis, ascari-
asis, pediculosis corporis and pubis (in other words nasty intestinal
worms, head-lice, crabs, and other such parasites) were inescapable
facts of life. These places weren't all utter shitholes, however. People
had effected what repairs they could. Joists had been buttressed.
Roofs had been patched. Doors had been remounted. Et cetera. A
lot of the kitchens had wood burning stoves, which were usually
ancient electric stoves that you gutted and lined with metal sheeting,
and ran some ductwork up the wall, across the ceiling, and out the
window. Some of them even had running water (most of the mains
in the Zone still worked), and power, which, if you knew what you
were doing, you could tap from a transformer out in the street.

16 Mulberry, Taylor's address (not that anyone really needed one)
had originally been 14-18 Mulberry, three adjoining red brick tenements wedged in together between other such tenements. At some
point during the course of history, the walls dividing the three original tenements had been demolished and the apartments expanded,
probably in order to form some kind of luxury lofts that you paid
through the nose for. Later, at some other point in history, the pro-

cess, apparently, had been reversed. The walls had all been bricked back up, and the original twenty-four shotgun apartments, converted to eight of these luxury lofts, had been chopped up into forty-eight units, fitted with miniature toilets and sinks, kitchen "areas," and private doors. Then, at some even later point in history, probably once the climate shifted and windows became a survival issue, the cheap-ass drywall whoever it was had used to create the forty-eight units, or detention cells, or whatever they were, had been mostly ripped out, restoring, sort of, the original twenty-four shotgun apartments, or at least some weird-ass cartoon version of something resembling the original apartments. The result of all this was that your typical apartment at 16 Mulberry was one long space with a kitchen and a makeshift bathroom at one end and then this series of odd little rooms (each of which rooms you had to walk through to get to the next, as there was no hallway), some of which still had the miniature toilets, which one was seriously discouraged from using, as the pipes no longer connected to anything, despite the fact that they looked like they did, but fed down into the apartments below and, well, I think you get the idea.

The point being, this is where Taylor lived. He lived there out of a greasy old duffel and a twenty-three year-old cardboard box he stowed beneath the plywood platform he had built for his flimsy futon mattress, the standard complimentary bedding provided by IntraZone Waste & Security. He lived there with people like Alice Williams, Rusty Braynard, Meyer Jimenez, Coco Freudenheim, Coco's cat, Dexter, and assorted other Class 3 Anti-Social Persons. They lived on the second floor, in 2E. It wasn't exactly the Ritz or anything, but at least it was better than up on 3, which was under the roof, and was like a sauna, the roof being flat and covered with tar, or some synthetic tar-like polymer substance, which had been in a state of permanent melt for as long as anyone could possible remember. Nobody knew who lived up on 3. You never saw them. They might have been dead ... except for the fact that you heard them sometimes, stomping around in circles, it sounded like, moaning or sobbing, and occasionally screaming. Only at night though. Never during the day. Days in Sector C were quiet. Or relatively quiet, in terms of scream-ing. In any event, the streets were deserted. Anti-Social Persons sat out the heat of the day inside their tenements. Nights were better. People went out. Or at least got up from their soppy futons and moved around, and drank, mostly. Or abused an assortment of illicit substances. Like Plastomorphinol. Or MDLX. Or maybe watched some In-Zone Content. Or ate. Or slept. Or fought. Or fucked. Whatever. Anything to break up the boredom.

Now, as vile and loathsome as this probably sounds (and definitely sounded to the Normals outside), it could have been worse, Taylor's life in the Zone. Or maybe it was just that Taylor was used to it. The way Taylor saw it, the heat was, yes, insufferably brutal, but it wasn't that bad. (The A.S.P. 3s, being mostly nocturnal, slept through most of the worst of it anyway.) The rats, roaches, and other insects were disgusting, sure, but they were mostly harmless. The acrid stench of rotting garbage, human sweat, urine, and feces, was what Taylor's world had always smelled like. Born and raised in the Zone as he was, he didn't even register the noise, which ranged from mildly annoying to deafening, and never ended, anywhere, ever, which to us would have been like a form of torture, but to Taylor it was just this background soundtrack of people talking and shouting and screaming and fucking and snoring and sirens and sometimes the rotors of Unmanned Aerial Vehicles ... not the bad ones, which no one ever saw, the small ones, which looked like giant mosquitoes. That, and the endless streams of Content they pumped into the Zone all day, which played, not only on people's Viewers (i.e. primitive homemade pirate-systems cobbled together out of salvaged materials) but also outdoors on the Public Viewers, massive digital video screens mounted on towers and the sides of buildings that ran all kinds of In-Zone Content ... music videos, cloudscape loops, game shows, SitComs, educational features, three hundred year-old Nature Content, all of this in no particular order, and interspersed on the hour and half-hour with one or more of the talking heads, a revolving line-up of ethnically diverse, spastic, over-enunciating morons whose out-of-synch borderline hysterical voices rang out across the sweltering rooftops like some incomprehensible call to prayer ...

Which all right, getting back to our story, at approximately 0530 that morning, as Taylor lay there on his moldering futon, staring up at that dot on the ceiling (which now he wasn't quite sure what it was, as it didn't seem to be moving or anything, so maybe it was just a spot on the ceiling), one of these talking heads, a woman, with tangerine hair and, it seemed, no eyelids, was wrapping up an InfoBreak.

The expected high was 46 Celsius. Heat advisories were in effect. Security Gates 15 through 18 were operating at reduced capacity. Quarantined Persons with travel passes were advised to use Gates 14 and 20. Quarantined Persons, regardless of class, were hereby reminded that animal husbandry, including, but not limited to, the breeding and keeping of feral pigeons, was strictly prohibited by Ordinance 40. And finally, due to the airing tonight of a special program celebrating the life of Jimmy "Jimbo" Cartwright, III, founder and CEO of Finkles, hosted by "Jimbo's" personal friends, SoniVerse/FaceWorld recording artists, Hootey Brewster and the Brewster Boys, regularly scheduled In-Zone programming was being preempted as of 2100. Today was Tuesday, 17 April, 2610, H.C.S.T., or it was Monday the something in the month of Iyyar, or Day whatever in the Year of the Lemur, or some other totally made-up date ... which everyone knew, or at least suspected, wasn't remotely when it really was.

Taylor couldn't possibly have given less of a shit when it "really" was. In Zone 23, it was Tuesday morning. In Taylor's world it was Tuesday morning. Taylor knew that because Taylor was awake. Taylor was awake because Alice Williams and Rusty Braynard, and some other person, had been stumbling around the room they shared, kicking at piles of crap on the floor, and they'd kicked over a glass, or a bottle, or something, and Rusty Braynard had stepped on some glass, and cut his foot pretty bad, it looked like, and now he was hopping around like a chicken calling Alice Williams a whore, and a fucking whore, and a cunt, and so on, and grabbing onto the back of her shoulders trying to get her to walk him around while he hopped behind her on his one good foot. Alice Williams was throwing elbows, trying to get him the fuck off her back, and twisting and jerking and bobbing up and down, and running all around the room in circles shrieking as if her skin was on fire. All of which together looked, at least in Taylor's peripheral vision, like one of those weird aboriginal rituals you saw sometimes in the Nature Content, which aside from being incredibly annoying, was making it impossible for

Taylor to think, which he hadn't been doing a lot of lately, at least not clearly, which was not good. Taylor needed to be thinking clearly. If he wanted to live through the day, he did. And even if he didn't, it didn't matter, because at this point it all came down to one thing ... he needed to get to Jefferson Avenue and up to Cassandra's by 0730. He needed to do this without getting shot, or taken out by a Godsend missile, or picked up by a Security team. To do that, he needed to do two things. One of which was start thinking clearly. The other of which was, get out of bed. At the moment, he was doing neither. What he was doing was lying in bed, staring up at what was now, beyond all doubt, a mutant cockroach, which was crawling aimlessly around in circles on the ceiling directly above his head ... off to one side of which, Taylor's head, Alice Williams and Rusty Braynard were dancing and hopping and flapping all around, doing whatever the fuck they were doing. His head, incidentally, was throbbing. His eyes were probably going to explode. Worse, it appeared his tongue had been coated with some type of post-industrial adhesive you used to glue things underwater that tasted not unlike the ass of a dog. Soon he was going to projectile vomit, or shit himself, one, or possibly both. Which, given the way the bed was violently spinning and dipping, was going to get ugly. What the fuck was he even doing there, back home, in his bed, on Mulberry Street? He did not know this. He could not remember ... or, OK, one thing he could remember was ... well, actually, not all that helpful. He remembered staggering down the embankment of what appeared to be the Dell Street Canal, gazing up at what looked like the moon, and what might, in fact, have been the moon, onto the phosphorescent face of which had been projected the Finkles logo. Nothing particularly idiotic or self-destructive occurred in this memory, or memory fragment, or whatever it was, but then, OK, another memory ... this one also not that helpful. Here was another Dell Street Canal scene, this one prominently featuring Taylor dragging what certainly appeared to be a body ... the body of what looked like a walrus, or dugong, or some other species of sea-going mammal, all of which had been extinct for decades, so OK, odds were, not a walrus, or any other sizable sea-going mammal, but definitely a blimp, as in a massive body, as in a king-sized, fat-assed, bloated, blubbery, conspicuously unresponsive body. Unresponsive, as in a lifeless body, wearing what looked like a Watcher's uniform ... a Watcher's uniform the size of a tent. Taylor, in this nauseating hungover flashback, is hunkered down at the bottom of the frame, dragging this elephant seal of a body backwards down a concrete embankment toward what appears to be the Dell Street Canal. He's got one hand around each ankle, or almost, because they're the size of his arms, Taylor's arms, the ankles are (his biceps, that is, not his forearms), or the size of two big joints of TōHam, and they look just about as pink and clammy, and he's gritting his teeth and heaving and snorting and using his legs and his back and jerking, and it looks like he's going to bust a hernia before he can get this enormous fat guy down the embankment and into the canal. The huge dead fat guy is just lying there, prone, very conspicuously not responding as the jagged concrete acts like sand-paper, grinding off what's left of his face. Which isn't much. The nose is gone, as are the lips, and cheeks and brow, and most of the chin, so the face is flattened, sickeningly flattened, and is sliding along, smearing this streak of blood and face meat down the embankment like the trail of a slug. Taylor, clearly totally shitfaced, jerks it down the concrete slope the last few heaves, grimacing, groaning, backs down into the bright green scum, dragging the fat-assed, flabby bulk of the non-responding Watcher with him, grapples with it, turns it, pushes ... the water up to his armpits now, the now completely faceless body floating, bobbing, finally sinking ... except he couldn't remember it sinking ... and, OK, now it was coming back to him ... the body belonged to one J.C. Bodroon, who he'd dumped in the Dell Street Canal, apparently, and had weighted him down with ... what? Fuck. What had he weighted the body down with? Nothing ... which meant it was out there now, lolling among the other garbage. Which meant it was just a matter of time before some satellite's camera spotted it, pattern-recognized the Watcher uniform, and flagged it for a Security team. Once that team ID'd the body and scanned his logs, they'd be onto Taylor ... unless they were already out there now, waiting for him to exit the building, in which case there would be IntraZone snipers up on those rooftops across the street, which if Taylor could just sit up and look out the window, odds were, he could probably see ... in any event, what it all added up to was that probably the last place he needed to be at 0530 that Tuesday morning was lying in bed on Mulberry Street watching some mutant form of cockroach crawl around on the fucking ceiling, while Alice Williams and Rusty Braynard, and some other unidentified person, reenacted some neo-aboriginal ritual to invoke the gods of ... whatever.

Taylor, in a feat of incredible strength that surely would have killed a lesser mortal, sat himself up on the edge of the bed and waited patiently to puke his guts out. Alice Williams and Rusty Braynard must have seen him, because they stopped in their tracks. They turned, took one look at Taylor, quickly plotted the likely vector of Taylor's potentially imminent puke stream, and skittered and hopped their way out of same. Taylor, however, did not puke his guts out. What he did was, he sat there a moment, making weird faces as he surveyed the room, which appeared to have been professionally ransacked, strewn as it was with dirty clothes, beer bottles, bags of worthless junk, burnt-out circuit boards, gutted Viewers, wires, knobs, plastic syringes, pages torn out of paperback books, assorted collections of cigarette butts, and all of this sprinkled with jagged shards and crunchy nuggets of broken glass, and spattered with blood, and what he did was, Taylor, as quietly as he possibly could ... he asked Alice Williams and Rusty Braynard exactly what the fuck they thought they were doing.

"The fuck are you doing?"

"Who? Uth?"

Rusty Braynard spoke with a lisp.

"Yeth. You," Taylor mocked him. "Thee anybody elth in here?"

"Asshole," Alice Williams interjected.

"I thlithed my foot on thome fucking glath."

"I can fucking see that. What's with the dancing?"

"Danthing?"

"Or whatever the fuck you were doing."

"I don't underthand."

Taylor gave up. They didn't know what the fuck they were doing. By this time they had probably forgotten how it started. They both had that Tuesday morning look ... the bug-eyed mono-maniacal stares, the lockjaw grins, the fluttering fingers that looked like they were playing scales on a pair of invisible miniature pianos. The other person was some greasy little punk who was missing some teeth, and was maybe Chinese, who Taylor had never seen in his life. He wondered if Taylor might have a cigarette. Taylor wondered if maybe the punk would like to suck one out of his ass. The punk didn't seem to want to do that, so Taylor went ahead and started getting his boots on. Meyer Jimenez was already up and cooking something pungent in the kitchen. It smelled like maybe pigeon paella. Claudia's Husband of the Week was snoring. Coco Freudenheim, who never really slept, was calling Dexter a silly belly and pleading with someone who wasn't there to witness what a silly little belly he was. Aside from the sappy funereal music, which the Public Viewer had gone back to playing, all this was just like any other morning. Somewhere in here Rusty Braynard had cleaned up his foot and found some shoes, which might have been Alice Williams' shoes, and he was down on their futon wedging them on, and Alice Williams was helping him tie them. The greasy little possibly Chinese punk, the only one currently in the bedroom who wasn't futzing with a pair of shoes, had moonwalked his way to the two big windows that looked out onto Mulberry Street. He was standing there, gazing out like a moron, his body bathed in the cool blue light that spilled from the screens of the Public Viewers, which lit him up nicely for the Intra-Zone snipers ... which, OK, probably weren't out there, because they hadn't mistaken the punk for Taylor and fired about two hundred high-velocity rounds through his chest in a tightly-grouped pattern.* Then again, Taylor reasoned, they might have been showing some discipline for once and just lying up there on those fucking rooftops waiting for him to exit the building. This, however, was extremely unlikely, snipers being notoriously twitchy, and not so discerning when it came to their targets, and ... whatever. He'd find out soon enough.

He tied off the laces of his jungle boots, peeled off his bloody, canal-stinking T-shirt, pulled on another odoriferous T-shirt that was lying in a ball at the foot of his futon, and that wasn't spattered

---

* *IntraZone Waste & Security Services had some kind of deal with UltraLite, Inc., makers of the classic UltraLite Rifle preferred by most Security professionals. They took this tiny .18 caliber Dum Dum ammo that looked kind of silly, until you watched them put about two hundred rounds into someone's back in just under four seconds.*

with a Watcher's blood, grabbed a half a beer off the floor, drained it, belched, got to his feet, and then lurched in a more or less John Wayne fashion down the submarine-like hallway. He staggered past Coco's and Meyer's rooms, Claudia's room, Dodo's alcove, Sylvie's nook, through the kitchen, and into the tiny makeshift bathroom, firmly intending to take a big dump. He felt like, if he took this dump, and maybe puked, and got another beer down, he might be able to clear his head enough to make a run for Cassandra's ... assuming, that is, he wasn't cut to shreds the moment he stepped out the door.

His progress was interrupted briefly by some female Anti-Social Person who was stretched out naked in the filthy bathtub, ankles and wrists draped over the rim, eyes wide open, staring at nothing. It looked like maybe she'd spent the night there, probably tripping on MDLX, which meant she was one of Claudia's friends, most of whom Taylor had fucked at some point, but this one didn't look at all familiar. She didn't seem to be going anywhere, so Taylor went ahead and took his dump.

Minutes later, he was back in the kitchen, where Meyer Jimenez, who was on Taylor's kill-list, was stirring a pot of pigeon paella, acting like he didn't know what was happening. He stood there blithely, ignoring Taylor, stirring away with his huge wooden spoon, as if he had never heard of Sarah, or Adam, and was just some random asshole Taylor had slapped around for no reason, who didn't have anything to do with anything. Meyer, as ever, was drenched with sweat from head to toe, and stank like rum, and the bottle of rum was there beside him, and his seersucker suit was sticking to him, and the kitchen smelled like garlic and saffron and only slightly of Taylor's dump. Taylor stood there glaring at him. Meyer looked up from his pot of paella. He peered out at Taylor through the sweat-streaked lenses of his glasses, which he wore on the tip of his nose. He seemed on the verge of saying something, or asking or possibly explaining something. Taylor, who had heard enough from Meyer (who was fortunate Taylor hadn't already killed him), turned and walked back down the hallway. If he somehow managed to survive the morning, he'd come back and deal with Meyer later. And if not ... well, it wouldn't matter.

Back in his room at the end of the hall, Alice Williams and Rusty Braynard, dressed in their neon yellow track suits, were down on the floor on their hands and knees, digging through boxes of "important papers." They were searching for their CRS IDs. They looked like giant yellow raccoons with some kind of neurological damage. The punk was standing just behind them, making this high-pitched whining noise that Taylor didn't need to be hearing at the moment, and was just about to put a violent end to, when the voice of bug-eyed, orange-haired woman, the talking head on the Public Viewer, informed the residents of Mulberry Street that the time at the tone would be 0600. That was it ... it was time to go.

Taylor got down on his knees, fished his backpack out of the duffel that was under the bed beside the box, opened it up, and there it all was ... the change of socks, the GoGo bars, brand new toothbrush, bottles of water, counterfeit Travel Pass, homemade pacifier ... all of which was useless now. He took the Travel Pass. That would be evidence. And the GoGo bars. He left the rest. He shoved the pack back under the bed, pushed himself up off the floor, staggered back down the hall once more, passing everyone's rooms as before, back through the kitchen, adrenaline flowing, scrotum tightening, anus contracting, past Meyer Jimenez, nostrils flaring, and out the door of Apartment 2E of 16 Mulberry Street, forever.

He didn't say goodbye to anyone, not even Alice Williams and Rusty Braynard, who he knew would wonder, in the years to come, what had happened to him, how he'd died, or whether, maybe, he hadn't died, and had made it out to the Autonomous Zones, which everyone knew didn't really exist, which meant, deep down, they would know he was dead. It wasn't that he didn't want to, badly (i.e. say goodbye, or something anyway), but he couldn't, and he couldn't even flash them a look, because that wasn't what he normally did. He had to stick to his normal routine. She had drilled that into him, Sarah had, back before the plan went sideways. And now, even if the plan had gone sideways and everything was basically fucked all to hell, that didn't mean it was time to get reckless. Assuming they hadn't yet found Bodroon, or at least hadn't yet identified his body, and that there weren't snipers all over the rooftops, odds were, he could still get to Cassandra's.

He made his way down the stairs in the dark, navigating by the glimmer of light that spilled in through the shattered windows that looked out onto the disgusting airshaft that rose up through the center of the building, the ledges of which were crawling with pigeons, cooing and shitting all over everything. Just as he reached the first floor landing, the corner of which some Anti-Social asshole had decided to use as a toilet ... KA-BOOM! Something exploded outside, or was taken out by a tactical missile, or something ... he couldn't be sure what it was, because now there were hundreds of panicked pigeons spiraling up the airshaft beside him, flying sideways, mid-air colliding, beating each other apart with their wings ... and OK, this was it, he guessed, because odds were they were walking them in, and they'd put the next one right down the airshaft, and that one he would never hear, and ...

Valentina

Meanwhile, twenty-three kilometers away, in a world of comfort and infinite abundance, which Taylor Byrd had never seen, except of course on the screen of a Viewer, Valentina Briggs was sitting quietly, doing nothing, trying to detach. Her half-closed eyes were focused on a patch of wall where there was nothing to see. She sat there, fixedly, kneeling on the floor, her buttocks resting on her upturned feet, hands forming an oval in her lap, thumbs ever so lightly touching, trying her best to think of not thinking. Thoughts were racing through her mind. It felt like her head was full of hamsters, soft, fat, fuzzy little hamsters, running in place inside one of those wheels, running and running, then stopping for a moment, then running and running, then stopping again, then running and running for all they were worth, then stopping again and looking confused, like the poor little things just could not fathom why they could never seem to get to wherever hamsters were always trying to go.

Valentina Briggs observed and acknowledged the running in place of the cognitive hamsters without judgment and allowed them to run. She did not attempt to prevent them from running, or impatiently wait for them to finish running, or pray that the One would stop them running, or judge them, or herself, at all. Instead she concentrated on her breathing, in through one nostril, out through the other, in through that one, and out through the other, and sat there silently staring at nothing, and tried again to think of not thinking. The more she tried to think of not thinking, the more aware she became of how the thoughts she was trying to think of not thinking were multiplying within her mind. A lot of these thoughts were not even thoughts. They were more like random furry blobs of meaningless proto-cognitive matter, the only conceivable purpose of which was to make it impossible for her to detach, and stare at nothing, and think of not thinking.

The air-conditioning was on some setting designed to simulate frostbite conditions. It had been on this setting for several hours. The tips of her fingers were turning blue. Her hands were numb. Her feet were freezing. Her paraspinal muscles were spasming. Her frontal and maxillary sinuses ached. She could see her breath. Her teeth were chattering.

Valentina Briggs observed and acknowledged her chattering teeth and throbbing sinuses, the pain in her upper thoracic region, and the cold-induced paresthesia in her fingers, and she stared at the wall, where there was nothing to see, and tried again to think of not thinking. Everything was happening for a reason ... a reason beyond our understanding. She, Valentina Constance Briggs, despite her present circumstances, was still a single grain of sand on the endless beach where time met space, an indestructible, eternal part of the infinite, interwoven fabric of the spaceless, timeless, oneness of the One ... the oneness of the unnameable One ... the multiplicitous oneness of the One ...

Valentina spoke the words, repeating the mantra on her breaths, but they did not produce that peaceful feeling of complete surrender, and she could not detach. She sat there, on the floor, on her knees, her teeth chattering, staring at a wall, sensing that, all right, whatever had happened, however it was that she had ended up here (which she'd recently remembered, but had once more forgotten), she would never be feeling that peaceful feeling of total surrender ever again. How long had it been since she'd felt it? Weeks? Months? She wasn't sure. She had taken it for granted, at some point, hadn't she? At some point in her former life? Yes. She had. She remembered that clearly. It had always been there, easily available, inexhaustible, or so it seemed. Nothing changed, and everything changed, once you detached. The world didn't change. What happened was, you'd lost your perspective, and once you detached you got it back. If you felt afraid, confused, or sad, or angry, or any other negative feelings, it didn't take those feelings away, but once you'd said your mantra and detached, you saw that they were only feelings, and the feelings had less to do with you somehow, and you were able to acknowledge them and let them go ... because you didn't have to feel those kinds of feelings, those negative, self-destructive feelings, those confusing, frightening, resentful feelings, and if you did ... well, that was your choice.

Yes. It was all coming back to her now ... again. She seemed to keep losing it and finding it. Everything happened for a reason. Everything always the result of a choice. You learned it as a child, this simple axiom, as you started down the Path of Responsibility. Later, you saw it bear itself out. The schools you attended, how you did, what you studied, the clothes you wore, who you married, your sexual preferences, the corporation for which you worked, the house you lived in, the state of your health ... everything always the result of a choice. Everything happened for a reason, and if you couldn't see the reason, that only meant that you couldn't see it, and you probably had some detaching to do. Remove the beam that is in your eye and the speck in the other's eye disappears. Anger is nothing but projected fear. Freedom grants us the freedom to choose but not the freedom not to choose ...

Valentina got off her knees and stood up and shouted at the video camera that was mounted to the ceiling in the corner of the room.

"My fingers are turning blue in here, asshole!"

The video camera panned up with her and auto-focused on her new position. The PA beeped. A voice addressed her.

"This is Barry. How can I help you?"

"You can turn the fucking temperature up! I'm losing sensation in my fucking extremities!"

Valentina was a healthcare professional, so she knew how to talk to people like Barry. The profanity, however, was unfamiliar. She didn't know why she was talking like that.

"Oh, my, that doesn't sound good. I'll see if we can't adjust the thermostat. Oh, and your transport is being arranged. Should be just another few minutes."

Valentina took another deep breath and clapped and rubbed her hands together. She hopped and danced around the room to try to improve her circulation. The video camera panned and tilted, monitoring her every movement, the little red light on its housing blinking.

"Was there anything else at the moment, Ms. Briggs?"

There wasn't anything else at the moment, so Barry switched off and left her alone to hop and dance around and clap, and do this kind of pursed-lip breathing thing. All of which, added to the state of her hair, which looked like maybe she had had it styled by someone with tremors who was totally blind, made her resemble a demented person, which, of course, technically, was what she was.

She was wearing the standard in-patient ensemble ... faux satin, lemon chiffon pajamas, matching grip-sole, ankle-length socks, and a plastic bracelet around her wrist with her name and a number, which she couldn't get off. She'd been in this room for several hours, seven or eight at least, she guessed, her sense was over the course of a night, but, the truth was, she had no idea. The room was a windowless holding cell, upholstered in pink, indestructible Naugahyde. There was some kind of rubbery padding behind it. The video camera and an intercom speaker were mounted out of reach in the corner of the ceiling.

Barry had advised her at regular intervals that her transport would be just another few minutes. He sounded like one of those teenage waiters you got at Giggles or the Salad Consortium who were always so happy to be your server and tell you all about the awesome specials. Valentina imagined Barry, sitting at a console in the nurses station, watching her dance around and clap, talking, seemingly to no one at all, but in actuality talking to his girlfriend on a Strauss-Chen Industries Cranio-Implant. The SCI 227.8 was probably out of Barry's price range, so Barry would be wearing a 226, which wasn't all that different from the 227s, except for a few superfluous features. Barry was likely still in school. Valentina put him in his mid-to-late thirties, which meant he was definitely Variant-Positive, and on some form of pharmatherapy, probably Zanoflaxithorinol H, or one of the earlier versions thereof. Something like seventy to eighty percent of the Variant-Positive population was on some version of Zanoflaxithorinol. The rest were on some other stabilizing agent, Lamictotegratol, Oxcarzenadrine, Olanzatriperidone, or one of the others. Barry was certainly on Zanoflaxithorinol. He spoke in that indefatigably cheery, slightly superior tone of voice, the hallmark of Zanoflaxithorinol patients. It made you sound, not totally obnoxious, but like you were privy to some secret wisdom you wished you could share with the others who weren't, but you knew, if you tried, they just wouldn't understand.

Valentina tried to remember how she had sounded when she'd sounded like that. She knew she must have sounded like Barry, and her husband, Kyle, and Susan Foster, but she couldn't play it back in her mind now ... her voice, in that supercilious tone. It wasn't as pronounced as that of the Clears, whose condescension was of a whole other order, but it was close, and it was causing her to grind her teeth, and to painfully clench her masseter muscles. She hated it now, that tone of voice. When exactly had she come to hate it? Hate ... hatred. That was the word ... it must have been, for what she was feeling. She imagined Barry with a sucking chest wound, flopping around on the floor like a fish, panicking, trying to cry out for help, but not being able to make a sound. The mental image of it made her sick. And yet she couldn't seem to erase it. What kind of monster was she becoming that imagined people with sucking chest wounds?

The day before, or whenever it was, before they transferred her into the waiting room, she had lain awake in four-point restraints and imagined gouging the tips of her fingers deep into Doctor Hesbani's neck, closing her hand around his laryngeal prominence, and ripping it clean out of his body. Doctor Hesbani was kneading her abdomen in different places with his first two fingers. He asked her whether it hurt ... there. And there. And what about there ... and there? Yes, it hurt. There and there. Valentina hurt all over. Doctor Hesbani nodded and smiled, like he'd just performed a magic trick, which he was waiting for Valentina to acknowledge. He looked like a giant badger or something. Valentina wanted to rip his throat out.

This part had happened in the S.I.C.U., or what they'd told her was the S.I.C.U. It didn't feel like an S.I.C.U. Then again, she was heavily sedated. She figured she'd been there about a week, or ten days maybe, or maybe longer. She'd woken up out of a dreamless nothing. Doctor Hesbani was hovering over her.

"Hello, Ms. Briggs. I am Doctor Hesbani."

It sounded like he was shouting, or singing. Droplets of mustard clung to his whiskers, which grew untended from below his eyes to the top of fleshy laryngeal prominence.

"You are in the Surgical Intensive Care Unit. We have managed to stop your internal bleeding. You are experiencing some severe discomfort. We are giving you palliative care for this."

Valentina remembered thinking whatever they were giving her wasn't working. She felt like she was trying to defecate something the size and shape of a toaster. She couldn't remember where she was, or why she was there, or what was happening. She opened her mouth to try to ask, but a pulsating pain that started in her bowels radiated through her entire body, and paralyzed her, and she must have passed out. The next time she woke it was much the same ... excruciating pain, fog of sedation, a few confused thoughts, then unconsciousness.

That's the way it went for a while, exactly how long she could not say. Then, one day, whenever it was, she'd woken up again, still in the restraints, and the Hadley Security Consultants were there. They were standing on either side of her bed, far enough up toward her head so that she had to turn from side to side to see the face of the one who was speaking.

"How are you feeling today, Ms. Briggs?" The one on the left, the man, asked her.

She rotated her head toward him, painfully.

"My name is Winston. This is Alicia. We're here to help arrange your transition."

Both of the Consultants had perfect skin, smiles full of flawless, bright white teeth. The whites of their eyes were utterly bloodless, the irises milky, infant blue.

"The doctors tell us you're recovering well ..."

Valentina rolled her head to the right.

"... which means it's time to start getting you ready."

Alicia smiled like a flight attendant who really needs you to return to your seat.

Valentina, although no longer in agony, was weak, and still quite heavily sedated. She fought to get her mind to focus, but she didn't know what to focus it on. She scanned the room as best she could. She was looking for something. She didn't know what. The S.I.C.U. room, or whatever it was, was painted this horrible Creamsicle orange, like the color of a ten-minute tan gone wrong. The visitors chair was stacked with clean sheets. The shelf on the wall above it was empty, except for a plastic water pitcher. There weren't any flowers or cards or anything. Apparently no one had been to see her.

"We've got some release forms we need you to sign. But first let's just confirm your vitals."

Winston read out her name and address, her husband's name, her place of employment, her Login IDs, and bank account numbers, each of which Valentina confirmed. Winston and Alicia were definitely Clears. Both of them were in their mid-to-late twenties. They looked like A-list fashion models and spoke like Human Resources people.

"All right, good," Winston said. "Once your doctors have approved your release, you'll be moved to an interim transfer facility. Your ID bracelet is being prepared. You'll receive your bracelet at the transfer facility. Your old ID card, and all your other cards, have been deactivated and are no longer valid."

"The ID bracelet is just for transit," Alicia interjected cheerfully.

Valentina rolled her head to the right.

"You won't have to wear it indefinitely or anything."

"Your network logins and related passwords," Winston continued, causing Valentina to jerk her head back over to the left, "have been deactivated and are no longer valid."

"You'll be issued one mid-sized bag of clothing, hygiene articles, and other personal items."

"Personal funds in any bank accounts bearing your name, and your name alone, have been transferred into an escrow account for disposition at a later date."

"Normally, any such personal funds are used to offset the costs of your transport and housing during the quarantine period."

"Personal funds in any bank accounts bearing both your and your husband's names are heretofore deemed the property of your husband, and no claims or liens shall be set against them."

Valentina was jerking her head from side to side as fast as she could as Winston and Alicia took turns spitting this verbal boilerplate back and forth at her. She felt like she was going to pass out. Fortunately, just as she started to do that, Alicia stepped toward her and started undoing the artificial fur-lined safety restraint that was pinning her wrist to the aluminum bed frame, which for some presumably legal reason Winston felt he needed to narrate.

"Alicia is undoing your right-hand restraint."

Valentina nodded gratefully. She smiled. It seemed like the thing to do. Alicia reached over, took hold of her wrist, lifted it up and out of the restraint, and pushed a plastic inkless pen the size of toothpick between her fingers. She held out a tablet with a screen at the top and an isolated capture pad at the bottom. The screen was displaying what looked like a contract. The print was way too small to read.

"This is a standard acknowledgment form. You, the Patient, hereby acknowledge your non-responsiveness to pharmatherapy, and freely elect to enter quarantine, effective as of your date of transfer."

Valentina signed the pad. Alicia smiled her Clarion smile ... warm, yet unmistakably superior. Then she clicked the tablet, producing another form that Valentina could not read.

"You hereby acknowledge that, in your present condition, you pose a danger to yourself and others, and hereby agree to remain in quarantine until such time as a medical doctor determines you no longer pose such a danger."

Valentina signed. Alicia clicked.

"You hereby indemnify, and forever release, the Hadley Corporation of Menomonie, Wisconsin, and all of its affiliates and subsidiaries and assigns, in respect to all claims of damage or injury arising from your treatment and quarantine period."

Valentina signed. Alicia clicked.

Valentina Constance Briggs, if one didn't count the last five months, had led a perfectly normal life. She'd enjoyed a perfectly normal childhood, had attended perfectly normal schools, and had blossomed into a perfectly normal if somewhat striking and buxom young woman with burnt orange hair and eel green eyes, which she got from her mother's side of the family. After university, she'd interned a bit, gone back and got her PhD, started her career, dated a while, and then met her future husband and married him. They'd honeymooned up on Hudson Bay, a popular, overcrowded resort for moderate- to fairly-abundant couples. Valentina's husband, Kyle Bentley-Briggs (he'd taken her name, she hadn't his) was the G-Wave Industries Associate Adjunct Semi-Permanent Assistant

Professor of Info-Entertainment Content at the Bloomberg Virtual Community College of Communications and Informatics. It wasn't Oxford or Yale or anything, but it wasn't anything to sneeze at either. They lived in a three-bed, two-bath condo at 3258 Marigold Lane in the Pewter Palisades Private Community, whose accent color was Persian green. Valentina, until a few months back, had worked in the Histopathology Department of the Breckenridge (Senior) Medical Clinic, a high-end, mostly geriatric outfit that made a killing on phenomenally expensive cancer screenings and advanced cancer treatments for the affluent over one hundred demographic, and was part of the Hadley Medical Group. She and Kyle were very happy. They owed about thirteen million on the house and ate out two or three times a week, usually on Pewter Palisades' Main Street, often with Bill and Susan Foster, who lived next door on Marigold Lane and had a time-share in the Arctic Circle. In addition to the more or less standard package of company-sponsored retirement vehicles, they maintained a diversified, if rather conservative, portfolio of primarily blue chip stocks, the usual mix of pharmaceuticals, Security, insurance, bioengineering, financial services and global re-development. Although quite young, being both in their forties, the trajectory of their lives was clear. Kyle, whose IQ was 101, or 103, depending on the test, but who compensated for his average intelligence with a natural gift for networking and politics, was a rising star at BVCC, and was already being aggressively headhunted by global educational and marketing firms, who were always on the lookout for bright, young talent. Valentina, although less ambitious, certainly enjoyed her work at the Clinic, which she planned to resume in some capacity, probably in her early seventies, once the children both she and Kyle wanted had reached the age of independence. They'd agreed on three, two boys and a girl, and had chosen a palette of traits for each of them, accentuating personal characteristics while preserving both filial and intra-sibling similarity. This was to be the year they started. The next six years would be the childbirth years, which would be followed by twenty to twenty-five years of childcare, education, and so on. Their youngest boy, Marlough, they thought, would be off to college at the age of twenty. Valentina would be in her prime, sixty-eight, or seventy maybe, and would still have a good thirty years ahead of her to pursue her histopathological career. Assuming their investment strategies were sound, and Kyle's career remained on track, they'd be able to cover the children's education, healthcare, and other basic needs, maintain a comfortable standard of living, prudently setting some funds aside to cover the routine joint replacements and organ transplants that everyone got, early-retire at ninety-seven, and move to a Flex-Care Seniors' Community somewhere north of the 50th Parallel ... or, at least, that had been the plan.

"You hereby consent to indefinitely forfeit, and hereby forfeit and waive any claim to, any and all rights, entitlements, and benefits accruing to Variant-Positive Persons as defined in the Cooperative Security Agreement, U.T.S. §1067, Paragraph 1 of the Global Civil Code."

Valentina signed the pad. Alicia lifted the tablet away, tucked it up into her armpit, and refastened the restraint around Valentina's wrist.

"Thank you for your cooperation," Winston said, examining his necktie. "Sorry to bother you with all this paperwork ... but, you understand, it has to be done."

Alicia had finished redoing the restraint, and now she appeared to be standing there staring fixedly into space at nothing. Her breathing had slowed. Her eyes were open, but her brain was in some meditative state, or semi-sleep state, or hibernation mode. She looked like a totally different person, or a perfect simulation of the person she was.

Winston glanced at his expensive wristwatch, and that seemed to snap Alicia out of it somehow. Valentina felt their energy changing. She didn't quite understand what was happening, or wasn't happening, but she thought was happening, but whatever was or wasn't happening, obviously, this session was coming to an end.

Valentina was glad it was. She was feeling tired, extremely tired, and confused, and her lower abdomen hurt, and she needed a nap before Kyle came to visit ... she wanted to be awake for that.

"Do you have any questions for us, Ms. Briggs?" Alicia asked, and smiled professionally. She seemed to be back to the first Alicia.

Valentina thought for a moment.

"When will I be going home?" she asked.

Alicia stared at her for several seconds.

"By home you mean to Pewter Palisades?"

Valentina nodded. That's what she meant.

Alicia and Winston looked at each other, the way that the Clears so often did, like they couldn't believe how stupid you were but they didn't want to say that and hurt your feelings.

"I'm afraid you're not going home, Ms. Briggs."

Winston turned away and cleared his throat.

"I'm sorry. We thought you understood ..."

Alicia's eyes were oozing compassion. The Clears could just turn it on like that ... like flipping a switch, that total compassion, an unbelievably creepy attribute that, once upon a time, centuries back, only enlightened sages had possessed. It was like they were looking right into your heart, and could feel the sadness, or pain, or fear, or whatever feeling you were currently feeling, and wished more than anything, at least in that moment, that they had the power to make you stop feeling it. The creepiest thing about it was, it wasn't fake. It was utterly genuine. So much so that you felt ashamed for even considering the possibility that it wasn't. You knew their hearts were just breaking for you (in some deeply profound and impersonal way) as they stood there staring into your insides, wishing they could give you their gift, the knowledge, the peace, of total detachment, but knowing, of course, that they never could, and that that too was all part of the plan.

Valentina looked up into Alicia's beaming, compassionate eyes ... she wanted to cry, but she didn't know why. Alicia gently placed her hand on Valentina's forehead and let it rest there, as if she were going to check her temperature. She smiled a beatific smile.

"Don't you remember how you got here, Ms. Briggs?" Alicia asked, in a childlike voice.

"No," Valentina answered, trembling. She was telling the truth. She didn't remember. Then ... maybe ... she was starting to remember ... which, OK, she realized almost immediately, she really did not want to be doing. It wasn't that she remembered details. It was more just this horrible, helpless feeling that rose up inside her like a wave of nausea, as if everything solid had begun to dissolve, like the simulated world of a defective Immersion ...

Winston took a few steps back.

"Are you sure you don't remember, Ms. Briggs?"

Alicia's hand was warm, dry, radiating heat into her forehead. Her hand wasn't moving and yet it seemed, to Valentina, whose eyes had closed, and who felt like her head and neck were paralyzed, as if its energy were entering her brain, tingling, stinging, pinpoint streams of microscopic electric needles, stabbing precisely into her synapses, redirecting their electrical processes ... and now she was flying through a shopping district where the streets were all coated with raspberry syrup, flying the way you do in dreams, so not really flying, more like floating, two or three meters above the ground, flanked by rows of faceless faces, featureless, eerily fetal masks ... flying past signs too fast to read them, gliding toward the massive screen of a video billboard running an ad for some new procedure where the doctors replaced your internal organs with synthetic linguine ... she flew right at and through the screen, and now she was in some dream environment that vaguely reminded her of Paul & Pomona, the upscale chain where she normally shopped for things like tablecloths and kitchen accessories, except that all the Sales Assistants were these gulping, brainless goldfish people with bulging fish eyes and goldfish mouths, some of whom were amputees, with sickeningly suppurating surgical wounds that were dangling fiber-optic ganglia, and these Sales Assistants had formed a circle around this screaming naked woman, who was down on her knees in the middle in the circle, and whose body was smeared with raspberry syrup ... and now, like it sometimes happens in dreams, Valentina became this woman, and she pushed one hand into her abdomen, right through her skin like a Hindu fakir, and pulled it out and held something out for the mutilated Sales Assistants to see and ...

A deafening buzzer, like the one that sounded when you got an answer wrong on Quandary, sounded. She was back in the padded pink room. The video camera swiveled toward her. The PA crackled. A voice, not Barry's, a colder, more professional voice, definitely Security, addressed her now.

"Step back from the door, Ms. Briggs."

Valentina froze in place, every muscle in her body contracting. The lights in the room appeared to be brightening.

"Step back from the door, Ms. Briggs."

She couldn't remember what she'd just been thinking. Whatever time and place this was was not where she was supposed to be. Something that had not happened had happened.

"Move to the wall. Face the wall. Place your hands against the wall."

Valentina assumed the position.

"Do not remove your hands from the wall."

She thought she'd dreamed but really what she'd dreamed had been the place she was, and this had always been the dream, which someone else she was was dreaming ... which didn't make sense ... unless ... maybe ...

The deadbolts in the door clacked open.

"Face the wall."

The oneness of the ...

"Do not attempt to turn your head."

The multiplicitous ...

"Do not move."

The loving compassionate oneness of the ...

Sex & Violence

One of the other hallmark symptoms of late-stage Anti-Social Disease was "an inability to form and maintain enduring social and professional relationships," the type of emotionally rewarding relationships the Normals, without even having to be reminded to do so by some app on their Viewers, formed and maintained with their families, friends, colleagues, clients, and online followers. According to the DSM XXXIII, Anti-Socials could "mimic" such relationships, and be "verbally facile" and "superficially charming," but they could never genuinely "empathize with others," whose pain and suffering they "viewed with contempt," or, in some cases, found entertaining.*

This "mimicking" (or "masking") of real emotions was usually employed to deceive their victims, or other unsuspecting persons they wanted to use for their selfish purposes, but occasionally it was also employed by Anti-Socials to deceive themselves. Now this had been proven in scientific tests. Bizarre as it sounds, there were documented cases where Anti-Social Persons had, through some weird form of self-hypnosis, convinced themselves they were capable of feeling genuine regard and fondness for others, and even something approaching empathy. Why they did this was not well understood.

Taylor, apparently, was one of these anomalies, these A.S.P.s who had hypnotized themselves ... because how else to explain this "feeling" of grief, or regret, or remorse, or whatever, Taylor, who, at that very moment (i.e. as Valentina was assuming the position), was feeling, or at least appeared to be feeling, crouching in the dark with his back to the wall on the first floor landing of 16 Mulberry? He'd been there, crouching, for about three minutes, during which teams

---

Due to their Narcissistic personalities, any "relationships" they did establish tended to be strictly practical affairs, i.e., based on common needs or interests, or some other form of exploitation.

of Security Specialists had not come storming up the stairwell after him. There had been no second detonation, or missile strike, or
whatever it was. Once the noise of the pigeons had faded, he'd heard
the voices of people shouting, but he couldn't make out what they
were saying, or whether they were actually saying anything. Then,
after a minute maybe ... nothing, just the usual din of the Zone, and
the Viewers playing that funereal music, which he still didn't know
what was up with that. He figured he would wait there another few
minutes, then, assuming the coast was clear, he'd make his way down
and see what had happened.

In the meantime, there was this pain in his chest.

The pain was like a knot, or cramp, or dull, throbbing, grief-like
ache. It was located near his solar plexus, and ... OK, if you didn't
know any better, like if you hadn't read the DSM, you'd suspect that
it might have had something to do with the thing he had to do that
morning, the thing he was going to Cassandra's to do, which was
going to be, no doubt about it, The Worst Thing He Had Ever Done.
Or, had it been an authentic feeling and not some pseudo-emotional
trick that Taylor was playing on himself (and us), that it might have
had something to do with all the unrelenting human suffering Taylor
had suffered, and inflicted on others, throughout his meaningless, violent life. However (and according to the DSM, this last explanation
was a lot more likely), it was probably just some sentimental crap
(Anti-Social Persons being notoriously sentimental toward themselves), like his not being able to say goodbye to Alice Williams and
Rusty Braynard, who he was certain he was never going to see again,
and who despite the fact that they were, by this time, useless fuckups
and a burden to Taylor, he had known and lived with for thirty-five
years, and basically regarded as ersatz family.

The three of them had all grown up together in a former section
of the Southwest Quadrant, way out west, on Walt Whitman Road,
where Alice Williams and Rusty Braynard had always lived, and
were probably born, and where Taylor's mother moved them after
they fled the Jackson Avenue Houses. This, of course, was back in
the old days, back when there were still kids in the Zone, so before
the Jackson Avenue Uprising, which left them all orphans at the age
of ten.

After the Uprising, and the purge that followed (which more on that later on in our story), they'd made their way as best they could, living at first with a series of relatives, like Alice Williams' uncle Seamus, until he died of liver cancer, then Rusty Braynard's aunt Louise, until she got stabbed and bled to death, then various other aunts and uncles, most of whom weren't really aunts and uncles, just people Taylor's mother knew, or at least whose names and addresses she knew, and wrote down on the scrap of paper she pressed into his hand that night (i.e. the night before the Uprising started) and told him she loved him, and would always love him, and kissed him and sent him down to the basement.

Taylor couldn't remember exactly how many nights he'd spent in that basement, camped out under those metal stairs, eating some kind of energy bars that were dry and tasted like moldy bananas. Mostly he remembered the sounds ... the pop pop pop of UltraLite rifles, the whir and boom of the RPGs, the grinding tracks of the APCs, and, weirdly, the sound of a woman's voice, repeating some phrase he couldn't decipher, over and over, which many years later, out of nowhere, without even trying, he realized must have been a recording. However many nights it was, once the noise had finally died down, he'd waited, two or three hours, he thought, climbed the ladder that led to the street, pushed open one of the metal drop-doors, and crawled out onto Walt Whitman Road, or what was left of Walt Whitman Road, which was just a strip of smoldering shells of burned out buildings and piles of rubble. IntraZone Waste & Security Services Sanitation Disposal Technicians, dressed in their orange HazMat suits, were loading the bodies into vans and buses, zipping them into big yellow bags, and stacking them one on top of the other. He wandered up as close as he could, but he couldn't get close enough to see their faces. He checked inside the ruins of his building, and some other buildings, and the old bodega, and he walked all up and down Walt Whitman Road, but the Techs must have already bagged his mother, or else she'd been burned be-yond recognition ... in any event, he couldn't find her. He poked all around up and down the street, looking for something that might have belonged to her, like her glasses, or one of those hair things she wore, and he found a few globs of melted plastic, and some

shattered lenses, and a couple of teeth, but the glasses could have
belonged to anyone, and the teeth were too yellow to have been his
mother's. He found Alice Williams and Rusty Braynard perched on
Rusty Braynard's stoop, their faces blackened with soot and blood,
eating stale marshmallows out of a bag. Rusty Braynard's building
was gone ... gone, as in it was not there. All that was left was the
concrete stoop, its steps rising up from the ground toward nothing.
The memory of the two of them sitting there, looking like a couple
of shell-shocked squirrels, eyes glazed over, mechanically chewing
cheekfuls of sugary marshmallow goo, made Taylor smile in the dark
of the stairwell ... because who would have guessed the three of them
would have stayed together all these years, or that they'd have even
survived that long?

Somehow, against the odds, they had. They'd done it living off
their rations, mostly, and scamming and stealing when times were
tough, and sharing whatever they had with each other, and sticking together, no matter what. They'd moved like nomads from place
to place, one shithole tenement after another, two years here, three
years there, until finally, circa ten years back, they'd lucked into
Coco's at 16 Mulberry. Along the way, they had, of course, fought,
tortured, and otherwise inflicted the gamut of senseless pain on each
other, just like real siblings, Taylor imagined, and that's how they
felt, just like real siblings, except for the fact that Alice Williams
and Rusty Braynard fucked sometimes ... or used to anyway, back in
the day. Taylor doubted either one of them could fuck themselves,
much less each other, strung out as they were by then. He wondered
what would become of them now ... how long they would make it
without him.

For some strange reason he remembered the time, back when they
were all in their twenties, when this gang of assholes trapped Alice
Williams and Rusty Braynard in a basement on Drake Street. Taylor
couldn't remember whether they had chased them down there or
had found them down there, but what they did was, they stripped
them naked, tied them to this set of pipes down there, and took turns
beating on Rusty Braynard with a piece of rebar until he bled from
the ears. They broke his jawbone in three or four places, fractured his
skull, fucked up his shoulder, did a number on his cervical vertebrae,

serious Class 3 Anti-Social stuff. Once they were done with Rusty Braynard, they took turns raping Alice Williams. They raped her in every hole she had. They did this several times a day, switching positions, for multiple days. The way they did it was, they bent her over this metal work table that was stained with oil, and the top of which was just about the length of her torso, and they raped her two at a time like that. Whichever asshole was standing in front of her would hold her head up by the hair with one hand, press the knife to her throat with the other, and warn her she had better not bite down ... which Alice Williams later said she wished she had, but never did.

After they didn't come home for a week, Taylor went out looking for them. He talked to some people who knew some people who'd heard some shit and, long story short, he found them down there in that basement on Drake Street, brought them home, and cleaned them up. Alice Williams couldn't walk for a month. Taylor had to pick her up and carry her down the hall to the bathroom. He held her head while she peed and shat, which made her scream just something awful, then he carried her back down the hall to the bedroom. After she had drifted off again, he went back down the hall once more and cleaned up the blood she had left on the toilet. He did this daily, for over a month. They had to spoonfeed Rusty Braynard until his jaw reset itself, kind of, which gave him that kind of bulldog look, and the exaggerated frontal lisp he spoke with. He never did get his hearing all back, but after a couple of difficult months, he started to be able to talk again, some, and Taylor and Alice Williams figured he made as much sense as he ever really had, which wasn't ever really all that much.

Once they were more or less out of the woods, Taylor went out and talked to some people, and found out who the assholes were, which it turned out they were some badass crew from the Douglass Morrison-Witherspoon Projects. He scoped them out for a couple three nights, laid in wait for them, one by one, whacked them upside the head to stun them, walked them down to that same Drake Street basement (i.e. as if they were drunk and he was helping them home) and tied them to that same set of pipes down there. It took him nearly a week in all, the last one being the hardest to ambush, but finally, early one Sunday morning, he had all four of them tied up together, side by side on that set of pipes, their arms stretched out and tied to the pipes and their asses on the ground in a seated position. He tortured them a while before he killed them, which normally wasn't Taylor's thing, but he made an exception for these particular assholes. He didn't torture them fancy or anything. All he did was, he found the rebar that they must have used on Rusty Braynard, and he used it, in kind of a surgical fashion, to shatter their knees and elbows and ribs, and crush their balls, and knock some teeth out, and to otherwise cause the asshole in question to experience prolonged and unimaginable pain. He did this to them one by one, working his way down the line of assholes. That way, he figured, the other assholes (not the first one, but that couldn't be helped) could see what they had coming to them, and maybe even reflect a little on what they had done to Alice Williams, which in Taylor's book was way over the line. He figured they had maybe reflected some, on account of how they got all quiet and just kind of sat there, shitting themselves, as he whaled on whichever asshole it was whose turn it was to get his balls crushed and elbows broken and knees turned to mush. After whichever asshole that was was all done blubbering and whining and begging, and looked like maybe he was going to pass out, Taylor got himself a good hold on the rebar, gripping it like a baseball bat (or on second thought probably more like a golf club, not that Taylor had ever held one), and he swung it into the asshole's face, over and over, just as hard as he could. He did that until he was fairly certain you couldn't tell who it was anymore, not so much to hide their identities, because nobody was going to miss these assholes ... it was more like he wanted to erase their identities, to erase who they were, or what they were, as if they weren't just these four assholes, but were parts, or nodes, of some fucked-up something Taylor hated, and had always hated ... something he couldn't put into words, something that had always been there, and would always be there, but shouldn't be there, and if he just swung that piece of rebar harder, and harder, and harder, and harder, he could kill that thing, or part of that thing, or hurt it, or turn back time ... or something. He remembered asking them some special question, chanting it each time he swung the rebar ... but now he couldn't remember what it was, or whether it was even words he was saying, or shouting, or screaming, or whatever he was doing ... whatever. It didn't matter what it was. All that had happened back in some other lifetime.

Now, the kicker was, a few years later, Taylor found out the whole misadventure had basically been about Plastomorphinol. Apparently, the assholes he'd killed in the basement were this crew of black market Plasto dealers, who were working their way up out of the projects, who Alice Williams and Rusty Braynard had ripped off two or three weeks before, which rip-off, according to Alice Williams, they had perpetrated purely out of desperation, and only after having been ripped off themselves by one of Rudy Rebello's associates, as to whose whereabouts Rudy Rebello swore he did not have a clue ... all, or most of which, coming, as it did, from Alice Williams and Rusty Braynard, if not a total crock of horseshit, was, at minimum, highly suspect. The thing that made it highly suspect, notwithstanding the well-known fact that Rudy Rebello was a spineless weasel and soulless scumbag of the lowest order, was that Alice Williams and Rusty Braynard, ersatz family and all that they were, were degenerate Plastomorphinol users ... and had been for going on twenty-five years.

Plastomorphinol, a semi-synthetic alkaloid derivative analgesic (also known as Diplastomorphinol), was sold throughout the Zone to registered users (in carefully regulated quantities, of course) at authorized pharmacies like CRS. They sold it in market-researched packaging with colorful graphics and fanciful brand names, but all it was was straight up Plasto. Something like ninety percent of the 3s in the Zone were registered Plasto users. Zero percent of 1s and 2s were, as registering as a Plasto user earned you a Class 3 designation and a relocation to Sector C. The 3s, however, were already 3s, and were already living in Sector C, and, basically, didn't have shit to lose, so anyone who could walk, limp, or otherwise get to their local pharmacy and sign their name, or their mark, or whatever, had registered as a Plasto user. Registered users who weren't actual users sold their allotments to the black marketeers, who marked them up and sold them on to registered users who were actual users, whose habits almost invariably exceeded their official allotments, and who were Plasto fiends.

Alice Williams and Rusty Braynard were registered users who were actual users. The way that worked was, once a week, so every Tuesday morning, officially, they would roll out of bed at 0530, dig out their CRS IDs, don their yellow polyester track suits, which hadn't been washed in several years, and which Taylor could smell from across the room, and set out walking, or steal a couple bikes, and set out riding, to the CRS. They would get back right around 0900 (or earlier if they pinched the bikes), their skin all red and dry from heatstroke, clutching their plastic CRS bags. They'd come in, not say a word to anyone, strip off their smelly neon track suits, get back into the bed they shared, another greasy old worn-out futon, exactly like Taylor's, except on the floor, and cook and shoot up Diplastomorphinol. Then they'd just slump there against the wall, mouths hanging open, hair all stringy, reeking something awful in the heat, and stare into space through their half-closed eyelids, just having the time of their lives, apparently.

Taylor had done his share of substances, amphetamines, mostly, and some MDLX, and he more or less regularly drank like a fish, but he'd never gone in for Diplastomorphinal, or any of the other synthetic opiates the In-Zone doctors indiscriminately prescribed. Despite its unimaginably euphoric and instantly addictive analgesic effects (which Taylor had experienced on numerous occasions, recovering from various lacerations, puncture wounds, fractures, and so on), the problem he had with shooting Plasto, aside from the lifelong addiction thing, was that it made you stupid and unable to fuck.

Taylor, generally, wanted to fuck. He wanted to fuck first thing in the morning ... OK, not like the second he woke up or anything, but generally pretty soon after that. And later, after he had rested a while. And then later, again, if he could possibly manage. And, OK, he wasn't a kid anymore, so that third round was mostly a thing of the past, and the second was kind of fifty-fifty, but unless he had gone out the night before and drunk himself into a walking coma, he was usually up for his morning fuck ... which was how this whole disaster had started. It was also why (and this made him laugh), had this been any other Tuesday morning, he'd have been, you guessed it, on his way to Cassandra's ... which he was, of course, on his way to Cassandra's, just not for the usual ruttish reason. But normally that would have been the reason. To get his rocks off. To get his nut. Because despite the fact that he'd been doing Cassandra for going on over ten years at this point, and that he mostly spent his days with Cassandra (because you couldn't go out in the daytime anyway), and, all right, he sometimes picked up her groceries, and they nursed each other when they were sick, and so on ... despite all that, which, were we not discussing a couple of Anti-Social Persons, might have resembled the two of them being in love, or even, you know, married, to Taylor that was all it was ... i.e., scoring, screwing, boning, fucking.

Which, OK, so much for Taylor's regard for women, or utter lack thereof, and his inability to maintain relationships. The point is, had this been any other Tuesday, that (i.e., sex) would have been the reason he was currently on his way to Cassandra's (which he wasn't ... he was still crouched down in the stairwell, pressing his finger into that pain in his chest). That, and because it was Tuesday, officially, and Alice Williams and Rusty Braynard would be lying around on the nod all day, stinking the place up something awful, and who could possibly sleep next to that? That, and the fact that Meyer Jimenez, if Taylor went out and sat in the kitchen, would want to sit across from Taylor, sweating all over the kitchen table, and lecture Taylor on the finer points of assorted topics of his expertise, which lecturing often lasted hours and involved going off on various tangents, which led to various other tangents that seemed to have nothing to do with each other, but then somehow invariably led to his theories on the definitely almost imminent purge of all Class 3 Anti-Social Persons by the Hadley Corporation of Menomonie, Wisconsin,* which hadn't been based there for several centuries, and maybe had never been based there at all ... all of which Taylor had already listened to Meyer rant about a thousand times.

That, and just Cassandra Passwaters.

Cassandra Passwaters was an A.S.P. 1. She was one of the "Thirties," which meant she was thirty, or rather, it meant she was under forty. In Cassandra's case it meant she was thirty. Due to Ordinance 119, the Thirties were last A.S.P. generation ... or, technically speaking, the last decennium. Cassandra Passwaters, born, officially, thirty

* _Wisconsin, or The Badger State, was one of the former federal states of the former United States of America._

years before, on New Year's Eve, had just made the cut and was, quite possibly, the best piece of A.S.-ass in the Zone. She was blond, full-lipped, ripe, luscious, had her own room in a shared apartment, and a weakness for A.S.P. 3s like Taylor. Taylor had been indulging this weakness, mornings, as soon as she got home from work, and afternoons, before she went back to work, on a more or less totally monogamous basis for going on over the past ten years. Which isn't to say he hadn't occasionally indulged the weaknesses of other women, like when he and Cassandra were fighting, for example, or when he was drinking, or Cassandra was working ... it was just that none of these other women whose weaknesses Taylor only occasionally indulged meant the slightest thing to Taylor. Certainly none of them even remotely approached Cassandra when it came to sex.

Cassandra Passwaters reeked of sex. Literally. It wasn't her fault or anything. It was some kind of weird pheromonal condition that made men want to just fuck her senseless if they got within three or four meters of her. Fortunately, this hadn't been a problem for Cassandra, who had no qualms at all about sex, or with using sex to get what she wanted, or manipulating 3s like Taylor with sex. Not that that was all it was ... no, Cassandra thoroughly enjoyed having sex. She didn't do drugs, or drink, hardly, so sex was her primary source of pleasure. It wasn't like she was addicted to sex, or some kind of nymphomaniac or anything. She wasn't. She was simply an earthy person, a sensuous person, with a carnal nature, a deeply wanton and lascivious nature, who wanted Taylor to fuck her brains out. Cassandra was very clear about this. She wanted Taylor to fuck her brains out in a totally Class 3 Anti-Social fashion, to finger and lick her until she came repeatedly, gasping, screaming, and ultimately laughing (she'd have these laughing fits when she came), and then fuck her from behind, and spank her, spanking her while he fucked her senseless, and not just because he liked it that way, but because she also liked it that way, and because that seemed to Cassandra Passwaters like one of the most natural ways to do it, and the way most other animals did it ... well, OK, maybe without the spanking, but rough, not like gentle, or nice, the way the Normals in the RomComs did it, and real, not all fake and show-offy, the way the ones in the pornos did it, the ones where they always kept switching positions, which it always seemed to Cassandra Passwaters like maybe they had somehow forgotten how it worked and were trying to remember through trial and error, and so were being, like, all deliberate about it, stopping and checking every few seconds to see whether maybe *that* was it, or *this* was it, or *that* was it, which it didn't ever appear to be it, the way they kept stopping and turning around and trying to get the angles just right, then going at it like that for a while, but no, that wasn't it either, and then switching back around to the other way again, which already hadn't worked before, and then finally looking into the camera plaintively, as if they were hoping the camera operator, or someone there on the porno set, would call a ten-minute break or whatever and explain to them how to do it already. It all seemed terribly complicated, and if there was one thing Cassandra Passwaters definitely was not, it was complicated. Which Taylor generally liked in a woman, not being all that complicated himself. Not that he was dumb or anything. He wasn't. Neither was she for that matter. They both just liked to keep things simple, and clear, and, well, uncomplicated.

So how, Taylor wanted to know, had everything gotten so fucking complicated, so unbelievably and hopelessly complicated, complicated to the point where now, there he was, on his way to Cassandra's, not to get laid, as he would have been normally, but to do this horrible fucking thing ... the very horrible fucking thing he'd been desperately trying to keep from happening for the better part of the last eight months? How did that make any sense ... in any version of fucking reality?

Fuck it, he thought. He forced himself up, groped his way down the stairs in the dark, stepped out onto the concrete stoop, and took a big whiff of rotting garbage. There, in the brume and din of the morning, was Mulberry Street in all its glory. Assorted Anti-Social Persons were pushing and dragging their carts of groceries ... cans of stew, soup, beans, sacks of rice, spoiling produce, and various other consumer products they had bought at the Jefferson Avenue market. Other Anti-Social Persons were out on the stoops of their buildings, smoking. Pigeons were perched on lintels, cooing. Rats of serious size were scurrying ... the usual mis en scène of the Zone. Up on the corner, Herman the Wino, who was well over ninety, and toothless, and blind, was hunkered down over a hole in the sidewalk, trying to defecate into the sewer. Off in the distance the Public Viewers were running what looked like archival footage of some old Normal business asshole who Taylor thought he vaguely recognized and didn't give two shits about. The funereal music they had been playing earlier had morphed into some sickeningly syrupy fascist sentimental horseshit ... the kind of horseshit they normally played when some rich Normal asshole died.

"The fuck's going on?" he inquired of Claudia.

Claudia was sitting on the stoop to his left, wearing some little nothing dress that showed off her enormous tits, which were still pretty good and not that saggy. Taylor hadn't noticed her at first, ghostlike, blending into the shadows, like you got after tripping on MDLX. Her gaze was fixed on the eastern horizon, where, now, against the predawn glow, a massive column of smoke was rising, and choppers and UAVs were circling ...

"Something blew up," Claudia stated the obvious.

People tended to state the obvious coming down from MDLX. The stuff was basically a tricked-out version of pharmahuasca, with a nitrating agent, that ripped your soul clean out of your body and showed it to you for forty-five minutes, after which, for the next six hours, you needed to fuck more or less continuously. It left you virtually dead in the head, as in reading random signs out loud, or saying the names of whatever you saw, which didn't make for such great conversation ... not that Claudia had ever been famous for her conversational skills or anything.

Taylor patted the top of her head as he slipped down the steps of the stoop and past her. He set out walking, north-northwest, into the tide of oncoming shoppers, just like every other Tuesday morning, and, weirdly, at least for those first few moments, as he dodged the carts and bikes and bodies, it almost felt like any other morning, except for the one significant difference. That difference being his acute awareness that he was never, ever, going to do this again (i.e. walk this stretch of Mulberry Street, or anything else he had ever done), because at some point on this particular morning, probably right around 0730, he was going to disappear from the face of the Earth, and presumably the rest of sentient existence ... and that would be the end of Taylor's story. First, he had to do this horrible thing, which he definitely was not looking forward to, after which he would have to run, and there wasn't anywhere to run but in circles, and hide, and you couldn't hide forever. No, sooner or later (probably sooner) Security Services were going to get him. They were going to detain him, and torture him, and kill him, and this was assuming they didn't spot him and shoot him down right on Jefferson Avenue, or vaporize his ass with a Godsend missile ... or whatever, the details didn't matter ... whatever happened, however this ended, whether he ended up making the news, another A.S.P. gone haywire and put down by Security Services, or just vanished without explanation, the only ones who would ever know the truth of what had actually happened, and how, and where, and why it had happened, were not his friends, or anyone he knew, but were whichever soulless fucks it was at the Hadley Corporation of Menomonie, Wisconsin that took care of all that kind of shit, the official accounts of what had happened, or hadn't happened, or might have happened, but then later would turn out not to have happened, which ... fuck it, by that time no one would care. Taylor could almost see them sitting there, in their ergonomic chairs in their air-conditioned offices, sitting there in their rows of cubicles, pushing buttons, following orders ... the meek who had inherited the Earth ... or who believed they had inherited the Earth, when, really, apart from their clothes, houses, haircuts, holidays, money, and gadgets, they were no more free than Taylor was, and were just as doomed as Taylor was ... so what did their haircuts and holidays matter? Because what did anything fucking matter? In a hundred years they would all be dead, the A.S.P.s, Variant-Positives, Homo sapiens sapiens, the whole fucking race ... at which point, what was left of the world, suffocating shithole that it was, would devolve to the Clears, and they were welcome to it. So what did it matter what he did, or who knew the truth, or who told his story, or what the point of any of it was ... or whether he even made it to Cassandra's?

It didn't.

It didn't matter to anyone.

Nothing fucking mattered to anyone.

Nothing mattered.

And yet it did.

And, see, here was another weird thing about Taylor that wasn't
covered in the DSM. Despite his Anti-Social nature, and inability
to form relationships, and empathize, and love, and all that, and in
spite of the crushing emotional weight of the utter pointlessness of
pretty much everything, Taylor felt he had to do this. He owed it to
someone, or something, to do this ... to Cassandra, yes, but not just
Cassandra ... something bigger than himself or Cassandra, something, or someone, who was looking down, or in, or out of some
other place, and keeping score, or track, or something ...

What?

Fuck if Taylor knew.

Something for which he had no words.

He knew a few things it definitely wasn't. It wasn't God, or the
One Who Was Many, or whatever nonsense the Normals believed
in, or The Fatal Contradiction of the Corporatist System, which
the morons in the A.S.U. believed in, or whatever impenetrable
mindfucking nonsense weirdos like Meyer and Sarah believed in,
or didn't believe in, as they liked to stress, because nothing was true
or real, or whatever, and everything always came down to faith, not
faith in some god or ultimate principle, like Fate, Truth, Desire, or
Power, but faith in some fucking unnameable something, which they
claimed, this faith, could alter reality, not virtual reality, actual reality,
which according to Sarah was not reality ... or was reality, was the
only reality, but was just as virtual as virtual reality, a manifestation of
collective will, or the current limit of our imagination ... which, OK,
was not remotely helpful, and was anti-helpful, and the opposite of
helpful, and none of which, not one fucking iota, had any bearing
whatsoever on staying alive for the next sixty minutes ... and see? It
was just this sort of thinking, this pondering the fucking meaning of
everything, of faith, and reality, and everything else, that had gotten
Taylor into this mess. Because what the fuck did it possibly matter
whether, or why, it mattered to Taylor, or to some unnameable spiritual something, or cosmic teleological principle, that you couldn't
even fucking talk about? It didn't. None of this fucking mattered.
All that mattered was the here and now. That fucking doorway. This
fucking step. These fucking rooftops, right fucking here. Not all this
ontological horseshit, but were there fucking snipers up there? Right

up there on those fucking rooftops. And whether that half-second flash of light that third-floor window across the street had just now reflected was a searchlight catching the lens of one of their high-powered scopes. And what about this fucking guy over here, with the sunflower shades, whose shoes were too good, who Taylor had never seen in the Quarter, and was he going to suddenly pull an UltraLite MiniMac 16 rifle out of that fucking cart he was pushing? Which ... OK, it didn't look like he was, because now he was heading up the steps of that building. Still, the point was, he could have, easily, anytime during the last few seconds, while Taylor had just been strolling along, his head going round and round and round with all these pointless thoughts and questions ... which, OK, this was it right here. This was the fucking problem right here ... all this fucking thinking about everything. This was how everything had gotten so complicated.

Taylor extracted his head from his ass, paused on the corner of Radisson and Mulberry, turned back and took one lingering look, a goodbye look, down Mulberry Street. It looked strangely smaller, like some kind of mock-up ... strips of tenements made of paper, a rendering half remembered from a dream. Claudia was there on the steps where he'd left her. It looked like she was just painted in there, a minor detail in some elaborate triptych. Coco was standing on the stoop behind her, waving hello or goodbye to someone across the street who Taylor couldn't see. Alice Williams and Rusty Braynard, unidentified punk in tow, were creeping, albeit in their bright yellow track suits, the two of which just about glowed in the dark, across the street to steal some bikes, trying their best not to look suspicious. They were weaving their way through the soft parade of shadows, shades, the shapes of shoppers, dragging their carts and bags up the street, making their way up the steps of their buildings, and into their doorways, and disappearing. Herman the Wino was down on the ground, pants and skivvies around his ankles, calling out to God, or someone, to help him up, which no one was doing. Off to the east, day was breaking ... the first malignant fissure of sunlight softening the hard rectilinear edges of rooftops, billboards, and Public Viewers forming a horizon across the Zone. The thick black column of oily smoke was rising over the Southeast Quadrant, mushrooming up into itself ... something was definitely going on. It was too much smoke for a missile strike, and those choppers were on the hunt for someone, the odds were just some random assholes who'd blown up a clinic and the fire had spread, but something about it didn't feel quite right.

Taylor stood there on the corner, sweating, and fighting down a wave of nausea, watching the smoke and the choppers and ... it felt like there was this hiccup in time, or maybe his mind just skipped a beat, or something, because now there was nothing but static, a blizzard of blinding blue-white light, and peals of piercing high-pitched feedback reverberating off of every surface ... it wasn't Gabriel's horn or anything. It was coming from the screens of the Public Viewers, and the video billboards, and PSA screens, and every other liquid crystal, and plasma, and light-emitting diode, and electroacoustic transducer in the Zone ... the entire IntraZone Content grid. It was all going haywire, all at once.

Variant Correction

Out in the Residential Communities, which, incidentally, also formed a series of more or less concentric rings, or circles, or semi-orbiculate shapes, radiating outward, away from the Zone, the Normals, those who were still at home, and whose condo balconies, or winter gardens, offered a view toward the Zone, watched the light show with rapt fascination. None of them had ever seen anything like it. Some of them tried to film it with their Viewers and fleep or tweak the pictures to their Friends. Others just stood there staring, baffled. Several people fleeped, or tweaked, that they thought it was some new form of lightning that emanated upwards out of the earth, or some kind of corporate art installation, or that they had not the faintest clue what it was. Whatever it was, it was certainly pretty, the way the lights kept flashing and flickering, but it didn't seem to be building toward anything, or at least not in any kind of linear fashion. After a few minutes, most of them tired, and turned their attention back to their Viewers.

The perspective was better from Center City, the innermost ring of Residential Communities, the one immediately surrounding the Zone, where the Variant-Positive manual laborers were loading their tools into the back of their work vans, prominently branded copolymer workshirts and coveralls already soaked through with sweat, and the hordes of baristas, stock clerks, checkers, packers, drivers, and healthcare aides were filing through the rows of body scanners in the metal doorways of their affordable housing, or making their way down the buckling sidewalks, their heads tilted upward to watch the light show, whispering guesses as to what it might be. Standing behind them, just off the sidewalks, safe from the sweltering morning heat inside their tubular ThermaSoak shelters, their physically perfect, immaculately groomed, serenely silent, blue-eyed children, Clarions all, observed their movements with an almost feline concentration, completely ignoring the lights in the sky ... which were obviously nothing but video static. One by one, the private school-trams glided to a stop in front of the shelters. The doors whooshed open, blasting the passing commuters with gusts of arctic air. The children boarded in an orderly fashion, single file, according to age, the younger ones turning and waving goodbye to their sweat-drenched Variant-Positive parents.

Meanwhile, in an undisclosed location, a team of three Security Specialists, outfitted in their matte black SecPro Systems lightweight, puncture-proof body armor, watched as Valentina changed into the off-white loose-fitting cotton pants and matching top they had given her to wear. She couldn't see their eyes through their visors, which were tinted black to keep out the sun, but they didn't appear to be terribly impressed with either her breasts or abdominal scar, which she noted appeared to be healing nicely. After she dressed, they fitted her wrist with a nylon In-Transit ID bracelet, and walked her down a long white hallway and into what looked like a service elevator, the walls of which were lined with the same material they had used in the pink padded room. They rode the elevator down to a sub-basement, walked her out, and loaded her into an unmarked black Security vehicle, a mid-size van with tinted windows and flip-down seats that were bolted to the walls. The Security Specialists climbed in with her. They strapped her in and slid the doors closed. The driver, who she could not see, drove them out of the underground garage and onto whatever street they were on ...

Wherever it was was somewhere down in the business district, where no one lived. It looked like early morning out there, an hour or so before sunrise, she guessed. Crews of sanitation technicians dressed in day-glow yellow spacesuits, some of them certainly Anti-Socials, were pressure cleaning the empty sidewalks, swinging their nozzles methodically back and forth through the mist like foraging insects. The video billboards were advertising some brand of extra-strength laxative for dogs ... or something, the van was moving too fast. They were speeding up some four-lane avenue, the mirrored façades of whose corporate towers were screening movies of other movies in which a series of flat black vans were driving past a number of glass and chromium buildings that all looked the same. The van slowed down and made a right and picked up speed and now they were on some other unknown four-lane avenue. They passed a Mister Victory restaurant, a Lucian's Luggage, a Big-Buy Basement, another long stretch of office buildings ... the movie of the van in the mirrors resumed. She sat there, strapped into her seat, watching a series of ever smaller silently speeding flat black vans, inside of each of which she was, recede forever into infinity.

Valentina knew that something was wrong with her head ... but she didn't know what. She knew who she was, and where she was. She was in an unmarked Security vehicle. At some point during the recent past, she'd thought she remembered remembering why she was in that unmarked Security vehicle, and where it was taking her, but now she'd forgotten. It felt like this was possibly not the most important thing she'd forgotten, but it was up there pretty high on the list. It wasn't so much that her memory was gone as that what was there was hopelessly scrambled. Also, she guessed, it came and went, so that what she thought she remembered now, later, she wouldn't remember at all ... by which time, of course, it wouldn't matter.

Two of the three Security Specialists, who were all still wearing their puncture-proof armor, were sitting across from her, staring right at her. Or at least it seemed like they were staring right at her. She couldn't see their eyes through the visors. The other one was sitting on the seat to her left. He appeared to be looking straight ahead. Maybe he was watching the movie. No one was talking. The driver was driving.

The van took a left onto Lomax Avenue, and ... OK, now she knew where she was. She was out on the northeast end of Lomax, numbers descending, so heading downtown. She also remembered where she was going, sixty kilometers south-southwest to the 23rd A.S.P. Quarantine Zone ... to live out the remainder of her natural life. She couldn't remember exactly why she was going to do that, but she knew she was. She remembered signing some digital forms, and the Clears ... yes, that was back in the hospital ... and dreams, but they didn't feel like dreams, and doctors, and her mother was in there somewhere, and there was something she was supposed to do and ... whatever, that was all in the past. She could sift through the broken pieces later. All that seemed to matter now ... was now ... now ... now ... now ...

Seventy-five kilometers west-northwest, at 3258 Marigold Lane, Kyle would be up and sipping his decaf. She could picture him there at the kitchen table, tie flipped back across his shoulder, scanning his morning Content stream ... sad, yes, but that would pass, with the healing power of time and the One, and by now their psychiatrist, Doctor Graell, would have upped his Zanoflaxithorinal dosage, and prescribed whatever else he needed to help him through this transition experience. In time, and with the love and support of Families of Anti-Social Persons Anonymous, he would process his pain, and eventually forgive her, after which, maybe a year down the road, he'd meet someone else, and life would go on. Could he forgive her? He had to forgive her, or the pain and resentment would tear him apart. She prayed to the One to help Kyle forgive her ... but for what? What had she done, exactly? Something that had gotten her wounded. She could feel the tightness around her scar. She closed her eyes and tried to remember. She was walking down some desolate boulevard, or outdoor mall ... there were stores ... bodies ... or mannequins ... no. She couldn't remember. She prayed to the One to help her remember. She couldn't remember. She opened her eyes.

The van slowed down and came to a stop at the intersection of Lomax and Rollins. Valentina found herself staring directly into the street-level entrance of 6262 Lomax Avenue, a two hundred story priapic monument to corporate and architectural excess. No one ever used this entrance. Spotless chromium escalator tubes ran down from the marbled lobby to the Lomax/Rollins WhisperTrain Station, which was served by the Orange, Blue, and Green lines. The exterior doors were mirrored, of course, but she knew, right at that very moment, legions of perfectly normal people, with normal haircuts and normal jobs, were streaming up out of those escalator tubes, the walls of which were running commercials for pharmaceuticals, hair conditioners, Viewers, readers, anti-aging crèmes ... spilling out into the main floor lobby, which looked like the nave of some Gothic cathedral, except that all the mosaics were screens and there weren't any pews or sanctuary ... swarming off every which way like ants, who thanks to some form of insect radar never seemed to collide with each other ... filing into Pauline & Proust, Lindtner's, Barnaby's Bagel Emporium, C.G. Woo's, and Coco Rico, to purchase their individually shrink-wrapped fat-free ChocoLite black bean muffins, decaf mochas, and soy-milk lattes, smoothies with plastic see-through dome tops, protein drops, IQ boosters, 10-packs of Tim's "Ye Olde" breathmints ... filing through banks of check-out scanners, body scanners, iris scanners, weapons and explosives detectors, data collectors, counters, sensors ... smiling into the faces of other smiling, talking, walking, swarming, fat-free muffin purchasing people, actual people, who were actually there, but to whom they were not actually talking, talking as they were to other people who were not actually there, where they were, but were crossing some other luxurious lobby, similarly smiling and walking and talking.

Valentina hiccuped violently, belched, in a squawking chicken-like fashion, and launched into an uncontrollable, inappropriate fit of laughter.

"Are we going to have a problem, Ms. Briggs?" one of the Security Specialists asked her, reaching for his can of mace.

She shook her head, and tried to answer, to tell him they weren't going to have a problem, but she couldn't speak, and she could barely breathe, and, worst of all, she could not stop laughing.

Four months earlier, so in officially December 2609, H.C.S.T., a considerably better-dressed Valentina Briggs had entered this very marbled lobby, navigated these legions of people, taken the express to the 200th floor, and was sitting on the end of an S-shaped bank of ergonomic, flesh-tone, faux leather seating in the lobby of Paxton, Wills & Huxley, a Limited Liability Company. Paxton Wills, a leading provider of assisted reproductive services, and a member of the Hadley Medical Group, boasted a nearly perfect success rate on variant-corrected IVF for its healthy Variant-Positive clients. Being a member of Hadley Medical meant they were able to variant-correct their human embryos right there, in-house, eliminating any possible risk of unwanted in-transit embryo incidents. The Fosters, longstanding Paxton Wills clients, were entirely satisfied with the overall service, satisfied with the helpful staff, extremely satisfied with the end results, and would recommend them to friends and relatives. Six months prior, over gluten-free scones, Susan Foster had done just that.

The Paxton Wills lobby was tastefully done in a range of gentle, complimentary earth-tones, the lighting low, warm, and slightly yellow, the temperature exactly 20C. The AmbiMood Systems viewing screens were running a series of time-lapse dissolves of orchids, hibiscus, and red amaryllis, delicate petals shuddering open, against what sounded to Valentina like surf washing up on a white sand beach. The Christmas season was in full swing. A crawler above the reception area was running the latest retail figures. Sales were up. Confidence was high. Now was the time to secure your future. Paxton, Wills & Huxley wished you a peaceful, prosperous holiday season and hoped that the Light of the One Who Was Many would guide you upon your chosen Path(s).

"Valentina Briggs," the receptionist said.

Valentina glanced up and smiled. The receptionist smiled. They nodded at each other. Another satisfied Paxton Wills client seated across from Valentina, a birdlike woman with bright blue hair, who looked to be about six months pregnant, turned toward Valentina and smiled. Valentina returned the smile. She checked around the lobby quickly. There didn't appear to be anyone else in her immediate vicinity she needed to smile at, so she quickly saved the histology article she hadn't even started reading yet, dropped her All-in-One in her purse, and headed up toward the reception desk. Behind the desk, a bank of screens were running loops of smiling, blue-eyed, cooing, variant-corrected infants. She was almost about to smile at the infants, but she caught herself ... they were just on the screen.

Kyle was late, which was inconsiderate. He'd called en route, feeling just awful. Something about an algorithm for some retroactive conversion or something. He thought he had snoozed the reminder on his Viewer, when it turned out he'd actually turned it off. Valentina had forgiven him, of course, but now Kyle would have to forgive himself before he could really let go of his guilt, which, being Kyle, might take a while.

Karen, one of the physicians assistants, who was slightly overweight, and had had some work done, was standing there in the open doorway just to the right of the reception area, smiling warmly at Valentina. "Oh, are you all by yourself today?" she asked, hoping that Kyle was all right and there hadn't been some kind of horrible accident. Valentina explained about Kyle and the algorithm ... or whatever it was. Karen nodded. She understood. Karen was also Variant-Positive.

As they made their way down the plushly carpeted hallway of the consultation wing, Karen explained that Doctor Fraser was in with another client at the moment, but he would be in to see her just as soon he could, and that all Valentina's recent tests looked good, and she said that she liked Valentina's new outfit, and she wondered what Valentina used on her hair, because it always looked so full and silky, and Karen's hair was always so dry, no matter which conditioner she used. Valentina smiled, thanked her, and told her the name of her hair conditioner, which you couldn't always find in stores, but which Karen could probably get online, and which Valentina just totally swore by.

By this time, Karen had ushered her into one of the cosy little consultation rooms, where the Muzak was always so tasteful and soothing. She smiled, Karen did, and Valentina smiled, and Karen thanked her, and more smiling ensued, and finally Karen told her that they would show Kyle in just as soon as he arrived. Then she stepped out and closed the door. Valentina had always liked Karen. She liked all the other physicians' assistants. She liked Doctor Fraser. She liked the receptionists. Everyone at Paxton Wills was so nice.

Kyle, however, was now seriously late, which regardless of whatever algorithm, or whatever it was that had gone kablooey and needed his undivided attention, was inconsiderate, and narcissistic, and was on the verge of becoming a pattern. The simple fact of the matter was, Kyle had chosen to snooze his reminder rather than stop whatever he was doing, or hand it off to one of his interns, and get to Paxton Wills on time. Whatever it was that needed his attention, Valentina also needed his attention. This appointment had been scheduled three weeks in advance. They had talked about it just that morning, about how happy they were to be pregnant again, and how it was going to take this time, and how Valentina just felt that it had, and how thrilled Kyle felt that she felt that way, because he did too, and how he knew, despite whatever struggles she'd been having, that

everything was going to be OK, and so much better, once they started their family. And now, here he was, late, and here she was, alone
with her feelings, which were definitely veering towards resentment
and away from detachment, compassion, and acceptance, which he
knew full well was toxic for her, especially given her recent struggles,
and her family history, and all the rest of it.

She closed her eyes and said her mantra.

"The loving, compassionate oneness of the …"

The reminder on her All-in-One went off … wind chimes in a
gentle sea breeze. It was time to take her Zanoflaxithorinal. She got
her pill bottle out and took one.

Three weeks earlier, the same Valentina, consciously sedated, her
feet in stirrups, had watched between her upraised knees as Doctor
Fraser carefully inserted his catheter into her cervical canal and
advanced it into her uterine cavity. The catheter was loaded with
three human embryos, which Doctor Fraser had grown in a dish.
Following a standard ten-day course of ovarian follicle stimulating
hormones, along with various hormone antagonists, all of which
were completely routine, Doctor Fraser had commenced ovulation,
transvaginally retrieved sixteen of her eggs, placed them into a culture medium, carefully added some spermatozoa technicians had
sperm-washed out of Kyle's semen, and allowed them to incubate
for eighteen hours. After confirming the appearance of pronuclei,
certified technicians had transferred the eggs into a special growth
solution, and allowed them to culture for another two days. Once
they had, Doctor Fraser, himself, had gender-selected and variant-corrected the three most promising XX embryos for manual
transfer into Valentina's uterus. This is what was happening now.

"Better to lie back and relax, Ms. Briggs. You're going to strain
your neck that way." Karen gripped and gently guided Valentina's
head down onto the table, so that now she was staring straight up
at the ceiling, which at the moment was out of focus. Doctor Fraser
was between her legs, working his catheter up inside her, trying to
get his angle just right. Real-Time footage of her uterine canal, shot
by a camera in the tip of the catheter, was running on the screen of
an instrument panel, which Valentina could not see.

"Beautiful," Doctor Fraser said. "Yes. OK. Here we go now."

Doctor Fraser was Valentina's age, tall, trim, a swimmer probably. He looked like a model in an underwear ad. His hands were warm, firm and gentle, even inside those neoprene gloves. He'd stand there, in his surgical outfit, between her naked, upraised legs, and explain what he was going to do to her, and how it was going to feel, and so on, which Valentina always enjoyed, not on account of what he was saying ... mostly just because she just liked Doctor Fraser.

Being a medical professional herself, Valentina understood the process, as did virtually every other Normal, even if they didn't quite get all the details or know all the Latinate names of things. It would have been rather odd if they hadn't. Assisted Reproductive Services, widely available to healthcare consumers for four or five hundred years at least, had, since the advent of variant-correction, become the virtually exclusive means of procreation for Variant-Positive parents throughout the United Territories. How that had happened went something like this ...

The year after Valentina was born, so 2569, 5282, or The Year of the Tapir, depending on the calendar, the team of Geiger, Chao, and Fournier, working on a grant from Pfizer-Lockheed, finally established a definitive link between sub-normal variants of the MAO-A gene and Anti-Social behavior in humans. The MAO-A (or "Warrior") gene had long been suspected as the primary locus of one or more genetic defects predisposing the human species to a host of Anti-Social disorders ... Oppositional Defiance Disorder, Anti-Social Personality Disorder, Borderline Personality Disorder, Negativistic Personality Disorder, Paranoid/Schizoid Personality Disorder, Conduct Disorder, Hyperactivity, the list went on and on, and on. According to the leading medical experts, generation after generation had suffered the effects of these various disorders. The history of the human race read like an in-depth pathology report. From its outbreak during the Early Bronze Age to its critical stage in the Age of Anarchy, the epidemic of Anti-Sociality had ravaged and emotionally crippled humanity, destroying entire civilizations, squandering irreplaceable resources, poisoning the seas, the land, and the air, wiping out countless species of animals, tearing apart societies, families, driving men and women alike to steal, murder,

rape, and torture, to senseless acts of political terror, civil unrest, malicious assembly, and other deviant and destructive behaviors ... but
now, finally, the link had been made, and finding a cure was just a
matter of time.

In the spirit of the scientific quest for knowledge, the team of
Geiger, Chao, and Fournier published the results of their research
online, foregoing any and all proprietary claims. Whereupon, en
masse, like a kettle of vultures, leading biotechnology firms, and the
bio-divisions of global conglomerates, like the Hadley Corporation
of Menomonie, Wisconsin, invested gadzillions in the race to de-
velop, patent, and be the first to offer, prenatal variant-correction
technology to the transterritorial consumer market. Given that
approximately ninety-nine percent of the global population had
sub-normal variants, the potential profits from variant-correction
were of a magnitude beyond calculation.

Valentina remembered the day that HH/BioTek GmbH, a formerly Austro-German subsidiary of the Hadley Corporation of
Menomonie, Wisconsin, announced the first successful correction of
sub-normal variants in human subjects. Naturally, no one understood
how HH/BioTek had achieved this success, their methods being
strictly proprietary, but that didn't matter, because a cure had been
discovered, and the all caps boldface BREAKING NEWS message ... CURE FOR ANTI-SOCIAL DISEASE, scrolled across
every screen in existence. Jubilant crowds poured into the streets,
celebrating like it was New Year's Eve. Prescheduled Content was
interrupted. Elated news readers sat there, live, interviewing anyone
remotely expert.

Valentina was only six years old, so she didn't understand all the
science at the time, but she knew that Anti-Social Disease was the
cause of everything bad in the world, and the reason that hundreds
of thousands of people had had to go live in the Quarantine Zones.
She had learned about the disease in school. She knew she had it.
Everyone had it. Her mother had it. Her father had it. So did her
teachers and her friends and their parents. It was why they all took
their medication, to keep them from doing and saying bad things,
and thinking bad things about other people, which the doctors
could tell if you were thinking those things. Mostly the medication

worked, but every once in a while on the news there'd be a story about some poor person who got real sick and did something bad and had to be sent away to the hospital, or sometimes to one of the Quarantine Zones.

"The disease is cunning," Ms. Johnston warned her.

Ms. Johnston was Valentina's first grade teacher. Valentina wasn't totally sure what "cunning" meant, but she knew it was bad, and she had to watch out, and take her medication, or she might start thinking and saying bad things. She didn't want to be sent away to the hospital or one of the Quarantine Zones. She wanted to stay with her mommy and daddy, and go to Playhouse Community Day School, and play with Zora, Tammy, and Gia, and not get sick and do something bad.

Sometimes Valentina's mommy forgot to give her her medication, and Valentina, who remembered religiously, would have to remind her mommy to do it. Other times it seemed like her mommy forgot to take her own medication, and she said these things to Valentina's daddy that seemed like maybe they were sick and bad. Whenever that happened, Valentina's daddy would hold his hands up in front of his chest and try to make her sit down and be quiet.

"Lower your voice," he'd whisper to her. Then he'd turn up the volume of their In-Home Viewer. He did that so the neighbors wouldn't hear and have to report her mommy to Security. Valentina was glad he did that. She wanted her mommy to take her pills, which it seemed like, eventually, she always did, because later she would seem to be happy again and wouldn't be saying those things to her daddy.

Then the doctors found a cure, and no one had to be sick anymore. Valentina asked her mommy when they could go and get their genes fixed.

"We can't, sweetheart," her mommy told her.

"Why?"

"Because it doesn't work like that."

"Why not?"

"Because of science, baby. We have to keep taking our medication."

"Forever?" Valentina asked her mommy.

"Yes, sweetheart. Forever and ever."

"Catherine," Valentina's daddy whispered.

"Catherine" was Valentina's mommy's name. Her daddy said it in that way he spoke when it seemed like her mommy was off her medication. They were sitting in the open kitchen area of the townhouse Valentina grew up in, in another Residential Community, almost exactly like Pewter Palisades, except with a different accent color.

"But the doctors cured the Anti-Socialty."

"Anti-Soci-al-ity, sunshine," Valentina's daddy corrected her. "Yes, they did. But what that means is, all the new babies will be born without it, and then their babies will be born without it, and then, one day, no one will have it."

"What about us?"

"We'll be just fine, hon. We'll just keep taking our medication."

Valentina's mommy coughed, or laughed, or some odd combination thereof. She pulled a used disposable tissue out of the pocket of her fuzzy bathrobe. The pockets of her bathrobe were full of those tissues.

"And then, one day, when you're a mommy, you can have corrected babies." She over-emphasized the word "corrected," smiling in that way that frightened Valentina. Then she hawked and spit into the tissue, and stuck it back into the pocket of her bathrobe. Valentina didn't get why she did that. Why didn't she just throw them away?

A few years after their historic breakthrough, HH/BioTek's bio-engineers perfected MAO-Variant Correction. Their techniques remained proprietary, but the basic science was something every medical professional learned in college. Valentina was no exception. In Anti-Sociality and Corrective Genetics, a sophomore-level survey course nominally taught by an adjunct professor with a Russian-sounding name who never appeared, and actually taught by graduate students, who sometimes got up on stage and lectured, but who mostly just streamed a lot of Content, Valentina learned the following: Monoamine oxidase A is a protein enzyme that degrades neurotransmitters, like norepinephrine, serotonin, and dopamine. The gene that encodes it, the MAO-A gene, lives on the short arm of the human X chromosome. People have different versions of this gene. These versions are commonly referred to as "variants." To tell one variant of the gene from another, you count the number of tandem repeats of sequences of genetic alleles, which are copies of your DNA, basically. People have different numbers of copies, two, three, four, five. Prior to HH/BioTek's discovery, geneticists believed that two to four copies was what was "normal" for the MAO-A gene. The geneticists believed this because two to four copies was what it turned out most people had. But then came the Pfizer-Lockheed research, and the findings of Geiger, Chao, and Fournier, which led to HH/BioTek's breakthrough, and the most successful biotechnology licensing franchise in human history.

What HH/BioTek's researchers had done, first in lab mice, later in humans, is copy and synthesize the MAO-A gene, lock in the number of DNA copies, knock out the gene in the Inner Cell Mass of some Day Six IV-fertilized embryos, insert their synthesized, variant-corrected MAO-A gene into the blastocysts, implant the embryos into a subject, and wait for nature to take its course.* The operation itself was simple, something that any competent genetic technician could handle in the space of an hour. What had taken so long in the lab to perfect was the synthesis of an encryptable gene which couldn't be copied by corporate rivals and that didn't cause some virulent strain of metastatic molecular cancer. They worked with the mice for a good ten years.

The final product was a perfectly healthy and otherwise normal common house mouse ... aside from several notable features. For one thing, this otherwise normal house mouse, which one of the geneticists christened "Leo," was exponentially more intelligent than your average beady-eyed laboratory rodent. They (there were twenty-six in all, so Leos 1 through through 26) navigated their little mazes in under half the time of a normal Mus musculus. Their reaction times and speeds were improved, as were their long-term memory functions. Their ability to follow simple commands and respond

---

* In addition to locking in the 4R allele, thus assuring a standardized variant sequence in association with the VNTR Region, a number of other adjustments had been made, all of which were proprietary, and so closely guarded corporate secrets. Isolated members of the scientific community had raised a few concerns at first, as had some members of the general public, regarding this apparent lack of transparency, but once the Internet and other mass media had been inundated with helpful features explaining how there was nothing to fear, these overly alarmist and borderline-paranoid naysaying voices soon fell silent.

to a range of meaningless stimuli, like flashing lights, was quite remarkable. All of which was certainly interesting, but given the state of bioengineering, IQ boosting, and genetic enhancement, was not exactly revolutionary.

What was, however, revolutionary, and changed the world as everyone knew it, was that HH/BioTek had engineered a creature completely devoid of aggression, and not just "active" or "predatory" aggression, but also "affective" or "reactive" aggression (i.e., elicited by fear or sense of threat, also known as "defensive" aggression).

Interestingly, this absence of defensive aggression did not mean that the Leo mice had been rendered incapable of self-defense. On the contrary, in batteries of lab experiments, the Leos, when predatorially aggressed by hostile uncorrected lab mice, exhibited a shockingly intelligent type of cooperative self-defensive behavior.

First, they formed an outward-facing circle, to keep the hostile intruders at bay. (Picture an impenetrable circular wall of raggedy yellow rodent teeth.) Then, by opening a gap in this "wall," which must have appeared to the less-intelligent predator mice as an exploitable weakness, they lured the aggressors, one by one, into the center of their defensive ring, then sealed the ring up tightly around them. Trapped inside and totally isolated, the aggressor mice were easily neutralized. Designated Leos chewed their throats out, while the other Leos maintained the defense, keeping the aggressors ignorant as to the fate of their now ex-comrades inside. Thus, the Leos gradually degraded the size of the hostile aggressor-mice group, eventually achieving numerical superiority, at which point they simply swarmed their remaining opponents ... and chewed their throats out as well.

But it wasn't the intelligence and cooperative behavior displayed by the Leos that was most remarkable. What was most remarkable was how the Leo mice successfully defended their phyletic social group (i.e. literally gnawing the aggressors' throats out ... in some cases actually severing their heads) without exhibiting any of the symptoms of predatory or affective aggression. In fact, during the entire experiment, their heart rate, blood pressure, and respiratory readings never once fluctuated, not one iota. The typical fight-or-flight response (or "stress response") was simply not there. They appeared to be utterly impervious to fear, and able to carry out acts of violence as calmly as one might flip a light switch.

Another interesting aspect of the Leos was their rather atypical sexual function. Which is to say, they procreated in more or less the usual fashion, but here, again, the behaviorists found, the typical neuro-affective activity accompanying coitus was absent or negligible. It wasn't that their pleasure centers weren't working. They definitely were. They registered pleasure. It was just that they registered sexual pleasure no differently than any other type of pleasure (feeding, for example, or grooming each other, or solving one of those spatial puzzles, or reacting to a sequence of flashing lights). Basically, they conducted the sexual act in the same Zenlike state of detachment they'd exhibited during the commission of violence, which violence, the behaviorists needed to emphasize, was initiated in reaction to a threat, so not aggressive, or in any way gratuitous.

And this, of course, was the point, after all. Left unmolested, fed and watered, the Leos were peaceful, cooperative creatures, highly sociable, easily trained, intelligent (although not terribly curious), and responsive to visual and verbal commands, and other types of exhortative stimuli. These traits were also the predominant features of the first generation of human subjects, which thanks to a global marketing effort soon became known as "Clarions" or "Clears."

The first few thousand successful births (i.e., outside the lab, to regular consumers) occurred when Valentina was eleven. She remembered the all caps BREAKING NEWS messages that appeared throughout the spring of that year. By summer, reports of additional births were appearing routinely in the normal news streams. HH/BioTek (now wholly-owned by the Hadley Corporation of Menomonie, Wisconsin's wholly-owned subsidiary, Clarion Corp., Inc.) began its global marketing campaign ... and the rest, as they say, was history.

By 2580, or 5293, or The Year of the Loris, depending on the calendar, when Valentina turned eighteen, variant-correction had become the norm throughout the United Territories. By the time she finished her medical studies and began her histopathological career, the number of births of uncorrected children had dropped to virtually zero.

Screens on the walls of the consultation room at Paxton Wills, where Kyle was late, and Valentina was waiting for Doctor Fraser, and for her meds to kick in, were running those loops of the infant Clears that the screens in reception had been running earlier. Their pallid, blue, equanimous eyes appeared to be staring directly at her. Other screens were running the standard archival footage of the Leo mice you saw on the science and medical channels. They were looking straight into the camera imperiously, wiggling their little rodential noses.

She took a deep breath and said her mantra. Any moment now the half a milligram of Zanoflaxithorinal she'd taken would go to work on her neurotransmitters and still the storm of thoughts in her head. Many of these thoughts were questions ... questions she had asked a thousand times, silently, safe in the dark of her mind, and had never been able to satisfactorily answer.

For example, the one that occurred to her now, as she watched two Leos placidly copulating, was what those behavioral geneticists had meant by the Leos' "atypical sexual response." This question wasn't haunting her or anything, but it occurred to her pretty much every time she saw this archival footage of the Leos, which she (and every other Normal) saw on a more or less daily basis. The atypical sexual response they'd described was what Valentina had always experienced while having sex with Kyle, or anyone. Of course it was. This was no mystery. Zanoflaxithorinal, if you stripped away all the added features, was basically an MAO-A inhibitor, which mimicked, as well as any compound could, the emotional state of the Clear Generation, and that of its progenitors, the illustrious Leos. She'd been on Zanoflaxithorinal forever. She'd been on it when she lost her virginity, and every time she'd had sex since then. She liked having sex. Sex was pleasurable. But then lots of things in life were pleasurable. Yoga. Meditation. Shopping. Work. Reading. Running. Eating. Watching Content. Seeing friends. Shopping. All of these things were pleasurable.

Any moment now the Zanoflaxithorinal would flood her brain with serotonin, and wave after wave of warm well-being would wash away all these negative thoughts, these obsessions, these phrases that stuck in her head ... like the one she'd first heard while watching the Leos copulating in that archival Content, years before, back at Gates University, which was playing inside her head right now ...

"Typical neuro-affective activity accompanying coitus absent or negligible ..." She could still hear the voice of whatever actress had done the narration, an Austrian woman, who she later suspected had done these ads for some kind of upscale carpet cleaner. She couldn't remember the name of the cleaner.*

Another question she could not shake, and which she swore her mother, Catherine, had asked her at some point during her early childhood (an event which Catherine had repeatedly denied), was why, if the One Who Was Many was infinite, indivisible, and multiplicitously molar, which meant that everything that was was perfect, and the infinite Paths of the Path(s) to Prosperity led one, not to some "higher" state of being, but simply to a state of Total Acceptance and Affirmation of what already was ... why weren't people already perfect? Why did their variants need correction? Why did anything need correction? She swore her mother had asked her this question. She'd asked it herself a thousand times. Here she was, asking it again. She did not want to be asking this question. She wished she'd never heard this question. She averted her eyes from the unblinking stares of the infant Clears in the video screens and prayed to the makers of Zanoflaxithorinal to hurry up and erase this question. The Austrian actress barked in her head.

"TYPICAL NEURO-AFFECTIVE ACTIVITY ..."

It wasn't that she didn't want this baby. She did. She desperately wanted this baby. Things were going to be so much better, once she had it ... her ... Zoey. It was just that, despite the fact she knew she needed to let all this go and surrender, she kept coming back to this irritating phrase, and wondering what it was, exactly ... or rather, wondering how it felt. She knew what it was. It was ugly, and sick. This TYPICAL NEURO-AFFECTIVE ACTIVITY was the type of neuro-affective activity Anti-Socials experienced when they had sex ... their brains were flooded with norepinephrine, serotonin, and

---

* Actually, she had read this phrase, as the archival Content was recorded in German. Later, having forgotten she'd read it, her memory had reassembled the moment, erasing the English subtitles she'd read and reinterpreting the German she'd heard as an Austrian accented woman speaking English.

other stress hormones, driving them into states of frenzy so that they didn't even look like people anymore. She'd seen enough lab films of A.S.P.s mating, their faces contorted into grotesque masks, the males just hammering away with their things, straining, grunting, the females screaming, gouging their fingernails into the backs of the males, occasionally drawing blood ... and the sounds they made as they reached their orgasms, and the way their eyes rolled back in their heads, obviously on the brink of seizure. She thought about the sex she'd had with Kyle, and, before Kyle, with his cousin, Greg Cramer. She thought about the sex she'd had in high school, with Donny Decosta, Cole Quintana, Sunil Walters, and Handrail Barkley, and a few other boys who she'd never mentioned to Kyle, and who didn't officially count. These boys had always been warm, gentle, and attentive to her sexual needs. They had kissed, caressed, and massaged each other, establishing physical and emotional trust, stroked or sometimes orally stimulated their respective genitals to sufficient states of genital arousal and lubrication, making eye contact at regular intervals, then inserted and performed the sexual act, which normally culminated in mutual orgasm, followed by a period of extended cuddling. All of it was textbook sex. Normal sex. Typical sex.

And this is what was eating at her. Not the sex ... the logic of it. Because what did the geneticists mean by typical? Typical in relation to what? If the Leos' neuro-affective activity during sex was somehow atypical, and the Clarions' genes had been modeled on the Leos' ... wasn't their neuro-affective activity during coitus also atypical? And what about her own neuro-affective activity, altered as it was by Zanoflaxithorinal? Didn't it follow that it was also atypical? But, again ... in relation to what? In relation to the A.S.P.s? No. That didn't make any sense. The only difference between the A.S.P.s and the Variant-Positives was pharmatherapy. They were all just Homo sapiens sapiens. They all had the same defective genes. The only difference was that the Anti-Socials were non-responsive to Zanoflaxithorinal, and every other MAO-A antagonist. So how could their neuro-affective activity during sex be considered typical and variant-corrected, or pharma-mitigated neuro-affective activity atypical?

Valentina did not know. Valentina was getting a headache. Her jaw was clenched. She was grinding her teeth. She suddenly felt extremely dizzy. Today was Wednesday ... Kyle was late. In addition to which she wasn't supposed to be asking herself these kinds of questions, or thinking all these negative thoughts. Not that there was any law against it. In the Age of the Renaissance of Freedom and Prosperity, everyone was free to think what they wanted, and ask whatever questions they wanted. It was just that some of these thoughts and questions, like the ones Valentina was entertaining, and had entertained more or less all her life, were extremely unhealthy, and were symptomatic of latent Anti-Social ideations ... which meant one's dosage of Zanoflaxithorinal, or whatever one was taking, should be increased.

Valentina went in her purse, got her pills out and took another one. Her hands were shaking. She closed her eyes.

"The loving, compassionate oneness of the ..."

Doctor Fraser burst into the room, reading her file, beaming warmly. He was wearing a watermelon Oxford shirt, which Doctor Fraser could get away with.

"All right. Looks like we got ourselves a winner."

Valentina opened her eyes. She smiled the smile she had, for months, been practicing in her bathroom mirror, alone, at night, while Kyle was sleeping. She felt like her chair had dropped into a hole that had opened in the fabric of space, down which she was being sucked by some bottomless black eternal nothing.

"The multiplicitous way of the One. The oneness of the ..."

Time had stopped.

Doctor Fraser, freeze-framed in place, was grimacing at her like a frightened baboon ... all of which were dead, of course. Half the planet Earth was dead. The Indian Ocean was probably boiling.

Valentina ordered time to resume its march ... it would not do this. Apparently she was now trapped inside some interdimensional transport capsule plummeting into some Boschian Hell where drooling animatronic infants materialized out of plasma screens gurgling horrible incantations in backwards Latin like demonic seraphim. It wasn't that she didn't want this baby. She did. She wanted it. She wanted it desperately. Everything was going to be OK, and so much better, once she had it ... her ... It. No. No, it was just this headache, and Kyle being late, and her mother, and her genes, and her family history ...

Doctor Fraser was grinning again. The masseter muscles in his face were moving. Apparently, time was back in business.

Valentina burst out laughing, laughing in Doctor Fraser's face. She had no idea why she was laughing. Nothing was even remotely funny.

Doctor Fraser grinned and beamed, mistaking her laughter for relief and joy. "Yes, I know, it's wonderful, isn't it?" he nodded, turning back to her file. "Let's see you again in a week, OK? We'll run a few tests, but don't you worry. Everything's fine. You're definitely pregnant."

The baby Clears were smiling at her. The Leos were wriggling their noses at her. Doctor Fraser was grinning at her. She heard a SNAP inside her head, and ...

The Heat

Meanwhile, approximately four months later, so back where we originally started, or shortly thereafter in any event, Taylor was still on his way to Cassandra's, or, rather, he was on his way there again. He was sticking to his usual route, as ordered, because despite that fire, or conflagration, that appeared to be spreading throughout the Southeast Quadrant, and those choppers swirling through the dirty column of thick black smoke that was rising out of it, and whatever, or whoever, had temporarily blown the entire Content grid ... no one was coming after him. No one was even tailing him. He hadn't seen Community Watcher one, which was kind of unsettling given that they'd been on him for weeks now, but he shrugged that off. The sky to the north, his current bearing, was quiet, as in dark, or relatively dark, as in there weren't any choppers, and nothing was burning. He could make out the glow of the massive Klieg lights they used at the markets in the early mornings, and the Public Viewers, and video billboards, and the corporate stores that lined one side of Jefferson Avenue, which was where he was going.

Cassandra Passwaters lived in this little cul-de-sac alley right off the avenue. It was back behind the big TōFish tent, which, thanks to some secret olfactory additive that mimicked the breakdown of triethylamine oxide, reeked like real decaying fish. During the pre-dawn shopping frenzy, if you didn't already know it was there, you'd never find it, hidden as it was behind the tables stacked with mounds of assorted brands of slimy TōFish. There was some kind of makeshift garage back there where two old guys with Yakuza tattoos repaired the scooters, beat-up old cars, work vans, golf carts, and other such vehicles that the A.S.P. 1s were allowed to drive, which, along with their jobs, better housing, and slightly expanded access

to Content, was one of the 1s' most cherished privileges. 1s with
Out-of-Zone Travel-to-Work passes drove their cherished motor
vehicles up to the boom arms of Gate 15, submitted to extensive
Security procedures, and then drove out to the specially-designated
"A.S.P. Only" commuter stations, where they boarded the specially-designated shuttles that took them to their specially-designated
jobs, mostly as sanitation technicians. 1s who worked for IntraZone
Waste, and were not allowed out, but were nonetheless privileged,
drove around the Zone all night, putting down poison, collecting
garbage, tagging unidentified bodies, and basically doing whatever
they were told. The rest just drove up and down the avenue, not really
going anywhere in particular, mostly just showing off their vehicles
and clogging up traffic something awful. They did this after sunset, of
course, but also in the predawn hours, inching, jerking, and honking
their way through the sea of pedestrians, rickshaws, bikes, wagons,
wheelbarrows, trolleys, carts, people shoving their way to the stalls,
vendors lugging crates of TōEggs, MREs, spoiling produce, gangs
of scoliotic old women, some of them cloaked in tattered burkas,
assless old men in their slippers and bathrobes, Transplants in their
Transplant whites, Plasto junkies, night-shift zombies, and pretty
much every other variety of Anti-Social human being ... all of them
streaming obliviously past the mouth of Cassandra Passwaters' alley,
which, once you made it through the throng of bodies, and through
the labyrinth of stacks of crates of stinking TōFish, was like an oasis.

Taylor's usual route to Cassandra's was north on Mulberry, west
on Jamesway, north up Ohlsson to Gillie's Tavern, where he'd usually
stop and grab a quick beer. After which he'd shoot up Collins, which
ran all the way through Sector B, take a left onto Transammonia,
bear right onto CostCo Place, cut up Speedway Motorsports Alley,
and come out right on Jefferson Avenue. The whole trip took about
ninety minutes, typically, that is, on a normal morning, when unidentified person or persons hadn't blown the whole IntraZone
Content grid, and IntraZone Waste & Security choppers weren't
swarming all over the Southeast Quadrant ... and possibly into the
Southwest Quadrant. Taylor thought he could hear them back there,
their rotors, off in the distance behind him, but he didn't want to
turn around to confirm, as you never knew when the BirdsEye was

ZONE 23   77

watching.* He turned onto Jamesway, and kept on walking.

Taylor, since he'd "settled down" with Cassandra and officially retired as a part-time robber of Plasto dealers, pimps, rapers, and assorted other unsavory scumbags, had done a fair amount of walking. It was mostly just a recreational thing, but it also helped him clear his head, and kept him from getting drunk too often. He walked at night, while Cassandra was working, usually around the English Quarter, but sometimes out to the far West Side, or along the bank of the Dell Street Canal, which snaked down into the Southwest Quadrant, but, generally, he stuck to the Northwest Quadrant. Not that there was any ordinance against crossing into other sectors or quadrants. The Zone was only eighteen kilometers across, so you could walk the whole thing from end to end in three or four hours ... but no one did. It wasn't exactly scenic or anything, and you were liable to get egregiously violated. The gangs came out around sunset, mostly, some of whom were rather territorial. Most people stayed inside their sectors, except in the mornings, when they went out to shop, or occasionally went for a beer or three at some makeshift bar like Gillie's Tavern.

Beer, liquor (i.e., full-strength liquor, not the stuff the Normals drank), tobacco, candy, and other foodstuffs containing harmful processed sugar, real caffeine, or dangerous trans-fats, although banned throughout the United Territories, were still manufactured and sold in the Zones. Groceries, drugs, items of clothing, Content discs, and other such essentials, were all for sale at the stores and markets. The quality of everything was crap, of course, but you could get whatever you needed, basically. You paid for it all with paper money, which hadn't been used outside the Zone for three or four hundred years, at least. The notes, which were issued by whatever company ran whatever Zone you were in, had pictures of famous CEOs, CFOs, COOs, and other illustrious Normals on them, industry titans like Vladimir Chiba, Theodore Hadley, and "Jimbo" Cartwright. IntraZone Dollars is what they were called. The 1s and the 2s, who worked in the factories, could earn up to IZD 2000,

---

* *The BirdsEye was what the Anti-Socials called the network of UAVs, satellites, and other forms of technology, that provided the corporate Security Services with Real-Time footage of pretty much everything happening everywhere, all the time.*

monthly, most of which they spent on rent, food, and drugs, and the
rest on Content. The 3s, who wouldn't dream of working, were issued
a basic subsistence allotment of IZD 486.20, all of which they spent
on food, which meager income they were forced to supplement by
stealing, robbing, dealing in substances, and other such Anti-Social
enterprises.

According to people like Meyer Jimenez, the corporations that
supplied the Zone had some kind of deal where they all got paid directly by the Local Territorial Authority, which was technically still
the municipal government, but nobody really knew for certain. It
was possible they all got paid directly by the Hadley Corporation of
Menomonie, Wisconsin, which billed the Local Territorial Authority
as part of their contract to administrate the Zone. According to
Meyer, the L.T.A. (and presumably the rest of the so-called government) was nothing more than a virtual entity the corporations used
to stockpile taxes, which were paid back out to the corporations in
the form of contracts and service agreements. Which meant, if Taylor
had gotten that right, that the Hadley Corporation of Menomonie,
Wisconsin was paying him 486.20 a month for nothing, which made
no sense. Apparently it did to Meyer Jimenez, who'd repeatedly explained how the whole thing worked (it was something to do with
taxes or fees), but Taylor, who didn't really give a shit anyway, hadn't
listened very closely, and couldn't remember.

In any event, there was cheap booze aplenty, and as long as you
didn't mind too much that the beer, which came in aluminum barrels,
was hot and flat and tasted like piss, and that the liquor burned your
throat going down, you could drink yourself into a bellowing stupor,
which most people did on a nightly basis. The produce they sold at
the outdoor markets was invariably bruised and wilted and spoiling, but at least it was actual food from somewhere.* You couldn't
grow anything edible in the Zone. People tried, but it was always the
same. Either nothing sprouted at all, or whatever did was all weird
and wrong, bright blue squash that had no skin, tomatoes in cloves
that resembled garlic, mutant ears of toxic corn, glowing broccoli ...
you get the idea. The markets, as well as the indoor stores, carried a

---

* Actually, most of the produce was grown in the Normals' indoor Agri-factories, but had been
rejected for aesthetic reasons, or had passed its optimal sell-by date.

decent range of TōFood ... artificial soy-based meat-like products, which sometimes smelled like, but never quite tasted like, whatever meat it was pretending to be. The stuff in cans, the MRE packs, the boxes of milk and flavored juice drinks, were totally synthetic and full of preservatives, so none of them really tasted like anything. The rice and the beans were usually OK, genetically modified, but real, technically. People made do with what they got, and washed it all down with beer, mostly.

The outdoor markets, where they sold the produce, along with most of the In-Zone stores, were located out on the very edge of Sector A, right across from Wall. One of the bigger ones was Jefferson Avenue. It stretched from Gates 15 to 16, and serviced the entire Northeast Quadrant. Weekday mornings, from 0500 to just before the sun came up, the 2s and 3s would make their way out there from wherever they lived in the inner sectors, do their shopping, and scurry back home. The 1s, who were already there, of course, stayed inside the Sector A ring, none of them having any reason or desire to venture any deeper into the Zone. IntraZone Waste & Security Services, Inc. maintained cleanliness and civic order with a regiment of Waste & Security Specialists armed with UltraLite automatic rifles. Most of them were stationed in Sector A, to protect the corporate stores and property, and also to protect the A.S.P. 1s, who worked at the In-Zone plants and factories, and while they weren't officially corporate property, were close enough to it to warrant protection. Units of Waste & Security Specialists, clad in helmets and puncture-proof armor, occasionally patrolled the inner sectors in their APCs and MRAPs, but mostly it was just the Community Watchers. The Community Watchers were A.S.P. 3s who'd turned Cooperator, and been issued truncheons, and in some cases cans of mace and stun guns, and answered to IntraZone Waste & Security, and were the lowest forms of life on Earth. At night, in Sectors B and C, you were constantly getting hassled by Watchers, but they didn't come out much during the day. Neither did anyone else for that matter, apart from totally burnt-out geeks, Plasto fiends, suicide freaks, and the Transplants, who, for some sadistic reason, they delivered just before dawn each morning. Sadistic, because at that time of morning, you had about an hour to get inside, and the

Transplants, of course, had no idea where they were, or where they were going. You would see them out there on a daily basis, staggering down the desolate streets in their Transplant whites with their rolled up bedding, desperately trying to find their housing before their brain cells fried completely and they sat down on a curb somewhere, passed out, and promptly died of exposure.

The thing was ... it was really hot.

Unlike up in the northern latitudes, where the weather was ... OK, unpredictable, snowing one day, scorching the next, but often quite pleasant, and generally mild, the average temperature in Zone 23 was 46 Celsius, in the shade. Out in the sun, your skin just sizzled. Your brain stopped working. Then you died. At night it got down into the upper 30s. Still, everyone sweated like pigs. You fell asleep in a pool of sweat and woke up in that same pool of sweat. Everything, everywhere, stank of sweat, and mold, and mildew, and general decay. Your skin was coated with a film of sweat that never washed off, no matter what you did. Your mattress stank of and was stained with sweat, and assorted other bodily fluids, which due to the unrelenting humidity never really completely dried. A steaming river of human excrement coursed through the sewers, which were open in places. It tasted like you were breathing in shit, or some sort of shit-scented air-freshener spray that was squirted out of some sensor-activated shit-scented air-freshener sprinkler system. A stifling heat haze hung in the air, viscous and thick, like petroleum jelly, distorting anything you saw at a distance. It looked like there were pools of water up ahead at the end of every street, but then, when you got there, there was no water. It was just a mirage, an inferior image, hot air rising off the molten asphalt. Clouds of filthy sweltering steam shot up out of the sidewalk grates, coming from ... no one exactly knew where, some vast infernal heating network that was somehow impossible to ever turn off. The iron railings on the stoops of buildings, the rusted-out gates of old underground stations, the metal chassis of stripped-down cars, anything metal burned to the touch. Everything trapped and radiated heat, which heat built up and trapped more heat, which process then repeated itself, creating this kind of multi-layered oven-inside-an-oven effect that never abated because there were no seasons ...

Basically, it was fucking hot.

According to folks like Meyer Jimenez, the Zone had only been the Zone for two, maybe three hundred years, and before that it had been part of the city, which must have been built back when there were still seasons and the cold was a bigger problem than the heat. Taylor subscribed to this particular theory. A person would have to be a drooling moron to build this way in this type of climate. These narrow streets lined with old brick tenements, built maybe seven, eight hundred years ago, jammed together side by side, their chimneys bricked up to keep out the pigeons, the ruins of an underground network of trains, the ancient radiators, the sidewalk grates ... everywhere traces of a colder age. This desolate patch of dirt and sawgrass (the one he was just now passing on Jamesway), strewn with garbage and crawling with rats, its crumbling stumps infested with woodlice, had once been a square where people sat, talking, he imagined, or smoking, or reading, or maybe just dozing on the long wooden benches that ran alongside this winding path here. The wood had rotted away long ago, or had been consumed by mutant termites. All that remained were the iron frames, snaking through the yellow sawgrass like the petrified spine of some giant serpent.

Back when Taylor and Alice Williams and Rusty Braynard were all just kids, there used to be a rainy season when it seemed like almost every day, usually in the late afternoon, you'd get these freak torrential rainstorms, where the sky would go black and crack with thunder, and the rain would beat down hot and hard, pounding down onto the streets and rooftops, blowing sideways into the windows, and the gutters would overflow, and flood, and the rats would come pouring out into the streets and run around in mindless circles, and up onto the stoops of buildings, but you couldn't hear them shrieking or anything, because all you could hear was the sound of the rain hammering down on the tar and stone and plastic awnings and sheets of metal, hammering like a million fists, the fists of a million invisible babies, and it seemed to Taylor and Alice Williams and Rusty Braynard, and all the other little kids, like maybe the world was finally coming to an end, and they'd run out into the street to see it (because who'd want to miss a show like that), shouting, squealing, peeling their clothes off, heads turned up, mouths wide open, to drink in the rain and the end of it all, their mothers shouting down out of windows to get back into the fucking house before they got hit by fucking lightning or bitten by one of those fucking rats and ... then, just like that, it would stop, as if God or someone had turned off a spigot, and two minutes later the sun would be out and ...

Here was Taylor's turn up Ohlsson.

He zig-zagged through the clots of shoppers coming the other way down the street, pushing and dragging their rickety carts, schlepping their plastic bags of groceries. They trudged along silently, soaked with sweat, shirts and dresses sticking to their backs, staring intently down at their feet, determined to beat the sun to their houses. A saggy-titted old Chinese lady who Taylor passed nearly every morning shuffled toward him, raised her head, and gave him that "what are you crazy?" look, like she did pretty much every time she saw him walking in the wrong direction like that. Taylor smiled and pushed on past her.

The Public Viewers were all back online. They were running the standard standby feed, synthesized strings and a glockenspiel, or something, over a montage of Security professionals protecting various innocent civilians from some unspecified, imminent threat. One of the talking heads came on ... a silver-haired man, looking "serious." The following, he said, was a Security Advisory.

Due to an incident of civil unrest in the Southeast Quadrant of Sector C, all Class 3 Anti-Social Persons were advised to return to their homes immediately. Class 3 Anti-Social Persons remaining outdoors in Sector C after 0630 would be deemed "uncooperative," and subject to immediate detention. Class 3 Anti-Social Persons unable to reach their homes by that time were advised to remain outside the Sector, move indoors, shelter in place, and await the issuance of further advisories. IntraZone Waste & Security Services regretted any inconvenience this caused, and thanked you for your cooperation.

Shoppers dropped their bags in the street, abandoned their carts, ran, walked, hobbled, limped, shuffled, skipped, hopstepped, and otherwise ambulated, as fast as they could toward their homes. Taylor turned and looked to the east. That column of thick black smoke was still rising, growing ... the fire was obviously spreading.

Choppers were circling, swooping, and banking. He turned to the south. Choppers there too. Sweeping the streets with their NiteSun beams. They hadn't yet made it to the English Quarter, but now it was just a matter of time. This was not some random firebomb set off by a bunch of bozos. He wondered whether ... no, fuck it ... there wasn't any time to wonder. According to the silver-haired talking head, he had, he guessed, about nine minutes to make it to Gillie's and out of the Sector.

Gillie's, on the corner of Ohlsson and Clayton, so right on the border of Sectors B and C, was strictly a Class 3 Anti-Social hangout. However, being located on the B-side of Clayton, Gillie's was technically a Class 2 tavern. Thus, even if they sealed off the Sector, which it certainly appeared they intended to do, Taylor would be all right at Gillie's. The only problem was, Gillie's Tavern was another fifteen blocks up Ohlsson. At a block a minute, that was fifteen minutes. Walking, at least. He would have to run. Which wasn't a problem in itself, running. The street was full of people running. Running in the other direction, that is, into the Sector, not out of the Sector, the direction that Taylor was going to be running. This was going to be a problem. One lone Class 3 Anti-Social Person running flat out, out of the Sector, while everyone else was running in, was definitely not going to look so kosher.

He took off running ... cursing himself, and whatever asshole had invented tequila.* An enormous specimen of Class 3 idiot, with a gang of other little idiots in tow, was running right at him, hooting and hollering, waving his fat, flabby arms all around. Taylor, who wanted to avoid this idiot, stagger stepped deftly and cut to the right. The big fat idiot cut to the right, to Taylor's right, the idiot's left, hollering something that sounded to Taylor like "OW-WAH-MAH-WAH-MAH," or something like that. The other little idiots followed suit, laughing hysterically, obviously drunk. Taylor cut left. The idiot cut left, closing the distance between them to nothing. The big fat idiot, idiot that he was, idiotically, raised his arms, as if he were going to tackle Taylor, and let loose with some kind of Gaelic war cry. Taylor head faked left, right, dropped his shoulder, accelerated, body checked the big fat idiot savagely in the xiphoid process,

---

* Which is what, he'd remembered, he'd been drinking the night before when he'd totally lost his shit.

broke it, along with several ribs, and possibly ruptured the idiot's
liver. He spun off the check and kept on running, through the gaggle
of other little idiots, none of whom seemed particularly interested in
getting in Taylor's way any more.

After he'd run the first few blocks, he felt like someone was twisting a burning metal fork up through his ribcage. He staggered to a
stop, doubled over, hands on his knees, gasping for breath. The voice
of Silverhaired Talking Head Man echoed out of the Public Viewers,
none of which Taylor was viewing at the moment, getting ready to
puke as he was. The following was a Security Advisory. Class 3 Anti-
Social Persons had less than five minutes to return to their homes, or
otherwise move their asses indoors and out of the sight of Security
Services. Class 3 Anti-Social Persons found out of doors in Sector
C after 0630 would be deemed uncooperative ...

Taylor slowly pulled himself up, wiped the sweat out of his eyes,
took a deep breath and ... something was wrong. Class 3 Anti-Social
Persons without a shred of human empathy were standing around
on the stoops of their buildings, and crouching out on their fire escapes, and leaning half out of their tenement windows, staring at
him like he was out of his mind, or was some kind of fucking circus
clown who was out there for their entertainment. The street was
now completely deserted, as in there was not one single person on
it, except, of course, for Taylor Byrd, who was standing right in the
middle of it. Ahead, in the distance, five blocks north, the orange
outline of the neon Gillie's sign winked at him faintly out of the
dark. Five long blocks on an empty street. There wasn't any way he
was going to make it.

He took off running, or, technically, jogging, the veins in his neck
and temples throbbing, cut up onto the sidewalk to his right, which
he figured was probably marginally safer than the middle of fucking
Ohlsson Street, caught his left boot on a crack in the sidewalk and
went down howling in a mound of garbage. He got up, cursing, and
took off again, ignoring the laughter and scattered applause from the
ass-wipes standing around on their stoops (who he hoped would die
of liver cancer), and made it another two agonizing blocks, and was
feeling like maybe he was actually going to catch a break, when he
heard the chopper.

The chopper, a standard StreetSweeper model, was coming in fast and low from the west, rotors running intentionally loud, flat black snout tilted menacingly downward. Two buildings up was an open doorway. He bolted for it, sprang up the steps, and made it in just as the chopper's NiteSun flooded the street with its blue-white beam. The chopper banked, came back around, and hovered there, right in the middle of the street, scanning for Class 3 Anti-Social Persons.

Taylor pressed back into the darkness. There wasn't anything to do now but wait. The chopper had either seen him or it hadn't ... and OK, he figured it probably hadn't, because it hadn't fired an AGM into the vestibule and blown him to pieces. Odds were, it was a routine part of IntraZone Waste & Security Service's rapid response to the civil unrest, which was either spreading into the Sector, or threatening to spread into the Sector, and which was somehow linked to the taking out of the Content Grid, which had either been sabotaged, or collaterally damaged in the rapid response ... or whatever the fuck it was that was happening.

Taylor had no clue what was happening. Whatever it was, it was definitely something. IntraZone Waste & Security Services didn't seal off an entire sector every time some gang of assholes set off an isolated IED. And whatever took out the Public Viewers ... Taylor hadn't even thought that was possible. No. This was coordinated. Which meant that it had to be the A.S.U. ... which it could not be, because they'd all been detained ... unless they hadn't ... which they obviously hadn't ... which meant ... no ... it couldn't be, could it? On the other hand, what the hell else could it be? If it wasn't the D.A.D.A., what else was it?

"No deviations, no matter what happens."

He could almost hear her voice in his head. She'd made him repeat it like he was some kind of moron ... Sarah.

"I need to hear you say it."

"No deviations."

"No matter what happens."

What if Sarah hadn't disappeared? What if she was out there now, on her way to the rendezvous point? What if she had always planned to synch up "the action" with the start of the D.A.D.A.? That would be just like her, wouldn't it? There'd never be a better diversion.

He reached down into the pocket of his chinos. There it was ... the counterfeit Travel Pass. Was it possible, remotely possible, that he might not have to go through with this thing ... this thing he was going to Cassandra's to do ... the Worst Thing He Had Ever Done? No, he told himself, it wasn't possible. He was going to do it. He had to do it. He had to prepare himself, mentally, to do it. He had to steel his heart to do it. To close his heart. To empty it out. He didn't have any more room in there for any more of Sarah's faith-based pipe dreams ... assuming, that is, they *were* her pipe dreams, and not some faith-based-sounding nonsense scripted by some corporate hack to lure him into some Corporatist plot to penetrate whatever actual faith-based Terrorist network was actually active, and had possibly finally launched the D.A.D.A. ... unless the D.A.D.A. was also part of it, in which case ... no, he'd confused himself now. The point was, even if she wasn't dead, or being detained and tortured somewhere, and was out there, on her way to the rendezvous, how could he possibly trust her now, or anything she'd said, after all that had happened? He couldn't. He shouldn't have ever trusted her. He shouldn't have ever trusted anyone. What was it Meyer Jimenez had said?

"Everybody infiltrates everybody."

Right.

"Everybody uses everybody."

Right.

And something else he'd said ... something Taylor couldn't quite remember, something to do with time, or power, or the unreality of reality, or something ... which didn't matter, and wasn't going to matter, unless Taylor made it out of the Sector.

At the moment, he wasn't making it anywhere. What he was doing was hiding in this vestibule, hoping that that IntraZone chopper out there was not equipped with Thermal Imaging, which Taylor, like a lot of Anti-Social Persons, mistakenly believed could see through walls. It couldn't, of course, but he didn't know that ... so one more thing that didn't matter. Or maybe it did ... just not to Taylor, who, again, like a lot other people, and not just Anti-Social people, could only believe what he thought he knew was real at the time was the way things were, which maybe it was and maybe it wasn't, or maybe it was both, or neither.

"At the core of every fact, my friend, is an act of faith."

That was it.

Fucking Meyer.

Whatever.

Anyway ...

"CLEAR THE STREET," the chopper ordered.

Whatever decrepit tenement Taylor was hiding in the dark of the vestibule of was definitely some kind of total shithole that seriously reeked of week-old dead guy. Taylor was suddenly acutely aware of this. His hangover was suddenly acutely aware of this. He stuck the tips of his first two fingers up his nostrils to keep from gagging. Peering around in the dark of the vestibule, with his fingers up his nose like that, he didn't see any sign of the dead guy, but what he did see was just as repulsive. There, on either side of his head, a few of them sickeningly close to his head, feral pigeons were nesting on the lintels, cooing and shitting down the sides of the jambs. Below the pigeons the ceramic tiles were cracked and broken and caked with guano, which had hardened into a greenish crust, which ran down to an enormous mound of human feces he had nearly stepped in. Across from him, also streaked with guano, a rusted-out panel of doorbell buttons displayed the names of long dead people who used to live there, who no one knew ... Chu, Mahmoud, Weber, Kupferberg. No one ever thought about these people, or knew their stories, or when they had lived here. Their names were etched in neat little rows in the vestibule of every building in the Zone ... a faded memorial from some other world.

He took a quick peek out into the street.

The chopper was starting to yaw and dance now, which meant it wasn't there for Taylor. This was just a routine maneuver, which would soon be over, which, as soon as it was, he would tear-ass the last three blocks to Gillie's, and find out if anyone knew what was happening. They hadn't yet set up a perimeter on Clayton when he'd ducked into this lovely vestibule, and he doubted they had managed to set one up in the last two minutes or whatever it had been ... which meant he maybe still had a chance. Or he would, if that chopper would just fuck off. It wasn't fucking off, however. Instead, it was kind of circling slowly, sweeping the street with its NiteSun

again, which it already had, illuminating nothing ... except for that
crusty old Russian-looking guy with his face jammed into the side
of a building, leaning into it, holding his dick in the classic drunken
two-handed grip, peeing all over his taped-up shoes.

"CLEAR THE STREET," the chopper reiterated.

The Russian-looking guy continued peeing. He removed his right
hand from his dick, which he seemed to be able to manage with his
left, raised it, his right hand, into the air, and flipped the chopper an
old-fashioned bird. The chopper ascended, ever so slightly. Taylor
winced and shook his head. He'd seen this movie many times before.
The Russian guy, who was obviously shitfaced, and not quite finished
peeing on his shoes, did this little shimmy-shake dance where his
head kind of bobbed back and forth real fast, and his arms kind of
flapped, and his fingers quivered, as the over-adrenalized chopper
gunner put about three hundred rounds in his back. He crumpled,
dead, at the base of the wall, down which most of his guts were now
dripping.

The voice of Silverhaired Talking Head Man, who really wasn't
kidding around now, informed the residents of Ohlsson Street that
the official time was 0630. The IntraZone chopper, its work done
here, swooped off in a southerly direction to maintain order and
cleanliness elsewhere.

Taylor bolted down the steps.

He got down low and took off running ... running in the street,
because fuck the sidewalk. At this point it was all about speed. One
block up he hit his stride. The street was empty. This was good. So
was the sky, which was also good. However, two blocks up ahead, at
the intersection of Clayton and Ohlsson ... popcorn lights, sirens,
headlights. So not so good ... but not over yet. The units, and presumably APCs, were closing in fast from both directions, but they
hadn't yet reached the intersection. If Taylor could get across the
avenue before they got there and dive down the slope that ran down
off the avenue to Gillie's, and get himself up and get into Gillie's,
which maybe he could with the streetlights out, which it looked like
they were, and if he stayed real low, and now there was only one
block to go and ...

Revelation

One thing every Normal knew, knew for a fact, and took for granted, was that Anti-Social Disease was cunning. They knew this because they had heard it repeated over and over throughout their lives, more or less since the day they were born. As children, they had heard it repeated by their parents, their kindergarten teachers, their grammar school teachers, high-school teachers, and guidance counselors. Later, they had heard it repeated by their friends, their professors, doctors, coworkers, and bosses. They heard it repeated in the Content they streamed. It was spoken by the actors in virtual Immersions, frequently quoted in corporate presentations, invariably recited in political speeches. It was whispered in the course of grave conversations, typically with friends or family members, concerning other friends or family members. Often it was lunchroom gossip, the news that someone had gone full-blown, and had behaved inappropriately, and had had to be hospitalized, which happened on a fairly regular basis. News like this was always sad (deeply sad ... very, very sad) for the person concerned, and their loved ones, of course, but hospitalization was for their own good and was hopefully just a temporary measure. Whoever delivered such distressing news, which in Valentina's case was usually one of the Histopathology Department's breezy administrators, would typically do so, pause for effect, sigh wistfully, raise their eyebrows, tactfully refrain from mentioning how they'd suspected whoever had gone full-blown had been "slipping away" for quite some time, loudly stir their herbal tea, which didn't need stirring, with a metal spoon, look Valentina squarely in the eye, and repeat the adage, "the disease is cunning."

And cunning it was, diabolically cunning (which Valentina knew only too well), the way it tricked you, toyed with you, lied to you, used your own thoughts and perceptions against you, twisting your interpretation of things to the point where you couldn't even trust your own mind. They had to stay vigilant, the Variant-Positives, as the threat was always there, lurking, even at times when it seemed like it wasn't, and especially at times when it seemed like it wasn't. Which was also part of its insidious nature. Human Anti-Social Disease was not just cunning, it was also patient. It might lie there dormant inside you for years, and then, one day (you never saw it coming), out of nowhere, for no discernible reason, some seemingly insignificant event, a dream, or memory, or some associative connection, would start you thinking, questioning, doubting. Once that happened, you were pretty much lost. Before you knew it your head was swimming with all kinds of Anti-Social ideations.

According to the DSM XXXIII, these "Anti-Social ideations" took any number of invidious forms: resentment, blaming, shaming, enabling, coveting, other-directed thinking, emotional sabotage of self or others, toxic remorse, future tripping, excessive grieving, pride, self pity, projection of fears and/or weaknesses onto others, emotional distancing, hostile questioning, manipulative simulation of illnesses ... the list went on and on, and on. Everyone had them to some degree, these ideations (not all of them, of course, but several, at least, in some combination), some more active, others more latent. On top of which, newer forms of ideations were being discovered on a daily basis, and older forms were often amended or merged into other umbrella designations. Which meant that trying to stay abreast of all the myriad forms of ideations was virtually hopeless. So no one did. No, the best you could do was become aware of the ideations you, yourself, were prone to, acknowledge, accept, and admit them openly, and keep them in check as best you could. The Clears, of course, whose defective genes had been corrected in a petri dish, were immune to this threat and thus free from the burden of having to monitor their every thought, as were the A.S.P.s, like Taylor, who were born full-blown, and according to the experts didn't even think they had the disease. But for Valentina, as for most of the Normals (and significantly more than for most of the Normals, in light of the history of disease in her family), the danger of slipping had always been there.

Valentina had done her best to deal with her latent Anti-Social ideations. She had diligently walked the Path(s) to Prosperity, and practiced its principles, for thirty-one years. She'd carefully adjusted her recommended dosage of each new version of Zanoflaxithorinal that came to market every two to three months, under the guidance of her doctors, of course. She had taken all the other pills they'd prescribed ... the serotonin reuptake inhibitors, the norepinephrine reuptake inhibitors, the norepinephrine-dopamine disinhibitors, the sedatives, tranquilizers, the anti-psychotics, the anticonvulsants, the psychostimulants. She had joined an array of anonymous support groups, Latent Anti-Social Persons Anonymous, Children of Latent Parents Anonymous, Verbal Abuse Survivors Anonymous, among many others, and had worked their programs. She'd taken up yoga, transcendental meditation, running, weaving, said affirmations, stared at candles for days on end, read entire self-help libraries, adjusted her diet and the hours she slept, and attended countless retreats and seminars, and individualized life coaching sessions. In her desperation, she had even tried the scheduled substance known as LTC9, a powerful supposedly dangerous hallucinogen that some in the alternative medicine community believed could cleanse the neural pathways, erasing latent Anti-Social ideations and simulating direct union with the One. Alison, a temp in the Records Department, who dressed a bit oddly, but who was generally nice, had slipped her the pill the day she left. "You only have to take it once," she whispered, "trust me, it'll change your life." Aside from giving her a three-hour migraine, and causing her to dream she was trapped inside an enormous hive of cancerous tissue housing an infinite number of other identical insect versions of herself, the LTC9 changed absolutely nothing.

So on they came, as they had forever, the negative thoughts, the doubts, the questions, the aural and visual hallucinations ... that very December morning, for example, the supposedly happiest day of her life. Valentina had been sitting in the kitchen, silently drowning in sunflower yellow, gazing out through the sliding glass doors into the silver predawn twilight, the poisonous sky alive with beacons, strobing, flashing, winking, twinkling ... the running lights of commercial airplanes, corporate choppers, and UAVs, pulsing, painting trails of light, webs of color, lines of flight, forming some faint, familiar pattern ... some half-remembered whorling maze. One of the Pewter Palisades gardeners, Joachim Maria-Torres Oakley, with whom Valentina was fairly friendly, was down by the pond behind the house, carefully trimming a hedge of Snail Seed. He was trying to trim the last few meters before the sun got all the way up. Sweat was cascading down his back, which Valentina was intently ogling. Joachim lived down in who knew where ... somewhere down in Center City, just outside the Quarantine Zone. He lived there with his wife and kids, his parents, her parents, and their other relatives. He and his wife (Kinshasha, was it?) and the older generations were Variant-Positives. The kids, two boys and a girl, were Clears. They lived in a three-bed, two-bath apartment in a low-rise complex on a big noisy street. They had a modern, if limited kitchen, a decent sized Viewer, wore clothes off the rack, paid their rent and bills on time, carried approximately a million in debt, and generally lived a relatively comfortable, paycheck-to-paycheck type of existence.

Valentina had no idea why she was thinking any of this.

Kyle was scanning his All-in-One, letting his morning decaf go cold. His mustard yellow Tucci tie was flipped up onto its face on his shoulder, the better to keep it from catching drips of the decaf coffee he wasn't drinking.

"Hot one today," he announced, clicking.

Valentina, elsewhere, eyeballed, out through the sliding glass doors of the kitchen, across the still surface of the artificial pond, down at the end of the hedge of Snail Seed, Joachim Maria-Torres Oakley's lateral muscles flexing like wings. Right at that moment ... now ... now ... billions of trillions of Globodollars were being transferred from bank to bank, purchasing stocks, corporate paper, covered bonds, repackaged debt, hedges, futures, anything, everything ... forty gadzillion transactions per second. Some of those virtual Globodollars were hers and Kyle's. None were Joachim's. Each and every one of Joachim's Globodollars were spent in advance. They were spent on rent, food, clothes, toys, Info-Entertainment Content, energy fees, water, taxes, medical bills, and interest on debt. She and Kyle were also in debt, but theirs was an altogether different equation ... an equation based on the price of money, interest rates, amortization, return on investment, inflation, and so on. They, and everyone else in their circle, were making money with other people's money. Which was what made the world go around after all, virtual streams of numbers, figures, flowing freely through fiberoptic cables, in and out of virtual accounts, feeding investment, producing returns, generating compound interest. This was the magic of other people's money, the Tree of Abundance, whose fruit was Wealth, the Wealth with which they would feed their family, pay for their schools, clothes, toys, Viewers, therapy, software, medicine, and personal growth-based corporate seminars ...

Valentina understood all this.

She understood the Path(s) to Prosperity. She understood that she and Kyle had chosen spiritual and material abundance, plenty, plenitude, affluence, assets ... it wasn't that she didn't understand all this. It was just that, gazing across the pond, sipping her ginger tea that morning, with all those trippy colored trails of light bleeding off the edges of everything, forming mandalas in the brightening sky, Valentina could not for the life of her shake the thought that those other people, those other people whose money it was that she and Kyle were making theirs with, were, basically, people just like Joachim. Not even like. They were Joachim ... who Pewter Palisades paid enough to house himself and his family, barely, feed everybody, and keep them distracted, buying products and servicing debt, the interest on which was paid to the banks, which owned the low-rise building he lived in, and her and Kyle's house, and Pewter Palisades, and virtually everything else in existence ... well, OK, not quite everything else. Some of it was owned by other people, or other corporations, which were owned by these people, who also held a stake in these banks, or who held a stake in some other business which held a stake in some other bank upon which the banks in question depended, the failure of which (the banks in question), or even the unwarranted fear thereof, would trigger a massive financial crisis that would quickly spread around the globe precipitating widespread social unrest and bringing an end to life as she knew it ... which basically, the way Valentina saw it, looking at it through the funhouse lens of her Anti-Social ideations that morning, made Joachim a glorified slave ... all right, granted, a glorified slave with

sixteen hundred channels of Content, health insurance, and air-conditioning, but nevertheless, essentially, a slave. Hanging in a physical
drawer in Kyle's study were various legal and official documents, the
signed, original copies of which it was still, even in this paperless age,
customary for people to retain. One of these documents happened
to be the lease for their house on Marigold Lane. Valentina had read
this lease. She had signed this lease. She'd had it scanned. This lease
consisted of sheets of paper. Sixty-three, if memory served. Sixty-
three sheets of A4 paper.

This was what made Joachim a slave.

"Val?"

Kyle was talking to her. How long had he been talking to her? She
raised her mug and faked a smile.

"What is it, honey?"

"What time's our appointment?"

OK. She was in the clear.

"Eleven."

"Eleven? I thought it was later."

"Why?"

"What?"

"Why did you think that?"

"What?"

"Why did you think it was later?"

"Uh ... I don't know. Are you OK?"

He was looking at her like she wasn't OK.

"Yes, Kyle, I'm OK."

He went back to clicking through screens on his Viewer.

"Did you see this comment on Friedman's Fleep?"

"What Fleep?"

"On the Kiki Brezinski piece."

"Kiki Brezinski?"

"What's her name's agent."

"I have no idea what you're talking about, Kyle."

"I'll forward it to you."

"I'm sitting right here."

He forwarded it to her. His Viewer bleated. He checked it.

"Hold on, I need to read this."

Valentina closed her eyes and tried to change the channel in her head. Let go and detach, she told herself. Joachim is not a symbol of anything. Joachim is a gardener. He chose his life. No one is enslaving anyone. Everything is all a series of choices. Everything is happening for a reason. Joachim went to school ... a public school, which everyone knows are ... NO. Stop it. The Oneness of the infinite One. The Multiplicitous Oneness of the ... He could have gotten a scholarship somewhere. People do. Some people do. OK, not many. Practically no one. Still, theoretically, he could have. Or saved some money. Or not had kids. Or invested ... or, all right, not that much, but if he'd set aside a little monthly ... in forty or fifty years he could have ... NO ... or started a business. With what? Nothing. See? That's how it works. The system ... NO ... the Oneness of the ... DETACH. Try to see the big picture. Someone has to do the gardening. Someone has to pick up the garbage. To pick up our garbage. Shine our shoes. NO. Please. PLEASE make it stop. PLEASE ... SHOW ME WHAT TO DO.

On the other side of the sliding glass doors out of which Valentina was staring again, the temperature was 42 Celsius and rising. Another suffocating day was breaking, which the Normals were all going to spend indoors. Across the pond, Joachim and one of the other gardeners were loading their gear into the back of a ten year-old hybrid work van, the side of which was prominently branded with the double "P" Pewter Palisades logo. The self-adjusting projectile-proof glass in the sliding glass doors in the sunflower kitchen where Kyle was now grunting and poking his Viewer was turning a soothing shade of green.

"I covered that in my memo, I believe."

Valentina's hand was shaking. Her heart was racing. Her teeth were clenched. She grabbed up an orange prescription bottle from among the collection that lived on the table, and took a pill, a Zypralexathol, an anti-convulsant, which sometimes helped. Please, she prayed ... please, make it stop. Help me, please, let go of these thoughts. She closed her eyes and slowed her breathing.

"Val?"

Kyle was staring at her. Yes ... she could definitely feel him staring. How long had he been staring at her? How long had she been lost in her thoughts?

"I'm OK ... give me a minute."

"Thoughts?"

"Uhuh. Give me a minute."

One of those endless silences followed.

"Anger?"

"Mostly guilt," she whispered.

He took her hand, and squeezed it gently.

"Try to let it go," he said.

"That's what I'm doing."

"I'm sorry ... I just ..."

A Fleep came in on his All-in-One. He glanced at it quickly. She could feel him do it. She pulled her hand back and opened her eyes.

"I think Graell ought to up your dosage."

"I know, Kyle. I'm seeing him tomorrow. I took another one. Just give me a minute."

"I wasn't trying to pressure you, sweetheart."

Another Fleep came in on his Viewer. She watched him resist the urge to read it. He gazed at her, radiating love and concern. She turned away and looked out the doors again. Joachim and the other gardeners were gone. Kyle got up, flipped his tie down, dropped his All-in-One in his pocket. He leaned down and kissed her on the forehead.

"I love you," he said. "I didn't mean to pressure."

"I know. I'm sorry."

"I love you, muffin. I'll see you there at eleven. OK?"

Valentina reached for his hand, found it, squeezed it, nodded, and smiled. He bent down and kissed her sweetly on the temple.

"I love you," she said. "I'm OK."

"You're really OK?"

"I'm really OK."

Valentina was not OK. Despite both her and Kyle's attempts to wish it away, and pray it away, and talk it away, and gloss it over, the ever more undeniable truth was, Valentina, in spite of all her efforts to keep her latent disease in check, was "Non-responsive to Pharmatherapy." This was becoming increasingly obvious, incontestably, embarrassingly obvious. The possibility had always been there, given her mother's medical history, and now ... here it was ... it was actually happening. She and Kyle had discussed this at length, back when they were both in their twenties, when it had all seemed very remote and abstract. Her mother, Catherine, after all, had made it into her early sixties before she had finally gone full-blown. Kyle and Valentina figured, worst case scenario, she would make it that long, and maybe, just maybe, with the right combination of medications and spiritual programs, she would never go full-blown at all.

Then, one summer, six years earlier, she'd had the first of her little episodes. It didn't seem that dramatic at the time, one random sarcastic remark in public, made to a server at Giggles, luckily, and not at work, or to one of Kyle's colleagues, which certainly would have gotten her reported. A few weeks later, another remark, this time to a Content Assistant in the Literary Content department at Finkles, which Susan Foster had clearly overheard, and had had no choice but to mention to Kyle.

Then, a few days later, another.

During the six long years that followed, Doctor Graell and her other psychiatrists had diagnosed her with a cornucopia of latent Anti-Social "conditions" ... Chronic Altered Reasoning Complex, Early-Onset Perceptual Disorder, Oppositional Logic Syndrome, Stage 3 Ideational Slippage, Werden's Disease, among many others, which together led to one grim conclusion ... Valentina was "very possibly" Non-Responsive to Pharmatherapy.

In light of the rather catastrophic personal, professional, and social consequences flowing from such a diagnosis, "Non-Responsiveness to Pharmatherapy, was never confirmed by laboratory testing, which entailed a significant margin of error. Confirmation was entirely based on observation of the patient's behavior, which, if the patient was Non-Responsive, exhibited certain hallmark symptoms, which once reported could not be ignored. Any type of violence was of course dispositive, but such behavior was extremely rare. Typically, much less dramatic eruptions (i.e., verbal abuse, aggressive gesturing, or disregard for private property) were enough to confirm the diagnosis and earn one an NRP designation. As long as a patient hadn't crossed that line and forced some doctor to enter the dreaded "NRP" in the patient's records, Non-Responsiveness to Pharmatherapy remained merely "possible" or "very possible," which meant that the doctors could continue treating, writing prescriptions, and billing for same.

Valentina Briggs, at this point in our story, had not yet officially crossed that line, but clearly she was inching up to it. Clinically, she was "decompensating." Her paranoid ideations were worsening. She wasn't reading reality right. She was suffering fits of delusional thinking. For example, the one she'd suffered that morning, gazing out at the lateral muscles of Joachim Maria-Torres Oakley, that had caused her to think all those Communist thoughts as she spiraled down into the destructive feelings of guilt she so obviously didn't deserve. Or the one that started, a few hours later, with her sudden outburst of inappropriate laughter in the consultation room at Paxton Wills ... and that continued now as she rode the elevator down from the 200th floor to the lobby. These fits were not full-blown psychotic episodes. They were simply extended delusions of reference, minor variations on a discordant theme, a twisted narrative her mind had created, which turned the real world upside down, not in terms of what it was, but, rather, in terms of how it worked ... for, whereas, now, and in all her fits, Valentina still perceived the world (i.e., the physical world) as you and I do (e.g., chairs were still chairs, cars were cars, toasters weren't alien listening devices), her perception, or, rather, her interpretation, of societal and interpersonal relations was disturbingly, pathologically skewed. Everywhere she looked she saw (or thought she saw) some bit, piece, evidence of some secret scheme, some deeply diabolical complot, in which, her intuition told her, everyone was implicated ...

Simply put, when the drugs were working, the world was ... OK, not quite perfect, but considering what the world had been like for thousands of years of human history, a brutal, ugly, savage place, where cruelty, violence, and sadism reigned, where torture, war, slavery, and genocide had become the norm, and were not just ignored, but were subtly integrated into society, and often even celebrated ... well, OK, compared to a world like that, the Age of the Renaissance of Freedom and Prosperity was something close to a textbook utopia. Seemingly unsolvable social problems (i.e., widespread poverty, homelessness, hunger, lack of access to medical treatment, illiteracy, smoking, traffic congestion, substance addiction, public rudeness,

war, naturally, but more than just war, violence itself, all forms of
aggression) had been eliminated, or virtually eliminated. Medical
advances had gradually increased the average life expectancy dramatically. Cancer, although not entirely eradicated, had become a
routine, manageable illness. Pharmaceutical breakthroughs enabled
the vast majority of Variant-Positive Normals to live fulfilling,
contented lives, free from anxiety, depression, boredom, envy, resentment, and other conditions that had plagued humanity throughout
the ages. Despite the fact that the Age of Anarchy had set the march
of progress back, who knew how many hundreds of years, technological development had now been resumed. Information proliferated,
and was instantly accessible around the clock. Crime was virtually
non-existent, apart from occasional isolated instances of fraud, insid-
er trading and such, which was almost always unintentional, and was
one of the costs of doing business. Thanks to the non-existence of
crime, there wasn't any need for jails or prisons, or any other type of
penal industry, most of the leading members of which had converted
over to Security Services, or A.S.P.-Management and Quarantine
Services, during the Age of Emergency Measures. Nations, although
technically still in existence, were nothing more than administrative
bodies, fiscally, financially, and in every other way, dependent on the
corporations. Which meant that they, these nominal nations,* would
never again be in a position to launch such wars as had brought the
world, over and over, to the brink of destruction, and the list went
on and on, and on. Clearly, to anyone thinking properly, the Age of
the Renaissance of Freedom and Prosperity, if not an ideal utopian
society, was ... well, things could have been a whole lot worse.

Or so it seemed when the drugs were working. The problem was,
when the drugs weren't working, this textbook utopia was just a veneer, a gleaming front for something sick, something far worse than
the wholesale slaughter, carnage and conflict that had led up to it,
something that wanted much more than to merely kill, enslave and
oppress its victims, because one could at least identify and fight that
... but no, not this, this simulation, which guaranteed "peace" and
called itself "freedom," but was really just about domination, not the

---

* No one ever referred to these nations, which everyone thought of as "former nations," although, on
paper, they did still exist.

kind that crushes your face with a giant despotic Orwellian boot, or
puts a bullet in the back of your head, despite the fact that everywhere you went was swarming with teams of Security Specialists,
surveillance cameras, biometric scanners, and other Counter-Terror
measures ... no ... this was far worse than that, smarter, infinitely
more efficient. This was the kind of domination that controlled your
MIND, and not just your thoughts, opinions and expressions, but
how you perceived, and what you perceived, controlled, not you, or
any individual, but REALITY ITSELF, not with some kind of fake
reality that you lived in like a video game, ACTUAL REALITY
... THIS REALITY ... such that someone, let's say, for example,
Joachim Maria-Torres Oakley, was, in fact, in reality, FREE, and
NOT a slave, and NOT exploited, and no one was stealing the value
of his labor, his time, his life, his very BEING, sucking it leech-
like out of his body and using it to enrich themselves. And this was
not merely some online pundit's or tenured academic's opinion,
but was actually a FACT, a provable FACT ... and such that, when
a doctor told you that what you were thinking was symptomatic
of Human Anti-Social Disease, this, too, was a FACT, a medical
FACT, a scientifically provable FACT, and not just a tactic to mar-
ginalize you, to separate you, to undermine you, and convince you
you were losing your mind ... and such that, when it wanted to kill
you, this vast conspiracy that didn't exist, in the end, when it decided it needed you dead, once it knew it couldn't control you, could
never quite get all the way inside you, and completely possess your
eternal soul, it didn't have to physically kill you ... all it had to do
was CHANGE REALITY, as in invent some new disease or condition, which wouldn't be a fake disease or condition, but an actual
REAL disease or condition, and write it up in the DSM ... or ... or
... and this was the HORROR ... genetically design some brand new
human, better-than-human form of human ... a perfect, blue-eyed
pseudo-human ... bred to obey and serve ... IT (this horrible something, whatever IT) ... feeding IT ... multiplying IT ... substituting
IT for everything ... until ... until ... eventually, one day, not one trace
of anything other than IT remained and finally no one would even
be able to ever imagine anything other than IT ... EVER!

Kyle was part of IT. Yes ... he was. Kyle was the one who wanted this baby. Yes, it was all so clear to her now. Kyle and the doctors were racing time. It didn't matter if she lost her mind. As long as they could keep her physically healthy until she delivered ... that's all they wanted. They would strip the baby's DNA of all her Anti-Social genes. They would rip them out like the spine of a fish and toss them into the yellow bio-bin ...

DING!

"YES, THAT'S R-I-I-I-GHT, VALENTINA!," boomed Big Bob, the host of Quandary.

DING!

WHAT ARE YOU IDIOTS LOOKING AT?!

Sixteen incredibly happy people in seasonally appropriate business attire who just couldn't wait to get up to their offices and start taking orders from their supervisors were standing in front of her, smiling at her, waiting for her to exit the elevator. One of them was waving his hand in front of the sensors to prevent the doors from closing. Each time he did that the doors went ... DING! Valentina wasn't quite sure how long she'd been in there, hallucinating, and how long they'd been out there, smiling, but it felt like maybe it had been a while. She blinked, coughed, took a deep breath, and stepped out into the brightly lit lobby of 6262 Lomax Avenue, a vast, vaulted, corporate cathedral muraled with 3D PlasmaTron screens. It was like a simulated Sistine Chapel ... the ceiling crawling with video footage, or possibly the actual reanimated corpses, of CEOs, CFOs, COOs and DHRs, the Lomax Industries' canon of saints, beneath which swarms of mid-level managers, key account managers, senior vice presidents, department heads, executive assistants, personal assistants, paralegal assistants, assistant archive retrieval technicians, copy technicians, and assistant receptionists were crisscrossing back and forth between the beams of camera crab eyes panning every which way on Styrofoam stalks, tracking Valentina's every step, firing their laser Ultrasound signals into her womb to monitor ... IT! They were feeding the data to relay units hidden inside ... THIS woman's purse ... THIS man's briefcase ...

"WHAT ARE YOU SMILING AT?!"

"Beg your pardon?"

"Where's the EXIT?"

"The exit to where?"

"Call Security."

"Exit! Exit! Do you speak English?!"

Lomax Security was onto her now, all darting eyes and earpiece whispers, her vitals up on their in-lens screens ... hairless murdering nametagged mannequins ...

RUN! NO! DO NOT RUN!

Walk.

Smile.

Blink out the tears.

Ten more steps to the escalator.

Will your lips to stop their quivering.

Hold the handrail.

Down she went ...

Down the tubeway, suctioned down the seamless, sterile, white intestine ... Valentina Funiculus Briggs, talking chrysalis, symbiont, host, the parasite within the parasite, feeding the seed of her own erasure ... way down there the tube was spitting picture perfect pellet people into a sea of writhing worms, while here, up here, its inner membrane, some reprogrammable digital skin, was running a stream of Content in which the CGI models, affluent people, with bleached white teeth and hairless nostrils, were gazing down into bowls of salad as if into the countenance of God ... and there, ascending, flowing past her ... whoosh ... whoosh ... other faces, smiling faces ... empty eyes ... single grains of necrotic ... NO! She gripped the handrails to either side of her, squatted slightly to keep from falling, blinded by the wave of light that hit her like a wall of wind and blew her brain out into pieces ... infinite, ever multiplying pieces, shattering, splitting, subdividing, spraying out through all eternity, drifting, floating ... throughout all time ... ever finer ... dust ... stardust ....
.... and .... then .... all at once .... the pieces ..... particles ... specks ... of her ... as if inhaled all fell together ... interlocking. CLICK. SNAP. SEAMLESS. ALL OF IT ... EVERYTHING ... ONE. She stood there, in the center of the station, smiling commuters streaming past her as if she were part of the architecture. Someone had turned off the sound in her head. All her life she'd had it backwards. All her life she'd been fighting the disease. Or

someone who she thought she was had. Someone she had never
been. Someone she had tried to be. For Kyle. For her parents, her
doctors ... everyone. But Valentina was not this someone. Valentina
was some other someone ... the ugly one, the one she'd been fighting
... or the simulation of her had been fighting. But if the One was
truly one, and truly infinite and multiplicitous, why was she fighting? What was she fighting? What was she fighting if not the One?
All her life she had seen the disease as something alien, attacking
her body. But what if it wasn't ... what if she wasn't ... something
alien, sick, and wrong? What if, actually, nothing was wrong, and
everything, as it was, was perfect? And she was perfect ... as she was.
Whatever she was. And the Path(s) were circles. All her life she'd
been running in circles, desperately trying to arrest a disease she did
not have, and no one had, except insofar as they all believed it, as
she'd believed it ... and now it was nothing ... and they had torn the
skin off the sky for nothing, and had boiled the seas and the lakes
for nothing, and had scorched nearly half the earth for nothing, and
they had killed the bears and the birds and the cats and the fish and
the snakes and the dogs and the frogs and every creature that had
walked the Earth except for the pigeons and the roaches and rats ...
and, OK, maybe a handful of dogs ... and had killed and tortured
and raped each other and beaten and bombed and enslaved each
other until there was no one left to enslave and rape and bomb and
torture and kill, until all that was left was to kill themselves, to turn
their hatred on themselves, which is what they were doing ... replacing themselves, remaking themselves in the image of IT ... human
beings, Homo sapiens, who they hated even more than they hated
the creatures who had walked the Earth, or the Earth itself, or the
even the black abysmal heavens in which it hung a dying world, and
the timeless winds of time itself ... existence itself ... this cosmic mistake ... this insult ... this sickness, this disease they would cure ... but
Valentina would not let them. Standing there, right in the middle
of the station, in the clearing the commuters were forming for her,
staring up at where heaven would be if up and down weren't totally
relative, arms outstretched and palms turned up like those statuettes
of the Virgin Mary, the muscles in her face and neck all tense, protruding through her skin, and twitching slightly, she saw her Path,

and she was already on it. They, the minions, the armies of IT, were on the verge of ... well, she wasn't quite sure, something unimaginably horrible, and almost definitely apocalyptic, and she, Valentina Constance Briggs, of 3258 Marigold Lane, Pewter Palisades Private Community, had been chosen by the One to stop them.

Ordinance 119

Four months later, Taylor Byrd, who when we left him was right in the middle of trying to make it across Clayton Avenue ahead of those teams of Security Specialists who were locking down the entire sector, was having his own little spiritual experience ... which all right, while it wasn't as dramatic, or as revelatory, or possibly psychotic, as Valentina's Lomax Escalator Vision, in its own way was probably just as spiritual ... or at least it had something to do with faith. Taylor didn't want to call it faith. But it was. It was basically a question of faith. It wasn't a question of faith in God (or The One Who Was Many), as it was for Valentina. No, for Taylor, it was more about faith in people, and the future of civilization generally, which as far as he could tell was on the verge of becoming the sterile, conformist nightmare it had always secretly dreamed of becoming, and was probably always destined to be.

Now this is a rather important distinction, because we're dealing with two different types of faith, each of which, in their respective ways, were deadly threats to peace and prosperity, but which were threatening in very different ways.

One of these threatening types of faith, religious fanaticism, was as old as the hills. The historical sites were replete with accounts of wars, pogroms, holy crusades, inquisitions, and other such atrocities, carried out in the name of God, which was what people used to call the One, and what some in the older generations still did. It wasn't only the Christians who had done this. Muslims, Jews, Hindus, Buddhists, and adherents of other, less popular religions, believing themselves to be the Chosen People, had slaughtered millions on account of their "beliefs." In reality, of course, these fanatical "beliefs" were nothing but the morbid fabulations of untreated late-stage Anti-Social minds, minds besieged by paranoia, hallucinations, delusions of reference, aggressive compulsions, and other pathologies ... like the kind Valentina was experiencing that Christmas. The difference was, in earlier ages, before the advent of modern pharmatherapy, ninety-nine point nine nine percent of the public was late-stage Anti-Social, which meant that their pathological delusions were not perceived as aberrations, but, rather, being shared by virtually everyone, were considered normal, and just the way things were. The fact that nearly everyone shared these delusions, and regarded them, not as irrational beliefs, but as axiomatic and self-evident truths, didn't make them any less pathological, at least not in the eyes of the Normals, for whom the idea of killing, or dying, for any such "beliefs" was inconceivable.

Which isn't to say the Age of the Renaissance of Freedom and Prosperity was religion-free. On the contrary, throughout the United Territories, Normals were permitted (and were actively encouraged) to belong to any of a number of religions, or to several religions, or to no religion, or to otherwise worship the One Who Was Many in whatever shape or form they chose.* Religion being a question of taste, the general feeling was, the more the merrier. The specific symbolic system one adopted was strictly a matter of personal preference. The One Who Was Many/the Many Who Were One (i.e., the ultimate referent of all such symbols) contained all faiths within Its infinite, multiplicitous singularity.

This liberal attitude toward religion was not just convention; it was written into law. The Tenth Amendment to the Global Civil Code guaranteed each individual the personal freedom to believe in whatever, and to worship whatever, in whatever fashion, as long as their personal religious beliefs did not infringe on, or offend, or threaten, or insult, directly or indirectly, the rights or property of other individuals, or corporations, or their subsidiaries and assigns. Thus, although religions abounded, and their followers exhibited a fierce brand loyalty (much in the way an HC Systems All-in-One user would never, ever, consider using a MultiMax Viewer), peace, acceptance, and tolerance reigned.

---

* *Christianity, Islam, Judaism, Hinduism, Buddhism, The Way of the Spirit, Hazeldonism, Astrotheology, Scientology, the Church of Being, the list went on and on, and on.*

This hadn't come about by accident … this novel "brand-based" approach to religion. No, the primary thing that had made it work was the privatization and wholesale restructuring of the hundreds of formerly powerful churches and other global religious bodies, first and foremost the Christian churches, but also the Jewish and Islamic unions, Buddhist and Hindu organizations, and every other such institution to which believers had once felt devoted.

This privatization and wholesale restructuring had occurred in the early 24th Century, so during the Age of Emergency Measures. Following the horrors of the Age of Anarchy, from which the world was then just emerging, fanaticism, in whatever form, but above all else religious fanaticism, was, it was universally agreed, something that needed to be done away with, now and forever, by whatever means. Priests, ministers, rabbis, clerics, religious leaders of every stripe, those who had somehow survived the chaos, were rounded up and made redundant, and replaced with teams of "interfaith consultants," who immediately set about the delicate business of re-positioning their respective brands. This repositioning was, of course, a meticulously coordinated intra-corporate effort, the goal of which was to preserve and strengthen the individual faiths (or brands) while simultaneously rendering them harmless … attractively distinct yet interchangeable multi-market lifestyle commodities.

And this is where the One Who Was Many came in.

The One Who Was Many was marketing genius. In one fell swoop, it put an end to thousands of years of religious conflict, united all faiths under one umbrella, and upended the whole personal worship equation. The One Who Was Many was not a deity, or not in the traditional deity sense. No, it was more like an aggregate meta-deity that contained all deities within itself, and so *was* all these deities, and was none of these deities, and was also the laws of space and time, and each physical unit of space and time, and each and every other physical and metaphysical aspect of being. In other words, the One Who Was Many was pretty much anything you wanted it to be, as long as you were able to keep in mind that it was also what other people wanted it to be, and that it was simultaneously all of these things, and none of these things, and was utterly unknowable.

And therein lay the marketing genius.

The One Who Was Many, being unknowable, omnipresent, and ... well, basically, everything, it went without saying, could never be explained, not in any authoritative way, so there were no priests or clerics or gurus to claim any kind of privileged knowledge of the fundamental nature of Its all-knowing being. However, some of Its infinite aspects were describable ... and thus highly marketable. For example, the fact that the One was Many, which it patently and indisputably was,* which meant that everything that was was one. Now, obviously, all of these many things (these things that were) were also themselves, and therefore, in that aspect, many, but at the same time, they were also one. Moreover, although each one of the Many (the Many Who Were One) was, in that aspect, a unique, nameable, knowable entity, taken altogether, in their unified aspect (i.e., as attributes of the One Who Was Many), they ceased to be nameable, knowable entities, being, as they were, merely parts of the One, whose Oneness was ipso facto unknowable. (How could a part of the whole presume to "know" the whole of which it was part?)

What all this nonsense essentially meant was that Jesus, Allah, Jehovah, Brahman, Vishnu (or whoever, take your pick), every major and minor deity, were simply aspects of the One Who Was Many, and thus merely parts of a larger wholeness ... a boundless, unimaginable Oneness, existing everywhere, containing everything, the will and essential nature of which were beyond the limits of human understanding.

The newly appointed interfaith consultants seized on this then revolutionary concept, called in their serious marketing guys, and went to work on the old religions with pretty much everything they had in their arsenals. The transformation didn't happen overnight, but after two or three generations of around-the-clock relentless messaging (and the summary arrest and indefinite detention of anyone deemed "fanatically religious") the overwhelming majority of people had successfully adjusted their faith-based thinking.

By the 27th Century, H.C.S.T. (or the time of our story, in any event), the very notion of religious intolerance was unimaginable and beyond absurd. The Normals, irrespective of their faiths, took for

---

* *This fundamental axiom being the opening line of the Path(s) to Prosperity.*

granted that their personal deities were nothing but symbols, work-alike signs, each one referring to the One Who Was Many, which could never be represented in Its Oneness. Thus, it made no differ-ence whether one prayed to Jesus, Allah, Jehovah, Vishnu, or to God as you understood Him ... whoever you prayed to, you prayed to the One. Likewise, the strictures of any one faith were just one Path (one Path among many) which led one onward, to other Path(s), each of which led one closer to the One. As all Path(s) led one closer to the One, the whole idea of forcing others to walk one's Path, or worship one's symbols (or otherwise adopt one's personal values, which had been the cause of so many of those wars, persecutions, pogroms, and so on), was not just Anti-Social behavior, and a Terrorist Act. It was also pointless.

Which didn't stop the faith-based Terrorists from plotting their devastating Terrorist attacks, which they did relentlessly, and un-der the threat of which everyone had lived for several centuries. But then, they were all late-stage Anti-Socials, not to mention religious fanatics ... we'll get into all that Terrorist stuff later. The point at the moment is, for the majority of Normals (i.e., those who weren't receiving personal messages from God, like Valentina), faith was a strictly personal affair. It didn't matter what other people did. All that mattered was walking their Path(s), and keeping the focus on them-selves, and meditating and praying for guidance, and for knowledge of the loving Will of the One. This, the Normals knew, was the key to successfully walking the Path(s) to Prosperity, not judging others, nor judging themselves, nor attempting to understand the One, or the inscrutable logic of Its cosmic plan, or questioning Its loving Will, but asking only, in a state of humility, to be shown what the One would have them do.

Taylor, of course, could have given a fuck. The One Who Was Many, the Many Who Were One, God as the Normals chose to understand Him, Jesus, Allah, Jehovah, Brahman, Krishna, Ahura Mazda, et al., each and every one of these entities, individually or together as a group, were welcome, as far as Taylor was concerned, to astrally travel across the universe, take human form at the bar at Gillie's, and suck foul wind out of his ass. And as for the so-called Cosmic Plan, it didn't seem much of a plan to Taylor. That is, unless the main objective was to wreak as much pointless suffering as possible on as many varieties of life forms as possible and then piss off to some other cosmos and nuke the ruins of the first from orbit. The way Taylor saw it, assuming there were some Higher Power, or Master Architect, He was some kind of twisted Über-Sadisto who got his rocks off torturing people, first in this life, just for kicks, then later, in earnest, for all eternity. Taylor had read *The Path(s) to Prosperity*, as well a number of older scriptures (i.e., the Christian Bible, the Torah, the Koran, the Way of Nature, and other such crap), all of which seemed to be variations on the same inspiringly jubilant message ... that people were basically pieces of shit. And it wasn't just that they were pieces of shit, and inherently worthless, and bad, and wrong, they were also selfish, stupid, and faithless, and, above all, they were disobedient. According to all these holy scriptures, God, or the Truth, or Reality, or something, was going to show them the error of their ways, and teach them a lesson, and punish them, and kill them, and fry their souls in Hell forever, or send them back to the Wheel of Karma, to suffer, until they got their minds right.

Which, what do you know, as it just so happened, God was about to do to Taylor. Oh yes, God was going to whale on Taylor. God was going to fuck Taylor up. God was going to rip Taylor's head off and take a big shit down Taylor's neck. First, though, He was going to torture Taylor, and not just any old type of torture, like having the skin peeled off your body or being boiled in oil or whatever. No, God had something very special in the way of torture in mind for Taylor. Before God smote him, and sent his soul to burn in the fires of Hell forever, God was going to make Taylor do The Worst Thing He Had Ever Done. He was going to make him do this sober, so Taylor could take the vivid memory, which would be like a Hi-Def replay loop, down into the Inferno with him, and suck on that for all eternity. According to these various holy scriptures, God was going to do this to Taylor, not because He hated Taylor, and all other human beings generally, and wanted to hear what they had to say now, as they roasted in the fires of Hell forever ... no, God was going to do this to Taylor because God was Taylor's spiritual Father, and the Father of Time, and of all Creation, who had conjured light from the primordial darkness, and whose essence was pure and infinite Love.

Taylor, who wasn't infinite anything (he was just an all-too-human being, and an Anti-Social human being at that), was sitting at the bar at Gillie's Tavern watching an ad for The Path(s) to Prosperity and nursing a pint of piss-warm beer. He'd been sitting there for about ten minutes. Casual Dad was talking over a series of shots of ecstatic children playing on swing sets and merry-go-rounds and other such cloying Normal treacle. The ad was running on the pirate Viewer that T.C. kept behind the bar, the screen of which was all warped and dusty. The time was approximately 0650. At this point, he had about forty-five minutes to get to Cassandra's and make a decision, which, all this faith-based bullshit aside, the decision he needed to make was simple. He needed to decide what he thought was happening, or believed was happening, which was one of two things. See, either whatever was happening out there, the sealed-off Sector, the choppers, et cetera, was the Day of Autonomous Decentralized Action, which meant there was still an outside chance that Sarah was out there, and on her way to the rendezvous, or it wasn't, which meant she probably wasn't. Simple either/or equation. Subject to the laws of probability. Nothing fuzzy, metaphysical or remotely fucking faith-based about it.

So, OK ... reason it out, he thought. What were the odds that this *was* the D.A.D.A., and that now, as in right at that very moment, autonomous factions of the A.S.U. were launching a series of militant actions, coordinated actions, as in bombings, and so on, and not just there in Zone 23, but in Zones throughout the Northeast Regions, and possibly the entire United Territories?

What were the odds that that was happening?

The odds were lousy. They were virtually zero ... virtually, but not definitively zero, which slim contingency was eating at Taylor, because, all right, unlikely as it certainly was, desperate pipe dream that it probably was, still, if Sarah *was* still out there, and hadn't disappeared, or been disappeared, the plan was still the best way to go. However, if she wasn't out there, and today was just Tuesday, and not the D.A.D.A., and whatever was happening was simply the work of some random assholes who had blown up a building, or worse (and this was definitely possible), some IntraZone Waste & Security scheme, and he went ahead tried for the rendezvous, and ended up out on Jefferson Avenue with nowhere to go and Security on him, there wouldn't be any other choice at that point ... he'd have to do what he'd have to do, and he'd have to do it quick and dirty. And he didn't want to have to do it quick and dirty. If he had to do it, which he probably did, he wanted to do it clean and painless ... but mostly he didn't want to have to do it.

Gillie's Tavern, at this time of morning, was usually quiet, but not this quiet. The air felt like it was charged with static. Sector C was locked down tight. The northern perimeter was just outside, running both ways on Clayton Avenue, bomb units, barricades, APCs, water cannons, robots, the whole fucking circus. Taylor, obviously, had made it across by the skin of his balls as they sealed off the border. Now, officially, he was sheltering in place, trying to get his thoughts in order (which, for how that was going, see above). Across from Taylor, behind the bar, Young Man Henry was washing glasses and telling Jim MacReady the story of T.C.'s dog, a Brazilian pit bull, name of Bullet, who'd been dead for years. MacReady, who had already heard the story of T.C.'s dog about a thousand times, and who'd been on a drunk for three days running, was squinting across the dark, dank, windowless basement that was Gillie's Tavern at a withered old hag named Coreen Sweeney, who looked like a starving chicken on speed. MacReady, who under normal conditions wouldn't have fucked a walking corpse like Coreen Sweeney with Taylor's dick, was smiling a kind of goofy drunken smile that was meant to look lascivious. Coreen Sweeney was smiling back at him, or she would have been, had she had any teeth. Across the barroom, at a table in the back, a gang of fairly nefarious-looking Class 3 Anti-Social-type Persons, most of whom Taylor knew from around, guys like Shane and Charlie Gilmartin, Estrellita Klein, and Vaclav Borges, and Palmer, it looked like, were playing poker. All these people, MacReady, Coreen, the nefarious poker players, Young Man Henry, as well as a lot of other people who'd had the sense to drag themselves home, had been there at Gillie's the night before when Taylor, having recently killed several people, and staring up into the Asshole of Doom, had put down all that fucking tequila and lost what little remained of his shit. He couldn't be sure what he'd said or hadn't, but he figured he hadn't said anything damning, or at least hadn't loudly announced his intention to go out and kill several other people, people whose names he had on his kill list, beginning with one J.C. Bodroon ... or no one had made any mention of it. He sat there, staring down into his beer, mentally cursing God and the One, and himself, and Adam, and the A.S.U., and Sarah, and Meyer, and the faith-based Terrorists, and the Hadley Corporation of Menomonie, Wisconsin, and trying to decide what the hell to do.

Gillie's Tavern, like all the taverns, was owned by IntraZone Waste & Security,* but was run by a one-legged half a Cajun named T.C. James, who had transferred north when the Zones down south got inhospitable. Young Man Henry, who was in his eighties, or possibly his nineties, or maybe even older, and was the blackest black man Taylor had ever seen, had transferred up with him. They were like a team. T.C. James was a straight out racist, but not in any kind of serious way.** He sported an impervious, silver pompadour, wrap-around glasses with elaborate frames, the lenses of which were as thick as your finger and made his eyes look way too big. He wore this second-hand prosthetic leg that strapped to the stump that was left of his thigh, the left one, just below the hip joint, which didn't fit right and was terribly painful. He'd cut loose with all these racist slurs, "nigger" this and "wetback" that, and would call people "Ivan" and "Jerry" and "Charlie," drawing upon some redneck lexis no one in the Zone had ever deciphered. An ancient American Confederate flag (a faithful reproduction, of course) hung on the wall behind the bar, which T.C. and Young Man Henry had built, as they had most everything else down there, and had run the electrics, fixed the plumbing, and rigged up the toilets to halfway work. They had done all this with scavenged materials, T.C. limping around on his leg, measuring lengths of wood and cursing, Henry swinging a hammer

---

* *Technically, everything in the Zone was owned by IntraZone Waste & Security, or by the Hadley Corporation of Menomonie, Wisconsin, or one of its agents, subsidiaries or assigns (except for the corporate stores and factories that were owned by other corporations, which were technically owned by those corporations, regardless of whoever actually owned them).*

** *Serious racists did exist in the Zone, but they were fewer in number than you'd probably imagine. Despite the fact that the gangs were race-based and that the Zone was somewhat racially segregated, classification overruled race, which meant that, generally, 3s hung with 3s, 2s with 2s, 1s with 1s, regardless of race, color, or creed.*

and singing, the two of them taking turns telling old stories, lies, and jokes, which they'd told for years, Henry talking in his "Sambo" voice, like some kind of weird old minstrel routine.

Henry was up to the part of the story where Bullet just stood there, saying "nnnnnnnnnnnnn." He was standing slightly to the left of Taylor. MacReady was sitting at the bar in front of him (i.e., in front of Henry, to the left of Taylor). Coreen Sweeney was off to his right. The poker players were at a table behind him. MacReady pulled himself off his barstool, downed the lukewarm dregs of his beer, took one step toward Coreen, fell face first onto a nearby table, rolled off, taking the table with him, and lay there on the floor, unconscious. It didn't appear to be Coreen's morning. Henry went on telling his story, exactly to whom now it was not clear, which didn't seem to matter to Henry, and definitely didn't matter to MacReady. Taylor turned back to T.C.'s Viewer, which was showing some sort of Edu-Content in which a team of enthused archeologists were reassembling the skull of a cow. This was the kind of Content they ran when they took the IntraZone grid offline, which meant there wouldn't be any more news until whatever was happening was over.

"You look like shit, boy," Henry said.

Obviously he was done with story.

"I feel like shit," Taylor told him.

"I expect you do, the way you was drinking."

"Any idea what the fuck this is?"

"Nary a clue," Henry said. "Last they locked down a sector like this was Jackson Avenue, far as I recall. You was just a kid then, probably."

"Yeah ... I was ten," Taylor said.

Henry sucked his teeth and snorted. Then he went down the bar to tend to Coreen. Taylor went back to staring at his beer. He shook a dash of Sansalt into it, trying to get it to bring up a head, which, of course, it wouldn't, and he sat there and watched as the crystals slowly sank and dissolved. Tiny circles of carbon dioxide rose to the surface and spread like ripples, growing, expanding, surrendering their forms ... something clicked inside his head.

Perfect, he thought, and he had to smile, because this was how this whole thing had started, these past six months with the A.S.U.,

Sarah, whoever she really was, Meyer, whatever his fucking deal was, the faith-based Terrorists, if they even existed, Dodo, Bodroon, the Community Watchers, Cassandra's bedroom sequestration, the kill list, Max ... the whole fucking mess. This was it. This image right here. This was how it all began, not with a glass of beer at Gillie's, but back at Cassandra's with a glass of urine ...

Seven months and week or so earlier, on a hazy, humid September morning, a particularly hot one if memory served, Taylor, having traveled his usual route, and having stopped for his usual beer at Gillie's, and having wound his way up the rusted-out fire escape that led to Cassandra's third-floor bedroom, crawled through her window and found her sitting there ... holding a glass of piss in one hand and a plastic pregnancy tester in the other. She was sitting on the side of the head of her bed, which Taylor had built the platform for, and which seemed to be floating in the sea of clothes, discs, books, plates, glasses and various other random items that she'd never once picked up off the floor in all the time that Taylor had known her. She looked like a mannequin, sitting there, staring. Or like she was dead. She wasn't breathing. Then she turned and looked at Taylor. She didn't say anything. Not with words.

Taylor stood there at the window a moment, looking like men often look at such times, which is kind of disbelieving and clueless.

"How the fuck could this have happened?" he asked.

Cassandra shot him a withering look. He knew exactly how this had happened, and when, and exactly why this had happened.

Six weeks earlier, so back in July now, she'd lost her Anti-Baby pills among the profusion of clothes, discs, books, and assorted other crap that was always strewn around her bedroom, and she'd had to go to the CRS and get a new package and start all over. By the time she did that, she had missed a few days (too many days, she explained to Taylor), which meant she would have to wait until she got her next period to start the new round. In the meantime, Taylor would have to wear a condom, which he wasn't used to and had always hated. He reiterated this fact to Cassandra. She was overcome with sympathy for him.

"Grow the fuck up. It's just for a month."

"I fucking hate them."

"Join the club."

"I'll just pull out."

"The fuck you will."

Taylor stood at the window and pouted.

"Have you ever even worn one?" she grilled him.

"Of course."

"When?"

"It doesn't matter."

"When?"

"It doesn't matter when."

"You fucking liar. You've never worn one."

OK, so he'd never worn one. Which was not as odd as it probably sounds. Guys didn't wear a lot of condoms in the Zone. Condoms were not a popular item. This was true for two good reasons, one of which being that there hadn't been a reported case of an STD for longer than anyone alive could remember ... the other being Ordinance 119.

IntraZone Ordinance 119, discouraging A.S.P. procreation, had been in effect for thirty years, during which an entire generation of A.S.P.s had been discouraged. Anti-Baby pills were widely available free of charge to A.S.P. women, as were a range of other options. For men, there were condoms, or sterilization, neither of which options were terribly popular. Sterilization was strictly voluntary, but strongly recommended for male 2s and 3s. 1s were deemed responsible enough to make their own contraceptive decisions. A.S.P. 2s, and especially 3s, were deemed as responsible as rutting billy goats, so the sooner the men were sterilized the better.

IntraZone Ordinance 119, among its numerous other provisions, had authorized IntraZone Waste & Security to found a subsidiary, IntraZone ConCept, whose mission it was to hasten this process. In addition to the Public Service Advisories that ran all day on the Public Viewers, there were ConCept posters all over the Zone extolling the virtues of "permanent contraception," which procedure for men was quick and painless, and available free at any ConCept clinic. The face on these posters belonged to "Candy," a buxom, blond, heavy-lidded, nineteen year-old nymphomaniac, who looked like maybe she was masturbating right there into the lens of the camera. Her lips were slightly parted and glistening. Her eyes had that pre-orgasmic glaze. "DO IT FOR ME!" was Candy's slogan. It stretched in bright pink all-cap letters across the space where her nipples would have been. Unfortunately, for IntraZone Waste & Security, and IntraZone ConCept, and their parent company, the Candy campaign had been less than convincing. Most of the posters had been defaced. (Guys struck out "for" and wrote in "to.") They weren't exactly lining up to get their vasa deferentia snipped either. The ConCept clinics in Sector B had dwindled in number to about fourteen, and the ones in Sector C had all closed. Class 3 Anti-Social Persons kept throwing objects through the windows.

Despite the disappointing response to the "Candy" campaign and other enticements, IntraZone ConCept had not given up on sterilization of the male 2s and 3s, but they'd pretty much written off Taylor's generation and were concentrating now on the under-40s. In the meantime, for the older guys, there were other contraceptive strategies. For one thing, there were always the women, who for one extremely compelling reason, the nature of which we'll get into shortly, tended to take their pills like clockwork. And if something went wrong, like, say, for example, you lost your pills in the piles of crap that completely covered the floor of your bedroom, which you'd never once cleaned in like ten fucking years ... well, OK, there were always condoms.

"How the fuck do you think it happened?"

She dropped the tester into the glass of urine and set it down on her bedside milk crate, nudging aside the other glasses of stuff that looked like but wasn't her pee. She smiled at Taylor in that way he hated, with that icy, condescending smirk that 1s reserved for Class 3 morons, which is how 1s generally regarded 3s, but was not how Cassandra regarded Taylor, at least not usually, not till today. She looked like she was getting ready to reach for something heavy to throw at him, then she broke down and burst out sobbing. Cassandra never burst out sobbing. She'd never once cried in all the years he'd known her. She was making this guttural keening sound. Her face was quivering. Her hands were shaking. Taylor had never seen like this.

He went to the bed and sat down and held her, which only made her sob even harder. She pushed him away and fumbled around in the sheets for something to blow her nose on.

"What are we going to do?" she moaned.

"This isn't your fault. This is my fault."

"I know."

"So ... I'll think of something."

"What?"

"I don't know. Something."

"You'd better or I'm fucking dead," she blubbered.

Taylor wasn't just saying shit he thought Cassandra wanted to hear. In some Narcissistic, self-serving way, he really believed it was his fault, or was mostly his fault, or was partly his fault. If he hadn't been such a big fucking baby, Cassandra wouldn't be sitting there pregnant, making those horrible wailing noises, and blowing her nose into her filthy bedsheet. But then again, he also believed, if Cassandra hadn't lost her pills, he wouldn't have gotten so fucking mad at her, and gone to Gillie's, and gotten so drunk, and ended up out in the Willoughby Projects, in which case (i.e., if he hadn't done that) he wouldn't have ended up back at Cassandra's, and they wouldn't have fought, and thrown shit around, and made up and fucked like savage beasts, all pent-up and desperate and angry, which was how they always ended up fucking after they fought ... so OK, sure, technically speaking, it was his fault, but partly it was also her fault. And mostly it was the condom's fault.

Taylor had never quite mastered the art of fucking with his cock wrapped in plastic. In Taylor's book it was almost worse than not being able to fuck at all. He did the best he could that month. He wore the condoms, grinned and bore it, but even when it worked, his heart wasn't in it. He didn't understand how the Normals did it. Never mind the question of why they did it. He figured they were all numbed out on their meds ... that, or maybe they had all been brainwashed and couldn't really tell the difference anymore. You'd see them in the Normal pornos, which were really just Sex-Education Content, gazing longingly into each other's eyes as they tore the condom packs open, slowly, licking their lips like they just couldn't wait to hermetically seal their cocks in plastic.

This didn't make any sense to Taylor. Wearing a rubber was like eating TōFood. You went through the motions of doing the thing you were actually doing, but weren't really doing, but weren't exactly not doing either, because there you were, in the flesh so to speak, eating or fucking, whichever it was, and it looked and worked like the actual thing, except for the fact that the chicken or fish was a bunch of genetically modified bean curd and your cock was wrapped in sterilized latex as if it was going into surgery or something. Which, frankly, for Taylor, just killed the whole mood, such that sometimes, after a minute of fucking, or Tōfucking, as he took to calling it, he'd start to get all tense and frustrated, and his cock would go limp and just hang there, sadly, wrapped in its little rubbery sheath. And at other times, when he didn't go limp, he'd fuck Cassandra like he normally did, fuck her into a screaming frenzy, and she'd come like crazy, two or three times, and run out of gas, and lie there, gasping, and Taylor wouldn't even be close to coming. All right, so they'd fuck some more then, and after a while Cassandra would reach another plateau and come again, hard and deep now, down in her soul, and Taylor, who normally, whenever that happened, would come so hard he'd hurt his prostate, would want so desperately to come along with her, but he couldn't come with the condom on, so finally he would just pull his cock out, tear the fucking rubber off, and Cassandra would finish him off with her hand ... which left him feeling all scrambled inside, like he'd just gotten laid, but hadn't, not really.

One night, after a couple of weeks of that, Taylor went down to Gillie's Tavern and got himself good and fucking shitfaced. He picked up a drunken little A.S.P. 3 with a snake tattoo by the name of Loraine, took her home to her shithole apartment on the 17th floor of the Willoughby Towers, drank her liquor and fucked her brains out from Friday night until Sunday morning. They dropped some MDLX she had, put some hypno on endless repeat, got out Loraine's collection of toys (most of which had been designed to inflict some form of pain on Loraine), and otherwise behaved like stereotypical Class 3 Anti-Social Persons all weekend. Which was fine with Taylor, as far as that went. The only problem was, as hard as he tried, he couldn't stop thinking about Cassandra. He thought about Cassandra the entire weekend. The more he thought about

Cassandra, the harder he spanked and fucked Loraine, which worked out pretty well for Loraine, but left Taylor feeling all numb inside, which wasn't exactly his favorite feeling.

Loraine's apartment was the size of a closet, and reeked of sweat and feet and pussy (and some unidentified mystery smell), however, being up on the 17th floor with nothing around it, the view was stunning. A strip of windows you couldn't open looked out as far as the eye could see. Taylor stood there, at some point, tripping, gazing into the gray, dimensionless sky alive with liquid trails of the lights of planes and commercial choppers and UAVs on their way to nowhere. He could see the whole Zone, or the northern part anyway, all three alpha-coded sectors, all the way out to Jefferson Avenue, and the markets ... and there, out beyond the Wall, the boundless sea of twinkling lights stretching endlessly off to the north, dropping down off the visible horizon ... cities bleeding into other cities, megacities, gigacities, thirty-something billion people packed into townhouses, corporate offices, condos, air-conditioned cocoons, sleeping, eating, working, breeding, churning out products and streams of Content, going forth and multiplying, choking what was left of the Earth like shimmering colonies of luminous algae ... what was the fucking point of it all? Down and off to the right of this vista, scattered through-out the Northeast Quadrant, the lights of the In-Zone plants and factories were winking and blinking and bleeding together like the synapses of some vast neural network. Down there somewhere, in one of those plants, assembling motherboards, or chipsets, or some-thing, was Cassandra Passwaters ... who he did not need. He didn't. Taylor didn't need anyone. He certainly didn't need *this* bullshit. This lame-ass condom-wearing bullshit. Fuck Cassandra and her fucking condoms. He'd wait until she got her new pills. She'd either have him back or she wouldn't. And if she wouldn't, he'd just find some-one else. (Not Lorraine, someone else.) It was probably time to do that anyway. Fuck Cassandra and her fucking monogamy. He'd never meant to "settle down" anyway, and so on, in Taylor's doped up logic.

Just before sunrise that Sunday morning, Taylor got up and got a shower in this plastic cold-water shower contraption that dribbled pathetically and had zero pressure. He was coming down from the MDLX, so his body felt like it was made of Jell-O. Loraine, who was nowhere near as attractive as Taylor remembered thinking she was, was passed out cold in the crusty sheets, the stench of which was past intolerable. He checked around for something to eat, but there wasn't anything even vaguely edible, so he got his boots on and tiptoed out, heading back home to 16 Mulberry, or the deep Inner Zone, or who knew where, Gillie's maybe, it didn't matter ... anywhere that wasn't Cassandra's.

He got to Cassandra's just before dawn, pushed and shoved his way through the throngs, cut through the fishmarket, climbed the fire escape, and crawled in through her bedroom window. She had just gotten home from her factory shift, and had changed out of her factory coveralls and into one of her see-through gown things. Her pirate Viewer was playing some Content in which a clown was trying to teach some other clowns how to drive a car. She asked him where the fuck he'd been. He informed her he hadn't been fucking anywhere. She asked him what the fuck he wanted. He asked if she fucking had something to eat. She said she thought she maybe had some powdered eggs, which he could shove up his ass. He wondered if she'd gotten her period yet. She told him she hadn't. He asked when she would. She told him it should be any day now, and either he could be patient and wait, or grow the fuck up and use the condoms, or go back to whatever whore he'd been fucking without a condom if he liked her so much. Taylor reckoned he might just do that, and he wondered if maybe she'd found her pills among all this crap all over the floor, which maybe she was waiting for the maid to clean up. She snatched a bottle from her bedside milk crate and hurled it at him. It missed, just ... shattering against the wall beside him and spraying shrapnel every which way. Taylor caught a shard in his cheek. He dug it out, examined it, briefly, dropped it in an ashtray, and started for the window. Cassandra leaped up off the bed, jumped on his back, knocking him over, got up, pounced on his chest like a cat, and punched him two or three times in the face before he could get a good hold on her wrists and roll her over and hold her down, and still she managed to get one knee up and into his nuts before it was over.

Later that night, they'd been going at it good and hard for a couple, three hours, not fucking for three hours straight, of course, but fucking, then lying around for a while, then fucking again, and so on, like that, and Cassandra was on her back for a change, folded in half with her legs in the air, and Taylor was pinning her wrists to the bed and was up on his hands and the balls of his feet in something resembling a push-up position, fucking her like there was no tomorrow (which, of course, technically speaking, there wasn't), and anyway, Cassandra couldn't take it anymore and started to shudder and come and shout, and Taylor pushed himself way up into her and shuddered and started to come and shout, and now the two of them were coming and shouting, and one of Cassandra's roommates was shouting, and banging the wall with the heel of her shoe, which neither Taylor nor Cassandra noticed, shouting at the top of their lungs as they were, their bodies convulsing in perfect synch, orgasms shooting electric currents up their spines and into their brains, rolling their eyeballs back in their heads ... and it wasn't until a few seconds later that both of them, more or less simultaneously, realized the condom had broken.

And so it was, on that late July or possibly early August morning, 2609, H.C.S.T. (the Year of the Mekong Giant Catfish), that a tiny unauthorized Anti-Social Person, who several months later Taylor named Max, began his strange and fateful journey toward the light of this dying world ... which, more about Max and the dying world later. We need to get back, or forward, rather, to that September morning, and the pee, and the sobbing ... or, technically, a few days after that.

Taylor spent those next few days (i.e., after the morning of the pregnancy test) doing exactly what he had promised Cassandra, namely, trying to think of something. He hadn't been able to think of anything. Except for what he'd eventually thought of, which was crazy, and was definitely not going to work. At the moment, he was sitting in a booth at Gillie's, drinking heavily, and reviewing the facts. And looking for a way around the facts. And there wasn't any way around the facts.

Cassandra was pregnant. This was a fact. She shouldn't have been, but there it was. And this was really eating at Taylor, because medically speaking it was virtually impossible. At 0500 on the Monday morning following the Sunday of the Broken Condom, they had gone to the CRS together, picked up a package of MorningAfter pills, and gone back to her place and followed the instructions. The pill, when taken within twenty-four hours, had a ninety-nine point nine nine success rate. And she'd definitely taken the fucking pill. Taylor had sat there and watched her take it. So, OK, there was another fact. Which didn't matter. Not one iota. The pill hadn't worked. The pill was shit. Which meant they were down to two or three options, each of which, individually, sucked.

For starters, according to paragraphs 3 and 4 of Ordinance 119, as of 01 January, 2580, or 12 Tevet, 6340, or something in the Year of the fucking Dugong, female Anti-Social Persons who had somehow gotten accidentally pregnant despite the employment of clinically tested and widely available contraceptive measures, were, upon discovery of said pregnancy, to report, in person, at their earliest convenience, to their nearest IntraZone ConCept clinic ... whereupon they would disappear.

While no one knew the official numbers, conspiracy theorists, like Meyer Jimenez, estimated that approximately two hundred thousand accidentally pregnant women had followed these instructions, and had disappeared. They'd walked into their local clinic, taken a number, had a seat, been shown through a door by a smiling assistant, and had never been seen or heard from again. According to Ordinance 119, these disappeared accidentally pregnant women had all been transferred to a specially-designated Females-Only Quarantine Area. They had been provided with prenatal care, had delivered their babies, and were living happily (albeit in a female-only environment) somewhere very far away. Their unauthorized infants had been transferred to a Juveniles-Only Quarantine Area, where doctors, psychologists, and other medical professionals, were treating their Anti-Social Disease with cutting-edge pharma- and behavioral therapies, many of which were experimental.

No one in the Zone believed a word of this.

The vast majority of the disappearances had happened during the two-year period following the issuance of Ordinance 119. It had taken a while for people to begin to put together what was happening, and even then, for the first few years, no one wanted to face what was happening. So, they didn't. Simple as that. They told themselves that it wasn't happening. They told themselves, and each other, stories, or chose to believe the ConCept story, the story about the "relocations" to the "other Zones" and all that horseshit. All of which was understandable, the implications being what they were. However, as more and more women went missing, and the sound of infants crying in the Zone gradually diminished, then entirely ceased (and history wonks like Meyer Jimenez correlated the date of the Ordinance to the births of the first generation of Clears) people began to accept the truth.

By January 2585, or Tevet 6345, or something in the Year of the Coronado Skink, the pregnancy rate in Zone 23 had been reduced to zero, or virtually zero. It had stayed that for twenty-five years. By now (i.e., the time of our story), there was no one left in the Zone under thirty. There were still, of course, the occasional accidents, but these were extremely rare events, and were invariably due to the inexplicable failure of the so-called MorningAfter pill, a powerful progesterone receptor antagonist, which, according to the label, was totally foolproof, and the last defense against accidental pregnancy.[*] According to Ordinance 119, the unfortunate women who suffered these accidents, or otherwise remained accidentally pregnant six weeks after their last menstruation, were required to report to a ConCept clinic.

So that was option number one.

Option number two was an abortion. It didn't get more Anti-Social than that. The Normals, obviously, had no qualms with contraception, IVF, or genetically modifying human beings. Abortion was an entirely different matter. Abortion was murder, plain and simple, the taking of a healthy human life. Like any other type of premeditated homicide, it earned you a Class 4 designation, which got you just as disappeared as if you walked into a ConCept clinic. Cassandra was willing to take that chance, or would have been, had there still been anyone able to perform an abortion safely, which, of course, by the time of our story there wasn't. IntraZone Waste & Security Services had disappeared anyone even halfway qualified. The only abortions still on the market were performed in the basements of

---

[*] *Oddly, these accidents only occurred among the A.S.P. 1 population.*

derelict buildings with a shot of Plasto and a hot piece of wire, by some ninety-year-old junkie sadist.

So, OK, option number three.

Option number three was Taylor's idea. It had come to him, more or less fully-formed, while he was lying in bed with Cassandra that morning. It was either a stroke of utter genius or the worst idea he had ever had. Option number three was, basically, to take Cassandra down to the basement, soundproof the basement with some egg crates or something, set her up with a bed, some cards, an offline Viewer, a box of Content, some kind of nasty makeshift toilet which Taylor would have to empty out, hide her down there for the next seven months, make up some story her roommates would buy explaining her sudden disappearance, let her have the baby down there, and then, assuming all that worked, get the baby out of the sector and into the hands of the A.S.U., which rumor had it was building some kind of underground army that would someday launch ... well, no one really knew what, exactly, some kind of global revolution or something. The A.S.U. would smuggle the baby out to the so-called "Autonomous Zones," which no one really believed existed, but which according to legend were isolated pockets of virtually uninhabitable wilderness scattered throughout the Recovering Areas, where tribes of mutants and free A.S.P.s lived some neoprimitive existence, drinking rain and cactus water and hunting skinks by the light of the moon.

Taylor and Cassandra had been over these options. Option number one was out. Cassandra was not going to walk into some ConCept clinic and disappear. Option number two was also out. Cassandra had heard too many stories of women who had ended up bleeding to death, and had been left to rot in some abandoned warehouse, or their bodies dumped in the Dell Street Canal.

So that left option number three. Crazy as it was, Cassandra reasoned, if she could just make it until the baby was born, and not get snitched on by one of her roommates, and somehow account for her absence at work, and if Taylor could contact the A.S.U., and assuming they would take the baby ... after that, it would all be over, and she could go back to work like normal, and the baby could go live with the A.S.U., and grow up to be a Terrorist or something, and they'd all live happily ever after. She wasn't going down to the basement, however, or shitting in any kind of makeshift anything. She would hole up in her bedroom, she said. The bathroom was right across the hall. And if one of her roommates did get wise, Taylor would have to deal with that.

Taylor didn't have any better ideas, so option number three it was. OK, there were no Autonomous Zones, not really, but the A.S.U. existed, and they probably had a network of safehouses, or tunnels ... or somewhere they could hide the baby. Certainly they would want to do that. They probably did it all the time. There were probably hundreds of unauthorized babies, and maybe entire unauthorized families, living in an underground network of tunnels, or hiding in a series of revolving safehouses ... or something like that. Sure there were. Which meant that all he needed to do, aside from all the logistical details, was get in touch with the A.S.U., which was easy ... however, there was one little catch.

The A.S.U. was notoriously paranoid. At least the more militant members were. It wasn't like he could just walk up to one of them and start blabbering about Cassandra and the baby. They'd make him for a Cooperator, or a moron, one, and probably kill him. No, if this plan was going to work, Taylor would have to earn their trust. And there wasn't any way to do that on his own, or not in the time he had available. He needed someone they knew to vouch for him. He needed someone to do that promptly.

He sat there, in that booth at Gillie's, and drank, and gave it considerable thought, and somewhere in the dead of night, or the dead of morning, or whenever it was, at approximately 0330, let's say, he determined, against his better judgment, and all his instincts, and his intuition, that that someone was probably Meyer Jimenez.

2.

Cramer

Now, before we get started with Part Two of our story, in the interest of fairness and objectivity, let's look at things from a different perspective, one that isn't so cynical and gloomy, or depressing, or whatever ours has been so far. It's good to stop and do that sometimes, because it's easy, when you're all immersed in a story, to forget that there's this larger world outside the world of the characters in the story, who are often in the midst of some dramatic crisis, and who you really can't help but identify with. For example, in our case, you might assume that everyone living in the 27th Century (or whatever century it really was) was miserable, and desperate, and totally confused. But that was not entirely true. No, despite whatever personal problems an unfortunate minority of troubled individuals like Taylor and Valentina were having, for the vast majority of individuals, life in general was pretty darn good in the Age of the Renaissance of Freedom and Prosperity.

OK, it wasn't any kind of utopia or anything, because, granted, there were still the Zones and all that, and Anti-Social Disease was still there, lurking in the folds of people's brains in its cunning and diabolical fashion, and there was always the chance of a weather event, or a sudden and devastating Terrorist attack, or cancer, or early onset dementia, and a host of other disturbing aspects ... but these were not things the majority of Normals walked around consciously thinking about, or made repeated inadvertent reference to, or lay awake in their beds at night with the lights off more or less totally obsessed with.

Life, for the most part, was pretty fulfilling. People, as a rule, were happy. People had choices. A lot of choices. People had nearly unlimited choices. This is what freedom meant, after all ... the freedom to make individual choices. Which is mostly what the Normals did all day. They went around making a lot of choices. They did this whether they wanted to or not. They didn't have much choice in the matter. The choices were there. They had to be made. Or not be made. Which was still a choice.

And it wasn't just all those streams of Content among which the Normals had to choose. They made all kinds of other choices, personal choices, professional choices, and ... well, a lot of other choices, mostly involving products and services. They made these choices day after day from the moment they woke until they passed out at night. Then they got up the next day and did it again.

Life was an endless series of choices.

Given all these choices they had, and the overall spirit of peace and prosperity, and entrepreneurial ingenuity, and fervor, omnipresent security, that prevailed throughout the entire U.T., how could the Normals not have been happy? They couldn't have not been. They were very happy. The Normals were very, very happy. And, OK, it wasn't only the choices, and the peace, and the other ethereal stuff. There were also lots of products and services ... an unbelievable amount of products and services. There were so many different products and services you'd have thought they couldn't come up with any more. And yet they did. There were always more. And when there weren't, there was always a way to privatize something that hadn't yet been privatized, and offer and relentlessly market that.

Now there were numerous bold and innovative and otherwise shining examples of this (i.e., the Globalized Proprietary Sewage System, Privatized Community Customs Services, Conversational Advertising, et cetera, the list went on and on, and on), but the boldest and shiniest example of them all, and the revenue-generating mother of them all, was the one that had gotten the whole thing restarted ... the Global Proprietary Calendar System.

The Global Proprietary Calendar System, commonly known as the G.P.C.S., and adopted throughout the United Territories in 2310, H.C.S.T.,* despite what you'd probably naturally assume, was not a retail calendar product (which is to say an actual calendar), or

---

* *Or 6070, I.T.S.T, or 1740, I.M.S.T., or 2231, R.A.S.T, or the Year of the Neotropic Cormorant (not to be confused, as it so often was, with the Year of the Double-Crested Cormorant).*

any type of calendar-related product, but an Interterritorial trade agreement completely deregulating and privatizing same. Despite the dire and hysterical warnings of 24th Century apocalypticians, professional naysayers, and other critics, the G.P.C.S. had been functioning smoothly for going on over three hundred years. Now this was totally revolutionary, because after nearly five millennia of government regulation of time, consumers were finally free to choose among a wide and ever-expanding array of proprietary annotated calendar systems, most of which were moderately priced or offered at competitive corporate discounts. By this time (the time of our story, of course, so 2610, H.C.S.T.), there were four predominant (i.e., widely used) calendars, and in excess of eighty "alternative" calendars, each of which generated spin-off products and assorted licensing and franchising streams. There were also a variety of open-source calendars, and amateur calendars, and vanity calendars, which consumers were equally free to choose among, and to use for business and personal purposes, and to personalize however they liked to express their individual tastes. The G.P.C.S. was extremely popular. The Normals just loved their proprietary calendars. The only minor problem was, no one knew when it was anymore.

This, however, if you asked Greg Cramer, was really nothing more than a technical glitch, and a temporary technical glitch at that. Gregory Cramer was Senior Vice President of Info-Management, Maintenance & Storage at the Hadley Corporation of Menomonie, Wisconsin's District 12 Northeast Regional Headquarters. He was forty-one years old, fit as a fiddle, and handsome in a completely unmemorable way. At approximately 0420 o'clock on a sleepy afternoon in officially March, he was staring into the physical screen of his HC Systems desktop Viewer, in the upper right-hand corner of which his biometric face was staring back at him. The face was smiling a becoming smile. There was nothing remotely reptilian about it. Its features were angular. Its forehead prominent. Its hairline was prematurely receding. It was receding right off the back of his head.

Cramer had an office on the 26th Floor with a view of some other 26th Floor office. There was nothing terribly wrong with his office, except that it was on the 26th Floor. Which meant that it was not on the 70th Floor, or the 71st or 72nd Floors, in Interterritorial Security

Management, which was run by Robert "Big Bob" Schirkenbeck. Cramer, of course, did not resent this (Zanoflaxithorinal relieved resentment) but he thought about it two or three times an hour as he read and responded to the thousands of queries that came up on his screen all day, most of which, in one way or another, concerned the question of when it was. Cramer did not resent these queries, and was perfectly content to sit there and answer them (it being his job to do that and all), but somewhere, way in the back of his mind, he wondered idly whether, just possibly, some of them might not be so vital.

This one, for example, from Jim Matsumura, of TeleDynamic Systems, Inc., asking, basically, when it was. Or this one, from someone named Aksel Torres, who appeared to be some kind of salesman of something (probiotic shampoo, it looked like), beating around the bush a lot, but essentially wondering if anyone at Hadley happened to know when it really was.

Which, all right, here was a prime example of the kind of thing that tempted Cramer to walk down the Path of Toxic Resentment, because obviously no one at Hadley did (i.e., happen to know when it really was), or why would Cramer be sitting in his office fielding queries regarding same, as opposed to sitting in some other office, on the 70th to 72nd Floors, let's say, doing something that might conceivably get him noticed by Big Bob Schirkenbeck?

What Cramer didn't actually consider doing (the hazy concept just drifted through his mind) was writing a boilerplate response-to-query message to send back to Jim and Aksel, and whoever, regretting the fact that neither he, nor anyone at Hadley, nor anyone else, was privy to when it really was (nor, as everyone plainly knew, would anyone be for quite some time), and wondering whether, on the next occasion they felt compelled to query him, again, regarding when it really was, they might refer back to this boilerplate message, or stop and think for a half a second (i.e., before they sent their latest query) about what they were about to do, and how utterly pointless and inane it was.

This hypothetical boilerplate message, which Cramer would never even consciously contemplate much less actually set about writing, would be written in terse, yet extremely professional, demonstrably compassionate, irony-free language, in compliance with both the letter and spirit of Hadley Communications Policy. But terse. The message would definitely be terse. Terse, in this case, would be appropriate. Because, seriously, Cramer thought to himself (and he made a mental note to up his dosage), what did it matter when it really was? Everyone knew when it was officially. The date was right there on the screen of your Viewer. Depending on which calendar you followed, it was 04 March, 2610, or 16 Sha'ban, 2049, or 17 Adar, 6370, or day Whatever in the Year of the Lemur, and all the other dates it officially was.

In Cramer's personal professional opinion, which he shared in his weekly online check-ins with Charmane T.R. Haverson-Cho, the fairly-abundant Department Head of Info-Management, Maintenance & Storage who was never going to help him transfer anywhere and had zero suction with Big Bob Schirkenbeck, the G.P.C.S. was running smoothly. The one little minor ongoing glitch (i.e., the one that people like Jim Matsumura and Aksel Torres were all worked up about), was that even there, in the Western Territories, where most people tended to use the same calendar, although you were free to choose, of course, the dates had been changed so many times that you couldn't work back from whenever it was to whenever it had been before they'd changed them, and even if you did, or thought you had, by the time you did, they'd have changed them again, which meant you would have to start all over, which would mean going back to whenever it was (i.e., the post-adjusted current date) and reentering the dates of whatever events you'd chosen to use as your set of variables, and then trying to rerun your algorithm, only to discover that one or more of the dates of your variables had also been adjusted, so you'd have to go back and adjust for that, and then start the entire process all over.

Naturally, one was free to do this. The system wouldn't prevent you from trying. All that would happen was, after a while, this no-reply message would come up on your screen reminding you that dates and events were tentative, due to the Reconstruction Project, and so really what you were sitting there doing was probably just a waste of time. The text of these messages varied slightly, but the essential content was always the same. One was advised to do one's best, and to plan for further, albeit diminishing, chrono- and philological adjustments, on a more or less randomly-occurring basis, out into the foreseeable future, and to otherwise, basically, have a nice day.

How had things gotten into such a state? No one really knew for certain, but the official story went something like this ...

Back in the early 24th Century, at the dawn of the Age of Emergency Measures, Future/Past-Continuous, Inc. (a not-for-profit corporation founded but neither owned nor controlled by The Hadley Corporation of Menomonie, Wisconsin, and run by a consortium of global corporations representing most of the United Territories) had been charged with the almost impossible task of reconstructing recorded history, the majority of which had been obliterated, or overwritten with malicious intent, during what was known as The Age of Anarchy, which most intelligent people agreed had, at some point, actually occurred.* Intelligent people agreed on this mostly because the official story (the details of which were subject to change as Future/Past-Continuous, Inc. unearthed new informational artifacts) consistently featured The Age of Anarchy, which preceded the Age of Emergency Measures, which everyone knew for a fact had occurred. The Age of Emergency Measures had ended in 2550, H.C.S.T., so anyone over the age of sixty had been alive then, and remembered it clearly, or at least well enough to be sure it had happened. Also, although the United Territories were enjoying a Renaissance of Freedom and Prosperity, a number of these Emergency Measures remained in effect in some remote locales.

According to the Reconstruction Project's current tentative historical timeline, the Age of Anarchy had officially begun sometime circa 2100, give or take a couple of decades, and had ended circa 2300 (these dates being H.C.S.T., of course). So it had lasted, at minimum, two hundred years, and possibly longer, no one was sure. At one point, back in the 2580s, the inception date had been tentatively listed as sometime circa 1940, but now, the general feeling was, that that couldn't be right, so it had been amended.

The point being, at least in the minds of the Normals, this Age of Anarchy (whatever the dates were) was like a temporal or historical bridge, stretched across a river of time, linking the present

---

* *This Herculean or Sisyphean effort was known as the Reconstruction Project.*

(i.e., the world they knew) to a distant pathological past, the facts of which were at best unproven and at worst were purely hypothetical. Unfortunately (and this was the root of the problem), at some point during the Age of Anarchy (in the mid-to-late 22nd Century, it was thought), this temporal bridge to the distant past had been tactically nuked beyond all recognition. In other words, nobody actually knew what had happened during this Age of Anarchy, or when, or where, or why it had happened, or not in any definitive way.

Thus, for over two hundred years, or as long as anyone alive could remember, the official dates of The Age of Anarchy (as well as the dates of the events it comprised, along with the facts of those events themselves) had been continually adjusted, revised, and rewritten, as Future/Past-Continuous, Inc. discovered and correlated new information, which adjustments, in turn, it went without saying, had triggered the adjustment of any and all dates prior or subsequent to the dates in question (and the events to which said dates referred), which dates (and often the events themselves), prior to the latest adjustment, had been based on the original dates in question (of events which had or had not occurred).

Which, OK, probably sounds confusing, but over time had gotten to be as routine as any other type of software update. You'd get this little message on your screen advising you that something that had always happened on 16 November, 2120, the Neu-Hohenschönhausen Unrest, in this case, had, it turned out, really happened on 23 June, 2119, pending official verification, of course. And sometimes something that had always happened on 24 August, 2183, in this case, the North Mississauga Massacre, had actually never happened at all, and Haley Dean Morrison, the alleged perpetrator, had never been born in Halton Hills, or anywhere else, and had never existed, and the whole thing had just been invented out of whole cloth by anonymous "persons of malicious intent," pending verification, of course. Pretty much every official date (and alleged event taking place on that date) was pending some kind of verification, or pending the results of the correlation of other dates of possible influence.

Now as Cramer was fond of reminding people (in a needless to say professional manner), this monstrous historico-calendrical clusterfuck was in no way the fault of Future/Past-Continuous, or the

Hadley Corporation of Menomonie, Wisconsin. It was entirely the
fault of the Cyberterrorists, the so-called "persons of malicious intent," who had generated veritable shitloads of nonsense and hacked
it into the historical records. These "persons of malicious intent" had
made up people who'd never existed, falsified records of their births
and deaths, and involved them, not just in major events, like the
non-occurent North Mississauga Massacre, but also in mundane
and meaningless events, which no one knew about, and which had
never taken place. They had dreamed up fake international conflicts,
insurgent struggles, earthquakes, floods, utterly useless consumer
products, financial crises, sexual practices, medical conditions, math-
ematical theorems, et cetera, the list went on and on. Then, when
whatever had actually happened during the Age of Anarchy happened, which regardless of the details (which were being verified)
was definitely some kind of global catastrophe, and with so much
information destroyed, or written over, or rendered unreadable,
whatever frame of reference there had been to help one distinguish
the real from the fake had been twisted so hopelessly out of shape
that no one could really say anymore, or not with any reliability, what
had or hadn't really happened.

However (and this was the crucial point, it being more or less the
core assumption upon which the whole Reconstruction was based),
the fact of The Age of Anarchy in itself (i.e., the fact that it had actually occurred, and comprised a sequence of actual events, however
subject to verification by Future/Past-Continuous, Inc.), while of
course one was free to say what one wanted, was not a fact that was
up for debate or inquisitive discussion by serious people. Not that
any such discussion, or debate, was in any way officially discouraged,
or censored, or anything despotic like that. No, the subject just never
seemed to come up. Future/Past-Continuous, Inc. was not, after all,
some malevolent autocracy intentionally falsifying historical records
to perpetually confuse and exhaust the public. On the contrary, it
was a global consortium of well-respected corporate partners working on a strictly not-for-profit basis while maintaining the highest
transparency standards. The entire Reconstruction Project was meticulously documented and available online. One could, if one was so
inclined, access the records of every adjustment considered, debated

and ultimately made, and the online discussions regarding those adjustments, and every advisory relating thereto, going back almost three hundred years, at the Reconstruction Project's website: www.recon.proj.

Hardly anyone was so inclined. The Normals had better things to do with their time than wade through zetabytes of digital records verifying the verification of obscure and irrelevant historical data, and anyway there were people who did that, oversight committees or whatever they were ... and the simple fact of the matter was, nobody really cared when it was. Well ... OK, sure, some people cared, professional historians, heortologists and such, and Future/Past-Continuous, Inc., and other corporations whose products and services depended on the Reconstruction Project, and investors in these corporations. But that was different, because all these parties cared in a strictly professional capacity. They understood that it might take centuries to figure out when it really was. And thus, in the meantime, what was the point of querying Cramer over and over? There was no point. That was the point. And was why these professionals didn't do that. Because they understood how pointless it was. As long as the folks at Future/Past-Continuous were in the process of working it all out (i.e., deciding what had actually happened and assigning specific dates to that stuff), and then posting it all on the World Wide Web in a way that made some narrative sense, what did it possibly matter to anyone whether the Neu-Hohenschönhausen Unrest had happened in 2119, or in 2120, or 2130, or when the Visigoths had entered Rome, or in which American Civil War the Battle of Port Royal Sound had been fought?

The answer was, it didn't matter, except to cognitively-challenged persons, like Jim Matsumura and Aksel Torres, and the thousands of other inveterate losers whose queries it was Cramer's job to answer ... rather than it being his job, for example, to assist in Regional Security Services, or even up in Regional A.S.P. Management, where Cramer's talents and exemplary soft-skills would surely be noticed by Big Bob Schirkenbeck. Info-Management, Maintenance & Storage was nowhere anywhere near the vicinity of Big Bob Schirkenbeck's radar screen, which Cramer needed to appear upon if he ever wanted to get anywhere at Hadley, at least within its Security divisions.

Security, Cramer sensed, was his Path, or was one of his Path(s), and he wasn't on it, or in it, or anywhere near its vicinity. He was forty-four floors below its vicinity. He'd been there forever ... nearly a year. During this year he'd surreptitiously downloaded, digitally copied and carefully analyzed every available Hadley organogram, and he had yet to find one viable route from Info-Management, Maintenance & Storage to any Schirkenbeck-run division. He'd transferred down there from Consumer Collections, mostly for the Senior VP title, but also because he had heard a rumor that Charmane T.R. Haverson-Cho, the fairly-abundant Department Head of Info-Management, Maintenance & Storage, had some kind of suction with Big Bob Schirkenbeck, which it turned out later she did not have. Cramer found out who had started this rumor, and he had prayed to the One for forgiveness, of course, because holding on to resentments was toxic, and borderline Anti-Social behavior, but he had not forgotten the name of this person, who according to the ironclad law of Karma would someday reap what he had sown. In the meantime, however, he needed out of Info-Management, Maintenance & Storage. And he needed out on a vaguely upward Big Bob Schirkenbeck-oriented vector. Which it seemed one could not locate from here, or from anywhere else one could locate from here. Wherever this vector originated was somewhere Cramer could not locate.

Another query came in on his screen, this one from someone named Meredith Moone, who claimed to be some sort of entertainer and needed to know when it really was. Cramer watched from outside his body as his finger reached toward the screen, and very nearly deleted the query ... but he caught himself at the very last second. He pushed himself back from his desk in horror. He couldn't believe he'd almost done that. Deleting a query, or any other form of written or verbal communication, was tantamount to professional suicide, and doing so with knowledge and forethought was technically an act of corporate sabotage.

Now, as terrifying as this moment was, this near total loss of control on his part, it was also a blessing, as Cramer knew, as it meant that he had now hit bottom. Which meant that any second now ... yes, here it came, his Moment of Clarity. He got out physical pen and paper (which he could carry out with him and dispose of later) and set about taking fearless inventory.

At some point in the recent past, weeks, or possibly months before (it didn't really matter when it had started), he had stopped surrendering to the Will of One and had started surrendering to his own Self Will, which had led him down a destructive Path, and now to this nearly self-destructive act. He hadn't consciously chosen to do this, but nonetheless he'd chosen to do this. He'd done this out of fear, of course (he wrote the word FEAR in upper case letters), RESENTMENT (ditto), SELF-CENTERED THINKING, FEAR OF INSUFFICIENT ABUNDANCE, ENVY OF THOSE WITH GREATER ABUNDANCE, and a number of other standard phrases he'd memorized from *The Path(s) to Prosperity*. He drew little circles around these phrases, and lines from these circles to other circles, in which he scribbled selected keywords referring back to events in his childhood that had triggered these negative fears and resentments, which every Variant-Positive experienced, but each in their own individualized way. Between, and around, and intersecting these circles, he drew another series of lines, which he labeled with the names of the destructive Path(s) that corresponded to his fears and resentments and to each of their respective triggering events. The upshot of all this scribbling was, through a series of resentment- and fear-based choices, he had wandered off his spiritual Path, and away from the light of unlimited abundance ... and that was why he stuck down there in Info-Management, Maintenance & Storage.

Now, at this point he had about forty-five seconds to take advantage of this Moment of Clarity and resurrender to the Will of the One before his own Self Will took over and set him back on some negative Path. Cramer knew this. He had been here before, and had weathered other such spiritual crises. The first thing he needed to do was surrender. He could not think his way out of this mess. His thinking is what had gotten him into it. Thinking was what he needed to surrender. What he needed now was not a plan, but was, rather, a miracle, an act of Grace, a transdivisional karmic intervention from one of the infinite Many of the One. He took out his personal All-in-One (i.e., not his Hadley-issued Viewer), pulled up his dog-eared digital copy of *The Path(s) to Prosperity* and clicked at random.

The following passage came up on his screen:

> The Unseeking Seeker, seeking the One, seeks but the Unseeking Self of the Seeker, mistaking the Unseeking Self of the Seeker for Seeking Self of the Unseeking Seeker. In so doing, the Unseeking Seeker, taking the Unseeking Self of the Seeker for one of the Aspects of the Oneness of the One, walks the Path(s) of Separation, Deprivation, and Spiritual Delusion, perceiving only the Multiplicity, and never the Abundant Oneness of the One. In contrast to the Unseeking Seeker, the Seeking Seeker, seeking the One, seeks but the Seeking Self of the Seeker, knowing the Seeking Self of the Seeker to be but one Aspect of the Oneness of the One. In so doing, the Seeking Seeker, perceiving the Oneness of the Multiplicity, and knowing this Oneness to be but one Aspect of the Multiplicitous Oneness of the One, walks the Path(s) of Surrender and Detachment, opening the Self to Infinite Abundance.

Believe it or not, this particular passage, which Cramer had chosen completely at random, and that to anyone unfamiliar with the Path(s) probably sounded like gobbledegook, was exactly what he needed to be reading at that moment. Not that he understood a word of it, but understanding was not the point. The point was, he needed to reopen his Self, abandon the Path of Separation, Deprivation, and Spiritual Delusion, and reseek the Path(s) of Surrender and Detachment, ideally in some sort of unseeking way. He needed to actively (i.e., physically) do this, immediately, right there in his office. He checked to make sure the door was locked, then he got down on his knees and prayed.

All of this was more or less standard procedure for Normals in states of spiritual crisis, i.e., reaching one's bottom, the Moment of Clarity, opening *The Path(s)* to some random passage, and interpreting whatever the passage said as instructions for how to get out the crisis. For the Normals (or at least the Variant-Positives) *The Path(s) to Prosperity* was not just another essentially useless sacred text, like the Christian Bible, the Torah, the Qur'an, the Sutras, the Vedas, or the Bhagavad Gita. It was more like a spiritual owner's manual (which came with a metaphysical roadmap), the vehicle in this case being your soul, or spirit, or purusha, or whatever you called it.

It didn't matter what you believed (you could stay a Christian, or a Muslim, or a Jew, or a Buddhist, or whatever it was you were) as long as you could also accept the fundamental revolutionary concept upon which *The Path(s) to Prosperity* was based, namely, that Abundance was infinitely available to anyone and everyone, without conditions, and that all you had to do was apprehend that, and reach out and take as much as you wanted. Abundance meant not just material Abundance (i.e., money, which it certainly meant), but also emotional and spiritual Abundance, which according to Chapters 1 through 9, 12, 15, and Endnote 40, were the sources from which material Abundance, despite all appearances, ultimately emanated. Opening one's Self to unlimited Abundance (or "partaking in the Infinite Oneness of the One") was the goal of the program, which one attained by following a series of simple Steps, meditating and praying regularly, and visualizing infinite Abundance. The Steps themselves were simple enough to be understood by a six year-old child, and were basically an extremely simplified version of the philosophy underlying the Path(s), and the multiplicitous Oneness of the One, which, for most people, was somewhat challenging to grasp, or was impossible to grasp, or was utter nonsense.*

---

* For example, according to The Path(s) to Prosperity, the One, an abstract singularity, did not contain but comprised the Many. The One was the Many, and the Many were One. Each of the Many were also One, each One of which comprised the Many, each and every One of which, when taken as a whole, comprised the One. Each One of the Many had infinite Aspects, each of which were also Aspects, not only of the One comprising that Many, but of every other One of the Many, which, of course, ultimately, were also One. And thus the Multiplicity of the One, notwithstanding the fact that each of its infinite Aspects was essentially singular, nevertheless retained its Oneness. All of these unique, singular Aspects, each no more than a grain of sand on an endless beach that stretched throughout the infinite fabric of Space-Time itself, beginning in its end, ending in its beginning, together comprised a meta-singularity, the Multiplicitous Oneness of the One, which after years of meditation and contemplation of The Path(s) to Prosperity one came to know by its other name, the Oneness of the Unnameable One. Later, after many more years of meditation, contemplation, and attendance at various retreats and seminars, one came to understand that all these "names" were really just provisional names, substitutes for the "Nameless Name," which no one knew, and could never be spoken. Consciousness being but one of its Aspects, how could one ever know the One? One couldn't, or not entirely, anyway. Even those with limited Knowledge, and one could always tell who they were, as Abundance flowed like a stream toward them, accepted the limits of their Knowledge, which acceptance then increased their Knowledge, which increased their Abundance, and on, and on.

In essence, what it all boiled down to was that every lack, or temporary shortfall, of spiritual and/or material Abundance could be ascribed to the same fundamental error ... misapprehension of the Oneness of of the One. For example, attempting to define the One led straight to the Path of Knowing the Unknowable, whereas questioning the infinite nature of the One, one walked the Path of Proving the Unprovable. Failure to meet the terms of one's debts, including, but not limited to, timely payment of interest thereon, was Walking the Path of Attaining the Unattainable. Making unauthorized copies at work was Walking the Path of Possessing the Unpossessable. And these were just a few of the negative Path(s). Walking any one of these Path(s) invariably led to diminished Abundance, and conversely, diminished Abundance proved that one was walking such a negative Path. And so on. The point was, diminished Abundance was never the result of external factors. It was always the result of some unconscious choice, which was based on some spiritual misapprehension. And thus the question, for the Seeker in crisis, was never how to change the world (i.e., something in the actual physical world), but how to change the way one perceived the world, and above all else the choices one made, not one's conscious choices, of course, but one's unconscious, or Karmic choices.

Cramer, down on his knees on the carpet, strategically positioned so as not to be seen by the person in the office across from his office (who sometimes glanced in Cramer's direction, and who looked to be about his age, but whose hairline was only slightly receding), knew all this, this stuff about choices, and the Path(s), and so on, to be the truth. This knowledge was not a matter of faith. This knowledge was fact. It was cause and effect. Choosing Abundance produced Abundance, as anyone abundant was living proof. Big Bob Schirkenbeck was a prime example. Here was a man who was clearly walking one or more of the The Path(s) to Prosperity. Here was a man who had chosen Abundance. Serious Abundance. Unlimited Abundance. Here was a man who understood the Game, who understood that winning the Game was never just a matter of defeating your opponent in a crushingly decisive and humiliating fashion, but was always, ultimately, an expression of your Self ... your Will to Win. Your Will to Abundance.

Which was what it all came down to, essentially, the Path(s), and the whole Abundance thing ... winners won, and losers lost, not because of random factors like physical strength, intellectual prowess, or access to readily available capital. No, winners won because they chose to win. They chose success. They chose Abundance. And in so doing they affirmed Abundance, and they affirmed the infinite Oneness of the One. The obverse, sadly, was also true. Losers lost because they chose to lose. They chose to fail. They chose to suffer. And in so doing they denied Abundance, and they denied the infinite Oneness of the One.

Cramer, whose ankles were starting to cramp, fervently believed in the Oneness of the One, and in the loving, compassionate Will of the One, and that everything that happened was a matter of choice. So somehow he had chosen this challenge. Somewhere in this trap he was in was some kind of karmic lesson to be learned. He prayed to the One to be taught this lesson, and for the One to guide him back onto his Path(s), and to make him more like Big Bob Schirkenbeck, and ...

His intercom rang.

"Yes? What is it?"

"Terribly sorry to bother you, Greg."

"What is it, Gloria?" he barked, from the floor.

"There's a Kyle Bentley-Briggs on line three for you, Greg."

Cramer's virtual assistant, Gloria, reminded Cramer of this dental hygienist he'd dated once, for like forty-five minutes. He'd been asking to have her voice reprogrammed, but the IT guys had been slow to respond.

"I'll call him back."

"All right, Greg."

"Thank you, Gloria."

"Oh, and Greg?"

"Yes?"

"He mentioned a Security matter. I thought you'd want to ..."

Cramer's heart stopped.

"Security?!"

He leapt up and reached for his phone.

"I'll go ahead and take that message for you, Greg."

"No! Wait! Gloria! Wait!"

"Yes, Greg?"

"Put him through."

"All right, Greg. Transferring now."

Cramer closed his eyes and prayed.

"Greg, it's Kyle."

"Kyle, buddy! How the heck are you?"

His eyes were still closed.

"Good. You?"

"Great."

"Good ... is this a bad time?"

"No. What's up?"

"Nothing ... well ... something, actually ... I need to talk to you."

"What's going on?"

"It's Valentina. She's ..."

Kyle choked up. Cramer was getting goosebumps now.

"I can't ... look ... I'd rather not talk on the phone. Could you meet me somewhere?"

"Sure. When?"

"How about tonight? I know it's short notice."

"No. No problem. I'm here for you, buddy."

Cramer took the call off speaker.

"Just tell me what we're dealing with here. Gloria mentioned a Security matter ..."

Several seconds of silence followed.

"Kyle? You there?"

"Listen, Greg ... I can't ... I mean ... they're recording this, aren't they?"

"What? This call?"

"Yeah."

"You serious?"

"No?"

"This is Info-Management and Maintenance. Nothing going on down here ..."

Another few seconds of silence followed.

"Still ... I'd rather talk in person."

"How about Rosie's? Twenty-one hundred?"

"Rosie's ... yeah. I can get there by then."

"Where are you now?"

"I'm on the train."

"The train?"

"Why? Is that a problem?"

Cramer winced.

"No, no problem. It's just ... it just doesn't sound like the train."

Another excruciating second of silence.

"Let's talk tonight in person, OK?"

"Sure, no problem, and listen ... Kyle?"

"Yeah?"

"Whatever this is, we'll handle it."

"Thanks, Greg."

"Don't mention it, buddy."

"I didn't know who else to call."

"Absolutely. You did the right thing."

Kyle clicked off. Cramer hung up. He sat there a moment, unable to breathe. He closed his eyes and said a quick prayer of gratitude to the One Who Was Many.

Another query came in on his screen.

Withdrawal Symptoms

Approximately forty-three kilometers away, rocketing north through its underground tunnel at three hundred ninety kilometers per hour, the CSR Bombardier Alstom Neumeyer V600 TVR WhisperTrain felt like it was standing still. Whether working or simply relaxing in comfort in your fully-adjustable faux-leather seat, available in First and Business Class coaches, the interiors of which were eerily silent,* you could not detect the slightest vibration, and even on the most precarious of curves there was absolutely zero roll. You could, for example, place a marble on the non-stick surface of your pull-down tray table (assuming, for whatever unfathomable reason, you happened to have a marble with you, and needed to take it our of your pocket), and let it rest there, and stare at it and smile.

The eerily silent Business Class coach of seriously abundant businesspeople featured in the WhisperNet on-board promos apparently felt they needed to do this. One of them, a particularly abundant executive, reached down into his trouser pocket, produced a jade green Cat's Eye marble, placed it on the surface of his pull-down tray table and sat there and watched it not moving, and smiled. The surrounding businesspeople saw him do this. One by one, they all followed suit. They reached down into their own trouser pockets, or into compartments inside their handbags, and took out marbles and set them down on their silicone-laminated pull-down tray-tables, which in Business Class featured a faux-wood veneer. Then they all sat there, smiling at their marbles, looking superior to other people who were fairly but not yet seriously abundant and so were not riding in the

---

* *The V600 had been equipped with an ambient-audio dampening system, which meant that, as long as you were in your seat, you could hear yourself, and your Viewer, of course, but nothing beyond your immediate radius.*

Business Class coaches of V600 TVR WhisperTrains moving at hundreds of kilometers an hour, feeling like they were standing still.

Valentina was one of these people, these fairly but not yet seriously abundant people who, for whatever reasons, found themselves without any marbles, and were thus unable to look superior to those who didn't but nevertheless could travel at hundreds of kilometers an hour and feel like they were standing still. Which at approximately 1053 o'clock on the morning of officially 27 February (so two weeks prior to Cramer's fortuitous phone call from Kyle, which of course was recorded) was precisely what Valentina was doing. That, and employing all her powers of concentration and mental discipline to act like a passably normal person and not compulsively masturbate in public. The previous night she had lain awake, with Kyle in bed beside her, snoring, devising an assortment of clever ruses to use that day to pass for normal, most of which, upon awakening, she'd realized she'd completely forgotten. She had, however, remembered to purchase the two adjacent single seats, one a window, the other an aisle, three rows aft of the mid-coach toilets. If all else failed she could reach those toilets in three or four steps, squeeze inside, lock the door, which was on a timer, and compulsively masturbate for up to ten minutes. This wasn't so much a ruse, really, as much as a kind of failsafe measure. The ruses had all been much more clever. She remembered there being an assortment of them, none of which she could remember at the moment. Except for the one about buying two seats, which she'd already done, so that was good. She sensed that a lot of the other ruses, of which there had definitely been an assortment, had had something to do with avoiding other people, most of whom would want to make conversation, and tell her all about their lives and families, and ask her her name and her husband's name, and whether she'd seen the latest episode of 15 Minutes, or Blowback, or Quandary, none of which episodes she would have seen, which would seem suspicious to these other people, and would make them nervous, which would make her nervous, which would make her want to compulsively masturbate.

Fortunately, even in her current condition, Valentina was not without resources. Sipping her raspberry tea that morning, with Kyle at the table beside her, scanning, she'd devised a simpler, if guileless strategy, which had worked thus far and to which she was sticking. This strategy consisted of gazing "out" of the "window" at which she was currently sitting, in Economy Class on the Northbound Orange, at Late Winter Landscape (Morning) 40. Out the window (which wasn't a window) bursts of sunlight were flashing between the ice glazed branches of a stand of birches that were reeling past at a distance of maybe fifteen meters ... or so it seemed. Across the aisle, out the opposite window, a second sun was rising over a distant stretch of desert mesas, turning the sky all red and orange. Valentina was watching this happen in the make-up mirror she was secretly using to check behind her every ten or twelve seconds while never once turning around in her seat.*

A slightly dampened simulated bell-tone sounded three times. Valentina glanced up. The LED creeper that announced the stops read, "Breckenridge Village - 15 minutes." She slipped the mirror into her purse, nonchalantly adjusted her sunglasses, and went back to gazing "idly" out the "window." Her All-in-One started bleating frantically. She snatched her purse up, thrust her hand in, felt for it, found it, and dismissed the reminder. It was time to take her Zanoflaxithorinal. She dug around in the bottom of her purse, found her pill bottle, popped the cap, fingered a pill out, palmed it deftly, pretended to take it, closed her pill bottle, and dropped both the pill and bottle into her purse. The depths of her purse, which were always a rat's nest of lipsticks, pill bottles, mirrors, swipe cards, tissues, brushes, hair-ties, and so on, was littered with pills she had deftly palmed and pretended to take, and had not taken. She needed to gather and dispose of these pills, but she hadn't decided how to do that safely. Flushing them down the toilet was out. She'd tried that early on, and it had worked, but one day one of the pills washed back and sat there down at the bottom of the bowl just waiting for Kyle to come in and find it, and fish it out, and bring it to her, holding it up in front of her face pinched between his thumb and forefinger, raise his eyebrows in that way she dreaded, and ask her what was going on. Other awkward questions would follow ... like what in the name of the One was she thinking, or had she maybe forgotten what happened to people who went off their medication?

---

* *The seats across the aisle were empty. Someone had left the "window" on.*

Seasoned medical professional that she was, Valentina knew what happened to people who went off their medication. Their nervous systems, suddenly deprived of the excessive levels of serotonin, benzodiazepine, and other substances, to which they had all become accustomed, melted down and eventually crashed. This meltdown was usually a gradual process, and was different for each individual patient. The result, however, was always the same, "extended loss of contact with reality," or full-blown, bug-eyed, raving psychosis. Along the road to shrieking lunacy, these patients experienced any of a number of extremely unpleasant withdrawal symptoms, among them, insomnia, nausea, confusion, dyspnea, tremors, excessive sweating, heart palpitations, hallucinations, and something known as cranial zings, which felt like electric shocks to the brain.

Eight weeks into her first trimester, Valentina was experiencing them all. Fortunately, up to this point in our story, her experience of all these various symptoms (and other symptoms, which we'll get to shortly) was mostly an interior state of affairs. Again, being a medical professional, she had known they were coming, and had steeled herself for them, and developed various strategies to hide them, most of which seemed to be working, so far. Following her transient psychotic episode (or spiritual awakening, as Valentina saw it) descending into the nether regions of 6262 Lomax Avenue, she'd pulled herself together enough to play the happy, expectant mother for Kyle, the Fosters, Doctor Fraser, the helpful staff at Paxton Wills, her father, her colleagues, random strangers, and everyone else who possibly mattered. Her nausea, insomnia, and even her sweating, which had risen to the level of profuse at times, had been attributed to her early pregnancy, hormonal fluctuations, and such. She'd even learned to grit her teeth and smile through the horrible cranial zings, which felt like lightning was striking her head, but they never lasted all that long. The much more serious problem had been (and continued to be) her hallucinations, or delusions of reference, and her paranoia, which were harder to conceal, and which were steadily worsening.

After the first few days off her meds (she had started flushing them that very day, the day of The Lomax Escalator Vision), it began to seem to Valentina (although she knew it wasn't real at the time) like all the other Variant-Positives, people over thirty, had disappeared. Well, OK, not quite disappeared ... there were, of course, still Variant-Positives, like Kyle, and Susan Foster, and so on, but there were also, suddenly, hordes of Clears. Droves, legions, multitudes of them ... or maybe they had always been there and she'd simply never noticed them before. In any event, they were everywhere now ... roving in perfect lockstep packs down Pewter Palisades' manicured Main Street, pouring down the aisles of stores toward her, their perfect hair and nails and skin tone, smiling like electric eels, blue eyes staring out of video screens, adolescent and teenage Clears, married young-professional Clears, pushing their double and triple load prams of cooing, blue-eyed baby Clears, who never cried or soiled themselves, and who looked right through her and saw her sickness ... saw what she was planning to do.

Nights, she sat home flipping channels (i.e., not even bothering to program a stream) ... and there they were, on every channel, staring at her, knowing, judging, speaking in code, emphasizing WORDS ... pretending they were talking to each other in some SHOW that had nothing to do with her, but what they were really talking about was whether she was experiencing PROBLEMS getting a clear and consistent SIGNAL or whether her RECEPTION of this secret SIGNAL was badly DISTORTED and needed ADJUSTMENT in which case they'd be happy to send A REPAIR CREW out to check her EQUIPMENT ...

Kyle was concerned. Which was inconvenient. Or whenever he was home it was. Not that he was home all that often. During the week it was mostly just to sleep a few hours and gulp down breakfast. Bloomberg Virtual Community College had just been acquired by EduSolutions, a market-leading Content Provider, and was undergoing serious restructuring. Entire departments were being marched out into the quad each morning and summarily streamlined. Squads of corporate efficiency consultants were roaming the halls with lists of names of associate professors they wanted delayered. Kyle was helping to point them out. Sometimes he was also helping to keep them as calm as humanly possibly as the squads escorted them down to the gym they had retrofitted for the mass delayerings. All of which was somewhat stressful, and involved a lot of face-time for

Kyle, which had made it easier for Valentina to hole up in the house all week, not go to lunch with Susan Foster, not take her pills, and compulsively masturbate.

Sundays were the major problem. Kyle was almost always home, and bent on making up for his absence and lack of attention to Valentina's needs by following her around the house all day listening to whatever she might have to say with demonstrably intense and unflagging interest. She had made it clear that this was not called for, and that she knew he loved her, and cared, and so on, and was busy at work, which she understood, and she knew he was generally more than happy to listen to whatever she had to say with demonstrably intense and unflagging interest, but she didn't really have that much to say, and she really wasn't feeling all that well, which was normal during the first trimester, and was probably just going to take a nap, so why didn't Kyle just watch some Content.

Which, early on, he had usually done.* However, as the hot winter weeks oozed by, and Valentina's symptoms worsened, and an unmistakeable tone of sarcasm gradually crept into her voice (a tone which now apparently accompanied every other thing she said), Kyle had become increasingly concerned. Now, no matter where she went to hide from him, after ten to fifteen minutes, he would appear in whatever room she was in, lean against the door frame and stare at her. This was meant to show concern, and not annoyance or disappointment.

"How are you feeling?" he'd ask her, gravely.

"You asked me twenty minutes ago, Kyle."

"Sorry, I just ..."

"What?"

"Nothing. I thought ..."

"What? That I was wrong before ... that I only thought I was feeling nauseated?"

This was meant to drive him away. It never worked.

"Can I get you something?"

"Something like what?"

---

* He'd sit there, on their faux-leather sofa, watching endless back-to-back reruns of KILL CHAIN LIVE! on Channel 16, which ran on Channels 726, 772, and 803, along with reruns of The News at Five, once they went into syndication.

"Have you eaten anything?"

"Nauseated, Kyle."

"Well, have you taken anything?"

"Like what?"

"A pill?"

"I took my pills. You saw me take them."

"I meant for your stomach."

"I'm pregnant, Kyle."

"I know. I know …"

Silence invariably ensued at this point.

"What?"

"Nothing. I'm just …"

"Concerned?"

"Yes."

"And?"

"I'm worried, OK? You're sitting in here in the bedroom again."

"Where am I supposed to be sitting?"

"Nowhere."

"I'm not supposed to be sitting."

"No. It's just … do you hear what you sound like?"

"Why don't you tell me what I sound like, again."

"You sound like …"

Another protracted silence.

"Say it, Kyle. Say it already."

"Forget it."

"Say it. I sound like my mother."

This is how it went most Sundays. Kyle was growing increasingly concerned. Despite her attempts to deflect, evade, avoid, and deny his non-accusations, Valentina did sound like her mother, or like what her mother used to sound like before she took up permanent residence at Breckenridge Village, "a Retirement Community." Her mother didn't sound like anything currently. She hadn't uttered one word for years, or otherwise attempted to communicate with anyone. She just kind of sat there and stared out the window.

Valentina understood Kyle's feelings, his mounting frustration, his disappointment. Here they were, finally pregnant (which she knew Kyle had always secretly assumed was the underlying cause of all her problems), and not only had this not fixed Valentina (which she knew was how he secretly saw it), somehow it had made things worse. He had missed her completely at Paxton Wills that fateful day in late December, the day of her Lomax Escalator Vision. By the time he got there she was locked in the bathroom of a northbound train she had boarded at random. He frantically messaged, and fleeped and tweaked, and buzzed and called, but she did not answer. Naturally, he'd assumed the worst. Once Doctor Fraser had told him the news, he'd breathed an enormous sigh of relief, and assumed Valentina wasn't answering her phone simply because she needed some space to process the emotional pain he had caused by unavoidably missing their appointment (which he knew was getting to be a pattern, and had already set a reminder to work on). He'd stopped in the lobby and picked up two dozen jumbo thornless long-stemmed roses and a magnum of non-alcoholic champagne. Then he'd hurried home to Marigold Lane, where Valentina was not waiting. She'd staggered in around 2200 looking like she'd been been been caught in a windstorm. She informed him she wasn't sure where she'd been, walking, thinking, she didn't know where. He gave her the flowers. She smiled wanly. Things had gone downhill from there.

She'd toughed it out at work through the holidays, maxing out her personal days, white-knuckled her way through the month of January, and had finally taken the standard unpaid maternity leave that everyone got, effective as of 01 February. This had come as a huge relief, to Valentina, as well as her colleagues. In early January she had botched a number of routine liver and colon biopsies, mutilating the tissue samples in ways that were somewhat hard to explain. Moreover, without the Zanoflaxithorinal to level them out, her emotions were raging. Any little thing would set her off. She would be in the middle of zapping dinner, or resecting a cancerous prostate or bladder, and out of nowhere she'd break down sobbing ... or the paranoia would rise up inside her, scaling her spine like a poisonous spider, and she would have to run and hide in the bathroom, often for extremely lengthy periods. Once inside she'd double over and wail and moan and make these faces that looked like she was undergoing an unanesthetized lumbar puncture, which was how the compulsive masturbation had started.

It started at work, the first week of January, she couldn't remember the date exactly. She was at her station in the BMC lab, dicing a section of malignant intestine, and two of her colleagues, whose names were both Bree, were down at the end of the stainless steel table slicing some dead person's brain like prosciutto while trying to remember the name of the actor who had played the handsome Security Specialist in some insanely popular Content series that Valentina had never heard of. They kept making reference to this actor's CAR, and to the SPECIAL RADIO he was always using to JAM THE SIGNAL of the TERRORIST SUSPECTS he, or rather, his character, was after, who were using some sort of SECRET CODE. These FAITH-BASED ANTI-SOCIAL TERRORISTS were unaware that the handsome actor had broken their code and was LISTENING IN ON EVERY WORD THEY SAID OR THOUGHT. Valentina, who was hyperventilating, and experiencing sudden abdominal cramps, set down her scalpel, rose from her stool, peeled off and binned her surgical gloves, and calmly fled in a state of panic. She hurried into the alternatively-abled private restroom that was out in the hall, locked herself in and doubled over, silently screaming at her pink rubber clogs. Her panic peaked and gradually subsided. The cramps in her abdomen and chest did not. She could not breathe. She was tachycardic. She slapped herself in the face, which hurt, but not enough to stop the series of muscle contractions that were wracking her body. Finally, out of sheer desperation, or acting out of some primal instinct, she loosened the tie of her bright pink scrubs, dropped them, pulled her panties down, perched on the edge of the lid of the toilet, one hand braced on the chromium handrail, spread her legs, grabbed her vulva, hooked two fingers up into her vagina, found her G-spot, pressed into it, mashed the transverse metacarpal arch of the palm of her hand down against her clitoris, and masturbated for all she was worth. Her orgasm shot up her spine like a missile, detonating deep in the base of her brain, rolled her eyes up in their sockets, knocked her sidewise off the toilet, and most importantly, stopped her cramps. She lay there on the floor for a minute, scrubs around her ankles, laughing. She was laughing more out of relief than anything.

Then she got up and did it again.

Unfortunately, she found, in the days that followed, the relief provided by masturbation, although reliable, was only temporary. It lasted an hour ... two at best. After which time her delusions of reference and physical symptoms returned with a vengeance. And thus she began what soon became a vicious cycle of panic attacks, masturbation, more panic attacks, more masturbation, and so on like that. By the end of that week (the second of January), she was sneaking off to alternatively-abled private restrooms throughout the department to compulsively masturbate four times a day. By the end of the month she was up to six. Shortly thereafter the inevitable happened ... alternatively-abled histologists complained. Which was understandable and to be expected. These restrooms were for the alternatively-abled, not for traditionally-abled people who claimed to have some kind of urinary problem that caused them to lock themselves inside and compulsively masturbate eight times a day. Luckily, just as her supervisor, Doctor Klemmer, having reviewed these complaints, was on the verge of having a word with her, her unpaid maternity leave took effect. She smiled, in a somewhat un-settling manner, apologized profusely to one and all, coded out, and fled the scene.

Once back home on Marigold Lane and safe from the Brees and the alternatively-abled, her compulsive masturbation frequency spi-raled totally out of control. As did her frequent panic attacks. And her aural and visual hallucinations. And all her other withdrawal symptoms. She threw herself into her spiritual practice ... yoga, breathwork, visualization, self-affirmation, the whole nine yards. She meditated for hours, fiercely, contemplating the epiphany she'd had, or rather (as Doctor Graell would have told her, had she ever actually told him the truth), reinforcing the structural logic of her psychopathological ideations, which seem to center on, or revolve around, some vast and nebulous cosmic antagonist that Valentina didn't have a name for.

Which ideations went something like this ...

IT (i.e., her cosmic antagonist) was after Valentina. IT wanted to kill her ... or no, not kill her, possess her, own her, consume her body, her mind, and her soul. IT was ... well, she did not know. She could not describe IT. But she sensed what IT was. And what IT wanted

... IT wanted to use her, to use her body, and everyone's bodies, to infinitely replicate and multiply ITself. This was the main objective of IT, this infinite replication of ITself, which insidious process IT had nearly completed. IT was everywhere. Everything. Everyone. Or not quite everyone, but almost everyone. Kyle was part of IT. Yes, he was. So was Susan Foster, probably. The way she kept asking, "are you all right, Val? You look like you're walking a little bow-legged." She kept stopping by with gluten-free scones, or to invite her out to lunch on Main Street ... but Valentina was onto her now. Once Susan got her out on Main Street, out in the open, with no-where to run, she would sit there acting completely normal, slurping her BioMax Ginseng smoothies, plastic proboscis sucking orange blood like sludge through her bright green lips, skin pinned back behind her ear flaps ... as if she couldn't see them coming ... YES ... CLEARS ... THE MINIONS OF IT ... watching ... listening ... smiling ... waiting ... sniffing at the air as they passed her table ... as if they could smell IT ... growing inside her ... THIS THING that belonged to THEM inside her ...

Now, obviously, what was going on in Valentina's brain at this point was extremely disturbing, and not at all normal. And, OK, there were several theories on that, but only one of them really counted ... the one in the DSM XXXIII (which we'll get to in just a couple of minutes). We don't have time to review all these theories (the other theories that didn't count), most of which were fairly complex, and were written in psychiatric-speak (and some of which were plain old silly), but let's go ahead and take a look at one of them.

According to this theory (which was probably the best, or at least the most lucid, of the ones that didn't count), what Valentina was undergoing was a process known within certain marginal and widely-dismissed psychiatric circles as Transmutation-Integration, a process during which the "repressive Subject" confronted and ul-timately accepted its "Shadow," integrating light and darkness, or good and evil, or health and sickness, or whatever dualistic terms one preferred. In the course of this process, the Subject's "Identity" (con-stituted as it clearly was to repress the very act of repression upon which its dualistic integrity depended) disintegrated and ... well, basically, died. The Subject (theretofore exclusively identified with its constitution-repressing Identity, and often projecting its Shadow externally), faced with the dissolution of its Identity, appeared to devolve into paranoia, and often, in practice, actually did. However, in some exceptional cases, the Subject undergoing Transmutation was somehow able to perceive the death of its repressive Identity not as *its* death (i.e., the death of the identifying Subject) but merely as the death of an abstract construct, the death of which revealed the "Self" (or God, or whatever one wanted to call it), with which the Subject then attempted to identify, and almost invariably failed to do.* During the early stages of this process, the Subject was rather abruptly confronted with its Shadow (i.e., the irrational matter the recently departed repressive Identity was originally constituted to repress), which it naturally mistook for the "Anti-Self" (or the Devil, or whatever one wanted to call it) and was either, as probably mentioned above, consumed, and its psyche smashed to little pieces, leaving the Subject in a catatonic state, or (and they weren't quite sure how this happened, the proponents of this particular theory), in order to avoid this horrible fate, the Subject identified with the Shadow, which it forthwith imbued with the authenticity it had once ascribed to the repressive Identity, which for unknown reasons usually worked. This created a whole new array of challenges for the "Shadow-identified Subject" to work through (which it sometimes did and sometimes didn't), which we don't have time to explore right now ... the point here being, according to this theory, that the Subject was actually undergoing an admittedly radical and inarguably dangerous, but nevertheless potentially positive neo-Jungian transformation of its constitution, or spirit, or soul, or whatever the Subject was, exactly.

Applying all this to Valentina in her then current state (which no one did), one might have interpreted the rearrangements her psyche was making in a different light. Clearly, her repressive Identity was shattered. Pieces of it were lying all over. Just as clearly, her assumed Identity (i.e., Valentina, the Destroyer of Worlds) was a desperate but arguably courageous attempt to integrate her enormous Shadow

---

* *The Self being almost ideally suited to handling transcendental matters, like defying the laws of time and space, and letting there be light and so on, but not so suited to practical matters, like tying one's shoelaces or discussing the weather.*

and focus its savage, mindless rage on whatever was left of her repressive Identity (i.e., this adversary she had labeled IT), which she unconsciously sensed was trying to possess her, and ultimately destroy her ... which, of course, it was. Or that was one way of looking at it.

The other way of looking at it, the one in the DSM XXXIII, was that Valentina was Phase 2 psychotic, and in immediate need of serious sedation, and hospitalization, and four-point restraints, and there wasn't anything neo-Jungian, or neo-anything, to debate or discuss. Her N-methyl-D-aspartate receptors were borderline functional and needed rebooting. Her mesolimbic pathways were flooded with dopamine. Her entire perceptual apparatus was a mess. Nothing she said or secretly thought was of the slightest etiological value. It was all just nonsense, disorganized thinking, the product of a brain in a state of crisis, desperately trying to make some sense of what, medically speaking, was pure neural chaos. What she needed, and never received, was pharmaceutical intervention. She needed her D2 receptors shut down. With Clozoprazoladine, probably, for starters. And if that didn't work, there was ECT, plain old electro-convulsive therapy, and a number of other powerful tools that could turn her brain off and give it a rest.

Unfortunately, Valentina was tough. Bull-goose loony as she was by then, some part of her mind was still cogent enough to hold it together and hide her symptoms, or at least her most glaring and dispositive symptoms. Being not just a medical professional, but the daughter of someone currently receiving pharmaceutical intervention around-the-clock in a residential setting, she knew precisely what awaited her if she lost it completely, and started raving, and gave away her secret plan. What, you're asking, was her secret plan? Valentina's plan was simple ... insane, perhaps, but essentially simple.

Valentina's secret plan was to find and contact the N.I.N., the most notorious and imminently-threatening Terrorist network on the face of the earth. She was going to find them, and approach them, and join them, the others like her, who had seen the light, or who'd been personally chosen by the One, as she had, the faith-based Anti-Social Terrorists, who were living in the so-called Recovering Areas, the badlands south of the 38th parallel, where the average temperature was 60 Celsius, and the scorching toxic skies of which were swarming with Anti-Terrorist drones.

Valentina had no illusions ... the life of a faith-based Anti-Social Terrorist was definitely not a party or anything. It was typically short, desperate and brutal, but there was a certain element of romance to it ... or so it seemed to Valentina in her current, deluded state of mind. The basic outlines of their bleak existence was common knowledge among the Normals, the subject being standard fare on the Terror and Anthropology channels, which Valentina had been studying, recently. According to the experts you saw on these channels, they (these faith-based Anti-Social Terrorists) slept by day in their underground tunnels, caves, cellars, and secret bunkers, and crept by night through the cremated waste of cities reduced to nothing but rubble, or overrun with impenetrable jungles of mutant formerly tropical plants whose putrid fruits all oozed this clotted yellow matter that stank like pus, foraging for anything vaguely edible, or convertible into deadly weapons, and conducting neo-primitive rituals, which typically involved some type of sacrifice to their bloodthirsty faith-based Terrorist god. Amazingly, in the course of all this, this creeping and foraging and ritual-conducting, they not only managed to somehow evade the inevasible orbiting network of state-of-the-art surveillance satellites and remotely-piloted aerial vehicles that bombarded their hives with white-phosphorus bombs and picked them off with laser-guided missiles the second they showed themselves above ground, but they also occasionally attempted attacks on innocent unsuspecting consumers, or at least they conspired to attempt such attacks, or planned to conspire to attempt such attacks, according to the various Terrorism experts. Valentina would live there among them, in those barren wastes and putrid jungles, naked, filthy, caked with crud, blood, semen, and other fluids, feeding on scraps of toxic garbage as she learned their neo-primitive rites. She would offer her foul and feculent body as a living altar for their psychotic rituals, which would certainly involve her being penetrated, over and over, by men in goat masks, as well as a lot of creepy chanting of pseudo-Egyptian-sounding names, all of which (along with the powerful psychedelic roots they would want to make her eat) would eventually purge her body and soul of every last living vestige of IT, transforming her from the wreck she was into what she knew she really was ... Valentina, Destroyer of Worlds.

All of which was, of course, ridiculous.

Take the N.I.N., for example, which Valentina was determined to join, assuming, that is, that it still existed, which officially it did, but probably didn't.

Which, all right, here's the story on that one ...

The N.I.N., or N.I.N.E., the Nihilist International Network, or "das Nihilistische International-Netzwerk der Erde," allegedly founded on 18 September, 2016, in a bar in Berlin, had been one of the most prominent Terrorist networks active during the Age of Anarchy. Now (i.e., the time of our story ... not whenever you're reading this), coming up on three centuries later, it posed the last remaining threat to the maintenance of peace, freedom, and prosperity throughout the United Territories.* According to the official story, inculcated into the Normals daily by an ever-expanding variety of media, in the final decades of the Age of Anarchy, facing assured annihilation at the hands of the corporate Security Services, elements of the N.I.N. had gone inactive, adopted covers, and blended back into Normal society. They had taken jobs as manual laborers,

---

* The circumstances surrounding its origins were, unsurprisingly, somewhat cloudy. Although most scholars and historians agreed that the core of the group had initially met on the eighteenth day of the month of September (according to the old Gregorian calendar), the year of the meeting had not been verified, and so remained the subject of academic debate. Presumably, given the N.I.N.'s fondness for memes of numerological significance, the year in question was either 2016, 2025, or 2034, or possibly even 2042, or some subsequent novenary permutation. However, one piece of compelling evidence supported the case for 2016, namely the existence of an early draft, carbon-dated back to 2023, of the seminal faith-based Terrorist Gospel, Norma's Raincoat: Cantos I-XCIX, which no one outside the Security Section of Future/Past-Continuous, Inc., had ever actually read, or seen. Attributed to one R. A. Wilder, an itinerant translator of technical manuals and amateur poet, then based in Berlin, Norma's Raincoat was actually written by an unknown number of anonymous authors. In all probability, "R. A. Wilder" (who the records suggested had actually existed, and had evidently lived for a time in what was then still the city of Berlin, but who had either had nothing, or very little, to do with the creation of the text) had, for some inscrutable reason, been used by its authors as a nom de plume. In any event, the impenetrable manuscript, all 8,667 pages of it, had clearly taken years to assemble. And thus, its existence in 2023, proved (to the coterie of forensic philologists at Future/Past-Continuous, Inc. who had been granted clearance to read such stuff) that the original members of the N.I.N. had known each other, and had collaborated, decades prior to 2023. So, sticking with the novenary permutation theory, that took them back to 2016. All of which was academic. The point was, among the literally thousands of Terrorist networks that had once plagued the Earth, most of them during the Age of Anarchy, but some of them, in a reduced capacity, on into the Age of Emergency Measures, the N.I.N., or N.I.N.E., was one the weirdest, and most tenacious. It was also, officially, the only one left.

or baristas, or sometimes temporary help. They had rented and in some cases purchased apartments, presumably down in the "Center Cities," and started little Terrorist families. Passing as Normals, their Terrorist descendents had survived the Age of Emergency Measures, and now, unimaginable as it seemed in the Age of the Renaissance of Freedom and Prosperity, a network comprised of their distant offspring, though mostly dormant, still existed. From time to time official sources unearthed evidence of possible links between this N.I.N. sleeper network and the faith-based Anti-Social Terrorists living out in the Recovering Areas.

And this was really the crux of the threat (i.e., this last remaining threat to freedom), because whereas, within the United Territories, there hadn't been a single incidence of violence, much less anything approaching Terrorism, for longer than anyone alive could remember (except for in the Quarantine Zones, among the A.S.P.s, which didn't really count), regrettably, out in the Recovering Areas, as well as a handful of remote Northern regions, deserts and mountainous expanses mostly, in faraway lands, which no one ever visited, the aforementioned bands of faith-based Terrorists (in addition to foraging, evading missiles, and conducting macabre rituals, and so on) were relentlessly plotting and sometimes actually attempting devastating Terrorist attacks. Not that they could do much damage, totally isolated as they were. Still, the threat was always there, and assuming the official story was true, and the N.I.N. was still in business, and was somehow in league with these afflicted souls (and maybe even with the A.S.U., which was active within the Quarantine Zones) ... well, who knew what kind of schemes they were up to? Suicide missions, with deadly nerve gas, anthrax, cholera, smallpox, plague, or improvised thermonuclear devices, anything was possible after all ... assuming, that is, one actually believed a single word of any of this.

Valentina had no choice. She had to believe. So, she did. Her only chance, insane as it was, of ridding her body and soul of IT was to locate and contact the N.I.N., announce her spiritual and political awakening, and beg them to take her in and train her, and use her for their sex-magick rituals, and so on. The way this would work (in Valentina's fantasies) was they would meet her in some safehouse basement somewhere, and would listen intently as she explained her epiphany, or her nervous breakdown, or whatever it was,* and how she'd been personally chosen by the One to carry out some portentous mission that would set off a global wave of insurrection that would change the whole course of human history. Once she had done that (i.e., explained all this, not carried out the mission, of course), they would smuggle her out, terminate her pregnancy (they probably had access to MifegyneX, or some other progesterone receptor antagonist), give her a few days to recover, hopefully, and then start right in with their salacious rituals. Valentina Constance Briggs would disappear without a trace, never to be seen or heard from again, until such time as her dental records identified her as the suicide bomber that had brought down 6262 Lomax, or 212 Jobs, or 16 Murdoch, or some other gleaming symbol of IT, launching a wave of insurrection that would someday end the reign of IT over people's minds and bodies and everything … or some other grim scenario like that.

Late Winter Landscape (Morning) 40 had just rebooted and started over. Valentina stared out into a snow white world that was not there. The muted bells rang. The creeper crept. "Breckenridge Village – 45 seconds." She prayed to the One to help her do this, to help her find the N.I.N., if they even existed, whoever they were … the details didn't really matter. All that really mattered now, now that the drugs were out of her system, was that Valentina was alive, awake, and seeing the world as it really was. It wasn't peace. There was no peace. There was only this never-ending fight. This fight for survival … for what one was. Valentina was ready for it. She was ready to do whatever it took. She would fight them all … she would go down fighting them, all the insidious forces of IT. She would tear them out of her head and fight them. She'd fight them in her organs and cells. And out in the world, in the streets and malls, and the offices of Paxton, Wills & Huxley. She would fight them to the very ends of the earth, around the Horn and the Norway Maelstrom, and into perdition's flames, if necessary, and spit her dying breath, and so on, whatever was called for, whatever it cost her … but first she needed to visit her mother.

_____

* _Which would someday be known in Terrorist circles as Valentina's "Lomax Escalator Vision."_

The Anti-Social Underground

Meanwhile, back in Zone 23, back in officially mid-October, Taylor was being subjected to torture.

A particularly excruciating type of torture.

"The Anti-Social Underground movement is a totally leaderless, decentralized network of autonomous militant revolutionary cells collectively employing a diversity of tactics to resist all forms of Corporatist oppression. The A.S.U. does not discriminate on the basis of race, gender, age, A.S. Class, or any other basis. Discrimination will ..."

This was Adam.

Adam was the leader of the totally leaderless Fifthian Cluster of the A.S.U. He was reading out the text of the Eighth Revision of "The Standard Preamble to All A.S.U. Meetings," which, before you could start an A.S.U. meeting, someone like Adam had to do.

Adam was a little pink sawed-off white guy who wore his hair in a dreadlock Mohawk and had that kind of white-guy skin with zero melanin that never really tans. He was reading out the text of the Standard Preamble to the hardcore members of Fifthian Cluster, a totally autonomous insurrectionist cell employing a diversity of militant tactics to achieve the liberation of all Anti-Social Persons and resist all forms of Corporatist oppression. The hardcore members of the Fifthian Cluster, who numbered thirteen, including Adam, and who also sported creative haircuts, and facial tattoos and copious piercings, were sitting around in a semi-circle, giving Adam their undivided attention. Taylor, who was bored, and detested Adam, was sitting near the door at the back of the meeting, an Actions Working Group Action Update, which Adam had convened in some airless basement winos used as a field latrine.

"Autonomous cells are free to plan and take what actions they deem appropriate. Such actions include, but are not limited to ..."

By this time Taylor could recite the Preamble, having heard it read out on a daily basis, by Adam or one these other idiots, at the start of each meeting for the past five weeks. The actions each autonomous cell was free and encouraged to deem appropriate, plan, and theoretically take, included, but were not limited to, educational and fundraising activities, property destruction, vandalism, theft, détournements of corporate Content, and other more militant types of actions, which up to then Adam had only alluded to. But those had all been general meetings, which were open to anyone with an honest desire to resist all forms of corporatist oppression, and where security culture was strictly maintained. This was Taylor's first Action Group Update, which one of the peripheral hardcore members, a woman named Sarah, had invited him to.

"Does anyone have any general issues?"

Nobody had any general issues.

"Good. Then I'll turn things over to Jamie."

Adam turned things over to Jamie, a gigantic, hairless, ethnically ambiguous, indeterminately gendered person, so as not to in any way reinforce the arbitrary race- or gender-based dominance of skinny little pink-skinned white guys like Adam, who were always trying to dominate everything.

"OK, everybody, listen up." Jamie took a pause for dramatic effect. "Word is in from the last few cells. This is it. The D.A.D.A. is on."

The hardcore members of the Fifthian Cluster sat bolt upright in their chairs and twinkled. Twinkling was when you raised your hands, palms toward the speaker, and wiggled your fingers. You did this to convey consent, or approval, or enthusiastic support, or something positive in any event.

"Before we break out into working groups, we need to discuss and consense around a preliminary Phase Two security culture ... which maybe Adam could facilitate that, and Maya and Dorian could handle the stack, and ..."

Another round of twinkling ensued.

Taylor, who could not believe these idiots were actually going to sit around and exhaustively discuss "security culture" for the fourteen fucking hundredth time, steeled his nerves for what he knew was to follow, which was probably going to take all night. According to their non-hierarchical principles, the hardcore members of Fifthian Cluster, before they could make a decision on anything, which could only be made by consensus, naturally, needed to sit around in a circle, typically for several hours at a stretch, and exhaustively discuss whatever it was they felt they needed to consensually decide. Now this was even worse than it sounds, because the hardcore members of the Fifthian Cluster, despite their clearly extensive knowledge of militant insurrectionist theory (or maybe as a consequence thereof), could not articulate a simple concept in plain fucking English to save their own lives. It was like they were all infected with some kind of polysyllabic lexical virus. Virtually every other thing they said was couched in this pseudo-militant jargon, as if there weren't already words for whatever the fuck they were trying to say. On top of which they had all these rules, rules about twinkling, and stacking questions, and checking one's race- or gender-based privilege, which they had to review before every discussion, and refer to, repeatedly, during discussions, which you couldn't just fucking have, of course, because they had to be facilitated, and someone had to "stack the speakers," and someone else had to "monitor vibes," so that no one's latent hierarchical or normatively privileged choice of words unintentionally verbally oppressed, or excluded, or otherwise offended anyone.

This was mostly what they did all night, the hardcore members of the Fifthian Cluster. They sat around in semi-circles, in the basements and attics of abandoned buildings, with their insurrectionist haircuts and piercings, not oppressing or offending each other. They did this in the course of discussing a range of vital revolutionary topics, like which corporate storefront to boldly vandalize, or which unpronounceable pronouns to use for non-hierarchically gendered persons. The general meetings, which it had to be assumed were being attended by Cooperators, and possibly even Corporatist agents, and where an atmosphere of total paranoia prevailed, usually began with a lengthy discussion of the ins and outs of "security culture," and the definition of "security culture," and the need to maintain "security culture," and then moved on to other more militant topics, like "report backs" on various acts of vandalism, or bake sales, or other fundraising efforts. Once these points had been covered in detail, and the lexis used to cover these points thoroughly scrutinized and challenged, and so on, and consensually revised for future discussions, they would set about discussing, at inordinate length, ways of inciting, or "calling out," the completely apathetic Anti-Social masses, and convincing them to join the hardcore members of the Fifthian Cluster, and other clusters, and other cells of the A.S.U, in the streets and the squares of Zone 23 on the Day of Autonomous Decentralized Action. According to Adam and his inner circle of hardcore militant resistance fighters, on the Day of Autonomous Decentralized Action (or D.A.D.A., and one pronounced it "dah-dah"), leaderless cells of the A.S.U. in every sector of Zone 23, and in Zones throughout the Northeast Regions, and presumably throughout the entire U.T., would rise up against their Corporatist oppressors, occupy In-Zone factories, stores, assembly plants, administrative offices, and seize control of the means of production, and eventually control of the Zones themselves. These occupied Zones would then be used as totally leaderless fortified bases from which to launch some globally-coordinated anti-Corporatist revolution, which would bring to an end all forms of oppression and establish a peaceful, non-oppressive, global economic and political system, the definitive nature and features of which had not yet been consensually decided.

Taylor wished them luck with all that.

In the meantime, what he was actually doing there (i.e., what he'd been doing for the past five weeks) was sitting in the back of their general meetings, listening, nodding, and twinkling along, as he kept an eye out for person or persons connected to whatever ultra-secretive baby-smuggling inner circle Meyer Jimenez had led him to believe was operating deep within the A.S.U. Theoretically, once he found them, and they agreed to take Cassandra's baby, and smuggle it out to the Autonomous Zones, or hide it in one of their underground safehouses, or tunnels, or whatever they did with the babies, Taylor's life could go back to normal. At this point, five weeks into his mission, he hadn't met any such person or persons. All he'd met were a lot of Transplants ... polysyllabic jargon-spewing, privilege-checking, twinkling Transplants.

The Anti-Social Underground movement, the old one, the one that Taylor remembered, had a long and rather apocryphal history. How and exactly when it had started were questions no one could possibly answer, and were thus the subject of heated debates at watering holes like Gillie's Tavern. Older guys, like Young Man Henry, T.C. Johns, and Jim MacReady, sat around drinking and told all these stories, stories they'd heard as younger men from older men in other such taverns, but everybody knew that that was all they were, tenth-hand, wildly conflicting accounts of people who had probably never existed doing things that had probably never happened.

Covert historians, like Meyer Jimenez, reasoned the original resistance had been founded back in the mid-to-late 2300s, so during the Age of Emergency Measures, which was when the Zones were first established, at least according to the corporate records. According to these records, the 24th Century had been a period of reconstruction, during which what was left of humanity, having clawed its way back from the brink of destruction, had moved above the 40th parallel, and established life as everyone knew it. Purportedly, the Age of Emergency Measures (which had officially ended in 2570, but in reality was still very much in effect) had been preceded by something called the Age of Chaos, or the Age of Anarchy, or whatever they called it. (Taylor could never keep that straight.) The dates of this age had not been confirmed, however, as far as Meyer could tell, it had spanned at least two (and maybe several) centuries, during which time a combination of sociopolitical and meteorological catastrophes, including, he wagered, a limited exchange of tactical thermo-nuclear weapons, had wiped out sixty to seventy percent of the sentient population of the planet.

Or maybe all this had happened earlier. Whatever. The point was, whenever it had happened, this Age of Anarchy, or Chaos, or whatever, had ended circa 2300, when the Age of Emergency Measures was declared, and Anti-Sociality discovered, and anyone even vaguely disgruntled, much less outright uncooperative, was herded into the inner cities, around which, possibly fifty years later, the Security Walls had been erected. Presumably, in fairly short order after that, the Anti-Social resistance had been born.

In any event, by 2565, or 6325, or the Year of the Blowfish, or any

of a number of other such years (all being the year of Taylor's birth),
the Anti-Social Underground movement had been around ... well,
if not quite forever, then longer than anyone alive could remember.
Jackson Village, the four-block quadrant of low-rise projects where
Taylor was born and lived until the age of five, back in those days,
was A.S.U. City. Virtually all of his mother's friends, and probably
his mother, had been involved, just how deeply he did not know ...
and he told himself he did not care. They'd lived in some tiny-ass
shared apartment with fifteen, maybe twenty other people, where,
exactly, he couldn't tell you ... those three-story red brick housing
units (and there were hundreds of them) were nearly identical. His
earliest memories were all just bits of scenes his mind had spliced
together into this kind of weird montage of kitchens crammed with
faceless people ... shirtless, bearded, smoking men with crude tattoos
and scars like his, sweat-haired, heavily-titted women, also smoking,
also tattooed, their featureless faces floating over tables piled with
pots, plates, bottles, the jar lids they used for ashtrays, talking, drinking, shouting, laughing, the salty stench of their sunburned bodies,
rice and beans and beer on their breath ... and somewhere in there,
in those kitchen memories, somewhere among those faceless faces,
one of those faces was the face of his mother, whose face he thought
he did remember ... or maybe it was just some random face his mind
had somehow linked to his mother, which maybe didn't even look
like his mother, which Taylor would never know for sure, as there
weren't any photos to help him remember, and mostly that's how
memory works. Sometimes, and more and more often recently, for
no clear reason, and at the oddest times (like right in the middle of
this fucking meeting), he found himself wondering which of those
faceless men in those kitchens had been his father, assuming one of
them had been his father, and not some other faceless face he had
never seen and so had never forgotten. Whatever, he thought. Who
cared who he was? Some hairy old guy who'd fucked his mother. The
point was, he was fucking dead, as was his mother, and the rest of
those people. Everyone in a nine-block radius of Jackson Avenue at
the time of the Uprising, or everyone over the age of ten, or all the
grown-ups in any event, and the older teens, and a lot of the younger
ones, all of them, they were all fucking dead.

And see, that was where resistance got you. It didn't get you out of the Zone. It didn't get you better conditions, or sympathy from the fucking Normals. It got you zipped inside a bag, and loaded into the back of a van by IntraZone Sanitation Technicians, and driven off to some crematorium. It got your whole neighborhood leveled by missiles, hammered to pieces by urban artillery, bulldozed flat, and left like that, as a warning to anyone stupid enough to not just sit around and talk about occupying, but to actually occupy corporate property, and take Community Watchers hostage, and make a series of hopeless demands on IntraZone Waste & Security Services, which is what the Jackson Avenue cell of the A.S.U. had done that summer.

They called it the Jackson Avenue Uprising, as if it were some great historic battle, when all it was was a couple hundred militant A.S.U.-type idiots setting fire to corporate stores, hanging banners, making speeches, and, OK, taking a couple of hostages, but mostly just barricading Jackson Avenue and dancing around in the streets all night.

Taylor had no idea at the time, but he learned from various people later (and Meyer Jimenez confirmed all this) that the spark that had set the whole thing off was the leaking of a draft of Ordinance 119, which wouldn't take effect for another five years. The author of this draft was one Nigel P. Gruber, Senior Vice President of A.S.P. Management, Hadley Corporation of Menomonie, Wisconsin. Although obviously still in the planning stages, all the basic elements were there ... the founding of ConCept, the walk-in clinics, the In-Zone Pro-Contraceptive Messaging, the Candy campaign, the whole nine yards. Someone had gotten a hold of this draft (it had to have been a 1 with a pass), smuggled it into the Zone on a chip, and had passed it on to the A.S.U. Their plan had been to "alert the world" to the Hadley Corporation of Menomonie, Wisconsin's unspeakably evil and genocidal scheme to rid the planet of Anti-Social Persons, according to Nigel P. Gruber's projections, by sometime circa 2720. The goal of the Jackson Avenue Uprising was to draw the attention of the Normal media, as well as the Anti-Social population, providing the A.S.U. with a chance to publicize this secret draft, which would horrify the folks in the Normal Communities and hopefully cause the Anti-Socials throughout the U.T. to rise

up en masse. Unfortunately, due to a scheduling error, the Jackson
Avenue Uprising started an hour before the opening ceremo-
nies of the Interterritorial quarterfinal rounds of "15 Minutes of
Superstardom," the most-watched Amateur Talent Competition in
the history of Talent Competition Content. And if that wasn't terrible timing enough, immediately after the start of the Uprising, they
streamed a new round of KILL CHAIN! LIVE!, which meant the
Normals were going crazy flipping back and forth between the two
"live" shows. And thus, though the Jackson Avenue Uprising was the
stuff of legend in Zone 23, virtually no one outside the Zone was
aware that it had ever happened. And as for the so-called Gruber
Draft, it must have been in the hands of someone who died that
weekend on Jackson Avenue, or Cromwell Place, or Walt Whitman
Road, or during the purge of the 4s that followed, which had also,
officially, never happened. In any event, the draft disappeared, and
no one remembered it had ever existed, except for covert historians,
like Meyer, and some of the people who were there, like Taylor, and
... whatever, that was all in the past.

In the going on thirty-five years since the Uprising, the A.S.U.
had primarily focused on education and network-building, and
had toned down the militant street-fighting thing. They had run
these underground schools for kids, but they had gradually phased
out during the 90s as the last few classes of A.S.P.s, and finally
the Thirties, came of age. For adults, they had offered clandestine
workshops on subjects like History, Microeconomics, Gardening,
Psychology, and Basic Chemistry, most of which had been poorly
attended. More militant members of the A.S.U., although fewer in
number, had kept themselves busy burning down ConCept walk-
in clinics, corporate stores, and Security vehicles. The vast majority
had been shot in the process. That, or else wherever they'd lived,
or Security Services had thought they'd lived, had been blown to
smithereens by a drone. Occasionally these had been surgical strikes,
where they put the missile right through your window, but usually
they'd just go ahead and waste the whole building, and everyone in
it. Or they'd drive a bus up in front of the building, march all the
residents out at gunpoint, load them in, drive them away, and they'd
never be seen or heard from again. For these, and other similar rea-

sons, the A.S.U. was not exactly popular among the Anti-Socials, at least not among the native Anti-Socials ... most of whom were simply trying to live through the day without getting wasted and had zero interest in resisting anything. Taylor had often wondered how they had kept the network alive all these years. Now, of course, it all made sense. The old A.S.U., the one he remembered, the one of his mother's generation, had faded into the mists of history. The new A.S.U. was being run by Transplants, jargon-spewing, twinkling Transplants.

Taylor scanned the faces in the meeting. There was Adam, Jamie (or possibly Jaimé), Flaco, and Chino, who were ops-type people, Bethany, Sean, and Maya, the hackers, Dorian, who Taylor didn't know what his thing was, Sarah, who stayed in the background, mostly, and appeared to be kind of an adviser to Adam (and who'd invited Taylor to this fucking meeting), Ahmed Niedermeier, who was totally paranoid, Ahmed's girlfriend, Ingrid or something, and some tattooed punk whose name he'd forgotten.

None of these people were baby smugglers.

According to Meyer, the A.S.U. had zero to do with smuggling babies. No, the way it worked was, the baby smugglers, who were members of some other more militant outfit (some much more se-cretive militant outfit, the name of which Meyer did not know, or if he did, would not divulge), were there, inside the A.S.U., and were technically members of the A.S.U., but the A.S.U. didn't know who they were, and neither did Meyer Jimenez, allegedly.

"So how do I find them?" Taylor pressed.

"Who?"

"These people ... these baby smugglers."

This was back at 16 Mulberry. The time was approximately 0430.

"Hypothetically?"

"Sure. Whatever."

They were sitting alone at the kitchen table, drinking rum and sweating profusely.

"A person would never find such people."

Meyer glanced around suspiciously, or maybe just drunkenly.

"How does it work then?"

Meyer reached across for the bottle.

"Hypothetically?"

"Hypothetically."

The stub of a candle was burning on the table. Their enormous German Impressionist shadows were looming above them on the opposite wall.

"A person would not approach such people. A person would wait to be approached by them."

Dodo Pacheco was snoring loudly.

"Yeah ... but how will they know I'm looking for them?"

Meyer poured a shot of rum.

"They'll know."

"How?"

Meyer drank.

"Faith."

"Faith?"

Meyer nodded.

"I don't understand. Do you get word to them?"

Dodo made this apnea-related plosive sort of puffing noise.

"How?"

"You obviously know who they are."

Dodo gasped, and went back to snoring.

"No one knows who these people are."

"Then how do you know they even exist?"

Meyer poured another shot of rum.

"Faith."

"Faith."

Meyer smiled. He slid the shot glass across the table.

"Faith in what?"

"Ah ... this is the question."

"No, Meyer ... this is not the question."

Taylor sighed, and threw back his shot. The conversation had been going like this for close to an hour. Taylor was frustrated. Meyer, who was never a font of clarity, was being especially vague, or cagey ... or maybe it was just that he was shitfaced drunk.

"You said this cell, this ..."

"Fifthian Cluster."

"They're in there."

ZONE 23175

"Who?"

"The baby smugglers."

"Possibly."

"But also other infiltrators."

"Certainly."

"Who?"

"Exactly."

"No ... I'm asking you that."

"Asking me what?"

"Who are the other infiltrators? Cooperators? IntraZone Waste?"

Meyer nodded.

"Security Services?"

"Everybody infiltrates everybody. Everybody uses everybody."

Meyer reached across for the shot glass. Taylor snatched it.

"So what do I do?"

"Do about what?"

"Focus, Meyer."

Taylor was about to blow a gasket.

"What?"

"How do I know who's who?"

"Exactly."

"What? Exactly what?"

"This, my friend, is what it all comes down to."

"What is what it all comes down to?"

"Faith."

Dodo choked, and snorted.

"In the end it all comes down to faith."

This was back in early September, before all the stuff that was going to happen, or appear to happen, in the months that followed (which would later, almost imperceptibly, although part of Taylor would sense it happening, totally over-complicate everything, and radically change his whole take on Meyer) had happened, so Taylor was still in the dark. As far as he knew at this point in our story, things were pretty much what they were. Cassandra was pregnant. The plan was the plan. The A.S.U. was the A.S.U. The baby smugglers were baby smugglers. And Meyer Jimenez was Meyer Jimenez. Unfortunately, the way it turned out later, things were not at all what they were, or what they seemed to be at the time (as opposed to what they would seem to be later), which Taylor, of course, had no way of knowing ... which is maybe what Meyer Jimenez was saying.

Taylor, on a fairly consistent basis, had no idea what Meyer was saying ... or, OK, he got the gist of it, generally, as in he understood the meaning of the words ... but there was always something behind the words, which Taylor, when he was concentrating, and Meyer wasn't so shitfaced drunk, thought he could sense when he heard the words ... because the words were like the shadow of it, this thing you could never express directly, which seemed to have something to do with faith, or how nothing was actually real, or true, or it was, but it was all just part and parcel of the story you were telling yourself, but you couldn't admit you were telling yourself, and so believed that you were being told ... or whatever the fuck it was exactly Meyer was always trying to allude to.

Meyer Jimenez (who was not A.S.U., but who knew some people who knew some people who knew where some other people hung out) had been in residence at 16 Mulberry, by this time, October, for just over a year. For reasons that weren't entirely clear, his arrival had not been announced to anyone. He seemed to have just materialized there in the kitchen one morning the previous summer. The story, it turned out, was Meyer's father, Chaim Santobal de something Jimenez, had been active in some militant cell with Coco Freudenheim's nephew, Maury, who along with Chaim, and a lot of other people, had disappeared during the Bain Street Riots, which had taken place down in the Southwest Sector in the run-up to the Jackson Avenue Uprising ... but the two things weren't connected, directly. Or maybe Chaim Santobal de something had made it through the Bain Street Riots, and had slipped up out of the Southwest Sector and joined the Jackson Avenue Cell, and so had died in the Jackson Avenue Uprising, and it was Maury who had died in the Bain Street Riots, or it was one of Coco's other nephews. All that history was kind of hazy, and mostly depended on who you talked to, which didn't really matter, because whatever had happened, Coco Freudenheim vouched for Meyer.

A few days following his mysterious arrival, Meyer assumed the title and duties of Chef de cuisine of Apartment 2E. He specialized in Cuban dishes, pigeon paella, frijoles negro, arroz con pigeon, arroz con maiz, fried plantains, yuca, malanga, depending on what they had at the markets. Meyer never visited the markets. In fact, he never left the apartment. No, the way it worked was, Meyer stayed home, drank like a fish and manned the kitchen, and everyone else took turns with the shopping, which worked out nicely for everyone involved, as nobody else could cook worth shit. Meyer made up the shopping list, which naturally people were free to add to ... the only thing was, no fucking TōFood. Meyer had a thing about TōFood. He would not eat it and he would not cook it. What he'd do was, if you brought it to him, he'd throw it down on the floor at your feet and kick it and curse it in Yiddish and spit on it, as if it were some kind of alien organism.* To Meyer, the entire TōFood concept was a personal affront to his culinary prowess. It wasn't like he was a meat freak or anything. Meals were often vegetarian. It was just that, to Meyer, meat was meat, the flesh of some formerly living animal, a cow, a pig, or a chicken, preferably, and not some non-meat meatlike substance made out of processed soy bean curd. The only problem was, there were no cows, or pigs, or chickens, or not real ones anyway. Fortunately, there were plenty of pigeons. Pigeons weren't always easy to catch, but people did, and they bred them in coops, which they covered with tarps and weeds and garbage to fool the BirdsEye and the roving drones. Killing pigeons, or rats, or squirrels, or any other species of sentient being, was, of course, technically, murder, and earned you an automatic Class 4, but people went ahead and did it anyway, and sold the meat to people like Meyer.**

In addition to his gastronomical activities, Meyer was something of an amateur philosopher, or a cultural theorist, or a conspiracy nut. Or at least he had all these crazy theories, which he would sit there, sweating, at the kitchen table, after he had finished whatever he was cooking, and had settled in for some serious drinking, and

---

* In addition to Standard Business English, the official language of the United Territories, Meyer was familiar with (or at least could read) a number of older, unofficial languages, Spanish, of course, which people still spoke, Arabic, Russian, Cantonese, Ancient Greek, Latin, German, Yiddish, something called Aramaic, and even a little Ancient French, which in spite of the fact that no one understood them, people still spoke in Region 16.

** According to Meyer, pigeons were kosher. People had eaten them for thousands of years. He drew the line at rodents, however. He'd sooner die than eat a rat.

recount, and explain, and lecture you on, all night long if you sat there and let him. Topics ranged from the nature of time, and being, and becoming, and the perception thereof, and other such standard philosophical topics, to other not-so-standard topics, like the formerly secret, now redacted, possibly totally made-up history of the Hadley Corporation of Menomonie, Wisconsin, or the structure of the Interterritorial government, which Meyer claimed didn't actually exist, except as a front for the corporations (which, OK, of course, he was right about that one, but everybody pretty much knew that already). If you sat there long enough, drinking with him, which Taylor, oddly, found himself doing, he'd end up shouting all this nonsense, red-faced, sweat just rolling down his cheeks, about how time did NOT equal space, no more than people's bodies were composed of variously colored biles and humors, which Meyer insisted people had believed for hundreds of years in the Middle Ages, and medieval scientists had been able to prove (at least at the time, while people believed it), until Enlightenment scientists discovered "the truth," that our bodies were composed of cells and enzymes, which according to Meyer was not "the truth," or it was the "the truth," but it was still made-up.

"At the core of every fact, my friend, is an act of faith," he'd shout, or slur, or sometimes "nothing does not exist," or the quote he would often end his rants with, "the will to nothing is the will to death!"

One of Meyer's more paranoid theories concerned the accidental pregnancies among the A.S.P. 1 population. According to Meyer, these were no accidents. Meyer's theory (which he hadn't named yet) was that Hadley and the other corporations were using the female 1s as livestock, sabotaging their Anti-Baby pills, their MorningAfter pills, and even the condoms. These "accidentally" pregnant women (who'd been selected by the corporations, who of course had access to their MedBase files), had been rendered to secure facilities, their babies harvested, psychologically conditioned (or raised) in some corporate training compound, and finally, once they had come of age, put into service as Security Specialists. The mothers had probably been killed and cremated, as once their babies had been safely harvested, there'd be no reason to keep them alive. Meyer suspected the corporations were breeding battalions of these brainwashed soldiers, who they sent out into the Recovering Areas to exterminate any faith-based Terrorists living in the ruins of the blasted cities, and in caves, and in fortified underground camps ... all of which sounded a bit far-fetched, if not just batshit crazy, to Taylor.

Meyer had a million of these theories, some of which actually made some sense. One of Taylor's particular favorites was the one about how the corporations were not really being run by the Normals, but were more or less running themselves at this point, operating like autonomous programs according to some systemic logic that the Normals, being part and parcel of, had lost the ability to even perceive. According to this theory (which Meyer called "The Fascist Decentralization of Everything"), the minds of the Normals were all controlled by this a priori perceptual paradigm that determined the parameters in which they could think, and even the questions they were capable of asking. This paradigm (which Meyer explained to Taylor was like the unconscious model, or matrix, in relation to which one interpreted everything) was not an ideology, or creed, which one could at least define and critique, but rather, was the unarticulated boundary establishing the limits of one's imaginative powers, and interpretative powers, and thus perception itself. Taylor couldn't follow that completely, but he thought he got the general idea, how what the Normals thought of as just "common sense," or obvious facts, or "the way things are," was as much a product of mental conditioning, or brainwashing, as anything else they believed, and that sounded more or less right to Taylor.

Another one of Taylor's favorites, which was also one of Meyer's favorites, was one called The Pathologization of Everything, which had something to do with the corporations replacing morality, and ethics in toto, with a much more effective and insidious means of controlling the Normals' thoughts and behavior. Here, according to Meyer at least, was the ultimate Corporatist tour de force ... the eradication of any surviving remnants of anti- or non-market values, along with the co-optation thereof by the healthcare and pharmaceutical industries. According to Meyer, the way this worked was, whenever they (i.e., the corporations) wanted to control or entirely eliminate some specific behavior or way of thinking, they didn't have to bother convincing people (as earlier, more despotic regimes had) that whatever it was was "bad" or "wrong" ... they simply invented some new disorder, or syndrome, or some other pseudo-illness, with a new set of symptoms that matched that behavior (or emotion, or undesirable way of thinking), and added it to the DSM. Then they sent out the appropriate press releases and let the media do their thing.

Being a Class 3 Anti-Social Person, this wasn't exactly news to Taylor,* however, there was this one little part of Meyer's theory that he found intriguing, and had sat around drinking and discussing with Meyer until they both passed out on numerous occasions. This was the part that was gnawing at him now (as he sat there in that airless basement while the hardcore members of the Fifthian Cluster exhaustively discussed "security culture"). According to this part of Meyer's theory, despite the Pathologization of Everything, the Normals, or at least the Variant-Positives, the products of nearly three thousand years of psychological and behavioral conditioning, even then, in the 27th Century, continued to perceive the world and people, not in medical or pathological terms (which is what you'd expect, given this theory), but in moralistic terms ... like "right" and "wrong." They didn't use these words of course. They used other words, like "healthy" and "unhealthy," and "positive" and "negative," and "balanced" and "imbalanced," but what they meant was right and wrong. If you asked them to explain these terms, and what they were based on, they couldn't, not really. They'd tell you it was something they just felt in their hearts, and knew intuitively, and was probably innate, something to do with fairness and kindness and treating others as one wanted to be treated. Of course, they had never been able to do this, and instead had killed and butchered and tortured and enslaved each other throughout human history, but that was on account of original sin, or the fact that carnate life was suffering, or it was some kind of test that God was conducting, or something ... there was always some tortuous logic that explained why humans were tragic miscreants, and why "good" and "bad" and "right" and "wrong" were not just concepts, like other concepts, but were a priori transcendent truths, which no sane person could every question.

The origin of all this moralistic thinking, according to Meyer (and

---

* One of the symptoms of Anti-Social Disease was denial that the disease was real.

Taylor concurred), was nothing transcendent or in any way spiritual. It was simply fear. Primordial fear ... fear of being killed and
eaten. Apparently, once, a long, long time ago, the earth had been
host to a variety of species, many of them larger and rather more
frightening than the rats, pigeons, mutant insects, and other forms
of unattractive fauna indigenous to the United Territories.* Tigers,
for example, or those really big sharks, man-eating lizards, snakes,
crocodiles, bears, wolves, panthers, jackals, vicious apes, enormous
weasels, and snorting, slavering pig-like creatures with mouths full
of horrible grinding molars ... which, the point is, if you came across
them, odds were you'd be killed and eaten. Human beings had lived
like this for thousands, possibly millions of years, scurrying about
like terrified monkeys, stuffing their faces with nuts and berries,
dashing in and out of caves, and so on, trying to not to be killed and
eaten. Then, according to Meyer's theory, something truly astonish-
ing happened. Sometime during the Paleolithic Period, for reasons
Meyer had never explained (at least not to Taylor, as far as he remembered), people got tired of being killed and eaten, and of living
in constant white-eyed terror of being killed, and dismembered, and
eaten. So what they did was, they banded into groups, groups of ten
to maybe twenty individuals, which reduced the odds of being killed
and eaten ... reduced, but unfortunately did not eliminate, the odds
of being killed and eaten. However, they were on the right course
now. So what they did next was, they enlarged these groups, these
so-called "bands" of up to twenty individuals (whose structure was
based on filial ties and was typically informal and egalitarian), forming "tribes" of hundreds of individuals, who were still pretty squirrely
and not very disciplined. So all right, good, they were making progress. However, at this stage, they encountered a problem. Due to the
growing size of these tribes, and the frequent disagreements among
their members (disagreements which were typically resolved by
bashing each other's skulls in with rocks), intra-tribal societal discipline became a necessity, or at least an advantage, and means were
soon sought to establish same. Warrior chiefs, with the aid of their
shamans, rose to prominence and established this discipline, and

---

*Actual species, that lived in the wild, not the genetically modified replicas the Normals designed for
their Wildlife Worlds, and Animal Kingdoms, and other such places.

codes of acceptable tribal behavior, and subjugation and allegiance to their tribes. Members of such tribes were called "the people," which (a) probably sounded nice, and (b) served to distinguish these members from the members of other disagreeable tribes, who lived across the river somewhere, and were not "the people," and were strange and frightening, and eaters of filth, who worshiped demons.

Morality was born. The rest was history. Tribes grew to chiefdoms, chiefdoms to states, states to empires, empires to superpowers, all of which relentlessly attacked each other, and blockaded, and financially strangled each other, until finally there was just a single superpower, i.e., the former United States of America, which had saved everybody from the Nazis and the Communists, and had established the global market economy and spread democracy throughout the world. And still, despite the spread of democracy, and equality, and individual liberty, and despite the fact that the world was finally united under a single signifier, and that there were no longer any outside enemies, because everything was one big market economy ... despite all that, this primordial fear, this fear of being killed and eaten, and the fear and hatred of "the other" it had led to, persisted, and threatened to ruin everything ... or so went the logic of the official story.

In other words, according to Meyer's theory (or as far as Taylor could follow the theory), according to the Normals' official story, by sometime in the mid-to-late 21st Century, or possibly early in the 22nd Century, the subspecies Homo sapiens sapiens had reached its evolutionary end point. Human beings had finally evolved (or human society had finally progressed) to the stage where we were all just one big tribe, happily living and working together in a peaceful, prosperous global marketplace. The irony was, according to Meyer, that the very thing that had made this possible, and that had driven all progress throughout human history, this fear that had given rise to morality, and ethics, and enabled us to form societies, the very fear that had originally saved us from those snorting, slavering pig-like creatures, was now, apparently, going to kill us ... unless we preventatively killed ourselves. All of which, of course, was patently absurd.

No, according to Meyer, the whole Clarion Project, including the phase-out of Homo sapiens sapiens, had nothing to with defective genes, or preventing aggression or violence per se. What was really happening was, the corporations were eradicating the last conceivable form of resistance to their Total Domination of Everything, which according to Meyer that last conceivable form of resistance was ... well, it was faith.

And this was the part that was eating at Taylor ... the notion that this living hell, this waking nightmare they had been born into, and had spent their whole lives in, and were currently living in (and the reason Taylor was sitting down there in that stinking basement thinking all this), was all the result of the corporations' sustained attempt to eradicate faith ... which according to Meyer they'd been trying to do since sometime during the Middle Ages. If Taylor understood what Meyer was getting at, it didn't even matter what kind of faith. What mattered was whether people acted on it ... whether they actually lived according to the values of whatever faith it was, rather than according to corporate values ... which it turned out, whenever people did that (i.e., not just mouthed whatever platitudes, but actually attempted to conduct their lives according to some sort of faith-based beliefs, they ended up opposed to the corporations, which made them Terrorists, or potential Terrorists ... or at least it made them Anti-Socials.

Which ... all right, Taylor was fine with all that, in terms of the basic logic, anyway, but then came the batshit crazy part. Meyer claimed that the Normal doctors had located some sort of faith-based gene, or faith-based center of the brain, or something, and that this was what they were actually modifying when they "variant-corrected" the Normals' embryos. They weren't editing out aggression ... they were systematically breeding a race of human beings incapable of faith, or any other type of non-rational thinking, a race incapable of ever resisting (or meaningfully questioning the nature of) the corporations' Total Domination of Everything.

Taylor, although he certainly appreciated the spirit of this part of Meyer's theory, felt that it was a probably bit of a stretch, and was somewhat paranoid, and was completely ridiculous.

And yet his whole plan depended on it.

Meyer had suggested, or intimated,* that the baby smugglers Taylor was seeking (or, rather, was waiting to be sought out by) were,

---

* Or Taylor believed he remembered he had.

in all likelihood, faith-based Terrorists (who presumably subscribed to Meyer's theory, or to some similarly paranoid version thereof), and that what they were doing was raising the babies in their underground camps in the Autonomous Zones, filling their heads with faith-based nonsense, and training them on weapons and explosives and whatever, and that someday they (i.e., the faith-based babies) would form the ranks of some guerrilla army of faith-based Homo sapiens sapiens that would storm the Normals in their private Communities, and ... whatever.

It was all a fucking pipe dream.

Sitting in the rear of the Action Group Update, as Adam and the rest of the Fifthian Cluster approached the midpoint of their exhaustive discussion of "a Phase Two D.A.D.A. security culture," it occurred to Taylor that it was highly likely that, in spite of his philosophical acumen, and taking nothing away from the thrust of his genealogy of morals in general, as far this thing with babies went, Meyer Jimenez was full of shit.

There were no fucking baby smugglers. Meyer had dreamed the whole thing up, not out of any malicious motive, but because it fit in nicely with his fucking theory. Which meant that Taylor was seriously screwed, as now he had wasted the last five weeks sitting around in these fucking meetings listening to a bunch of dipshit Transplants trying to outstupify each other with their jargon, and otherwise militantly jerking off.

So, excellent, this was just fucking beautiful. What was he going to tell Cassandra? The truth? That his plan had gone belly up? That now she was fucked? That the baby was fucked? No. He couldn't. He would have to lie to her. Which that was OK. He'd make something up, something to keep her calm for the moment. He didn't know what, but he'd think of something. Then he'd come up with another plan. First, however, he needed to determine where, when, and exactly how, to egregiously violate Meyer Jimenez, whose fault this fucking fiasco was. Just as he was mulling over the various in and outs of doing that, someone leaned up and whispered in his ear.

"Pussyhorse Lounge, 2200."

He turned around slowly. The someone was Sarah. She'd moved up and taken the chair behind him, which he hadn't noticed, which wasn't like him. Now she was sitting there, eyes on Adam, who was designating something a "need-to-know" subject. He leaned back toward her and started to ask ...

"Shhhh," she whispered. Her eyes never moved. She raised her hands and joined in twinkling. Her neck was beaded with droplets of sweat. Taylor, who at this point was totally focused on his mission with an almost laser-like intensity, hadn't even hardly noticed until then how dark, sleek, strangely feline, and otherwise incredibly fuckable she was.

"Turn around," she whispered, twinkling.

Taylor turned back around in his seat.

"Twinkle," she whispered.

Taylor twinkled.

Whatever, he thought. Life was short. He'd deal with the baby problem tomorrow. He'd deal with Cassandra and Meyer tomorrow. He would deal with all his problems tomorrow. Tonight, apparently, he was going to get laid.

Billy Jensen

Six months and a few days later, Billy Jensen, who lived somewhere else, and who had never even heard of Taylor Byrd, or Valentina Constance Briggs, or any of the other people in our story, was ... well, basically, he was watching TV. He was doing this on the JumboMax screen of his Tannhäuser Systems In-Home Viewer, a Model 60, Series K, which covered one entire wall of his studio ... or, rather, *was* one wall of his studio. The Model 60, which he had bought on credit, and owed about GD 400,000 on, was patched into his Tannhäuser Systems In-Home Professional Gaming Console, which resembled the cockpit of a military aircraft and took up most of the rest of his apartment.

Serious gamers like Billy Jensen didn't mess around when it came to their Viewers, or their In-Home Professional Gaming Consoles. They shelled out for the seriously high-end Pro-stuff, which was optimized to support whatever professional-quality gaming platforms the company in question designed and marketed, or had the exclusive rights to distribute, or some other kind of lucrative deal. Tannhäuser Systems (a partly-owned subsidiary of another subsidiary of another subsidiary of the Hadley Corporation of Menomonie, Wisconsin), in addition to being the market leader in the seriously high-end Viewer market, and Professional Gaming Console market, and offering an extensive and affordable line of professional quality gaming accessories, and T-shirts, and caps, and branded coffee mugs, was also the maker of the wildly popular interactive simulated MercyKill game, KILL CHAIN, which was Billy Jensen's game.

KILL CHAIN, despite its aggressive-sounding name, was nothing like the horribly violent Anti-Social first-person shooter games people used to play in the bad old days. The violence involved was in no way gratuitous; it was strictly clinical, and compassion-based. The Targets were all Class 4 Anti-Socials, who were needlessly suffering late-stage disease, and whose quality of life was non-existent when measured on the HRQOL scale. Most of them were dangerous faith-based Terrorists, who posed potentially devastating threats, possibly with improvised nuclear devices, or horrible chemical or biological agents that would kill you the second they touched your skin. KILL CHAIN players (or "Operators") targeted these poor lost souls remotely, neutralizing any threat they posed, and putting them out of their pointless misery.

KILL CHAIN VIII: Compassionate Hammer, released online the previous December, just in time for the Christmas holidays, was, in Billy Jensen's opinion, one of the best in the KILL CHAIN series. It was sitting there, loaded, in his gaming console, ready to go when he logged off work. KILL CHAIN VII: For Their Own Good had been a serious disappointment. Too much focus had been placed on the Targets, on their personal lives and medical histories, had been the general critical consensus. Billy Jensen had to agree. It felt like maybe the narrative talent had gotten a little carried away with themselves, building in all these endless layers of exposition and mood and whatever. It was like they wanted you to work your way through some interminable, rambling Russian novel (or some pseudo-academic sociological text) before you could even sight the Targets, much less put a missile down on them. You sat there, stick in hand, for hours, watching them unnecessarily suffering ... which, all right, granted, definitely got you all pent-up and, like, itching to tag them, which of course when you did, after all that build-up, certainly heightened the sensation of the kill, which was obviously what the designers were going for, but it left you with this weird kind of empty feeling, which after a while got rather tiresome. KILL CHAIN VIII: Compassionate Hammer had cut way down on patterning time. All that boring background stuff had been relegated to a single window that displayed down in the corner of your screen. Average acquisition-to-action time (or "ATA time") was under an hour. Veteran players, like Billy Jensen, could get a perfectly decent kill in during their lunch or dinner breaks, which Billy Jensen routinely did.

Billy Jensen was a Junior Online Customer Service Solutions Specialist. He was twenty-seven years old ... a Clear. He worked for a firm called Kierkegaard/Bose, designers of some kind of software solutions that had something to do with the needs of business that Billy Jensen did not understand. This wasn't because he was unintelligent. Billy Jensen was extremely intelligent. He could have understood. He just didn't care to. It wasn't his job to understand. Billy's job was to virtually chat with K/B's transterritorial clients, trouble-shoot their myriad problems according to a detailed algorithmic script, and get them off the Live-Chat network, in less than seven to eight minutes, ideally. Like most OCS reps, he did this from home (a totally modern single's unit on the 98th floor of TransCom Towers in Northwest Region 228) while logged into K/B's global network, which auto-monitored Billy's keystrokes.

Billy worked the lobster shift, from 2300 to 0700, which didn't bother Billy one bit. He kept to a relatively rigid schedule, which, apart from doing his OCS job, primarily consisted of playing KILL CHAIN six days a week, up to six hours a day. He logged in as soon as he logged off work, and played until just after 1500, after which he worked out, ate, slept a few hours, got up, showered, ate a light breakfast, viewed some Content, and logged back onto the K/B network.

The Content Billy religiously viewed while drinking his micronized-glutamine breakfast was KILL CHAIN LIVE! on Channel 16, hosted by Dr. Roger P. Greenway and Susan Schnupftuch-Boermann Goereszky. And thus, it being a normal day, and the time being circa 2150, was exactly what Billy was doing at the moment.

The screen of his Tannhäuser Model 60 was running the standard Real-Time feed of what appeared to be a Quarantine Zone, shot from the nose of a UAV holding at an altitude of twenty-three kilometers. Crosshairs were sweeping a four-block grid of empty streets of unlit buildings. They looked like maybe former warehouses ... nothing terribly fascinating.

"Any idea where we are now, Roger?"

"Susan, we're looking at Zone 18, Southeast Region 423. Looks like a sultry night down there. Not much to see at the moment, I'm afraid."

"It does look pretty desolate, Roger."

"Like I said, Susan, hot one down there."

"Shall we introduce Target Number One then, Roger?"

"Susan, looks like Target Number One is a subject name of Carlos Witherspoon. Designated Class 4 Anti-Social Person. Late stage disease. History of violence. Hiding in one of those buildings there, Susan."

"Any idea which building, Roger?"

"No, apparently not, Susan. We seem to be standing by at the moment."

An unflattering photograph of "Carlos Witherspoon," bug-eyed, grimacing, needing a shave, appeared in the lower left corner of the screen.

"Here's a photo of Witherspoon, Susan."

"Wow."

"Yeah. Obviously in pain."

"Breaks your heart to see them like that."

"Yes, it certainly does, Susan."

"No way to hide that kind of suffering."

"Hopefully, we can get him some relief tonight."

Billy Jensen hoped they could too. He disliked watching anything suffer, any form of sentient being, even a dangerous faith-based Terrorist. Being a Clear, he could not help this. Compassion was coded into his genes. His heart went out to Carlos Witherspoon, and all the other Carlos Witherspoons out there, suffering their needless pain and suffering. He meticulously peeled the foil away from his Happy Henry's low-glycemic, gluten-free instant energy bar and tried to imagine their pain and suffering. He couldn't ... or not entirely anyway. The desperate and unfocused rage, the hatred and envy of everything normal, and above all the unrelenting fear that ruled their existence and governed all their actions, were emotions Billy had never felt, and thus could never completely conceive of, except in some purely intellectual way. The Variant-Positives were challenging enough, with their inner conflicts, and doubts, and questions, and their constant struggle to stay detached. Billy's heart went out to them too, more so even, as he understood them, and how they thought, and he felt their pain.

They wanted to be healthy, the Variant-Positives. They never would be, but they tried their best. The medications they took were crude, but they did seem to slow their disease progression, or at least reduced the worst of their symptoms to something approaching manageable levels. The drugs, however, could never stop them from forming their Anti-Social ideations, or clear away the fog of primitive drives and emotions that shrouded their brains. As uncorrected Homo sapiens sapiens, the best they could do was attempt to maintain a constant state of hypervigilance (i.e., paying close attention to their thoughts and feelings, writing them down, analyzing them, and then verbalizing them to "make them real"). They did this in their support group meetings, and with friends, family, colleagues, and doctors, and whoever was sitting beside them on the train, soliciting feedback from all and sundry, which they then evaluated and processed with others, who gave them feedback on this feedback, which brought up other thoughts and feelings, which they diligently processed, analyzed and verbalized, and meditated on at considerable length. All of which left them totally exhausted and no longer certain what they were feeling, or thinking, or exactly what they wanted, or what they had just been talking about.

Billy's Variant-Positive parents, Woody and Carmen, were perfect examples. They could hardly get through a conversation without stumbling over some thought or emotion that triggered some anxious observation of some possibly symptomatic reaction that they needed to process, accept, and detach from, and otherwise discuss at considerable length. Billy loved his parents dearly, and he empathized with their pain, of course, but he couldn't help feeling that they would both be so much happier once they had reincarnated.

Whatever, Billy reasoned, chewing, in another hundred years or so the endless trials and tribulations of the Variant-Positives would all be over. In the meantime, they had done as much as any defective strain could do to tackle the problem of Anti-Social Disease in a rational and scientific manner. To use a systems-based trouble-shooting analogy, which Billy did whenever possible, they had tracked and found their system error (the aberrant variant of the MAO-A gene), effected repairs to what they could (medicated the Variant-Positives), effectively quarantined what they couldn't (segregated the A.S.P.s), and had taken appropriate long-term steps to eliminate any future recurrence (developed the variant correction technologies, which had produced the Clarions, like Billy Jensen). All of which steps were perfectly logical, and thus, to Billy, complete no-brainers. However, he reflected, swallowing, for the Variant-Positives in charge at the time, these must have been rather difficult decisions, entailing as they did the making redundant, or phasing out, of their entire subspecies.* Cognitively challenged as they were, he had to admire those Variant-Positives, those of his parents' generation, who had made those decisions and who were trying their best to ensure a smooth and peaceful transition to a healthier world they would have no part in.

The A.S.P.s were a different matter. The poor things didn't even know they were sick. Their brains were so gone, so riddled with disease, that they actually believed that *they* were normal, and that the Variant-Positives and Clears were the freaks. Which, one good look in the mirror should have told them, was not just wrong, but completely ridiculous. All right, sure, there were exceptions, but overwhelmingly, the Anti-Socials were simply ... well ... unattractive. They looked unhealthy, and congenitally so. And this was true of even the least afflicted and most cooperative among them, the ones they allowed outside the Zones to work in the Residential Communities, who Billy sometimes saw in passing on his way to Finkles or Big Buy Basement. The ones they didn't let out were worse. Their skin was terrible, either dry and cracked or overly oily, and probably stank. Their hair was all greasy, clumped, and matted, or it was powdered with dandruff and crawling with lice. Most of them seemed to be missing teeth, which was certainly caused by periodontitis. They bathed infrequently, clearly never flossed, didn't use condoms, and smoked tobacco. Something like sixty percent, it was said, were chronic Diplastomorphinol users. The rest were mostly alcoholics, or were killing themselves in some other fashion. Billy could not begin to fathom what went through their tiny, enfeebled minds. How they went on, what they lived for, why they didn't just euthanize themselves, were questions he had never been able to

---

* *The Clarions, taxonomically speaking, constituted a separate subspecies, which the biologists were calling "Homo sapiens consentiēns."*

answer. Still, despite his instinctual revulsion (which any healthy organism felt when confronted with some obvious abnormality among the members of its potential gene pool), he was, above all else, a Clear ... so whenever he saw their photos appear on the screen of his Viewer on KILL CHAIN LIVE!, or even when he was just playing KILL CHAIN, and was confronted with their unrelenting pain, and pointless physical and emotional suffering, he felt himself overcome with compassion, and not just for the Target at hand, but for every living, needlessly suffering, uncorrected sentient being ... that, and an irresistible urge to take them out as quickly as possible.

KILL CHAIN LIVE! on Channel 16, had been on the air for some twenty-five years. It ran at 2300 nightly, except for Sundays and major holidays.* Billy Jensen had been watching the show, religiously, since the age of twelve, which technically his parents should have prevented, but nobody ever checked that stuff. The production elements had changed through the years as styles went in and out of fashion and new technologies came online, but the basic premise remained the same. Targets posing imminent threats, usually in some Recovering Area, but occasionally in one of the Quarantine Zones, were acquired, locked on, and taken out, typically by a laser-guided AGM 660 Godsend missile, the classic air-to-surface munition manufactured by Pfizer-Lockheed, which was one of the major sponsors of the show. The 660 Godsend, a solid fuel rocket, equipped with either a standard condensed or "indoor" thermobaric warhead, and a Semi-Active Laser Homing guidance system that was totally unrivaled, was the ordnance of choice of Security Services throughout the United Territories. Not only was the Godsend a first class weapon suitable for use in both open and urban Emergency Threat Containment environments, but by licensing the use of its in-flight footage to KILL CHAIN LIVE! on Channel 16, Security Divisions of leading corporations, like the Hadley Corporation of Menomonie, Wisconsin, were doubling and tripling their profit margins. Hi-Def Real-Time NoseCam feed provided PixelPerfect

---

* In addition to the regular nightly show, there were also various special editions, like KILL CHAIN! OUTBREAK! and KILL CHAIN! PANDEMIC!, which ran unannounced at irregular times, and which were really all parts of the same competition, which was kind of like the KILL CHAIN! playoffs, the Interterritorial quarterfinal round of which Billy Jensen had just qualified for.

footage of the Godsend's dizzying Mach 2 descent through diaphanous webs of fluffy white clouds like some monomaniacal avenging angel. Average flight time was 26 seconds, during which the Operator needed to hold the crosshairs steady, painting the target, which was often moving, for the Godsend's onboard laser seeker. The last few seconds were always a blur, so you had to wait for the slow-mo replays and satellite footage from other angles to see all the details and determine the score. For the overwhelming majority of Targets, death was instant, and presumably painless, unless a Target was exceptionally good, or whoever was manning the UAV screwed up somehow, or something malfunctioned. Normally, the Targets, whoever they were, males mostly, but sometimes females, and sometimes groups, or "hives" as they called them, were vaporized never knowing what hit them. Before the strikes, you'd get their backgrounds, names, photos, medical histories, ages, associates, whatever there was. Then came a ten-minute call-in segment, when they read out people's Fleeps and Tweaks, followed by some kind of medical expert, who Billy Jensen generally ignored. The current hosts, Dr. Roger P. Greenway and Susan Schnupftuch-Boermann Goereszky, were fairly attractive Variant-Positives whose job it was to look "concerned" or "deeply interested" or "wildly excited" while talking into the camera continuously as their line producers talked in their ears, telling them what to do and say.

"Susan, I think we're getting the yellow."

"I've got that here as well, Roger."

Susan Schnupftuch-Boermann Goereszky, who sometimes did the news on Sundays, was "live" at her desk on the KILL CHAIN LIVE! set, a technological phantasmagoria officially located in Studio B of the Channel 16 Broadcast Center. Dr. Greenway was hunkered down in an undisclosed secure location, probably somewhere down the hall, surrounded by screens and wires and panels of buttons that nobody knew what they did.

"Susan, we're definitely yellow here, Susan."

"Still no sign of Witherspoon, Roger?"

"Nothing yet, but there must be something, or we wouldn't be getting the yellow, Susan."

"Roger, we're going yellow in the studio."

The infinity cycs in Studio B slowly faded from orange to yellow. Susan Schnupftuch-Boermann Goereszky cleared her throat and adjusted her posture. An ad for Anabastastic Plus, a painless anal bleaching compound, popped up right in the middle of the screen, which didn't have anything to do with anything, so Billy minimized and stacked it with the others.

"Susan, it feels like something's happening."

"Is something happening?"

"Feels like it, Susan."

"Still no sign of Witherspoon, Roger?"

"Susan, we're getting ... hold on, Susan. Someone's talking ... yes, good. We've got a location."

"Which satellite, Roger?"

The feed from various orbiting satellites was flipping past in one corner of the screen ... overhead shots of abandoned buildings on nearly identical empty streets.

"Do we have a number on that satellite, Roger?"

"Hold on, Susan. It's coming in now."

Susan Schnupftuch-Boermann Goereszky rolled her neck and flared her nostrils.

"2230. 2230. Satellite 2230, Susan!"

Dr. Greenway wrenched his neck now, rolling the tension out of his shoulders. Billy smiled and scanned his messages. Nothing that couldn't wait ten minutes.

"Got him, Roger! There he is now!"

Satellite 2230 was up and feeding a beautiful tracking "god shot" of Carlos Witherspoon barreling out of some random building which was now on fire.

"Looks like that building's on fire there, Roger."

"Yes, it certainly does, Susan. It appears we've got some boots on the ground. They seem to have flushed him out there, Susan."

"Oh no. Are they going to take him themselves?"

"Possibly, Susan. We just don't ... wait. Wait. Yes. I'm getting something."

Consummate professional that she was, Susan Schnupftuch-Boermann Goereszky went straight to Real-Time Operator Feed, a risky move, but she just had a feeling. Carlos Witherspoon ran for his life, across an avenue and into a field, heading for a grove of crumbling buildings.

"We're getting something ..."

"I'm on it, Roger."

The RTO Feed came up sharply, crosshairs groping and feeling for Carlos, who was doing a crazy zig-zag pattern across the field where there was no cover.

"Green, Susan. We've got a green here."

The cycs in the studio went to green.

"Going green in the studio, Roger."

Operator 225 was up. A silhouette showing his operator number and season statistics, which were all exemplary, appeared in the lower right corner of the screen.

"What can we say about our operator, Roger?"

"Susan, Operator 225 has 93 kills, 15 collateral, EEA of 2.1."

"Pretty incredible numbers, Roger."

"That's right, Susan, and it's only April."

Operator 225 was good. Really good. Like circus shot good. Billy had seen him bank a missile off one moving vehicle and into another, wasting an entire family of Targets with virtually zero collateral damage. Another time he'd flown one down a stairwell and into the lobby of this building, vaporizing everyone hiding in the lobby while the others upstairs went on with their breakfasts. What he was doing with Carlos Witherspoon was dancing the crosshairs back and forth against the direction and matching the speed of his zig-zag pattern across the field. Billy gave him, like, another twelve seconds before Carlos reached the safety of the buildings.

"This operator is amazing, Susan. He's leading the target."

"We're watching it, Roger."

The Foxtrot button on the RTO screen lit up suddenly.

Billy smiled.

"FOXTROT, SUSAN! FOXTROT! FOXTROT!"

Dr. Greenway leapt to his feet, bringing his crotch up into the camera. Billy chuckled. Carlos ran. Susan Schnupftuch-Boermann Goereszky kept her composure and went to NoseCam.

Southeast Region 423, wherever that was on the planet Earth, was rushing up into the screen ... a blur of shuddering white and red and orange lights with squiggly tails, the patchwork grid of endless cities bleeding into other cities, indistinguishable, like a storm of stars, as the Godsend missile screamed down out of the night from twenty kilometers up. In a window in the lower left corner of the screen, Operator 225 was sweeping the delicate crosshairs back and forth, back and forth, back and forth, dancing with Carlos, intersecting him ... now ... now ... now ... and finally ...

"WHOA! Unbelievable precision!"

"Absolutely textbook strike!"

"That's got to be one for the highlight reel, Susan!"

"Let's take a look at the replays, Roger."

The screen was already subdividing into an assortment of slow-mo replays of the kill from sixteen different angles. Billy froze one in which the missile hung in the air over Carlos Witherspoon, ten or twelve meters above and behind him, its cherry red nose cone pointed at the spot the stride he was taking would carry him into in approximately 0.06 seconds. In another window, he pulled up and readied the login screen of the K/B network. His shift began in forty-three seconds.

"Never knew what hit him, Susan."

"His needless suffering is over now, Roger."

"Not to mention the threat he posed, Susan."

"Any details on what that was, Roger?"

"I'm afraid not, Susan. Definitely serious, though. Oh, look at that shot on Satellite 60! You can almost see the expression on his face."

Billy pulled up his algorithmic script.

"Roger, we're getting some breaking news in."

"That is a dead center hit there, Susan!"

"Roger, we're breaking away for a second."

"Say again, Susan."

Susan was gone. The picture had cut to a stock montage of Jimmy "Jimbo" Cartwright, III, founder and CEO of Finkles, who had been battling cancer for several decades, and who had suffered some sort of major setback. Senior News Anchor Chastaine Chandler, a stunning young Clear with designer lips and no hips at all who Billy had a crush on, appeared in a window in the upper right corner. Sadly, Jimbo's condition was grave. The family had gathered at the

Cartwright compound, filming on the grounds of which was not permitted, and had issued a statement thanking Jimbo's millions of loyal customers and fans for their millions of emails, and Fleeps and Tweaks, and prayers, and ongoing customer loyalty. Chastaine Chandler took a beat, shook her head in disbelief, and wiped a tear from the corner of her eye.

"I'd like to play a Fleep we received from a Finkles customer in Region 220 ..."

Billy Jensen swiped her away and logged onto the K/B network.

"K/B Customer Service Solutions. This is Billy. How can I help you?"

Long-Term Relaxation

Six weeks earlier, Valentina, who, as you may or may not remember at this point, was on her way to visit her mother, had no idea where she was anymore. She knew she was somewhere in the underground labyrinth of Breckenridge Village, "a Retirement Community," but she didn't know where that somewhere was, or how, exactly, she had ended up there, or how one got from wherever that was to wherever it was one had to go to get back to the place she had started in order to take a different route and hopefully end up where she was going.

Breckenridge Village, "a Retirement Community," was a city-sized glass and chromium cluster of geodesic dome-like structures that rose up out of the surrounding suburbs like a squadron of alien Mayan spaceships. Home to just over two hundred thousand cognitively compromised Long-Term clients (and their doctors, aides, and insurance adjustors), it provided the finest in Healthcare services, assisted living, and social activities, in a thoroughly stimulating yet relaxing environment to which most of the clients were completely oblivious. The Breckenridge Group of HealthCare Companies had spared no expense on design and furnishings. The sumptuous lobbies, with their wall-to-wall mirrors, marble floors, recessed lighting, atrium gardens, fountains, et cetera, had all been individually appointed to reflect the various tastes and budgets of the clients' loved ones when they came to visit, which they tended to do on Sunday mornings, approximately 8.6 times per year. The Residential Units themselves, which were slightly less sumptuous and much less mirrored, were segregated according to the clients' or the clients' loved ones' abundance levels, the Weston Unit for the super-abundant, the Greenwich Unit for the seriously abundant, the Henley Unit for the very abundant, and so on down the abundance scale.

Valentina's mother, Catherine Briggs, was a Breckenridge Village "Special Needs" Client. She shared a "semi-private" room (with adjoining dayroom and shower facilities) in Breckenridge Village's "Seaview Unit" with thirty-two other Special Needs Clients.

The Seaview Unit, which currently offered one hundred and twelve such semi-private rooms, was a twenty-eight story concrete tower out on the southernmost edge of the complex that was almost totally impossible to get to and which most people thought was a parking garage. Its windows (which were all on the southern side, so facing away from the rest of the Village) looked out onto a fake lagoon, the surface of which was a solid layer of bright green algae and stagnant slime. Around the lagoon were some artificial palm trees, plastic herons, and a couple of flamingos, which due to the heat had melted slightly. Catherine was up on the 20th floor. Up there with her, gumming their tongues, the wispy remnants of their burned-out hairdos jutting out at unfortunate angles, medicated past all need for restraints, were Dotty Drinkwater, Cindy Chu, Katja McGruder, Latonya van Buren, and the rest of Catherine's Special Needs roommates, except for those whose turn it was to get their weekly bath and grooming, which was pretty much the highlight of everyone's week. Due to their troubling medical histories, Special Needs Clients didn't get many visitors. By the time their loved ones finally consigned them, usually after years of grief, stress, and social stigmatization, to Long-Term Care in the Seaview Unit, these loved ones felt they had done their duty and now, finally, it was time to let go. On top of which, no one was entirely sure that the clients even recognized visitors, or the aides, or even their fellow clients, preventatively medicated as they were.

For Special Needs Clients like Catherine Briggs, the Seaview Unit was the end of the road ... a warehouse for the afflicted abundant. Virtually every Retirement Community operated one of these Special Needs units. They weren't featured in the online brochures, but for those whose loved ones could afford the service, they offered around-the-clock Long-Term Care to drug-resistant family members who were facing an A.S.P. designation and relocation to a Quarantine Zone. As long as the patient-in-question's symptoms hadn't progressed to attempted violence, and one was carrying the proper insurance, or could otherwise demonstrate ability to pay, Special Needs clients could live out their days, in relative comfort and anonymity, in a pharmaceutically stabilized state, and spare their loved one the disesteem and embarrassment flowing from "designation." Loved ones could choose from an assortment of levels of accommodations, menus, Content, and personal hygiene and grooming options, creating customized Patient Care Packages according to their budgets and the patient's needs.

Valentina's father, Walter F. Briggs, a Junior Partner at Pincus, Sarkovsky, so fairly, but not quite comfortably abundant, had chosen the "Seaview Standard Plus," one step up from the basic package, and even that had been a bit of a stretch. He'd had to liquidate most of their assets to cover the Up-Front One-Time Pre-Pay (GD 26 million after rebate), and now, even with Valentina and Kyle helping out as much as they could, every year, come 15 January, he found himself struggling to make the deductible (thirty-eight percent of the annual fees). In order to bump up his billable hours, he'd relocated, ten years back, to F.E. Region 124, learned a few words of Japanese, and bought a small condo with bamboo floors and a partial view of Lake Shikotsu, which during the winter you could sometimes swim in. Valentina hadn't seen him for years, except of course on the screen of a Viewer. He'd fleeped her during the Christmas holidays, back when she was suffering those cranial zings. They'd chatted, briefly, about her pregnancy, and how happy Walter was for the two of them, and she'd casually inquired about her mother.*

Walter reported she was doing well.

In order to get to the Seaview Unit and pretend to visit and interrogate her mother, Valentina was forced to navigate the maze of the Breckenridge Village complex, which had clearly been designed to intimidate visitors and discourage any unnecessary wandering. The WhisperTrain ride from Pewter Palisades had taken approximately ninety two minutes. She'd detrained smoothly on Level 12, ridden the escalator up to 11, slipped into the nearest private Ladies room and compulsively masturbated for less than ten minutes (after which the door automatically opened). Once she was done, and the coast

* You had to assume Security Services was listening in on any Fleeps involving the families of Special Needs clients.

was clear, she'd ridden the escalator up from 11 and entered the main reception area, which was lit like the ballroom of a luxury cruise ship. One of the helpful Security Staff at a circular station in the center of the lobby bodyscanned her and gave her directions.

"You'll need to go through Day Room 7. Stay to your right. Look for the signs. You'll see one leading to Corridor D. Take that past the Roger and Marjorie Bainesworth-Bradley Breakfast and Games Room to Corridor 30. It'll be on your left. Follow the yellow footprints on the floor. You'll pass a big double door on your right. Don't go through that. Keep on going. All the way down at the end of the corridor you'll see a bank of unmarked elevators. Any one of those will take you to Seaview."

Outfitted with these precise instructions, Valentina set out on her odyssey ... ten minutes later she was hopelessly lost. She'd circled around the Security station, traversed the expanse of the lavish lobby, and started up the central concourse, which seemed to be the only way into the complex. Weaving her way through the oncoming streams of doctors, nurses, healthcare aides, administrators, and other visitors (most of whom were deeply engaged with their Viewers, or talking to the back of other people's heads) she found her way to Day Room 7, an overly lit, acoustically savage "daytime active recreation area" roughly the size of an airplane hangar, where everything was done up in iris-punishing primary colors that gave her a headache. The day room was packed with Breckenridge Residents dressed in cheerful daytime attire and arranged in various "active" poses at tables of board games they were not playing. It looked like some kind of wax museum for affluent zombie golfers and their wives. Several of the more responsive Residents were pushing colored plastic pieces around in random patterns on their boards, or were picking their noses, or at scabs on their arms, but mostly they were just sitting there staring. Their cannula tubing had been discreetly taped into the folds of their flaccid skin, which appeared to have been sprayed (or possibly painted) with some kind of orange pancake substance to enhance their overall "active" look. A few of the Residents saw her coming and reached toward her as she passed their tables, clawing the air with their bony fingers. She drew her arms in close to her chest, dodged them, and crossed as fast as she could. She made it across, out the doors, quickly located and took Corridor D, passed the Roger and Marjorie Bainesworth-Bradley Breakfast and Games Room on her right, completely forgot which corridor came next, took a wrong turn into Corridor 6B, descended an almost imperceptible downward incline that went on forever, went through yet another set of doors, down a hallway, which she knew was all wrong, turned a corner without any doors, and ended up in something called the "Long-Term Relaxation Area."

Valentina, who was not at all squeamish, and who had seen a few things in medical school, and in her many years as a healthcare professional, had never seen anything remotely like the Long-Term Relaxation Area. Formerly active Breckenridge Residents, hundreds if not thousands of them, were lying in rows of single beds that stretched off past the visible horizon. They were lying supine, eyes wide open, arms at their sides, completely naked, their mechanically-ventilated rib cages heaving, section by section, in synchronized waves. Strands of plastic translucent tubing dangled down from the ceiling like vines, disappearing into mouths and nostrils, reappearing out of abdomens and genitals, finding their way to plastic reservoirs of dark brown urine and citrine excrement, which were fastened with clips to frames of each bed. She backed up into the wall behind her, closed her eyes, and repeated her mantra. The multiplicitous oneness of the ...

Wherever this was (assuming it was real), it was definitely somewhere deep underground, some sub-subterranean network of caverns that ran beneath the entire Village. What were these people doing down here? Maybe they simply stored them down here until their loved ones called and scheduled a visit, then took them upstairs and arranged them somewhere and sprayed them with that orange stuff. Or maybe they were offering a time-share deal for clients whose loved ones were aspiringly abundant. Or perhaps these clients didn't have any loved ones, but they had insurance, which was paying the bills.

A Viewer overhead and to the right of Valentina switched on suddenly. A face appeared ... a blue-eyed nurse, obviously a Clear.

"Can I be of any assistance, Ms. Briggs?"

Valentina nearly wet herself.

"Yes. I'm lost. I'm trying to get to ..."

"The Seaview Unit. You took a wrong turn. Walk back up the way you came. Take a left at the end of the corridor. Walk straight ahead to Corridor 30. Follow the yellow footprints from there."

The image on the screen sort of flickered for a second.

"Thank you," Valentina stammered.

"The Long-Term Relaxation Area is a Residents-Only Restricted Area."

"I know ... I'm sorry."

"There's a door to your right."

Valentina bolted for it. She staggered out into the corridor. The nurse was there on another Viewer, the screen of which was also flickering, or maybe she was just a software program. She cocked her head and smiled professionally.

"Enjoy your visit, and have a nice day."

Valentina retraced her steps, took a left at the end of the hall, found her way to Corridor 30, and followed the yellow footprints from there. They led to a bank of unmarked elevators. She took one up to the 20th floor, and stepped out into another day room. This was definitely the SeaView Unit. Scores of female Special Needs Residents were seated in rows of sofas and recliners, facing south, toward the lagoon, a wall of tinted, unbreakable glass reflecting their peaceful, expressionless faces. They looked like an audience of elderly mannequins awaiting the start of an outdoor performance. A handful of professional Healthcare aides, dressed in cheerfully-colored scrubs and those perforated rubber hospital clogs, were huddled together in the nurses station, watching what like sounded liked a Finkles commercial.

Valentina tiptoed past them. She stood against a wall at the back of the day room and scanned the reflections of the faces in the glass. The women, despite their disparate ages, appeared to be minor variations of each other. Each of them had the same beige pallor, EasyCare haircut, pale blue pajamas, bright pink lipstick, and matching nails. One of the aides, an older woman, coming toward her with with a kidney-shaped pan, noticed Valentina and raised her eyebrows.

"Catherine Briggs?" Valentina inquired.

The aide took a look around the floor. "Third one up from the end," she said. She smiled at Valentina like a shop assistant who knows you're in her store by mistake, because you can't afford whatever she's selling, and headed back off to wherever she was going.

Valentina peered across at the group of Residents down at the end, three nearly identical older women staring blankly out the window. Apparently, the one on this end was her mother, unless the aide had made a mistake. Valentina studied the woman, waiting for something to jog her memory. Nothing did. She looked like a stranger. Had she changed so much in fifteen years? Or maybe it was just that she was so far away. She took the long way across the Day Room, hugging the wall around the periphery, and tiptoed up to the group of women.

On closer inspection ... yes, in fact, it was her mother, or what was left of her, or at least the body that had once contained her. Her dominant features were all intact, but they were inexplicably softened somehow, as if Valentina were looking at her through a sheet or filter of transparent gauze. Her hair had gone completely white. Or maybe it had always been white. She had dyed it any number of shades of blonde and red throughout the years. In any event, it was snow white now, which went with her eel-green eyes quite nicely. Oddly, although in her early eighties, she seemed somehow younger than she had in her sixties. She had gained some weight. Her skin was softer. The tension was gone from the muscles of her face.

Valentina pulled up one of the straight-backed chairs they left out for visitors. She sat down directly across from her mother, and stared into her bright green eyes.

Catherine smoothly switched her gaze from some random focal point out the window to Valentina's face, two meters in front of her, much like a camera auto-focusing. Her peaceful expression did not change. The other two ladies, Dotty and Katja, turned and adjusted their depths of focus. The three of them sat there staring at her. Their eyes, though obviously responsive, were vacant ... they appeared to be simply tracking movement.

Valentina smiled.

Catherine smiled.

"Mom? It's me. It's Valentina."

Dotty and Katja were also smiling.

"Mom," she asked, "do you recognize me?"

She checked Catherine's eyes for any reaction.

Nothing. Not one flicker. Zero.

Valentina, truth be told, from an early age, and throughout her childhood, and continuing into her teenage years, and on into her twenties and thirties, although, of course, she loved her mother, had never really liked her mother. It wasn't just that she blamed her mother for her lousy genes (which of course she did), or even that she had always believed that, contrary to her perfunctory denials, her mother had always secretly relished the fact that the doctors could never find the right combination of medications to arrest her latent Anti-Social symptoms and stop her being a drain on her family ... no, the simple truth was, she just didn't like her. And neither did most other people.

Catherine, on her better days, was, to put it mildly, acerbic. On her not-so-good days, she was out and out cruel, often bordering on verbally abusive. The woman physically radiated hostility. You felt it the moment she entered a room, lips curled up in a permanent sneer, eel eyes brimming with accusation, searching out a target for her scorn. That target, when it wasn't Valentina's father, which it usually was, was Valentina, or at least it had been throughout her childhood. As a child Valentina had not understood this. She had never been anything but kind to her mother, as had her father, excessively perhaps, which had prompted Catherine to be even more acerbic, and cutting, and borderline verbally abusive. Later, of course, in her decades of therapy with Doctor Graell and her earlier therapists, where she had worked through most of her childhood traumas, and the emotionally debilitating effects thereof, she had come to understand and had forgiven her mother, in an abstract, intellectual fashion. Catherine's inappropriate behavior was not her fault ... she couldn't help it. It was caused by her drug-resistant condition, which was caused by her defective genes, which she'd inherited from her infamous father, the mysterious Terrorist, Stanislav Barnicoat, whose shadow loomed over Valentina's family like a toxic cumulonimbus cloud, and regarding whose nefarious Terrorist activities Valentina now needed information ... which was why she'd come to visit her mother.

This was her only chance, she thought. In order to approach the N.I.N. and join their faith-based Terrorist struggle against the maleficent minions of IT, and the corporations, and society generally, and offer her naked blood-smeared body to their well-hung priests in those salacious rituals ... well, first she needed to find them somehow, and her grandfather seemed like the best lead she had. She needed names, dates, locations, anything Catherine might possibly remember, because there wasn't really anything else to go on. She had searched online with her Viewer, of course (which probably wasn't such a great idea), but the public records surrounding the life of Stanislav Barnicoat were rather sparse.

Born to one Everlina Tompkins Barnicoat, on 7 February, 2480, during the Age of Emergency Measures, deep in what was then Region 7, the southeast corner of North America, technically one of the "Privatized Regions" nominally administrated by Graham McKenzie,* but in reality a virtual no-go zone (i.e., a hotbed of insurgent Terrorist activity), Stanislav's life from the time of his birth until his detention at the age of sixty remained a subject of speculation ... which is to say, there were no records. Nothing. The official records were blank. For sixty years the man had managed to stay completely off the radar, an inconceivable feat of subterfuge, particularly in the Age of Emergency Measures, when the corporations were surveilling more or less everyone and everything around the clock. Then, at approximately 0140, on the morning of officially 21 August, 2540, H.C.S.T. (retroactively the Year of the Bactrian Camel), a BREAKING NEWS SECURITY ADVISORY interrupted individual streaming, and Stanislav Barnicoat's name and likeness appeared on the screen of every Viewer throughout the United Territories. Charged with Conspiracy to Aid and Abet the Furtherance of Acts of Organized Terror, Attempted Evasion, and Resisting Detention, and a host of other lesser charges, Stanislav was suddenly page one news.

Here was a man, an absolute cipher, a Class 4 Anti-Social cipher, deranged and dangerously paranoid, certainly, but highly intelligent and obviously educated, who had just materialized out of the ether. Where had he lived? How had he lived? He had never held a job in

---

* A market-leading global Security/Logistics contractor that no longer existed.

his life, had never attended a day of school, had never purchased a single product. Where did he come from? Where had he been hiding? Obviously right under everyone's noses. This was not some poor, malnourished, late-stage Anti-Social savage, some cave-dweller from the Recovering Areas. No. He had been there all along, hiding right in plain sight, apparently, passing as normal, or relatively normal, as he went about plotting his nefarious activities, and aiding, abetting, and furthering, and so on. All of which led to one grim conclusion ... somewhere, and very possibly everywhere, burrowed into civilization like disgusting hives of diabolical termites, was an underground network of Anti-Social Persons, and a rather sophisticated network at that, which was probably linked, or cooperating closely, or loosely affiliated with the N.I.N., and was conceivably even an offshoot thereof, or an offshoot of some other Terrorist network that was somehow linked to the N.I.N., or that had followed in the latter's nefarious footsteps, or vaguely had something to do with it somehow ... in any event, an underground network about which, in exhaustive detail, each and every Security Division of every corporation was eager to learn.

Throughout the autumn of 2540, and continuing into the following winter, a crackerjack inter-corporate team of Information Extraction Specialists extraordinarily interrogated Stanislav more or less around the clock. And came up with exactly nothing. Aside from a litany of verbal abuse, a lot of it having to do with their mothers, and unorthodox things that they could do with mothers. Or so the official statements read. After which, again, officially, Stanislav was relocated to a "MegaMax" Isolation Facility, where eventually, at the age of ninety-seven, he died, allegedly of kidney failure.

And that was it for the official records.

But here's what Valentina remembered. She must have been eight, nine, maybe. They came in person, the Security Specialists. Hadley men. Four of five of them. Sitting around in their suits in the living room. Their haircuts. The skin above their ears. Her father smiling, talking too much. The men not smiling, looking all around. Her mother smiling, but like a snake, asking questions the men couldn't answer, or maybe weren't allowed to answer. The cardboard box on the coffee table. Inside it, disks, books, MemCards, ID badges, and assorted papers. And a plastic bag of dark gray ash ... all that was left of Stanislav Barnicoat.

On Valentina's sixteenth birthday, they sat her down and told her the story. Her father, Walter, did most of the talking. Her mother just sat there, smirking and nodding, and occasionally coughing into her wadded up tissues. The story was, Catherine's mother, so Valentina's maternal grandmother, Constance Rosenthal, had, it turned out, lied to the Hartford HealthCare Company regarding the identity of Catherine's father, who, according to lines 16 and 20 of Catherine's corporate birth certificate, and thus officially, remained unknown. Unofficially, and thus in reality, Catherine's father, Valentina's grand-father, was the mystery Terrorist, Stanislav Barnicoat. Constance Rosenthal's lie had somehow held up for almost fifty years.* None of the family had ever been informed (or not in so many words at least) how the truth had finally come to light, but the only feasible explanation was that the Information Extraction Specialists had, at some point, broken Stanislav, and had learned all kinds of inter-esting things, one or more of which had led them to Constance, who they promptly detained and extraordinarily interrogated. Again, the details were rather sparse here, but apparently Constance had been uncooperative, because nine months later they received a Fleep from Hadley Global Security Headquarters advising them that Constance had, regrettably, been extraordinarily interrogated to death. Three years later, a Mister Zippy's normal delivery COD parcel addressed to Catherine arrived at the house. Inside the parcel were assorted papers, jewelry, credit cards, ID badges, and various other personal items, and a plastic bag of dark gray ash ... all that was left of Constance Rosenthal. Incidentally, the following year, on 16 December, 2568, or 25 Kislev, 6329, or the Year of Nepalese Large Eared Pika, and a host of other proprietary dates, Valentina Constance Briggs was born.

Valentina had lived with the shame of her family background for twenty-five years, and probably even longer than that. Sitting up there, beside her mother, as the lights came on in the Seaview Unit,

* In the Age of the Renaissance of Freedom and Prosperity, this kind of thing could never happen, but back in the Age of Emergency Measures, Security Specialists had better things to do than pour through random corporate records verifying people's patrilineal descent.

watching the pink and purple sunset off to the right of the toxic lagoon, remembering back, it had always been there, back before she knew what it was, before that fateful sixteenth birthday when they'd sat her down and told her the truth. All her life it had clouded her vision. It had shrouded her mind since the day she was born. It had hung in the air in the house she grew up in, on Chestnut Court in Sturgeson Falls, like one of those noxious egg-smelling farts you can't believe the person you love and have lived with for years is capable of cutting ... basically, it had ruined everything. Certainly it had ruined her mother. There she was, beside her ... ruined. Valentina had never known the woman her father sometimes described, the one who loved to dance and sing, who read voraciously, and loved to travel, who laughed until she choked sometimes, laughed at silly things he couldn't explain, misspoken words that didn't mean anything, archival clips of baby sloths, and cats, and other exotic creatures, in short, the woman he'd fallen in love with, married, and lived with, more or less happily ... until the day her mother, Constance, was picked up by the Security Specialists at the makeup counter of her local Finkles.

She had heard this story from her father as well. He told it wistfully, staring off into some subjunctive hole in time that had closed forever, sealing him in, molding him into the man she knew. He appeared, at those times, to want to believe (and very possibly did believe) that they might not have ever found out what happened, had Constance, who was seventy-six and spry, not put up a bit of a fight at the counter, during which she had managed to blurt out Catherine's name to the Finkles Assistant. Once the Specialists got Constance bagged and dragged her out by the elbows and ankles, the Assistant called and told them what had happened. At the time, of course, they'd had no idea why or by which Security Division of which corporation she'd been detained. However, it being Northeast Region 709 of the United Territories, the odds were in favor of the Hadley Corporation, whose local Security Services hotline Catherine proceeded to call incessantly. Helpful Customer Service Representatives with made-up names and impenetrable accents took Catherine's calls, put her on hold, left her there for several minutes, then switched her to other Representatives who regretted that they were unable to help her. This went on for weeks, and months, during which Catherine did not sleep. She locked herself in the upstairs bathroom, called the hotline, and cried, and drank. According to Walter, who would pause at this point, everything went to hell from there. During the course of the rest of that year, she quit her job at Friendly Frank's Real Estate, stopped taking most of her medication, stopped going out, stopped seeing friends, and returning their messages, and generally decompensated. Her drinking worsened, as did her insomnia. On the rare occasions that she was able to sleep, she woke him up shrieking, or sometimes cursing. The neighbors started smiling at Walter in a way that made him distinctly uneasy. Worse, the Security Services Division of the Hadley Corporation of Menomonie, Wisconsin started sending Walter a series of messages asking him, personally, and all those in his household, to please refrain from calling their hotline and screaming (in what some might have construed as a borderline Anti-Social manner) at their Representatives at all hours of the night.

Something had to be done immediately. Sanjay Upton Douglass-Solomon, a senior partner at Pincus, Sarkovsky, made a call to a friend whose wife was on the board of the Halloran Center, a high-end facility in Region 3 that offered a range of interventional therapies to minor and former minor celebrities on a strictly semi-anonymous basis.

Catherine was admitted, and treated, repeatedly.

Six weeks later, a heavily medicated and much better rested Catherine Briggs was returned to Walter on Chestnut Court and took up residence on the living room sofa. A few weeks later, the Fleep arrived informing them of Constance's regrettable demise. Catherine read it, set it aside, then went back to viewing her day-time Content.

Throughout the twenty-eight years that followed, she had alternated between this much more manageable state, in which nothing mattered, and much less stable and more frightening states resembling, to greater and lesser degrees, the total breakdown she had suffered earlier. This was the woman Valentina had known, the one who had raised her, fed her, dressed her, bathed her, read her bedtime stories, who had stood in the dark and watched her sleep, or pretend to be sleeping, humming softly, whose kisses on her forehead felt so soft and warm and right and tender ... whispering, "I will always be with you, no matter what happens, I will always be with you" ... and who sometimes grabbed Valentina's hand and squeezed it so hard it hurt her fingers, staring wildly into her eyes, her daughter's eyes, her mother's eyes, as if she were trying to keep from falling into some vacuum Valentina could never see but could feel beneath them, some horrible, bottomless, boundless abyss, some infinite nothing within which all that was was somehow floating suspended. This was the mother Valentina knew, the mother, who, despite the demons that tore her apart from inside out, clearly loved her so much it hurt ... and more than just hurt, had damaged her somehow, had forced her to fight with all her will against herself to twist herself into some acceptable version of herself, some smiling, seething sham of herself ... the ad hoc semblance of a normal mother that Valentina had tried for years, for twenty-six years, to forgive, and love, and had, in spite of everything, loved ... and yet, just after her twenty-sixth birthday, when her father called and she came and found him slumped out on the stoop that night, and he looked up at her through his swollen eyelids and shook his head, and his lips were trembling, and she knew that he had finally done it, had made the call to Breckenridge Village, every muscle in her body relaxed.

Finally, she was able to breathe.

She sat there now beside some mother who wasn't the mother who wasn't her mother, watching the sky go red and orange, their mirrored faces staring blankly back at them out of the tinted glass, each on one side of vertical strip of riser that ran up the window between them. They looked like before-and-after pictures of some green-eyed woman they both resembled, but neither of them actually was. She had been there for almost six hours at this point, sitting beside her mother's chair, staring out at whatever Catherine was staring out at in the dead lagoon. Catherine hadn't said one word. Valentina hadn't eaten. Her butt muscles ached. Muzak played. The P.A. wanted Pedro to please report to Room 7. The light was fading. She didn't know what she'd thought was going to happen there in the Seaview Unit (as in some kind of medical miracle or something), but whatever it was was not going to happen. Catherine was not going to tell her anything.

Valentina slipped her hand beneath the downturned palm of her mother's. She interlocked her fingers with Catherine's. She levered her forearm up like a drawbridge, raising Catherine's hand to the light, steadied it there, and opened her fingers. Nothing happened. The hand just lay there, resting lightly against Valentina's palm, its fingers open, slightly bent, a plastic non-removable name tag fastened securely around its wrist. The skin of her mother's hand was brown, paper thin, and webbed with thousands of intricate kind of diamond-shaped lines. They looked like scales or patterns made in the sand by the wind, or like waxed brown paper someone had taken and crumpled up, then uncrumpled and stretched around the bones of her hand. There were blotches of blue and purple bruises, and faded patches of old adhesive left by the strips of tape they used to hold the IV needles in place. Valentina wanted to cry. She lowered her arm, and her mother's arm, her fingers still interlocked with Catherine's, and sat there watching the sky turn violet.

"I love you, mom. I'm sorry," she whispered.

The words came pouring out in a torrent.

She spoke in frantic, breathless whispers, watching the reflection in the window for aides, who were shuffling about the dayroom behind them collecting Special Needs Clients for dinner. She told her everything, or nearly everything … everything she had never told her. She filled Catherine in on her life, her marriage, her job, her resistance to medications, her latent Anti-Social ideations, Kyle, the baby, Doctor Fraser, and finally her Lomax Escalator Vision. Somewhere near the end of all this, she realized why she had actually come. It wasn't to clandestinely interrogate Catherine (which deep down she had known would be fruitless). She had come to tell her mother goodbye. She realized this as she was begging her mother for help, a hint, a clue, anything … anything Constance might have said, or left behind, or that might have belonged or somehow related to Stanislav Barnicoat. She explained this to Catherine, knowing that Catherine didn't understand a word she was saying. She had to get OUT, she whispered desperately, or else she was going to end up there, in one of those chairs with Catherine and Dotty and Katja, and all her other roommates, staring out at that dead lagoon on who knew what medication they gave them … which Valentina was so very sorry, and she wished that she could get her out of there, but she couldn't, because she had to get out herself ... she had to get OUT, she reiterated, before they detained her and took her somewhere, and kept her alive on feeding tubes until they could harvest her Clarion baby, which was one of those THINGS that were part of IT, and were taking over, and were not human, and she told her she understood it all now, her mother's inappropriate behavior, and her anger, and God ... why was it like this? Why did everything have to be like this? And if she was in there, if Catherine was in there, if any part of her was in there somewhere, hearing this, hearing these words, she wanted her to know that she had always loved her, that part of her had always loved her, and would always love her, no matter what happened, and ...

No one was in there hearing anything.

Catherine was staring off into the sunset.

Valentina was talking to herself.

The P.A. announced that dinner was going to be Salisbury steaks with peas and potatoes. The P.A. was extremely pleased about this. Valentina was trying to keep from standing up and incoherently screaming. She started to reach inside her purse to get out a tissue and dab at her tears (which she didn't think any of the aides had seen yet), but she couldn't, because Catherine was squeezing her hand ... which OK, this was likely just some autonomic metacarpal spasm. Except that it wasn't a muscle spasm. Catherine was definitely squeezing her hand. Or rather, she was squeezing her finger. At some point during Valentina's confession, she'd slipped her wrinkled, leathery thumb covertly under Valentina's palm, and now she was pinching, and using the tip of her yellow thumbnail to gently tug at, the edge of Valentina's wedding band.

Valentina shifted in her chair, turned and looked into Catherine's eyes. They were just as blank and vacant as before. Her finger was still involved with her ring. She leaned in close.

"What is it?" she whispered.

Nothing. Not the faintest flicker.

She gently pried her mother's fingers off her ring and retracted her hand. Catherine's forearm pivoted upwards. Her pointy elbow was resting firmly on the padded arm of the white recliner, but her hand was reaching, groping, clutching, her fingers grasping, as if she were trying to ... wait ... Valentina remembered this feeling. This feeling of dread ... her dread of the Hand.

"What are you doing? Is that the Hand?"

Catherine's fingers tilted toward her. She recoiled from them ... as she always had. She could almost hear her mother laughing, cackling, coming toward her with the Hand. She could hear herself screaming, laughing, squealing, her mother laughing, smelling like liquor ...

A smiling aide was coming toward them, presumably to drag her mother off and stuff her full of Salisbury Steak.

"I understand," Valentina whispered.

The aide was almost there by then.

"I love you, mom. I will always be with you."

"Salisbury Steaks for dinner, ladies!"

Slowly, as the aide approached, as if it were just another random muscle contraction that didn't mean anything, Catherine's fragile fingers closed like wilting petals into a fist.

The Terrorists

Now, before we go any further with our story, we probably need to take a moment and address this ... well, this Terrorist business. Because as much as we might be tempted to, you know, call it by some other name, or otherwise sugarcoat it or weasel around it, what we're looking at here is our two protagonists, one of whom was trying to become a Terrorist, and the other of whom already was one, the latter being Taylor, of course. Which was rather ironic given the fact that Taylor, unlike Valentina, had no desire to become a Terrorist, or to join any fictive Terrorist networks, or to knowingly associate and conspire with Terrorists, or provide material support to Terrorists, or aid or abet them by word or deed. He didn't want anything to do with Terrorists, or with any of their Terror-related activities. All Taylor wanted was to save Cassandra, and her baby, from IntraZone Waste & Security, and the Hadley Corporation of Menomonie, Wisconsin, preferably without getting wasted in the process. Unfortunately, it didn't really matter what he wanted, or how he perceived what he thought he was doing. What mattered were the facts ... and the facts were clear. The moment he entered the Pussyhorse Lounge and sat down across the table from Sarah, Taylor, officially, became a Terrorist.

And, all right, now you're probably thinking ... a Terrorist? What did that mean exactly? Wasn't that just an essentially vacuous fear-inducing catch-all term for anyone the corporations didn't like and wanted to harass, or indefinitely detain, or summarily execute with complete impunity? And, fair enough, that's a legitimate question, or it would be in some kind of ideal world where people weren't living in constant fear of sudden and devastating Terrorist attacks, and were allowed to seriously ask such questions, but that's not the world where our story takes place. On the contrary, for completely understandable reasons, in the Age of the Renaissance of Freedom and Prosperity, where people were aware that a Terrorist attack (possibly involving some sort of home-made nuclear device or chemical agent) could happen anywhere, at any time, this question was not a legitimate question, or ground for philosophical inquiry, not even in some purely etymological way. The meaning of the term was not up for discussion It meant what it meant. Plain and simple. There was nothing ambiguous or equivocal about it. Terror was Terror. Terrorists were Terrorists.

Which isn't to say this was some kind of ill-defined label that could just be slapped onto anyone, this "Terrorist" label, because it wasn't, at all. The meaning of the term was clearly defined. There were people who were Terrorists and people who weren't. You had to meet a certain set of criteria, the wording of which had been carefully chosen by leading Security and Terrorism experts, and which was posted on some website somewhere. Valentina was a perfect example. Valentina was not a Terrorist (or at least not up to this point in our story). Valentina was sick and confused. For all her Anti-Social ideations, and paranoid fantasies, and inappropriate emotions, she was still, officially, a Variant-Positive, and Variant-Positives were not Terrorists. Taylor on the other hand was not a Variant-Positive. Taylor was a Class 3 Anti-Social Person. A Class 3 Anti-Social Person who had, with clear intent, and knowledge and forethought, sauntered into the Pussyhorse Lounge and involved himself with person or persons who were members of an actual Terrorist network,* which made him a member of this Terrorist network, or at least an associate of this Terrorist network, which ipso facto made him a Terrorist. This was not just a question of semantics or half-assed tautological reasoning. Taylor had actually, physically, done this. This was a fact, ergo the truth, the undeniable and self-evident truth.

And, all right, now you're probably asking ... the truth? What did that mean exactly? Weren't there a lot of different truths? Wasn't the meaning of "truth" subjective? And yes ... absolutely, in one sense it was, but it another sense it absolutely wasn't. Which wasn't quite as paradoxical, or sophistical, as it probably sounds. See, even in an

---

* Not just a bunch of jargon-spouting, pamphlet-distributing graffiti artists.

unimaginably tolerant, semiotically sophisticated age like the Age of the Renaissance of Freedom and Prosperity, where the vast majority of signifiers floated, and values other than commodity value were generally seen as totally arbitrary, some things were simply what they were. The truth, for example. The truth was the truth. And facts. Facts were pretty much facts.

Now this is true of any age. Despite what people discover later, the prevailing facts of that age, or epoch, or civilization, or global empire, at the time, have got to be regarded as facts, undeniable, indisputable facts, or else how could the people living in that age determine what was real, or true, or make decisions about anything at all, like their medical treatments, or what to eat, or how to build things, or what to invest in, or who the actual Terrorists were? They couldn't. They would all be walking around reading their own preconceptions into things in a kind of perceptual feedback loop, or otherwise ... you know, just making stuff up.

Which, of course, was not the case here at all. No one was making anything up, at least not regarding this Terrorism thing. The facts here were the actual facts. There was nothing epistemologically contentious or in any way subjective about them. People who were Anti-Social Persons who joined notorious Terrorist networks, the overarching objective of which was to perpetrate a series of globally-coordinated, senseless and devastating Terrorist attacks, were not romantic revolutionaries.* Such people were Terrorists ... actual Terrorists. People who were Variant-Positive Persons who had gone off their meds, and were sick and confused, and who thought they were Terrorists, or who wanted to be Terrorists, or provide material support to Terrorists, were clearly in need of immediate treatment, and were ... OK, potential Terrorists, but for the time being were not actual Terrorists.

And yes, before you even ask, there was an actual meaningful difference between "actual" Terrorists and "potential" Terrorists. Look, let's not get all hysterical here and blow this up all out of proportion.

---

* Like the progenitors of the corporations who had overthrown the ancient monarchies by admittedly violent but necessary means, and had slaughtered, enslaved and tortured millions in order to consolidate and maintain their power over the course of several centuries, all of which was, of course, regrettable, and which the corporations had apologized for, not for the revolution itself, but the subsequent slaughtering, enslaving, and torturing.

The Age of the Renaissance of Freedom and Prosperity, whatever its drawbacks and shortcomings were, was not some kind of Orwellian dystopia. Thinking thoughts didn't make you a Terrorist. At least not the thoughts Valentina was thinking. On the contrary, they proved she was still a Normal. You had to be a Normal, a Variant-Positive, to even be able to think such thoughts, or to entertain concepts like "overthrowing IT," and "purging your body and soul of IT," or to decide one day to renounce your status and privileged lifestyle in your gated community for the sake of some moral or ethical belief, and set out to become a Terrorist.

This was not a type of thinking your actual Terrorists ever engaged in, this moral or spiritual type of thinking ... except for the so-called faith-based Terrorists, also known as the N.I.N., who may or may not have actually existed, and who nobody really knew what they believed in, some kind of hodgepodge of quasi-Gnostic neo-Kabbalist sex magick nonsense, Tantric Yoga, Chaos Theory, and possibly something to do with Spinoza.

No, according to the leading Security experts, your actual Terrorists, who *did* exist (most of whom would have jumped at the chance to eviscerate you and your entire family, especially the kids, on general principle), had zero interest in this type of thinking. They certainly weren't setting off on any kind of half-baked spiritual quests to "free their minds" and "become what they were" so they could join in some ultimate Armageddonish battle (which was clearly unwinnable and probably eternal) against the Corporatist manifestation of some primordial nebulous demiurgic force. On the contrary, to these actual Terrorists, everything was all about power. And not any kind of spiritual power. Actual power. As in physical power. Economic and political power. The way these actual Terrorists saw it, the Normals had this actual power, this economic and political power. They, the actual Terrorists, did not. They wanted to have it, and they would kill to get it. Morals and ethics did not enter into it.

According to these learned Security experts, who had researched all this stuff extensively, these actual Terrorists subscribed to the theory that right and wrong, and healthy and unhealthy, and all the other moralistic, dualistic terms that those in power had used forever to define themselves and their allies and enemies (and with

which Valentina was so desperately struggling as she contemplated
the life of her gardener, and her and Kyle's investments, and so on,
and which Taylor was not really struggling with at all), were tactical terms, with no inherent meaning. They did not believe in these
meaningless terms, or in any other moralistic, dualistic terms, or ax-
ioms, or precepts, or articles of faith. Which didn't really leave them
that much to believe in ... and there was the heart of the problem
right there.

According to these same Security experts, who you saw online
on a daily basis, these actual Terrorists, despite whatever vision of
a better world they were selling, in their heart of hearts, believed
in nothing. They worshiped nothing. They stood for nothing. They
honored nothing and respected nothing. They clearly didn't respect
other people, who they wanted to murder, maim, and eviscerate, or
private property, which they wanted to steal, or destroy, or at minimum senselessly damage, and not for any rational reasons, or to
further any cause or ideology, or to free themselves and their fellow
Anti-Socials from any invisible post-despotic regime of Corporatist
domination ... no, oh no, it was simply to feed their nihilistic lust for
destruction, which stemmed from their envy and hatred of others,
and their desire for power and control over others, which stemmed
from their Narcissistic personalities, which stemmed from their
Anti-Social Disease, which rendered them incapable of ever leading
normal productive lives in society.

Oddly (and this was never entirely satisfactorily explained by the
Security experts), in spite of their envy and hatred of others, and
Narcissistic personalities, and so on, these actual Terrorists worked
in groups, secretive, highly-disciplined groups, autonomous cells
with inscrutable names, like ZF2, A:::A, the B/O3 Fraktion, and
the Bond Street Bombers (OK, the latter being probably not that
inscrutable*), and it was all these autonomous militant cells, or working groups, or factions, or whatever, working in coordination with
each other (and not some molar, hierarchical structure, which would
have been a whole lot simpler), that the various corporate Security
Services with all their hi-tech weapons systems were somehow never

_____

* _Or no more so than that of the Fifthian Cluster, which took its name from Jean Luc Fifthian, a_
legendary figure in Terrorist circles whose story we don't have time to get into.

able to eradicate ... which given the fact that these Terrorist groups were all based within the Quarantine Zones (so it was kind of like shooting fish in a barrel), if you thought about it, was kind of weird.

Another small item in the Weird Department was the fact that (and this had been officially verified) although each member of these Terrorists groups, or cells, or factions, was an Anti-Social, only a very small minority of Anti-Socials were actual Terrorists (significantly less than one percent). Fortunately, for IntraZone Waste & Security, and anyone else who wanted to find them, this negligible minority was known to frequent a number of extremely unhygienic, off-the-radar drinking establishments located down in the deep Inner Zone, an Anti-Social no man's land, where you did not go unless you belonged there, and into which not even the Watchers ventured (out of fear of having their balls cut off and stuffed down their throats, and other such antics).

One of the least hygienic of these places was ... you guessed it, the Pussyhorse Lounge. It was hidden way down at the assward end of this no-name alley off Muybridge Lane, which you got to via this other alley, which nobody really knew where it went, but a stretch of it ran through this desolate tunnel where people got raped and killed, and so on. In spite of its somewhat suggestive name, the Pussyhorse Lounge was not a whorehouse, or a sex club, or a makeshift S&M dungeon. There were plenty of those around, of course. The Pussyhorse just didn't happen to be one of them. The Pussyhorse Lounge was a straight-up tavern ... which apparently no one ever went to anymore. The place was empty, except for Taylor, Sarah, Adam, of all fucking people, and the facially-tattooed bartender, Eoghan, who Taylor remembered from the bad old days. The three of them, Adam, Sarah, and Taylor, were sitting in this plywood booth in the back, that term being relative, the place was so small. It was just the bar, a couple of tables, and the booth where they were currently sitting, speaking in conspiratorial whispers and ignoring their mugs of luke-warm beer.

Taylor had found his way to the Pussyhorse, in which he hadn't set foot for nearly ten years, and had walked in just past 2200 with a song in his heart and half a hard-on, all prepared to get himself laid. Sarah was sitting there waiting for him. Sitting there beside her was Adam, which meant ... OK, he wasn't getting laid. However, one look at their faces told him, and the absence of any other patrons told him, and the way that Eoghan had nodded at him told him, he'd finally found his baby smugglers, or technically, they had finally found him.

He slid into the booth across from the two of them, Sarah, who was clearly attracted to him (she had that unmistakeable look), and Adam, who just as clearly wasn't. A mug of flat beer was sitting there waiting for him. He ignored it, and checked out Sarah's tits.

"You know who we are ... we know who you are." Adam whispered to someone in his beer. "You talk about any of this shit to anyone," he looked up at Taylor, "you disappear."

A cockroach with some kind of cranial deformity zig-zagged up the wall beside him. Another one was leisurely traversing the ceiling on its way to the bar to visit with Eoghan. Taylor, who was not that terribly impressed with Adam and his new and more hardcore persona, was staring across the booth at Sarah. He had moved up from her tits to her eyes, which were staring back unblinkingly at him. He was also keeping half an eye on Eoghan, who back when they were both in their twenties had wasted three people that Taylor knew of.

"Cassandra Passwaters disappears."

Now Adam had Taylor's full attention.

"Yeah, genius, we know who she is."

Everyone sat there looking at everyone.

Eoghan looked up.

The cockroach stopped.

Sarah was steadily eyeballing Taylor.

"All right, so you know what's happening," Taylor fished.

Sarah nodded.

"So ... what's happening?"

Sarah smiled. Then she told him. She went into detail. Cassandra, the baby, the whole nine yards. Taylor sat there, deadpan, listening, holding her gaze, watching for signs, but he couldn't read her, which was disconcerting, because normally he could read a woman. Whatever. He was quickly connecting the dots. Obviously they had talked to Meyer. Because how else would they know all this? Which meant that Meyer was probably one of them ...

Sarah finished. Taylor nodded.

"OK," he said, "so how do we do this?"

"How we do this is *we* fucking do this. You don't do this. *We* fucking do this." Adam had clearly rehearsed this shit.

Taylor flashed Adam his total-lack-of-anything-resembling-a-conscience look.

"You see this? The eyes? What did I tell you?" This time Adam was talking to Sarah, who ignored him completely, so he turned back to Taylor. "Look, asshole, we know all about you. We know your whole story. We've seen your file ..."

Sarah adjusted her posture slightly.

"My file?"

Taylor didn't like the sound of that.

He reached for his beer mug.

Eoghan glanced up.

The cockroach was on the move again.

Sarah reached over and gripped Taylor's forearm. She did it casually, as if to get his attention.

"You think we could run this kind of operation if we couldn't hack their system?" she asked.

Yeah, OK, that made sense. He relaxed his arm. Sarah let go. Eoghan went back to washing glasses. Adam, who appeared to have no idea how close he'd just come to having the side of his skull caved in with the bottom of a beer mug, sat there trying to look intimidating, which was pointless given his ridiculous haircut.

Sarah hadn't taken her eyes off Taylor.

"You don't exactly fit our profile."

"Your profile?"

"We don't get a lot of 3s. Or fathers. We usually deal with the mothers."

"Who are mostly 1s."

Sarah nodded.

"3s tend to be ... a little unpredictable."

"Which doesn't fucking cut it," Adam piped in.

Taylor ignored him.

"So what do you need?"

"We need to believe we can work with you ... safely."

"So what do I do to make you believe that?"

"Nothing. We either will or we won't."

The cockroach had paused and was reconnoitering. Sarah studied him for several seconds ... Taylor, that is, not the cockroach.

"You grew up out on Jackson Avenue."

"Around there."

"What used to be Walt Whitman Road."

"Yeah."

"So you were there when the purged the 4s."

Taylor nodded.

"But you've never been active."

"Thought you said you read my file."

"Why not?"

Taylor gave her the eyebrows.

"She asked you a fucking question, slick."

"Guess I never got the point."

"The point of what?"

"Resistance. Whatever."

"Nothing in it for you personally, right?"

Adam was intentionally trying to goad him, possibly as some kind of test ...

"Your file goes dead about ten years back."

Sarah's eyes were locked onto him.

"I settled down."

"With the mother."

"Yeah."

"Why?"

"Smell the roses, you know ... play a little golf."

"Keep it up dickhead."

"You used to run with Vaclav Borges."

"Did I?"

"A particularly nasty character."

"I don't know anyone by that name."

"You remember Eoghan?"

Eoghan glanced up. Taylor kept his eyes on Sarah.

"He remembers you. From back in the Nineties. You and Borges. The Gilmartin brothers. He describes you as somewhat ..."

"Unpredictable?"

"Volatile was the word, I think."

"People change."

"Do they? Really?"

There was that look again.

Taylor smiled.

"I haven't done shit in forever, OK?"

"We know. We checked."

She stroked a strand of hair back out of her face with one finger. The two of them sat there looking at each other.

"Why don't you just blow him already?"

Adam was obviously getting restless, or jealous, or maybe he was playing a game. He drained his beer mug and sucked out the dregs. Sarah's eyes were still fixed on Taylor. The look was gone, though. She was back to business.

"Look, if we do this, we do it our way. It goes by the numbers. There's no discussion. We tell you to do a thing, you do it. We say something goes this way, that's it. It goes that way, or everything's off. We abort the action, clean up the mess ..."

"Including you," Adam clarified, just as the cockroach came into range. Taylor got it with the palm of his hand, squirting its guts in Adam's direction.

"Motherfucker."

Taylor ignored him. He hadn't taken his eyes off Sarah.

"Agreed?" she asked.

Taylor nodded.

"Then say it," she said.

"Agreed," he said.

"OK. You're on."

"Good ..."

"For now. Listen carefully. Here are the ground rules. One. Starting now, tonight, you and the mother do nothing unusual. Nothing. Zero. Nothing changes. Both of you stick to your normal routines."

"No deviations from your normal routines," Adam reiterated, as if she hadn't just said that.

"You realize she just said that, right?" Taylor asked, just wanting to confirm.

Adam glared.

Sarah sighed.

Eoghan was watching them all in the mirror.

"Do I have to keep coming to meetings?" Taylor wondered.

"No deviations," Adam spat.

"The meetings are infiltrated," Sarah explained.

"Cooperators?"

Sarah nodded.

"They'd notice if you suddenly stopped attending."

"You know who they are."

"Some of them, sure. Why?"

Taylor shook his head.

Sarah studied him.

"You think we should waste them."

"For starters, yeah."

Adam smirked.

"We'll take care of the Cooperators, killer."

"Maybe you can fucking twinkle them to death."

"Two. Anti-Baby pills. The mother picks them up like normal. She brings the package home like normal. She flushes the pills on her normal schedule ..."

Taylor sat there, pretending to listen, and nodding every now and then, and mostly ogling Sarah's breasts, as she and Adam ran down the ground rules. All right, he thought, step one accomplished. Baby-smuggling Terrorists located. Assuming that was who they were. It certainly appeared to be who they were. At the same time Taylor was acutely aware of the fact that he had no proof who they were, and that theoretically they could have been anyone, and that he didn't much like the vibe he was getting. Not from Sarah, who seemed OK, but from Adam and Eoghan, who seemed a bit jumpy, but he had no choice but to go ahead with this. Whoever they were, they had his number. They knew who he and Cassandra were, knew she was pregnant, they knew the whole story. Which meant they had to have talked to Meyer. Which meant that Meyer was definitely one of them. The question was ... one of who? An A.S.U. within the A.S.U.? Another Terrorist network entirely? Faith-based Terrorists? He didn't think so. They didn't come off particularly faith-based ...

or, OK, Sarah was a little spooky. She sported a number of runic tattoos, some of which might have been triple sixes, or inverted nines,
or triskelions, or something. He could see them through the fabric
of her flimsy tunic, but he couldn't make out the artwork completely.
He could also see her tits through her tunic. They weren't as luscious
as Cassandra's but still ... and her nipples were poking up under the
fabric ... dark ... like her hair, and her eyes and ... wait ... what was
that shit about his file? Was that just a slip, or had they meant to
say that? And what was Adam's game, exactly? Was he simply the
puffed-up dickless punk with delusions of grandeur he appeared to
be, or was he needling Taylor as some kind of test, trying to taunt
him into losing his shit?

Everybody infiltrates everybody ... everybody uses everybody.

"Seven. Paranoia Control."

"What?" Taylor asked, snapping out of it.

"The closer we get to the launch of the D.A.D.A., the more
Security is going to be on us. We're going to need to keep our shit
together ..."

"When?" Taylor asked.

"You'll know when you need to," Adam answered, "like everyone
else."

"Look," Taylor addressed this to Sarah, "she won't have the baby
for another six months, so if you're planning to, you know, start the
revolution before then ..."

"He thinks it's a fucking joke."

"No, I think it's fucking suicide. But knock yourself out."

"So what if it is? You think they're going to let us die of old age?"

"That seems to be their plan at the moment."

"You have no fucking clue what's happening."

"And what ... you do?"

Adam smiled.

"We're getting off track," Sarah interrupted. "Look, we'll take
care of the timing, all right? You need to trust us. Can you do that,
Taylor?"

Taylor nodded.

Adam looked away.

"Eight. Sequestration of the mother ..."

Now, officially, this was 30 October, 2609, H.C.S.T., and the Year of the Mekong Giant Catfish, and several other totally made-up dates. Valentina, who Taylor didn't know, had just spent the day at Paxton Wills undergoing various hormone treatments to get her uterus to stop rejecting the Clarion embryos it kept rejecting. Cassandra, who Taylor knew quite intimately, was ten, maybe eleven weeks pregnant, which gave them another five, six weeks to deal with shit before she started showing, at which point things were going to get hairy. The plan was, she would hole up inside her bedroom, away from her nosy and annoying roommates, who, as Taylor now explained to Adam and Sarah, he was relatively sure he could probably handle, as the roommates were all scared shitless of him. The only really serious danger, in Taylor's opinion, was Cassandra's bathroom, which the roommates were always going in and out of, and which was right across the hall from Cassandra's door. However, if you put your ear to her door, you could usually tell if one of them was in there, or out in the hallway waiting their turn, or just nosing around and being annoying. No, their major problem, as Taylor saw it, was not the roommates, but Cassandra's job, which was soldering mostly touchscreen controllers and accelerometers, and things like that, into the chipsets of assorted models of indispensable consumer products, the names of which she was not privy to, at the GCH Components factory from 1900 to 0500.* At some point before officially December, they needed to get Cassandra out of there, and keep her out for the next five months. And they needed to do this in such a fashion that, once Cassandra had had the baby, and Taylor had delivered it to Adam and Sarah, Cassandra could go back to work at the factory, and their lives would go on as if nothing had

---

* *The vast majority of A.S.P. 1s, and a fairly high percentage of 2s, worked at some factory like GCH. Due to the climate, they worked the night shift, which cut down on air-conditioning costs. They worked at rows of assembly tables, ten hours a night, six nights a week. Or they worked at one of the metals factories, at rows of massive precision presses, or CNC lathes, or milling machines, breathing in a permanent mist of water-soluble cutting coolant that looked like milk and tasted like oil and gave you these painful, boil-like pimples that stank something awful whenever you popped them. Or they worked at vats of nitric acid, or at rows of high-speed sewing machines, or at industrial looms, or chemical mixers, or in labyrinths of vacuum packaging machines, smelting, plating and polishing machines, froth flotation plastic separators, or at bottling, slitting, slicing machines, filling machines, cartoning systems, or machines that treated human sewage, the point being cushy jobs like Cassandra's (i.e., in an air-conditioned Clean facility) were highly coveted, and hard to come by.*

happened. This, Taylor was explaining at length, would be tricky, yes, but not impossible. He'd already worked out most of the details, which he now related to Sarah's tits.

See, according to paragraphs 2, 4, 6, and 12 of Ordinance 3, In-Zone employment was strictly voluntary. Officially, no one was forced to work. Anyone was free to quit their job on two weeks notice, no questions asked. The only catch was, quitting your job, or not showing up, for whatever reason, without some kind of authorization in writing, clearly demonstrated "failure to sustain a consistent pattern of work behavior," which immediately got you knocked down a class, and earned you a spot on the IntraZone watch-list. So Cassandra quitting was out of the question. No, the plan at the moment (Taylor's plan) was that Taylor would bribe Cassandra's foreman, Santobal Prosky, or threaten him, one. Or maybe threaten him first, then bribe him. Or maybe not even bother to bribe him. In any case, however he did it, get this guy to put Cassandra on the Temporarily Work-Disabled list. Which, he figured, that wouldn't be hard to accomplish. Taylor didn't know this Prosky asshole, but Cassandra made him sound like one of your typical A.S.P. 1-type weasels. Taylor had no doubt that he was. Most of the 1s, and especially the foremen, were spineless little brown-nosing punks, which was why they had been promoted to foremen. The trick with sniveling cowards like that was making them more afraid of you than they were of IntraZone Waste & Security, which wasn't going to be a big problem for Taylor.

Adam and Sarah listened patiently to Taylor's plans to intimidate Prosky, or bribe him, or some combination thereof, and informed him that he was out of his fucking mind and that all that shit was out of the question. They'd take care of Prosky, they informed him, as well as all other "operational details," most of which Taylor would not be privy to, and the rest of which he would be advised of on a need-to-know basis as time went by. Taylor's job was to deal with Cassandra, to keep her fed, entertained, and otherwise physically and emotionally healthy during the "sequestration period" (so officially December to officially April). That, and discourage her nosy roommates from sniffing around outside her door, and knocking and asking if she needed anything ... as if they possibly gave a shit. If the roommates somehow detected her pregnancy, Taylor was instructed to "take no action" and "not to deviate" from his normal routine, other than to promptly report said detection to Adam and Sarah, who would deal with it themselves.

They could not over-emphasize this point. Taylor was to take "no independent action," was not to "engage with any threats," and was not, for any reason whatsoever, to "deviate from his normal routine."

"I got to take a shit," Adam announced. He slid out and presumably went to do that. Sarah waited until he was gone.

"Questions for us?"

Taylor couldn't think of any. She reached across the table and took his tobacco.

"You haven't asked what we do with the babies."

"Everyone knows what you do with the babies."

"Do they?"

"Yeah. You smuggle them out."

"Out to where?"

"The Autonomous Zones."

"And you believe they exist?"

Taylor smirked.

"This isn't about the baby," he said.

"What's it about then?"

"It's about the mother."

She licked the glue on the rolling paper. Her eyes were probing him.

"Why not abort it?"

"She doesn't want to."

"*She* doesn't want to."

"We don't want to. What difference does it make?"

She struck a match and lit her cigarette.

"I'm just trying to get to know you, Taylor."

"What's to know?"

"Why you're doing this."

She exhaled smoke through both her nostrils.

"Most of the fathers just walk away. They're mostly 1s with factory jobs."

"1s are a bunch of candy-asses."

"The mother's a 1."

"She's an exception."

"What about you? Are you an exception?"

"To what?"

And there was that look again. She leaned in towards him and lowered her voice. "This isn't just about the mother. There are other ways to deal with babies." She pushed his tobacco across the table. "You came to us because you don't want to kill it."

"Yeah. So?"

"So why does it matter?"

"It doesn't. What are you trying to get at?"

"What you want."

"You know what I want."

She smoked.

"What you *really* want."

Taylor took the cigarette from her.

"It ain't that fucking complicated."

A second passed. Then she smiled. Her upper lip was beaded with sweat. Taylor took a drag off the cigarette. Then he handed it back across the table. He reached down and slid the sleeve of her tunic up her arm to expose her tattoos, a series of spiral Celtic triskelions, way too good to have been done in the Zone. She gave him time to get a good look, then pulled her arm back and shook her sleeve down. She did it calmly, staring right at him. He could smell her sweat from across the booth. He couldn't quite put his finger on it, but something about her was definitely off. Or something about her reminded him of someone. Or something. There was definitely something about her. Something foreign yet somehow familiar. He knew he wanted her. He knew that much. But then Taylor wanted, or thought he wanted, pretty much every other woman he saw, assuming she wasn't totally toothless or some kind of giant sea cow or something. In Taylor's experience, more often than not, these women also wanted Taylor. He could tell by that look they got in their eyes, not that look that some women gave him, the one designed to make him want them, which didn't mean anything other than that they wanted to see if they could make him want them* … that

---

* Taylor had learned at an early age to avoid these women, who were dead in bed.

other look, that serious look, the one that came from deep inside their brains where they weren't even consciously thinking. He could also tell these women wanted him by the way the vast majority of them dug their fingernails into his back and screamed while Taylor fucked their brains out. This was usually a telltale sign, and what he was thinking he would do to Sarah, who definitely wanted him ... she had that look. He was sitting there across from her, looking right at it. However, although she had that look, something about it was somehow off. It wasn't that she was faking it or anything, because you couldn't fake it, not that look, but rather, that what it looked like she wanted was sex, yes, was serious sex, sweaty, desperate, back-straining sex, but was more than just sex, which was making him nervous. It felt like she was using her eyes, or some power that she controlled with her eyes, to pry him open, to force her way in ... as if she wanted unlimited access to some deeper or ultimate level of Taylor, which Taylor himself had never explored, and which he wasn't even sure was down there. Maybe it was something about her eyes, which he had sworn were brown, but which were actually hazel ... or maybe they had changed to hazel ... which he knew was impossible, so that wasn't it. Her irises had these imperfections that looked like miniature spiral galaxies ... gold at the pupil, shot with sinuous streaks of dusky greens and blues. The longer Taylor stared into them, the less he felt he could read what was in them. Except for that look. He could read that look. But it wasn't just her eyes, or her tits, or her lips, which he could tell were unbelievably soft. No, there was something else that was less specific, and that wasn't physical, or wasn't merely physical, or was some kind of purely pheromonal-type thing ... whatever it was, she radiated some irresistible female something that in spite of the fact that she was obviously a Terrorist, and possibly even a faith-based Terrorist, he felt he needed to put his dick in ... but no, he told himself, not this time.

Sarah sat there watching Taylor, nostrils ever so slightly flaring, nipples hardening through her tunic, as all these thoughts raced through his mind in the space of maybe three or four seconds.

"You sure?" she asked.

"Sure about what?"

"That it isn't that fucking complicated."

Walking home that night from the Pussyhorse, reflecting back on what had just happened, and the now current status of the baby problem, Taylor was feeling pretty good about himself. His plan, or at least this part of it, was working. He'd established contact with the baby smugglers, and had passed his interview, or whatever that was. Now, assuming he could follow all their rules, and not deviate from his normal routine, in six months they would take the baby and smuggle it out to the Autonomous Zones ... which, OK, there were no Autonomous Zones, but they would hide it in one of their safehouses somewhere, or their underground tunnels, or whatever they did with them ... after which life could go back to normal and it would be like nothing had ever happened. And as far as this thing with Sarah went, Taylor decided, right then and there, as he came to the end of Muybridge Lane, Taylor, despite his Anti-Social nature, and his deeply ingrained lack of restraint, and his total absence of impulse control, and generally goatlike inclination to disperse his seed as profusely as possible, Taylor Byrd, the Class 3 Dog, made the clear and conscious choice to, once, just this once, he resolved, to forgo this spooky but fine piece of ass, about whom there was definitely ... something ... something seductive, or irresistible, something that maybe scared him a little, and that he sensed would scare him a whole lot less if he could hold her down and fuck her, forcefully, not like to hurt her, but to ... what? own her? to control her? tame her? ... he did not know ... he couldn't even put this stuff into words ... all he knew was what he wanted to do, or what some part of him wanted him to do, which was what he was not going to do this time ... because no, he owed Cassandra that much ... not to fuck this whole thing up by fucking Sarah, and pissing off Adam, who wasn't in charge of the baby smuggling thing, because pretty obviously Sarah was, but who was either fucking her, or wanted to be fucking her, or in any case wouldn't want Taylor to be fucking her, and also for a host of other reasons, which Taylor couldn't quite remember at the moment, all of which led to the same conclusion, which was, basically, no spooky ass for Taylor. No sir. Uh-uh. Not this time. No, this time, he was going to act like a grown-up and do the right thing for once in his life. He would keep this on a businesslike basis, and tolerate whatever Terrorist bullshit he had to tolerate to see it all through. Yes, this was how it would go. By the numbers. Until the day. Upon which he would deliver the baby, thank them kindly for all their efforts, wish them well with their totally decentralized autonomous revolution or whatever, and, OK, after all that was over, go ahead and throw a quick fuck into Sarah, who regardless of whatever shit she was into looked like she could really use one. She looked like she either wasn't getting laid, or was getting laid by Adam, poorly, which was why she was so wound up and intense and involved in all that faith-based bullshit, and whatever that was she did with her eyes ... it was all that pent-up sexual hunger. She'd probably come in, like, ninety seconds, gasping and hyperventilating, which Taylor would go ahead and get that over with, after which he would fuck her properly, making her come again and again, relentlessly, until her brain stopped thinking ... but afterwards, once he had handed off the baby, because what could it possibly hurt at that point? All right, good, so that was settled. Just one quick one. Nothing serious. One hot fuck and sayonara ... or two or three nights at the absolute most. After which they would both agree that getting involved would be a bad idea, and would get dressed and go their separate ways, after which life would go back to normal ...

He turned up out of the deep Inner Zone and headed north on Wallace Lefferts, a desolate former business thoroughfare lined with gutted office towers, low-rise stores and residential buildings, the ruins of some ancient city center. Someone was walking along the rooftops off to his right, but that didn't mean anything. People walked along on rooftops. This was no time to start getting paranoid. Up ahead, at the end of the avenue, a Public Viewer was running some Content in which a middle-aged Normal couple, whose names apparently were Tom and Tina, were being accosted by a leering host who looked like an android with too much make-up. Tom took hold of this enormous roulette wheel (or a simulation of such a wheel) that was mounted on a stand that faced the camera so the viewers at home could see the series of concentric circles comprised of panels lit up in alternating primary colors and covered with arcane letters and symbols that only the fans of the show understood ... and pulled it, Tom did, and sent it spinning. Tina hopped up and down in place and smiled insanely and clapped her hands and squealed hysterically into the camera with her protuberant eyeballs and rictal grin like maybe she was going to just shit herself from joy. Tom reached over and took her hand and joined in hopping, and smiling, and squealing. The host stood just behind them, grinning. The wheel kept spinning, faster and faster ... round and round, round and round, colors bleeding into other, symbols blurring, disappearing, and ...

Severance

On rare but emotionally scarring occasions, back in that three-bed, two-bath condo on Chestnut Court where Valentina grew up, when her mother, Catherine, was off her meds, she would chase Valentina around with the Hand, waving it at her, laughing and cackling, as Valentina shrieked in terror and hid behind furniture and feared for her life. Valentina never saw it coming. Her mother would storm into the living-room, where Valentina was coloring or something, or loom out of a doorway suddenly, as she was trying to walk down the hall to her bedroom, clawing the air with the hand, and cackling. Valentina would pee her jammies and run as fast as she possibly could. Catherine would be right on her heels, cackling, groping for her with the hand as she ran. She'd reach with it under the dining room table, driving Valentina out the other side. She'd chase her down the hallway with it. Valentina would hide in the bedrooms, wait for Catherine to come inside and clear the door, then run out behind her, and look for some other place to hide. Catherine would be wearing her filthy bathrobe and those big fuzzy hamster-like slippers she wore. Her hair would be sticking out every which way, her eyeballs bulging like hard-boiled eggs. She'd chase Valentina around with the Hand, laughing and coughing, until she started to choke. Then she'd sit down at the dining room table, or sometimes on the living room sofa, and disgustingly spit into one of the wadded up tissues she always kept in her robe.

Catherine, in the condition she was in back then, found this game uproariously funny. Valentina did not find it funny. Valentina found it emotionally scarring. For years she'd had these recurring nightmares in which her mother, who was white-eyed psychotic, was chasing her down a series of hallways clawing at her with her black plastic hands. She'd discussed her deep emotional scarring in her expensive sessions with Doctor Graell, who'd knowingly nodded for several seconds, and then upped her Zanoflaxithorinal dosage. Somewhere in her mid-to-late thirties, the recurring nightmares had finally stopped, and at some point she'd forgotten the Hand.

That is, until Catherine's pantomime in the Seaview Unit remind-ed her of it, and the memories all came flooding back. She knew exactly where to find it. She knew that because she had put it there herself. The week after Catherine took up residence at Breckenridge Village, "a Retirement Community," she'd wrapped the Hand in sev-eral sheets of recycled plastic translucent bubble-wrap and sealed the ends up with cellophane tape. She'd done this in her mother's bedroom, while her mother sat and stared out the window of the Seaview Unit at the toxic lagoon. Her father had sat, alone, in the living room, watching some purported Historical Content regarding the Early Age of Austerity, which he didn't appear to be watching as much as staring forlornly at the screen and drinking. She'd stripped the dreaded Hand of its rings, and the chains that were draped be-tween the fingers, then bubble-wrapped it and carefully packed it into a 10-cube EasyStore Storage box. Then she'd packed up the rest of Catherine's things. Later that day, the EasyStore Storage men had loaded the box, Box 1 of 13, into their bright blue EasyStore Storage van. They'd driven it out to 1317 N.E. Corporate Perimeter Road, dollied it into the EasyStore storage complex, and stacked it neatly in Storage Cubicle 6344923. There it had sat for fifteen years, until that humid February evening when Valentina, upon her return from her visit with Catherine in the Seaview Unit, called the EasyStore Emergency Hotline at a cost of sixty-three cents per second and requested overnight delivery of the box to 3258 Marigold Lane.

The box arrived the following morning, at 0530 the invoice said, just as Kyle was leaving the house on a three-day trip to Region 20, where the Hakuhodo Chayevsky Foundation was holding some kind of Informatics seminar where Kyle was giving a presentation about which Valentina couldn't have cared less.

"Uh ... what's this?" Kyle wanted to know.

"Nothing. A box of my mother's things," she answered, casually, signing the invoice, for GD 743.60.

"Nothing? An Overnight Delivery of nothing?!"

"Emergency Overnight Rush Service, technically," the EasyStore driver offered, helpfully, printing out a copy of the digital invoice.

"Honey, listen ... we need to talk."

"You're going to miss your plane," she said.

The Pewter Palisades Airport Shuttle, which was parked there, waiting, flashed its headlights.

"I'll call you from the hotel tonight."

Kyle was using his extremely concerned voice.

"OK, honey," she answered mechanically. "Have a nice flight."

"Tonight ... OK?"

"OK, you folks have an awesome day now," the EasyStore driver chimed in cheerfully. "And thanks for going with EasyStore Storage."

He turned and sprinted back down to his van.

Kyle just stood there, shaking his head. The Airport Shuttle hit him with the high-beams.

"Keep your phone on."

"OK, honey."

Valentina clutched the box.

She carried the box into the kitchen, set it down on the kitchen table, cut through the tape, flipped up the flaps, dug down into the sea of little indestructible Styrofoam peanuts, felt around, and found the Hand. She carefully cut free the tape on the bubble-wrap, pried it out and set it on the table. There it stood, all black and shiny, its ophidian fingers reaching heavenward.

Valentina thought she might faint.

She thrust her hand down into her pajamas and compulsively masturbated for two and half minutes, imagining she was being ravaged by Joachim Maria-Torres Oakley, the well-built Pewter Palisades gardener, except that Joachim was a Terrorist shaman whose body was oiled, or slick with sweat, and all around them other Terrorists were dancing naked by the light of a bonfire, and chanting something backwards in Latin and ...

After she came, and got her breath back, and made a quick cup of ginger-lemon tea, she turned her attention back to the Hand.

The Hand, a ring and bracelet holder, was a family heirloom ... a real antique. It was probably over one hundred years old, definitely worth a lot of money. It wasn't real ebony, but some kind of glass, or glazed, seamless, glass-like material, heavy, but fragile. It didn't feel hollow. She picked it up and gently shook it. No. It definitely was not hollow. She stood there at the kitchen table, sipping her tea and staring at it.

What had Catherine been trying to tell her? The particular way she'd bent her wrist, and extended her fingers, reaching, straining, and the way she had pinched Valentina's ring ... that had to have something to do with the Hand ... or, then again, maybe it didn't. Maybe it had all meant nothing, and Catherine had just been having a spasm, and her eyes had simply been drawn to the ring as they were to any other shiny object.

No, she told herself, it wasn't nothing. It didn't mean nothing. Nothing meant nothing. Everything meant something. Everything counted. Either everything counted ... or nothing counted.

Valentina was coming to know this, and not in the purely abstract way she had always known it, and everyone knew it, but experientially, to *really* know it, to know it in the very core of her being. Ever since that fateful day, the day of her Lomax Escalator Vision, the One had been guiding her, showing her things, teaching her how to see the world, not as it had always appeared, veiled, or shrouded, or clouded over, but to see it as it *really* was, sharp, clear, charged with meaning, brimming with meaning, oozing signs. Everything, every word, gesture, advertising slogan, random comment, everything, every detail was part of it. This was what was really meant by the infinite aspects of the One Who Was Many, which *was* The Truth, which IT had twisted, and bent, and spindled, and mutilated, and stripped of its meaning, and made to conform to its own perverted demiurgic logic, which was all a lie and ...

She caught herself. She repeated her mantra, and tried to refocus. Examine the Hand, she ordered herself. Look at it. Look at what it is. Not what you expect it to be, or want it to be, or remember it being. It isn't the Hand that is there in your head. It's not in your head. It's here on the table. The Hand is this actual, physical object.

She examined the actual, physical object.

The skin of the Hand was black and shiny. Nothing was etched, scratched, engraved, or otherwise written on the seamless surface. It bore no trademarks, no dates, names, no artist's signature, no initials ... nothing. Nothing that might have been a coded message, or a hint, or clue. There had to be something. Maybe it wasn't the Hand itself. Maybe the Hand was a sign ... a symbol. A symbol for what? For some other hand?

No. That didn't make any sense.

Valentina sat there, staring. She stared at the Hand. She said her mantra. She emptied her mind. She made it a blank. The jabbering of her thoughts subsided. She sat there, empty, desiring nothing, looking ... listening for the voice of the One.

She sat there like that for twenty-three minutes.

Something was hidden inside the Hand.

Valentina got up from the table, fetched a solid sky blue dish towel from the drawer where she kept the sky blue dish towels, spread the towel out flat on the table, wrapped the hand inside the towel, tucked the ends of the towel in neatly, and hurled the hand down onto the floor with every ounce of strength in her body. She heard it shatter, or crack at least. She knelt and felt it. There were three big pieces. She grabbed it like a shank of TōLamb and slammed it against the floor repeatedly. Once she'd decided it was thoroughly demolished, she carefully placed it back on the table, opened the towel, and examined its contents. There, among the shiny black shards and nuggets of whatever material it was, sealed in a plastic Ziploc packet, was what looked like an old-fashioned 3x3 MemCard. She ripped the packet open with her teeth. It *was* an old-fashioned 3x3 MemCard, which of course was totally obsolete, having been replaced by a series of other identical MemCards of other sizes ... but being the wife of an Associate Professor of Info-Entertainment Content at the Bloomberg Virtual Community College of Communications & Informatics, at least in this case, had its upsides. Among the prodigious assortment of crap Kyle kept in the bedroom he used as his office were a number of fairly antique Viewers and other ancient, out-of-date gadgets, some of them twenty or thirty years old, including, Valentina now wagered, something that would take a 3x3 MemCard.

The Viewer she found was an HCS60, a cumbersome proto-All-in-One that she vaguely remembered from her early childhood and that barely fit in the palm of her hand. She dropped it into its power station, connected the station, and plugged it in. The HC Systems welcome message appeared on the screen ... which was seriously primitive. An eternity later a series of little red indicator lights started flashing, frantically, indicating that the HCS60 was attempting to connect to the Internet, and failing. This was just as well, she noted. Whatever was on that ancient MemCard, she didn't want to be connected to the Internet, which was monitored, when she booted it up.

She popped the card in. Nothing happened. She sat there and waited ... nothing happened. She popped the card out. She popped it back in. She sat there and waited ... nothing happened. That was OK, she told herself. There were probably other Viewers she could try. The HCS60 was the first one she'd found that looked like it took a 3x3 MemCard. She would just keep digging through the drawer until she found one. She took a deep breath and said her mantra. The loving compassionate oneness of the ...

Before she could finish, the MemCard loaded. A textfile directory of files appeared. It took forever, ten full seconds. It started like this:

    aleph/spokework/statement/ver/ar-2265-12-01-77723
    clownfish/manifest/dever/ar-2420-09-09-2247885
    disinf/spargel/erklaerung/ver/ar-2210-04-04-1138540

And ended like this:

    regen/mantel/response/unver/urar-5512-2027-3341
    wachowski/statement/ver/ar-2315-10-08-3375-9919
    wilder/gedichte/unver/ar-9999-88-42-3547-000

And somewhere near the middle was this:

    norma/vangelium/barnicoat/ver/ar-2550-02-08-4368

Valentina clicked on the file. A prompt appeared and asked for the password. She sat there, staring at the message, thinking. The prompt was there on the screen, blinking. She keyed in CONSTANCE, which was not the password. She keyed in ROSENTHAL, which was not the password. She keyed in CATHERINE, which was also not the password. The password prompt screen disappeared.

The screen went blue. There was nothing on it.

She took a breath and said her mantra.

Everything happening for a reason ...

The screen went black, flickered briefly, then came back to life. A message appeared. The message was in a different typeface.

WHO ARE YOU?

Valentina froze.

Time slowed down. The room got brighter. She closed her eyes, inhaled through her nostrils, pursed her lips, and exhaled slowly. She did this until her panic subsided. Then she opened her eyes and looked at the screen.

WHO ARE YOU?

She checked the readouts. The online indicator light was red. Which meant she was definitely not connected. Which meant the message could not be live. It was probably just another password prompt. Which theory she decided to test.

She typed in the following:

WHO ARE YOU?

The screen responded:

YOU KNOW WHO WE ARE.

Valentina suddenly felt the need to move her bowels extensively. She stared at the online indicator light. Maybe the indicator light was broken. She snatched the device up out of its station and tried to access online Content, weather, news, markets, whatever. She couldn't. Because she was not online. And now the screen read:

WHAT ARE YOU DOING?

NOTHING, she typed.

Nothing happened. Then she typed:

ARE YOU STILL THERE?

All of this could have been preprogrammed. But now it read:

THIS IS NOT PREPROGRAMMED.

The following exchange of messages ensued:

I DON'T BELIEVE YOU.

YES. YOU DO.

WHAT TIME IS IT?

WHERE?
WHERE I AM NOW.
0720. THERE'S A CLOCK IN THE VIEWER.
The Viewer was right. Stupid question. She tried again.
WHERE AM I NOW?
3258 MARIGOLD LANE.
Which could have been some kind of GPS trick. She desperately tried to think of a question to stump the possibly pre-programmed software. A question having to do with history. Recent history. That would do it. The MemCard had been inside the Hand since before she was born. A lot had happened. Forty-one years of her life had happened. Why then couldn't she think of anything ... one single significant historical event? Then it hit her. Variant Correction. The Clear generation. That was it. She opened her eyes, and was about to type, but now the screen read:
CAN WE SPEED THIS UP?
HOW?
USE YOUR LIVING ROOM VIEWER. GO TO CHANNEL 313. THERE'S A LITTLE BLUE GNOME, OR SOMETHING, WITH A FLUTE.
Valentina sat there in shock ... the HCS60 could not know this. Channel 313 was a children's channel. The little blue gnome was Peter Pitpatrick, the roly poly pansexual spokes-being that taught the children to respect private property and to pay back the interest on their loans on time. Peter Pitpatrick's PreSchool Playhouse was eight, maybe nine years old, on top of which Channel 313, back in the days of the HCS60, had been an Asian women's channel. A software program could not do this.
And now the HCS60 informed her:
THE GNOME IS RIDING A FERET OR SOMETHING.
Valentina went into the living room, leaving the HCS60 in its dock. She switched on the Viewer, keyed in the Channel, and there he was, Peter Pitpatrick, playing his trademark magic pan flute. His magical ferret, Gibby the Ferret, was licking the tears off the face of some kid who had just learned one of life's valuable lessons. Valentina clicked off the Viewer. She stood there staring at herself in the screen. There was no other explanation ...

Someone was live on the HCS60.

Someone, either a Security Specialist, or possibly a member of the N.I.N., was sitting at an online console somewhere typing the messages she had just received. This someone, who was probably a Security Specialist, had been alerted when she had tried, and failed, to open the file she had tried to open. Probably when she'd blown the password. Or maybe the moment she had loaded the MemCard. It didn't matter. What mattered was, whoever it was on the HCS60 was sitting there, right at that very moment, waiting for her to return from the living room. Something told her not to do that. It told her, explicitly, never to do that, to never, ever, return from the living room.

Valentina returned from the living room.

And now the screen read:

WHO ARE YOU?

She typed her name in, VALENTINA BRIGGS, reasoning, if it was Security Services, they probably already knew who she was, and were on their way to Marigold Lane ... and would be there in approximately three and a half minutes.

HI VALENTINA. WAIT ONE MOMENT.

She listened for the sound of Security units screeching up into her driveway, bolting up to the house in force, setting their mini-Semtex charges, blowing her front door off its hinges and ...

VALENTINA CONSTANCE BRIGGS?

YES.

DAUGHTER OF CATHERINE AND WALTER?

YES.

CATHERINE ROSENTHAL BRIGGS?

YES.

GOOD. WAIT ONE MOMENT.

Out the window of the bedroom office the sun was up and baking the orange "Spanish"-tiled roofs of Pewter Palisades. No one was out there. Nothing moved. Not one leaf. There was no breeze.

VALENTINA? ARE YOU STILL THERE?

YES.

LISTEN.

Valentina listened. The HVAC unit was humming softly. Other than that there was nothing to hear. No one was screeching up into the driveway, or blowing the hinges off her Persian green door, or otherwise storming the house in strength.

WE CAN'T STAY ON THIS LINE MUCH LONGER.

OK.

WHAT DO YOU WANT FROM US?

Valentina's thumb was paralyzed She willed it to work.

I WANT TO HELP.

ARE YOU SURE?

YES.

ABSOLUTELY SURE?

YES.

YOU HAVE TO BE TOTALLY SURE.

I AM.

OK. DO YOU WANT TO MEET?

YES. WHERE?

LEAVE THE HOUSE. EJECT THE MEMCARD. TAKE THE MEMCARD. TAKE THIS VIEWER. FIND SOMEWHERE SAFE.

WHERE?

GO TO CENTER CITY. RELOAD THE MEMCARD. WAIT FOR INSTRUCTIONS. OK?

OK.

EJECT THE MEMCARD!

Valentina ejected the MemCard. The screen went blank. The HVAC hummed. She sat there for a moment, stunned. Her heart was hammering against her sternum. She closed her eyes, recited her mantra, and did her pursed lip breathing thing.

The infinite, unknowable Oneness of the ...

One of two possible things had just happened.

Either the MemCard, her grandmother's MemCard, maybe even Stanislav Barnicoat's MemCard, and in any event an obsolete MemCard, had been equipped with some kind of feature that whenever someone loaded the MemCard sent a ping to the N.I.N. (i.e., to some underground safe house or basement, which would have to be manned around the clock, because how would they know when someone would load it? But why would they do that ... unless ... wait ... maybe there were hundreds or thousands of these MemCards

hidden in horrible, ugly hands, and other seemingly mundane objects, scattered throughout the United Territories, waiting for people
like her to find them ... which, OK, that was totally nuts ... unless
some earlier generation, as in Stanislav Barnicoat's generation, of the
N.I.N., facing capture, had, in a desperate last ditch gambit, hidden
their files inside such objects, hoping that one day, many years later,
people like her might stumble upon them, just as she had ... and
she had, after all ... which would mean that her mother, Catherine,
knew ... which of course she did, she knew it was in there, and had
always known, and had always been waiting, waiting for Valentina to
awaken, and visit her in the Seaview unit ... all of which seemed to
Valentina, even in her borderline delusional state, highly unlikely, to
put it mildly), or else (and this was rather more likely) what had happened was, she had loaded the MemCard, and Security Services had
picked up its signal with some kind of covert surveillance technology that could monitor devices that weren't online (which she'd never
heard of such technology, but that didn't mean it didn't exist), and
now they were simply toying with her, leading her on, setting her
up, possibly trying to lure her away from Pewter Palisades Private
Community in order to avoid unsavory publicity, and detain her
elsewhere, and render her off to ...

Valentina got up from the desk and looked around the bedroom
office. There, in the corner, was the faux leather easy chair Kyle had
had since their days at college, the stuffing poking out of a hole in
the seat. Standing behind it were Kyle's father's golf clubs, which
neither Kyle nor anyone played with, not even on the air-conditioned indoor courses. Against one wall was the sleeper sofa nobody
ever came to sleep on. The walls were adorned with photos of Kyle
and assorted other smiling professors standing around with assorted
groups of assorted smiling corporate executives. Valentina had no
idea where Kyle was or who he was with. She stared at the faces of
the men in the photos. Who were these men? She didn't know them.
They looked like all the other men you saw in all the other photos of
abundant white men in their forties to sixties with receding hairlines
and expensive watches who were on the boards of corporations, or
institutions, and were interchangeable. They stared back out of the
photos, smiling ... no ... impossible, they could not know ...

She gathered up the HCS60, its power station, cords, case, and switched off the light in the office as she left. She walked down the plushly carpeted hallway, passing the glossy color photos of exotic animals that no longer existed ... the Bengal tigers, Boa constrictors, African lions, leopards, cheetahs, gazelles, zebras, antelopes, elephants, sea lions, herons, pelicans, partridges, penguins, parrots, birds of paradise, dolphins, whales, treefrogs, toads, catfish, redfish, sharks, rays, bighorn sheep, cave shrimp, crayfish, Barrington iguanas, hairy armadillos, Andean condors, sportive Lemurs ... there were literally hundreds of these photos in the hall, crowded together, frame to frame, floor to ceiling, obscuring both walls, a virtual gauntlet of gaping eyes ... staring at her like the eyes of children ... exterminated ... for the sake of ... what? She couldn't remember. There had been a reason, or an explanation ... hadn't there, once? Why had she framed and hung these photos? She'd done it because that was what everyone did. Everyone had these walls of photos ... these shrines, or were they trophy walls? She cupped the Viewer and the gear to her breast and ran the last few steps down the hall, away from the eyes and into her bedroom. She closed the door behind her and locked it. She dumped the Viewer and the gear on the bed and went back to the door and unlocked it. She changed her mind, and locked it again. Then once more, and unlocked it, and opened it.

A voice in her head said, "someone's coming."

"No one is coming. No one is coming."

She packed her Charles Vittorio suitcase, the mid-sized blue one with the wheels that swiveled. She did this quickly, and not very carefully, telling herself that no one was coming. After she had finished, and no one had come, she stared down into the tangle of clothes and the random assortment of hygiene products she had jammed into its crème compartments, which she couldn't even remember doing. Then she sat down on the bed, and wept.

Once her sobbing finally subsided, she looked around the room in a daze. The bedroom set was three years old, dark, faux mahogany was it? She couldn't remember who she'd been when they'd bought it, or whether she'd liked it. She didn't now. But she didn't exactly dislike it either. She wasn't quite sure how she felt about it. It didn't have anything to do with her somehow, and neither did anything else in the room. It wasn't that they weren't her things. Most of the things in the bedroom were hers ... the antique mirror that had been her mother's, the family snapshots, of both of their families, that Valentina had arranged on the dressers, her jewelry boxes, her medicine cases, the artificial flowers, orchids, begonias ... objects, things, alien things. There, on her night stand, were stacks of bottles of Pregadrel, Luprocene, Fertex, Ovitrol, and other such hormones and anti-rejection drugs. She picked one up and read the label: BRIGGS, Valentina Constance (VP) - 3258 Marigold Lane. She slipped her hand up under her blouse and felt her abdomen. She wasn't showing. Her nipples hurt, though, and they itched something awful.

She was almost exactly ten weeks pregnant.

She left her KeyCard and her All-in-One Viewer, both of which were easily trackable, on the table in the foyer, where Kyle would find them, wheeled her suitcase out the front door, which locked automatically, and pulled it shut. The official time was 0730, the temperature 39C and rising. She walked the ninety-three steps to the MoveWay, stepped into the air-conditioned tube and onto the conveyor, pulling her suitcase, looking like any innocuous Normal on her way to somewhere for a two-day trip. She'd put on her blue Matsumoto pantsuit, which set off her hair and eyes quite nicely, or would have had she not been wearing the enormous SeaSyde wraparound sunglasses she had snatched up at Shade World for twenty percent off. The MoveWay was empty, which was normal at this hour, most people having left for work between 0530 and 0600. Montages of Pewter Palisades' Main Street were streaming past her on the walls of the tube. The Muzak was the usual cheerful nightmare ...

Main Street, a ten-block "outdoor" shopping loop, was the heart of the Pewter Palisades Community. All the MoveWays brought you to Main Street, in the central landscaped garden of which was the Pewter Palisades WhisperTrain station, where people caught their trains to work. Radiating out from the WhisperTrain station were hundreds of quaint little simulated lanes that were lined with quaint little simulated shops, which were really all outlets of eight or ten chains, like Finkles and BuyWorld and BigBuy Basement. Many of these shops had quaint little names like Zena's Travel, or Ye Olde

Shoe Repair, or Happy Time Cleaners, or Paolo's Beans, as if they weren't corporate outlets, but family businesses, owned by people. Their interiors were usually decorated with authentic-looking "ethnic" objects, and the sales assistants wore fanciful uniforms, and spoke with various "ethnic" accents, all of which was quaint and charming and not at all cheap and completely impersonal. Surrounding the central landscaped "garden" was an endless array of stores and restaurants ... stores like Finkles, Big Buy Basement, CRS, and the Content Warehouse, and restaurants like Giggles, Salad Emporium, Fair Trade Burgers, Woo's, Twannika's, and Brewster & Cuttlestons, a simulated pub chain. All of this, of course, was hermetically sealed within an immense translucent SkyDome, which tinted gradually throughout the day, creating a virtual "outdoor" effect that studies had proved was almost natural. The MoveWay's exits were strategically positioned to deposit the residents of Pewter Palisades, not in or outside the WhisperTrain station, but down at the east and west ends of Main Street so that they had to walk past the stores and restaurants to get to the station and catch their trains ...

Which is what Valentina was doing now, dragging her Vittorio suitcase behind her. She was weaving in and out of the streams of smiling, well-dressed Pewter Palisades residents, who were already shopping, or were standing around outside the windows of Finkles and BigBuy, or sitting at tables in the "outdoor" section of Salad Emporium, or the Giggles "Café," sipping neon green and purple breakfast smoothies through their bendy straws. A veritable arsenal of surveillance cameras were pivoting around on their slender stalks. Pewter Palisades Security professionals were patrolling in their battery-operated go-carts, biometrically scanning people at random as they strolled up and down the pristine sidewalks or huddled outside the windows of stores. Valentina contorted her lips into some semblance of a Normal smile and snaked her way through them, her technical neighbors, none of whom she actually knew. The voice in her head said, "everyone's watching."

"No one is watching you ... no one is watching."

A grinning formation of teenage Clears was coming right at her on the sidewalk ahead, laughing in their all-knowing, all-feeling way, their wind-blown hair and blinding teeth ... and now, in one sicken-

ingly synchronized movement, they turned their eyes on Valentina.
"Smile, nod, breathe, walk ..." The two in the center, a girl and a boy,
parted to let Valentina pass through, blue eyes tracking her, nostrils
smelling her, some pea-sized bud in their neocortex telepathical-
ly alerting the others ... she nodded, smiled, walked right through,
keeping her own eyes fixed on the station, four blocks ahead and ...
"Walk ... don't run."
Passing the coveted sidewalk tables at Content Warehouse's Café
de Flore ... all of them packed with young professionals, sitting together in twos and threes in total silence scanning their Viewers, or
talking into space on their Cranio-Implants while they nodded and
smiled at the people they were with, to whom they presumably had
nothing to say, as they scanned the faces of passersby, like Valentina,
to see who was looking, and held up their fingers to the servers and
smiled ... and here came the mothers with their prams and strollers
and slings and wraps and beaming faces and nannies and aides and
personal assistants, who probably lived in cramped apartments in
Center City, where Valentina was going ... and here came the windows festooned with products, the Viewers, Readers, Memcards,
implants, scanners, sticks, chips, clips, the dishwashers, sweepers,
dusters, drainers, the steamers, strainers, the temperature regulators,
the processors, players, signal distributors, toothbrush sterilizers,
palm oil recyclers, the walls of cosmetics and hygiene products, lipstick, gloss, rouge, eye liners, skin crèmes, eye crèmes, hemorrhoid
crèmes, wrinkle-removing revitalizing agents, anti-aging nipple
decolorizers, mouthwash for people with sensitive skin, genital
shavers, penis straighteners, anal buffers, fingernail planers, taste bud
shrinkers, dyes, pastes, gels, salves, powders, pills, drops, mists, cul-
tures, solutions, applicators, syringes, suppositories, fifty-two lines of
clothing each year, jewelry, accessories, decorative items, products,
services, gadgets, gizmos, which everyone owned, or wore, or used,
or wanted to wear, or own, or use, the wearing and owning and using
of which, and the virtually interminable discussion of which, was, in
large part, what made them normal ...
"Three more blocks ... hold it together!"
How many nights had she sat across from Susan Foster, or Lydia
Fishbeck, or May Pei Gonzalez, or Rachel Greene-Morley, or one

of the cheerfully tranquilized wives of one of Kyle's colleagues at
BVCC, none of whose names she could remember at the moment,
discussing, actually discussing products ... comparing products,
praising products, fondly remembering former products ... that,
or recounting the content of Content that one, or both, or all of
them had seen, or wanted to see, or had heard was worth seeing?
Why? Why was there nothing to talk about, other than products,
and Content, and work? Valentina knew the answer ... she almost
lost it and screamed it into the face of the woman walking right at
her ... IT! IT had done this to them! YES, it was all so clear to her
now, how you couldn't begin to talk about anything, anything that
actually mattered to anyone, whatever that might possibly be, unless
you were ready to talk about IT, which of course no one was, or ever
would be ...

"Hold it together. Two more blocks."

Faces streaming past her now, normal faces, smiling faces, pausing,
turning, sniffing, wincing ... asking each other, "what is that smell?"
That smell, of course, was Valentina, who in her haste had forgotten
to shower and reeked of compulsive masturbation. She breezed right
past them, pulling her suitcase, smiling, baring her big white teeth.
"CUNT," she wanted to scream, but she didn't. She wanted to stick
her sticky, stinking fingers up their manicured nostrils and shove
them up into their ethmoid sinuses. The muscles in her cheeks and
forehead were twitching. Why had she thought of that disgusting
word, a word she had never uttered in her life? Then it hit her ...
she was not scared. She was feeling ... well, she did not know. Her
heart was pounding, and she had that metal adrenaline taste in the
back of her throat ... but her mind was calm, clear, detached. It felt
like a switch had been flipped in her head, and now, after months of
confusion, or possibly after years of confusion, she was able to think,
and see, and hear, and she could feel her body ... which was walking
too fast.

"Slow down, walk ... one more block."

The WhisperTrain station was directly ahead, perched on its little
green hill in the "garden." She felt like if she took one leap she would
fly through the air in a single arc like an astronaut bouncing in zero
gravity and float across the flowered slope and ...

"Valentina?"

She knew that voice. Susan Foster. She kept on walking.

"Val?" the voice called out behind her.

"Do not turn around … do not turn back."

The surveillance camera at the southwest entrance panned and filmed her as she entered the station, smiling insanely, her unbrushed hair, the mess of her lipstick, her misbuttoned pantsuit, a bit of a bra sticking out of her suitcase … two point seven four seconds of footage, which Security Services, six weeks later, would play for Kyle in a windowless cubicle, once, and then erase the disk.

3.

Mister Normal

All right ... here comes the horrible part. Part Three, that is. Or a lot of it, anyway. This is the part where Valentina and Taylor, each in their own horrific way, indulge in some seriously deviant behavior, which neither my publisher, nor its parent company, nor any of its agents, subsidiaries, assigns, affiliates, or employees, promotes or condones. Nevertheless, it is what happened, so I need to tell you about it somehow.

First, though, we need to get something else straight.

That something else concerns "normality," and the Normals, and what it meant to be normal, and the way things worked in normal society (i.e., 27th Century normal society), which was weirder than I've probably been able to convey. I may have even given you the false impression that being "normal" was something akin to being a member of a political party, or something that was printed on your ID card, or coded into your subdermal chip. It wasn't.

Actually, it was just the opposite.

In the 27th Century H.C.S.T., despite the fact that Normatology was an established field of academic study, which various august and elite universities offered a smattering of extremely competitive and insanely expensive post-graduate degrees in, "normality" was not some rigidly defined, or in any way officially codified, concept. There weren't any rules or sets of guidelines articulating what made one "normal." There certainly wasn't any Ministry of Normality issuing edicts on individual behavior, or arresting people for non-conformance, or any other type of nonsense like that.

On the contrary, the meaning of the term "normality" (as well as that of its various derivatives), which the normatologists were still debating, was of negligible to zero interest to the Normals, most of whom never even gave it a thought, as it didn't directly affect their lives, which, all things considered, were pretty darn good.

The Normals, for example, didn't call themselves "Normals," or think of themselves, and their families and friends, and everyone else they knew as "Normals." Most of them had never even heard the term, which was mostly used by Anti-Socials in a pejorative and flagrantly aggressive way. Variant-Positives referred to themselves as "Variant-Positives" in contrast to Clears, and Clears the other way around, naturally, but this was strictly a medical distinction, as opposed to any kind of caste system thing.* The Normals referred to the Anti-Socials as "Anti-Socials" or "A.S.P.s," but they didn't refer to themselves as anything (i.e., in contrast to Anti-Socials). Being the overwhelming majority, and the unarticulated normative standard, which no individual could ever attain, and which the Anti-Socials deviated from, they thought of themselves as ... well, as normal.

Now, of course, there were varying degrees of normal, which the Normals semi-consciously perceived, and instinctively recognized in themselves, and each other, and measured each other, and themselves, naturally, and everything else, in relation to. The way this worked was, more often than not, they would see some Content on their All-in-One Viewers that would somehow start them questioning whether what they were doing (not at that very moment, more in regard to their lifestyles in general, as in what they were wearing, or eating, or reading, or the vehicles they were investing in, or the medications they were currently taking, or their body mass indices, or sexual techniques, et cetera, it didn't really matter what it was, as it could have been any aspect of their lifestyles, and usually was) was entirely appropriate.

More often than not, the Normals discovered (according to this Content they had seen, or heard about from their friends or families), there was something about this particular aspect of their lifestyles they needed to re-examine, or to further examine, or otherwise examine. Unfortunately, on a fairly routine basis, upon examination of whatever aspect of their lifestyles this Content had inspired

---

* In the Age of the Renaissance of Freedom and Prosperity, everyone was equal, basically. Their rights were enshrined in the Global Civil Code, which the corporations had written and ratified. The Clears didn't have any special status, apart from their obvious biological advantages.

them to question, they discovered there was room for significant improvement, in terms of their spiritual and material growth, and their physical, emotional, and financial health, and their attitude and performance at work, and their level of personal happiness, generally.

Now, normally, what the Normals would do at this point was they would fleep and tweak and otherwise alert (and in some cases actually physically meet and share this most recent discovery with) their friends, colleagues, family members, therapists, sponsors, and random strangers, many of whom, as if by magic, or due to some recent realignment of the planets, would just happened to have made the same discovery (i.e., regarding their lifestyles and the appropriateness thereof, and their levels of personal happiness, generally). Information would then be exchanged, much of it involving products and services that could help the Normals achieve these improvements in their lifestyles and experiences of personal growth ... which, of course, would then lead them to, or make them aware of, other areas (or lifestyle aspects) which needed examining, and upgrading, and so on.

All of which (i.e., this perpetual process of continually examining themselves, and each other, and identifying areas for potential improvement, and then scanning the web with their All-in-One Viewers to locate affordable ranges of products and services to hopefully effectuate same ... all of this) was entirely normal. It was what the Normals did all day, except when they were actually working, contributing to the productivity and profitability of the corporations that provided the aforementioned products and services.

Persons who declined to engage in this process of ongoing lifestyle and personal improvement (also known as the pursuit of happiness), or who questioned or appeared to scoff at this process, while by no means Anti-Social or anything, were looked upon as ... well, not quite normal. It wasn't like they were branded with a big red "N" in a circle with a line drawn through it, or punished, or oppressed in any way. They just didn't tend to get invited to parties, or important meetings, or bonding weekends, or learn they were being groomed for promotion, or considered for some prestigious accolade, or otherwise emotionally and professionally validated ... or whatever. You know how all that works.

This happened to more people than you would probably imagine, as all it took was one carelessly-worded Fleep or Tweak, or email, or comment, sent in haste, which someone saw, and took offense to, or was emotionally triggered by, and commented on to that effect, which comment was then refleeped, or retweaked, or otherwise streamed out into the ether, along with the original offending Fleep, or Tweak, or email, or whatever it was, and then sat there on the Internet forever casting aspersions on one's degree of normality, or outright condemning one as "not quite normal." This happened to untold numbers of people, otherwise perfectly normal people, with normal jobs at normal corporations, who were otherwise pursuing their personal happiness, and who had just slipped up in a moment of weakness and had said or done something inappropriate. It could happen to almost anyone, really ... well, except for someone like Kyle Bentley-Briggs.

Kyle Bentley-Briggs was so utterly normal that other Normals thought of him as normal. It didn't get any more normal than Kyle. Kyle Bentley-Briggs was the epitome of normal, the quintessence, the apotheosis of normal. The man was virtually normal incarnate.

Kyle was a man of normal height and normal weight, with a normal build. All of his features were remarkably normal. The size of his hands and his feet were normal. The size and shape of his head was normal. His ears were normal. His nose was normal. His chin and jawline were entirely normal. His eyes were not piercing, or steely, or dreamy, or bright, or dull, or ... well, anything, really. He wasn't thin-lipped, nor especially full-lipped. He wore normal clothes, had a normal haircut, bore no distinguishing marks or scars, and exhibited no memorable physical traits. His appearance in toto was profoundly normal.

And it wasn't just physical, normality, with Kyle. Every aspect of his life was normal ... was a reification, an embracement of normal. His palate, for example, while, of course, eclectic,* was impeccably and definitively normal. His tastes in Entertainment Content, whether visual, literary, musical, tactile, interactive, or fully-im-

---

*He got it mostly from the "Dining" sections of prominent online periodicals, where they ran these features on whichever restaurants the excessively abundant were currently fond of, and the ridiculous dishes they were paying through the nose for.

mersive, while in no sense lowbrow, were equally as normal.* His
political views were exceedingly normal (e.g., stability, freedom, and
peace were healthy, extremism and social unrest were unhealthy).
He worked normal hours, took normal medications, and attended
normal social functions, where he made normal small-talk on normal subjects that never caused anyone to question anything. His
aspirations were normal aspirations (material security, professional
advancement, and emotional, spiritual, and personal growth), and
thus, like pretty much every other Normal, he diligently read *The
Path(s) to Prosperity*, and basically believed in the tenets thereof, but
not in any overly literal way, and certainly not to the point of fanaticism. While he was ambitious, to a normal extent, he didn't aspire
to any level of greatness, and had no desire to leave a mark on the
field of Informatics, or anything, or to otherwise etch his hyphen-
ated name into the annals of recorded history. At the same time, he
had warmly and graciously welcomed the minor recognition he'd
received (which he knew was minor, and did not overestimate, or
tediously crow or go on about) from his peers in the Informatics
community, as well as, of course, from G-Wave Industries, who were
sponsoring his position as Associate Professor at the Bloomberg
Virtual Community College, which had just been acquired, and
was being delayered, and streamlined, and otherwise totally re-
structured, by InfoEducation Solutions, which rumor had it was in
turn being looked at by G-Wave Industries' parent company, U.A.
MedEon Content, Inc., who were possibly merging with Hadley
Entertainment, none of which negatively affected Kyle, who was
more than happy to work with whoever. As far as Kyle Bentley-
Briggs was concerned, a corporation was a corporation. Each had its
own unique identity, corporate culture, policies, and so on, but the

---

* *Kyle was an avid reader of novels. He read normal novels about normal families with normal characters, with whom he identified, in the course of which various normal things happened, more or less as they really happened to actual people in their actual lives. These characters fell in love, died, overcame challenges, confronted hard truths, had love affairs, suffered accidents, and did all the oth- er things normal people do. This was extremely comforting to Kyle, i.e., having normality represent- ed this way, in a way that was hauntingly and poignantly familiar, and that confirmed his view of what was normal, and how people normally thought and felt. It made him feel like the authors of these novels, despite all their training, and extraordinary talent, which enabled them to perceive what others couldn't and copy it all with such amazing accuracy (which was what the business was about after all), were really just normal people like he was, experiencing the same reality he was.*

bottom line was always the same. The bottom line was the bottom line ... profits, for the corporation and its shareholders.

During Kyle's tenure as Associate Professor, the Bloomberg Virtual Community College had been bought and sold by a host of corporations, each and every one of which determined to increase the profits of its shareholders. A variety of meticulously thought-out strategies had been employed in pursuit of this goal, most of them involving the complete restructuring of every department and its staff and curriculum. While providing a first-class private education to its virtual and, in some cases, physical students remained the college's number one priority, this constant restructuring did create some challenges. For example, whenever the college was acquired by a new corporation, its marketing divisions would immediately survey the courses on offer, identifying any academic Content referencing, citing or otherwise relating to the products and services of its proprietary predecessor, and then, unless that predecessor was a non-competitive subsidiary or assign, would delete that Content and replace it with Content referencing or citing its own products and services. Which, as you can probably imagine, unless properly managed, which it hardly ever was, rendered the curriculum of every subject, if not entirely incomprehensible, then muddled and confusing to the point of absurdity. Nevertheless, it had to be done. Because imagine the ire of the company's shareholders if they learned that one of the corporation's assets (e.g., the Bloomberg Virtual Community College) was actively marketing, or otherwise promoting, the products and services of one of its competitors.

This Review and Revision of Academic Content (or "RRAC") was a lengthy process, and one that was never entirely completed, as inevitably, at some late stage of the effort, the college, or the corporation that owned it, or the parent of the corporation that owned it, would be acquired by yet another corporation, which, naturally, would start the process all over. The result of all this was that BVCC was usually crawling with marketing analysts, Content reviewers, and delayering specialists, roaming the halls with digital clipboards, vivisecting lectures, eviscerating syllabi, hacking entire canons to bits, and making redundant any faculty members they deemed unwilling or unready to cooperate.

Kyle was more than happy to cooperate ... it was probably his most distinguishing feature, and his cardinal virtue, and his spiritual center, and what made him so exceptionally normal. Kyle, unlike a lot of academics, understood the logic of business. And the ways of business. And the needs of business. And the need to set the needs of business against the needs of education, and weigh those needs, and balance those needs, and, basically, to do whatever he was told. And not just in the professional sphere. Kyle, routinely, followed directions, and generally did whatever he was told. He did this in every realm, province, domain, and sector of his normal existence. He routinely followed the directions of doctors, lawyers, accountants, financial advisers, fitness consultants, management gurus, celebrities, experts, and online pundits. He carefully read and followed the instructions of installation and operating manuals, prescription labels, product inserts, those tags they sewed on the sides of mattresses ... anything that came with a set of instructions. He switched off his Viewer and gave his attention to flight attendants before departure. He scrutinized the terms of service agreements. He was not ashamed to be witnessed doing this. He was proud of doing this. It was good to do this. It was prudent, practical, and wise to do this.

This was the kind of person Kyle was, and had always been, and intended to remain ... and thus he could not begin to fathom how he had ended up sitting there, alone, on their overstuffed faux-leather eggshell sofa, in the suit he'd been wearing for the last three days, staring into the dead white screen of their HC Systems In-Home Viewer as if into a dimensionless abyss, trying to come up with one viable alternative to pressing "Security" on his All-in-One Viewer.

Which was what he knew he had to do. Which was what one was supposed to do. And was what Valentina would want him to do. And what she'd expressly told him to do. How many times had they talked about it?

"If I ever lose it ... really lose it, you make the call," she had told him, tearfully, time after time, and he had nodded and kissed her, never actually believing it could happen.

"Don't you ever do that, OK?"

"I'm trying, Kyle."

"I know. I know."

Her mother had made it well into her sixties. Valentina was only forty two ... or forty one, Kyle couldn't remember. He'd taken a lot of Zanoflaxithorinal. More than the recommended dosage. And a few Nembutrixafil. And some Thorochlorazadine. None of which had done the trick.

Two nights earlier, at 1940 in the evening of officially 02 March, he stood in the tasteful, teal green foyer of 3258 Marigold Lane, staring gravely at Valentina's Viewer, which she had not answered for the prior three days. It was resting on the spotless, smoked glass surface of their Coleman & Waterston landing strip table with the unfinished "rustic" wrought-iron legs. Her KeyCard was lying there right beside it. He'd just returned from a fascinating seminar ("The Informatics of Info-Entertainment") nominally sponsored by something called the Hakuhodo Chayevsky Foundation, but actually run by the Branding Division of InfoEducation Solutions, and convened at their luxurious corporate headquarters, a city-sized complex in Region 20. Bob Sandusky, an IES bigwig, had given a talk on Saturation Strategies, which Kyle had attended, but hadn't quite followed, distracted as he was by the series of messages he'd left for Valentina, which she had not answered. There they were, all sixteen of them, logged on the counter of her All-in-One. He'd called out her name when he came in the door and saw her Viewer and KeyCard lying there ... and received no answer. Which didn't make sense ... unless ... perhaps ... yes, that was it, she'd locked herself out, and had gone to Susan Foster's, and was sitting there waiting for Kyle to get back, and figure it out, and come and get her. However, that didn't begin to explain why she hadn't answered when Kyle had called her sixteen times from Region 20. She hadn't been sitting at Susan Foster's waiting for him for the last three days. If she had locked herself out the day before, or the day before that, she would have called Security and had them come and let her in. Which she hadn't done. So that wasn't it ... whatever. He keyed in the Fosters' number.

Susan Foster answered cheerfully.

"Foster residence!"

"Susan, it's Kyle."

"Kyle ... oh."

This was not good. "Oh" was not good.

"Is Valentina there?"

Valentina wasn't there. Susan Foster didn't know where she was. On top of which Susan sounded funny, not quite normal, more frightened than usual, and slightly sad, which made Kyle nervous. He steeled his nerves and asked her whether there had been some kind of horrible accident. Susan Foster said no, there hadn't, or at least not as far as she knew at that time. She said they needed to talk right away. She told Kyle she would be right over.

Susan Foster came right over and told him how she thought she'd spotted Valentina entering the entrance of the WhisperTrain station with her wraparound glasses and Vittorio suitcase and her hair all a mess. Actually, she was sure she had spotted her. She'd called out her name, but Valentina hadn't answered. "She looked upset," was how Susan put it, "or agitated ... definitely agitated."

"Agitated" was really not good. "Agitated" was "off her medication." "Agitated" was NormalSpeak for borderline Anti-Social behavior.

"Should we call somebody?" Susan suggested.

Susan Foster was Valentina's friend, so she knew the details of her medical conditions, and her family history to some degree, and was naturally concerned for her personal welfare. In addition to which, the way it worked was, if someone you knew went off their medication, or behaved in an otherwise unstable manner, you needed to get them some help right away, to prevent them from harming themselves or others. You needed to do this by alerting Security, which was who Susan Foster meant by "somebody."

"I will," Kyle assured her, "I'll call tomorrow."

"Tomorrow?"

"Look, let's not overreact here. Maybe something happened to Walter."

"Her father?"

"Let me make a few calls."

"I wanted to wait until I talked to you, Kyle."

"I appreciate it, Susan."

"But it's been three days."

"I know."

"It's just."

"I know. Don't worry. I'll talk to Walter. I'll handle this, OK?"

"Call me tomorrow?"

"I will. I promise."

"Because."

"I know. I will. I promise."

The next two days were Kyle's worst nightmare ... there was nothing to do but sit and wait. He knew he couldn't call her father, or anyone else on her contact list. If he had, the Network would have picked up his KeyWords, run the recordings, and alerted Security. He couldn't go out looking for her either, because where would he start? He had nothing to go on ... except for all that shattered black glass, or whatever it was all over the kitchen, the jagged, pea-sized fragments of which he had tried in vain to reassemble into whatever object it had originally been, which he speculated might have been a vase, except ... whatever, it was totally hopeless. He'd ransacked the house and was relatively certain that she had been in his desk and had taken some Viewers ... some ancient, seriously obsolete Viewers, which wouldn't even connect to the Internet. Which rendered them useless. Which didn't make sense. Nothing made sense. He was losing his mind. He needed to sleep. He could not sleep. He called in sick and sat there and waited. He swallowed more pills, and imagined scenarios, flipped through six hundred channels of news, ransacked the house again, and ground his teeth. He scoured the Internet for "preemptive detentions," and poured through the records, which numbered in the hundreds, but none of them sounded like Valentina. He knew this was risky, as they would correlate his searches and flag his account for suspicious activity. But what else could he do? He had to do something. Hour by hour, minute by minute, the crisp clear image of his normal existence, *their* normal existence, his and Valentina's, and the baby she was finally carrying, was breaking up, dissolving, warping, the pixels bleeding into each other, meaning collapsing into chaos, which he wasn't prepared to just sit there and watch. Whatever had happened that had set her off, which had something to do with that mess in the kitchen, wherever she was, whatever she was doing ... clearly, Valentina had lost it. Based on Susan Foster's description, it sounded like she had lost it completely. Where did she think she was going with the suitcase?

She couldn't get on a plane like that, with her hair a mess and those big black sunglasses ... no, she had to have taken a train. To where? Kyle had no idea.

The thing was, it had been five days, or nearly five days, since Susan had seen her ... five whole days since she'd gone full-blown, during which Kyle had not called anyone, not Pewter Palisades Community Security, not Hadley Security, not any Security. He hadn't even contacted Doctor Graell, who he knew would immediately call Security. He hadn't even called back Susan Foster, who at this point had possibly called Security. This was not at all like Kyle, this lapse in judgment, this failure to act, to do what one did in times of crisis. His All-in-One fleeped. It was Georg Borovsky, Dean of Marketing at BVCC, hoping Kyle was feeling better. He wasn't. He flagged and saved the message. The time on the screen was 0840. The time was time to make a decision. He could not go on sitting on the sofa praying to the One Who Was Many to save him. He needed to do what needed to be done ... which was press the "Security" key with his thumb. Once he did that, that would be it. They would plug her into the SkyNet system and GPS her and track her down. They would track her down and find her and help her. Men in puncture-proof armor would do this. These men would turn her over to doctors, who would diagnose her, and help her further. They would help her with sedatives, serious sedatives, and possibly even four-point restraints, to prevent her from harming herself or others. They would do this in a locked facility, with visiting hours, for an indefinite period. This would happen no matter what. He could not save her. He knew he couldn't. Whether he, or Susan, or some fellow passenger, or random pedestrian made the call, or she flipped and started raving in public ... or whatever, the details didn't matter, this ended with Valentina in the hospital. So why not simply press the key and get it over with? Why was he waiting? Did he think she was going to walk in the door, collapse at his feet and beg him for help? She couldn't even get back into the Community ... not without her KeyCard she couldn't.

"Press the key," he told himself. "Press it already."

He could not press it.

Every minute he delayed the inevitable increased the danger he was already in. Even if he pressed it right this minute, this second

... now ... now ... now ... he was going to have to answer a lot of questions, questions he could not begin to answer. Beginning with why he'd been sitting around over-medicating on his eggshell sofa and not calling anyone for five whole days. He hadn't, of course, he'd been at the seminar, but that wouldn't matter, and was no excuse, because what did that say about his ability to function as a normal, responsible person, a caring husband, a soon-to-be father, an Assistant Professor of Info-Entertainment at the Bloomberg Virtual Community College? How, if he couldn't even monitor his wife, could he be entrusted with the education of his virtual and in some cases physical students, much less with raising and nurturing an infant, a child ... a Clarion, all by himself?

"Press it. Press it now ... now."

The sooner they got her into the hospital, the sooner she'd be safe, at least. And the baby ... it would be safe at least. And the sooner he could answer all those questions. He'd do his best. He had nothing to hide. He'd tell them the truth. He'd cooperate fully. He'd let them search the house if they wanted. They could search his office ... whatever they wanted. He'd ask his doctors to send in his records. He would call on his colleagues at BVCC (those few who were left), who would all attest to his unimpeachable and unswerving normality. They'd likely put him on supervision, and up his meds, but that was OK. He would make it through this, and so would she. She would have the baby in the locked facility, and Kyle would take a leave of absence, and raise her himself, which ... he could do that. His mother would probably fly in and help him, and Susan Foster would certainly help, and eventually Valentina would improve, and they would let her out and she would come back home, probably even better than ever, and life ... and life ... could go back to normal.

"Press it. Stupid. Press it. Now."

Why? Why was this happening to him? How, and when, had he chosen this Path? Was all of this some kind of spiritual test, some trial by fire, or initiation, the One Who Was Many was putting him through? He couldn't remember asking for it. He'd never prayed for insight, visions, evolution of his mind and body, or initiation into the Mysteries. He didn't want it. He liked who he was. He liked his life exactly as it was. All he wanted, and had ever really wanted, was what the majority of people wanted ... a normal life. A normal family. A normal townhouse in a normal Community. A normal job at a normal college, owned by a series of normal corporations ...

His All-in-One tweaked. It was Susan Foster, wondering whether he'd made that call.

"Press! Press the fucking button!"

Kyle Bentley-Briggs could not press the button. Something deep inside him couldn't. Something Kyle did not understand, and did not want to understand, and feared, and wished would go away, or wither up and die inside him. He broke down sobbing. Heaving. Convulsing. He switched on the HC HomeSystems Viewer and turned up the volume to mask the sound. He pushed his face into a puffy pillow and sat there on the sofa and screamed. He wailed. He wept. He keened and whined, the muscles in his face contorting as if they were taking massive Gs. It felt like maybe his ribs were breaking. His hands were coiled into fists, and the pain ... and he cursed the One and the fucking Many ... and the tears ran down his face like rain.

He called Greg Cramer at 1640 from his Business Class seat on the southbound WhisperTrain. He was on his way back from Breckenridge Village, where he had visited Catherine, who had told him nothing. However, one of the Seaview aides had been kind enough to check the logs and confirm that Valentina had spent the day (i.e., the day before he left on his trip), or the better part of that day, with Catherine ... doing what, exactly, Kyle couldn't imagine. Catherine was completely uncommunicative. It wasn't the kind of thing you could fake. Kyle had studied her for five or six minutes. She was not in there. No one was. No, whatever Val had gone there looking for, she hadn't gotten it, not from Catherine ... and yet, she'd come home and ordered that box of whatever it was from EasyStore Storage. Maybe she had hallucinated something. Something which had set her off. Whatever it was had something to do with all that broken black glass in the kitchen, which Kyle had sealed in a Ziploc bag and locked in a drawer in his desk in the office. That was after he took a quick shower ... by which time he had already decided to definitely probably call Greg Cramer

Kyle had decided to call Greg Cramer shortly after he awoke on the sofa, where he had finally passed out and slept for two hours after weeping convulsively for who knew how long. He awoke with a headache. The Viewer was blaring. He clicked it off and sat there trying to remember who he was and what had just happened. Then he remembered his cousin, Greg Cramer, who worked in some Info-related department of the Hadley Corporation of Menomonie, Wisconsin, and who the odds were probably knew somebody who knew somebody who worked in Security. It wasn't much, but at least it was something. If he contacted Greg, and Greg was willing, and he knew the right people, and had any juice, strings could be pulled, corners cut, possibly even blind eyes turned, and Valentina could be delivered to Kyle, and not to a locked-down hospital facility. In any event, it was worth a shot. However, before he took that shot, he wanted to ride up to Breckenridge Village and talk to Catherine, or the staff, at least, and gather what information he could ...

He called Greg Cramer from the southbound Orange at 1640, and got his assistant, Lorie, or something, who was not a real person, and who asked if she could ask what it was regarding, which she did, then promptly put him on hold. After a minute, Greg picked up. Kyle couldn't say very much on the phone, but he told Greg it was a Security issue involving Valentina, and Greg was no dummy. He seemed to be willing, even eager to help. He suggested they meet that night at Rosie's. Kyle agreed, and rerouted accordingly.

Rosie's was one of these exclusive upscale simulated downscale cocktail lounges where the scuz on the tiles in the restrooms was fake and a blue-gray haze of certified-harmless pseudo-cigarette smoke hung in the air. It was down at the bottom of the business district, right on the border of Center City. The bartenders all had spray-on tattoos. The waitresses dressed like aging prostitutes. The bar was festooned with emerging executives, Variant-Positives with designer stubble, loosened tie-knots and perfect teeth, shouting into their Viewers and implants and drinking their non-alcoholic beers out of dirty glasses that weren't really dirty. Everyone in there was over thirty.

Cramer was waiting in a booth in the back. He waved Kyle over. They ordered their drinks, HalfLife whiskeys, which were alcoholic, but the buzz wore off after twenty minutes. They switched off their Viewers, and Kyle laid it on him. He spilled his guts. He told Greg everything.

"Wow. Man. I'm really sorry."

"I didn't know who else to turn to, you know?"

"Totally. No, you did the right thing."

"Is there anything ... anyone ... what can we do here?"

"I don't know. Let me think for a minute."

Cramer sat there and thought for a minute, or just stared across the room intently, looking like he was thinking for a minute. The Viewer behind the bar was running some soft-core porno, or an ad for condoms. A Swedish android with gargantuan breasts stared into the lens of the camera and cooed and drooled as she licked her own nipples.

"OK, listen. Here's what we'll do. I know a guy who knows a guy in Domestic Security who owes me a favor."

"The guy in Security?"

"No, the guy who knows him. Let me talk to him."

"OK, good."

"Maybe my guy can get his guy to flag her as a drug reaction."

"A drug reaction?"

"Happens all the time. Somebody takes the wrong combination, temporary psychosis ensues. You get 'em, sedate 'em, no muss, no fuss. Released to a doctor or family member."

"Really?"

"Yeah, but, look, don't get your hopes up. It's worth a try, but it's not a sure thing. Drug reactions stay domestic. That's what we want. Domestic is good. If it goes Territorial, forget about it. Hospital stay, then Special Needs City. If we can get my ..."

Cramer stopped mid-sentence. A derivatives trader with an eyebrow piercing was passing their booth on his way to the men's room. Cramer waited until the coast was clear.

"Let me talk to my guy tomorrow. The only thing is, technically speaking, the incident report needs to come from a doctor. Who's your psychiatrist?"

"Graell, at Cleveland."

"Cleveland Medical."

Kyle nodded, gravely.

"Forget about that then."

"So, what? That's it?"

"No, but we'll have to work around that. We're going to need copies of both your prescriptions."

"I'll send them tonight."

"Send them tomorrow."

Cramer sipped his whiskey slowly.

"How many people know about this?"

"Me, you, one of the neighbors."

"A neighbor?"

"Susan. Susan Foster."

"Married?"

"Yeah. It's her and her husband."

"She told the husband?"

"No. Well ... maybe."

"OK. We assume she told the husband. Kids?"

"No. They're grown. They're gone. Why?"

"It's nothing."

"Why? What are you thinking?"

"Nothing. It's nothing. Drink your drink."

Kyle hadn't touched it. He picked it up. His hand was shaking. He set it back down. Cramer leaned in and whispered to him.

"Look, stuff like this. It happens all the time. To all kinds of people. Hadley people ... or not to them, but to family, you know. Wives, kids. Arrangements get made. Thing is ... it's got to be handled cleanly."

"Cleanly?"

Cramer didn't respond.

Someone up at the bar was laughing.

"I'll do whatever is necessary, Greg."

"I know you will, buddy. But let me handle it. You go home and get some sleep. Clean yourself up. Go back to work."

"What do I say to Susan Foster?"

"Nothing. Tell her you called it in."

Cramer scanned the room a moment, waved down a waitress and gestured for the check. Kyle automatically reached for his wallet.

"No. I got this."

"You sure?"

"Yeah."

Cramer had his company card out ... the Hadley slogan embossed at the bottom. He was watching the Viewer behind the bar, or staring off in that direction at least.

"Everything happens for a reason, right?"

"What?"

Kyle turned and checked the Viewer. The nipple-licking Swedish android was walking through a tunnel that went on forever ... or no, it wasn't the Swedish android. It looked like ... was it Kiki Brezinski?

"Everything happens for a reason."

The tunnel wasn't a tunnel either. It was just a MoveWay in a mall somewhere.

"Right ... I guess. I mean, sure ... yes."

"How far along is she?"

"Who?"

"Val."

"Oh. Three months ... three and a half."

Kyle was having trouble concentrating.

"Boy? Girl?"

"Girl."

"You name her?"

"Zoey, we think."

"Zoey. Nice."

The screen dissolved to an aerial shot ... skimming across an endless field of bright green genetically-modified soybeans. The smiling face of "Jimbo" Cartwright faded in above the horizon. The waitress arrived and took Cramer's card. Neither one of them looked at the waitress. Her name was Tamara. She was in her forties. She lived in a studio in Center City and worked the night shift six nights a week. The moment Cramer walked into Rosie's and took a six-top booth in her station, she'd made him for a lousy tip.

Sarah's Game

Three months earlier, so back in December, presumably right around the time Valentina was having her spiritual awakening in the lobby of 6262 Lomax after finding out she was finally pregnant with the Clarion baby both she and Kyle wanted, and that was going to make everything so much better, Taylor was starting to begin to believe (or at least he was starting to begin to suspect) that getting involved with whatever faith-based, baby-smuggling Terrorist outfit he'd unknowingly gotten himself deeply involved with had maybe not been such a brilliant idea. Things were getting complicated ... or maybe they had always been complicated, and Taylor, in his fervor to save Cassandra, and dump this baby on the baby smugglers, and get a little action on the side in the process, had seriously misjudged the whole situation.

For starters, he'd been wrong about Sarah. She didn't come in ninety seconds. It took her about twenty-five minutes, actually, the first time at least, back in early November.

What had happened was, a few days later (i.e., after their initial Pussyhorse meeting), while Jamie, or Jamé, or whatever her name was, was reading the Standard Eighth Revision of the Standardized Preamble to all A.S.U. meetings, she'd leaned up, Sarah, who in some kind of seriously special ops fashion had snuck up behind him, and whispered in Taylor's ear again. She wanted to meet alone, she whispered ... which Taylor figured, here we go. By this time, of course, he'd completely forgotten his vow to keep things on a businesslike basis, and he was looking at another five excruciating months of sitting around in the back of these meetings pretending to resist all Corporatist oppression, and he was bored, which Anti-Socials were prone to, and up for a little sexual distraction. He figured Sarah was also bored. She didn't seem all that engaged with the D.A.D.A., which was clearly mostly Adam's thing.

They met that night at a bar called Frankie's, down in the thick of the deep Inner Zone, took a few sips of their lukewarm beers and retired to one of the rooms upstairs, where Sarah promptly sat him down on the bed and did not rip his clothes off. Instead, she said they needed to talk. Which was fine with Taylor. Taylor could talk. Taylor was more than happy to talk. Taylor knew how to talk to women. He had no problem talking to women. It wasn't like he was some heartless hard-on whose only interest was in getting his nut. Taylor had sat and talked to Cassandra (or at least he had sat and listened to Cassandra) on several occasions, for nearly an hour. No, Taylor could definitely talk to women. Just normally not at a place like Frankie's. People didn't go to Frankie's to talk. People went to Frankie's to fuck. They also fucked at home, of course, and up against walls, and ... well, wherever, but if you wanted some privacy, you went to Frankie's, or one of the other sex clubs like Frankie's, and so, naturally, when Sarah suggested Frankie's, Taylor figured that's what she wanted, which it turned out it was, but after they talked, which, if Taylor had known, he'd have brought his beer up.

The thing was, for Sarah, unlike for Taylor, sex was not a simple, physical, animalistic, instinctual act, but, rather, was a complex, quasi-spiritual, ritual experience involving "levels" and "stages" and assorted "states of surrender" that one "attained" and "explored" and "heightened" through the use of certain fairly common but nonetheless deviant sexual practices, about which Sarah was very specific. She told him exactly what she needed, how she needed it, how long she needed it, how she'd probably act when she got it, and what would probably happen if she didn't. She said of course she'd understand if Taylor wasn't into such practices, and couldn't provide her with what she needed, and so wanted to call it off right then, in which case there would be no hard feelings, and it wouldn't affect their baby-smuggling plans, which deviantly fucking Taylor at Frankie's in any event had nothing to do with. Taylor, bless him, was undeterred.

By late December, 2609, the Year of the Mekong Giant Catfish, and 6370, and 2049, and all the other years it officially was, they were meeting three, four times a week, and going at it like a couple of fuck monkeys. They met at places like Frankie's, Henry's, and Hardcore Carla's, and the original Darkside, which were sleazy, deeply Inner Zone dives with rooms upstairs you could rent by the hour, or (as in the case of the original Darkside) straight ahead old-fashioned BDSM clubs, the ones with the swings and slings and cages, and the antique dentist chairs, and all like that, but also with private rooms you could use, because Sarah, whose deviant sexual behaviors were very specific, was not an exhibitionist.

Now the thing you have to keep in mind, in terms of deviant sexual behavior in the Age of the Renaissance of Freedom and Prosperity, is that among the Normal population (where Sarah had begun her sexual activity, and had likely discovered her deviant proclivities), sex was somewhat complicated, or fraught ... or was like a potential minefield. It wasn't that the Normals didn't have sex. They did. The Normals enjoyed having sex. Sex was a healthy, pleasurable activity. There was absolutely nothing wrong with sex. On the contrary, sex was strongly encouraged, and openly celebrated, and widely marketed, and constantly discussed and fleeped and tweaked about, and taught in schools and workshops, and so on. And it wasn't like the Normals didn't get kinky. They did. The Normals got totally kinky, but they did so in a non-aggressive, loving, mutually respectful manner that had nothing to do with, and bore no resemblance to, anything approaching sexual abuse, or sexual assault, or rape, or torture, or that "potentially stimulated ideations or sexual fantasies involving same." According to the DSM XXXIII, sexual practices which crossed that line (wherever it was, which wasn't that clear) and led to such ideations or fantasies (of being raped, say, or sexually tortured, or of performing such acts on another person) were clearly symptoms of late-stage disease, and sexually deviant, and designateable. Which meant the Normals had to be careful, very careful, extremely careful, as all it took was one complaint by a sexual partner, or husband or wife, that one was possibly having such fantasies, and that would be it, they'd be off to the hospital, and eventually off to a Quarantine Zone, where rumor had it rape, abuse, and other somewhat more consensual but no less violent sexual practices, although officially forbidden, were fairly rampant ...

Which, all right, in this case, the rumors were true. It wasn't that the Zone was a non-stop rape-fest, or some kind of year-round S&M orgy, but people did tend to get raped a bit, and the deep Inner Zone was definitely home to a staggering number of seedy establishments where Anti-Social Persons could go and indulge in a variety of deviant practices.

Class 3 Anti-Social Person that he was, Taylor was not entirely inexperienced when it came to deviant sexual practices. In fact, prior to "settling down" with Cassandra (as Taylor had taken to calling it at some point), his sexual adventures had been of a nature some might describe as indiscriminate. In his wilder days, with a head full of whiskey, or sometimes tequila, or rum, or gin, but mostly just good old DMLX, he would hop in the sack with just about anyone, and do whatever, or almost whatever (everyone has their limits, naturally). During the course of these dissolute decades, Taylor had been with tops, bottoms, switches, witches, yankers, spankers, electrical sadists, shavers, ravers, garden variety garment fetishists, women who want-ed to whip or be whipped, to call him names, or to be called names, to pee or be peed on, poo enthusiasts, asphyxiophiliacs, needle freaks, and a couple of women who could only come if you tied them upside down and did this jackhammer thing while they masturbated.

Sarah was nowhere near in that league. Actually, once she let go of her head, or attained her state of surrender, or whatever, she wasn't all that deviant at all, or at least not in Taylor's professional opin-ion. The thing was getting her to that point, which took some time, which was fine with Taylor, as long as it eventually led to the two of them screaming together at the top of their lungs as their heads exploded with violent orgasms that shot up their spines like electric currents, and not to Sarah convulsively sobbing in a fetal position for thirty-five minutes. What usually worked was binding her wrists and ankles to the rusty old wrought iron bedposts (or, if available, the stainless steel eye-bolts some helpful person had attached to the wall) and then teasing her mercilessly for twenty-five minutes. Halfway through this, she would start to beg in a half-hearted "listen-to-me-begging" kind of way, which Taylor had learned to ignore completely. When the begging didn't work, and the teasing continued, she'd get aggressive and order Taylor to stop with the fucking tongue already, or the wax, or ice, or nipple clamps, or pinching fingers, or nibbling teeth, or whatever he happened to be using at the time, and fucking untie her ankles and fuck her. Then, when Taylor did not untie her, and the merciless teasing with the tongue, or fingers, or the Pyrex dildo with the clitoral stimulator, or whatever he happened to be using, continued, she would lose it completely, her body convulsing and shuddering in waves as she had this series of mini-orgasms that punched little holes in the wall in her head that she had to get through. Now, the crucial thing at this stage of the process was to not let up and untie her too soon, which would leave her hanging and plunge her into The Pit of Despair and Uncontrollable Sobbing, which once that had happened she wouldn't be able to move or speak for extended periods. Occasionally, this was unavoidable, but usually it was if Taylor kept on teasing her until her eyes rolled back in her head and she finally let go utterly. Then, and only then, he'd untie her, which he normally managed in just under four seconds, pulling the cords of the quick-release knots he'd had to relearn, and practice tying, at which point Sarah would spring up off the mattress in a state of animal frenzy and throw him down on his back and mount him and just fuck them both completely senseless.

Which OK, technically, made her a switch ... but that wasn't what it was with Sarah. No, with Sarah it was all about "surrender." And not just sexual and emotional surrender. Spiritual surrender. Complete surrender. The way she'd explained it to Taylor, repeatedly, was that what she needed was to let go utterly, as in to lose her self (by which she meant her identity, or ego, which ideally needed to be shattered to pieces) and fuse with some unnameable something, which Sarah insisted was not God ... but which sounded a lot like God, to Taylor.

According to Sarah, this unnameable something was neither God nor The One Who Was Many (which Taylor didn't get the distinction), but, rather, was something virtually identical, yet essentially different in every way. She had tried to describe this essential difference (or differences, as they were apparently infinite), unsuccessfully, to Taylor, repeatedly. All of it sounded suspiciously like the Normals' bible, *The Path(s) to Prosperity* (except for the part where spiritual enlightenment made you rich, or the other way around).

For example, whereas the Normals believed that "everything happened for a reason," Sarah, and whatever group she was with, believed that "everything happened as it had to." Whereas the Normals trusted in the "Will of the One," Sarah trusted in the "Wheel of Becoming," which was what she claimed her triskelion tattoos with the sixes or the nines were supposed to be. "Surrender" wasn't giving up, or having faith in any deity, it was some kind of radical affirmation, "affirmation without judgment," of life and death, love and hate, joy and suffering, and … well, basically, everything.

And OK, that was fine with Taylor … affirmation of life, or whatever. He didn't quite get what it had to do with resisting all forms of Corporatist oppression, or the smuggling, or hiding, of unauthorized babies, but it wasn't like he really gave a shit either. No, the thing that was starting to gnaw at Taylor by late December 2609 was … OK, it was actually several things.

The first of these several things was Sarah, who (Taylor wasn't a total idiot) was almost certainly a faith-based Terrorist, and all this convoluted crap she was spouting, and whatever her real agenda was. See, the thing was, while Taylor was perfectly willing to help her surrender whatever it was she needed to surrender, without judgment, and affirm whatever, and fuse with whatever, and slip one finger up his ass and bounce up and down at lightening speed on his cock as if possessed by whatever … all this faith-based Terrorist hooey was starting to make him a little nervous.

Another one of these several things (these things that were starting to make Taylor nervous) was the fact that, as far as the baby smuggling went, nothing, or virtually nothing, was happening. Taylor, apart from fucking Sarah, had been sticking to his normal routine as ordered. There'd been a few further clandestine meetings at the Pussyhorse Lounge to go over "logistics" and "coordinate" various "action contingencies," but these had all been perfunctory affairs. Taylor wasn't privy to operational details, like how they were going to "transport" the baby (or the "package," as Adam was calling it now), or where they were going to "transport" it to, so there wasn't much for Taylor to do until Cassandra actually had the baby, at which point he would "collect the package," "conceal the package" in a Transplant bag, and "transport it to the rendezvous point." The rendezvous point had not been determined, but logistics dictated it was going to be one of the covered alleys off Jefferson Avenue. It wouldn't be Cassandra's alley, of course, as it didn't lead anywhere and was thus a deathtrap, but one of the other covered alleys that snaked back into the warren of lanes that lay to the south and west of Cassandra's, like the one behind the little Fruity Juice stand ... or wherever. They'd tell him whenever they told him. It wasn't like he had any say in the matter.

Yet another one of these several things that were making Taylor uncharacteristically nervous (in addition to whatever Sarah's game was, and the dearth of movement on the baby-smuggling front) was the timing of the tentative projected launch of the Day of Autonomous Decentralized Action, "stage three preparations" for which, according to Adam, were now well underway. Although the launch date remained a secret (or hadn't been consensually decided on yet), based on the more or less totally made-up inception date that Taylor had provided, Cassandra's "projected delivery window" over-lapped the "base parameters" of Adam's "projected D.A.D.A. launch window," which meant that it was entirely possible that whatever debacle these idiots were planning would have already started when Cassandra gave birth, and theoretically might be in full swing. If it was, and assuming the D.A.D.A. was actually anything resembling what these morons were envisioning, IntraZone Waste & Security Services, and possibly even Hadley Domestic Security, would, by the time Cassandra delivered, have (a) locked down the entire Zone, (b) declared an indefinite curfew, (c) dispatched Security Specialists to occupy the streets and quell the disorder, and (d) otherwise made it impossible for anyone to smuggle out unauthorized babies.

Taylor, at one of their Pussyhorse meetings,* had shared these concerns with Adam and Sarah, who had smiled at him like he was some kind of idiot and advised him to stick to his normal routine. This was Adam and Sarah's mantra, "No deviations ... stick to the plan" ... which OK, one, they hadn't told him the plan, and two, what were they ... fucking parrots? How many times did they need to say it? Taylor got it. "No deviations." Adam would say it extremely

---

* Which Taylor had lately come to dread ... he couldn't have told you why, exactly, the place just felt all wrong somehow.

slowly, then he'd give him that condescending look. Taylor fucking hated that look. Who did this dickless Transplant asshole think he was with his fucking looks, and his jargon, and his over-articulation? So he had read some fucking books. Taylor had read some fucking books. Taylor had read a lot of fucking books, and he didn't much care for Adam's attitude. He was thinking maybe, when all this was over, assuming Adam wasn't a bug splat, he would take him down to the Dell Street Canal and deviate his face a little ...

Oh yeah, and another one of these things, these multiple things that were making him nervous, the primary thing that was making him nervous, was how he was now, on a routine basis, having to evade the Community Watchers who appeared to be trying to incompetently tail him every fucking place he went. Oh yes, they were definitely all over Taylor ... and had been since back in early November. And it wasn't just an A.S.U. thing either. (There were always a couple of Community Watchers hanging around outside of meetings, taking down names to feed to their handlers, but they didn't tend to follow people home or anything.) No, oh no, this was definitely personal. The Watchers were all over Taylor, specifically. Not that the Watchers were a problem in themselves, totally incompetent at surveillance as they were.* No, the problem was, if the Watchers were on him (which they were, they were seriously all up his ass, as in they knew where he lived and his patterns, and so on), that meant that IntraZone Waste & Security had taken an ongoing interest in him, and had him on some kind of Terrorist watch-list, and at some point were going to want to detain him, and anyone who even vaguely knew him, which would inevitably lead them straight to Cassandra.

Now at this point it never occurred to Taylor that the increased heat he was feeling from the Watchers had anything to do with Adam and Sarah, or their baby-smuggling operation, directly. Whatever he thought of each of them personally, they were clearly dedicated hardcore Terrorists, who had been doing this stuff for quite some time (as in without getting caught and detained, and liquidated). Adam was Mister Security Culture. Weasel that he was, he ran a

---

* They didn't exactly blend in or anything, walking around in their khaki uniforms, which were really just matching khaki work clothes, rubber rain boots, and faux-leather belts.

ZONE 23   283

tight ship. His Chinese walls, need-to-know-bases, and the other extensive security measures the Fifthian Cluster routinely took, intensely annoying as Taylor found them, he had to admit, were extremely effective. And Sarah moved around like a ninja. You never saw her coming or going. She seemed to just appear and disappear. He would sit around somewhere, waiting for her, turn his head, and there she would be, as if she had just materialized next to him. He didn't understand how she did that. No, this heat was coming from somewhere else, somewhere closer to home, Taylor thought ... closer, as in from Apartment 2E.

Someone he knew was cooperating.

Taylor hated Cooperators. He hated them with a thick black bile. He hated them more than he hated the Normals, who he hated, but who he still regarded as people. Cooperators looked like people, walked like people and talked like people, but actually they were a sub-human species of slimy fucking bootlicking sycophants who would rat you out for a pat on the head from anyone in anything resembling a uniform. The Zone, of course, was lousy with them, mostly in Sectors A and B. They got their name from the tag that ran at the end of all the IntraZone Content and was printed at the bottom of the forms and posters.

THANK YOU FOR YOUR COOPERATION!
... IntraZone Waste & Security Services, Inc.

Due to his Anti-Social condition, Taylor could not begin to fathom what the fuck it possibly was that made a person want to cooperate. He figured they were probably born that way. It had to be some kind of neural malfunction. Logically speaking, it made no sense. It wasn't like it got you out of the Zone or reclassified Normal, cooperating. It didn't get you anything, really, aside from better housing, maybe, or a better shit job in one of the plants, which, OK, granted, was more than nothing, but hardly justified the risks they took. Cooperators, as you can probably imagine, lived in a permanent state of fear of egregious violation at the hands of the 3s, most of whom, if given the chance, would summarily waste them on general principle. No, it had to be a serious mental short circuit, was the only way that Taylor could explain it, because why else would a human being (or any other type of sentient organism) cooperate with an occupying force of cheerfully sadistic ravenous parasites who were living off the fruit of his labor, and who clearly, eventually, meant to kill him?

But whatever ... all that was academic. The relevant question at the moment was, who was fucking cooperating on him? Meyer? No. It wasn't Meyer. Meyer was somehow in league with Sarah, who Taylor was right on the verge of deciding was not only Adam's direct superior (at least regarding the baby-smuggling), but was likely part of some whole other network that Adam had little or nothing to do with, and that the A.S.U. was just one small part of, or was possibly just an elaborate front for.* Claudia? No, it wasn't Claudia. Claudia was harmless. She always had been. Plus, she didn't know Taylor's patterns. She hardly knew her own fucking patterns, ripped out of her fucking gourd on various substances as she was. Coco Freudenheim? Not a chance. Coco would sooner cook and eat Dexter than cooperate on her worst fucking enemy (not that Coco had any enemies ... or not any living ones, or not anymore). Alice Williams and Rusty Braynard? Taylor couldn't even entertain the thought. OK, sure, they were all strung out on Plasto, which technically made them likely ... but the two of them were basically ersatz family. Sylvie? OK, possibly Sylvie. Sylvie had always made him nervous, mostly on account of she was so nervous, which Taylor didn't get what the fuck was wrong with her. Dodo Pacheco? Very possibly. Dodo Pacheco was a spineless weasel, and a degenerate Plastomorphinol fiend, and a known associate of Rudy Rebello, a ratfaced scumbag of the lowest order who Taylor wouldn't put anything past him, but he hadn't seen Dodo Pacheco for weeks.

---

*Taylor, on a lark one night, while Meyer was passed out drunk in the kitchen, had snooped around in Meyer's papers, which were filed, in no immediately apparent order, in cardboard boxes stacked in his room along one wall from floor to ceiling. He'd found, among a wide assortment of Meyer's scribbled notes on his theories, a faded print-out from who knew when, from some currently non-existent website, with pictures of various triskelion designs, sun wheels, ancient Hindu swastikas, and Greco-Roman and Byzantine swastikas, and runes, and snakes that were eating their tails, and other suspicious faith-based symbols. He'd also found maps. A lot of maps. Not just maps of the United Territories, upon which Meyer, or someone, had noted the locations of various corporate headquarters, but also maps of the Recovering Areas, upon which patterns of dots and lines and numbers, which Taylor interpreted as distances, had been penciled in by Meyer, or somebody. The maps must have been from different ages, as the geography of the Recovering Areas didn't quite match on any two maps. You didn't notice that right away. You had to really examine them closely.

Oh yeah ... and if all that wasn't enough, Sarah's game, whatever it was, and whatever faith-based Terrorist network she was probably almost definitely with, and whatever their ultimate agenda was, and being left out of the baby-smuggling plan, and Adam and all his condescending bullshit, and the D.A.D.A. launch date, and the fucking Watchers, and whoever was fucking cooperating on him, there was also the whole Cassandra Situation involving her nosy and annoying roommates.

At this point, Cassandra had been "sequestered" (otherwise known as locked in her bedroom) for over a month, and was four months pregnant, and bored out of her fucking mind. She'd been locked in there since mid-November, peeing, mostly, and occasionally puking, into a little blue child-sized plastic bucket that Taylor had to carry across the hall to the bathroom and empty out. He did this just before sunrise each morning, legs still shaking from his sessions with Sarah, brain misfiring from lack of sleep, having dragged himself there from the Darkside, or Carla's, or some similar sleaze-pit in the deep Inner Zone. The bucket was Taylor's brilliant idea, and was meant to prevent Cassandra's roommates from getting suspicious, which they already were.* Prior to Cassandra's sequestration, and Taylor's deployment of the plastic bucket, she'd been in the bathroom half the day, peeing, or being convinced she had to pee ... which all right, was already fairly suspicious, but was back before she started showing, so was mostly just inconvenient for her roommates, who took to standing in line in the hall, wondering in loud annoying voices whether Cassandra was all right, and so on. What was even more suspicious, the way they saw it, was that one day everything was relatively normal (except for Cassandra's excessive peeing) and the next day she was locked in her bedroom, and no one could see her, except for Taylor, who Cassandra's roommates lived in fear of and did their level best to avoid. It wasn't that they were all friends, the roommates. They weren't. Well, OK, a few of them were, with each other, that is, but not with Cassandra, who they also did their best to avoid. The reason there being, if they knocked on

---

* He'd intended to purchase a normal-sized bucket, but all they had the day he went to the CRS were these child-sized buckets, the kind the Normals gave their kids to play with at the indoor beaches.

her door, wanting to converse about roommate stuff, like missing food or neglected garbage or whose hair this was in somebody's soap, Cassandra would often be in there with Taylor, a giant Class 3 Anti-Social Person with scars on his face and crude tattoos they made by hand with sewing needles all over his arms and chest and back, and they'd both be in there grunting and shouting, and punching holes in the wall with the bed ... and sometimes Taylor would answer the door and stand there, naked, with his scars and tattoos, and his drooping but still half hard-on, grinning, and ask them how he could possibly help them.

Or at least this is how it had frequently gone ... until that day in mid-November when Cassandra was suddenly locked in her bedroom and wouldn't come out, or even open the door, and the only sounds they could hear in there now were the Content disks she was always watching, which didn't sound like In-Zone programming, and so were probably some kind of pirate Content that Taylor had killed some helpless Class 1 Anti-Social Person and stolen.

Now the cover story was that Cassandra had caught this strain of mutant Hepatitis or something, which Taylor was somehow totally immune to, but Cassandra's roommates probably weren't, and so basically, what they needed to do was to not come knocking on her bedroom door inquiring as to whether she had eaten some roommate's fucking Egg-o-Likes or GM tomatoes, and to stay in their rooms, or the kitchen at least, and out of the fucking hallway entirely. Unless they were using the bathroom, that is, which they really shouldn't have been doing anyway, due to the risk of serious infection from the mutant Hepatitis ... and so on. Taylor had told this ridiculous story to two of the smaller and more timorous roommates, Tawanda Rae and Fyodor, or something, who'd nearly lost control of their sphincters being in Taylor's presence for two minutes. He'd instructed these two to tell the others, but not to tell anyone else they knew, unless they wanted to get evicted, and possibly isolated, and possibly worse. A few days later, one of the larger, not-so-timid and more annoying roommates, Jules, or Joel, or whatever his name was, who wore these tribal earlobe rings that Taylor found particularly asinine, had apparently made some smart-ass comment casting aspersions on the Hepatitis Story, which Cassandra had heard another roommate repeating in the hallway with her ear to the door, which the following morning, upon his arrival, anxiety ridden, she'd reported to Taylor. Taylor promptly stomped down the hall and into the kitchen, identified this Jules, took him aside by the throat and scrotum, and strongly dissuaded him from making such comments. Taylor, as Fyodor would later attest in his official statement regarding the failure of Jules, or Joel, to report to work at his factory job, could be very dissuasive. Unfortunately, he could also be rather transparent, which wasn't a serious disadvantage when it came to lying to Cassandra's roommates, who were only half-listening to what he was saying, and were mostly just trying to discern what he wanted them to do so as not to get egregiously violated ... but it didn't fly at all when it came to Cassandra, his transparency, and bald-faced lying, and so on.

Cassandra, in addition to feeling bloated, and to thinking she had to pee all the time, and to being bored out of her fucking mind, was also getting increasingly nervous, and suspicious, and was asking a lot questions, which was making it impossible for Taylor to sleep, and was building towards an ugly breaking point regarding Taylor's deflections and lies.

Just that very morning, for example, Cassandra, having woken up in one of her moods, and the bedroom being an airless cauldron that stank like sweat and fish and pee, had been less than enchanted with Taylor's bullshit.

"So what is it, now you're in love with this whore?" she inquired as she peed down into her bucket. She was holding her skirt up and clear with both hands, squatting directly over the bucket. Taylor was staring at her mid-term belly. It was round and small, but it was definitely there. He hadn't seen one for thirty years.

"All I'm saying is, they took care of what's his name ..."

"Prosky."

"Whatever. They did what they said. You're safe."

"Am I?"

"You got your sick time."

He lay back on her futon, exhausted.

"What if somebody checks?" she asked.

"They won't."

She wiped herself off with a rag.

"How do you know?"

"They won't, all right? And even if they do, it doesn't matter. It's in the system. You had an accident. Fuck ..."

Cassandra got up off the bucket, let her skirt down and joined him on the bed.

"You don't know anything about these people."

"It's the fucking A.S.U., all right?"

He'd spared her the faith-based Terrorist details.

Cassandra drew her legs in and crossed them.

"They've done this hundreds of times," he continued. "All this shit is standard procedure."

"And fucking the fathers. Is that standard procedure?"

"I'm not fucking Sarah."

She laughed in his face.

"Please. I know when you're fucking someone."

"When this is all over, you'll meet them, OK?"

"When this is all over, we'll probably be dead."

She pulled her skirt up and curled and tugged at her pubic hairs, which Taylor hated.

"Stop."

"What?"

"Stop pulling them out."

"It doesn't hurt."

She yanked one more out, then pushed her skirt down and sat there pouting.

"All they want is the baby, right?"

"Right. So?"

"So *think*, dummy. You know their names. You know their faces. Why would they leave you walking around ... someone who could identify them?"

Taylor had been having the same thoughts recently, but he didn't want her to get all hysterical.

"And how could they fake an accident for me? They'd have to hack the MedBase system. Who can do that?"

"They can, apparently."

"A.S.P.s ... from inside the Zone?"

Cassandra was right. Taylor knew it. He reached for her hand. She pulled it away.

"What?"

"We never should have tried to do this."

Later that night, while fucking Sarah in a particularly redolent room at Carla's, Taylor remembered his conversation with Cassandra that morning, and lost his erection. Fortunately, by this time, Sarah had already achieved her "levels" and "states of surrender," and was nearly worn out, having come several times. Taylor, who'd been holding back and had screwed up his timing, had not come once, and so was now, officially, sexually frustrated.

Sarah reached over and took hold of his cock. It flopped around limply. She worked it a minute.

"What's going on," she asked him, finally.

"Can I ask you a question?"

"OK," she said.

Some kind of aircraft was rumbling overhead.

"What happens to us when this whole thing's over?"

"You and me?"

"Me and Cassandra."

"Oh."

"Yeah."

He was taking a chance here.

"Nothing. As long as it goes by the numbers."

She sat herself up.

"What are you thinking?"

"You're going to leave me walking around ... knowing who you are?"

"Oh, you know who we are now?"

"I know your names."

"Names are nothing."

Someone, maybe two rooms over, screamed like an animal being slaughtered.

Taylor sat up and turned to face her.

"I'm serious. What are we doing here?"

"Fucking, I thought."

"Cut the crap."

"What are you asking me?"

"The MedBase records. Cassandra's accident."

"What about it?"

"Who can do that? Who are you people?"

Sarah looked into his eyes for a moment.

"It's complicated."

"Simplify it for me."

Taylor waited.

"I can't," she said. "But I can tell you what I know, or some of it."

"Go," he said.

"Roll me a smoke."

Taylor reached over and grabbed his tobacco.

"Number one, there is no us ... not like you mean. There's no central structure. There are people who work with certain people, who work with certain other people, who work with certain other people ..."

"Yeah, I get the decentralized thing."

"The people who hacked the MedBase files, who got us your files. I don't know those people."

"Then how the fuck do you know who they are?"

"Because I know a person who knows a person ..."

"What about Adam?"

"What about him?"

"He's one of your people ... who know other people?"

"Adam has his things. I have mine. I help him with information and what not. He helps me with the babies from time to time."

"The babies are your thing."

Sarah nodded. Taylor handed the cigarette to her. She lit it with the candle beside the bed.

"What do you do with them?"

She smoked her cigarette.

"We send them out of the Zone in vehicles. The drivers are 1s with Travel passes. The drivers drive them out of the Zone. They meet up with other people outside. They meet at different rendezvous points. The drivers wait there. These people show up. They take the babies and drive away."

"Drive them where?"

She exhaled smoke.

"I don't know."

"Who are the drivers?"

"I told you, I have no idea."

"You don't fucking know who these people are?"

"No."

"Well, OK, how do you contact them?"

"We don't, directly. We contact someone ..."

"Who contacts someone ..."

"Who contacts someone. That's how it works. That's as much as I know."

Taylor sat there processing this.

"So you're saying you have no clue what you're doing. You have no idea where the babies end up."

"We have an idea."

"But you don't fucking know. How do you know you're not handing them off to Security Services?"

"I know."

"How?"

"I told you, it all comes down to faith."

"You going to start with the God shit again?"

"You know that's not what I mean by faith."

"Faith in what then?"

"Other people. Faith in ourselves. Faith in something."

"Something."

"Does there have to be words for everything?"

"And the Autonomous Zones?"

Sarah smoked.

"Fuck."

"Why are you doing this, Taylor?"

"What?"

"This baby is not your problem. Why do you give a shit? Why are you doing this?"

"For Cassandra."

"You love her."

"Sure. Whatever."

"You love her. You feel responsible for her."

"So?"

"So you're willing to risk your life to save her life, and the life of the baby. You could have aborted it. You still could, probably. Or just wait until it's born and drown it. Why did you come to us for help?"

Taylor didn't have an answer for that.

"What do you think the corporations do with them?"

"I don't know."

"Neither do I. You think it's something sweet and nurturing? You think they rock them to sleep at night, dress them up in little Corporatist onesies?"

She flicked her ashes onto the floor.

"Meyer says they condition them or something, turn them into Security Specialists."

Sarah laughed.

"What?"

"Nothing. Imaginative, is all. Who's this Meyer?"

Taylor studied her eyes for a moment. She looked on the level, but what he did he know?

"No one. Conspiracy theorist friend of mine."

"You trust him, this Meyer?"

"I don't trust anyone."

"Yes you do. Or you wouldn't be here."

"Gee. You got me all figured out."

They sat there a moment, facing each other, naked and wet as the day they were born. The candle was throwing their shadows onto the wall across from the foot of the bed.

"How do you think the corporations perform their little magic trick?"

"Magic trick?"

"Maintain their power. How does a minority control a majority?"

"With guns."

"No. Not with guns. Think, Taylor. About the Zones. Hundreds of thousands of A.S.P.s are controlled by a couple of thousand Specialists?"

"Specialists with guns, and gas, and missiles. Which we don't have."

"Give me a break. If we all rose up and attacked them at once? How many of us do you think they could kill before we overwhelmed them and took their weapons?"

"Never happen."

"There it is."

"There what is?"

"The magic trick. That's their power."

"What is?"

"You. Your mind. Let me ask you something."

She took a quick drag off her cigarette here.

"What do you believe in?"

"What do you mean?"

"You don't even know."

"But you're going to tell me."

"You believe in the same thing the Normals believe in."

"The One and the Many."

"No."

"Then what?"

"Nothing."

"Nothing?"

"That nothing matters. That we're out here in space on a big ass rock spinning on its axis for no real reason. That all this is some kind of cosmic accident. That life is a competition for survival ... until we all fucking die, and the planet dies, and the universe dies, and sucks back up into its own asshole and returns to nothing."

She took another drag on her cigarette here.

"How does that sound? Sound familiar? That totally meaningless and depressing story? Because that's what it is. It's a fucking story."

"A story."

"Yes. A creation myth. Every age and empire has one. They're the lenses we're issued to look at the world through. This morbid little myth is their fucking story."

"The Normals."

"No. The corporations. The Normals are no different from us, essentially. Except for a few material comforts. Their lives are just as empty as ours are. They're just as hopeless and doomed as we are. They're not our enemies."

"No? Who is then?"

"I don't know. The story itself. It begins with nothing, and ends with nothing. Or the logic, or something there aren't words for. Something that gets inside our brains and breaks our spirit and starts us thinking, 'fuck it, we're never going to change things anyway, and nothing really matters anyway, so we might as well give up and go along.' People don't start out hopeless, Taylor. It happens to us. They do it to us. They do it to most of us when we're kids."

"The babies."

She nodded, and took a quick drag.

"You think that someone you know is cooperating? You want to know who's cooperating? You are. We are. Everyone is. Believing their story. Watching their movie. But to most of us it doesn't look like a movie."

"What does it look like?"

"It looks like this. It looks like just 'the way things are.' Most of us don't even realize it. We don't even remember when we started doing it. Do you? Do you remember, Taylor?"

"Remember what?"

"When you gave up?"

Taylor's head was spinning slightly.

"By the time we reach the age of ten, or twelve, and start to think for ourselves, we're already trapped inside their story ... we're thinking their thoughts, asking their questions, perceiving the world within the narrow limits of their sad little Corporatist myth ... which is just like any other myth, or faith, or body of faith-based beliefs, except that it denies its existence as such, and passes itself off as scientific fact ... medical fact ..."

Taylor laughed.

"What?"

"The Pathologization of Everything."

"Right. Wait. Where did you hear that?"

"I don't remember."

She snorted out smoke.

"You're lying. Whatever. It doesn't matter. Pathologization is just the latest form. We've been doing it since the dawn of the species. 'The first and most cardinal means of controlling the masses is the mental conditioning of the children.' That's a quote. I didn't make it up. It comes from a book I'd like to show you. It all comes down to faith, and the children. Am I freaking you out now?"

"A little, yeah."

She offered the rest of the cigarette to Taylor. He shook his head. She took it back. He was staring past her at the wall at nothing.

"So ... the babies ... what are you saying, exactly? You're saying the Autonomous Zones are real? You're ... what? You're raising them ... you're teaching them ... what?"

"I told you, I don't know all the details. I've never been out there. My work is here. But yes, basically, that's what's happening."

"Or what you want to believe is happening."

"What I choose to believe is happening."

"I don't get it. What's the point? There can't be that many."

"Babies? No. That's only part of it. There are other projects."

"The D.A.D.A."

"Sure, the D.A.D.A. is one of them."

"It's suicide. You know that."

She smiled sadly.

"What can I tell you? Diversity of tactics. It's more a recruiting tool than anything else."

"It's going to get a lot of people killed."

"Like I said, there are other projects. Keeping the resistance alive in the Zones is important, but it's never going to be enough. It's the Normals that are really the key to everything."

"The Normals."

"Yes."

"You're going to wake up the Normals?"

"The Normals are the only hope we've got."

"You're kidding, right?"

"They're people, Taylor. The Variant-Positives are still people, anyway."

He studied her eyes. She seemed to be serious.

"How could we have hacked the MedBase? Who got us your files? Who are the drivers? These are your questions. The ones you asked. Who could do that?"

"Normals, you're saying."

"They're people, Taylor. They still have souls. I should know. I was one of them."

He'd forgotten for a moment that she was a Transplant.

"And the Clears?"

"No. The Clears aren't people. Or they are ... people, but not like us. Whatever they do to them seems to be permanent. They don't respond to ..."

She exhaled smoke.

"Have you ever talked to one?"

He shook his head. Most of the IntraZone Specialists were Clears, but they didn't exactly engage in conversation.

"I grew up with some of them. I think I did. They were regular kids in a lot of ways. In other ways ... I don't know ... something's missing. Nothing bothers them."

"Because they're fucking robots."

"No. They're not. It's weirder and more fucked up than that. They're just like people. They have emotions ... certain emotions, like love and sadness, but it's like they're in total control of their feelings. They can cry, but it's not like actual crying. And they don't get angry. And they do not hate. And I don't think they can really feel fear. They can do these things, or some of them can ..."

She trailed off and stared into space, reflecting, remembering.

Taylor sat there and watched her.

"So what's the plan for dealing with them?"

She stared down at the roach of her cigarette.

"Yeah ... well, we're working on that."

Borderland

Ten weeks later, in the sunless depths of a phantasmagorical cosmic sea of apparently timeless, spaceless space that had no beginning and went on forever, the Undead Thing that had no name, but which was clearly the malificent spawn of IT, or IT incarnate, or both at once, was coming to murder her, and eat her brain. The monstrous macrocephalic head of it (the prehensile octopoid beak of which was going to chew right through her skull and slurp out her brain like cottage cheese) was slowly turning, or revolving, toward her, its own amphibian brain expanding ... the black, blind monocular fish-eyes shifting slowly from the sides to the front of its pinkish, piglike mask of a face. Its ears were empty, soundless pinholes, portals back to some inconceivable muteness that was even more horrible than silence, because there'd never been a single sound, or surface off which sound could resonate, or time for sound to travel across that utter nullity from whence it came. It floated toward her, the unseen seer (because she was somewhere in there as well, in that timeless, spaceless void, or whatever), this wormlike, phylogenetic freak. She could see inside it, the Undead Thing. It was not breathing. And yet it lived. Its neurons were firing, its organs budding, its shriveled pollywog heart was beating, follicles sprouting, intestines rotating, its fingered flippers flapping, groping, reaching, and just as they were going to touch her ... Valentina woke up screaming.

Fortunately, no one in the immediate vicinity could hear her screaming, or much of anything else, other than the roar of the turbofan engines of JiffyJet Airlines Flight 43, which had just taken off and was thundering across their rooftops at three hundred kilometers an hour. Plaster dust was wafting down from the ceiling. Light bulbs were flickering. Windows shaking. The AC was definitely still not working. The vent was farting fetid bursts of humid air down into the room, which already stank of mildew and sex and something else she couldn't identify. The temperature in the room was 36C. Outside it was well over 40. Blades of sunlight were stabbing in through the gaps in the curtains, which didn't quite close, and were made of some cheap kind of tangerine orange heat-absorbing synthetic material. Everything in the room was orange. Or it was yellow. Or some feculant shade of brown. She sat there, naked, dripping sweat, the sweat-stained sheets and scratchy old blanket dangling down from the foot of the bed where she'd kicked them off in her sleep, apparently. The roar of the jet engines peaked and faded.

Ten seconds later, it started all over.

She'd had the dream for three nights running ... or three times in succession anyway. They weren't all nights, the times she'd slept, or hadn't slept, or had kind of slept, or had drifted in and out of semi-consciousness wearing her wraparound SeaSyde shades. The first night she'd spent on the aisle of a row of sticky seats in an AllNite Cinema, her suitcase wedged in firmly beside her. There were fourteen other patrons in the theater. She vaguely remembered bits and pieces of the family-friendly animated features ... stories based on super-heroic action figures, or talking animals, the voices of which were read by actors that everyone knew and loved and followed, household names like Brad McGrueder, Gigi Duprey, XR7, Beatrix Nivens, and Thor Esposito, who all had family-friendly images and lived on their private islands in the North. These were all standard formula pictures (with indistinguishable plots and settings designed to appeal to the broadest possible family demographic of the global audience) in which some murderous virus-like villain menaced some obvious representation of Normal society and its democratic values, and was either vanquished by the superheros or spiritually enlightened by the talking animals. Valentina did that thing where you keep passing out for two or three seconds, and your head droops down, chin to chest, then jerks back up and your eyes shoot open. Every time she drifted off, there it was again, coming toward her, the Undead Thing, to eat her brain.

The second night she spent in a series of Cocoa Rococo Co. Free Trade coffee shops nursing an array of undrinkable beverages with fanciful Cuban- and Italian-sounding names. She hadn't been able to sleep in these places, but at least she'd been able to relax a while in those comfy, mass-produced faux-leather easy chairs (which they had at every Cocoa Rococo Co.) and stare out the window as if waiting for someone (and do that nodding off head-bobbing thing), and occasionally ask the helpful staff, who she'd told she had a bladder infection, for the KeyCard to the customers-only restroom and slip in there and compulsively masturbate.

The third night she broke down and got the hotel room, by which time she could barely walk. She could hardly think. Her thoughts kept drifting. Two and a half days she had been wandering aimlessly, dragging her Vittorio suitcase behind her, doing her best to avoid the cameras, and compulsively masturbating only when necessary. Days she had spent at the Northside Mall, which was air-conditioned, and where she felt anonymous, periodically pretending to shop in low-end stores like Bullseye Bazaar, but mostly just resting on the podlike benches beside the old ladies with their aluminum walkers. On several occasions she'd slipped into the public restroom, which anyone could use, and had loaded the MemCard, as instructed, and the files had come up, but that was it. Whoever she'd established contact with, back at home on the HCS60, and who had sent her down there to Center City, whether it was actually the N.I.N., or just one of the corporate Security Services, she'd had no further contact from them.

Finally, at approximately 2100 in the evening of officially 02 March, 2610, H.C.S.T., she'd checked into the Skyline Motor Lodge, a stainless steel and concrete atrocity down at the end of a former strip mall that had been converted to residential use. Families of non-abundant Normals were living in the spaces that had once been stores, pizza restaurants, lottery kiosks, or discount dental and medical practices. These were the people, Variant-Positives, who did the jobs that no one else wanted, construction workers, plumbers, fitters, servers, cleaners, window washers, taxi drivers, scanners, painters, gardeners, inventory clerks, and the like. They lived down there in Center City, a rundown but basically liveable area where the airport, warehouses, waste facilities, reactors, and a lot of light industry was located.

Center City, which was not a real name, but was what the Normals called the area, completely surrounded the Quarantine Zone and so served as a sort of protective barrier between it and the Residential Communities. Affluent Normals did not go down there, except on very rare occasions, like if they happened to own a business down there and for some reason needed to stop by in person, which they almost never needed to do. They definitely did not wander the streets with ostentatious designer suitcases. Not that it was in any way dangerous. These people were, after all, Variant-Positives, and took their medications like everyone else. It was more just the general scarcity of affluence, and the overall shabby look of the place, the downmarket stores, the tacky restaurants, and the way people dressed, which was, frankly, embarrassing.

The Skyline Motor Lodge offered a view of a parking lot lined with waste receptacles. The only motor vehicles in sight were HVAC and other service-type vans, the sides of which were stenciled with names like Chavez HVAC, Associated Plumbing, Donny's Pest Control, and Wally's Burritos. Milton Hadley Memorial Airport was just down the road, or its runways were. Flights took off every forty-five seconds, mostly massive commercial aircraft (all of which were biofueled, of course), but also fleets of corporate jets, and UAVs, and Security fighters, which barely seemed to clear the rooftops as they pulled up into their initial ascents. Checking into such a hotel, or any hotel, was a bad idea.* However, she simply had to sleep. She'd taken the tram to the end of the line ("Industrial Boulevard," she thought it read) and staggered into the Skyline lobby, an odiferous, orange-carpeted space where poorly dressed people with unusual haircuts were sleeping, or were trying, on sofas and chairs, in front of an ancient wall-mounted Viewer that was running the Evening Market Report. She'd smiled at the desk clerk, whose name she'd forgotten ... Kim, or Kham, or Khun, or something, mumbled some nonsense about "visiting relatives," paid in advance with Kyle's Endeavor Card, took the KeyCard, dragged her suitcase up the stairs

---

* The details of the Normals' purchases were instantly transmitted to DataWorld, Inc., or to one of the lesser demographic aggregators, who then sold the data to their corporate clients, who distributed it to their marketing divisions, who shared it with their Security divisions, or sold it to outside Security Contractors. All of which of course was perfectly legal. Data sharing was a proven deterrent to potential Terrorists, and Terrorist plots, and a powerful marketing tool, and so on.

to Room 303, stumbled in, pulled the curtains, peeled off her pant-suit, collapsed on the bed, and dreamlessly slept for eleven straight hours. Early that morning, so 03 March, and Day 555 in the Year of the Lemur (and all the other dates it supposedly was), she awoke from the dream of the fetus, screaming.

At ten weeks, technically, it was a fetus. An organism. A human being. An incredibly small and slimy human being, but nonetheless a human being. Which is to say a human fetus, as opposed to just a fertilized egg. An egg was ... well, it was just an egg. An egg was not a human being. An egg was part of a woman's body, like any other part of a woman's body. This was not a part of her body. This was a body in and of itself ... a body attached to her, from her, of her, but not a part of her, growing inside her. She wasn't showing, or not to speak of, so she couldn't see it, but she could feel it in there, forming, hatching, feeding on her. It was not hers, this thing inside her. No. They had put it in there. Doctor Fraser, Kyle, all of them. The smiling men with rubber gloves who said relax and spread her legs and shoved their plastic tubes up into her. They spurted their mutant seed inside you and grew these things that looked like people but weren't people ... or maybe they were ... in another sixty, seventy years, they, the Clarions, would be the majority and people like her would be the minority, the abnormalities, the mutants, the freaks ...

"Everything's relative," the voice in her head said.

"No it isn't," Valentina replied.

The voice in her head was just a tape. This one was. There were other voices.

"They aren't human."

"What is human?"

She wasn't supposed to talk to the tape.

Repeating her mantra on her breaths to drown out the tape of the voice in her head, she forced herself up off the sweat-soaked bed, her naked body coated with a film of plaster dust that was streaked with sweat, staggered into the filthy yellow bathroom, which smelled like toe jam, and turned on the shower. Her doubts were fear. That's all they were. Fear was OK. Fear was normal.

"Not this kind," the tape in her head said.

"The loving, compassionate oneness of ..."

The lukewarm rotten egg-smelling water dribbled in rivulets down her body, backing up out of the rusty drain and into the slippery mildewed basin. Another plane was flying overhead, knocking tiny chunks of moldy grout out from between the tiles. She reached out and pressed her palms against them and closed her eyes and tried to recall the devastating, irreproachable clarity she'd received in her Lomax Escalator Vision. Time, or something, was stealing it from her ... sucking the essence of it out of her. What had seemed at the time so incontestable, so undeniably revelatory, so utterly profound and epiphanic, looking at it now from a different perspective (i.e., that of the voice on the tape in her head), was possibly nothing but paranoid nonsense. She turned the plastic knob on the faucet, making the shower as cold as possible, and stood there under it, breathing deeply.

"The multiplicitous oneness of ..."

What if the tape in her head was right? What if she had simply lost it due to some weird hormonal reaction and had abruptly ceased her meds for no reason, exacerbating her already probably pretty advanced dissociative state, and had run away from Pewter Palisades, leaving behind her All-in-One, and was pointlessly standing in this slimy shower having an acute psychotic episode? No, she wasn't. She hadn't done that. She couldn't have done that. This was real.

"None of this is real, darling."

Yes it was. All of it was. The tape was a liar. She knew what was real. The MemCard inside the Hand was real. It was right there in her Vittorio suitcase, along with the HCS60 Viewer ... physical objects, ergo real. The files were on it. They were real. The conversation she'd had with the Viewer ... someone was there, on the other end. But then why had she not received a message from whoever it was when she'd reloaded the MemCard? She'd reloaded it here, in Center City, in the public restrooms at the Northside Mall, and here in her room at the Skyline Motor Lodge, which was what they had told her to do, was it not? Yes. It was. She remembered that clearly. She wasn't dissociative. The tape was a liar ... she couldn't remember when the tape had started.

She switched off the shower and exited the bathroom dripping cold (or coldish) water, lay down on the uncomfortable bed, and compulsively masturbated for fifteen minutes. Turbines roared through the sky above her, drowning out her moans as she came. Her orgasms helped to untangle the thoughts that were tendrilling through her mind like vines, leaving just the essential questions.

Focus, Valentina, focus ...

What if it wasn't the N.I.N. who had sent the message when she'd loaded the MemCard? What if it was Security Services? No. It wasn't. She wouldn't be lying there. She would be in a bag in the back of a van. So, OK, if it wasn't Security, then it had to have been the N.I.N. But then why would they leave her hanging like this? It didn't make sense, unless ... unless ... no. Yes. She had to consider it. What if there had been no message? (Her heart rate was steadily elevating now.) What if the HCS60 was real, and the MemCard was real, but not the message? Was it possible? Yes. It was. Not very likely, but certainly possible. In which case Kyle would have called Doctor Graell, who would have called Security, who would be here by now ... which they weren't, so that didn't make sense either. Nothing did. Nothing made sense. She lay there, naked, hyperventilating.

"What if none of this is really happening?"

Listen.

Still your thoughts and listen.

Ignore the tape in your head and listen.

What if she got up off the bed and got her clothes on and took her suitcase and went back home to Pewter Palisades and confessed to Kyle, who loved her dearly? Could things go back to the way they'd been? No. They couldn't. Of course they couldn't. Things never went back to the way they had been. Whatever you did was done forever. Time proceeded pitilessly forward. Whatever was or wasn't real, Kyle, by now, had called Security, if nothing else to report her missing. They were out there, right now, looking for her. What could she do then? She couldn't stay here. They were likely on their way here already. No, she had to keep moving, but where? She couldn't just drift from hotel to hotel, circumnavigating Center City, not indefinitely. She had to go somewhere. But there wasn't anywhere to go ... except home.

She sat up and bent down and opened her suitcase and got out the Viewer and loaded the MemCard. The files came up, as they had each time. She clicked on a file. It would not open. The prompt came up and asked for the password. She did not have it. She sat there and waited.

Nothing happened. Absolutely nothing.

She set the HCS60 aside, got up and got the remote control, and switched on the wall-mounted Courtesy Viewer. The Morning Market Report was playing. An attractive young Clear named Pei Lin Moreno was chirping about a new edition of some kind of software you apparently needed to run some other important software. Valentina muted Pei Lin and read the news that was always running on the creeper at the bottom of every screen.

The expected high was 44C. Extreme heat advisories remained in effect. Due to a massive low-pressure system that had formed below the 40th Parallel and was slowly, ominously, drifting north, viewers below the 50th Parallel were advised to stay tuned for further advisories. Consumer confidence, however, was high. Shares and factory orders were up. And, sorry Chip, this was just in ... Jimmy "Jimbo" Cartwright, III, was back in the hospital receiving treatment for the metastatic intestinal cancer that had spread to his liver, and several other organs, but that according to his team of leading oncologists, cardiologists, gastroenterologists, and assorted other medical experts, was under control and was definitely treatable.

Valentina stared at the screen.

"What if this is also treatable?"

"Stop it."

"This is probably very treatable."

The tape in her head was trying to confuse her. It was trying to get her to subscribe to the theory that whatever it was that was wrong with her brain, and had caused her to totally lose control and inappropriately raise her voice in the lobby of 6262 Lomax after inappropriately bursting into disturbing peals of demented laughter as Doctor Fraser grinned down at her like some kind of frightened cartoon baboon, then violently experience spiritual enlightenment on the escalator to the WhisperTrain station, and go off her meds, and begin a cycle of compulsive and excessive masturbation, and then disappear from Marigold Lane, and not even take her Viewer with her ... that maybe whatever had caused all that was not a legitimate spiritual awakening, nor any other type of bona fide enlightenment, nor the sudden, catastrophic progression of her latent Anti-Social Disease, but was some anomalous chemical reaction that had something to do with early pregnancy and that was probably, if she simply got up now and walked back to the WhisperTrain station, and took the train back to Pewter Palisades, and confessed to Kyle, and sought help now, was something simple ... something treatable.

Virtually everything, at this point, was treatable. The vast majority of pernicious diseases, debilitating ailments, chronic complaints, dysfunctions, deficiencies, and so on, were treatable. Eating, sleeping, and sexual disorders. Sadness, anger, insecurity, envy, jealousy, boredom, fear ... all these negative emotions were treatable. Most of the organs of the body were replaceable. Traumatic or distasteful memories were erasable. Even Anti-Social Disease, although incurable, was certainly treatable. Surely whatever she had was treatable.

Valentina stared at the screen.

"Jimbo" Cartwright was descending the steps of one of his fleet of private jets. Pei Lin Moreno was looking "confident."

Life was treatable.

Death was treatable.

Treatable ... if not yet entirely preventable.

Just last year, Kenneth Bainsbury, another illustrious giant of industry, had succumbed to complications of Leukemia, or Hodgkin's Lymphoma, or Myeloma, or some other hematological malignancy. The year before that it was Ariel Harrington, the powerful InstaMedia magnate, who had died at the age of one hundred and twenty of an astrocytoma, or some other glioma, or some kind of anaplastic something.

The screen, which it looked like someone had sneezed on, had gone to black for a half a second, and now it was running the opening sequence of that classic Mister Mango commercial where the children all gather in the field at dawn and await the return of Mister Mango.

Valentina stared at the screen.

She could feel it in there ... feeding, growing.

The aluminum frames of the windows were rattling.

"Jimbo" Cartwright was dying of cancer.

Everyone was dying of ... something.

In the Age of the Renaissance of Freedom and Prosperity, nobody ever died of old age. When people died, and they did, eventually, often well into their fourteenth decades, unless there'd been some horrible accident, they died of something, something specific, something with a medical-sounding name. Which was usually cancer, but was not always cancer.

Nine times out of ten it was cancer.

People died of a variety of cancers, intestinal, lung, and liver cancers, colorectal and prostate cancers, bladder cancers, pancreatic cancers, bowel, blood, and bone marrow cancer. Or, if they didn't die of cancer, and there hadn't been some horrible accident, they died of some other disease or condition, like bronchopneumonia, or Alzheimer's disease, or vascular or frontotemporal dementia, or chronic obstructive pulmonary disorder, or myocardial or cerebral infarctions. Occasionally, they died of renal failure, or pulmonary thromboembolisms, or sudden cerebrovascular accidents, or any of a number of other diagnoses. They never simply died of old age.

The field, or steppe, or endless expanse of digitally-generated golf course green upon which the shamelessly naked ranks of cherubic Clarion children gathered side by side in symmetrical rows and all held hands went on forever.

Valentina stared at the screen.

They died of diseases, genetic defects.

Mister Mango appeared in the heavens.

They died of mistakes, unfortunate accidents.

The children raised their arms in unison.

They died of infections, invasive organisms.

Valentina stared at the screen.

Mister Mango pursed his lips and blew a beam of orange light down onto the upturned faces of the children.

The mango-colored Oneness of the ...

Valentina was a histopathologist.

Death was, theoretically, treatable.

She lived in a house on Marigold Lane.

Death was theoretically treatable.

The screen dissolved to an ad for Jammys, the anti-oxidant breakfast fruit bars, which came in a range of natural flavors.

In the Pewter Palisades Private Community.
Valentina, the Destroyer of Worlds.
Orange, pineapple, kiwi, banana.
The screen dissolved to the dream of the fetus.
The mother who wasn't her mother was Death.
A message came in on the HCS60.
It beeped, once, then vibrated briefly.
Valentina snatched up the Viewer.
TURN THE TV OFF.
She clicked it off. A paroxysm of spastic texting ensued.
CURRENT LOCATION IS NOT SAFE.
I KNOW.
RELOCATE IMMEDIATELY.
WHERE?
SOMEWHERE SAFE.
WHERE?
OFF THE NETWORK.
Where was that?
OK, she texted. THEN WHAT?
Nothing.
She stared at the screen.
Nothing. Then ...
DO YOU TRUST US?
YES.
YOU SURE?
YES.
Nothing. She sat there, waiting.
THEN TRUST YOURSELF.
I DON'T UNDERSTAND.
YES YOU DO.
Yes ... she did. Or some semi-conscious part of her did. But how did they know that? Wait a minute. Were they watching her through the HCS60? Watching her sleep? Watching her masturbating? They knew she'd been hallucinating.
I THINK I'VE BEEN HALLUCINATING.
HOW CAN YOU TELL?
STOPPED MY MEDS. WITHDRAWAL SYMPTOMS.

Nothing.

PLEASE. CAN YOU HELP ME?

MAYBE. DEPENDS.

DEPENDS ON WHAT?

ON WHAT YOU WANT.

She sat there paralyzed.

WHAT DO YOU WANT?

I WANT TO GET OUT.

OUT OF WHAT?

OUT OF HERE.

AND THEN DO WHAT?

JOIN YOU. FIGHT.

FIGHT ... WHAT?

She hesitated. Then she typed it.

IT.

Nothing. She sat there and waited.

WHAT IS IT?

I DO NOT KNOW.

YES YOU DO.

CAN'T EXPLAIN.

WHAT DO YOU WANT?

I TOLD YOU ...

NO.

Something was wrong. They didn't trust her.

SOMETHING ELSE.

YES?

She typed it.

TEN WEEKS PREGNANT.

No response.

ARE YOU STILL THERE?

VARIANT CORRECTED?

YES.

Nothing. She thumbed the keypad.

ARE YOU STILL THERE? HELLO?

YES.

CAN YOU HELP ME?

NO.

WHY?

YOU KNOW WHY.

NO I DON'T.

Yes she did. She typed the question.

BECAUSE I NEED TO DO IT MYSELF?

YES.

Her stomach clenched like a fist.

I CAN'T. WHY?

IT CAN'T COME WITH YOU.

Of course it couldn't. She knew it couldn't.

HERE?

NO. SOMEWHERE SAFE.

"You realize that's Security, don't you?"

"Shut up."

She had to ignore the voice. She texted frantically.

I CANNOT DO THIS.

YES. YOU CAN.

She couldn't type. Her fingers were shaking. Her head was spinning.

CAN'T YOU DO IT ONCE I GET THERE?

NO. YOU HAVE TO DO IT THERE.

The room appeared to be titling sideways, trying to spill her off the bed. She lay down flat on her belly on the mattress and fingered the keypad.

HOW SHOULD I DO IT?

YOU KNOW HOW TO DO IT. YOU'RE A MEDICAL PROFESSIONAL. DO IT. THEN RELOAD THE MEMCARD.

She lay there staring at the message on the screen.

IN OR OUT?

"What are you doing? Are you out of your mind?"

She could not do this.

IN OR OUT?

"Do you know what you'll be?"

IN ... OR OUT?

She fingered the keypad.

IN.

GOOD. NOW EJECT THE MEMCARD.

Valentina ejected the MemCard. She tried to sit up, which did not go well. Her elbows buckled. Her arms gave out. She collapsed face first onto the bed, curled up into a fetal position, and lay there staring at the orange carpet. She wasn't actually staring at the carpet as much as into a sea of orange acrylic water in which she was drowning, and had been pretty much all her life. Tired. She was so terribly tired. Every muscle in her body was tired. Her teeth were tired. Her hair was tired. Words could not convey the crushing magnitude of how tired she was. She dragged the fusty sheets up from the foot of the bed and pulled them toward her. She slithered and wriggled around in the bedding, writhing like an unearthed worm. Flurries of orange plaster flakes were floating down on her like toxic dandruff. The bed was shaking. The vent was sputtering air like gas from a cancerous colon. Her vulva was red and raw and swollen. She got her hand around it and squeezed. The pain was good. The pain was real. The pain was what was keeping her going ... whoever she was, whatever she was ... whatever she was now becoming ... Valentina Destroyer of Worlds, prophetess of the One Who Was Many ... Terrorist ... suicide ... filicide ... freak ... there were too many words and names for everything ...

"Baby murderer," the voice in her head said.

No. No. It was just a tape.

Transplant Blues

Part of Taylor's normal routine, from which he was absolutely not to deviate, was that shortly after the sun began to drop below the western horizon, or at 1830, whichever came first, or whenever Cassandra left for work, he'd slip back out of her bedroom window, down the fire escape, into the alley, which, although the TōFish tent was closed, continued to intensely reek of TōFish, turn left onto Jefferson Avenue, and walk back home to Mulberry Street. Jefferson Avenue, at this time of day, was nowhere near the teeming mass of Anti-Social humanity it was in the mornings when the outdoor markets were open, but it wasn't exactly tranquil or anything, because the corporate stores would be back in business and the sidewalks packed with sweat-drenched 1s on their way to work in the plants and factories, which were located out in the Northeast Quadrant where hardly anyone officially lived, and they would all be wearing their variously colored, color-coded company ensembles, which looked like pajamas, except for the footwear, and prominently featured the company's logo, as they walked right at him staring blankly ahead at nothing like a herd of zombies. Also, by this time, the Security gates would be processing the line of returning vehicles, and the Security Specialists with their UltraLite rifles milling around outside the little bunker-style Security stations, where they sat out the heat of the day in comfort, and the Public Viewers would be booming out whatever time it would be at the tone, and running ads for beer and liquor and tobacco products and Plastomorphinol, and the avenue crawling with company shuttles, which were also color-coded and prominently branded for ease of identification purposes, and IntraZone Waste & Security vehicles, and assorted tricked-out A.S.P. cars and go-carts and scooters, and other such vehicles, and Remotely Piloted Aerial Vehicles, would be hovering overhead, and so on.

Cassandra, under normal circumstances, would be walking east on Jefferson Avenue, lost in that herd of pajama-wearing zombies. She'd be making her way to her privileged job at the GCH Components factory, where she and hundreds of other equally privileged 1s all sat in rows of contaminant-free assembly tables from 1900 to 0500 and contributed to the manufacture of various highly-advanced components of the state-of-the-art consumer products the Normals could not live without … but these were hardly normal circumstances.

Officially, Cassandra had suffered an accident and had hairline-fractured a lumbar vertebra, and was absent from work with a doctor's approval, which would stand up to scrutiny, according to Sarah. In reality (whatever that meant anymore), Cassandra was locked inside her bedroom, with her cravings, and her abnormally massive gravidity, and her heightened sensitivity to the heat, and mood swings, and general irritability, peeing into a plastic bucket. So she wasn't exactly in the best of moods. Neither was Taylor, who had just about had it with being the exclusive human being she had had to take her shit out on for the last three months of this fucking nightmare. On top of which, now she was totally paranoid about how much her nosy and annoying roommates (who were taking turns tiptoeing down the hall and listening at her door all night, then conferring with each other in secret in the kitchen, about her) knew, or strongly suspected. They worked at different plants, she'd explained, so one of them always had the night off. She suspected they had worked out some kind of rota by which to monitor her every movement. She could hear them out there breathing, she swore, their ears pressed up against her door, noting how often she got up to pee, or moan, on account of her massive gravidity, or what she was watching for the hundredth time on her shitty little offline pirate Viewer. Oh, and also, forget about sex. Sex was out. There was no sex. The baby was crushing her internal organs. The last thing on her mind was sex. Technically, she was now six months pregnant, but Jesus fucking Christ she was big. Way too big, in Taylor's opinion. He was starting to worry that they had screwed up somehow and had seriously miscalculated her inception date.

He slipped out the side of the TōFish tent and headed west through the oncoming 1s, scanning faces in the crowd for Watchers. And OK ... good, there they were, the same two that were on him yesterday, standing around outside the entrance of Discount City like a couple of dipshits. He waited until one of them finally spotted him, then he slipped into the CRS. He waltzed them around the aisles for a while, and up and down the non-working escalators, then he dumped them in the feminine hygiene section.

Back outside on Jefferson Avenue, he caught a brief ride on the back of a van that some Mexican guy was already riding, and scanned behind him for additional Watchers. There weren't any, so he hopped off the van. He stayed in the street for half a block, dodging a series of oncoming vehicles, then cut across the throngs of 1s and ducked into Speedway Motorsports Alley. He was heading home to 16 Mulberry to try to steal a few hours of sleep before he hooked up with Sarah at Frankie's at midnight and she started in on his head again. He wasn't getting much sleep at Cassandra's. He hadn't been for several weeks now. He wasn't getting much sleep nights either, as he was spending most of them fucking Sarah, and then lying beside her until 0430 as she interminably whispered in a quasi-monotone (which after a while got seriously hypnotic) about the corporations and the Normals and the babies, and the Autonomous Zones, and the stories and myths, and a lot of other faith-based Transplant nonsense that Taylor by this time had heard enough of. Off to the west the sun was setting like a fifteen megaton nuclear strike, painting the sky in radioactive shades of yellow, red, and orange. Ahead, in the south, the light was fading. Somewhere down there, among the blasted ruins of the cities and suburbs and strip malls, and industrial parks and wilderness preserves, and whatever else was allegedly down there, cells of Sarah's Terrorist comrades were rousing in their caves and tunnels, and presumably underground parking garages, and who knew where else, the sewers, probably, and suiting up for a night of foraging in the undergrowth of some mutant jungle ... or this was the crap she would have him believe. She couldn't say how many were out there, thousands at least, maybe tens of thousands, or maybe even more, no one knew. How these neo-primitive Terrorists were surviving below the 40th parallel, where the average temperature was 62C, and the landscape was either arid desert, where nothing could live for hundreds of years, or the charred and melted and twisted wreckage of former megalopolian areas, where hideous groves of mutant flora (and possibly fauna) grew untended, and the rivers, streams, and lakes were toxic, and anything you ate or drank would cause this form of hyper-aggressive cancer that killed you in the space of a week ... Sarah had no answer for that. She wouldn't even honestly address the question.

"You're watching their movie," she had taken to repeating, whenever he even broached the subject. "We have no idea what it's like down there."

"Yeah, it's probably like 18 degrees and breezy."

"Don't be an asshole. Of course it's hot. If it's this hot here, it's worse down there. But toxic? All right, sure, toxic. But exactly how toxic?"

"What, like mildly toxic? Partly scorching throughout the day with periods of intermittent toxicity?"

"All these numbers you see on the news, caesium levels, strontium levels, anthrax, ebola, pneumatic plague, where do they come from? The corporations. You're telling me you believe their data?"

This, in the wake of Sarah's bombshell.

She'd dropped it on him back in December, a week or so after he'd pressed her for all those details about the baby-smuggling, and who she really was, and all that.

They were lying in a puddle of bodily fluids on a bed in a private room at the Darkside.

"What if we could get you out?"

He'd been playing this back in his head for a month now.

"To the Autonomous Zones."

Sarah nodded.

"If they even exist."

She let that go.

"Me and Cassandra?"

"You and the baby."

He wasn't going anywhere without Cassandra.

"Cassandra is safe. They need the 1s. The 1s are their workforce."

He knew that already.

"So what are you saying?"

"Nothing ... just ... things are changing."

They lay there staring up at the ceiling, watching each other in their peripheral vision.

"Things?"

She nodded.

"What kind of things?"

Seconds passed.

"Serious things."

"Could you maybe be a little more fucking vague."

"I'm saying, you don't have much future in here."

So, OK, that was fairly ominous. He'd pushed her, but she wouldn't go into details. All she would say was that she'd heard from someone who had heard from someone who'd heard from someone that, allegedly, one of their Normal sources (which Taylor still doubted actually existed) had noticed a reduction in purchasing orders for foodstuffs and other consumer items normally allocated to Zone 23, beginning as of the following quarter. The conclusion Sarah drew from this was that some kind of partial purge was coming ... the logical explanation being that IntraZone Waste & Security Services (or maybe even Hadley Domestic Security) had gotten wind of the unbelievably extensive preparations being made for the D.A.D.A.* and was planning to take preemptive measures and, basically, kill a whole shitload of people. Sarah reasoned that the Fifthian Cluster, and anyone demonstrably involved therewith, including Taylor, would be among these people, unless they could smuggle him out with the baby. Him ...Taylor ... not Cassandra, who he would never see or hear from again.

Taylor had numerous problems with this strategy, which now, as he made his way back home (because, suffocating oven-like dump that it was, 16 Mulberry *was* his home), he was running through in no particular order. One of these problems was the Autonomous Zones. Because even if they did exist, and there were a few areas that weren't so toxic, where maybe you could grow bananas or something, and whatever cancer you got from the water wouldn't kill you for several decades, how was he supposed to live down there? He and

---

* *The date of which, as of then, late January, had still not been consensually decided.*

the baby. What would he do? Zone 23 was all he knew. He'd been born in the Zone and had spent his life there. And also, assuming she was on the level, Sarah, and could smuggle him out as she promised, and assuming the Autonomous Zones were real, and there were some sweltering swathes of land, or remnants of cities, or wilderness areas, that the Normals hadn't scorched with white phosphorus, or tactically nuked, or negligently poisoned, or otherwise sucked the last drop of life out of to fuel their vehicles and color their hair, what would Taylor do with the baby? He didn't know how to raise a baby. He didn't know the first fucking thing about babies. The whole idea was fucking nuts. Did she really expect him to believe they were running a network of underground baby orphanages? How was that supposed to work? Were they feeding them bottles of toxic formula? Singing them little Terrorist lullabies? Training them on little baby explosives?

Bullshit. There were no Autonomous Zones. Whatever whoever was doing with the babies was happening above the 40th parallel.

The rest of it was all a Transplant pipe dream.

Taylor had recognized Adam and Sarah as Transplants the moment he laid eyes on them, of course, them and the rest of Fifthian Cluster, back at his very first general meeting. Adam, for one, just reeked of Transplant. Sarah less so, but still he knew. Or at least he'd had that feeling about her, which the first time they'd deviantly fucked had confirmed. Transplants were Variant Positive Normals who went "Non-Responsive to approved medications," or acted weird, or fucked up somehow, and got themselves designated and sent to the Zone. They brought them in on a daily basis, for some reason always in the hour before sunrise, one or two a day, typically, so five or six hundred a year in total. All in all they probably made up two or three percent of the population. Most were designated A.S.P. 1, and went right to work in the plants and factories. Same with the small percentage of 2s. Transplant 3s were extremely rare, and were pretty much left to their own devices.

Taylor could always tell a Transplant. It didn't matter how long they'd been in, or how Anti-Social they tried to act. They had this air of detachment about them, which most of the natives mistook for arrogance, but Taylor knew it was something else. It faded over time in the Zone, but they never really lost it completely. Taylor could always spot it, anyway, from the way they talked, or looked at you sometimes. You got the sense that somewhere, deep down, no matter how long they'd been inside, some semi-conscious Normal part of them believed that, really, this was all just temporary, and that someday they'd be going back home to their nice little houses, families, jobs, streams of Content, flavored condoms, and all that other Normal shit. Long-time Transplants, like Adam and Sarah, who'd both been designated in their teens, learned to blend in and went unnoticed, by most people anyway, but not by Taylor. Recent Transplants, as well as the unfortunate few who'd been designated later in life (over the age of thirty, say), who could never completely make the adjustment, might as well have been wearing big red TRANSPLANT signs around their necks. Some of them didn't fare too well. They tended to get egregiously violated, often in a violently sexual manner, usually by the gangs for sport, or else by some predacious sicko. Other simply turned up "missing," as in they never made it to their housing assignments, or showed up to work at their factory jobs, and officially nobody knew what had happened to them. Unofficially, their bodies were rotting in some dead-end alley off Muybridge Lane, or they were down at the bottom of the Dell Street Canal, or else, if Meyer's theories were right, they'd joined the Anti-Social Underground, dropped off the radar and got lost in the Zone, which Taylor surmised was the story with Sarah, who was definitely living off the radar.*

Nobody really knew for certain what the corporations did to the Transplants' brains before they transferred them into the Zone. They probably used some variation on electroconvulsive shock or something. Whatever it was, it left them kind of scrambled and foggy for about a year. It didn't erase their memories as much as mix them all up, or estrange them somehow, such that they couldn't be sure anymore whether something they thought they remembered from their childhood had actually happened or had been implanted, or

---

* *Dropping off the IntraZone radar was not particularly difficult to do. There were plenty of 1s to work the factories, so it wasn't like they would come looking for you. As long as you didn't need your job, or your subsistence allotment in the case of 3s, and you didn't need to see a doctor, and didn't get stopped by the Community Watchers, you could live off the radar pretty much indefinitely.*

was just some totally random scene their brains had copied from some stream of Content and used like putty to plug a hole in the leaking wreckage of the stories of their lives. Meyer Jimenez reasoned they'd have to zap the whole brain (repeatedly, probably) to fractionate all those long-term memories, which weren't so easy to locate precisely. Which would also explain the tics, fits, and speech impediments some of them suffered, which involved a lot of blinking and snorting, which fortunately Sarah had mostly been spared ... except when she melted down in bed and was sucked down into The Pit of Despair and Uncontrollable Sobbing for extended periods. However they did it (whatever they did to the Transplants' brains before they brought them in), it didn't appear to affect their ability to think in general or to form new memories, and the longer they spent inside the Zone, the less it mattered what had happened outside. Life went on. New things happened. The continuity of their narrative shattered, the shiftless traces of the past they had lost, and could never recover, lost their luster, were gradually eclipsed by new events, and finally just slipped away forever.

That was how Sarah described it anyway, like the image in your mind of a house you once lived in, the one you thought you would spend your life in, the rest of your life in, and the person you were there, and how it all fades, that image, that person, and is imperceptibly written over, until one day you can't even remember the color of the walls of the bathroom, or where the soap went, or the bed you slept in, or what you dreamed there.

According to Sarah, she and Adam, prior to being designated, had (assuming these were accurate memories) been deeply involved with some underground network that operated out in the Normal Communities, which neither one of them could clearly remember, and so possibly didn't actually exist. This alleged network they had been involved with (assuming they had been involved with anything) may or may not have been connected to the larger, definitely more clandestine, and probably purely apocryphal network the Normals referred to as the N.I.N., which few in the Zone had ever heard of (outside of the A.S.U., of course), and which Sarah claimed was actually just a catch-all name the Normals used for any type of organized resistance that didn't already have a name, or a sinister-sounding three-letter acronym. They hadn't known each other as Normals, or at least they didn't believe they had. Based on what details they could remember, they had grown up in different Residential Communities. They'd both been designated late in their teens, Adam for aggravated vandalism to some Corporatist statue, or icon, or something, and Sarah for attempted falsification of historical records and literary Content. She couldn't recall all the details, of course, but she thought she'd been involved with some cell (i.e., part of this probably fictive network, not the network she was now involved with, which was also not the N.I.N., she stressed) that sabotaged the official Content the Normals were perpetually brainwashed with. This Content, Sarah was quick to add, was not so much intended to fill their heads with lies as just fill their heads, as the corporations were intelligent enough to recognize that deceiving people was much less effective than unrelentingly bombarding their brains with irrelevant nonsense.

Taylor didn't quite follow all that, or get the actual point of their mission, the mission of Sarah's former network ... it was something to do with attention spans, and with the Normals' almost total inability to think through anything that didn't immediately synch up with some other thing they recognized.

"The fuck are you trying to say?" he said.

"We made shit up," Sarah clarified, "people, places, historical events, and slipped them into the official records, online histories, wikis, whatever. We changed the dates of things that had happened, invented things that had never happened, some of which looked like falsifications of other made-up things we'd invented, which then, by virtue of having been falsified, appeared to be what had actually happened."

"Why?" Taylor asked, confused.

Somewhere off in the northern distance, a Public Viewer was playing a rerun of Brandon Westwood's third Immersion, The Long and Winding Road to Valhalla, not the fully-immersive version, the one you could watch on a Public Viewer.

"What is today?"

"What? The date?"

"Mm hm."

Taylor had no idea.

"I don't know. January something."

"Hadley Corporation Standard Time."

"Right."

She started to roll a cigarette.

Taylor post-coitally farted.

"And where are we now?"

"Here. At Carla's."

"Where is Carla's?"

"Here, in the Zone."

"And where is the Zone?"

"You want the coordinates?"

"How do you know?"

"How do I know what?"

She licked the edge of the cigarette paper, sealed it, tore the ragged ends off, and lit it with the stub of the bedside candle.

"Where did the information come from?"

"What information? It's fucking geography."

"Is it? How do we know for sure? You've never been out of the Zone in your life. And I can't remember where I've been. How do we know this isn't Siberia? Or somewhere in Europe? Or the South fucking Pole? Do we even know which continent we're on?"

"We're on the North American continent."

"Why? Because you saw it on a screen? Because you saw a picture with some words at the bottom? An interactive map or something?"

"The fuck were we even talking about?"

"Don't change the subject. Stay with this. Where did the information come from?"

"The Normals get in planes, all right? They fly across the Atlantic ocean." Taylor made his hand into an airplane and flew it across the Atlantic Ocean. "They land in Oslo, or Leicester, wherever. Cities that have been there for hundreds of years."

"How do they know that Oslo is Oslo?"

"Give me a fucking break, will you?"

"What if Oslo is actually Hanko? Or was Hanko? Or there was no Hanko? What do the Normals actually do? They ride to the airport. They board a plane. The plane takes off. They look out the

ZONE 23   321

window. They see an ocean, a coastline, houses. They land in some
other so-called Region that looks exactly like the Region they left.
The weather is the same. The Private Communities, office towers,
malls, everything. What's the largest historical city in Northeast
Region 709?"

"Magog."

"A name, on a map, on a screen."

"So what are you saying ... it isn't there?"

"All I'm saying is, how do we know? How do we know that Hadley
Time remotely resembles what they say it does?"

Taylor reached over and took her cigarette.

"What if this isn't the Twenty-Seventh Century? What if this
is the Twenty-Third Century? Or the Sixty-Sixth Century? How
would we know? What if even they don't know? What if they just
made it all up ... invented timelines, dates, and facts? The wars, ep-
idemics, migrations, the shifts in climate, did they really happen?"

"Yes."

She took the cigarette back.

"Maybe the planet was always like this."

"It wasn't. They wouldn't have built like this."

"And what about all these animals they worship, the Thompson's
gazelle, the giant rice rat, the tongo bongo, the Siberian tiger, the
curlew, the snipe ... did they really exist? How do we know?"

"Who gives a shit?"

"What if I told you we made up animals, falsified biological records, detailed data, photos, everything."

"You did, or they did?"

"What's the difference?"

"All right, whatever."

"No. Not whatever. We made up cities. Companies. People. Family
histories. Births. Deaths. We hacked them into the official records.
We wrote whole books on popular subjects, and attributed them to
authors who never existed, then created references to those books by
other authors who did exist. Scholars based their research on this.
We made up archeological digs ..."

Taylor got up from the bed abruptly.

"Where are you going?"

He didn't know where he was going.

"Why?" he asked, for the second time.

"Because it's all made up ... it's just stories, Taylor. You go online. You read the news. Look up something on the history sites. You sit there and read it as if it were true. Why? Because someone with money wrote it? Because it has some corporation's name on it? Why don't you believe in the Autonomous Zones?"

"Because there's nothing out there."

"How do you know? Because they showed you some pictures? Told you some stories? The people in suits?"

"Look, I get it, all right?"

"No, Taylor. You *almost* get it. You're still thinking in terms of lies and truth, as if there were some kind of actual truth that someone who knew it was going to tell you."

"It's just fucking words. It doesn't matter."

"Everything matters, or nothing matters."

"Is there some little book of these fucking platitudes?"

Sarah laughed.

"What? Big word? I know a few more. They're fucking words."

This was the type of convoluted, obscurantist Transplant crap that Sarah had been subjecting him to, relentlessly, for going on the past two months. His head was reeling from all this malarkey, from her pseudo-profound ontological riddles, aikido-conversationalist tactics, and all the other manipulative strategies she could not have been more blatantly employing to get him to (a) accept her offer to let her smuggle him out with the baby, and (b) attain satori, or whatever, some sort of spiritual and political awakening, and surrender to her unnameable something. Taylor thought he had made it clear that he wasn't about to surrender to anything, and certainly not to some sketchy-sounding non-god God of Multiplicity, which Sarah sometimes referred to as "Mystery" and at others times as the "Being of Becoming" and at still other times as the "Archon Abraxas," which was some kind of neo-Gnostic hooey which Sarah was welcome to blow out her ass. He wished, when the Normals had zapped her brain, before they brought her into the Zone, that they'd zapped the region some pretentious clown had filled full of all this magical thinking, or neo-post-structuralist epistemology, or hermeneutics, or whatever it was, because whatever it was, his head was full of it.*

By the time he got back to Mulberry Street, his brain misfiring from lack of sleep, and from going around and around and around with all this stuff, and getting nowhere, the sun had been down for over an hour, so the daytime heat was finally breaking. The dickwad on the Public Viewer said it felt like it was 38C. People were out on their stoops getting drunk, and smoking, and generally smelling like oxen. Herman the Wino was making his rounds, bumming cigarettes and assorted change. He had picked up another pair of Watchers (Taylor had, not Herman the Wino) as he'd turned southeast off Transammonia and onto Collins into Sector B. They'd followed him down to Clayton Avenue, where he'd stopped for his evening beer at Gillie's. He left them out there while he drank his beer, knowing they'd never set foot in Gillie's (for fear of testicular amputation, and so on), then he came back out, waved them over, started down Ohlsson as he usually did, then cut through a series of service alleys that looped back around and promptly lost them. Sarah had ordered him to ignore the Watchers, and not to jerk them around like that, but he couldn't help it. He was sick of the Watchers, and of being followed everywhere he went.

Actually, now that he thought about it, ascending the staircase to Apartment 2E, the list of things he wasn't sick of, or getting sick of,

---

In addition to enduring these verbal onslaughts several times a week for the past two months after fucking Sarah in a series of rooms that stank of other people's genitals, Taylor had been reading a 12-page excerpt of an obviously significantly longer document that he had stolen from Meyer Jimenez's bedroom when he was in there snooping around one night, the content of which did not exactly match the crap that Sarah was spouting, but it sort of did, which was close enough. Whoever had originally authored this text, which was written in an overly florid style that Taylor needed to reread several times to make any sense of, which was really annoying, they appeared to be into the same kind of puerile spirituo-political garbage as Sarah. There were several references to "being" and "becoming," and to "Mystery," who was clearly some kind of goddess, and to some other woman whose name was either Norma or Irma, or possibly both (or maybe that was just a typo). There were also references to this god, Abraxas, or Abrasax, who was either this Mystery's father, or was just another name for Mystery (who according to these pompous occultist morons was "invoked by any number of names," and who was either both male and female, or neither), who appeared in a drawing with the head of a chicken (i.e., as a chicken-headed Gnostic god, as opposed to brandishing a severed chicken head), above which was printed a cryptic inscription, "Wer geboren werden will, muß eine Welt zerstören," which was German, which Taylor had to translate. Mixed in with all this infantile nonsense was a lot of anarcho-revolutionist theory, parts of some of which Meyer had obviously based a number of his theories on, as well as a host of other totally impenetrable passages Taylor, by this time, had given up trying to make heads or tails of, but that were rattling around in his head all day like the marble in an empty can of spray paint, which was causing him to walk around grinding his teeth.

was shrinking quickly. He was sick of Cassandra's endless bitching, and crying, and her fits of paranoia, and of emptying out her plastic bucket, and her lack of interest in his lack of sleep. He was sick of Sarah and all her bullshit, her Transplant pipe dreams, her deviant sex, which wasn't even all that deviant, really, and her states and levels, and all the rest of it. And the Watchers. He was seriously sick of these Watchers, these bozos in their fucking rubber rain-boots who couldn't have tailed their own bowel movements if their useless lives depended on it. What else was he sick of? He was sick of meetings. General meetings. Action Updates. D.A.D.A. updates. And Security meetings. And every other type of A.S.U. meeting. He was sick of sitting around in basements and lofts and attics, and wherever the fuck, listening to Adam, or Jamé, or whoever (Dorian was one of his particular favorites), pontificate in their obtuse argot to congregations of twinkling Transplants who were stupid or just ass-ignorant enough to believe that they were part of some coming revolution that would save the human race from extinction. But mostly, or at least at the moment anyway, the thing he was feeling acutely sick of, the thing he was sick to fucking death of, was not deviating from normal routine, and leaving everything to Adam and Sarah, and not taking any independent action ... for example, to identify, and exhaustively question, then take somewhere dark and egregiously violate, whoever the fuck was cooperating on him, and had put these fucking Watchers on him, because he felt like ... well, like hitting someone, like hitting someone hard, repeatedly. Also he needed to get some sleep. He desperately needed to get some sleep.

He hauled himself up to the second floor landing and stumbled into Apartment 2E. The door was standing open, as always, in a futile attempt to ventilate the kitchen. Meyer Jimenez was cooking his famous andouille pigeon jambalaya, which was basically Meyer's pigeon paella, except when the markets were out of saffron. Taylor had been avoiding Meyer, who he knew was somehow in league with Sarah, and was probably part of her overly garrulous network of baby-smuggling Terrorists. He hadn't come out and asked him directly, because Meyer would have just denied it of course, but Meyer was the one who'd sent him to Sarah, and he'd found those maps and that 12-page excerpt, and Taylor wasn't a total moron. He hadn't been home for several weeks, except to change T-shirts, and sleep, and bathe, and to peer into Dodo Pacheco's alcove and verify he was still not in there.

Alice Williams and Rusty Braynard were twitching like fiends at the kitchen table. Their protruding eyeballs locked onto Taylor.

"Fifteen minutes," Meyer announced.

Taylor dug into the pocket of his chinos, and came up with IZD forty and change ... enough for a black market hit of Plasto.* Some ancient jazz recording was playing. He handed the money to Alice Williams.

"Fucking Tay!" Rusty Braynard sputtered, watching Alice Williams count out the money, "Fucking lifethaver! Ith that all you got?"

"I'll have more tomorrow," Taylor said.

They leapt to their feet, spilling their beers, and dashed down the hall like Olympic sprinters. Meyer stood there, sweating profusely.

"You couldn't have waited until after dinner?"

Taylor shrugged.

"Sit. Eat."

Taylor sighed.

"I need to sleep."

"A person also needs to eat."

Taylor was also sweating profusely.

"It's like a fucking sauna in here."

Meyer had been cooking for several hours.

"A sauna? And you would know this how?"

Coco Freudenheim emerged from the hallway, Dexter prancing along behind her. She waved Taylor out of her way with her little bird-bone hands and started past him. He grabbed her shoulders, turned her gently, and planted a noisy kiss on her forehead. She pushed him away and made the little puffing noise she frequently made. She was wearing the ratty old yellow bathrobe she wore whenever the pink one was drying.

"One for dinner," Meyer announced.

Claudia bellowed something utterly incomprehensible from down the hall. She sounded like she was having a boil lanced.

---

* Authorized pharmacies, like CRS, didn't sell individual hits. You had to buy at least a Ten-Pack, which went for something like IZD Eighty.

"Two for dinner," Meyer noted.

Dexter hopped up onto the table and yowled and hissed and slapped with his paw at the puddle of beer that Alice Williams and Rusty Braynard had recently spilled, and otherwise showed that puddle who was boss. Coco sat and adjusted her hair, which she'd teased up into a frightening bouffant. The saxophonist on the jazz recording (which by the way belonged to Coco, who was something of an aficionado) completely abandoned what was left of the melody and went off on some honking, squeaking, squealing type of atonal run. Alice Williams and Rusty Braynard, outfitted now in the latest line of Plasto-copping evening wear, streaked through the kitchen and out the door as if the apartment was about to explode.

Taylor staggered down the hall in a last-ditch effort to make it to his futon before he passed out on his feet in the hall and fell on his face and broke all his teeth. Along the way he threw a quick glance into into Dodo's alcove, where Dodo was not, and had not been for quite some time, and Sylvie's nook was also empty ... whereas Claudia was in her room with some enormous conceivably Cuban fellow, who Claudia was riding like a mechanical bull, apparently trying to fuck him to death.

Taylor dropped down onto his futon and lay there staring up at the ceiling ... at those quasi-concentric rings of mold, which had always been there, and were who knew how old. He set his mental alarm clock to go off at 2200, or thereabouts. Just as he was drifting off, he got that feeling you get sometimes, lying in bed, where it feels like you're falling, falling forever through endless space, which technically speaking, you always are. All his worries, cares, and woes, his suspicions, the questions he couldn't answer, the filmy images his mind kept conjuring of neo-primitive desert outposts, the face-less faces of the nameless dead that floated just beyond the visual periphery of whatever half-conscious state he was in, entering his dreams, which he wouldn't remember, were fading like the receding waves of an almost out-of-range radio signal ... Sarah, Cassandra, Dodo, the D.A.D.A., the Autonomous Zones that didn't really exist, Alice Williams and Rusty Braynard, the face in his mind he called his mother, or some other woman, making his bed, lighting a candle to set in the window of the house that he had never seen but had visited repeatedly, all his life, Coco laughing, Dexter yowling, music wafting up from the street, the indistinguishable murmur of voices talking, shouting, laughing, singing, blending into the bending notes that weren't even musical notes anymore, running, the rising sun at his back, burning through the paper skin of the sky, across some featureless desert of salt that stretched off forever in all directions, the baby, the time it would be at the tone, the time it would never be at the tone, the time it would always be at the tone ...

The One Who Was Many

It wasn't supposed to be like this ... the world. Not at this stage anyway, not at the dawn of the 27th Century, or whatever century it actually was. Where were all the flying cars, the household robots, the magic foglets, the TV dinners you could zap into being in a nanotech-oven right there in your kitchen? Where were the squadrons of nanobot-operated, self-replicating interstellar spaceships, the supercomputers the size of planets, the obsolescence of work as we knew it, and all the other wonders they'd promised?

All right, sure, there had been advancements. The world was finally at peace and all that. And there were All-in-One Viewers and Info-Streams, and Immersions and other Entertainment Content, and life expectancy was dramatically up. And there were Cranio-Implants and virtual screens, and nearly everything was solar-powered, or nuclear-powered, or bio-fueled, and everyone was either vegetarian, or vegan, or they were intravenously fed. And thanks to the miracle of ThermaSoak skin there were outdoor domes and pedestrian tunnels, and the trains and planes and trams and taxis were mostly unmanned, or remotely-piloted, and even if there weren't any android servants, there were all kinds of other nifty gadgets, like self-cleaning kitchens and programmable clothes, and anything plastic was totally recyclable, and up around the Arctic Circle the weather was still for the most part fine. And there were artificial limbs, and joints and organs, and menageries of cloned and artificial animals, and artificial wilderness areas, and satellite-assisted senior golfing, and there were IQ-boosters, and orgasm drops, and do-it-yourself cosmetic surgery, and there were apps where you could spend your weekend navigating lifelike fantasy realms that you completely controlled like some kind of god, the inhabitants of which were being threatened by fanatical Terrorists, or deadly pandemics, or whatever projection of groundless fear you felt you needed to face and conquer ... and there was market data around the clock.

So it wasn't like there hadn't been progress. There had. There had been phenomenal progress. And not just on the material front, with respect to products and gadgets, and so on, and the basic amenities and creature comforts that everyone mostly took for granted, also on the knowledge front, with respect to philosophy, and stuff like that, like universal rights, and ethical behavior, and on pretty much every other front involving the betterment of human nature. Certainly, in evolutionary terms, looking back across the ages to the dawn of human civilization (which according to the Reconstruction Project had emerged in a then quite fertile region extending northwestward from the Persian Gulf that was now an enormous radioactive desert in Recovering Area 3), there had been nothing short of mind-blowing progress. In the space of a scant six thousand years, which in cosmic time wasn't even a blip, we'd progressed from crafting primitive metal implements out of copper and tin to devising thermonuclear weapons that could scorch the entire surface of the planet. We'd progressed from scratching rows of wedge-shaped pictographs into slabs of clay to authoring, not just representations (i.e., stories, movies, maps, and so on, which were mere interpretations of the world), but fully-immersive simulations, copyrighted little worlds of our own. We had progressed from magical herbs and shamans to redesigning our genetic code, from peasant farming to agrifactories, from slavery to gainfully rewarding employment, from countless forms of discrimination to a totally free and equal society, from despotism to cooperative corporatism, or democracy, or whatever this was, exactly.

Looking back even farther than that, back to our rather humble origins as inorganic matter, or dirt (which at some point, billions of years ago, had somehow gotten electrically-stimulated, or catalyzed, into proto-molecules, which proto-molecules had evolved into cells, which cells in turn had gradually evolved into these slimy, disgusting spongelike creatures, which evolved into worms, then fish, and so on, up the evolutionary scale, which was clearly like a ladder leading somewhere upward, or onward, or outward, or in any event away from the Earth, and the dirt and filth from whence we came, toward some terminal goal or stage, or ultimate, possibly godlike knowledge the universe was concealing from us, and maybe even taunting us with, the attainment of which knowledge, which was ours by right, would be worth all the horrors we had perpetrated, and the mindless devastation we had wreaked, in our quest to obtain and exploit this knowledge, which we deeply regretted, all the horrors, and so on, and swore on a stack of *The Path(s) to Prosperity* we would never, ever repeat, again) ... in light of how far we had come from then, who could claim we were not making progress?

And yet, if you actually sat down and read (i.e., not just skimmed in a cursory way as you searched online for some celebrity's birthday, but actually consciously read the words of) the voluminous online historical records at the Reconstruction Project's website (not all of them, of course, but a representative portion) and thought about them, and drew little graphs, and timelines, and so on, as Valentina had done, and even after you took into account the setbacks during the Age of Anarchy, which were kind of like the Middle Ages that followed the fall of the Roman Empire, and during which dark and savage period there'd been no technological advances, nor accurate historical records kept, or they had all been destroyed or maliciously altered beyond all hope of reconstruction ... something cardinal did not make sense.

According to these records, the Age of Anarchy officially began in 2101 (H.C.S.T., it went without saying) and ended at the dawn of the 24th Century. So it had lasted a mere two hundred years. Prior to which technological progress had been increasing exponentially. It had been doing this since the Age of Enlightenment. By the end of the Second Thirty Years War, when the United Territories of the Earth were established, in 2076 H.C.S.T.,* people were already scanning streams of more or less individualized Content (not on All-in-One Viewers, of course, but on a range of earlier, more primitive devices that were basically the same as All-in-Ones). Human Anti-Social Disease had not yet been officially discovered, so of course there were no Quarantine Zones, but people lived in

---

* *Officially, the Second Thirty Years War, sometimes referred to as the War on Horror, or Operation Global Resolve, but never referred to as World War IV, not by educated people anyway, had ended in the Winter of 2072, so four years prior to the actual signing of the Declaration of Global Unity.*

Residential Communities, which in those days were much more heavily fortified, and were also known as "gated" communities. Also, it appeared, in these historical records, that people, by the end of the 21st Century, were taking a variety of differently labeled but pharmaceutically virtually identical medications to control their aggression, and depression (which was epidemic at the time), and there were high-, if not quite Whisper-speed trains, and solar power, and nuclear power, and GM food, and UAVs, and biometrics, and corporate Security, and bioengineering, and the Internet, of course, and there were all sorts of staggering medical advances, and it seemed, at least to Valentina, that in purely technological terms, nothing ... or, all right, very little, had changed in any meaningful way.

People, sadly, were still just people.

Mammals.

Animals.

Even the Clears.

As far as she understood the science (or what parts of it weren't proprietary secrets), even with all their genetic enhancements, the Clears, biologically, were still just people ... OK, creepy, synthetically enlightened people, attractive in a sterile, airbrushed way, with perfect teeth and hair and skin, who went around beaming inner peace and boundless love and well-being at you, but nonetheless people, in human bodies, physical bodies ... mortal bodies. Here it was, whenever it was, late in the game in any event, and we were all still chained to these physical bodies (like the body growing inside her body). Weren't we supposed to have arrived at some sort of technological singularity, or have evolved into some numinous form of super-intelligent spirit-entities? Wasn't that supposed to have happened by now? Where was that gentle master race of cybernetic sentient beings who were going to descend like a rain of angels and bear us up out of the physical world and all its senseless pain and suffering and up the stairway to haptic heaven?

Valentina did not know. However, she knew where they definitely weren't. They weren't out there by the pool. Valentina had been out there for hours ... and she hadn't encountered any haptic beings.

The swimming pool of the Skyline Motor Lodge, which was poured concrete and kidney-shaped, and the deep-end of which was

full of garbage, hadn't been used for at least several decades, except
as a kidney-shaped waste receptacle. The deck, or poolside patio area,
which was also vaguely kidney-shaped, was cracked and buckled and
chunks were missing and saw grass and other species of weeds were
growing up through it in various places. Valentina was stretched out
on a rusty aluminum reclining lounger, the sagging plastic strap-
ping of which was starting to kill her lower back, gazing up into a
constellation of spastically twinkling satellite beacons, or she was
whenever the monstrous sharklike soot-streaked metal underbellies
of assorted private and commercial aircraft weren't screaming across
the sky above her scaring the bejesus out of the colony of rats that
apparenty lived in the courtyard ... so you'd think they would have
been used to the planes flying over all the time like that, but they
weren't. The planes flew over every two or three minutes, so much
less frequently than during the day, and every time one did the rats
would scramble up out of the pool en masse and scurry off into the
dark somewhere in a state of abject rodential panic. Once the noise
of the turbines had waned, they would all creep back and crawl down
into the pool and into the mound of garbage and get right back to
nocturnally feeding on the greasy bits of disgusting, gooey, processed
non-cheese cheese-like substance and the streaks of waxy, tasteless
chocolate that were smeared all over the shiny wrappers that apparently the people who lived down there, or people who visited the
people who lived there, couldn't be bothered to recycle properly and
just threw down into this horrible pool as if they didn't all have to
live in such close proximity to all these rats.

Valentina wasn't scared of the rats. She sliced up cancerous organs
for a living. And naturally, being a histopathologist, she'd euthanized her share of rats.* They scrambled across the courtyard in
waves, flowing like currents of fur around her, as she lay there on
her caved-in lounger, gazing up between the satellites (the majority of which were geostationary, and so were always there, whatever
the hour) and out into the charcoal gray expanse of the seemingly

---

* It wasn't something she particularly enjoyed ... but it had to be done from time to time. You stuck
them in a little rodent guillotine, which you had to manually push down on, because it wasn't the
kind where the blade just drops, and chopped their squeaking little rodent heads off. This wasn't
considered murder, of course. Exceptions were made for medical professionals, and for anyone else
involved in any merciful type of euthanasic activity.

334 C. J. HOPKINS

starless sky ... somewhere (technically speaking everywhere) within the ever-expanding expanse of that very same seemingly starless sky, approximately fourteen billion years ago, give or take a billion years, everything had exploded out of nothing, all at once, for no discernible reason. Precisely what this nothing had been doing prior to its propitious explosion remained, even now, at the time of our story, an intransigent and thus somewhat embarrassing mystery. In addition to all the above-mentioned things that were supposed to have happened but hadn't happened, the theoretical physics community, in spite of all the groundbreaking work it was doing with its very (and extremely) large particle colliders, had still not been able to solve this quandary. They had proposed a number of intriguing theories, which served, among the physicists at least, as grounds for constant and lively debate (and which were promulgated to the general public in simplified versions, with lots of special effects), but as far as any actual knowledge went, none of them had the slightest idea ... and neither, of course, did Valentina.

Nights, as a child, when the heat was bearable and there weren't too many hungry mosquitoes, often when Catherine was off her meds and she and Walter were having a "discussion," Valentina had gone outside and stretched out on the reclining lounger that no one ever used on account of the heat and so sat out there on the concrete dock, or massive untreated slab of concrete, beneath the glassed-in concrete patio, overlooking the man-made pond (which was almost exactly the same as the pond behind her house on Marigold Lane), and she peered up into the sky for hours and fervently prayed to the One Who Was Many. She prayed for patience, and forgiveness, and guidance, and blind acceptance of the Path she was on, which was what little girls were supposed to pray for ... but sometimes, also, she prayed for knowledge. Not for knowledge you could learn at school, or find online in two or three seconds, and then more or less immediately forget, deeper knowledge, secret knowledge, like of what that theoretical nothing was doing before the beginning of time. She didn't know why she wanted this knowledge, or what this knowledge was, back then, but she knew she wanted, or needed, or craved it, in some unhealthy, selfish way. She told herself she shouldn't want it. She tried to will herself not to want it. It didn't work. She wanted it anyway. She lay on the lounger on the dock in the dark and desperately prayed to the One to be given it, the blue-white bits of broken images emanating from the streams of Content running on the screens of the neighbors' Viewers dancing like flames in the frames of the windows of the nearly identical houses surrounding the artificial pond in which nothing lived. Whatever it was, this knowledge she had craved, or needed, as a child, and had never received, and had later, at some point, given up hope of ever receiving, and had given up praying for, and had totally forgotten she had ever needed (at some point grown-ups stopped asking such questions, and focused on more important things) ... whatever it was, she needed it now.

The probably mostly adrenaline-influenced sudden clarity and utter certitude with which she had been completely possessed at the time of her Lomax Escalator Vision was gone. She was currently out of clarity. She was running dangerously low on certitude. What completely possessed her now was fear.

She could not do this. She simply could not. She had told them she could, but now she couldn't. She could not terminate ... abort ... kill ... Kill? How she could possibly kill? She'd euthanized rats, but that was different. This was an actual human being. A child. A baby. This was her daughter ... Zoey, or whatever they'd decided to call her. She had to do it. Did she have to do it? No. She did not have to do it. If she wanted out, she had to do it.

Did she still want out?

Yes. She did.

But why did they need to make her do it? And why in this horrible, unclean place? Couldn't they come here, and take her away, far away, to their Terrorist camp, or cave, in some remote Recovering Area, and anesthetize her, and do it there? No. Of course not. She had to do it. She knew why they needed to make her do it. They were testing her. This was all a test. Because how could they trust her if she couldn't do it ... if she couldn't commit an act of violence, intentionally hurt, or horribly maim, or murder, another human being, or any other type of sentient being (which healthy Normals could never do)? How could she possibly be entrusted to perpetrate (or otherwise materially participate in) a horrific series of sickeningly violent and senseless and devastating Terrorist attacks on unsus-

pecting innocent consumers if she couldn't even summon the inner
fortitude (and the cold-hearted totally fanatical hatred of everything
Normal society stood for) required to abort the tiny defenseless ten-
week-old fetus of the Clear she was carrying?

No ... she either had to do it, or go back up to Room 303, flush the
MemCard down the toilet, hastily repack her Vittorio suitcase, toss
the HCS60 into the garbage at the bottom of the pool in passing,
slink back home to Pewter Palisades and selectively confess to Kyle
and the doctors.

"Show me what to do," she prayed.

A corporate jet screeched past overhead, driving the rats up out of
the pool and frantically off into their bunkers. She closed her eyes
and tried to recall the revelation that had started all this. It was right
there ... right on the tip of her mind, but the words wouldn't come.
Then they came.

"Everything, as it is, is perfect."

But everything as it was was not perfect. Everything as it was
was wrong. This was wrong. It felt so ... wrong. She could feel its
wrongness deep in her body. It was something that had always been
there ... this sense, or awareness, or whatever it was. This wasn't an
intellectual exercise, a game, or some essentially harmless fantasy
(like her fantasy about the men in goat masks). They wanted her to
get up and actually do this. They wanted her to actually kill her baby.
Which was wrong, and bad, and sick, and evil, in some axiomatic,
a priori way, which she couldn't explain but just knew was true, and
could feel in every fiber of her being.

Killing other creatures was wrong. Violence was wrong. It accomplished nothing ... and yet what else had brought about all that
progress, and enabled us to crawl up out of the slime and eventually
(i.e., after two thousand centuries of killing, torturing, and raping
each other) establish a peaceful and prosperous society? Hadn't violence accomplished that? Was that also wrong? No ... it wasn't. Or
yes, it was, but that was before, before we discovered Anti-Social
Disease, so that didn't count, but now it did, now that there weren't
any foreign enemies, or despotic regimes to be violently deposed,
and that the last remaining threat to peace was not the Terrorists,
or not per se, but rather, the Anti-Social Disease that distorted their

thoughts and made them Terrorists, which was also the same Anti-Social Disease that everyone had had for thousands of years while they'd made all that revolutionary progress and defeated all those foreign enemies and …

Valentina couldn't keep it all straight.

Sometimes back on the dock on the pond (in another body that no longer existed, so for all intents and purposes was dead, but whose memories she had inside her brain) she had dreamed, or possibly just imagined, that she, and her mother and father inside "discussing" her mother's latest symptoms, and the neighbors viewing their streams of Content, and the Security guards at the entrance gate, and her friends at Playhouse Community Day School, and her teachers, and doctors, and everyone else, were all just figures in an endless dream … a dream the One Who Was Many was dreaming, and had always been dreaming, and would always be dreaming, and which had never begun, and would never end. The One Who Was Many was not the dreamer, or not like she was when she dreamed (which was more or less like watching an Immersion, because even though you were in the Immersion, part of you wasn't, and was only watching, and knew that it was only watching, and it was like the part of you in the dream that was going to wake and remember the dream …), because the One Who Was Many *was* the dream, from which there was no one (no dreamer) to wake.

Lying out there in the stifling heat with the bugs and the flick-ering lights in the silence, except for the hum of the HVAC units (because you couldn't hear anything from inside the houses, and the fountain out in the middle of the pond, which Shaniqua Goldin and Carly Gomez thought was simply a decorative feature, but was actu-ally to keep the water moving, automatically switched off at night), this other Valentina, who no longer existed (or who only existed inside the mind of the Valentina who now existed), lying out there with her whole life ahead of her, pinned by the curvature of phys-ical spacetime to the surface of a rock that was orbiting one of the countless suns that were out there somewhere, burning out, for no real reason, lying out there, supine, on the lounger, facing up or out at what her teacher claimed was like a giant ice cream cone that was made of time (and that's how it looked in the pictures he showed

them, like a cone, or a tube, inside of nothing), little Valentina, lying out there, waiting for her father to appear on the patio and rap
on the glass with his first two knuckles, which he would do when
they had finished "discussing," Valentina, this earlier version, who
had replaced a series of earlier versions who had disappeared and so
were technically dead, and who was already taking 20 milligrams of
Zanoflaxithorinol daily (she was probably six or seven at the time),
knew, or believed, or at least suspected (not that she could have explained it back then), that what she was learning at the Playhouse
Day School in an ostensibly meticulously-structured manner, and
was otherwise soaking up like a sponge in the course of just being an
exceptionally intelligent and inquisitive child at a formative age, and
was being bombarded on a more or less moment by moment basis
on her Viewer with (but not at that particular moment, because she
had left it inside when she went outside to lie on the dock in the heat
with the insects), was not as much knowledge, or facts, or whatever
(this stuff she was learning, or was being spoon fed), as it was an
attempt to extract her from, or otherwise forcibly pry her out of, the
dream the One Who Was Many was dreaming (i.e., the aforementioned beginningless, endless dream) and imprison her within some
other dream (which was like an almost identical copy or simulation
of the aforementioned dream) where something was always wrong
with something, and everyone was always scared and confused and
sleep deprived and gritting their teeth (though they did their best to
pretend they weren't), as if they were somehow strangers there (in
the only place there was to be), as if they weren't all perfect parts of
the one and only thing there was (which wasn't bound or contained
by anything ... especially not some endless nothing), and she didn't
understand that, not one bit.

This was how her thoughts were flowing poolside now at the
Skyline Motor Lodge, memories flowing along the cognitive streams
of the infinite lines of flight that were spreading like a web of hairline fractures across the seamless plane of the world they had coated
her spirit, her energy, with, as if she'd been dipped in a vat of translucent liquid plastic, which had frozen and cracked ... and what she
was was seeping out of it. What she was was not what she was. She
wasn't just a middle-aged Variant-Positive who colored the streaks

of gray in her hair and whose breasts were starting to sag a little ...
or OK, more than just a little, whose genetically-inherited medical
condition was causing her to blow her unconscious terror of bearing
and raising a brood of children she had never even wanted in the
first place (which would claim like thirty years of her life, and most
of what was left of her sanity, and would leave her fat and loose and
dumb and probably depressed to the point of suicide) up into some
phantasmagoria involving fictive Terrorist networks and some nebulous quasi-demiurgic force, when actually all that was happening
here was that she didn't really want to have this baby ...

No ... this was not what this was. Why was she even thinking it
was? All that was just the film, or glaze, or imperceptible, immaterial membrane the child on the lounger on the dock in the dark (if
Valentina had actually done that, and hadn't just made the whole
thing up) got sealed inside of and couldn't get out ... which was all
she had ever really wanted, ever.

The problem was, there was no out. The world was one. It was
all one place. There were many places inside that place, but there
wasn't any place outside that place. Or anywhere to hide within that
place. Anything that happened to anyone anywhere was immediately known by everyone everywhere. Everything was connected
to everything. It was all one seamless inescapable network. And it
wasn't just here on what was left of the planet. There wasn't even
anywhere to go in space. They had probed, sampled, mapped, and
modeled, and assigned little correlated numbers to, every last fraction of every second of every light-year of Minkowskian spacetime
extending backwards in a conelike pattern to the vanishing point of
that original nothing. It was like they were trying to sketch out a
prison with the exact dimensions of the physical universe. Or maybe
that was just how it looked through the film (or imperceptible immaterial membrane) that was stretched like a layer of skin around
her (whichever one of her she was), which she needed to tear, or
rupture, or puncture (her intuition, or something, told her), because
possibly where she really was (i.e., the Valentina she really was, not
the one who lived in her forehead and that was still, despite all the
trials she had been through, trying to make sense of the circuitous
logic that every Normal was conditioned to employ) was floating

right there in the middle of it all (that dream she was, or was in, or was dreaming, and that knowledge she had prayed for but had never received, because maybe you didn't receive this knowledge, because you started out with it all inside you (and also somehow inside of it), but they wrapped you up from the day you were born in so many layers of immaterial membrane that you looked out through this film (or lens) at what passed for facts and truth and the world and what was real and common sense (which actually made no sense at all, but you never had time to think about it) ... but sometimes, if let's say you screwed up your meds, or suffered some kind of ischemic incident, you got this infinitesimal glimpse of it ... the fleetingest glimpse, which you couldn't hold onto ... of what it was like when you knew all that, in some it went without saying wordless way, before they turned you into this unique fucking godforsaken individual who was trapped in the core of a big glass onion) ... and so maybe what she needed to do at this juncture (if she really wanted out of all this) was snake a pointy metal object up into her uterine canal and stab it into her amniotic sac with a force sufficient to rupture same.

That would probably do it, she figured. One good jab, to start the process ... then a few (or possibly several) hours of excruciating pain, and it would all be over. She tried to imagine actually doing it. The cramps. The tissue squirting out of her. The blood. The sweat was pouring off her. She was wearing the Gina Lewinsky ensemble that she'd bought last summer and that was totally ruined. The voice on the tape in her head was shouting orders at her that she couldn't make out. The plastic straps of the lounger felt like metal blades cutting into her back. She remembered the grainy archival Content they showed you in school about the horrible past when women routinely murdered their babies, not for legitimate medical reasons (which of course that still occurred sometimes), but because their disease had rendered them void of any shred of human empathy. The Content they showed consisted of close-ups of sickening surgically dismembered fetuses, intercut with women smiling these satisfied, sociopathic smiles ... as if they'd gotten pregnant purely in order to be able to have their fetuses cut into pieces while they were still inside them, and then loudly vacuumed out their uteri and filmed for some reason that was never explained.

Valentina wasn't that far along. Her fetus was about the size of her thumb … the cuticle of which was a total disaster. For a half a second she was utterly convinced that she had known all along it was Hadley Security. Then it was gone. That knowledge. That thought. She would flush it down the toilet or something. Someone would. One of her would. Whoever or whatever she would be by then. Apostate. Monster. Stranger. Martyr. She couldn't string her thoughts together. They weren't her thoughts. She'd made a mistake. A big mistake. An enormous mistake. A series of seriously sizable mistakes. Other words that began with S. She had run out of breath mints. She had to decide. Or just lie there and wait for them to come and get her. She said her mantra. Or someone did. The One Who Was Many. The Many Who Were One. The dock. The dark. She prayed for knowledge. Sucked up into the tunnel of time. Born dead out of the asshole of nothing. The folds of her brain were crawling with words that sounded good but didn't mean anything. Good. Bad. Right. Wrong. Sick. Healthy. Hair conditioner. Comfort soles. Truth dispenser. She could feel the skin around the skin around the skin they had pasted onto her. How many Valentinas were there? How many had there been by now? The roar of the silver metal fuselage dribbling foamy streaks of grease that ran out of its flaps and hatches. The rats that raced in circles beneath her. Swarm. River. Water. Blood. Tides. Breath. Wordless current. Everything revolving counter-clockwise. The sweat was running down into her eyes. The dead girl's memories inside her mind. Her mother. Kyle. Hives. Cells. Cancer. Fingers up her cunt. The one she was was already dead. The sound of her voice on the tape in her head. All these thoughts she had already had uncountable times and would always have … in this moment in time that went on forever. She had to kill … to kill that voice. Kill the One and become the Many. Become the voices. The many voices … speaking … no … no, they were singing, singing together, all at once, as they always had been, and always will be, forever, and ever, and ever …

Listen.

No Deviations

The morning of officially 15 March, 2610, H.C.S.T., or 24 Phalguna, 2531, or 27 Sha'ban, 2049, or Day 565 in the Year of the Lemur, began, for Taylor, like any other morning, or at least like any other morning of late. It began in Room 3 at the Darkside Club, where he woke with a seething and painful tumescence. He also awoke with a throbbing headache that felt like someone had been hammering concrete nails into his eyes all night. Oh, and also with a generalized queasy-type feeling that, not immediately, but relatively soon, something terrible was going to happen to him.

He remembered dreaming that he was lost in a maze of infinite mirrors where, whichever way he turned, an infinite series of identical Taylors, or Taylor-like entities, were staring back at him, opening and closing their mouths like fish. He wasn't sure what kind of fish, but he thought maybe grouper, or possibly sea bass, or something large and ugly like that. He slid himself off the slimy bedsheet, staggered across the room in the dark, and pissed in the sink for about two minutes. Bladder empty, his tumescence wilted. His throbbing headache, however, did not.

Sarah was gone … which was standard procedure. So that wasn't what was bothering Taylor as he fumbled around in the dark for the candle, which wasn't on the shelf above the sink. What was bothering Taylor was the fact he couldn't remember much of the night before. However, he figured, given this headache, he must have gotten drunk, and was now hungover, which a couple of beers downstairs would fix. The only problem with this theory was, he didn't appear to be hungover … or at least his mouth didn't taste like hangover. It tasted like Sarah. And like he'd been snoring. And his headache wasn't a hangover headache.

Horribly cheerful Morning Show Muzak was playing on the Public Viewer outside, which meant that it was just past 0500, and he had overslept and fuck ... fuck, he needed to get out of there and get to Cassandra's. He raised the blind to let some light in, found his clothes, got them on, staggered out and down the hall, down the stairs that led to the basement, through this soundproof door they had there, and walked face first into a sonic wall of pounding Afro-Aztec music that made his internal organs vibrate.

The Darkside "playroom" was in full swing. Walls of contraband PlasmaTron screens were running loops of hardcore Content, repeatedly rephotographed lube-smeared reels of unidentified individuals sexually violating other individuals in every conceivable manner possible. Most of which acts were also being perpetrated live on the floor of the Darkside's playroom, a cavernous, red-lit, hangar-like dungeon you had to walk through to get upstairs, or in Taylor's case to get downstairs and get to the bar and get a beer.

He squeezed and pushed and pried his way through the clutches of naked and vinyl-clad lovers, ducking floggers, sidestepping dancers, steering clear of the heavier players, and finally made it across to the bar, a ragged slab of rusty metal that would slash your fingers down to the bone if you ran your hand along the razor sharp edge of it. He caught the eye of the bartender, Nilo, who was reapplying his blood red lipstick, and made the gesture for "emergency beer." Then he went in his pocket and fished out ... uh oh ... six IZ dollars and assorted change, three of which he now owed to Nilo. So great, this day was shaping up nicely. Not only did he have this fucking headache, and had overslept, and was going to be late, which Cassandra was going to have his ass for, and the dream, and the fish, and the sense of dread ... on top of that now he needed money.

Cassandra was down to the last of her rations and in desperate need of TōHam, Yogurt, Seaweed Chewies, Pineapple oatmeal, and those instant Chinese noodles that came in a variety of flavors in the 10-Pack boxes. She was also in somewhat less than desperate but fairly immediate and ongoing need of a particular brand of flavored potato chips, and TōSardines, and pickles, naturally, and Zwizzlers, and anything containing chocolate. All of which was going to cost money.

On top of which, there was the Content Problem. The Content Problem had now gone critical. Cassandra had been watching the same ten discs, the original pirate discs he'd brought her, Normal RomComs and SecFlics mostly, over and over for the last four months, and basically, if Taylor didn't get her some new ones, and soon, she was going to go fucking apeshit.

Taylor did the math in his head. It turned out he needed somewhere in the vicinity of IZD two hundred eighty-three fifty. Which neither he nor Cassandra had. Which meant he would have to rob somebody, or get back home to 16 Mulberry by 0600 at the very latest and borrow two hundred eighty-three fifty from Alice Williams and Rusty Braynard, assuming, that is, they had any money, which they probably didn't, it being a Thursday. In which case, maybe he could borrow it from Meyer, or Coco, or ... wait. What was he thinking? He could borrow it from Dodo, who was sitting right there in a recessed booth across the playroom sipping some neon green concoction and trying not to get spotted by Taylor.

Taylor experienced one of those moments you've probably seen in a lot of films where they dolly the camera away from the subject, while at the same time zooming in on the subject, so that the subject (in this case Dodo Pacheco) seems to just sit there utterly frozen, as the rest of the world goes whooshing past him ... which they do to convey the kind of experience Taylor was having at precisely that moment. Dodo, presumably sensing Taylor was having this type of cinematic experience, turned away and made this furtive move with his hand that was meant to look casual, but which ended up looking like just what it was ... a pathetic attempt to not get spotted.

Other people were in the booth. They were sitting on either side of Dodo, some pierced-up whitebread PKP freak, who looked on the verge of a grand mal seizure, another scumbag, who was probably his dealer, and a couple of regular Darkside dancers, one of whom was jerking off some fatso with a rubber ball in his mouth. None of these people were there with Dodo. They all just happened to be sharing the booth. This was obvious, at least to Taylor, and beside the point, because the question was, what the fuck was Dodo Pacheco doing in a booth at the Darkside Club at 0500 on a Thursday morning? Dodo Pacheco, who had never once been to the Darkside Club in his drug-addled life. Dodo Pacheco, the Plasto fiend, who had as much interest in deviant sex as he did in anything other than Plasto, which in case you were wondering was less than none.

Taylor quickly scanned the playroom, looking for anything else suspicious. The dance floor was writhing with naked, sweat-soaked, DMLX-fueled all-night dancers, their glistening bodies gyrating, whirling, circumnavigating stations of stocks, cages, splitters, racks, prangers, and other machines of unspeakable torture. Off in an al-cove, a trio of Machos was ganging what looked like a Nordic Nancy. Screens were running bootleg loops of tropical fish that swam in circles intercut with close-up footage of male-to-female sex change surgery. People were getting whipped, paddled, branded, pinched, pierced with needles, shocked, suffocated with bags on their heads … in other words, nothing out of the ordinary.

He turned his attention back to Dodo, or rather, to the booth where Dodo had been. Dodo was gone. Where the fuck was he? Wait … OK, there he was, creepy-crawling toward the exit, trying to use those dancers for cover.

Taylor drained the rest of his beer and fought his way through the crowd in pursuit, shoving, elbowing, and otherwise physically clearing a path through the wall-to-wall dancers. Any second he was going to go blind, or suffer a series of massive strokes, or oth-erwise die of this splitting headache, which was probably some type of mid-brain tumor, and here came that nebulous feeling of dread again, which he didn't have time to contemplate, currently. He made it to the rickety metal staircase, took the stairs two and three at a time, sprang out the street-level door of the Darkside, which opened onto this dead-end alley that terminally reeked of piss and garbage, and into the blue-white megawatt beam of an IntraZone chopper's NiteSun searchlight … which, OK, that was the end of his chase scene, and everything else, because now he was dead.

Or … no … OK, he wasn't dead.

What had happened was, he had frozen in place, and now, slowly, he raised his hands (the rotors of the chopper rustling his clothes), interlocked his fingers and very slowly brought his hands down on top of his head. Extremely slowly, he lowered his eyes out of the blinding beam of the searchlight, knowing that any sudden movement might cause whatever Security Specialist was up there aiming the .50 caliber armor-piercing armament at him to go berserk and splatter his guts all over the frontage of the Darkside Club. He'd seen this happen a hundred times, not at the Darkside, but other places. All it took was the slightest twitch, a fidgety finger, the flick of an eyelid, and they would blow your intestines, and adjacent organs, and the splintered bits of your spinal column, out through the gaping hole in your back that they had made with the armor-piercing armament.

Taylor, hoping to avoid all that, and who still had his nerve, and in spite of his headache, stood there like an inanimate object. He knew, odds were, he was probably dead anyway (you usually were with the NiteSun on you), but he stood there like a statue, waiting ... for death, or instructions from the crew in the chopper, until, oddly (as in this *never* happened), after what felt like an hour to Taylor, but was actually only five or six seconds, the chopper shuddered, rose, banked, killed its NiteSun and swooped away.

Once the sound of the chopper's rotors had faded into the ambient noise, Taylor slowly raised his head and scanned the alley, as best he could. Bright white floaters were occluding his vision, after-effects of the NiteSun beam. Even so, he could see well enough to see that Dodo Pacheco was gone. He must have made it around the corner before the chopper switched its light on, which didn't seem possible, given the geography, and ... whatever. He would deal with Dodo later.

By 0530, or thereabouts, he had made it back to 16 Mulberry and up the creaking, piss-reeking stairs and through the door and into the kitchen, where Meyer was slumped at the table, drunk, a half-empty bottle of rum in evidence. He went through Meyer's jacket pockets and came up with IZD ninety-two twenty. Meyer watched him through bloodshot eyes, mumbling something in what might have been Yiddish, but at this point Taylor didn't give a hairy fuck. The muscles in his neck were spasming. He was dripping sweat. His head was pounding. He took a quick swig of Meyer's rum, dug through the cupboard over the sink, found a packet of Ibucedrin in the secret spot where Meyer kept them, and gulped down five with a liter of water. Heading down the hall to his room, he threw a glance into Dodo's alcove, knowing that Dodo would not be in there, which, no surprise here, folks, Dodo wasn't. Sylvie's nook was also empty, which didn't mean anything, or not anymore. Wherever she was, she was off the hook. Taylor had found his Cooperator. Dexter was in with Coco, purring. Claudia, or someone in her room, was snoring. Out the front windows, on the Public Viewer, one of the female Talking Heads, not the one with the orange hair, was blathering on about the greatly improved but still officially guarded condition of some rich-ass Normal, Jimbo something, who was valiantly battling intestinal cancer, and who Taylor wished would just fucking die. Alice Williams and Rusty Braynard were half on the nod in front of a Viewer that was running their pirate bootleg copy of this ancient movie called Planet of the Apes, the hero of which, played by Marlon Brando, Taylor's mother had named him after.

Taylor squatted on the floor beside her (Alice Williams, not his mother, of course), fingered her hair back out of her face, kissed her on the forehead softly, and told her he needed some money, right now. Alice Williams (in super slo-motion) retrieved a bag that Rusty Braynard was holding in his lap, dug down in it, and pulled out a handful of IZD bills. She sprinkled the bills over Taylor's feet. She did this by feel, as her eyes wouldn't open. "Look," she mumbled, eyelids fluttering. She nodded toward the screen of the Viewer, where the apes were riding horses across a field of wheat or barley or something. "It's yooooooo," she cooed, and giggled, and drooled.

Taylor gave her another kiss, and counted out the cash he needed ... he took three hundred, just to be safe. He peeked inside the paper bag. It was stuffed with bills, fifties and hundreds, and pharmaceutical Plastomorphinol, several hundred hits, it looked like. He gathered up the leftover bills off the floor, stuffed them back into the bag, pushed it up under the greasy old blanket Rusty Braynard was halfway sitting on, and high-tailed it out of 16 Mulberry.

The time was approximately 0540.

Alternately walking and jogging to Cassandra's, he made a mental list of the people he would need to find and convince (or otherwise encourage) to divulge the whereabouts of Dodo Pacheco. The list consisted of Rudy Rebello, and Rudy Rebello's scumbag associates, who Dodo wasn't officially one of (he was more like an adjunct scumbag associate). Rudy, and his gang of slimy scumbags worked the streets off Zuckerberg Square, dealing Plasto, pirate Content, and anything else they could get their hands on. Last Taylor knew they were using the vault of a former bank as their daytime head-quarters. They sat out the heat of the day down there, copping Zs, shooting Plasto, and taking turns anally raping each other, then came out at night and worked the square. They mostly catered to the totally desperate, emaciated half-dead Plasto fiends, those with serious suicide habits, who the other dealers wouldn't deign to sell to. Taylor hadn't spoken to Rebello, whose guts he hated, for several years, but he figured Rudy would want to help him, once he had dis-located his elbow, or one of his scumbag associates would. The point was, whoever gave Dodo up, and after Taylor took Dodo somewhere and asked him a series of incisive questions regarding who he was cooperating with, and how much they knew about Cassandra, and the baby, and anything else he could think of ... Dodo Pacheco was fucking dead.

Now, the thing was, technically, before he brought an egregious and incredibly painful end to Dodo's worthless cooperating life, he needed to clear it with Adam and Sarah, because "no deviations" and all that shit. But that would be just a formality, he thought, because certainly, having heard his story, and having done some sort of "risk assessment," or whatever ridiculous operational procedure they would have to perform to make a decision, they would both agree that the Dodo situation was something that needed to be dealt with ... fatally. He figured he would probably find them down in the Branson Avenue basement that they mostly used for Action Updates but which also served as a daytime place to crash for some of the Fifthian Cluster. Or Adam would be down there, anyway. (Sarah had never told him where she slept, or how she spent her days, exactly.) So, OK, that's what he'd do, immediately ... after he did Cassandra's shopping.

Cassandra, at this point, was seven months pregnant, and miser-able, and peeing like twelve times a day, and getting up every hour or two while she was trying to sleep, in the heat, to pee. Which of course every time she got up to pee, or thinking she had to, she woke up Taylor, who hadn't slept for more than maybe ninety minutes at a stretch for weeks. Her nausea had passed (boy, that had been fun), and now it was only the total exhaustion, and the unrelenting physical discomfort, and the mood swings, and cravings, and the constant peeing, that were making her existence a living hell. That, and the ongoing Content Problem, and the fear of her nosy and annoying roommates, who were quietly freaking completely out over how she refused to come out of her bedroom, and who were probably going to cooperate on her ... oh, and also how Taylor now routinely showed up reeking of whatever her name was's cunt, as if she couldn't smell it all over him, while she, Cassandra, was a virtual prisoner, trapped inside her own fucking bedroom, peeing into a plastic bucket and watching the same ten Content discs, which were crap to begin with, for the last four months.

Taylor, at approximately 0650, bags of groceries and Content in tow, sleep deprived, headache throbbing, thoroughly sweat-drenched and pussy redolent, crawled in through Cassandra's window. He found her crouching beside the door, listening to one of her nosy roommates, who, apparently, if Taylor was correctly interpreting Cassandra's frantic series of gestures, was out there in the hallway right now, doing the same thing Cassandra was doing (i.e., crouching and listening through Cassandra's door). He set down the bags as quietly as possible and waved Cassandra away from the door. She crawled into bed and pulled up the sheet, assuming the infectious Hepatitis position. He tippytoed to the door (in his boots), gripped the doorknob, turned it silently, and yanked it open ... revealing nothing. No one was out there listening to anyone. Cassandra was obviously losing her shit.

"He was fucking out there," she assured him angrily. Jules (or Joel) was who she meant. Taylor told her he'd deal with that later ... and, oh yeah, they were out of Chewies, so he had gotten her these seaweed stick things instead. She reminded that him she hated those fucking stick things, which, if Taylor had ever actually listened to a fucking word she fucking said, he would have remembered she fucking hated, so now he could shove them up his ass. He told her she didn't have to fucking eat them, although, if she read the fucking box, she'd find out they were just like the Chewies, with a different name, but the same fucking shit. She informed him that he had no idea what the fuck he was talking about, and inquired as to whether he had finally managed to remove his dick from whatever her name was long enough to buy, or steal, or otherwise find her some new fucking Content, or whether she had to go fucking apeshit. He said, as a matter of fact, he had. He'd bought these fucking discs right here, and no, before she even asked, he didn't know what was fucking on them. He threw the discs onto the bed. She gave him that condescending Class 1 look, and wondered aloud if maybe she shouldn't just throw herself out the fucking window and put an end to this whole fucking nightmare, which Taylor was not making any easier by acting like a typical Class 3 asshole and talking to her like she was some kind of idiot, which if anyone was, it was fucking Taylor. Taylor apologized (not like he meant it) for saving her fucking life and all that, grabbed up her bucket, stormed across the hall, and emptied into the disgusting toilet that none of her nosy and annoying roommates had deemed it necessary to clean for weeks. One of the roommates (not Jules, or Joel, or whatever the fuck his fucking name was) was standing down there at the end of the hall, seriously contemplating coming down there. Seeing Taylor in the hall with the bucket, wild-eyed and not having slept for months, she changed her mind and got the hell out of there, which, OK, probably good decision. Taylor stalked back into the bedroom, put down the bucket, and started for the window, whereupon Cassandra immediately inquired as to where the fuck he thought he was going. He told her he had to take care of something. Cassandra replied that if he went out that window, that would be it, it would all be over, because she'd walk out onto Jefferson Avenue, seven months pregnant and (why not?) naked, and what did Taylor think about that?

Taylor, wincing, headache throbbing, sat her down on the edge of the bed and tried, as calmly as he possibly could, leaving out how he'd been at the Darkside deviantly fucking Sarah all night, to explain the recent Dodo sighting, and how he needed to get with Adam and Sarah and deal with same, which ... Cassandra didn't care.

"You're getting more paranoid than I am," she told him. "Which is saying something, because I'm losing my shit. I'm sitting here every night hallucinating roommates, and choppers, and goons out the window, while you're out fucking whatever her name is ..."

"Stop," he grabbed and held her wrists. "This is no joke. Dodo could burn us. If he knows about you …"

She twisted her wrists free.

"Listen to yourself. What actually happened? You saw a guy in a club somewhere … and what? What else?"

There was nothing else. Other than Taylor's sense of dread. That, and the Watchers, who were following him everywhere … or the Watchers he thought were following him everywhere.

"The fucking Watchers follow everyone everywhere. If they knew anything, we'd be dead already. You're freaking out."

OK, that … and Sarah, and her offer to smuggle him out with the baby, which he didn't want to burden Cassandra with. Or not at this particularly moment.

"I need to handle this."

"No. You don't. You need to stick to the plan like they said."

"The plan you keep saying is not going to work."

"Look at you. Look at both of us, will you? Please. Look at the shape we're both in. Stay. Help me get some sleep. You get some sleep. We'll both get some sleep."

"I need to …"

"Please. Please don't blow this."

"I'm not going to blow this."

"Yes. You are. And after all this … look, we made it this far. Two more months. We can make it two months. We can hold it together for two more months."

Taylor didn't know what to say.

"Close the curtains and get in bed. You can't go out in the heat now anyway. What were you thinking?"

He wasn't thinking. His head was throbbing. He could hardly see. Of course he couldn't go out in the heat. The expected high was 52 Celsius. His sleep-deprived brain would fry like halloumi before he even made it out of the sector. He closed his eyes and sat there in agony. What if she was right about all of it? What if Dodo was just a coincidence? What if he was just getting paranoid? He didn't know what to believe anymore.

"Sorry," he mumbled, and this time he meant it.

"Lie down," she ordered him.

Taylor did.

She sat there a moment watching him breathe. Then she used both hands to grab her gravidity, pulled herself up, waddled to the window, and drew the curtains to keep out the heat.

During the four weird weeks that followed, while the Normals were celebrating Easter, Passover, Resurrection Day, Egg-white Omelet Day, and the scores of other vernal holidays no one could remember why they were celebrating, Taylor's paranoia mounted. It wasn't just the sloppy tails he'd been shaking routinely since the end of October. He was seeing Watchers everywhere now, and he couldn't find Dodo Pacheco anywhere, and Sarah was still at work on his head, and there was still no go-date for the fucking D.A.D.A., and the thing with the chopper outside the Darkside ... what the fuck was up with that?

Or maybe it wasn't paranoia. Maybe it was just the insufferable heat. The daytime temperatures were up in the 50s. The humidity was one hundred percent at least. The talking heads on the Public Viewers were tracking some sort of cyclonic activity that was out in the Atlantic and moving this way. They were running all kinds of Doppler images, and impenetrable graphs, and generally panicking. The barometric pressure was dropping. Joints were aching. Moods were souring.

Or maybe it was lack of sleep. Sleeping in intervals of ninety minutes for months on end will do that to you. It will make you irritable, and moody, and jumpy, and overly suspicious, and totally paranoid.

In any event, whatever it was, he was seeing Community Watchers everywhere ... about which there was nothing imaginary. One day, two of them strolling down Clayton, right across from Gillie's Tavern, at 0600 in the fucking morning ... glancing into random doorways and making notes on their digital logs, as if a transparent ruse like that would fool a hardcore 3 like Taylor. The next day, another two, corner of Conolly, pretending that they weren't just fucking standing there waiting for Taylor to come up Mulberry, which what the fuck else would they have been doing there? A few nights later, three on Ohlsson, ostensibly checking Plasto scripts. And so on. Everywhere he fucking went. It was like some kind of Watchers convention.

As suffocating March turned to suffocating April, and the temperature rose, their numbers increased. Hordes of them now, all over the market, watching him out of the corners of their eyes as he shopped for Cassandra's morning groceries. Were they tracking his purchases? They might have been. He took to alternating stands more frequently. He also started noting the movements of Security cameras along his route, when they panned, or racked their focus, and comparing the number of Watcher sightings, those on any given morning, to those on any other given morning, and mentally logging the number of passes of low-flying drones and Security choppers, and checking the packaging of everything he bought for tracking devices, or listening devices, or miniature cameras or ... he wasn't quite sure.

Another thing he wasn't imagining was the disappearance of Dodo Pacheco, who had either gone into hiding somewhere far away across the Zone (which Taylor felt was extremely unlikely, given that Dodo never left the quadrant) or into some type of protective custody, and was sitting in an air-conditioned IntraZone facility ratting out Taylor for all he was worth. He'd gone down to Zuckerberg Square as planned (i.e., Taylor had, not Dodo Pacheco), and had had a few words with Rudy Rebello, who had sworn, between his agonized shrieks, that he hadn't seen Dodo Pacheco for weeks. He'd dutifully reported the Dodo sighting to Adam and Sarah that night at a meeting, an Action Group Update concerning the wording of the presumably final call-out for the D.A.D.A., the date of which (as of now, mid-April) had still not been consensually decided. They didn't seem too terribly concerned.

"We'll look into it," Adam told him.

"When?"

"When I fucking get around to it."

And that was wrong. That was not the right answer.

"If Dodo knows about Cassandra ..."

"We heard you the fucking first time, Chief."

"Yeah, well ... I thought you were maybe auditorily challenged or something.

"You're getting paranoid," Sarah whispered.

"Stick to the plan," Adam admonished him. "We'll take care of the Cooperators."

Taylor, as the weeks and months crept by, was growing less and less comfortable with Adam. Not that he had seen that much of him, except at meetings, which was fine with Taylor. But, see, there was another thing that was wrong, because despite the extensive preparations that according to Adam, and Jamie, and Dorian, and several other members of Adam's inner circle, had been ongoing on a sub rosa basis in various locations for the past five months, nothing visible was moving forward, or firming up, regarding the D.A.D.A., in terms of a date, or concrete plan, or anything else that anyone else at the Action Group Updates was privy to. No, it seemed (to Taylor, in his current state) like Adam, and his hardcore inner circle of jargon-spewing Transplant comrades, like Jamie, or Jamé, or whatever her name was, and Dorian and Maya, and two or three others, had just been using the D.A.D.A., which was never going to happen, as a means of recruiting as many new gullible militant Transplant idiots as possible, and then dividing them up into totally-autonomous working groups, which Adam controlled. The working groups, which were all allegedly hard at work on their respective projects, none of which could be discussed at meetings, in keeping with the tenets of security culture, were working in isolation from each other. No one, aside from Adam, apparently, knew what anyone else was doing.

And if that wasn't already suspicious enough, there was Sarah, and her fucking Unnameable Something, which was sounding more and more to Taylor like a dressed-up version of The One Who Was Many, and her ominous warnings, and Meyerish theories, and her constant pressuring Taylor to let her smuggle him out of the Zone with the baby ... all of which (apart from being highly fishy) was really starting to get on his dick. Every time they met now it seemed, after they'd done their deviant sex thing, which, frankly, was getting a bit routine, she would start in pressuring him to make a decision ... which Taylor had already strongly implied he wasn't going anywhere without Cassandra, but he hadn't categorically said he wasn't, so Sarah just kept needling away.

Two nights back, at Hardcore Carla's, he'd finally convinced her to tell him the plan ... or maybe she had always intended to tell him. More and more it felt to Taylor like everything that Sarah did was calculated, or was happening according to some sort of timeline, and that possibly every word she said was written down in a secret script, which she knew the end of but Taylor didn't.

In any event, on the day of the "action," which they figured would fall in the second week of May, the plan was, Taylor would go to Cassandra's, arriving at exactly 0630, pick up the "package," place the package in a towel inside a Transplant bag,* walk the package down Jefferson Avenue, turning, at exactly 0650, into an alley across from the stand where they sold the sun screen and other skincare lotions, at the far end of which some unspecified vehicle would pull up and wait for exactly two minutes.

"Where do I find you when she has the baby?"

"You don't. We'll know when she has the baby."

"How?"

Sarah gave him a look. So ... OK, they had someone watching her. And see, there was another thing that was wrong, because why the fuck were they watching Cassandra? More importantly, *how* were they watching her? Did they have a miniature camera in her room? Taylor wanted to know all this.

Sarah asked him to try to trust her.

"Oh, yeah, and one more thing ..."

Taylor was not to mention the plan, or anything remotely related to the plan, and definitely not the rendezvous point, to anyone, she stressed, including Adam.

What was he supposed to make of that?

"Nothing," she told him. "This is just how we do it."

Which Taylor knew was total bullshit. Sarah had been avoiding Adam. Or she had missed a lot of meetings recently. And the vibe between them had subtly changed, maybe on account of how Sarah was getting tied up and deviantly fucked by Taylor, which Adam was clearly not a big fan of, or maybe on account of something else ... but wait, the next part was even better.

After Taylor had verbally acknowledged that he understood and would follow the plan, she grabbed her backpack from beside the bed, set it on her belly, unzipped a pocket, reached in and took out

---

* One of the standard unmarked duffels they issued to every incoming Transplant, which then got bought and sold repeatedly, such that pretty much every A.S.P. had one.

a laminated card. She handed him the card. He held it to the light. His photo was there in the upper right corner. Printed beside it in IntraZone typeface:

WORK/TRAVEL CLEARANCE
BOYD, TYLER, A.S.P. (1), ZONE 23
0820.2565.709.Z23.
SANITATION SERVICES, RESIDENTIAL

"In case you change your mind," she said. "We'll activate it on the day of the action. You'll have about twenty-five minutes to use it before the sys-scan picks up the hack."

Taylor sat there, staring at the pass. His picture, the typeface, the IntraZone logo ... every little detail was perfect. Which was totally fucked. Because how could they do this? No one could do this. Who were these people? He turned to Sarah.

"Who are you people?"

Meyer's warning flashed through his head.

Everybody infiltrates everybody. Everybody uses everybody.

Sarah was staring off into space.

"Listen," she said, "if anything happens, no matter what happens, the vehicle will be there. Get to the rendezvous point with the package."

"What's going to happen?"

"Did you hear what I said?"

"Yeah. I heard. The rendezvous point. What's going to happen?"

She didn't answer.

"What are we going to do about Dodo?"

"Forget about Dodo. Forget the Watchers."

"If they're on to Cassandra ..."

"Forget the Watchers."

"Dodo Pacheco knows her name."

"Dodo Pacheco has nothing to do with this."

"To do with what?"

"With any of this."

He came around and squatted in front of her.

"What's going on?"

She looked into his eyes. She looked like she'd looked the first time he saw her, back before he knew who she was ... or whoever she wanted him to think she was.

"What's wrong?" he asked.

She smiled, sadly.

"Nothing," she said. "Nothing is wrong."

Something was wrong. Taylor was sure of that. He didn't know what, but definitely something ... something about how Sarah was acting, and the pass was wrong, was seriously wrong. Even if she was on the level, and a few of her faith-based Terrorist network were Normals, who were helping her to smuggle out the babies (which Taylor had reluctantly begun to believe), this was an IntraZone Travel-to-Work Pass ... an authentic pass, or a perfect forgery, which there was no such thing as a perfect forgery.* And why weren't Sarah, and Adam of all people, Adam, who was fucking security-obsessed, concerned in the least about all these Watchers, and Dodo, and ... see, that was also wrong. And what about Cassandra's annoying roommates, in particular this asshole, Joel, or whoever, who'd been snooping around Cassandra's door, which Taylor had also reported to Sarah, who'd seemed like she was only half listening, which made no sense ... unless ... unless ...

At some point during the first week of April, while elderly Anti-Social Persons were dying of heatstroke inside their apartments, and "Jimbo" Cartwright, who was in a coma, bravely fought his final battle, Taylor faced the possibility that the last six months, this whole misadventure, the entire baby-smuggling operation, Adam, Sarah, the Fifthian Cluster, the Day of Autonomous Decentralized Action, the defective condom, the MorningAfter Pill, all of it, right from the very beginning, had been one big byzantine IntraZone trap ... a trap that he and Cassandra had stumbled, or rather, had carelessly fucked their way into, the inexorable Corporatist jaws of which were now in the process of closing on them. Because ... OK, the extra heat from the Watchers, and even Dodo's cooperation, and disappearance, could be reasonably explained, because certainly IntraZone Waste & Security, or conceivably even an Intelligence Unit of the Hadley

---

* *IntraZone passes were impossible to counterfeit. They had all these watermarks and holograms and so on, which you couldn't reproduce inside the Zone.*

Corporation of Menomonie, Wisconsin, would have picked up chatter on its listening networks strongly suggesting that the A.S.U. was planning some kind of utterly futile but nonetheless highly disruptive action, which Adam, and by extension Sarah, and thus, by association, Taylor, were obviously up to their eyeballs in, and would have ordered the Watchers to order their Cooperators to rat out anyone who might be involved, which Dodo had done, which made perfect sense, and the condom was just a defective condom, and the MorningAfter Pills a bad batch of pills, or Cassandra had just had a bad reaction, and the D.A.D.A. would actually happen, someday, as soon as a date had been consensually decided ... each and every piece of the puzzle, obsessed about in isolation, theoretically, could be explained.

Or almost every piece of the puzzle.

The counterfeit travel pass could not be explained ... not to Taylor's satisfaction. And why was Sarah, or whichever outfit Sarah (if that was even her name) was involved with so invested in Taylor ... in smuggling Taylor out of the Zone? Was the whole thing one big Terrorist mind game, an elaborate psychological experiment, or was it simply an IntraZone Waste & Security (or a Hadley Domestic Security) set-up? And if so, why? To achieve what end? To track him out into the Autonomous Zones? Surely, with all their advanced technology, they would never resort to such primitive measures. Was it possible Sarah was on the level, and was hooked into some secret network that was not only active in the Normal Communities, but that had also somehow infiltrated the Hadley Corporation of Menomonie, Wisconsin, and could generate perfect travel passes for A.S.P. 3s whenever they wanted? He tried to get his mind around that. But now he was back to where he'd started ... why would they have chosen him?

Taylor, having faced all this (i.e., all these questions that he could not answer and scenarios he could not rule out), did not know what the hell to do. And so, he decided, he wouldn't do anything ... not without some confirmation as to what was what and who was who (and as to whether he was now completely paranoid, or was really as fucked as he thought he might be). In the meantime, he stuck to his normal routine, spending his days in bed with Cassandra, who was going through a gassy phase, and his nights with an ever more distant Sarah, or just wandering aimlessly around the Zone, which by this time was like a open-air sauna, his head going round and round and round ...

He got the confirmation he needed in the wee hours of officially 16 April, a particularly oppressive and ignominious morning. He was sitting alone in a booth at Gillie's, chasing shots of Dusky Grouse with piss warm beer and sweating profusely. Everyone at Gillie's was sweating profusely, and drinking heavily, and those who weren't were sitting around in semi-fugue states stinking like goats with their mouths hanging open. T.C. Johns was down in the head, trying to get the water to work enough to fill up the drain in the floor and stop it reeking like an open sewer. Young Man Henry, who was running the bar, was taking bets from the White Street Boys, and sundry other Class 3 scoundrels, on when and exactly in which direction Jim MacReady was going to pass out and fall off his stool and knock all his teeth out. In a booth across the room from Taylor, Charlie Gilmartin and Vaclav Borges were talking some totally shitfaced 2 with an eyebrow ring and a harelip scar out of whatever money he had wandered in with. Coreen Sweeney was sitting by herself at her usual table, staring into space. She looked like some kind of wax figurine, as in she hadn't twitched, coughed or blinked for five or ten minutes, and was probably dead. A din erupted from around the bar as Jim MacReady swayed southwest, and looked like he was going down, until Walter Dupree, who had a hundred on north, straightened him up with a vicious uppercut. MacReady started to teeter northeast, but now the rules were out the window, and one of the other White Street Boys, who must have had his money on south, caught him on the bridge of the nose with a roundhouse, knocking him off his stool to the floor. At some point during the melee that ensued, and lasted almost a full two minutes (which in terms of bar fights is like an eternity), and that was brought to an end by T.C. Johns, who waded in swinging this giant pipe wrench, someone, a spindly, spiderlike person, bearing an uncannily close resemblance, in Taylor's opinion, to Dodo Pacheco, slunk into Gillie's and up to the bar, the far end, steering clear of the scrimmage, which had now winnowed down to Walter Dupree, who was up in the face of T.C.

Johns, waving his arms all around and shouting, which shouting was spraying the massive lenses of T.C.'s glasses with flecks of spittle, which T.C. promptly put an end to by grabbing Walter Dupree by the scrotum and squeezing his balls as hard as he could, as if he were trying to crack one walnut by squeezing it against another walnut.

Taylor was relatively drunk at this point, so he couldn't be sure, but the longer he stared at this gangly Dodo Pacheco-like person, who had now gotten Young Man Henry's attention and summoned him over to the end of the bar, the more convinced he became that he was actually staring at Dodo Pacheco. Which made no sense, and couldn't have been right ... that is, until Dodo turned and smiled.* Then he walked right up to Taylor's booth and sat down across from him and started talking.

Dodo it appeared was the under the impression that Taylor had somehow come to believe that Dodo was in some way cooperating on him, and had been asking around the Zone about him (i.e., Dodo's current whereabouts and so on), and wanted to find him, and talk to him, and kill him. Which, OK, Dodo understood how Taylor could've come to believe that about him, because technically, in a sense, it was true ... but not like Taylor thought or anything, on account of how Dodo hadn't told them anything they didn't already know, or think they knew, or suspect about Taylor, who he had always had, like, the most respect for, despite whatever ugly history Taylor might have had with Rudy Rebello, who Dodo had never trusted, personally. The thing was, see, the reason he was there, Dodo, sitting there across from Taylor, in spite of the fact that Taylor wanted to gouge out his eyes with a spoon or something, was that he wanted to, you know, come clean with Taylor, and, you know, warn him, and tip him off, like. Apparently, the deal was, according to Dodo, this Community Watcher, one J.C. Bodroon, had taken a personal interest in Taylor, and was trying to gather enough information to take to IntraZone Waste & Security to prove that Taylor was up to something ... something involving the A.S.U., and some Terrorist uprising, or attack, they were planning, and oh yeah, Dodo just remembered ... possibly also an unauthorized baby. According to

---

* It was one of those classic obsequious smiles that Dodo employed at every opportunity to try to ingratiate himself with whoever.

Dodo, this Watcher, Bodroon, who Dodo swore held some kind of senior rank in the risible Watcher hierarchy, was all over Taylor like white on TōRice, and had been for weeks, and probably months, and knew he had a woman somewhere in the general vicinity of Jefferson Avenue, but he didn't know exactly where, because Taylor had been losing his men at the markets. Allegedly, six weeks back, approximately, this Watcher, Bodroon, and a few other goons, had collected Dodo from some Plasto pit, and forced him to, like, cooperate on Taylor, which Dodo was only, like, pretending to do, because really, he was acting as a double agent, and was working on Taylor's behalf ... and so on.

Taylor sat there, utterly stone-faced, still quite drunk, but sobering quickly, as Dodo, shifting back and forth on his ass cheeks, and continuously fidgeting with his clothes and hair, expounded this extremely improbable bullshit. He let Dodo get to the point in his tale where he swore on his life (and whatever Taylor wanted) that this Watcher, Bodroon, as far as he knew, not only had not identified Cassandra, but had also not reported back regarding Taylor to his IntraZone handlers. He hadn't done this, Dodo explained, because his plan was, once he had the whole case, Bodroon (who Dodo described as "humongous"), all wrapped up with a bow on top, he'd be better positioned for some serious suck-up ... at which point Taylor interrupted him. He said he wanted to know one thing.

"Where can I find this fucking Watcher?"

Dodo said they had this place on Broad Street.

Taylor nodded.

"Good," he said.

"So, are we OK?" Dodo wanted to know.

"Yeah," Taylor said. "We're OK. Just one more thing."

"Anything, bro. Whatever you need."

"Take me down there."

"To Broad Street?"

"Yeah. Show me the place."

Taylor, who already knew the place, and had no intention of going down there, walked an increasingly twitchy Dodo, who was obviously due for a Plasto fix, west on Clayton toward the canal. Coming up to the corner of Broad, he grabbed Dodo by the back of the neck

and steered him into this service alley that didn't go anywhere, which
Dodo knew. The alley stank of liquified garbage, that, and the scum
in the Dell Street canal, which was two blocks down and a right
off Broad, the north end, a long way away from the station where
the Watchers, and probably Security Specialists, were waiting in the
dark to pounce on Taylor.

"Oh, no … no," Dodo moaned, as he lost voluntary control of his
sphincter. He went all rubbery and started shaking. "Please …"

Taylor pushed him on.

Taylor hadn't egregiously violated anyone to death in over ten
years, not since he'd settled down with Cassandra. It wasn't that
he'd gotten religion or anything. He simply hadn't had any cause to.
Somewhere around the age of thirty, the Plasto gangs, the barroom
brawlers, and all the other predatory assholes who had plagued his
youth started leaving him alone. This was one of the interesting features of the ecosystem, as it were, of the Zone. You take your average
Class 3 hardass, a guy like Taylor, or Charlie Gilmartin, or Vaclav
Borges, or any of these guys, their odds of living to the ripe old age
of forty were like two hundred thousand to one. Thus, if they did, by
the time they did, there were two or three things you could pretty
much count on … one, they had killed a lot of people, two, they had
gotten away with killing them, and three … whatever … the point
here being, these were not the kind of guys you fucked with. These
were guys to whom your life, and the agonized high-pitched shrieks
you made as they took it from you, meant less than nothing. Some
of them, Vaclav Borges, for example, would stick-and-twist you as
a kind of sport, just to see if he could hit your liver, which by this
time Vaclav was pretty good at. Which isn't to say that Taylor was
all gung-ho to stomp Dodo's skull all to pieces. He'd never gotten
off on wasting people, even back in the bad old days. It was just …
well, sometimes it had to be done. And in this case it definitely had
to be done. And it had to be done tonight, apparently. The only plau-
sible explanation for Dodo's appearance and confession at Gillie's
was that IntraZone Waste & Security Services (or possibly Hadley
Domestic Security) wanted Taylor to walk down Broad Street, in
search of this alleged Bodroon, and into the sights of their UltraLite
rifles … which Taylor had no intention of doing.

Once they got far enough into the alley that no one would see or hear them from the street, Taylor grabbed Dodo from behind by the shoulders, spun him around so they were facing each other, and kicked down diagonally through Dodo's right knee joint, severing several ligaments crucial to standing upright and not screaming in agony. What happens when you do this is you hear this POP and the person whose knee you've just destroyed collapses, usually in the direction of your kick. Dodo did this, and as soon as he did, and was just about to start screaming in agony, Taylor stomped down on the bridge of his nose, ripping the cartilage clean off the skull bone. Now, this is just as painful as it sounds, and is often accompanied by temporary blindness, which in Dodo's case it definitely was, so that now he lay there, staring at nothing, crying, shaking, sputtering blood, his hands upraised in supplication, wrists together, fingers fluttering, begging Taylor in a gurgling whisper to wait … wait … wait … and so on. "No deviations," Sarah's voice said, as he stomped down on Dodo's skull, repeatedly, as if he was trying to drive his heel through Dodo's head down into the pavement. And here came that taste in the back of his throat, that familiar metallic adrenaline taste, which he hadn't tasted for all these years, and Dodo wasn't saying anything … and everything was finally getting simple.

There wasn't any thunder at first … just the sudden, deafening roar of the rain as it came down pounding hard and hot on all that heat-baked concrete and metal and melting asphalt and synthetic tar and liquified garbage and shattered glass and discarded hypos and feces pretzels with an uncontrollable inhuman force. Taylor stepped back, away from Dodo, who could not hear or feel the rain or the pain or anything else anymore, and closed his eyes and tilted his head back and let the rain beat down on his face. He stayed like that for close to a minute. He looked like one of those Roman statues, except that he happened to be wearing chinos and a filthy old T-shirt and combat boots, and was moving his arms incredibly slowly in backwards more or less S-like patterns. He didn't know why he was doing that, exactly, standing there in the rain like that, doing whatever he was doing with his arms, and with his hands, with all his fingers extended. He didn't care. He wasn't thinking. He was drunk, but in that weird sort of lucid way. At some point, while he was doing this, this modern dance-type thing he was doing, the thunder started, because now it was booming and echoing down the dark of the alley, and the night overhead was flashing shades of lipstick pink and TV blue ...

Taylor walked around in the rain, going nowhere, for close to an hour. The temperature dropped like ten degrees. The wind was blowing bits of paper, cellophane, rags, plastic bags, pages torn from old paperback books, scraps of old IntraZone ConCept posters, and anything light enough to rise on the currents, into the air like swirling confetti. Sidewalk gutters overflowed and rats came pouring up out of the sewers and flooded basements and holes in the ground and scrambled up stoops and into buildings, and anywhere they could to keep from drowning. People were sticking their heads out of windows, and crawling out onto their fire escapes, and walking out into the rain in the streets, which were coursing with water like reborn rivers. Webs of lightning ripped through the sky like shatter patterns on an enormous windshield. Teeth-rattling claps of thunder followed. It sounded like an aerial bombardment.

Taylor walked up out of the Sector, and around in circles in Sector B, and he sat down on an empty stoop, and he sat there in the rain and the wind with the lightning striking the tops of buildings and the thunder cracking and people shouting. He sat there like that for several minutes without a single thought in his head.

Shortly after 0600, he wandered back up to Jefferson Avenue and did Cassandra's morning shopping. He did this in the torrential rain, and the gale force wind that was ripping the canvas awnings off the fruit and vegetable stalls, and the signs off of buildings, and rattling windows, and blowing money out of vendors' hands. He wasn't the only one out there shopping. The markets were packed with Anti-Socials, every last one of them soaked to the bone, happily wading from stand to stand. They poked little holes in their plastic bags to keep them from filling up with water. People were standing around in the downpour, laughing, actually talking to each other. The Security Specialists had taken cover inside their stations outside the gates. The talking heads on the Public Viewers were breathlessly squawking into cameras, repeatedly declaring a weather-related state of emergency throughout the Region. Apparently, every available resource was being immediately brought to bear.

When he finally climbed through Cassandra's window, clutching his soggy bags of groceries, he found Cassandra on the floor by her bucket. She was crying. It looked like she'd peed on the floor. She hadn't, of course. Her water had broken. She was sitting there in the puddle, sobbing. She looked up at Taylor with a look he knew but had never seen on the face of Cassandra ... let's go ahead and call it white-faced terror.

"The fuck are you doing?" he asked her, stupidly.

"What does it fucking look like," she blubbered.

A bolt of lightning struck outside, splashing the bedroom with bright orange light.

"It's not supposed to be for a month."

"I know. It's coming now," she told him.

"Stop it."

Apparently this was funny, because Cassandra immediately burst out laughing. She sat there in her puddle of water, staring at nothing, laughing hysterically. Then she doubled over and screamed ...

Mission Abort

Meanwhile, back in officially March, on some made-up date that didn't matter anymore, as had a procession of outwardly normal-looking but inwardly ruthlessly methodical killers that snaked like some macabre parade along the margins of the annals of history, whose ranks she was about to join, Valentina made a shopping list. On it were the following essential items.

> Isopropyl alcohol, 500 ml.
> IbuFlam Plus, 100 tablets.
> Antimicrobial soap, liquid.
> Laminaria, dried, sticks.
> Latex gloves, sterile, powdered.
> Plastic garbage bags, heavy-duty.
> Packing tape, 1 roll, transparent.
> Ziploc bags, X-large, 4 count.
> Sanitary pads, super absorbent.
> Assorted hand towels, any color.
> Barbecue scissor tongs, dishwasher safe.
> Barbecue skewer, metal, stainless.

Valentina purchased these items at different stores in Center City, paying for them with different credit cards, some in Kyle's name, some in hers. She combined the more suspicious items with other fairly innocuous items. She did this in a futile attempt to throw off the programs that logged and analyzed every Normal's purchasing patterns on an ongoing, more or less Real-Time basis. She did this in the middle of the night, mostly at stores at the Bowlingbroke Mall, but she also stopped at a couple of places between the mall and the

Skyline Motor Lodge. This, she hoped, would prevent the programs from flagging her already rather dubious series of "contextually random" purchases as "geographically inconsistent," and placing holds on all her cards, and sending Security Services after her.

Before setting out on her shopping mission, she placed the HCS60 inside an airtight Ziploc plastic bag, the one that held her travel-size lotions, sealed it securely and dropped it into the reservoir tank of the old-fashioned toilet. She watched it slowly sink to the bottom, then she gently replaced the porcelain lid. She zipped the MemCard into the pocket in her purse where she kept her other cards, switched off the lights and the Courtesy Viewer, checked the peephole just to be safe, and then slipped out into the deafening roar of a JiffyJet CRL-9000 that was screaming across the sky overhead. She pressed the palms of her hands to her ears and tiptoed down the concrete balcony, past 301 and 302, both of which appeared to be vacant, down the yellow concrete stairs, across the parking lot, past the receptacles, and came out onto Industrial Avenue, a desolate stretch of former garages, garment factories, and small machine shops that looked like maybe it extended off to the north forever, though she knew it didn't. She walked to the corner, turned onto Commerce, and walked due east, the way she'd come, successfully avoiding the throngs of families and Security cameras in the Skyline lobby. Something told her to eschew the tram and walk the fifteen, sixteen blocks, which the GPS on the Courtesy Viewer had said would take about nineteen minutes.

She made it to the mall a half hour later, drenched with sweat, her hair a mess, in desperate need of air-conditioning and somewhere to sit down and drink a lot of water. Unfortunately, the only way into the mall was through a set of ever-revolving glass and chromium carousel doors that accommodated up to ninety-three people and advanced at a pace of one meter a minute, presumably for reasons of personal safety. She squeezed her way into the horde in the doors and shuffled toward the air-conditioning. The carousel smelled like body odor, polyester clothing, and cheap shampoo ...

Finally inside, she purchased a bottle of Ellesmere Island organic water for fourteen fifty at the Bunga Bunga, an organic juice place with a Polynesian theme. She shuffled toward the central concourse.

Her legs weren't working. She needed to rest. She collapsed down into one of the slots in this podlike "courtesy seating unit" where people could sit for up to ten minutes, after which an alarm went off and the slot they were sitting in started vibrating. She didn't plan to be there that long. She drank her water and scanned the terrain.

Herds of less-than-abundant Normals, most of them wearing synthetic track suits emblazoned with garish corporate logos, were drifting in and out of the low-end stores, dragging humongous transparent bags of prominently branded downscale products and obsessively checking the screens of their Viewers for news of the next big half-off sale. Many of them seemed to be humming along with the upbeat inspirational Muzak that was oozing out of the doors of stores, the walls, the ceiling, the thing she was sitting in, and pretty much every other object and surface you could hide a set of speakers in. Valentina listened closely, but she couldn't detect the subliminal messages IT had embedded inside the Muzak. It didn't matter ... she knew what they were. She hadn't noticed this subliminal Muzak at the Northside Mall, but it must have been playing. How many nights ago was that now? Two, three? She couldn't remember.

Another thing she hadn't noticed during her first few days down here, but noticed now, was the absence of Clears ... Clears above the age of twelve. The vast majority of the Bowlingbroke shoppers were either in the thirty-one to forty demographic or the forty-one to forty-nine demographic, and those who weren't were even older. Their children were either infants in strollers, or toddlers in strollers, or pre-adolescents. None of them were over the age of eleven. Valentina knew why this was, but she had never seen the effect in the flesh. The corporations offered a range of low- and variable-interest rate loans, and other generous financial assistance, to non-abundant Variant-Positive parents of Clarion children in need. This assistance enabled them to send their kids to technically-oriented boarding academies located out in the Residential Communities, where they learned any number of high-tech skills that led to financially rewarding careers, and where their parents could visit them once a month, but not in their brightly-colored track suits.

Valentina finished her water, wiped was left of the sweat from her face, said her mantra, pushed herself up, checked her shopping list, and got down to business. She stuck to the more familiar chains, CRS, Big Buy Basement, Family Farm, Whipple's, and Finkles, and avoided the smaller, more specialized places like Ollie's Ointments and Gadget City.

By 0020 she was out of the mall and walking west with her bag of items. Up ahead was a cluster of stores in what looked like a former office complex, one of which was an all-night Quik Shop. One of the others was definitely a pharmacy. She could make out the little green illuminated cross. She had passed it on her way to the mall, and thought she remembered it being an Albrecht's, but it could have been a Brecker's, or Vedder's ... not that it really mattered which it was. Overhead, the sky was screaming with commercial and corporate aircraft as usual. A driverless tram was whisking up the middle of the empty road to her left ... or the almost empty road to her left ... because there, meandering along just behind her, was a totally inconspicuous-looking unmarked four-door passenger vehicle, which being the only passenger vehicle out on the road was extremely conspicuous. Less-than-abundant Variant Positives did not tend to have their own passenger vehicles. What vehicles they did have were normally work-vans, which were loaded with plumbing or gardening equipment, and more often than not belonged to whatever Community or company they happened to work for.

"Now they've got you," the tape in her head said.

Valentina's anal sphincter clamped shut like an emergency airlock. She turned her head away from the vehicle and commanded her body to keep on walking. She guessed she had about three or four seconds before they screeched to a stop in front of her, leaped out, wrestled her down to the ground, plasti-cuffed her, and shoved her in the back. After which they'd inspect her bag, deduce what she was planning to do (that is, if they hadn't deduced it already), go through her purse, and find the MemCard. She briefly contemplated reaching down, pulling out the barbecue skewer, shoving it into her optic canal, through her frontal lobe and into the midbrain, which she thought she might be able to accomplish if she did it all in one violent motion. However, just as she was calculating the angle of entry into her mid brain, the car sped up and drove on past her. She watched its tail-lights recede in the dark, then turn off somewhere

up ahead, which might have been into the Skyline Motor Lodge ...
or not, she couldn't quite tell at that distance.

She picked up her pace and arrived at the Quik Shop, where she
purchased the roll of plastic garbage bags (the white ones, which
were all they had at the moment), and some sugarless gum and a disposable bottle opener, from a person of indeterminate gender with
bleached-white hair that just reeked of ammonia. She stopped next
door at (it turned out) the Albrecht's, bought the bottle of IbuFlam
tablets, and a box of extra-large edible condoms that came in assorted flavors and colors.

Walking the last six blocks to the Skyline, she mentally rehearsed
the scheduled procedure, a slight variation on a standard D&E.
She'd worked it all out in her head that morning, the morning following her crisis of faith, or whatever it was she'd experienced out
by the pool the previous night at the Skyline. She'd gone back up to
Room 303 and run through a number of desperate scenarios. She'd
briefly entertained the idea of swiping in at Breckenridge Medical,
sneaking into the heavily-guarded pharmacy down the hall from her
lab, stealing a bottle of MifegyneX (or some other type of aborti-
facient), rushing up the emergency stairs as BMC Security closed
in on her, and leaping off the sixth floor roof and into the hedges
surrounding the complex and ... all right, that was out of the question. As was vacuum aspiration, which would have been her next
best option, except that your standard vacuum cleaner was twenty
times weaker than what she needed. No, she was going to have to
do it the hard way, which she wasn't particularly looking forward to.
However, she was a medical professional. The only really significant
risk was perforating her uterus, or cervix, or potentially even her
small intestine, and uncontrollably hemorrhaging to death, or developing sepsis, a blood infection, or septicemia, a related condition, or
potentially even bacteremia, each of which, if left untreated, led to
multiple organ failure.

Stepping into the neon orange spill of the Skyline Motor Lodge
sign, which was mounted at the mouth of the empty parking lot, so
facing the empty street beyond, Valentina just had a feeling ... she
squeezed up against the cinder block wall that bordered the lot and
peered around it. There it was, the black sedan, idling just outside the

lobby. A man was sitting in the passenger seat. She couldn't make him out in the darkness. Where was the driver? There he was. A way-too-abundant man in his thirties in a dark blue suit with a jar-head haircut, standing at the desk with perfect posture, asking Kim, or whatever his name was, to bring up a digital map of the grounds which would show him the various approaches to her room. She drew her head back around the corner.

"Walk in there and surrender to them," the voice on the tape in her head suggested. "Tell them what happened. They're here to help you." She clutched the bag of items to her chest, closed her eyes, took a deep breath, opened her eyes and ... there was the tram, gliding silently up beside her. Well, OK, technically not right beside her, but fifteen to twenty meters away ... pulling past her now, another twelve meters, and up to the empty concrete platform in the median in the middle of Commerce. The tram was empty. The lights were on. Industrial Avenue was the end of the line. It slowed and stopped. The doors whooshed open. If she ran right now, she could probably make it.

"What are you thinking? You'll never make it."

She crouched down low and crossed the street, staying out of the line of sight of the man in the car, at least this far, got to the walk-way that led to the platform ... but now she had to get to the tram, which was more or less directly across from the lobby. She dipped her head and raised her bag, hoping it might distract from her face, and walked, calmly, or relatively calmly, resisting the urge to turn her head and ... she just made it in as the beeper beeped. The automatic doors whooshed closed behind her. She took a seat behind a panel between two windows, where he couldn't see her, clutched her bag and stared straight ahead. As the tram slid silently away from the platform, she risked a glance back into the parking lot. The car was still there, lights on, idling. She didn't have time to check the lobby.

She sat there, alone, on the driverless tram, heading east with her bag of items, the clothes on her back, and the things in her purse. The rest of her belongings, the Vittorio suitcase, and most impor-tantly the HCS60, were back in the room ... which meant they were gone. She quickly checked inside her purse. Yes, she had. She'd kept the MemCard. But now, of course, she couldn't use it, not without

the HCS60, which was down at the bottom of the reservoir tank of
the toilet back in Room 303.

She rode the tram to the Bowlingbroke Mall, got out, crossed a
plaza, or square, or an strip of cement in any event, took a seat in an
open-air kiosk, waited two minutes, then got on another tram. This
one appeared to be heading north, to somewhere known as Evanston
Square, which Valentina had never heard of, but which was probably within walking distance of the Southern Cross Station on the
Yellow Ring line ... the Ring line being the unofficial inner border of
the Business District. The trams that ran through Center City were
connected to each another, of course, but they didn't connect to the
WhisperTrain network that serviced the Residential Communities.
The only way to get from the Communities to Center City was the
Airport Express. The Express didn't stop in Center City. It took you
directly to the airport. Once you were there, there was nothing stopping you from walking outside and taking a tram to anywhere you
wanted in Center City ... but no one had any reason to do that. As
for getting out of Center City, well, OK, you could take a tram to the
airport and buy a seat on the Express, assuming you could afford a
seat, which most of your Center City Normals couldn't, or you could
take a tram out to the periphery where Center City sort of ended
and the Business District sort of began, and then walk the twenty
or thirty blocks from the end of the line to a WhisperTrain station.

All of which was academic, because Valentina had no intention
of availing herself of any of these options. She wasn't going back to
Pewter Palisades or anywhere else in the Residential Communities.
All she wanted to do at this point was to get as far as possible away
from that black sedan, and get her bearings. Which wasn't as easy as
you might imagine. The Center City trams, unlike the WhisperTrains,
were not equipped with built-in Viewers with interactive GPS, but
rather with these ratty old laminated maps displaying an indecipher-
able graphic that bore no resemblance to the actual geography and
that looked like some kind of circuitry schematic.

She sat there in the back of the tram, in the hollow of her molded
fiberglass seat, bag of items between her feet, desperately practicing
Nadi Shodhana. Five rows up, a withered little man in a pea green
suit who was sitting backwards was glancing at her every five or

six seconds, smiling to himself, then looking back down and typing on the screen of his All-in-One. Valentina didn't like the look of him. The other four passengers looked innocuous, a sweet-looking octogenarian couple with matching coral and chartreuse sweatsuits, a thirty-something student type, and a fiftyish woman who was probably a prostitute. Valentina pinched her nostrils and focused her attention on the man in green. She didn't want to stare directly at him, so she kept him fixed in the corner of her vision, pretending to be looking out the window as she inhaled left, pinched, held it, exhaled right, inhaled right. Out the window, whooshing past her, the brightly painted brick facades of stores with pseudo-Spanish names and gated appliance and hardware shops and chains of artificial chicken places were replaced by strips of peeling posters of beautiful models (all of whom were dead) holding up former haircare products with ragged chunks torn out of their faces.

The tram pulled up to an empty platform in the middle of something called J. Hoople Plaza, which looked like maybe it had been some kind of shopping complex a thousand years ago. The man in the pea green suit got out. He limped across the desolate square toward an indistinguishable shape in the shadows, which might have been a Security vehicle, an unmarked sedan, or it might have been nothing. She turned and tried to make out the shape as the tram pulled out of J. Hoople Plaza but there wasn't time and it passed out of view as the man blended into the surrounding darkness.

She got off the tram at Mecklenburg Mews, seven stops up from J. Hoople Plaza, and one stop short of Evanston Square, the end of the line of the tram she'd been riding. She left the tram at Mecklenburg Mews not because she knew where she was (she didn't ... she had never heard of the place) but because, as the tram was approaching the Mews, she had seen a string of "antique" shops, which she knew were really just worthless junk shops. But here's what Valentina was thinking ... one of these so-called "antique" shops might have, if not an HCS60, then some kind of obsolete Content Viewer, or some other device that could play the MemCard. She didn't know whether she could trust the MemCard, but logic told her she probably could. If the messages on the HCS60 had been sent by one of the Security Services, they'd have stormed Room 303 in force.

They wouldn't have sent a couple of agents in a black sedan to snoop around, talk to Kim and find out her room number ... or whatever it was they were actually doing.

At approximately 0230 that morning, she checked into the Hotel Huffington, which wasn't really a hotel as much as some kind of execrable, ad hoc boarding house. It was down this unmarked lane, or alley, which it smelled like people defecated in. Before she checked in, she had walked back down to the "antique" stores she'd seen from the tram. She couldn't see in through the pull-down gates, but they definitely looked like going concerns.

The reception area of the Hotel Huffington was under the bottom of an iron staircase that took one up to the rows of filthy airless cubicles they passed off as rooms. The reception desk was in a hole in the wall, which you wouldn't even want to call an alcove. The night clerk looked like the pictures they put on the warning labels for alcoholic beverages.

Valentina inquired as to the availability of an en suite room. The night clerk mumbled something in Spanish and held out his hand, which was missing two fingers. Valentina handed him a card that Kyle hadn't used in over three years. The night clerk scanned it and handed it back, along with a greasy plastic KeyCard.

Valentina's en suite room was a windowless cell on the second floor with a central AC vent that didn't work and a formerly cream-colored wall-to-wall carpet that was made out of some type of itchy acrylic. The bed, which took up half the room, was a worn-out futon dressed with a sheet prodigiously stained with sweat and semen. Across from the bed, on top of the carpet, men with cognitive disabilities had installed a plastic shower basin, a miniature sink and a miniature toilet. Several genera of toxic molds were growing up the wall behind them. Bolted to the wall beside the bed was an ancient Azimuth flatscreen Viewer. Valentina switched it on. She manually scanned through several channels, most of which were nothing but static, but one of which was trying to display some scrambled Content she couldn't make out. Twisted melting demonic faces leered at her out of the visual chaos. She punched the power and switched them off.

"The loving, compassionate oneness of ..."

Once she felt herself detach, she sat down on the edge of the
futon and took quick stock of her situation. Her situation was not
at all good. Security Services were definitely onto her. Either Kyle
had called her in missing, or Susan Foster had called her in, or her
recent purchases had thrown up a flag ... or whatever, it didn't really matter what had happened. Whatever had happened, they had
found her at the Skyline. And eventually they would find her here.
Whether they found her in a matter of minutes or a matter of hours
was the salient question. The answer depended on how long it took
for the Huffington to upload its batched transactions, which they
clearly were not doing in Real-Time. From what she had seen of the
infrastructure in that hole down there at the bottom of the stairs,
she figured she had at least a few hours ... time enough to complete the procedure. After she'd recovered enough to walk (which if
all went smoothly wouldn't be that long), her plan was, she would
go downstairs, rifle through the shelves of those junk shops, find a
replacement for the HCS60, reestablish contact with N.I.N., and
advise them that she'd completed the procedure, and had passed
their test, and murdered her baby, at which point they would come
and rescue her, at which point this would all be over.

She didn't actually believe in this plan, or, OK, maybe some part of
her did, but most of her didn't, which felt kind of weird, because the
part of her that knew, or was fairly sure, that she was either going to
wind up dead, or hospitalized for the rest of her life, was telling the
other part of her that didn't (i.e., the part that had to believe in this
plan) that it didn't know what it clearly knew ... which was totally
schizoid, and technically impossible.

She dug into her bag of items, extracted the roll of plastic garbage
bags, and the roll of transparent packing tape, and covered everything
she could in plastic. She covered the floor and the bed completely,
and the base of the toilet, and under the sink. She taped the ends of
the garbage bags together and taped them down onto every surface.
She went into her bag of items, found the package of IbuFlam Plus,
the maximum recommended dosage of which was one to two tablets
every six to eight hours, and swallowed five tablets with a handful of
water. Just for good measure, she went in her purse, found a bottle
of Xanelax 7, an old prescription, which she hadn't refilled, and took

the last two tablets that were left. She got her clothes off, went to the sink, squatted down and washed herself out as best she could with the lukewarm water and the liquid antimicrobial soap. Then she lay back onto the plastic sheeting she'd taped down over the futon mattress. She bent her knees, spread her legs, inserted her finger into her vagina and pushed it up until she felt her cervix. Holding one finger at the mouth of her cervix, she used her left hand to tease her nipples. She did this patiently, for several minutes, until it felt like maybe she had dilated slightly.

Now it was time for the laminaria. This part was going to be a little tricky. The laminaria sticks she had purchased were not the kind routinely used for unavoidable terminations of pregnancies threatening the life of the mother. What they actually were, these sticks she'd bought and was now inserting into her cervix, one at a time, four of them in all, was a bunch of dried-up yellow seaweed rolled into handy "Natural ChewSticks" and sold at various Asian-themed stores, like Satōs Herbal Health Emporium. Now ideally, if you had to use such sticks, you wanted to shove them all up in there, and leave them in there overnight, during which time they would fill with water and gradually expand and dilate your cervix. However, if, say you were ten weeks pregnant, so just past the end of your first trimester, and loaded up on muscle relaxers and a couple of extra-strength Xanalex 7s, you could probably get by with six to eight hours ... which Valentina did not have. Still, she figured, gritting her teeth as she wedged stick three in and rode out the cramps, an hour or two would be better than nothing. Certainly it would be better than this. She got stick four in between the others and collapsed back onto the plastic garbage bags, soaked with sweat and tachycardic.

"The unconditional forgiveness of ..."

The readout on the broken Viewer said 0320. She noted the time. She lay there, cramping, taking the pain, willing herself not to piercingly scream, or panic and desperately pull the sticks out. Shortly thereafter, she must have passed out, because the next thing she knew it was 0730, and Kyle was on the screen of the Viewer, saying something, and his face was melting. She tried to sit up and tell him she was sorry, but her wrists and ankles were strapped to the bed, or the slab, or whatever it was she was lying on. Her voice was speaking

without her somehow. It sounded like an old recording of a tape of
an even older recording. She lay there, listening, terribly confused.
Kyle was gone and now the Viewer was running a sitcom in which
her mother was coughing these tiny people out into one of those tissues she kept in her robe. Every time she coughed one out, there was
canned applause, or sometimes laughter, and she'd open the tissue
to see who it was, but Valentina couldn't see who was in there. She
pressed the "live in studio" button and told her mother and Kyle she
was sorry ... she wasn't sure for what, exactly ... for everything, she
said, that should cover it. She hadn't intended to become a Terrorist.
She swore she hadn't. She had not lied. She had wanted the baby,
Zoey, whoever. The only thing was, she explained to the audience,
IT had seeped into her brain and her organs and into her DNA and
had made her someone else she wasn't before she was even born a
fake that had had to pretend she was who she was. She had never
had a chance, she went on, to become who she was but had never
been. IT hadn't let her. IT would never let her. IT wanted her for a
talking catheter. There, in her hospital bed in the studio, surrounded by members of the N.I.N, who were wearing their goat masks
and sporting erections, reciting the Twenty-Fifth Affirmation, she
watched from the top of the nosebleed seats as she, the one she was
on the sound stage, dowsed herself with a kidney-shaped bedpan of
rapeseed oil and lit a match and ...

She came to (as you do sometimes) without a clue as to who she
was or where she was or what was happening. Wherever she was
was covered in plastic. A vent in the wall was blowing a stream of
humid armpit-redolent air down into this cell, or dungeon, or tomb,
or whatever this was she was lying in ... assuming this was actually
anywhere and not just somewhere else she was dreaming. Whoever
she was was definitely someone someone had jammed a lot of rocks
up into, or pieces of metal, or broken glass. When it was was 0350. A
clock on the screen of the Viewer said so. Above the clock the screen
was playing this retro-animatronic Content in which a gigantic mutant squid, or some species of monster with the head of a squid,
was terrorizing all these Japanese farmers, who weren't Japanese and
who were wearing pajamas embroidered with the face of Mister
Mango. The tentacles of the monster squid (boneless rubbery tubes

with fingers), were multiplying like glioblastomas, shuddering out
of the slime smeared bowel of the brainless dead-eyed cephalo-
pod torso like the time-lapse footage of those feeding corals you
saw sometimes on the Nature channels, hideous blood-red polyps
opening, fingers reaching in through the doors and the windows of
the Japanese cardboard farmhouses, wriggling up the farmer's asses,
their intestines, and bursting out of their mouths ...

Valentina forced herself up, got to her feet, and switched off the
Viewer. The screen went black. A message appeared.

YOU DON'T HAVE TO DO THIS.

She stared at the message.

She closed her eyes.

"There is no message."

She opened her eyes. The message was gone. The face of a woman
she vaguely resembled stared out of the dead black screen. Her name
was Valentina Constance Briggs. She lived in a house on Marigold
Lane ... in the Pewter Palisades Private Community. Somehow she
had ended up here, on a screen in a room at the Hotel Huffington,
naked, everything wrapped in plastic, preparing to perform a D&C
with salad tongs and a metal skewer. This was real. This was actually
happening ...

She pulled out the laminaria sticks and flung them into the shower basin. She checked her dilation as best she could. Two or three
centimeters. It would have to do. She went in her bag and found the
skewer. She forced herself up and stood at the sink. She washed her
hands, put on the gloves, used the bottle of isopropyl alcohol to ster-
ilize the tongs and the skewer, took another four IbuFlam tablets,
then she lay down and began the procedure.

She opened her vagina and inserted the tongs. She pulled them
open as wide as she could. She inserted the skewer and eased it in
until she felt it touch her cervix. She wiggled it around until she was
certain she had the tip in her cervical canal. She advanced the skewer
into her uterus, probing for the feel of the amniotic sac. She felt a
... what? A mass. A bump. A bubble. It didn't feel like muscle. She
probed it with the tip of the skewer. That had to be it.

"That's not it."

That was it.

On the count of three.

She took a deep breath and let it out slowly, emptying her lungs, two, three … and jabbed up hard and fast with the skewer, missing the amniotic sac completely, and stabbing into her uterine wall. Her pelvic muscles went into spasm, locking down around the skewer and squeezing the salad tongs out of her vagina.

She lay there for a moment, convulsing.

"Told you. Now you're going into shock."

No she wasn't. Not if she could help it.

She lay back onto the garbage bags, closed her eyes and focused on her breathing, gradually slowing, deepening her breaths, willing her body to relax, open … breathing, floating, weightlessly riding the rising swells of the waves of pain.

The pain is just pain … it isn't punishment.

"Yes it is."

All right. Again.

It took her a while to pry herself open and get the tongs back into her vagina. Her arms were weak. Her hands were shaking. Holding her head up was making her dizzy. The fingers of the latex gloves she was wearing were covered in dark red syrupy blood. Which meant she probably hadn't hit the artery. She probed once more with the metal skewer. And felt the sac.

"That's not it."

She probed around again, just to be sure, comparing the feel of the surrounding tissue. Uterus. Uterus. Sac. Uterus. Uterus. Sac.

That was it.

She jabbed up into the amniotic sac, which was roughly the size of a small avocado, but the previous attempt having made her tentative, she wasn't certain she had ruptured the membrane. She jabbed again, harder this time, and definitely pierced it, impaled it, she thought, and possibly drove the skewer right through it and up into the roof of her uterus. The wave of pain that hit her now was not the kind you can ride out breathing. This was a tsunami … a mega-tsunami, rising up her spinal cord and radiating out in all directions, frying her neurons, melting her synapses, stripping the myelin sheaths off her axons … and then … nothing … nothing at all … nothing but timeless, dreamless black.

Shortly after 0430, she awoke to find she was lying naked on a sheet of plastic in a fleabag hotel. She was lying in a puddle of urine or something. Urine and blood. Mostly blood. Which seemed to be emanating from her vagina. Out of which something metal was protruding. She pulled it out. A barbecue skewer. She sat herself up, and nearly passed out, mostly due to the pain in her loins, but also partly due to the fact that she could not get enough air in her lungs and was obviously having an anxiety attack. That, or maybe she was going into shock. She stripped the gloves off and checked her pulse. Sure enough, it was up near a hundred. And based on the way she was hyperventilating, her respiratory rate was right around thirty. OK, so ... there it was then. Textbook Class II hemorrhagic shock. She checked the puddle of blood on the bed, depressing the plastic with her hand to pool it, and guessed she had lost about a liter in ... what? Seventy, maybe eighty minutes. She quickly did the math in her head, reminded herself of the last two stages of hemorrhagic shock, confusion and coma, and determined that she was going to die here ... unless she could get up and get downstairs and get the night clerk to call an ambulance. Once she did that, if she did that, that would be it. End of story. Certainly, Security Services would save her. They would save her in order to interrogate her. They would want to know where she had gotten the MemCard, and everything she knew about the N.I.N. They'd probably want to interrogate Kyle, and maybe even Susan Foster, and Doctor Fraser, and possibly her father. They might even want to interrogate her mother. After they had finished interrogating everyone, they would lock her away in a secure facility and pump her full of medication, or send her away to a Quarantine Zone ... or in any event, whatever happened, one thing she knew was absolutely certain, this was as far as she was going to get. There would be no neopagan rituals, or random bombings or suicide missions ... but maybe this was her suicide mission. Maybe it was better to die right here ... to go out like a proper Terrorist. Maybe that was always the plan. Who was she to presume to know the Path(s) the One had chosen for her? If everything, as it was, was perfect ... hadn't she already struck a blow against the infernal forces of IT by aborting the fetus ... the Clear ... Zoey ... or whatever the fuck its fucking name was? She'd probably driven the skewer right through IT, right through its little froglike face, or through its tiny unformed ... wait. Where, exactly, was the fetus? She hadn't seen it in the puddle of blood that had pooled on the futon and in which she was sitting. She used her hands to dredge the blood puddle, smearing blood all over the sheets of taped-together plastic garbage bags, and her arms and legs and breasts and belly, and spattering blood up onto the walls. She found and sorted and closely examined a series of stringy globs of tissue. They were pieces of ... what? Gestational sac? It didn't matter. None were the fetus. She checked the floor, the shower basin, smearing blood all over the room. It should have been about the size of a fig, a fig-sized, probably mutilated, but nonetheless recognizable fetus. She couldn't find it. It was not there. Then it hit her. It was still inside her. It was in there, clinging to the wall of her uterus. She had to get it ... to get it out of there. She groped around in the blood for the skewer. She had to dislodge it and scrape it out of her ... IT. No. She could hardly breathe. She was squirming around in the blood on her belly. She pushed herself up, and collapsed immediately. No. She didn't want to die like this, sprawled out naked in her blood and feces. It didn't matter where it was. Whether the fetus was still inside her or somewhere she had missed in her search, the Security Specialists would surely find it when they found her blue-white bloodless body, and took their pictures ... which they would show to Kyle. She rolled herself over onto her back. She pushed herself up onto her elbows. All that was left to do at this point was choose the position she wanted to be found in ... lying on the bed, hands folded on her chest, lips curled into a smile of victory? Or what about cross-legged on the floor, sitting up in the lotus position? Or here, on her back in the blood on the floor, her arms outstretched, Christian-style, or ...

None of the above.

She could not do it.

Her body would not let her do it.

She lay there on the blood-smeared garbage bags praying to the One for the strength to do it.

"Please grant me the strength do this ..."

Hyperventilating. Heart-rate racing.

"Grant me the strength to walk my Path ..."

"Get up now," the voice in her head said, not the voice on the tape in her head, another voice, which she didn't recognize.

"Get up now or you're going to die here."

She pushed herself up off the floor.

"Open the door and get down the stairs."

She stumbled out and down the staircase, naked, blood running down her legs, dragging the piss-stained blood-soaked sheet in her wake like the bride of some abomination. Some other part of her was watching her do this. She didn't understand how her legs were still working. She turned the corner that led to the "office" and looked inside. The night clerk was gone. The desk he'd been at was coated with dust that looked like it had been there for decades. She opened her mouth and tried to scream ... but nothing came out, or she couldn't hear it. And neither could anyone else, apparently, because no one came running into the "lobby." She checked for a phone ... there was no phone. There wasn't anything ... no jacks, no lines, no sign that anyone had ever been here. The "office" was just a hole in the wall beneath a rusty old iron staircase. The Hotel Huffington was an abandoned building in the middle of absolutely nowhere. Or maybe she was already dead ... and this was some antechamber of hell. She looked down the derelict, unlit hall. It stretched off into the dark in the distance. Down at the end was a sliver of light. She started toward it. She was not going to make it. She was leaving a trail of blood on the tiles. The hallway seemed to go on forever. Seconds ... or minutes ... or hours ... passed. Her legs were wired into her brain stem. She made it to the door that led to the street. She staggered out wrapped in the blood-soaked sheet. She walked. She wasn't sure where she was going, maybe just out into the middle of the street to flag down a tram, or a passing van, or anywhere someone might possibly see her. Or maybe she was setting out, naked, on foot, for the 40th Parallel, and beyond, in search of the N.I.N., who were down there, somewhere, waiting for her on the border of that non-existent frontier ... or maybe, in the disoriented state she was in, she was heading for the nearest WhisperTrain station, heading back home to Marigold Lane, in the Pewter Palisades Private Community, where they picked up the recycling on Tuesday and Friday, and whose accent color was Persian Green ...

Max

Valentina missed hurricane ViviCo ... or whatever hurricane ViviCo was. One thing it certainly wasn't was a hurricane. It might not have even been a tropical storm. However, ViviCo Medien AG, a subsidiary of Spinner SE, "providers of quality Online Content for adults and children for over 200 years," was not in the mood to quibble over details. ViviCo had paid a pretty penny to plaster its name all over anything vaguely resembling cyclonic activity, and this tropical storm, or atmospheric depression, or lengthy period of heavy rain, contractually qualified, or close enough.

Whatever it was, Valentina missed it. It blew through the heart of Northeast Region 709 in the early hours of 16 April, 2610 (and all the other dates it was, of course), cutting a swathe of minor damage to color-coordinated patio awnings across the central Residential Communities, while she was being bathed, groomed, and otherwise processed for immediate transport.

Taylor was delivering Cassandra's baby ... or at least he was kneeling on the floor beside her, providing emotional support and encouragement by saying things like "push" and "breathe," and other things he had heard on television, and panicking, as Cassandra screamed in agony. Cassandra was experiencing the miracle of childbirth, which nothing had adequately prepared her for. She was squatting, sort of, at the foot of the bed, biting down on the rolled-up dish towel Taylor had stuffed into her mouth, and screaming as piercingly as she possibly could with the towel jammed into her mouth like that, as her uterine muscle contracted violently. In addition to the pushing and the breathing and screaming, another key part of the delivery procedure was gouging her fingernails into the backs of Taylor's hands as the contractions hit her. That, and squeezing his hands like a vice, and grinding the bones of his fingers together, which wasn't the cause of Taylor's panic ... no, the noise was the cause of Taylor's panic. As soon as Cassandra went into labor, and started producing these howling sounds that Taylor had never even heard a person make, he'd grabbed up a Content disc at random, shoved it into her pirate Viewer, and cranked up the volume as loud as it went, hoping that that, and the roar of the rain, and the gale force wind that was shaking the windows like some mindless monster that wanted in, would prevent her roommates and the neighbors from hearing her. As it just so happened, the disc he'd selected was *Dhalia the Dancing Dolphin, Part Three,* which was mostly a lot of old archival footage of dolphins, and other large oceanic mammals, in the wild, from back when they still existed. The score, which was somehow simultaneously nauseatingly upbeat and playful and depressingly maudlin and sentimental, was making the floor and the door frame vibrate. On top of which, even with the towel in her mouth, Cassandra was screaming to wake the dead. One of her nosy and annoying roommates was out in the hallway, pounding on her door. The sky outside was strobing lightning. Thunder was cracking. The windows were leaking. Cassandra was screaming. Max was crowning.

"Push," Taylor told her.

Cassandra pushed.

A few hours later, as she lay there, sleeping, with Max wrapped up in a blanket beside her, also sleeping, exhausted, the two of them, Taylor sat on the floor and watched them. He sat there, watching, for close to an hour. Nothing was happening. They were lying there sleeping, which Taylor found just endlessly fascinating, which is one of nature's better tricks. Max, who resembled a giant, rubbery, wrinkled specimen of week-old TōShrimp, was the sweetest, most adorable creature Taylor had ever seen in his life. Cassandra was not just stunningly beautiful, and radiant, and oddly, irresistibly sexy (her sweat-soaked hair was stuck to her face, her lips were all cracked, her eyes were swollen), but had been imbued with some mystical power that turned the brains of men to oatmeal.

Taylor sat there watching the two of them, making the occasional goo-goo noise, and putting his finger into Max's hand, so that Max's fingers would close around it, and grip it softly, which was some kind of miracle. He sat there watching ... what was he watching? He wasn't quite sure. Did babies dream? He didn't think so. What would they dream? He sat there watching a human baby and the woman he had just pulled it out of sleep.

Taylor also needed to sleep. He needed to sleep for several hours, or for several days, or possibly weeks. However, that wasn't going to happen yet, because first he needed to kill some people. Starting with Cassandra's roommates. Or at least whichever of Cassandra's roommates had been out in the hallway pounding on her door while Cassandra was experiencing the miracle of childbirth ... which the roommate might or might not have heard. The thing was, if this door-pounding roommate (which Taylor was praying was this Joel or whoever) had heard Cassandra delivering Max, or had heard Max crying, and wasn't just out there pounding on account of the dolphin music, and had rushed back down the hall in a panic and informed the other annoying roommates ... well, OK, the logistics were going to get tricky, regarding the disposal of bodies and so on. If memory served, there were three or four of them, whose bodies he would have to get downstairs, and into the trunk of a stolen vehicle, whose owner he would probably also have to kill, and drive them down to the Dell Street Canal, or somewhere the hell away from Cassandra's, without getting spotted and stopped by a team of Security Specialists, which was going to be challenging. Then again, if it was just the one roommate who had heard (or had possibly heard) Max crying, and Cassandra screaming like she was being gutted, and this roommate hadn't told the others, then it was just the one body, or two, with the driver, which would make things a hell of a lot more manageable. But that was assuming he could somehow be sure that this roommate hadn't told the others ... which how was he supposed to determine that to any acceptable degree of certainty? No, the whole thing was getting overly complicated. He gave it another few seconds thought, and decided the safest course of action was to go ahead and kill the entire household and deal with the body problem later.

Other people Taylor needed to kill were Dodo's Watcher, this J.C. Bodroon (assuming such a person actually existed), and anyone else Bodroon had talked to regarding Taylor, and Cassandra, possibly.

Taylor's instincts told him Dodo had been telling the truth, or most of it anyway, and that there probably was a J.C. Bodroon, in which case Dodo definitely hadn't told Bodroon Cassandra's name. If he had, Bodroon would have already run, or waddled, to IntraZone Waste & Security, which by now would have sent a Security team to scoop up Cassandra, and Max, and everyone ... and, OK, Taylor reasoned deftly (Max was squeezing his finger here), if Bodroon hadn't done that (i.e., delivered Taylor up), odds were, he hadn't told his underlings (i.e., the other Watchers who had been following Taylor) why he had had them following Taylor, and yes ... it was starting to come together now. Bodroon (who, according to Dodo Pacheco, was supposed to be some kind of high-ranking Watcher, whatever the fuck that meant exactly) was hoping to deliver the entire package (i.e., Taylor, Cassandra, Max, Sarah, Adam, and maybe even Meyer) to whoever it was whose boots he licked at IntraZone Waste & Security Services. A fat fucking bag of sadistic obeisance like this J.C. Bodroon would want to do that. He would want to serve the whole complot up like a steaming hot turd on a silver platter. So maybe this was getting a whole lot simpler, and Taylor only needed to kill Bodroon ...

But here was the thing about killing Bodroon. You didn't kill Community Watchers ... not and get away with it, you didn't. IntraZone Waste & Security Services took it as a personal affront. Taylor knew this. Everyone knew this. Every Class 3 cutthroat knew this. Killing spineless cooperating scumbags who nobody liked or gave two shits about, and who were A.S.P. 3s, like Dodo Pacheco, was one thing ... OK, sure, it was murder (and if you were dumb enough to get caught in the act, you would get Class 4ed and disappeared), but it wasn't the kind of murder anyone actively pursued, or cursorily looked into.* Killing a Watcher was a whole other thing ... a thing that attracted a lot of interest. For example, teams of Security Specialists, who expressed their interest by storming into whatever shithole their suspect lived in and cutting down anyone and anything

---

* Killing a few annoying roommates, who were A.S.P. 1s, and were gainfully employed, and who presumably someone somewhere liked, was a bit more risky, but not all that much, again, unless you got caught red-handed. Security Services would interview witnesses, and people who had known the victims, and so on, and enter these interviews into a database, which no one would ever look at again.

that moved with their UltraLite rifles on full-automatic (or detain-
ing the suspect's friends and acquaintances, associates, neighbors,
and random bystanders, and extraordinarily interrogating everyone
to death). The suspect, assuming someone they knew hadn't ratted
them out to avoid all that (which in this case wasn't deemed cooperating, it being a matter of self preservation), could rest assured
that IntraZone Waste would comb the crime scene for DNA, and
would pore over every frame of footage from every satellite camera
in existence, and would otherwise utilize every resource available to
ascertain their identity, and their current whereabouts, and go there
and kill them, and everyone within their immediate radius.

All of which meant ... well, it just wasn't done. Unless it was absolutely necessary. Which Taylor felt, in this case, it was. But first,
he needed to locate Sarah, and tell her to set the "action" in motion,
on account of the premature arrival of Max, who at the moment was
blowing a series of little saliva bubbles with his fat little cheeks and
groping for Taylor with his chubby little fingers, and generally being
ridiculously adorable ...

In the world outside of Taylor's head (also known as physical reality), the storm had brought the daytime temperature down to a
pleasant 31 Celsius. Anti-Socials were out in the streets, playing in
puddles the size of lakes, or just standing around in the pouring
rain laughing like packs of demented children. Columns of towering
cumulonimbi were crawling westward across the horizon, obscuring
the sun and sky and everything. Chutes of rain were cascading down
off the lips of the buckling roofs of tenements. Anti-Socials were
standing under them, sewer water up to their ankles. It looked like
an outdoor aquatic theme-park in some medium-security section of
Hell.

Taylor, thoroughly soaked to the bone, sploshed his way through
the throngs of revelers. He was heading for the former library, or archive, or bookstore, or whatever the fuck it was, where the hardcore
members of the Fifthian Cluster gathered in secret every Monday
morning. He'd left Cassandra with explicit instructions to keep her
piece of shit pirate Viewer turned up as loud as reasonably possible
to drown out Max, if he started crying, which being a baby, he was
likely to do, and additionally, under zero circumstances, to open her

bedroom door for anyone. He didn't feel it necessary, currently, to
share his intention to kill all her roommates. He figured she probably had enough to deal with, given the ordeal she had just been
through ... and now with the nursing, and crying, and burping, and
terror of being disappeared, and so on. He told her, promised her,
swore up and down, got on his knees and begged her to believe, that
everything was going to be OK, and that all they needed was twenty-four hours, because as soon as Sarah learned that Max (and yes,
he'd named the baby Max ... he wasn't entirely sure when he'd done
that), that Max had been born, prematurely, she would contact her
network of baby smugglers, who would put the "action" into motion,
the details of which would go like clockwork ... after which, once
little Max was gone, and on his way to the Autonomous Zones, and
Cassandra safe (and her roommates dead), everything was going to
be OK.

Cassandra had sat there, Max on her tit, doing his impression of
the cutest, sweetest, most adorable baby that had ever been born, listening to Taylor desperately trying to keep her from suffocating the
kid with a pillow more or less the second he went out the window.
Nothing was going to be OK. Everything was going to be not OK.
Everything was going to be totally fucked, until they got rid of the
fucking baby. And not in like twenty-four hours either ... like now,
before it started crying again, and got them both disappeared, and
killed, was the basic thrust of Cassandra's input.

Now this is a rather delicate point, so please don't get the wrong
idea. Cassandra, despite her Greek-sounding name, was not some
sort of baby-murdering psycho freak that had no feelings. Cassandra
had a wealth of feelings, an abundance of feelings, a surplus of feelings. Basically, Cassandra had too many feelings. Her heart, her loins,
her swollen breasts, every last cell in her voluptuous body, was dancing to the same hormonal tune that plays in the post-parturitional
brain of all post-parturitional women, commanding them to feed
and protect their babies. She wanted to feed and protect her baby.
And she was. She was lying there nursing her baby. She was stroking
his head. His hair was beautiful. Her baby was beautiful. She loved
her baby. At the same time, she did not want to die. She wasn't at
all confused about this. She did not want to cease to exist, to never,

not for one moment, ever, in the course of all time and all timeless eternity, be, feel, know, remember ... because, now, see, for Cassandra Passwaters, death was no longer just an abstract concept (i.e., an inconceivable absence of everything, or erasure of everything, which we all know is coming ... someday, yes ... but never today). Death, for Cassandra, was not at all abstract, or remote, or in any way the-oretical. Death was out there right fucking now, right out there in the fucking hallway, waiting for one of her annoying roommates to report the sounds of a crying infant ... which OK, it wasn't crying currently (it was gumming her nipple like a moray eel), but it would be soon enough, she predicted, at which point, blammo ... eternal nothing, followed by more eternal nothing. So there she was, pulled, as it were, this way by her maternal instincts, and that way by her survival instincts ... and so far her survival instincts were winning.

Taylor did not judge her for that. He had his own survival in-stincts. He just didn't want to her to suffocate the baby. He wanted to fix this. He believed he could.

He bounded up the spiral stairs of the former library, or archive, or whatever (where someone would know how to contact Sarah), pushed through the secret door in the wall, and into the secret room in the attic ... where absolutely no one was. The milk crates and met-al folding chairs the Fifthian Cluster used for meetings, and to sit around in semi-circles and talk a lot of militant crap all day, were strewn about the floor haphazardly. One of the dormer windows was broken. Rain was blowing in sideways through it. Either the Cluster had fled in a hurry, or the place had been raided, or, well, something had happened.

He ran back down the spiral staircase, out into the torrential rain, three blocks south, to Eckards Place, up another two flights of stairs, and into this loft-like warehouse space where the Fifthian Cluster normally ran their "Intro to Basic Vandalism" workshops. Two or more of the hardcore members of the Fifthian Cluster were always up there, guarding the stolen cans of spray paint and the plastic jugs of hydrofluoric acid, and other such highly corrosive chemicals, and the tools, and hardware, and other equipment ... not today, though. No one was up there. Moreover, the workshop had been disman-tled. The makeshift cookers, the beakers, burners, every last piece of equipment was gone. The racks where the paint went were standing there empty. Cabinet doors were hanging open. Nails, screws, wing nuts, washers, and various other shrapnel-type items were scattered like seeds on the paint-spattered floor.

Taylor ran, trudged, and waded through the flooded streets in the pissing down rain from meeting location to covert workshop to daytime safehouse to underground depot ... every place he checked was the same. And these weren't just Fifthian Cluster places. He checked the hangouts of virtually every cell of the A.S.U. he knew ... ZF2, the B/O3, he even checked the bar on Bond Street where the Bond Street Bombers always hung out. Could IntraZone Waste & Security Services have taken down all these cells at once? No, he reasoned, because if they had, someone would've have seen something somewhere. Taylor, in the course of his soggy reconnaissance, had interviewed all the usual thugs, dealers, thieves, whores, and dope fiends that hung out anywhere near the proximity of the places someone should have been, but no one was, and the word on that was, no one had seen anything, anywhere. Which made no sense. None whatsoever. How could the entire Anti-Social Underground vanish into thin fucking air? Not that Taylor gave a shit about the fate of the Anti-Social Underground ... but how was he going to locate Sarah and get her to set the plan in motion?

At approximately who knew fucking when, sometime later that afternoon, he bolted up the stairs of 16 Mulberry, his combat boots going squish squish squish as he took each flight in three or four steps, dripping water down the stairs behind him. He was on his way up to talk to Meyer, who was pretty much Taylor's last hope at this point. On the second floor landing some total wino was standing there, not a care in the world, pissing intently down into the corner, as if there were maybe a big "pissoir" sign with an arrow pointing into the building out front. Taylor, perhaps a wee bit on edge, grabbed the wino by the back of the head and slammed his face through the air-shaft window, precipitating multiple facial lacerations, and scaring the bejesus out of the pigeons that were weathering the storm out there on the ledge. The wino collapsed into his puddle of pee, groped at his face, and shrieked incoherently ... but by that time Taylor was up the stairs.

Meyer Jimenez was asleep in bed, which was weird, because Meyer was never in bed. There he was, though, lying there, snoring, his bottle of rum on the floor there beside him. Taylor took hold of the crinkled lapels of his seersucker suit and sat him up. Bleary, Meyer blinked, moaned, muttered something having to do with Taylor fucking his mother in Spanish, and fell back asleep in a sitting position. Taylor went ahead and slapped the living shit out of Meyer several times, explaining how he needed him to wake up and focus before Taylor ripped his balls off, and so on. Meyer, appearing much more alert now, inquired as to what Taylor's fucking problem was. Taylor told him, stressing the part where he needed to locate Sarah, or Adam, or any other member of the A.S.U., which Meyer needed to help him accomplish if he wanted to continue to be able to walk. Meyer listened, nodding, belching and saying "mmm" at the appropriate places. He said only had one question.

"Who are these people, this Adam and Sarah?"

Taylor, slapping Meyer's head from side to side to side repeatedly, which made him look like someone watching a tennis match being played on amphetamines, explained how he, at the present time, was the last person Meyer wanted to fuck with. He reminded Meyer that he was not a moron, and that he had known all along, from the very beginning, that Meyer was somehow in cahoots with Sarah, and was probably some kind of faith-based Terrorist, which he didn't give a shit as far as that went, but he needed to be able to reach her ... now, which Meyer was going to assist him with, or experience extensive internal bleeding. Meyer, after he finished vomiting and soiling himself and begging, and so on, swore on his life that he was telling the truth, that he had no idea who this Sarah was, or where she was, or who she was with, or whether the A.S.U. had been raided, or what he had ever done to Taylor to make Taylor want to abuse him like this. Taylor looked around for something metal to crush the bones in Meyer's hands with, but the room was mostly just full of old books ...

"Leave him alone," Coco said.

Coco Freudenheim was standing in the doorway glaring at Taylor with her hair on sideways. Dexter was riding shotgun beside her. His spine was arched, his pupils dilated. "What is wrong with you? Look at the man. Can't you see he doesn't know anything?"

She shoved Taylor out of her way. He let her. Nobody fucked with Coco Freudenheim.

"Don't just stand there," Coco ordered, helping Meyer back onto his bed, "go get a washcloth."

Taylor just stood there.

"Go already."

Taylor went.

Where did Taylor go exactly? He went out and walked around in the rain. He wasn't going anywhere, exactly. He just needed to think, and walk, and think, and figure this out. Which he could not do. His head kept asking variations of the same set of questions, which he could not answer. Like where was the fucking A.S.U.? And was it possible they all been raided? All at once? No, it wasn't. Had they gone into hiding? Why would they do that? Where would they do that? Where would they go? Technically, they were already in hiding. Were they down in some underground bunker somewhere, a staging area with a cache of weapons? Was this the D.A.D.A.? No. It wasn't. No one was rising up against anything. People were walking around in the rain, playing in puddles and laughing and drinking. And they hadn't even consensually decided on a date yet ... or at least not as far as Taylor knew. But then what did Taylor really know? What did he really know about anything? About Sarah? Or Adam? Or any of these people? He knew what they'd told him. And what he'd seen, or thought he'd seen, which could have all been bullshit. What if Meyer was telling the truth, and he didn't know what was happening either? Taylor had never mentioned Sarah, or Adam, or not by name, to Meyer. What if Meyer really didn't know them? What was it Meyer had said that night, back in October, when this whole thing started?

Everybody infiltrates everybody. Everybody uses everybody.

And Sarah, with her ominous allusions to the future, or the lack thereof ... what was that? Did she know this was coming, whatever this was? He reached in his pocket and felt for the pass ... which was not there. No ... that's right. He had stashed the Travel Pass deep in his backpack, along with some other travel-type items, including a homemade pacifier, a squishy little rubber sack with holes that you could stuff full of fruit that Max could chew on. When had he done

that? Why had he done that? He wasn't going anywhere without
Cassandra ... so what was he packing his backpack for? And where
was Sarah, who had sworn she would know when Cassandra delivered, which Cassandra had, and was waiting back there on Jefferson
Avenue with Max on her tit, freaking out? So where the fuck was
she and her faith-based comrades, assuming she hadn't just made
them up (because nothing was really real or whatever), and that
they weren't just a bunch of Corporatist agents running some sort of
complicated sting?

And on and on with the fucking questions, and scenarios he could
not make sense of ... and Christ he was tired of even trying, which
he had given up doing decades ago, trying to make sense of fucking anything, which they would never let you do completely (he
wasn't quite sure who he meant by "they" ... the corporations and
the Normals, sure, but there was also some sort of cosmic "they"),
because every time you thought you had, or had started to, anyway,
to make sense of anything, or begin to grasp what was really happening, as in who was really doing what to who, or running whatever
game on someone for reasons you could never begin to understand,
or was filling your head with some made-up nonsense that was actually only meant to distract you from what they were or weren't doing
... every time you thought you had maybe halfway started to figure
that out, it turned out you were just being played, manipulated, or
just flat out lied to, and the truth was, you didn't have a clue what was
happening ... and probably no one, anywhere, did.

Taylor sloshed around through the puddles, the rain beating mercilessly down on his head, asking the same unanswerable questions
over and over and over and over, and occasionally stopping in the
middle of the street and staring up into the Asshole of Doom. He
had wandered south, for no conscious reason, away from Cassandra
and Max and everything (and what it was gradually dawning on
him he was probably going to have to do), and was crossing Wallace
Lefferts Avenue and about to walk past Muybridge Lane, when he
realized the one place he hadn't checked, it being the middle of the
day and all, was back where this whole fiasco had started ... which
given the circuitous nature of everything was where he'd been heading all along, apparently.

He turned and walked down Muybridge Lane, cursing God and life and Sarah, veered off into the secret alley and went through the tunnel that led to the alley that no one knew how you got there otherwise ... and there it was, the Pussyhorse Lounge.

A nondescript work-van was parked out front. The pull-down metal gate was up. Someone was in there. Security? Possibly. He stood there across the alley, watching, running the scenarios in his head. He had to be extremely careful, because one wrong step and it would be all over and ... fuck it, he thought. He crossed the alley. The door was unlocked. He walked right in.

Eoghan was clearly surprised to see him, as was his enormous ugly friend, who was helping him pack the last few bottles of booze, beer mugs, and other accoutrements into a collection of Transplant bags, duffels, and taped-up cardboard boxes that were stacked up against the front of the bar and were obviously meant to go into the van. The two of them turned and stared at Taylor, and not in an overly amicable way. Another fairly mean-looking fellow was sitting in the booth where Taylor had sat with Adam and Sarah that night in October. Taylor had him in the peeling old mirror mounted on the wall behind the bar. He had never seen either of these guys in his life.

"The fuck you doing here?" Eoghan asked him.

"Looking for Sarah," Taylor said.

"Sarah who?" Mister Ugly asked. "He don't know who the fuck that is."

Mister Ugly was coming around from behind the bar. He was doing it slowly, as if he was going to sneak up on Taylor, who was standing right there in front of him, watching.

Taylor had never understood that move.

"What's going on?" Taylor asked Eoghan.

"The fuck's it look like?" Mister Ugly answered.

"Did we get raided or what?" Taylor pressed on.

"We? Who is we, motherfucker?"

Eoghan glanced below the bar. The mean-looking dude in the booth was just sitting there. A chair stood right-side up on a table to Taylor's right. The door was open.

"Why don't you just get the fuck out of here?" Eoghan wondered.

Taylor didn't move.

"I need to find Sarah," he reiterated.

Mister Ugly was coming toward him.

"She's gone. Everyone's gone," Eoghan said.

Four steps away, three, two. Mister Ugly was the talkative sort.

"Listen asshole, whatever the fuck you ..."

Taylor grabbed and swung the chair ... fracturing most of Mister Ugly's left molars, and his jaw, and the socket of the guy's left eye. He let the follow-through take him around, reversed, and lobbed the chair at Eoghan. Eoghan ducked. The chair sailed past him ... into the mirror behind the bar. Shards of glass rained down onto Eoghan, who had just been hit in the head by the chair, and on top of whom Taylor, who had vaulted the bar, landed, savagely, with both his boots. The mean-looking guy who'd been sitting in the booth was up now and, wisely, had his knife out. He was holding it backwards (in Taylor's opinion) and moving all Kung Fu and shit. Taylor didn't like the look of this asshole, nor was he in the mood to fuck around here. He groped around under the lip of the bar, where Eoghan had glanced, and found the zip-gun. Taylor had never trusted zips. They generally misfired and blew off your fingers. This one, however, looked pretty decent. Heavy tubing. Solid chamber. He raised it, aimed, snapped the band, and shot Mister Kung Fu below the left eye.

Taylor stood behind the bar, his boot jammed down on Eoghan's neck, and watched as the guy kind of waltzed around, groping blindly for something to sit. He found a chair, eased himself into it, and sat there, blinking, looking confused. A dribble of blood leaked out of the tiny .18 caliber hole in his cheek. He yawned, or tried to breathe through his mouth. Blood trickled down out of both of his nostrils. He didn't appear to understand what was happening.

Taylor rolled Eoghan onto his back and stomped on his genital area, repeatedly. This wasn't purely gratuitous cruelty. He needed Eoghan to stay where he was while he went out and dealt with his friends for a minute. He stepped over Eoghan's convulsing body and came out from behind the bar. He retrieved Kung Fu Guy's knife from the floor, went over to the guy, who was coughing up blood now, got behind him, grabbed his forehead, tilted his head back and slightly to the right, and cut across his left carotid artery. He held the guy's head against his own abdomen, aiming the spurts of blood away. He did this for maybe ten or twelve seconds, then he stepped back and let the guy fall to the floor.

Mister Ugly was down on all fours, crawling toward the door, it looked like, or maybe he was trying to collect his teeth, which were lying around on the floor in pieces. Taylor went over there, got behind him, straddled him, squatted, pulled his head back, and cut his throat from ear to ear. Then he stood up, and stepped back, and watched him bleed out. It took just under fifteen seconds. Then he went to the door and pulled down the metal gate from inside and came back in. He closed the door and flipped the deadbolt. Then he went back to talk to Eoghan.

He walked around behind the bar, stomped Eoghan once in the face to stun him, took him by the wrists and dragged him out. He dragged him to a spot in the back that wasn't covered with blood and teeth, and propped him up there to have this talk.

Now this was not Taylor's finest hour, this part of our story where he physically motivated, and, all right, let's face it, tortured Eoghan in what turned out to be a completely futile attempt to get Eoghan to tell him something. Eoghan didn't tell him anything. Or nothing that helped, or made any sense, or didn't further complicate everything. According to Eoghan, these guys he'd just killed were part of some secret A.S.U. cell that Eoghan claimed he didn't know the name of, but that allegedly Adam, and presumably Sarah, were apparently secretly deeply involved with. They had shown up earlier, the two dead guys had, and ordered Eoghan to pack the place up. They said they would help. They had given no reason. Eoghan hadn't pressed the matter. He insisted (to Taylor) that he was only a bartender. He wasn't involved with operations. Adam had been there the night before, but he hadn't seen Sarah for days, he swore. He didn't know where the two of them were. He didn't know where anyone was. Or what was happening. He didn't know anything. All he knew, and kept repeating, was whatever this was, it was something big, bigger than Taylor and whatever his thing was ... which yes, he said, like he'd said before, he had heard Adam talking about his thing, and his woman, Calliope, or whatever her name was ... Cassandra, sure, that was it, and yes, he'd heard the name "Bodroon," or something like that, or thought he had, but he swore he didn't know what any of that meant ... he'd heard a lot of names and numbers, and if Taylor would stop ... just stop for a second ... and go and fucking *look* at these guys ... look at their faces and ...

Taylor did. Kung Fu guy was lying face up. Taylor walked carefully through the blood and squatted down looked at his face. He didn't know what he was supposed to be looking for ... then he saw it. The guy was too young. Or maybe he wasn't. No. He was. He was in his late twenties, or maybe thirty. There wasn't any way to tell for sure. He got up and went back to talk to Eoghan. Eoghan was dead. So that was out. He walked back over to Mister Ugly, flipped him over onto his back and checked his face, which was all smashed up, and covered with blood, so not so helpful. He checked the guy's eyes. He wasn't a Clear. Unless they had changed his eyes somehow. He went back and checked Kung Fu Guy's eyes. Blue ... but not quite Clarion blue. Or maybe they were. He couldn't be sure. It wasn't like Taylor had ever gotten up close to any Clears in person. He went back over to Eoghan's body. He stood there, looking down at it, thinking.

"The fuck is going on?" he asked it.

So, lovely, this was just fucking beautiful ... because now he had killed a bunch of people, two of whom were Class 3 Anti-Socials, so that didn't really matter all that much, but the other two of whom were either Clears who had had some kind of ocular surgery, or grown-up faith-based Terrorist babies, which would make them either part of Sarah's network or Meyer's theoretically brainwashed babies, who the corporations had sent to the Zone as undercover Security Specialists ... or some other type of covert agents in some other scenario he couldn't imagine. In any event, whoever they were, he had killed them ... and accomplished nothing. Or virtually nothing. Or next to nothing.

What, you ask, was next to nothing? Nothing. Nothing was next to nothing. Nothing was flanked, on both sides, by nothing. And facing nothing. And backed by nothing. Nothing was basically surrounded by nothing. And was more or less floating in an ocean of nothing. And was drifting in a boundless, spaceless, timeless, infinite, immeasurable quantity of nothing. Somewhere right in the middle of this nothing, his cumbrous boots going squish squish squish, the front of his rain-soaked fortunately dark-hued T-shirt and chinos soaked through with blood, trudging back up Wallace-Lefferts Avenue out of the deep Inner Zone, forever, forcibly anally penetrated by God, or the One Who Was Many, or someone, was Taylor.

Yes, oh yes, our boy was fucked. In every figurative sense of fucked. And he knew he was fucked, monumentally fucked, epically, cosmically, colossally fucked. Oh yeah, and as fucked as he already was, that wasn't it for the fucking. Oh no. No, the serious fucking was just beginning. This was just like the warm-up fucking. This was the part where the ancient gods, or whoever was running this twisted show, first sent in the apprentice deities, whose job it was to loosen you up, after which the entire pantheon (hell ... probably all the pantheons) descended onto your upraised ass and got down to some soulful fucking. No, this, this mess, this raid, or sweep, or whatever the fuck this actually was, or in any event the extremely ill-timed disappearance of Sarah, and Adam, who now, purportedly, according to Eoghan, for reasons unknown, wanted Taylor dead, while Max, the sweetest little baby in the world (if Cassandra hadn't already snuffed the kid), was back in Cassandra's bedroom, crying, and Cassandra's roommates and no ... see ...

Taylor needed to figure this out. He needed to get out of this fucking rain, and get a fucking drink, and think. Just one drink, though, to sharpen him up. Because he needed all his wits about him, and all his powers of reasoning, and so on, and his faculties ... sure, he needed those too. The last thing he needed was to cloud his mind, to give in to some weak-ass impulse, or compulsion, or self-protective need, to dull the pain (i.e., the Worst Pain Ever) that was down there somewhere, throbbing, festering, impacted deep inside the sense, the realization that was taking shape, resolving now into a readable image, the way old analog photos used to, of what he probably had to do.

So that's what he'd do then, one quick drink, a shot of tequila, or possibly two. Then he'd just sit there, at Gillie's (where else?), and face this, and figure out what to do.

Half a bottle of Gillie's tequila, several beers, and a few hours later, Taylor, on a strip of actual paper, with an actual pencil he'd borrowed from Henry, who for some reason still kept tally that way, wrote out a list of three scenarios, ranked according to descending likelihood.

Scenario Number One (likely). The Fifthian Cluster, and the entire A.S.U., were locked in some underground corporate facility, being extraordinarily interrogated to death. That is, if they weren't all dead already. Odds were, they were all dead already. Sarah was dead. There was no Sarah. There wasn't going to be any rendezvous. No one was coming to pick up Max. Adam, who had somehow eluded capture, was running some desperate clean-up action, which Taylor had walked in on back at the Pussyhorse. Sarah had not eluded capture. Sarah had not eluded anything. Sarah had drawn on all her strength, inner resources, and faith, and so on, to hold out against interrogation, and had given up everyone and everything she knew. She had certainly given Taylor up, which meant she had also given up Cassandra. Which meant that he and Cassandra were dead. Which meant that Max was also dead. So that didn't play out all that well for anyone.

He paused to throw back a shot of tequila, which he promptly chased with a mouthful of beer.

Scenario Number Two (less likely). The A.S.U. had still been raided, and were being (or had been) extraordinarily interrogated, and so were just as dead, or would be soon, but Sarah had somehow eluded capture and was out there somewhere, in a safehouse, probably, working with Adam (and possibly also a skeleton crew of faith-based Terrorists) to damage assess, and clean things up, and above all not get captured and tortured. She hadn't given Taylor or Cassandra up. Still, the baby-smuggling was off. The D.A.D.A. was off. Everything was off. So no one was coming to pick up Max. No one was smuggling anyone anywhere.

So, all right, Scenario Number Two was slightly less grim than Scenario Number One. At least for Taylor and Cassandra, and Sarah. However, it didn't do much for Max. According to Scenario Number Two, Max was still an unauthorized baby, a ridiculously adorable unauthorized baby, who definitely strongly resembled Taylor, but nonetheless an unauthorized baby, who was going to get Cassandra killed. Even if Taylor killed all her roommates, and killed Bodroon (and possibly Meyer), and otherwise ruthlessly covered his tracks, keeping a crying unauthorized baby in Cassandra's bedroom was ... well, out of the question. So Max had to go. He had to go somewhere. Somewhere that wasn't Cassandra's bedroom.

It was time for another shot, and more beer.

Scenario Number Three (unlikely). This was Taylor's least favorite scenario, but he had to consider the possibility, depressing and paranoid as it was. Eoghan had informed him, back at the Pussyhorse, that he had overheard Adam discussing (with someone) the recent demise of Dodo Pacheco, and mentioning Cassandra by name, and so on,* and there wasn't any rational way to explain that, except for Scenario Number Three.

According to Scenario Number Three, Adam and Sarah, who were posing as members of this inner circle of baby-smuggling Terrorists that had infiltrated the A.S.U. (or that was using the A.S.U. as a front) were actually, the two of them, Corporatist agents, who had infiltrated the infiltrators, i.e., the actual baby-smuggling Terrorists, who Taylor had never actually met. Or worse yet, maybe there were no infiltrators, no actual faith-based baby-smuggling Terrorists, and the whole thing was just some Corporatist scheme to dupe the mothers of unauthorized babies, and detain them, and kill them, and use their babies for undercover agents, or suicide Specialists ... or whatever it was in Meyer's theory, the particulars of which had slipped Taylor's mind (he was getting a little tipsy by now).

No, he told himself, that didn't make sense. Why would Sarah, if she were an agent, conceivably go to all the trouble of deviantly fucking a Class 3 thug like Taylor on a regular basis in dives like Frankie's and Hardcore Carla's (not to mention the Darkside Club) for going on something like five fucking months? No. That didn't add up at all ... but wait (and OK, let's go ahead and call this Scenario Number Three Point One), what if everything was as it was according to regular Scenario Number Three, except that Sarah really was involved with the faith-based Terrorist baby-smuggling outfit, and was only posing as a Corporatist agent, and had infiltrated the infiltrators who had infiltrated the Fifthian Cluster? (Taylor was clutching at straws here, and he knew it. He threw back another shot of tequila.)

---

*OK, he had gotten her name wrong, but that could have been due to the extraordinary level of physical discomfort he was in at the time

And where did Bodroon fit into this picture? Was it possible he was nothing more than some random Watcher who had stumbled into this? What were the fucking odds of that? They were pretty fucking slim, in Taylor's opinion. No ... Bodroon was being run by someone. Someone was feeding him information. Someone higher up the food chain than some junkie scumbag like Dodo Pacheco. But who? IntraZone Waste & Security? The Hadley Corporation of Menomonie, Wisconsin? God? The One Who Was Fucking Many?

By this time Taylor was totally shitfaced, and beyond confused, and approaching depressed. None of his three and a half scenarios offered any hope regarding Max. He sat there, drinking, thinking, and sort of talking incoherently to himself ... and somewhere near the middle of the homemade "Gillie's Quality" tequila label, which Young Man Henry personally glued to all the top-shelf liquor bottles, he decided he needed to simplify everything. On his slip of paper, just below the scenarios, he drew up a kill-list, which looked like this:

> Bodroon
> Adam
> (Sarah)
> (Meyer)
> Joel ... Jules?
> Fyodor
> Tamara?

He couldn't remember the names of the roommates. Whatever. He wrote down "Cassandra's roommates." He gulped down another shot of tequila. He needed to add one name to the list. He gulped down another shot of tequila. And another. And yes ... it was better this way. Better than what was bound to come at the hands of IntraZone Waste & Security, and the Hadley Corporation of Menomonie, Wisconsin. No. See, the thing of it was ... he vacuumed up two shots in succession. The important thing was ... and then the beer. The thing was ... they weren't going to fucking get him. He wasn't going to let them fucking get him, and warp and twist and condition his mind ... one more shot here ... and own his mind ... his empty, beautiful, curious mind ... which Taylor, if he had the chance, in some alternate reality or parallel universe where he and Cassandra and Max would live in a little stone house in the woods somewhere, and Taylor would take Max out in the woods and teach him things he had never been taught, and thus didn't know, but had read about somewhere ... or even just here, in this reality, in some underground camp in the desert somewhere, or even if there were somewhere to hide and raise an unauthorized kid in the Zone, which there wasn't, but if there were, he'd teach him ... because even as fucked as everything was, there were still a few things ... like music, and books, and pirate films, and other things, which people hid and passed around ... and he could teach him how an engine worked, and how to make things out of wood ... and women, he could teach him all about women ... and maybe, out there in those Autonomous Zones that were not there there were other babies, who would grow up someday to be women his age ... and what if Sarah was right about the animals? Maybe there were actual animals ... beavers, bears, or something with a "b," and not just rats and fucking insects and ... fuck ... fuck ... fucking ... fuck it ...

He wrote the last name down on his list. Because this was how it had to be. Because either he did it or they would do it, or they would turn him into one of their killer sheep. Taylor would not let them do that. He would not allow these motherfuckers to take him and raise him and make him like them. No matter what happened, that was not going to happen. He took a swig straight out the bottle. No sir. That was not going to happen ... not to this baby ... not to Max.

4.

The Overlook Café

So here we are then, back where we started ... or, all right, circa ninety minutes later, in any event on that same Tuesday morning, 17 April, 2610, and all those other proprietary dates. Taylor was on his way to Cassandra's, having slipped out the back of Gillie's Tavern, where we left him, staring down into his beer. Cassandra was locked inside her room, with Max, who hopefully she hadn't snuffed yet. Valentina was in the back of a van, recovering from being pepper-sprayed in the face at more or less point blank range. Jimmy "Jimbo" Cartwright was dead. His mortal remains were lying at rest in a body bag (or cadaver pouch) in the cabin of a Finkles corporate jet that was screaming across the lower stratosphere toward an undisclosed location where the Cartwright family's personal mortician was waiting to pump them full of formaldehyde. The Normals were on their way to work, or they were already there, or were working from home ... clicking, stroking, pinching, poking, or verbally, visually or mentally cueing the keys and icons on their All-in-One Viewers, on which there hadn't been any more BREAKING NEWS, and which were streaming, tweaking, and fleeping frantically, filling their feeds with urgent messages, memos, updates, half-off offers, reminders to bookmark and comment on comments they had apparently read but didn't remember. By this time, most of them had totally forgotten whatever it was they were really only halfway paying attention to as they simultaneously only halfway paid attention to several other things that they didn't have time to reflect at any length on and two hours later wouldn't even remember having read or seen or heard in the first place (i.e., before some other item on their screens distracted them from whatever it was, and they clicked, or stroked, or poked, or verbally or visually prompted the screens of their Viewers,

and ended up viewing whatever they were viewing when it was in
terrupted by whatever they were viewing), which some of them were
actually viewing again, and experiencing a little déjà vu, which didn't
matter, or not at the moment, because the point was ... whatever.
There was no point. Or if there was (which there probably was),
the Normals were not privy to it. Or they didn't have the time or
energy for it. Most of them were way behind at work. And they
were doing their best to provide for their families, and to maintain
their physical and emotional health (i.e., to not start thinking destructive thoughts, or asking a lot of unanswerable questions). And
they were desperately trying to get enough sleep. And meet their
financial obligations, which primarily consisted of servicing their
debts. And to remain available around the clock to their friends and
families, and coworkers, and bosses, on their All-in-One Viewers,
which they never turned off, and which were logged onto their companies' networks, or one of their companies' clients' networks, or
some other corporation's networks, all of which were interconnected
and streaming katrillions of bajillions of bytes of information back
and forth and around and around in an endless circle at seven times
the speed of light like the brain of some spastic Kurzweilian god in
the throes of acute amphetamine psychosis ... and they were being
bombarded with this information, with facts, figures, images, words,
conjurations, simulations ... projections of a perfect, peaceful world
inhabited by happy, productive people, who were always on their way
to work, or were already there, or shopping from home, or enjoying
some type of leisure activity ... and they smiled down like goliaths
at you (out of whatever fictional world they lived in, these perfect
people you would never be), selling whatever it was they were selling
(which probably wasn't the product they were holding, or gazing
ecstatically happily at), and feeling overwhelmingly positive about
the future of pretty much everything generally ...

Kyle Bentley-Briggs was feeling unwell. He was feeling less than
overwhelmingly positive ... significantly less than overwhelmingly
positive. He was feeling this way about the past, and the present,
and the future, and ... well, pretty much everything. He'd been feeling this way for about three weeks. Kyle was having breakfast with
Cramer on the 110th floor ("the top of the spire") of the Morloch-

Malikov Broadcasting Tower, in the retro-trendy Overlook Café, which looked like a giant Christmas-tree ornament and was not quite imperceptibly revolving, widdershins (i.e., right to left), which for some reason felt incredibly weird. Cramer, who was sitting across from Kyle (so facing in the forwardly-traveling direction), and who was dipping into his bowl of Soygurt and assorted genetically-modified berries, was well on his way to completely forgetting those incessant and arguably unnecessary queries, and the constant Fleeps and Tweaks and emails, and calls, and other forms of media, people whose names he had already forgotten had routinely employed to interrupt him (while he was responding to some other idiot's query) and ask him when it really was. Such queries were no longer his responsibility. They were someone else's responsibility ... someone down on the 26th floor.

Cramer, immediately pursuant to his meeting with Kyle at Rosie's back in early March, where he had promised Kyle he would contact the guy who knew the guy in Domestic Security and attempt to back-channel the Valentina problem, had fleeped a taxi and high tailed it back to District 12 Northeast Regional Headquarters. He'd taken the express to the 70th floor, submitted to a battery of Security procedures, clipped his pre-prepared Visitor's Pass to the breast pocket of his Paul Pratt suit, marched right up to Big Bob Schirkenbeck, and right there, right in the middle of the floor, with everyone peripherally looking at him around the sides and over the tops of their identically personalized workstation cubicles, informed him, Schirkenbeck, that he, Cramer, had a situation that needed his attention. Now this was a seriously ballsy move on Cramer's part, which Schirkenbeck noted, the situation being somewhat sensitive, involving as it did a personal friend, and technically part of his extended family, or in any event his cousin's wife, who Cramer felt he should probably mention he'd slept with once or twice at college, back when they were all in their twenties and no one was technically married to anyone. What Cramer needed to carefully convey, in a seemingly unpremeditated way, was how his fervid and complete devotion to the vigilant 24/7 maintenance of Domestic and Interterritorial Security had overcome his natural reticence (being a human being and all) to report the extremely suspicious behavior and disappearance without explanation of his cousin's wife, who as it just so happened (and he looked straight into Schirkenbeck's eyes here) was the daughter of Catherine Rosenthal Briggs, the illegitimate daughter of Stanislav Barnicoat, whose story of course was the stuff of legend in Interterritorial Security circles. Schirkenbeck bought it hook, line and sinker, or at least he admired Cramer's acting skills, and his initiative, and his ruthless sense of priorities, and he elevated Cramer from the 26th floor to the 70th floor, where he clearly belonged.

Kyle was seated across from Cramer, so revolving backwards (i.e., right to left) at a pace that was slow, incredibly slow, but not quite slow enough to be imperceptible, which Kyle was finding increasingly unsettling, in both an emotional and physical way. His tie was hanging down into his bowl of gluten-free antioxidant oatmeal, which he hadn't touched and which was hardening into a disgusting, gray cement-like substance. He was staring across the table at Cramer, who was checking in on his All-in-One for the sixteenth time since the pretty young hostess had sat them at this rather prestigious table, after complimenting Cramer several times on the cut of his new designer suit.

"Sorry, buddy, just one second," Cramer mumbled, thumbing the screen.

Their table was one of several such exclusive Executive Dining tables positioned on the narrow spiraling tiers that ringed the upper reaches of the dome so that diners with Executive Dining cards could simultaneously gaze out over the endless sprawl of the megalopolis as the sun rose over the eastern horizon like a dazzling thermonuclear deathstar and look down on the other less-prestigious diners on the floors below. It was nestled right up to the curve of one of the massive ThermaSoak window panels, so that Kyle was forced to lean to his right, and hunch down over his juice and gruel, whereas Cramer was leaning slightly to his left, keying the screen of his Viewer with one hand and dipping into his Soygurt with the other. All along the tier they were on other presumably Executive diners at other tables in designer suits were similarly slightly leaning and hunching and keying their Viewers as they drank their smoothies through plastic straws with bendable necks and ate their bowls of

Soygurt and fruit, or oatmeal, or other gluten-free cereals. Suspended on a set of invisible wires from the stationary apex of the vertical axis of this giant revolving sphere they were supposed to be sitting there eating their breakfasts in, an orbicular array of video screens floated in space at different levels (i.e., the levels of the upper tiers), so that they seemed to be not quite imperceptibly revolving clockwise, so against the almost imperceptible counterclockwise revolution of the table itself, all of which (i.e., this nearly constant diametrically circular movement, which also included the antipodal rushing back and forth along the tiers of the servers as well as the pretty hostess) was making Kyle increasingly sick. Many of these seemingly revolving screens (which of course, in reality, were not revolving, it was just a matter of Kyle's perspective) were running special Real-Time footage of various members of the mainstream media reporting from the lawn of some Cartwright estate, and they were intercutting other footage of people placing candles and flowers and pictures of Jimbo and hand-written prayers at the gates of his various other estates, and in the elevator bays of corporate offices, and in the entrances of Finkles retail locations. Other screens were running OUTBREAK!, a special edition of KILL CHAIN LIVE! wherein KILL CHAIN! players throughout the U.T. competed live on a regional level, pitting their skill-sets against each other to take down dangerous Terrorist targets (who were threatening to maliciously breach their quarantine) for the chance to advance to the global finals and win an assortment of valuable prizes. Susan Schnupftuch-Boermann Goereszky was jabbering frantically into the camera, and going live to nose-cone footage, and interactive maps, and hologram gizzies, and handheld or possibly helmet-mounted right-in-the-thick-of-it action shots, and bringing in Dr. Roger P. Greenway to incomprehensibly holler nonsense whenever an operator took out a target. The obviously delirious Anti-Socials, whose end-stage Anti-Social disease had driven them to senseless Terrorist acts, and had filled their brains with rage and hatred, and whose suffering one could not imagine, were darting in and out of burning buildings, which were taking fire from Security forces, and were mounting pathetic and futile attacks on armored vehicles with stones and bottles, some of which they were filling with gasoline, or some other type of flammable substance, and igniting and lobbing into the ranks of Security Specialists marching toward them like a herd of identical faceless robots. Other Specialists (i.e., snipers or "Marksmen," and the gunners in the bays of Security choppers), were taking aim at the needlessly suffering Terrorists fleeing the advancing infantry, leading them slightly to account for the desperate zigzag patterns they were running away in, and finally mercifully cutting them down as quickly and as painlessly as humanly possible. Against the backdrop of all this chaos, and carnage, and agonized shrieking and so on, regional KILL CHAIN! quarter-finalists were laser-guiding precision missiles down out of the cloudless sky and into the open bedroom windows of high-ranking Terrorist leaders' apartments, and down into their basement bunkers, and through the walls of what looked like either torture chambers or nightclubs, or both, and down through the roofs of random buildings and various other high-value targets.

None of which of course was actually happening.

OUTBREAK!, like the rest of the KILL CHAIN franchise, was just an elaborate video game, a phenomenally expensive, interactive, "multi-player simulation," which aside from being insanely popular, and generating mondo revenue streams,* helped to relieve the chronic anxiety stemming from the constantly imminent threat of a sudden and devastating Terrorist attack with a nuclear device, or bio-agent, that the Normals were forced to perpetually live with. Basically, it let people blow off steam. Variant-Positives, despite the fact that most of them were medicated up the wazoo, and meditated two to three hours a day, and walked the Path(s) to Prosperity, and so on, were still just Homo sapiens sapiens, who sometimes needed to blow off steam. KILL CHAIN! allowed them to blow off this steam in a healthy compassion-associated fashion, as the virtual end-stage Terrorist targets whose bodies were being ripped to pieces, or vaporized into a pinkish mist, were beyond any sort of palliative care, so really this was the best thing for them.

Kyle was feeling increasingly unwell. Physically unwell. As in nauseated. As in he was going to uncontrollably vomit, in a sudden and shockingly projectile manner, either across the table at Cramer, who was smiling down into the screen of his Viewer, or off the tier and

---

* *There was spin-off Content, sporting apparel, little action figures for the kids, and so on.*

onto the heads of the non-Executive diners below. He turned away from the KILL CHAIN! horror and gazed out at the twinkling sea of lights stretching off into the horizon. He was moving backwards, north to west. He picked out the beacon of a tower in the distance and gave it his undivided attention.

"Sorry, man, what were we talking about?"

Cramer had finished whatever he was doing. He beamed across the table at Kyle like an infomercial appliance salesman.

"Valentina."

"Oh. Yeah." He switched to his deeply concerned expression. "So … how you doing with all that?"

"Not so good."

"But better, right?"

"Actually no."

"You're taking your meds, though."

Kyle nodded dutifully.

"What'd they give you?"

"Tribenzoline-something. I've got them at home."

Cramer had a piece of berry in his teeth.

"And you're walking your Path."

"Yeah. It's just …"

"Because that's the main thing."

"I know. I am. I …"

"Letting it go. "

"Right. I just …"

"What happened to your tie?"

"It's just a spot."

"Tonic water."

"No, it fell in my bowl."

"No. Tonic water will get it out."

The planet Earth was rushing up into a screen in Kyle's peripheral vision.

"Oh."

"Something wrong with your oatmeal?"

"No. It's fine. My stomach's just funny."

"Send it back."

Cramer scanned the tier, spied the server and eyeballed her over.

"No. It's fine. It's just a little … it's just a little motion sickness."

"Seriously?"

"I'm just not feeling that well."

The server was standing there smiling at them.

"You sure?"

"Yeah. Everything's fine."

"Is there something wrong with your oatmeal, sir?"

The server's name was Hyancinth Wong. It said so on the display she was wearing. Her lips were bright red shapeless blobs. You could see all her bones beneath her skin.

"No. I just …"

"I can warm it up for you."

She was also wearing latex gloves.

"Thanks, but …"

"Let her warm it up for you."

As were all the other servers.

"Fine. Sure."

"I'll just warm this up then."

A woman was sobbing on a screen behind her.

"Thanks. Great."

"Was there anything else?"

"Not just now."

Kyle retched, just slightly. He reached for his glass of mineral water. Cramer quickly checked his Viewer.

"Anyway, great to see you, buddy."

"Yeah, I …"

"I meant to call you sooner, but then … well … you know how it is. This whole promotion thing happened so fast."

"Congratulations."

"Long time coming. Shame it had to happen this way. Weird how things work out sometimes."

"Yeah."

"The Will of the One and all that. Anyway, I thought we should probably talk. Process what happened. You know what I mean."

"Thanks for your Fleeps."

"Hey, don't even mention it. What can I say? I'm just so sorry."

"You don't have to keep apologizing."

"I know. I didn't mean it like that."

"Oh."

"I just meant ... I know you're hurting. But we did everything we could for her, right? You know this disease. It's like they say ..."

Hyancinth was back with Kyle's warmed-up oatmeal.

"Here we go, nice and warm now."

Kyle grimaced and nodded.

"Was there anything else?"

A message tone beeped on Cramer's Viewer.

Kyle hadn't seen or spoken to Cramer since they'd met at Rosie's on 04 March. He'd rushed back home to Pewter Palisades, checked in quickly with Susan Foster to tell her everything was under control and that his cousin Greg, who worked at Hadley, had been advised, and was handling everything, then he collapsed onto the living room sofa. A few days later he'd received a Fleep, SORRY ... WE MIGHT HAVE A PROBLEM. Two days later he'd received another one, REALLY SORRY ... DEFINITE PROBLEM HERE. Two days later, INCREDIBLY SORRY ... VAL DETAINED & DESIGNATED, followed by an animated sad-face emoticon.

The day after that he'd received a Fleep from someone by the name of Joralamon Gomm, who apparently worked in the Records Department of the Family and Loved Ones Services Division of the Hadley Corporation of Menomonie, Wisconsin District 12 Northeast Regional Headquarters, informing him that he was now divorced. A few hours later he received an invoice from the Family and Loved Ones Services Division for GD 984.50 for "processing fees and related services." Other communications followed. Most of which were also invoices, mostly for various Healthcare services and sundry legal and administrative fees. There was one for GD 16,000, the deductible for "emergency medical services," and another for GD 4,000.20, for "mobile emergency transport services." There were two in the GD 5,000 range for "aggregated medical services," and one for GD 9,060.00 for "aggregated miscellaneous products of a non-exclusively medical nature related to in-patient care and comfort (including, but not limited to, disposable backless hospital gowns, non-slip footwear, moisturizing tissues, adhesive and non-adhesive dressings, nylon and/or dynaflex tubing, polyglycolide

suture, et cetera)." There were charges for various records amend-
ments, title transfers, releases, waivers, affidavits, statements, and
so on. Finally, on or about the morning of Differently Mentally-
Abled Persons Day, he'd received official confirmation of Valentina's
designation as a Class 3 Anti-Social Person and her transfer to an
undisclosed Quarantine Zone. Also attached to this official email
was a florally-embroidered digital greeting card extending the personal heartfelt condolences of the Board of Directors, Executive
Management, Legal Department and Administrative Staff of the
Hadley Corporation of Menomonie, Wisconsin on the loss of Kyle's
unborn Clarion daughter, and praying that the One would take
Kyle's hand and swiftly guide him down his hopefully short-term
Path of Unimaginable Grief.

Throughout all this, he'd repeatedly called and fleeped and tweaked
and texted and emailed his cousin Greg, to no avail. His Tweaks and
Fleeps all went unanswered. His calls got routed straight to voicemail. Doctor Graell had prescribed a veritable pharmacy to help him
through his grief, which he warned Kyle not to let himself wallow
in, lest it mutate into clinical depression. The pills didn't seem to be
doing very much, other than making him nauseated, so he was also
taking all these antiemetics, which made him drowsy, so he was also
taking several extra doses of Methylphenidril, and Benzehexophaline,
and other stimulants, and drinking like three pots of coffee a day.
He was quite a mess. His work was suffering. The Dean of Info-
Entertainment Content had called him in to extend his condolences
and suggest he take a few weeks off (or however many unpaid weeks
he had to) to work through his unimaginable grief, and then come
back refreshed and ready to work, and resembling his normal, cooperative self. He assured the Dean he'd be OK and doubled up on
his Methylphenidril (which he was already taking way too much of,
and walking around the BVCC campus audibly grinding his teeth
and grimacing). He went back home and sat in the empty sunflower
kitchen on Marigold Lane, where he muffled his agonized guttural shrieks, and his stomach-cramping convulsive weeping, with a
dish-towel that smelled like Valentina, and that went with the color
of the kitchen perfectly, and prayed like a child alone in the dark for
some magical power to turn back time.

"Are you OK, man," Cramer was asking him.

He was moving backwards from west to south.

"Yeah. Why?"

"You were talking to yourself. Muttering kind of."

"Was I?"

"Yeah."

"Sorry."

"This is really messing you up, huh?"

"Yeah. I guess."

"I'm here for you, buddy. Try to remember, this too shall pass."

"I know. I ..."

"Listen. About your messages."

"Messages?"

"The ones you left on my phone."

Way way off in the southern distance, out the window, or the wall, or skin, or whatever one called this kind of structure, some weird formation of enormous rain clouds was coming into view in the corner of his eye.

"On your Viewer you mean?"

"No, my voicemail. At work. That wasn't such a good idea."

"I'm sorry. I didn't ..."

"No. I know." He looked straight at Kyle as he reached for his Viewer. "You were probably overcome with grief" He positioned the Viewer on the table between them. "You didn't even know what you were saying, right?"

"I guess not. The truth is, I don't remember ..."

"Course not. You were still in shock at the time."

Something exploded on a screen to his right.

"But you're much better now. You're thinking clearly."

Kyle was putting the pieces together.

"You're on your meds. You're seeing your doctor."

Kyle nodded. A woman was running, on fire.

"You're letting this go. You're getting through this."

Kyle leaned forward and spoke to the Viewer.

"Yeah. I am. I'm feeling much better. I feel like I'm starting to turn the corner."

"Good."

Cramer switched off his Viewer. Kyle took his out and switched it off too. Jimmy "Jimbo" Cartwright, III was smiling and waving from the deck of some vessel that looked like a floating block of apartments.

"How bad?" Kyle asked.

"Semi bad. Fixable, probably. I'm working on it. The main thing is, no more messages. Or searches. You got to stop with the searches."

"The searches?"

"All that stuff is logged. You're typing in the names of persons ... Terrorist networks. What were you thinking?"

"I've been trying to research her family is all ..."

"Constance Rosenthal? Stanislav Barnicoat?"

"I didn't ..."

"The Nihilist International Network? Have you lost your mind?"

"I thought ... I mean ... it isn't secret ... it's all right there ..."

"Of course it's there. *Why* is it there?"

"It's history."

"Yeah, but that's not the point. You can't just search for stuff like that and not expect ..."

A waitress was passing. Cramer dipped into his Soygurt. That cloud formation was off to Kyle's left.

"I don't think you get what's really at stake here ... look, I can't get into operational details, but this was not just a standard flip-out. She was referencing certain parties, OK?"

"Valentina?"

"Keep your voice down."

"Who? What? What did she say?"

"It doesn't matter. Look ... Kyle, you're family, all right, and I love you and all, but you need to get your ducks in a row here."

"She ordered something from her mother's things. The paperwork said a jewelry holder ..."

"It doesn't matter. Let it go."

"I'm trying. I just need to understand ..."

"No. You don't need to understand. You need to stop with the calls and searches. Look at you. Take some time if you need it. You could go on one of those bereavement retreats ..."

Kyle was staring out into the distance.

"What is that?"

"What is what?"

Kyle nodded toward the clouds of smoke that were rising up out of the southern horizon. Cramer looked.

"That's Zone 23."

"It's burning."

"So?"

"Is that where she is?"

"Kyle, come on."

"Is that where they sent her?"

"Even if I knew, I couldn't tell you."

Kyle turned abruptly, spilling his water, and watched a screen on which a former factory, or something, was taking a missile strike. He spun back around and thought he saw a flash of orange in the smoke out the window. He turned to Cramer.

"Is that really happening?"

"What?"

"That."

Cramer glanced to his left. He turned back to Kyle.

"That's KILL CHAIN LIVE!"

Kyle turned to his right and watched the screen. The palms of both his hands were sweating.

"Where is that?"

"Lower your voice."

He turned to his left.

"Is that out there?"

Cramer reached over and squeezed Kyle's hand.

"It's Content, Kyle. Get a grip."

Kyle turned back to the screen to his right, but now it was running some heartbreaking footage of Jimbo Cartwright in a hospital bed smiling unflinchingly into the camera. He turned back to Cramer.

"I'm losing it, Greg."

"I know. I see that. We'll get you some help."

Hyancinth Wong was approaching the table.

"The other night I was searching around ..."

Cramer smiled, or winced, and made a gesture with his hand to ward her off. She smiled and breezed on by their table.

"And I found this site where someone had posted all this paranoid stuff about Hadley, and other corporations, and other stuff ..."

"See this is exactly what you need a break from."

Executive Diners all around the tier were sitting at their exclusive tables across from whoever they were sitting there with talking into space at no one, or they were staring down into the screens of their Viewers. Cramer was pretty much done with his Soygurt.

"And I knew I shouldn't be reading it, right? But I couldn't seem to stop myself."

"I'm going to call a guy I know."

Cramer switched his Viewer back on.

"I sat there, reading, for three or four hours."

Some kind of country music was playing.

"His wife's on the board of some bereavement outfit on an island up in Baffin Bay."

Kyle was sweating excessively, for Kyle.

Cramer was pinching and stroking his Viewer.

"I must have fallen asleep at some point. I woke up on the couch with my Viewer."

"You know we log how long you spend on those sites."

"I don't remember falling asleep."

"Wait ... I think I've got her number."

Hootey Brewster and the Brewster Boys were making some kind of official statement. Other eminent persons were involved.

"Here it is. Hold on, I'll fleep her."

It looked like comets were arcing down through the clouds of smoke onto Zone 23, which was slowly revolving away from Kyle, and had become the visual background for Cramer, who was fleeping this alleged woman he knew ... or in any event was fleeping someone. Kyle was now excessively sweating to such a profuse and flagrant extent that one or two Executive Diners, as well as possibly Hyacinth Wong, were surreptitiously glancing over at him.

"I haven't seen or heard from the Fosters."

"Who?"

"Susan Foster, our neighbor."

Cramer was finishing up his Fleep.

"They're probably on vacation somewhere."

He swiped away an ad for something. Kyle couldn't see what was on the screen.

"They have this time-share in the Arctic Circle ..."

"There you go."

"No, they go up in August. They do it every year like clockwork."

Selected revolving video screens were displaying the enormous bug-eyed face of Susan Schnupftuch-Boermann Goereszky, who was shouting something directly at you, but you couldn't hear it because the sound was muted. They cut to a satellite aerial shot of a Terrorist running with the crosshairs on him. Other screens had gone to commercials ... a Clarion mother with her Clarion baby, smiling beatifically into the camera ... hair conditioner ... cancer screenings ... an app you could run on your Cranio-Implant that simultaneously composed and played your own individualized orchestral score based on your mood and sensory input and ...

The Purge

Meanwhile, back in Zone 23, the endless column of APCs, MRAPs, UUSVs, AATVs, MCVs, medical units, craft services buses, flatbeds bearing porta potties, and assorted other support-type vehicles that Taylor wasn't quite sure what they did, clattered south down Collins Avenue like a herd of robotic ant-like insects that had awoken from a dormant ecdysial phase and embarked on some mindless foraging raid. Taylor was watching through the hole in the wall of the ruins of the former auto-parts factory into which he had hauled his ass and taken cover when he heard them coming. He wasn't hungover, not anymore. He had sweated most of the toxins out. No, the thing that was twisting and tying his large intestine into the shape of a giraffe, like one of those squeaky colored balloons that party clowns used to make things out of, was not a hangover; it was plain old fear. Good old, primordial, ass-puckering fear.

He'd never seen so much Security. And he hadn't seen this type of Security since the days of the Jackson Avenue Uprising. And that was, shit, thirty-five years ago ... when he was nine, going on ten years old. Apparently there had been some advances. The new and improved AATVs (i.e., Armored Anti-Terrorism Vehicles) had projectile-firing weapons turrets. Their NavPods were grinning with gunnery slits. The Urban Unrest Suppression Vehicles were monsters the size of lunar tractors, and were equipped with seriously heavy ordnance, like .60 caliber mounted machine guns, 120 millimeter cannons, rocket launchers, gas dispensers, flame throwers, some kind of sonic pulse weapon, and lasers, and who knew what else was in there. IntraZone Waste & Security Services did not stock this type of equipment. Not this much of it. This was bad. This was Hadley Domestic Security.

To the south, the sky above Sector C, or the part of it Taylor was able to see through his hole in the wall, which faced southwest, looked like they were halfway through a Security Services aerial trade show. Choppers were swooping in out of the sunrise, launching air-to-surface missiles, or laying down suppressing fire, then banking up into perfectly executed and completely pointless evasive maneuvers. Mosquito-like swarms of UAVs were circling in the sky above them, relaying Real-Time targeting data to other UAVs that were up in the stratosphere launching GodSend missiles down like falling stars onto Taylor's friends. Down there somewhere in the flames and smoke and the screams and panic was Mulberry Street, and Alice Williams and Rusty Braynard, and Coco, and Meyer, and Sylvie and Claudia, and assorted other Class 3 Anti-Social Persons, or the charred and bloody remains thereof.

All right, so ... this was it. The Day of Autonomous Decentralized Action. The D.A.D.A. It had finally begun. It didn't appear to be going that well, at least not during the initial stages. IntraZone Waste & Security Services, and the Hadley Corporation of Menomonie, Wisconsin's dreaded Domestic Security Division, were aggressively quelling whatever unrest the A.S.U. had been able to foment. Judging by this column of Security vehicles, the rear of which was finally approaching, and by the overwhelming superiority of aerial assets they were currently enjoying, they intended to quell the unrest completely, as in liquidate the entire sector. Which, OK, meant that Meyer was right, at least about one of his paranoid theories. This wasn't just a rapid response ... this was a purge.

They were purging the 3s.

Taylor crept back down the stairs and dropped out a window at the rear of the factory, landing in the trash-strewn service alley that paralleled Collins for a couple blocks. The column of heavy vehicles had passed, but who knew what was coming next? Collins was clearly their transport route, so best to stay the hell off that. Also, there was shade in the alley. The brief respite from the scorching heat that the storm had brought with it was officially over. The sun was up above the horizon, getting ready to start frying everything.

The rain had finally stopped the night before at approximately 0130, as Taylor was pounding the gigantic face of J.C. Bodroon into mush with a toaster. He'd already pounded Bodroon's face with a chunk of concrete and a cast iron stew pot, and was just about to call it a night, but then he saw the toaster lying there. (This, you'll recall, was down on the bank of the Dell Street Canal, where a few minutes later Taylor, several sheets to the wind, and having lain in wait for and ambushed Bodroon, macing him blind with his own can of mace, and extracting what little information he could,* and having walked him down to the western embankment, and broken his ankle to put him down, and pounded his face in with various objects, had dragged Bodroon down into the water and floated him out into the scum, and hadn't weighted him down with anything.) The way the rain abruptly stopped as he raised the toaster up over his head reminded Taylor of his childhood days, when storms like that had been more frequent. He couldn't remember exactly how frequent. He was sitting there, straddling Bodroon's chest, which hadn't moved for several minutes. He was resting the toaster on Bodroon's forehead. The rain was still pissing down at this point. He was saying something that made no sense to God or himself or whoever it is you unconsciously mutter and sometimes plaintively moan and confess to when you're shitfaced drunk. He couldn't remember the last time he'd cried. He wasn't now, but his face was all contorted like the face of a person crying. It wasn't that he didn't accept his fate. He did. He knew what he had to do. He knew it had to be this way, ... that it was better this way, so it wasn't that. It was just that, back on Walt Whitman Road, or in what was left of Taylor's memories of his memories of back on Walt Whitman Road, back when the sky would sprout these massive mushroom clouds of cumulonimbus that would pour down rain for hours like this, and the sound of it hammering down on the rooftops and streets and sidewalks and tapping the panes of windows like pebbles was all you could hear, and Alice Williams and Rusty Braynard and Taylor, and all the other little kids, because back then the Zone was full of kids, ran down out of whatever sweltering airless ratholes they

---

* *The information Taylor extracted turned out to be less useful than he had hoped. Bodroon had largely corroborated Dodo Pacheco's version of reality, and had denied any knowledge of Adam or Sarah, or Cassandra, or any Corporatist plot. Taylor was inclined to accept these denials, as he had broken Bodroon's elbow by then, and was kicking Bodroon in the balls repeatedly, and Bodroon was weeping and begging him to stop.*

were normally forced to spend all day in on account of the heat and went hydroplaning through the flooded streets on sheets of siding they tore off of buildings, and sloshed like monsters through the ankle-deep water making like they were going to catch and drown the even littler kids in the lakes of rain that formed on the corners, and just ran around playing grab-ass generally, and at night his mother would sit beside the cot in the hall where he slept back then and read him stories, not off a machine, stories from actual paper books, which stank like mold and water damage, and his mother smelled like sweat and cigarettes, and her voice was like a song in the dark, because his eyes were closed, and the words didn't matter ... and it was just that, back then, life, or the world, or Taylor's world, hadn't seemed so totally fucked beyond all recognition somehow ... but then again he was just a kid. He brought the toaster, whose housing was metal, down with both hands into Bodroon's face. He did this over and over and over. Because Max would never get to play in the rain. Or hear *The Adventures of Homer the Monkey* read to him in the dark by Cassandra. Or hunt down mutant monster rats in the ruins of scary abandoned buildings his mother had threatened to slap him senseless if he even thought of sneaking into ... or anything. Max would never do anything. Taylor hoped Bodroon understood that. He raised up one more time with the toaster. As he brought it down the rain ... stopped. All of it. Everywhere. All at once. It did not dwindle down to a trickle, or let up, or thin out, or taper, or wane. It was pouring down rain. Then it just stopped.

Now it was like it never happened. The heat and humidity were back with a vengeance. The muscles in his neck were cramping. His chinos and T-shirt were sticking to him. His skin was basting in a glaze of sweat. He could hear the bombardment off in the distance. He zig-zagged through the warren of narrow lanes and backstreets south of Jefferson, keeping to the shade wherever he could. A.S.P. 1s were scurrying toward him and into their doorways like panicked mice. There weren't any Public Viewers back here, but one of them in the general vicinity was explaining how Sector C was now closed on account of unrest, which was being suppressed, and how any remaining A.S.P. 3s in Sector A at the present time were to report to the following designated checkpoints, at which various refreshments

were being provided, and shelter in place until ... et cetera. Taylor
followed an A.S.P. 1, who was on his way home from his factory
night-shift and was nearly but not quite Taylor's size, into a doorway
and took him by the throat ...

Three minutes later, a better-dressed Taylor, or at least a more sec-
tor-appropriately dressed Taylor (1s didn't tend to wear ratty old
chinos, filthy T-shirts, or combat boots), emerged from that doorway and resumed his journey. He felt rather strange all dressed in
beige, or khaki, or whatever color this flimsy pajama-like corporate
uniform was, but at least he still had his combat boots. He'd left his
filthy old clothes in the hallway, so when the 1 woke up, he'd have
something to wear, which he realized now didn't make much sense,
as the 1 presumably lived in the building and so would probably
just walk upstairs in his underwear. He didn't quite understand why
he'd done that. He'd squeezed the 1 unconscious with a choke hold.
He was going to keep squeezing until he'd killed him. But then, for
some unknown reason, he hadn't. Now he was back outside in the
heat. He was heading north, or as north as possible, cutting from
backstreet to lane to alley, keeping the rising sun to his right. He
didn't know this part of the sector, which wasn't laid out in the usual
grid, but one of these streets had to come out on Jefferson. That was
where all the 1s were coming from.

Taylor, as he pushed his way through the streams of frightened
1s in their colored pajamas who were scuttling toward him through
this idiotic maze of winding lanes and circuitous alleys that were not
coming out on Jefferson Avenue, was trying to get his head around
the completely inconceivable concept that everyone he even vaguely
knew, except Cassandra Passwaters, was dead ... or they would be
by the end of the day. Alice Williams and Rusty Braynard, Meyer,
Coco, Sylvie, Claudia, Young Man Henry, T.C. Johns, Vaclav Borges,
the Gilmartin brothers, Jim MacReady, Coreen Sweeney, most of
the other regulars at Gillie's, the vast majority of whom were 3s,
random residents of Mulberry Street, like the people upstairs who
no one ever saw, Herman the Wino, the Chinese woman who always
made that face at Taylor when she saw him walking in the wrong
direction, all of them ... all of these people were dead. Taylor couldn't
be certain of course, but he reasoned, if he were IntraZone Waste,

and the Hadley Corporation of Menomonie, Wisconsin, areas like
the English Quarter, Stokely Fields, Little Damascus, and certainly
the entire deep Inner Zone, would have to be high-priority targets,
which meant they had been leveled with missiles already, and even if
they hadn't, it didn't matter, because they would be, because this was
a full-out purge, and Taylor, unlike a lot of people who had heard the
stories but hadn't been there, remembered the last one. He remembered it vividly ...

Following the Jackson Avenue Uprising, after Taylor, who was
only ten years old, had crawled up out of his basement bunker,
and couldn't find his mother's body, but found Alice Williams and
Rusty Braynard sitting on the stoop of their former building eating
stale marshmallows out of that bag, the three of them had wandered through the ruins of the streets that ran both ways off Jackson
Avenue. They weren't sure where they were heading at first, other
than away from Jackson Avenue ... as far away as possible, ideally.
Somewhere where Security Specialists weren't making people lie
down in the street, then shooting them all in the back of the head.
The way they did it, these Security Specialists, who were certainly
Hadley Domestic Security (Taylor believed he remembered seeing
Hadley logos on their body armor) was they stormed into whatever
tenement building they wanted to "sweep and clear" or whatever,
shot a few people inside the building so that everyone inside would
know they were serious, then they marched the others out into the
street. They made them lie face down in the street (or sometimes
stand against a wall, facing the wall, if they were doing it that way),
then they went down the row and calmly shot the tops of their heads
off, one by one. Taylor remembered all this vividly ... the pop ... pop
... pop ... of the pistols, as they moved down the row at a 4/4 pace,
and the way people's bodies would jerk, just once, and how the one to
their right would tense all their muscles ... pop ... pop ... pop ... pop.
He also remembered wondering why they didn't jump up (or just
turn around, if they were facing the wall) and run, or fight. Because
why would you just lie down in the street (or just stand there staring
at a fucking wall) and wait your turn to have your brains blown out?
Taylor, as a child, had not understood that. He continued to not
understand it now. Meyer Jimenez had tried to explain how people,

once they knew they were dead, or were going to be dead in another few seconds (or sometimes weeks, or months, or years; it depended on the person and the situation), when they faced the inescapable fact of it, and gave up hope, the last little shred of it, not some type of grandiose hope, like for revolution, or salvation, or something, but simply the hope that they would live through the day, or the morning, or just the next ten minutes, when people finally let go of that, according to Meyer, and surrendered to Fate, or to God, or whatever it was they believed in, there wasn't any point in trying to run, and there was no one to fight, because the fight was over. The fight was over ... and Death had won. The man who was steadily coming toward them ... pop ... pop ... pop ... pop ... and who was going to reach them in just another few seconds, and point his pistol at the back of their heads (exactly as he was doing now, as he blew their friend's or their lover's brains out) was not their enemy. It wasn't personal. It didn't have anything to do with this man. He didn't hate them. He didn't even know them. He was just, like, Death's employee, or something. It was like he wasn't even really there, because this, this final conscious moment, was strictly between the person and Death, who had always been there, who had always been coming ... pop ... pop ... and now he was here and this was it, that inconceivable moment, that final pointless flash of memory, the erasure of everything ... the end of time. Taylor had listened as Meyer explained this, and he had understood the words and all, but he didn't get it ... he just did not get it. He got the philosophical part, about the inconceivable nature of Death. What he didn't get was the other part. Because regardless of what you believed about Death, or to what degree you feared the erasure of every last shred of thought and memory that constituted who you thought you were, you didn't lie down in the fucking street or stand up against a fucking wall and let some corporatist lackey asshole blow the back of your fucking head off. No matter what happened, you did not do this. It wasn't any kind of personal statement, or ethical stance, or militant tactic, or anything that needed explaining to anyone. It wasn't ... it was fucking simple. If someone attacked you, you attacked them back. You attacked them with everything you had. You fought, or, OK, if the odds were against you, you ran, if there was somewhere to run ... and if there wasn't, then you killed as many of the motherfuckers as you possibly could. You did this until the moment they killed you. You did this because they were going to kill you, and you hated their fucking guts for that.

Some of the 4s had shared Taylor's sentiments. Not very many, but some of them at least. And not just the bozos who had started the uprising. Other people. People fought back. They didn't have a chance. They fought back anyway. Taylor remembered a little old lady who had climbed out onto to her fire escape and was throwing pots and pans and dishes down onto the helmets of the Security Specialists who were ordering people to lie down in the street. She was wearing a ratty old bathrobe like Coco's, except with an elaborate paisley pattern. Someone was handing them out the window, the pots and plates, and she was hurling them down at them, these soulless scumbags who were following orders, who had knowingly volunteered for this shit. She was using both hands to improve her aim. She wasn't doing this with quiet dignity. She was doing this screaming at the top of her lungs, red-faced with hatred and uncontrollable rage. She had to have been eighty, ninety years old, her skin was all wrinkled and blotched and bruised, her fingers all twisted up and arthritic, like the claws of a pigeon ... she was utterly beautiful. The Specialists shot her to pieces, of course, along with whoever was helping her inside. They blew her body back in through the window, then shot up every other window on the floor. Then they finished killing all the people they had there ... pop ... pop ... pop ... pop.

Whatever. The 4s were all history now. And so was history. History was history. An immeasurable stream of unreliable data scrolling across a network of screens, upon which the purge of the A.S.P. 4s in 2575, H.C.S.T., when Taylor was ten, was a tiny blip. There was surely an online record of it, because everything that happened was recorded somewhere, and then officially examined, and revised and corrected, and commented on to the point where either whatever had happened hadn't happened, or there were so many different conflicting accounts that no one could possibly be certain what had happened ... and who was left to say any different? The only ones who had made it out of the old Sector D, and so had witnessed the purge, witnessed it all up close and personal, were orphaned little kids like Taylor Byrd, and Alice Williams and Rusty Braynard, and a handful of other such damaged souls, like Rudy Rebello and Vaclav Borges (who, rumor had it, had had his mother's brains blown out into his face, and had walked around for days like that, covered in her blood and cranial matter). Older folks, like Coco Freudenheim, remembered the A.S.P. 4s, of course, and had a general idea of what had happened, but the few little kids who'd made it out hadn't been all that eager to discuss the details. To pretty much everyone else in the Zone, the Purge of the 4s was folklore, legend, another drunken story to tell, a story which everyone knew, or assumed, was primarily based on made-up bullshit. And of course, to the Normals, Taylor imagined, it had been just one more wonderful weekend, streaming their Entertainment Content, and playing with their little medicated kids, in fucking Shangri-La or wherever ...

Back in the present, or whatever it was, a detail of Hadley Security Specialists were working their way up the alley toward him, checking IDs against biometrics in a random and totally professional manner. Taylor walked directly at them, reaching into his pocket as if he were going to produce a legit ID card, then took a quick left the fuck up out of there, up this lane that wound around, taking him south, but he had no choice, and down these steps and through this tunnel, which it felt like maybe he was under Collins now, and then up this ramp and out into some other little labyrinth of lanes. He took his first available right, and now his bearing was north northwest ... which, OK, that was somewhat better, except that he was completely lost. He paused outside this weird-ass little two-story townhouse, or cottage, or something, where the shit-for-brains 1s had actually put some potted plants in the fucking windows. Morons. He stood there listening a moment. There ... yes, there it was. It was one of the jumbo Public Viewers, two, maybe three blocks north, so maybe this alley was taking him out to the far west end of Jefferson Avenue ... which, OK, that would do in a pinch. He couldn't make out what the Viewer was saying, but that didn't matter, except for the time, which he sensed was something like 0710, or possibly later, but he couldn't verify. He set out walking. Yes. Good. The alley was definitely taking him north. The sun was over the rooftops to his right. The Public Viewer was also to his right. And up ahead it looked like maybe ... yes ... there was Jefferson Avenue.

Taylor stepped out into the throngs of morning shoppers and
stood there, baffled, drawing a series of exasperated looks as people
pushed and shoved their way past him. Produce vendors were shouting out their end-of-the-morning cut-rate prices, desperately trying
to unload the last of their wilted wares before 0730. 1s and 2s were
rushing from stand to stand with their plastic bags and carts, hoping
to score a last-minute deal on a couple kilos of liquifying squash,
or rubbery carrots, or moldy mushrooms, or something equally
disgusting and inedible. Apart from the absence of A.S.P. 3s and
the heightened presence of Security Specialists, who were moving
through the crowd in twos and threes, checking IDs and scanning
irises, it looked like any other Tuesday morning.

Taylor's detour had taken him all the way down to the far west
end of the markets. Across the avenue, off to his left, was this field,
or lot, where there were no stalls, or tables, or corporate stores, or
anything. It was just this stretch of dirt and weeds that extended
all the way to the wall to the north and off to the roofless shells of
some buildings that had probably once been a school to the west. A
block up ahead was Gate 14. It looked like it was open for business.
IntraZone Waste & Security Specialists were processing the line of
outbound vehicles, mini-buses packed with manual laborers, work
vans, a couple of pick-up trucks. The Hadley Domestic Security
forces had probably used Gates 8 through 12, which no one used, as
there was nothing down there. They couldn't have entered the Zone
up here ... not with the avenue packed like this. He turned around
and looked to the south. Minarets of oily smoke were curdling up
into the cloudless sky.

Riding the currents of eastbound shoppers, he set out for
Cassandra's alley ... which was way the hell down at the other end of
Jefferson. Which meant he had a serious problem. See, he needed to
be there by 0730, as that's when the markets officially closed, and his
plan was, if he could get up to Cassandra's and back down into the
street with Max by 0740, or thereabouts, the vendors would be closing up their stands and hauling away their perishable items ... which
was good, as that was always chaotic, and he would still have the last
of the shoppers for cover. He wasn't going to make it. Not at this
pace. But it wasn't like he could start shoving his way through the

crowd, or even walk any faster, not without drawing the unwanted attention of the roving teams of Security Specialists. Up ahead, the gigantic face of the Orange-Haired Woman on the Public Viewer, the one he'd heard and had guided him out here, was informing the residents of Sector A that the time at the tone would be 0720. Down in the lower right corner of the screen, a window was running Real-Time footage of the manicured lawn of some Cartwright estate upon which members of the corporate media were filming Real-Time footage of each other, and repeating, every fifteen seconds, how Jimmy "Jimbo" Cartwright was dead.

Taylor snaked his way through the shoppers, squeezed between two Content stalls, and shot down the little strip of sidewalk the vendors used to stack their empty crates and boxes and barrels and whatever, and occasionally step out the back of their stands when no one was looking and pee down the gutter. He made good time for about a block. Then his secret passageway ended and he had to cut back out into the mobs. He drifted left, avoiding a pair of Security Specialists coming toward him, and got behind a pack of old Turkish ladies who had formed a V and were viciously pushing the prows of their carts into the people ahead of them. He passed a number of cooking oil stands, exotic soap stalls, and an auto parts tent, all of which smelled exactly the same, then the grannies turned off toward Haloumi Heaven, and he was out there on his own again. During all this, his brain was running an emergency cognitive clean-up program that deleted all extraneous abstract thoughts (like whether the D.A.D.A. was actually happening or was just a pretext for the purge in progress, and whether Adam was a corporatist agent, and who, what, and where Sarah was) and locked his mind (the program did) into this sort of tactical mode where everything simplified down to a series of instant decisions he made by instinct. Likewise, all the intense emotions Taylor had been debatably feeling (i.e., his grief for his probably now dead friends, and his fondness, or love, for Max and Cassandra, not to mention the fear, or mind-numbing terror, accompanying his likely imminent death) ... all of these emotions had been shut off. He was feeling nothing. He was like a machine. His eyes were scanning the terrain ahead for possible vectors, probable threats, he was calculating times, distances, speeds ... tobacco kiosk, produce stall, discount shoe store, sun-screen stand ... and yes, that was the sun-screen stand, the one where ... there it was ... just past it ... the little alley where he was going to rendezvous ... back in some other version of reality ... no, delete that ... stay in the moment ... Security Specialists off to the left, so veer right slowly, turn your head and ...

Two blocks down from Cassandra's place, he ducked behind the line of stalls, and into another service passageway, and was glancing over his shoulder quickly, and he walked right into this clueless Transplant and knocked her onto her ass in the gutter. He stood there a moment, looking down at her, some green-eyed, totally zapped-out redhead. On top of whatever else they'd done to her, the Normals had seriously fucked up her hair. She sat there, staring up at him, goggle-eyed, clutching the straps of her Transplant bag, as if he were going to take it from her. Her bedroll was lying in the muck beside her. Something about her looked familiar ... or maybe it was déjà vu ... or whatever. He didn't have time to wonder. Off he went, into the stream of shoppers ...

Coming in through Cassandra's window, he caught the tip of his boot on the sill, lost his balance, lurched, rolled, narrowly missed Cassandra's bucket, and ended up down near the foot of her bed in the pile of clothes, Content discs, and other assorted crap she kept there, including, apparently, several squeezable packets of bar-becue-flavored mayonnaise. Cassandra was sitting at the head of the bed nursing Max like the women did in those paintings from some earlier Renaissance period, back before there were digital cameras, the dates of which Taylor could never remember ... in any event, they looked beatific (Cassandra and Max did, not the women in the paintings), except for Cassandra's excessive sweating, and her eyes, which were swollen and red from crying. They looked across the bed at each other.

"What's going on?" Cassandra asked.

"I don't know," Taylor told her.

The pirate Viewer was lying beside her.

"They shut down the network. All you get ..."

"I know, he said.

"They're bombing."

"Yeah."

"They sealed off the sector. I thought ... "

"I know. Listen to me. We don't have time. After I'm gone, you clean all this up. You don't know me. You don't know anything."

"Wait ..."

"No. Don't talk. Just listen. I got to go. There isn't time. They'll be here later. They'll go house to house. They're purging the 3s."

"IntraZone?"

"Hadley. Look ... I don't have time to explain all this. Stick to the cover. In a couple of days, you go back to work like nothing happened. Wrap him up in a towel or something."

"Wait."

"No. Where's the bag?"

"I don't know. Taylor, wait ..."

Taylor tore through the crap on the floor and found an old towel and the Transplant bag. He threw the towel across to Cassandra.

"Wrap him up."

"No. Talk to me ..."

He sat down on the bed beside her, and pulled the hair back out of her face. Max was finished nursing for the moment. He was lying there in Cassandra's arms, squinting and making adorable faces, and just generally being helpless and innocent.

"We don't have time. There isn't time," Taylor babbled, not knowing what to say. "They're purging the 3s. I saw the units."

"Purging ... what are you talking about?"

"I don't think anyone knows about you. You'll be all right. But I got to go. I need to get him out of here, now."

"They're still going to take him?"

Taylor hesitated.

"Yeah," he lied.

"No they're not."

He reached for Max. Cassandra recoiled, tightening her grip on him.

"No," she said.

This was the part that just destroyed him. He was all shut down and ready to do this, then she goes and pulls this shit.

"Give him to me."

"No," she said. And now she was sobbing. And now he was sobbing. And this was the last fucking thing he needed.

"Give me the fucking kid already. You want to die?"

"No," she said.

Snot ropes were dangling out of both their noses. Their chests were heaving. This was so stupid.

"Do not do this," Taylor begged her.

Max went ahead and joined in sobbing. Now the three of them were sitting there, sobbing. The markets were closing. The clock was ticking. He stared at the floor between his boots.

"I love you," he told her.

"I know," she said. "I love you too."

They had never said it. They hadn't had to. Now they did.

He took her head with both hands, gently. Her head was so small. He looked in her eyes. He held her that way until she focused.

"Help me do this. Make him stop crying."

She nodded. Then she started sobbing again.

Taylor got up, went to the window, and pretended to check the alley below. He needed them all to stop fucking crying, which they weren't going to do with him sitting beside them. Cassandra started humming some little tune he had never heard her hum before, and rocking Max back and forth in her arms, which seemed to magically stop his crying. Taylor kept his back to the two of them. He used the sleeve of his stolen outfit to wipe the tears and snot and sweat and the remnants of mayonnaise off his face. His knees were all rubbery. He was going to shit himself. His thoughts were racing. He could hardly breathe. Leaning halfway out the window, he could see the back of the TōFish stand. They were packing the leftovers into crates, loading the vans, breaking down tables. He closed his eyes, clenched his asshole, and silently prayed that God, or the One, or whoever it was that wasn't out there, was looking down into his heart right now, and knowing the depths of Taylor's hatred ... for Him and His whole fucking sick little game.

When he opened his eyes and turned around, Cassandra was curled up into a ball with her face pressed down between her knees. Max was lying on the bed in front of her ... lying on the blanket on the bed in front of her. Taylor quickly wrapped him up, leaving his head sticking out of the blanket, and stuffed him into the Transplant bag. He padded it out with another blanket. He zipped up the bag, but not all the way, so that Max could get a little air in maybe. Cassandra, who was still curled up in a ball, lost it again, and started shaking and wailing. He picked up the bag, turned his back on her, staggered to the window like a broken robot, crawled out onto the fire escape, down and into the fish-stinking alley, and walked back out onto Jefferson Avenue.

Max was already crying again, but not very loudly, and the noise of the last of the shoppers and the stands being taken apart was apparently enough to drown him out, as no one was turning and looking at Taylor as he started back the way he had come, using what stalls remained for cover. The markets were all officially closed now, the crowds dispersing, and the avenue swarming with carts and vans and flatbed trucks that transported the stalls and stands and products back to wherever it was they came from. Taylor didn't know where he was heading, exactly. Step One was to get well clear of Cassandra's. Step Two was to find some isolated place. He'd fig-ure out the rest whenever he got there. The sun was broiling the back of his neck as he drifted from group to group of shoppers until they peeled off left and headed south, and he drifted up to another group, acting like just another A.S.P. 1 on his way back home with his bag of groceries. The only problem was, his bag of groceries was a Transplant bag, which was rather unusual, and also his groceries were squirming around and ... oh yes, now they were crying louder ... people were starting to look around and try to identify where it was coming from ... so, OK, time for a different strategy.

He drifted away from the groups of shoppers, most of whom were turning south anyway, and slipped back into that service passageway that ran along behind the stalls that were left, which there weren't that many and those there were were being disassembled quickly. IntraZone Specialists were making their rounds, motivating vendors and meandering shoppers to move their asses and vacate the area. Taylor scanned the avenue ahead and determined that after another two blocks he was going to run out of cover completely. The stalls were coming down too fast. There'd be nothing up there but a smat-tering of shoppers, Security Specialists, and empty avenue.

He let his instincts take him south, into some alley that veered southwest, which he took for all of fifteen seconds ... dead ahead was a makeshift checkpoint, where Security Specialists were checking IDs and scanning irises, looking for 3s. He doubled back and came back out onto Jefferson Avenue. Max was crying. He cut up behind a couple stands, then left, and into another little alley, halfway down which another team of Security Specialists were checking IDs. He backed up into a 1 with a cart, some exhausted-looking middle-aged guy whose pores were all clogged with grease or oil. By this time Max was caterwauling. He sounded like a cat on fire. The 1 looked down at Taylor's bag. He looked up at Taylor. He looked away. Taylor pushed past him and out onto Jefferson. Security units were cruising toward him. Fuck. He scanned. OK ... there. If he could just get behind that van right there, the one that was inching up the avenue, some kind of HVAC sign on the panel ... and wait, the driver looked familiar. No. That didn't make any sense. He looked like Cassandra's roommate, Joel, or Jules, or whatever the fuck his name was, the one with the ridiculous tribal earrings ... but why would he be driving some van ... with a woman beside him in the passenger seat ... a woman who looked a lot like ... Sarah? No. That was completely insane. Still, Taylor picked up his pace, walking quickly, skipping, jogging, trying to get alongside the van and get a better look ... and now he was running, and Max was howling like a fucking banshee, and this artificial banana vendor with the Panama hat was pointing at Taylor and shouting something and ... fuck ... fuck ... a Security Specialist across the avenue was talking into his lavalier mike, and fuck ... two more Security Specialists were walking toward him, pointing at the bag ...

"BAG ON THE GROUND!" one of them shouted.

The other Specialist was going for his sidearm, which the Specialists preferred for close encounters.

Taylor walked directly toward them.

"BAG ON THE GROUND! BAG ON THE GROUND!"

These weren't the most articulate Specialists, nor were they suited up for battle. They were just the everyday market Specialists, whose job it was to clear the avenue.

"BAG ON THE FUCKING GROUND, ASSHOLE!"

Taylor closed the distance with them just as Specialist Number Two was bringing his weapon out of his holster ... which Taylor promptly relieved him of, after driving one of his testicles up into his groin with a vicious knee kick. The shouty Specialist raised his rifle, which Taylor quickly grabbed the barrel of, and jacked the butt into his face, breaking off most of his upper front teeth. The firearms were bio-coded to the Specialists, so useless to Taylor, so he tossed them away. He picked up the bag of Max off the sidewalk, did a 360 to confirm that he was now totally and irrevocably fucked, which he was ... as now, behind him, to the east, a number of other, more formidable Specialists were running toward him with their UltraLite rifles, shouting down into their collars, and gutless fucking cooperating 1s were standing on the sidewalk pointing at him, and Security Units were executing U-turns, and poor little Max was hollering his head off, and God and the One and Fate were up there jacking each other off and laughing, and fuck them, fuck them all, he thought ... he tucked Max into his chest like a football, like American fullbacks used to do, locked his left arm over his right, and he took off running down Jefferson Avenue ...

Zone 23

Valentina had never actually seen the wall ... not up close. There were pictures of it online, of course, and you could see it from the upper floors of a lot of the corporate towers in the business district, 6262 Lomax among them, but Paxton Wills didn't face that way, and neither did any of the other offices she'd frequented in her previous life. She had seen it out the windows of planes, and now and again from the hills of the more abundant Residential Communities where she and Kyle had been invited to dinner at the homes of the various corporate bigwigs who were always restructuring BVCC, but none of those views had done it justice. Now, walking directly toward it, walking through the shadow of it, she could feel the unrelenting mass of the series of identical concrete slabs stretching away in both directions like an echelon of neo-brutalist monoliths standing out on the edge of the world.

She had glimpsed it out the window between the helmeted heads of the Security Specialists as they were traveling east on the perimeter road that formed the inner boundary of Center City. By that time her eyes had recovered from the mace, or the pepper spray, or whatever it was. The van turned onto an access road that traversed the two-kilometer stretch of no man's land surrounding the Zone. Strapped in her seat and facing west, she couldn't see it, but she had felt it down there, looming up out of the southern horizon, drawing ever nearer as the van approached. She closed her eyes and repeated her mantra, and there, in the dark of her mind, she saw it ... and she realized that it had always been there, out there on the abscissa of everything, blending invisibly into the depth of field of all her thoughts and dreams ... but those were only thoughts and dreams, apparitions, symbols, signs. This was the sensate thing itself.

Dead ahead was Gate 15. The Security Specialists were walking her toward it, two of them flanking her, one behind her. They were walking on the scorching asphalt path that led to the gate from the parking area. The blacktop was trapping the oppressive heat, which was worse down here than in Center City, where she had spent some nebulous period of time in some half-remembered cheap motel. It felt like the path was melting beneath her, sticking to the rubberized soles of the flimsy slip-on sneaker-type shoes she was wearing. The lightweight, loose-fitting clothes they had given her were soaked through with sweat. She was struggling to breathe. She squinted into the blinding glare that was bouncing off of every surface directly up into her eyes and staggered along like a broken rag doll someone had just fished out of a lake. The Security Specialists, whose body armor must have been coated with a ThermaSoak skin, and were safe from the glare behind their visors, marched her on, completely unfazed.

Gate 15 was a fortress type gate with a big red painted "1" on one of the doors and a big red "5" on the other. The doors were almost perfectly square, and opened outward, and were made of iron. Excessively armed Security Specialists wearing uniforms she didn't recognize were processing vans with mismatched fenders, mini-shuttle buses, and other odd vehicles, in the space between a pair of boom arms, one on either side of the gate. Other Specialists were standing off to the side with their matte black UltraLite rifles held in the classic "sling ready" position, staring implacably in various directions and generally looking intimidating. Just to the right of the door with the "1" was a bungalow-style Security Station, which looked like it was probably attached to the tower that rose up the wall behind it. At the top of the tower was a mirrored enclosure with a metal catwalk running around it. The sun was shining directly into it. Valentina looked away from it.

They veered to the right and walked her up a slightly sloping ramp to the station. The automatic doors whooshed open. They walked her into what felt like a freezer, and up to an elevated processing counter that stretched across the length of the interior and came up to the level of her eyes and the shoulder level of the Security Specialists. An older Specialist was seated behind it, a balding, middle-aged

Variant-Positive, typing something into a keyboard as he smiled down into a recessed screen. Stenciled on the wall behind him in a big red sans serif corporate font ...

INTRAZONE WASTE & SECURITY SERVICES, INC.
SPECIAL RESIDENTIAL AREA 23, N.E. REGION 709

He held one finger up to the Specialists, smiled at his screen, and went on typing. Her escorts stood there, waiting patiently. Valentina scanned her surroundings. The lobby, or whatever this was exactly, was an all-white rectilinear space, with the counter running across one side and a row of fiberglass seats on the other. The seats, in alternating primary colors, so red, then yellow, then blue, then green, which technically wasn't a primary color, then red again, and yellow, and so on, were affixed to a heavy metal bar that was bolted into the wall behind them. Down at the end of the row of seats were three other persons with unfortunate haircuts. They were wearing the same white, loose-fitting outfit that Valentina was currently wearing, each of which was in one or another stage of having been soaked through with sweat. They were staring fixedly down at the the toes of their shoes, or the floor just in front of their shoes, or something down there, and hugging themselves, and rubbing their hands together desperately, and shivering, and basically freezing to death. The dark-skinned man and woman in their sixties, who Valentina assumed were married, unless they were simply seated together, were whispering prayers in some non-English language. A few seats away was the younger woman, thirties, early forties maybe, rocking back and forth in her seat, whispering nothing in any language. This younger woman looked familiar, but Valentina could not quite place her. For a second she thought she was someone from work ... but no, she wasn't, or she didn't think so. She was foggy, but she still remembered her colleagues, their faces at least, or she thought she did.

The Security Specialist behind the counter pressed a button she couldn't see. A voice came over the PA system, "six four three ... six four three." The older man and woman stood up. They held out little squares of paper, extending their arms as far as possible, squinting at them without their glasses, determined that the woman had 643, and set about whispering about this fact. The man at the counter pressed the button. The PA system sounded again, "six four three ... six four three." The older couple continued whispering. The man at the counter sat there waiting, approximately fifteen meters away from them. Finally, the older, dark-skinned man convinced his wife to approach the counter, which, once she had, she couldn't see over, so she had to get up onto her tiptoes and pull herself up with both of her hands. The Security Specialist behind the counter reached across and took her number. He examined it, disposed of it behind the counter, and handed her down another slip of paper with something on it she could not read. She peered up over the edge of the counter with a desperate look of total confusion. During all this, Valentina's escorts hadn't moved one centimeter.

The man at the counter leaned out toward her.

"This is your housing assignment," he said. "Pick up your bedding at Gate 15. Your bedding, along with your hygiene kit, are provided as is, free of charge. You can upgrade them later at your own expense."

He handed her down another slip of paper.

"This is your temporary work assignment. Report to work tomorrow morning at that address at 0730. Once an evaluation has been made, you'll be given a permanent work assignment. Do you understand?"

The woman nodded.

"Exit out the doors to your left."

The woman staggered away from the counter, back to her husband. They whispered briefly. Then he walked her down to the doors to her left, the ones at the opposite end of the room. The doors whooshed open. The woman stepped through and out into the blazing sunlight. She stopped, turned back toward her husband, blinking, obviously blinded by the glare, and opened her mouth as if to speak ... the automatic doors whooshed closed in her face.

Valentina stood there watching, shivering herself now, completely baffled, as the husband shuffled back to his seat and went back to staring at his shoes or whatever, and to fingering his numbered slip of paper. No one seemed to be guarding these people. They just walked into the Zone on their own ... then again, what were they going to do, run for it up the access road, or across that stretch of no man's land, with all those Security Specialists out there, and those snipers up in that mirrored tower? And there were probably landmines, and who knew what else …

"What can I do for you gentlemen today?" the Specialist behind the counter asked.

"Level 3 transport," one of them said, and he handed the man at the counter a MemCard. The man at the counter took the card and inserted it into a port up there.

"Level 3?"

The Specialist nodded. The man at the counter pulled up a screen. "Walk-in?"

"Right."

He smiled at his screen and started typing on his keyboard again.

"Give me a couple, three seconds," he said, scanning his screen as he typed and clicked. "Housing is going to be a little tricky. We've got a bit of unrest in the sector. Mostly contained in the southern quadrants, though. HDS is in there now. You may have noticed as you were coming in."

"Right," one the Specialists said.

Valentina hadn't noticed, but then she hadn't been able to see out the windshield. Back out on Perimeter Road she had thought it had looked like it was going to rain.

"All right, this should be OK. It's way up in the northwest quadrant."

He handed her down a slip of paper.

7747 Calumet Avenue.

"That's your new address, Ms. Briggs. You won't be able to get down there currently. Sector C is in a lockdown until we neutralize this Terrorist threat. It shouldn't take more than a couple hours. After that, they'll let you right in. You may want to shelter in place for a while, somewhere inside, out of the heat. You're entitled to apply for a work assignment. You can do that at any job service center. Details on that, and everything else, you'll find in your orientation kit. You pick up your bedding and kit at the gate. These gentlemen are going to walk you in. Do you understand everything I've just explained to you?"

Valentina said she did.

"All right, gentlemen, have a nice day."

Valentina's Security Specialists walked her past the older man and the younger, possibly familiar-looking woman, and on through the other set of automatic doors, and out into the unbearable heat. They walked her past who she recognized now as the IntraZone Waste & Security Specialists who were scanning the interiors and undercarriages, and in some cases also the engine blocks, of the procession of vans and mini-buses that were waiting to be scanned and enter the gate, and on, past others who were taking and scanning what appeared to be the old-fashioned ID cards (as in physical laminated cards you carried) that the drivers were proffering out of their windows, and on, past the others, who were scanning people's irises, and faces, and teeth, and the tips of their fingers, and whatever else they could think of to scan, or just standing around with their UltraLite rifles looking like highly-trained professionals, and they walked her on, past still other Specialists, and through the gate, and into the Zone, the entire southern horizon of which appeared to be burning out of control.

Her body wanted to stop for a moment, but the Specialists walked her relentlessly on. Squinting out at the conflagration, she could make out the menacing shark-like shapes of remotely piloted aerial vehicles, and choppers, which looked like dragonflies, darting in and out of the columns of smoke. She saw the orange flaming tails of air-to-surface missiles streaking down from somewhere up in the stratosphere, and she heard their distant rumbling booms, and she saw the fiery mushrooms they made, like miniature suns, or sea anemones, and she saw the tentacled midair bursts of the dust-white blistering phosphorus bombs ... the Security Specialists tightened their grips, and turned her away from the fireworks show.

They walked her to another station, exactly like the one where she had just been processed, except that part of this one was an outdoor booth where a sweaty, red-faced, bored-looking man was waiting under the metal awning with a duffel bag and a rolled-up futon propped up on the counter for her. The red-faced man was an A.S.P. He was wearing a pair of old mirrored sunglasses, the lenses of which were flaking badly. His hair was buzzed like a Security

Specialist. Silk-screened across the front of his T-shirt in big block letters ...

COMMUNITY WATCH

"Look into the scanner," he said. An out-of-date-looking iris scanner mounted on the counter scanned her iris. Stacked on racks in the depths of the booth were other duffel bags and rolled-up futons. Something behind the counter beeped.

"That's it. You're done."

"Hold out your arm."

This was one of her Security Specialists. She held out her arm.

"The other arm."

He meant the one with the ID bracelet.

She held it out. He snipped it off ... the ID bracelet, not her arm. He slipped it into a pocket in his pants. The Specialists turned and walked back through the gate and out of her life forever.

Valentina watched them go. Then she turned back to the man at the counter, who had stepped back into the darkness of the booth and was sitting on a metal stool back there watching some sort of archival Content on the screen of an ancient desktop Viewer. She leaned in over the top of the counter.

"Excuse me."

"Step away from the counter."

"I was hoping you could ..."

"What are you, fucking deaf? Step the fuck away from the counter."

Valentina stepped away from the counter. She stood there, awaiting further instructions. The man went back to watching his Content. It looked like the Archeology Channel. After a moment he turned and glared at her.

"The fuck you waiting for?"

"I'm sorry. I just ..."

"Get your shit and get the fuck out of here."

Valentina did as instructed. She gathered the canvas handles of the duffel and pulled the duffel off the counter. Objects shifted around inside. The duffel weighed six, maybe seven kilos. She stood there staring at the rolled-up futon, which was tied at the ends and the middle with twine. She set the duffel down on the ground and wrestled the futon up onto her shoulder. Then she squatted down and picked up the duffel. She stood there, judging the weight in the heat.

Along the side of the access road that led to the gate was a blacktop path that led down to a four-lane avenue that followed the course of the Security Wall to the east and west as far as she could see. Across the avenue were rows of tenements, on the ground floors of which there were various stores ... stores she knew, like Big-Buy Basement, Content City, and CRS, and other stores she'd never heard of, like Lilly's Late-Nite Liquor Emporium, Ray's Original Famous Pizza, Chaim's Footwear, and ConCept Drop-In, and here and there were just boarded-up storefronts. The avenue itself was lined with stalls and booths and tents and crowded with people. It looked like ... yes, it actually was. It was one big endless outdoor market, like the ones they had on Main Street on Sundays, only ten times as big, and completely revolting. The stalls, and the vendors running them, were filthy. Garbage was strewn all over the avenue. People were blithely wading through it, dragging these horrible wobbly carts, which also appeared to be full of garbage, and some of them were balancing sacks on their heads. They were pushing, shoving, and otherwise physically moving each other out of their paths, attempting to get to the heaps of produce (which were clearly past their expiry dates) that the vendors were stuffing into plastic bags (or some bio-material that looked like plastic) with their bare (as in ungloved) dirty hands, shouting the prices of things per kilo in an inexplicably aggressive way ... a woman, who was bidding on some kind of orange vegetable that conceivably could have been carrots, pressed her finger against one nostril, and strenuously blew her nose on the shoe of a man beside her, who appeared to be blind. Other indecencies were occurring elsewhere. An unnecessary amount of spitting was involved. Everyone was shouting. People were smoking. An inebriated man was stumbling in circles, moaning incoherently. His head was bleeding. No one was paying him any attention. Across the avenue a parade of people in colored pajamas was apparently in progress. Two old women were slapping each other with bags of some kind of leafy vegetable while a group of old men stood by and laughed and spat and scratched and pulled on their scrotums. People on bicycles were trying to ride through the throngs and were getting knocked to the ground. It looked like one of those reenactments of the way people lived in the Middle Ages that you saw sometimes on the history channels, except that the props and costumes were wrong ...

She made her way down the path in the heat, futon draped across one shoulder, duffel clutched in her other hand, down the slope of a gentle incline that ran down to a row of stalls, sat down on a plastic crate that was stacked on another plastic crate, wiped the sweat off her face with her sweat-soaked sleeve, and bent over and unzipped the duffel. The first thing she found was a ConCept brochure, on the front leaf of which was a glossy photo of an actress she thought she vaguely recognized, extolling the virtues, convenience and ease of "permanent surgical contraception," available at any ConCept Clinic around the clock on a drop-in basis. The next thing she found was a booklet entitled "IntraZone Waste & Security Services – Codes of Conduct & Community Ordinances," which was printed in some ridiculously miniscule font-size that you needed an electron microscope to read. Next were a variety of corporate fliers advertising various two-for-one specials and half-off deals at the corporate stores, some of which included coupons. At the bottom, buried under all this literature, were some yellowed bedsheets, a miniature pillow, and what looked like a personal hygiene kit. She fished all around among the contents, but she couldn't find anything that looked like a map. She took out the paper with her new address, and memorized it fairly easily. Her short-term memory appeared to be working. It was more that most of her past was a mess. It wasn't that she couldn't remember anything ... there were pieces, scenes, names, faces, and she definitely remembered her old address ... she just couldn't seem to fit it all together, or not in any detailed linear way. And yes, there were definitely gaps in there, days, or weeks, or months she had lost, and ... whatever. She could deal with her memory later. At the moment she needed to get out of this heat.

She tugged out a corner of the sheet from the duffel and used it as a towel to dry off her head. When she'd finished, and extracted her head from the sheet, a disreputable man was standing over her. He looked to be in his early sixties, but something told her he was really much younger. He was wearing a pair of greasy lightweight trousers that were several sizes too big, and flip-flop sandals, and a tank-top undershirt. He smelled like he hadn't bathed for weeks.

"Jew look like jew could juse some help." He smiled. His upper incisors were missing. The rest of his teeth were brown or yellow.

"Thanks. I'm OK," she said.

"Where they put jew?"

She didn't answer. Other people were walking past.

"Jew one or two?"

"I'm fine, really."

"I know jew fine. Is not what I ask. What jew name?"

She hesitated.

"Catherine."

He held out his filthy hand.

"Domingo."

She reached up and shook the hand.

"Mírame Catherine," Domingo said, "relax, OK? I not gonna hurt jew. I gonna help jew."

"I'm really OK."

Domingo pronounced his Ys like Js.

"No, chica, jew not OK. Check jew head out. Is all focked up. Jew don't even know where the fock jew are, forget about where the fock jew going."

"I do."

"What, jew think I a rapist?"

He also dropped his auxiliary verbs.

"No."

"Jew think I a focking rapist."

"I don't."

He squatted down in front of her. He leaned in close. She could smell his breath. "I not a focking rapist, OK? If I a rapist, I take jew back there, to one of those alleys ... jew see those alleys?"

Valentina looked. She saw the alleys.

"I take jew back there. No one would stop me." He gestured toward the Security Specialists, or possibly all humanity in general. "They no care. They no give a shit. If I take jew back there and focking rape jew. Is that what I doing?"

She shook her head.

"Scumbags left and right who would do that. Fine looking piece of ass like jew. But I not one of those focking scumbags. My name is Domingo. I gonna to help jew. Jew understand me?"

Valentina nodded.

"OK, good. Jew got a little paper is got your housing. Jew got that paper?"

Valentina nodded.

"Show me that paper."

Valentina, who suddenly felt she needed a toilet more or less immediately, shook her head.

"Jew don't want to show me."

She shook her head again.

Domingo spat. There was blood in his sputum. He wiped his mouth with the back of his hand.

"Fock it. Jew see that CRS? The one over there?"

Valentina nodded.

"Jew get up, now, jew go in there. Right by the door is a screen with a map. Jew put the address in. It show you the place. This," he gestured east and west, "this is focking Jefferson Avenue. Sector A, Northwest Quadrant. Jew housing is probably close to here. Or else jew in Sector B somewhere ... but jew don't look like no two to me. Jew see that shit?" He pointed to the south where the sky was now a wall of smoke and the drones and choppers were banking and diving and GodSend missiles were raining down.

Valentina nodded.

"Jew don't go there. Motherfockers wasting the sector. Jew go to jew housing. Don't talk to no one. Don't go in no focking alleys. Jew go to jew focking job like they said. Jew brain all scrambled. That shit will pass. Couple weeks and jew be OK. Jew need something, anything, jew come here and find me. I out here almost every day. Say my name."

"Domingo," she said.

Domingo nodded. "Now get the fock out of here. Jew can't stay out in this focking heat. Jew got like thirty, forty-five minutes ... then jew brain is gonna fry like eggs. Here," he handed her an IZD Five note, "buy jewself a bottle of water."

She took the note from him ... some kind of currency. Domingo stood up and extended his hand. Valentina took it. He pulled her up. They stood there a moment, looking at each other. Then he hoisted her futon up onto her shoulder.

"Go ... get out of here." He coughed tubercularly. "Don't get raped." He turned and spat again. She wanted to thank him, but her head was spinning, and before she could speak he had walked away.

Duffel in hand, futon on her shoulder, IZD fiver in her front pants pocket, she gazed across the endless river of sweat-soaked Anti-Social humanity that was flowing both ways up and down the avenue. She looked for anything resembling a crosswalk, or any kind of designated place to ford. There wasn't anything remotely like that. It was every man for himself down there. The CRS was across and roughly thirty meters off to her right ...

She stumbled down the last of the path, squeezed through a passage between two stalls, and waded out through the ankle-deep garbage and into the bedlam that was Jefferson Avenue. She elbowed her way through the streams of shoppers, and bikes, and quasi-rickshaw things, being cursed and jostled and spun as she went, and across the avenue and up through another narrow passage between two stalls, and made it into the entrance vestibule of the CRS, and found the map. There was one of those digital "you are here" things, which, OK, good, that's where she was. She put down the futon and used the keypad, found her address, in Sector C, made a mental note of the major arteries, estimated distance and time, and quickly determined she would never make it. Not before she died of heatstroke. No. She would have to shelter in place ... somewhere in the immediate vicinity.

She stepped out the door of the CRS, futon back up on her shoulder, and now she spotted the Public Viewer, an enormous monitor across the street, just to the east of Gate 15, on the screen of which some redheaded Clear was informing the inhabitants of Zone 23 that the time at the tone would be 0720. Down in the lower right corner of the screen a window was running what looked like footage of the lawn of some Cartwright country estate, upon which members of the corporate media were breathlessly jabbering into their cameras. Valentina stood there, stunned. No one had told her that

"Jimbo" was dead. She also wondered how she had failed to notice this humongous outdoor Viewer, which was less than fifty meters from where she'd sat on the crates and talked to Domingo. What else had she failed to notice? She turned abruptly, to find that out, slapping some female Anti-Social Person full in the face with her futon. The woman pushed her out of the way and into the path of another Anti-Social walking the other way behind her, who pushed her back the other way, into the path of someone else, who was dragging a cart, who also pushed her, and so on, for ten or fifteen seconds.

After she had finally regained her footing, she headed west down Jefferson Avenue, humping her futon, clutching her duffel, sticking to the sidewalk behind the stalls, her mouth all dry, her hair a mess, her entire body just dripping sweat. She wove through the streams of oncoming 1s, noting their color-coordinated work-clothes, but of course she didn't understand who they were, or where they were going, or how anything worked here. She stopped at a little outdoor kiosk and bought some water with Domingo's money. She took a swallow, then one more, then she capped the bottle and put it in her duffel. She pushed on, heading for Collins Avenue, where the map had said she should take a left, catching dirty looks and elbows in her ribs, and being touched by sweaty hands, and occasionally having her toes run over by the wheels of shopping carts heavy with groceries. And now, to her right, just off the sidewalk, she noticed a passage the vendors were using to move back and forth between the stalls, where they had stacked their crates along the sidewalk to form a kind of protective wall. She scanned for an opening between the crates, saw one, and ducked into this passage, where before she could even get her footing in the mud and muck and cauliflower greens some enormous heavily-muscled person moving at thirty kilometers an hour slammed into her like a crash-test vehicle, knocking her backwards off her feet and down onto her back in the gutter.

She pushed herself up into a seated position, found and pulled her duffel toward her, and sat there in the sludge and leafage, staring up at him, gasping for breath. He stood there, straddling her, squinting down at her, his forehead furrowed, looking perplexed. His knuckles were covered with crude tattoos. There were scars in his brow and down the side of his face. He was wearing one of those colored uniforms, an unfortunate shade of taupe, or ecru, that was dripping sweat and did not fit him. His biceps were pulling apart the seams. Valentina was terrified of him. He shook his head and stepped on over her and disappeared down the narrow passage.

After a moment, she pushed herself up, retrieved her futon, which was covered with muck, wrestled it back up onto her shoulder, and made her way west through the service alley. She pushed on that way for a couple of blocks, dodging the occasional surly vendor, until the path dead-ended at an intersection, and she had go back out to the sidewalk. It seemed like the crowds were beginning to thin now, and the stalls were fewer and farther between, and she passed a place called Haloumi Heaven where a group of old men with thick mustaches were drinking hot tea out of little glasses, which were all the shape of hourglasses, and she passed some sort of auto parts tent where the vendors, whose arms were covered with grease, and several of whom were smoking cigarettes, which it looked like maybe they had rolled themselves, were shouting at each other in Chinese and Spanish, and she passed a string of perfumed soap stalls, and palm oil stands, and she flowed along with the streams of shoppers with their plastic bags, and the packs of scoliotic old women with their bags and carts, and the people on bikes, and everything was new and strange, and her brain was skipping like a blown transmission, and her scalp and the back of her neck were frying, and people were spitting and shouting and sweating, and the sun was rising, and the sky was brightening, and off to her left she heard the rumble of the bombs exploding, and here she was ... here, all alone, in the Zone, where she realized now she had always been headed. She thought she'd been headed to ... she couldn't remember. Where had she believed she'd been headed? She didn't know, but wherever it was, it wasn't here, to this horrible place, where she could hardly breathe for the heat and humidity, and everything smelled like sweat and feces, and her head was pounding from the heat and the noise of the cars and the scooters and people shouting and music blasting out of the doors of stores and people's windows and banging metal bins and shattering glass and all around her were sweating, stinking, coughing, spitting, nostril picking, dirty, toothless, lice-infested Anti-Socials, and now she was one of them ... and yet she wasn't.

What had she done? She knew what she had done. She had run away from Pewter ... something ... something, something Marigold Lane. She meant it more in the classic sense of, "Oh my God, what have I done?" She knew what she had physically done. She'd aborted her fetus with a barbeque skewer in some fleabag hotel in Center City. She had actually done that. She had killed her baby. Her variant-corrected baby, a Clear. Or had she? She couldn't remember, exactly. She remembered the blood, the pain, the skewer, but she couldn't remember seeing the fetus. She remembered Kyle, and Doctor Fraser, and Paxton something, on Lomax Avenue, but she couldn't remember when all this had started, or where, or what it was she had wanted. She was losing little pieces of her past at the same time she was recalling others. The connections between the fragments were fraying. It was thirty-three something ... Marigold Lane. She'd woken up in a hospital room. When? She was wearing a C-Section scar. And Doctor Hesbani, and the Clears with their forms, and some other doctor she couldn't remember, and Barry ... that was back in the all-pink room. And now she was here, in Zone 23, but if she had actually killed the fetus, the Clear, why was she still alive? And when had all that even happened, assuming any of it had actually happened? She stopped on the sidewalk and racked her brain. She couldn't be certain of anything, really.

She wasn't even sure what day it was.

Directly ahead another Public Viewer (apparently they were all over the place) was running some kind of homage to "Jimbo" that began with his chubby little baby pictures and then dissolved through his life ... in linear time. Down at the bottom, a crawler was running what was clearly an official advisory loop advising anyone viewing the Viewer that Sector C was in a lockdown and that any Class 3-designated Persons outside the sector should shelter in place. In the lower corner was the time and date. Apparently it was 17 April, 2610, H.C.S.T., as well as an assortment of other dates that were totally irrelevant to Quarantined Persons. Beyond the Viewer was another gate, identical to the gate she had entered, except that this one was Gate 14. Mounted on the wall above the gate was some sort of digital countdown clock that was counting down the minutes to something ... of which there remained exactly twenty.

Out ... yes ... that was what she had wanted. She had desperately wanted out of ... something. She didn't know what, but definitely something. Something that was suffocating her, coating her body like a second skin ... something she was drowning in. She had had a name for it, but now it was gone. The name didn't matter ... because IT was gone. Which meant she was out, but she wasn't out. She was locked in here, inside the Zone, where she didn't belong ... except she did. Apparently this was where she belonged ... because everything, as it was, was perfect. She had wanted out, and she had ended up in, but maybe in was actually out, and everything was backwards somehow. She stood there on the sidewalk, swaying, closed her eyes and repeated her mantra, "the loving, unknowable Oneness of ..."

A klaxon sounded somewhere behind her. When she opened her eyes, the sidewalk was empty, or nearly empty, or it was much less crowded. The avenue itself was devoid of shoppers, except for a few disabled stragglers. The vendors in the smattering of stalls still standing were packing up their products hurriedly and securing the wooden flaps of their booths. The roll-down metal gates of the stores that lined the sidewalk were clanging down. Padlocks were being clacked into place. Dead ahead, behind a stand where they sold what looked like sunscreen and hand crème, there was some sort of little service alley that was covered with corrugated sheets of aluminum, which appeared to provide some modicum of shade. Domingo had warned her to avoid such alleys, but she had no choice, she had to go somewhere. She adjusted her futon and started toward it, keeping to the outer edge of the sidewalk, in case there were rapists lurking in there. There weren't. It was just an empty alley, leading to another street to the south. Just inside the mouth of the alley was a stack of flattened cardboard boxes, which she figured she could mostly hide behind while she waited out the heat of the day and maybe even slept for an hour or two. After she slept she could try again to remember the things she knew she couldn't remember forgetting, but sensed were still there ... were somewhere back there, or down there, or somewhere, buried under the layers of twisted wreckage they had made of her mind, or that were mixed up with all her other memories, the ones she was sure were in fact her memories, or were simply misplaced in the skein of time ...

Outbreak

Meanwhile, hundreds of kilometers away, in a world of comfort and infinite abundance from which Valentina had been banished forever, Billy Jensen was on a roll. He was taking out Targets left and right, as fast as the Target Acquisition Specialists at KILL CHAIN Command could throw them at him. BOOM! He took out a former library, or archive, or some kind of school or something, the interior of which was swarming with Terrorists. BOOM! He took out a Terrorist vehicle, a tricked-out mini-van, or shuttle-type bus, that was zig-zagging down a four-lane avenue trying to evade the heavy fire a Security chopper was laying down on it. He didn't even pause to watch the chopper take out the few surviving Terrorists who were crawling away from the smoldering wreckage, most of whom were missing limbs, because BOOM! He took out a Terrorist building, or the top two floors of a Terrorist building, but he only got points for the uppermost floor, because that was the designated Terrorist Target. A few seconds later, other Terrorists, several of them dressed as elderly women, all of them bleeding, and badly disoriented, ran out through the building's entrance and into a Security Services crossfire. The Target Acquisition Specialists fed him yet another Target, a concentration of suspected Terrorists attempting to breach the Lockdown Cordon. This one was going to be a little tricky, as there were Specialists in the immediate vicinity ... he switched from anti-structural ordnance to anti-personnel and BOOM!

He took a second to check the scoreboard. Operator 225 was still leading, but Billy, who was Operator 262, was six points behind and gaining steadily. BOOM! He took out another domicile, slipping his missile right through the window and into what looked like a Terrorist kitchen ... but by this time Operator 225 had clocked him

coming up from behind and he had stepped up his already devastating game and was taking out designated Terrorist Targets with just
unbelievable skill and precision.

Billy Jensen, Clear that he was, did the math and faced the facts.
He wasn't going to make the semi-finals. Operator 225 was too
good. Billy was good, extremely good, very, very good ... but he was
not this good. Operator 225 was a player the likes of which Billy had
never seen. The guy was a veritable crosshair artist. A joystick wizard.
He could not miss. This was not a conflict for Billy, as the Clears
were incapable of envy, or jealousy, or of taking any type of personal pleasure in others' defeats, or humiliating failures, and in the
final analysis all the operators were all just members of one big team
whose competition against each other (i.e., as individuals, to win
the game) ultimately served to make the team stronger, and proved
the wisdom and superiority of the convoluted pseudo-cooperative
competitive philosophy underlying it. So it wasn't like he was be-
grudging Operator 225 his success or anything, or yearned to defeat
him in any sort of professionally or personally humiliating way, but
as long as Billy was still in the game, he felt he owed it to the other
players to maximize his full potential, if only to keep the competition honest. There wasn't any way he was going to win it trading
Targets with 225, however, if he could keep it close, he knew there
was still one outside chance. What Billy needed (and what some
subconscious part of his Clarion brain had been praying for) was
the "Special Bonus Terrorist Target," for triple or even quadruple
points, depending on the value of the Target. He'd never gotten one
in competition, but he had seen it happen for other players, pushing
their scores up over the top, often in the closing seconds of a round.
It wasn't something you could ever count on or allow yourself to be
distracted by. Distractions degraded your reaction time, and were
the bane of every KILL CHAIN! player. He erased the thought of
it from his mind, which he made a placid, featureless blank, aimed,
fired ... and missed a Target, obliterating an adjoining tenement, and
twenty to twenty-five Anti-Socials, none of whom had been designated Terrorists, or probable Terrorists, so zero points. He forgave
himself for losing focus, acquired the next Target, a moving Target
(a Terrorist male on a motor scooter with a female Terrorist riding

behind him), plotted his vector, fired ... and got it! He couldn't afford any more mistakes now, as 225 had pulled well ahead, and was picking off Targets ten a minute. The guy was a MercyKill machine. He was going nuts on a group of Terrorists the Specialists had flushed out into the open. They were caught out in this lot, or field, with nowhere to go. It was bug-splat city. But by this time, Billy was deep in "no mind" and locked into his groove and ... BOOM! He got a lucky three-for-one, two Terrorists helping a wounded Terrorist, and BOOM! What looked like a Terrorist restaurant, or take-out place, and ... BOOM! Whatever.

Now, according to the official rules of KILL CHAIN!, which were set forth in the KILL CHAIN! Players Online Terms of Service Agreement that everyone had to scroll down to the bottom line of and digitally sign, anyone of the age of majority (or any minor who could get his parents to digitally sign an online waiver) was entitled to become an Official Player, and compete with other Official Players in Interterritorial Special Events like KILL CHAIN! OUTBREAK! or KILL CHAIN! PANDEMIC!, or any other name the producers came up with, regardless of their variant-correction status. In reality, of course, all the players were Clears. This wasn't the result of any ingrained form of subtle discrimination or anything. There was nothing preventing Variant-Positives from signing up and trying to compete. It was just that the Clears were so vastly superior, and handed the Variant-Positive players their asses in such a demotivating way, that playing against them significantly lowered the Variant-Positives' self-esteem, and left them feeling deeply inadequate, and comparing themselves to archival footage of drooling mentally-challenged persons, which took all the fun right out of the thing. The psychomotor aspects of the game (i.e., target acquisition, tracking, accuracy, and collateral damage to target ratio) were nothing to the Clears. They smoked that stuff. The same went for their rational metrics, which the Variant-Positives were just no match for. But it wasn't only their peerless intellects and athletic abilities that set them apart. No, the thing that really gave them the edge, collectively over the Variant-Positives, and individually against each other, was an unquantifiable attribute, which they all possessed to some degree, but that was more pronounced in some than in others (for example, in Operator 225), and which due to its delusory and numinous nature is almost impossible to accurately describe, but let's go ahead and try it anyway ...

OK, remember Meyer Jimenez's theory about the evolution of civilization, and those bands of nomads, and those tribes with their shamans, and peoples with their kings and priests, and so on, and his whole genealogy of morals and ethics, and how all that purportedly stemmed from people's fear of being killed and eaten? Of course you do. And you know he was right. Because of course it all goes back to fear. Everything. It all traces back to fear. To our fear of snakes and bears and lions, and those giant pigs with their grinding molars, and storms and earthquakes and fires and floods, and falling stars, and the gods, and time, and other people who are not like we are, or anything bigger and stronger than we are ... because anything we cannot understand, and name, and tame, and control, we fear.

See, what Meyer, in his inebriated way, was trying to get across to Taylor, is that, essentially, people are ruled by fear. That fear is our master. That we are slaves to fear. And that being these excessively self-aware creatures, the thing we fear most of all is death ... because of how we are going to be dead forever, and we can't seem to get our minds around that.*

According to Meyer, this certain knowledge, or depressingly morbid ontological model (i.e., that of our own individual deaths, as well as the inevitable erasure of everything), which of course is based in scientific fact, and is not just groundless superstition, or wish-

---

* Take a minute and try to imagine it. Seriously ... try to imagine being dead. You can't, because you won't be there then. None of us will. We will all be dead. Everyone and everything that ever existed, and that is going to exist, it will all be dead ... and here's the part where time gets tricky, because once you are dead there will be no time. There will be no you to experience time, or to hang around waiting for the end of time. The end of time will have already happened. You will already be where we all are going ... or, actually, you won't, because no one will be there, because there won't be anywhere there to be. Now this is going to happen to all of us. One by one, we are going to die. Time is going to continue without us. All kinds of things are going to happen, amazing things we can't even imagine, which we will miss out on, because we will be dead. Once we are dead, we will keep being dead. We will never, ever, stop being dead. And the worst part is, we won't know we are dead. We won't know anything. We won't be anything. It will be like it was before we were born. Remember that? I didn't think so. Once we are dead it will be like that, like it was like before the universe was born, and what it will be like once it is dead, and time has finally come to an end. As in there'll be nothing. Not one thing. Not one single shred of memory. It will be like none of this had ever happened. As if time itself had never begun. And it will go on being that way forever ... go ahead, try to imagine that.

ful thinking, or some convenient belief, like some fairy tale about heaven or whatever, just terrifies the bejesus out of us. Knowing (or believing) that we are going to be nullified, and be nothing, forever, scares us shitless, and is the impetus driving all our efforts to solve the riddle of space and time, and our desire to control and dominate everything ... in order to control and dominate death. What we're dealing with here (according to Meyer, who probably spent too much time on this stuff) is nothing less than what makes us human ... this awareness, or knowledge, or concept, of death,* and the total unfairness and cruelty of death, and our crippling fear and hatred of death.

And now here comes the kicker, because oddly enough, despite our terror and hatred of death, and our feeling that death is unfair, and wrong, or is some sort of flaw that we need to correct, or disease we need to treat, or something, we are also rather enamored of death, and of reading or hearing accounts of death, and of watching representations of death, and of killing other creatures just to watch them die. We've got this ambiguous thing about death. We hate it and love it. We fear it and crave it. We're ashamed of it even as we bow down before it. We're fleeing from it as we rush toward it. You could almost say, in some twisted way, that all we've done and built as a species, since the dawn of human civilization, generation after generation, empire upon the dust of empire, is all just one big monument to it ... one big weird-ass monument to death.

Billy Jensen did not get this. Death was just not a big deal to Billy. This whole ambiguous relationship we have (and the Variant-Positives had) with death ... the Clears didn't have that. It just didn't register. They understood it in an abstract way, but it did not move them, at all, emotionally. For Billy, watching a human being fight for its life as it slowly died, watching the shock and terror in its eyes as the last of its life was extinguished forever, would have been about as fascinating as watching someone delete an email.

This is the part that's so hard to describe, because as far-fetched as this is going to sound, Billy had no fear of death. None of the Clear generation did. Now this had been proved in batteries of tests. It was

---

* As a spaceless, timeless, eternal nothing out of which we are born and to which we return, which renders our lives completely meaningless.

something to do with their lateral amygdalas. It wasn't like when people tell you, as some people will, or possibly have, that they have "overcome" their fear of death, or have "faced," or "conquered," their fear of death, or have made some other transcendent form of accommodation with their fear of death, which (a) is a load of horseshit, basically, and (b) the Clears didn't have to do, as they had no fear of death to begin with, so there was nothing to overcome or conquer.

No, for Clears like Billy, this utter lack of fear and fascination with death was nothing unusual or in any way extraordinary. It was simply part and parcel of their genetically-modified state of enlightenment (which was, and wasn't, what you and I would consider a bona fide state of enlightenment ... which also deserves a little explaining, then we'll get right back to the action, I promise).*

Spiritual enlightenment is actually not as complicated as it often sounds, like when people are trying to sell you their books, or workshops, or intensive weekend seminars. It all comes down to lack of attachment (or identification) with what we call the ego. This ego is what we think we are, this individual material vehicle we drive around through space and time, usually in an endless series of circles. Now your sages, gurus, fakirs, mystics, and living embodiments of God, and so on, understand that this ego thing, this individual we believe we are, is really just one of the Many Who Are One (and, it goes without saying, the One Who Is Many), which is, was, and always will be ... which is why there's no such thing as death. Or time. Time is also a trick. Because everything that ever was, and ever will be, also is ... and always has been, and always will be. The whole idea of the end of time, and the time before time began, is nonsense. It's just our egos projecting the fear of their individual ego-deaths onto the fabric of what we call "reality." Check with any enlightened being, or incarnate god, and they'll tell you this.

Of course, it's one thing to be able to say this, or to understand it in an abstract sense, and it's a whole other thing to actually know it

---

* Look, I'm not trying to be cute or annoying. I'm well aware that we're right in the middle of this nail-biting round of KILL CHAIN OUTBREAK!, which Billy Jensen is currently losing, and here I've come (i.e., the narrator) and taken us off onto this esoteric tangent, but we're almost to the end of our story, and we've mostly focused on Valentina and Taylor, and, OK, Kyle and Cramer a little, and Cassandra and Sarah to some degree, and we haven't spent as much as time as we could have on the Clears, who represent our future ... so indulge me a little, is what I'm saying.

... to perceive the world we live in that way. Which is why your bona fide sages, and mystics, and prophets, and actual gods made flesh, tend to end up walking the earth in rags and speaking in riddles, and so on. And why normally the first thing they tend to do, shortly after they become enlightened, is give all their money to the poor and hungry, and give away all their earthly possessions, and reject their families, and renounce their names, because all that stuff just gets in the way of the light of truth, and is all illusion, and the ego's attachment to this illusion, the illusion of its own individual existence, is the root of all human fear and suffering.

All of which we have known for ages.

Now, the Clears were not like GM versions of Jesus or the Dalai Lama or anything. They were engineered by corporations and grown in little petri dishes. They were, however, unattached to their egos, as well as the egos of other persons, who were all just parts of a greater wholeness, and whose individual lives meant nothing.

Life, the way the Clarions saw it, was one big spiritual ecosystem, or holistic, quasi-Spinozist organism, governed by basic free market principles, the goal of which was perpetual expansion, and the generation of unlimited abundance, and growth, and progress, and all that stuff.* At the same time, life was also a story, the story of this never-ending expansion, the protagonist of which was life itself. Evolution was the plot of this story, because progress, growth and technological advancement were the driving forces of the spiritual economy, and the raison d'être of all existence. Evolution and progress were going to continue until the universe sucked back up into whatever impossible hole in itself it was born out of and disappeared forever.

The point being, the Clears were looking at life through a fairly seriously fisheye lens, and tended to think in terms of aggregates, and conglomerates, and enormous spans of time, which, along with their unattachment to their egos, and the egos of other living persons, is what gave them the edge when it came to KILL CHAIN!

---

* Individual living persons, or consumers, were of course essential components of this cosmic market economy model that the Clears understood the universe as, as obviously the system couldn't function without them, and would, if they ever stopped consuming, collapse into itself and die, but individual individuals, in and of themselves, were less essential.

(not to mention the broader social context). While Variant-Positive KILL CHAIN! Players, looking down through their digital cross-hairs, saw other people, who looked like them, or their wives, or mothers, or brothers, or friends, and hesitated, just a fraction of a second, the Clears saw Targets they had been ordered to strike, and did not hesitate, not one tick. Their GM brains were operating on a molar (or metasystemic) level. They were like Arjuna in the Bhagavad Gita (after Lord Krishna becomes Death, of course), chopping down trees with the axe of detachment ... walking the Path of Karma yoga. Actually, given that all of their parents and older relatives were Variant-Positives, some of whom had, it was very likely, considering the odds, been designated, had KILL CHAIN! not been just a game, an incredibly lifelike simulation, and had they really been doing what they were sitting there doing, some of their Targets might have been their mothers, or their fathers, or uncles, or aunts, or cousins, which would not have made the slightest difference. Once a suspected Terrorist Target had been cleared for a kill by whoever did that, whoever they were no longer mattered. It was all just attachment to ego anyway. You took out the Target in a professional manner, collected your points, and that was that.*

Billy's last target was a perfect example.

Billy, during the preceding digression, had stayed locked in and was on his game. He was right on the heels of 225, averaging eight to ten points behind him. It was down to the two of them, mano a mano. They had pulled away from the rest of the pack and were matching each other Target for Target, pulling off crazy-ass circus shots and driving the viewing audience nuts. Susan Schnupftuch-Boermann Goereszky had lost her composure and was screaming into the camera with her blood red, spit-flecked lips, which Billy

---

* On top of which, assuming, as most people did, that KILL CHAIN! was, in fact, just a game, and not a twisted Corporatist invention where they utilized bright young Clears like Billy to take down Terrorist A.S.Ps (or just random Class 3 Anti-Socials who refused to work and were totally useless and an unjustifiable drain on profits) and streamed the entire sick proceedings "live" to the normal viewing public, the consensus among the players was that the names and biographical details they loaded on your screen on regular KILL CHAIN! (i.e., KILL CHAIN LIVE! on Channel 16, not special events like KILL CHAIN! OUTBREAK!, where the studio talent took care of all that) were made-up names and biographical details, created by teams of Content writers, who amused themselves by slipping in references to certain obscure historical Terrorists who no one except such writers remembered. So, in a sense, they weren't even people.

had her sound switched off so as not to be annoyingly distracted by.
They were coming down to the end of it now. Billy could sense the
tension peaking. The terrain they were working was littered with
bodies. Available Targets were rapidly dwindling. He wasn't going to
win it, he'd accepted that, but the thrill of going head to head with
225 was enough in itself ...

Then it happened.

A bell-tone sounded.

The top of his screen displayed the message:

SPECIAL BONUS TERRORIST TARGET
AHMED VOSBIGIAN, CLASS 4, ACTIVE

Billy Jensen took a deep breath. He held it a beat, did a quick
Mūla Bandha, relaxed his anus, and slowly exhaled. His screen went
blank for a half a second, then came back up on a different terrain,
out on the edge of this Quarantine Zone. The wall was right there.
He could see both sides of it. He zoomed in on the perimeter avenue that ran along the course of the wall to the west. He checked
coordinates, altitude and wind speed, as the T.A.S. team droned in
his headset. He didn't have a visual yet, as they hadn't synched him
up with a driver, so he was looking down at a twelve block radius out of the nose of some random satellite. On the right-hand,
or eastern, side of his screen, orderly processions of Anti-Socials
were walking eastward, into the sunrise, looking unthreatening and
generally cooperative. Behind them, so roughly in the center of his
screen, groups of collateral Anti-Socials were packing up the last of
their wares, loading them into the back of their vans, and locking
down the doors of their plywood kiosks. All of which was S.O.P.
These simulated Zones were all the same. The perimeter avenues,
open-air markets, pedestrian rush hour, were standard features. On
the left-hand, or western, side of his screen, it looked like there was
a concentration of friendlies by one of the Security Gates. Across
the avenue, a block behind them, a MedTeam was half deployed on
the sidewalk. As Billy was taking all this in, the female voice of the
T.A.S. in his headset was briefing him on the ball game. She spoke
in an utterly emotionless monotone, and used a lot of impressive

jargon, which conveyed a feeling of professional calm in the face of imminent personal danger. Target was on the move with a package. Contents possible IED. Target vector west northwest. Stand by for Target details. And so on. His screen went black then came back sharp and tight, which meant they'd found him a driver. The T.A.S. confirmed as much. He got the coordinates, punched them in, and obtained a visual on the Target.

Billy had her sound turned off, but folks at home, or enjoying their breakfasts in some massive revolving spherical restaurant, like Kyle and Cramer in the Outlook Café, or wherever they were sitting there glued to their Viewers, in addition to the deadpan military-speak and the tension-building Techno score, were being treated to the piercing tones of Susan Schnupftuch-Boermann Goereszky, who was totally out of her mind with excitement and screaming meaningless sentence fragments into the camera at the top of her lungs.

"262 ACCESSORIZED TARGET!"

Roger P. Greenway was helpfully clarifying.

"Yes, it looks like he's acquired the Target. Here come our Target details, Susan."

"ROGER GOING TO TARGET SATSCREEN!" *

The Target details appeared onscreen.

"Susan, our Target, Vosbigian, Ahmed, is presumed to be in his early forties, and in pretty bad shape from the looks of it, Susan. Class 3 up to the time of the incident. Extremely aggressive. Casualties involved."

"DEAD?! HOW MANY? CASUALTIES COUNT?!"

"No details yet on those casualties, Susan. The Target is apparently armed, however, and in possession of an IED."

"POSSIBLE   IMPROVISED   NUCLEAR   DEVICE?! ROGER?!"

"We don't have any details. Susan."

The screen was showing an overhead shot of Ahmed Vosbigian, who didn't really exist, running for his life up the empty avenue, a nondescript duffel bag clutched to his chest. Billy maneuvered the

---

* To give poor Susan Goereszky a break, her producer, a Clear in his early twenties, who looked like he was maybe thirteen, was shouting similar bursts of nonsense into her ear throughout this segment.

crosshairs onto him, coolly tracking his vector as he ran. He selected his asset, nothing too heavy, a 30-kilogram laser-guided anti-personnel-type GodSend missile.

"WHY AREN'T THEY GIVING HIM THE GREEN YET ROGER?!"

"They haven't given him the green yet, Susan. If he makes this shot, he could pull this out. Unbelievable quarterfinals, Susan."

"WHAT IS HE DOING?! HE'S STOPPING. ROGER!"

"He appears to have come to a stop there, Susan."

"WHY WOULD HE DO THAT?!"

"Unclear, Susan. Maybe he's come to his senses a bit. Sometimes even the bad ones, Susan, those suffering seriously late-stage disease, they have ... like a moment of clarity, Susan."

"HE'S JUST STANDING THERE DOING NOTHING ROGER!"

"That's definitely what he's doing, Susan. It looks like there's some kind of alley to his left. He might be considering fleeing into it."

"WHAT IN THE NAME OF THE ONE ARE THEY WAITING FOR?!"

"I couldn't begin to tell you, Susan. If he gets in that alley, 262 will need to switch to a larger ordnance, and he'll need to do that on the fly, which is no mean feat, I assure you, Susan."

"I DON'T UNDERSTAND WHAT'S HAPPENING ROGER! SHOULD WE GO TO ANOTHER ANGLE OR SOMETHING? I THINK WE SHOULD GO TO ANOTHER ANGLE!"

Susan's producer was screaming at her to calm down and try to milk the moment. Normals all over the United Territories were staring transfixed into the screens of their Viewers. The tension couldn't have been any been higher. One of these top-notch Operators was going to advance to the semi-finals. It all came down to this one last shot ... and the Target was not cooperating.

Billy Jensen was holding his crosshairs dead on the Target, awaiting the green. His finger was on the initiate button, ready to fire the second he got it. He wasn't impatient. He wasn't tense. He was breathing evenly. His heart-rate was normal. He wasn't thinking or wondering anything. He was totally relaxed ... completely focused.

He was in that magic place or state that every athlete knows and loves, where there are no distractions ... the world disappears, the sound drops out, time slows down, your mind goes blank, and you cannot miss ...

"ROGER?! ARE YOU STILL WITH US, ROGER?! WE'RE GOING TO ANOTHER ANGLE!"

Billy Jensen was in the zone.

Hail Mary

Taylor had run a couple of blocks, dodging the stacks of plastic crates and hastily abandoned carts and trolleys and tins of TōHam and cans of soup and the sacks of rice and beans and whatever that littered the sidewalk like an obstacle course, and he was passing a Mister Mango emporium, out of the door of which people with jumbo containers of genuine fruit-flavored beverages were staring with unabashed prurient interest ... when he finally realized no one was chasing him.

This realization occurred in his stomach, which suddenly felt like it was full of something terribly heavy, like a bag of cement. He glanced back over his shoulder awkwardly, into the blinding glare of the sun, and saw them all back there.

He kept on running.

Max was with him ... Max was his son. Max lived in a Transplant bag. He couldn't hear whether Max was crying. He couldn't hear anything. He was too busy running.

Taylor was running ... well, he wasn't sure where, somewhere else. It didn't really matter. Somewhere he could put Max down, and take him out of the bag, and kill him. Because no matter what happened in the next few minutes (which Taylor had a pretty good sense what that was), he wasn't going to let the corporations get him. He was going to take Max out of the bag, kiss him once on his adorable forehead, then press the towel down onto his face until his little lungs stopped breathing. He was going to do this somewhere else, somewhere close, but not just here, and soon, any moment actually, but not just now ... or now ... or now ... no ... because see, he needed more time ... not much more, just a few more minutes, or seconds, or just ... well, a little more time.

Three blocks back on Jefferson Avenue, Security Specialists were standing around, or were leaning up against their Security units, like parents at a softball game in which their kids had already trounced their opponents, but they had to play out the final innings, blithely watching Taylor run. This was bad ... but it was also good, because now he was not going to have to do it. Because they were going to do it for him ... and all he had to do was run.

See, the reason no one was chasing Taylor, or firing their UltraLite rifles at Taylor, or in any way attempting to prevent his escape, was that somewhere up in the merciless sky an invisible Unmanned Aerial Vehicle was preparing to fire a laser-guided GodSend missile down onto his head. The Security Specialists had been advised of this, which was why they were hanging back like that ... which meant they didn't know about Max. They probably thought he had some kind of IED in the Transplant bag, which the GodSend missile was meant to detonate when it blew Taylor into a thousand bits.

Good, he thought. Let them think that. Cassandra was going to be OK. There wouldn't be anything left of Max, or Taylor, once the missile got them. So no DNA tests ... or any other tests. They would hose what was left of them into the gutter. They would never even know there had been a Max. Cassandra was going to be OK.

Taylor was not going to be OK ... or maybe he was, because what did he know? Maybe he was going to join his mother, and his father, and all the people he had killed, and all the people he had seen being killed, in heaven, but that was rather unlikely. Or maybe he was going to undergo some form of spiritual transformation that he couldn't even begin to imagine ... or maybe he was going to be nothing ... which he also couldn't begin to imagine. In any event he was going to find out, in approximately two or three seconds, he figured. He vaulted a crate of some kind of squash, slipped, careened into a kiosk, righted himself, and kept on running.

Just up ahead was that covered alley that ran back behind the sunscreen stand, which back in some other fucking lifetime, before whatever had happened had happened, and everything had gone so fucking sideways, Taylor was going to walk into and hand Max off to whoever it was that was waiting down there in that HVAC van ... a glimpse of which Taylor now caught in passing.

He stopped dead in the middle of the sidewalk.

An HVAC van at the end of the alley? Had he just imagined it, or was it actually there? Sarah's voice was in his head ...

No matter what happens, the vehicle will be there.

He staggered backward and looked down the alley. There it was, an HVAC van. He couldn't see inside the cab, or tell if it was parked or the engine was running. It couldn't be Sarah. It had to be Sarah. It wasn't Sarah. Of course it was Sarah.

Sitting just inside the mouth of the alley, taking shelter from the morning sun, was ... wait ... that was that zapped-out Transplant, the one he had knocked onto her ass behind the stalls on his way to Cassandra's. She was perched, in what looked like a yoga position, on a stack of flattened cardboard boxes, her Transplant bag and her futon beside her, her eyes half-closed, her upturned hands resting lightly on her knees and ... no ... she couldn't be ... yes ... she was meditating. And now it was Meyer's voice in his head ...

In the end, it all comes down to faith.

Taylor, who had no faith in anything (or thought he didn't, when of course he did, because no one has no faith in anything), did a rather funny thing. All he had to do was stand there, perfectly still ... and wait for the missile. He knew it was coming. He couldn't hear it. He wouldn't hear it. He would never hear it. He and Max would both just be there ... then, one second later, they wouldn't. Max was definitely crying his ass off, wrapped in the towel inside the bag. Taylor could hear him distinctly now, howling, inconsolably wailing, even over his own labored breathing and his heartbeat pounding inside his head. All he had to do was stand there ... a few more seconds. The missile was coming. He could sense it coming. It was almost there ... and even if he broke and ran, ran up the alley toward the van, ran with everything he had left in him, cursing and crying and begging the fucking God he hated and didn't believe in for one last burst of fucking speed, to just let him do this one fucking thing, to let him save this one little baby, he would never make it to the end of the alley. And even if by some miracle he did, and got Max into the van in the bag, and turned and ran back down the alley, or down the street at the end of the alley as the van sped off in the other direction, these motherfuckers would just take out the van, as well as

Taylor, which would accomplish nothing. All these words are badly distorting the time this moment was actually taking. In reality less than a second had passed since the second Taylor turned back and stopped and heard Max crying and looked down the alley. All these thoughts were coming at once, were coming at some incalculable speed that was warping Taylor's perception of time, which had not merely slowed, as it had seemed at first, but had stopped, and now ... and there was only now, it was like the spaces between the times that were the moments had disappeared, or had fused into some indivisible space of time that went on forever, and where the mind that Taylor knew as Taylor, but wasn't Taylor, or wasn't only Taylor, was looking out over this spatiotemporal plane in all directions at once, which was totally disorienting, and completely impossible, so maybe he was already dead ... but no, he wasn't, because Max was crying. The redheaded Transplant had opened her eyes and was sitting there, cross-legged, staring at him. She was ten or twelve meters from the mouth of the alley. The van was still there at the end of the alley. Max was still crying. The missile was coming. His heart was racing. The avenue was empty. The sun was up and to his left. The Transplant bag was to her left. The van was waiting. The shrapnel radius. Fifty meters. Twenty seconds.

He bolted into the mouth of the alley and pushed the Transplant down off the stack of cardboard cartons and onto the ground. He shoved his bag into her arms. It squirmed. She grasped it. The bag was crying. "His name is Max," Taylor told her, as he tore the plastic cords off her futon. "Max," he said it one more time. He threw the futon over the two of them. He pushed a few cardboard cartons on top of it. He did all this in a blur of movement. Then he grabbed her identical Transplant bag and ran back out of the mouth of the alley, and into the middle of Jefferson Avenue ... counting his strides from the mouth of the alley ... five ... six ... they were beautiful strides ... his quadriceps were pumping pistons ... the sky to the west insanely blue ... seven ... eight ... nostrils flaring ... devouring air ... he threw his head back ... there were tears in his eyes ... but he wasn't crying ... not exactly ... nine ... ten ... thirty meters ... he was going to make it ... it was just ... yes ... thirty five ... it was all just ... it was just so fucking ...

Tinnitus

The sound was like the sound of something sucking everything out of existence through a pinhole punched through the skin of the sky. She never actually heard the explosion, or the whoosh of the wave of the million bits of shattered glass and asphalt and bricks and ragged shards of twisted metal blown back into the alley around them, and into the futon and the cardboard on top of them ... all of which had happened in less than a second.

Now there was just the ringing sound, or more like a buzzing or humming than ringing, and the faraway sound of a baby crying ... but she could feel it squirming right there in her arms.

She couldn't remember where she was at first, which by now she was getting used to that feeling, but she knew there was all kinds of stuff on top of her, some of which appeared to be burning.

She wormed her way out of the smoldering cartons, and out from under the shredded futon, and sat there clutching her duffel bag. No. This wasn't her duffel bag. The Anti-Social had given it to her. She unzipped the zipper ... and there was the baby, bawling away with the sound on mute. Its little pink face was twisted into the classic outraged baby face, the one where you know there's nothing you can do to immediately assuage its intense displeasure ... a face Valentina had not seen in the flesh for over thirty years. Then it hit her. It wasn't a Clear. Of course it wasn't. She was in the Zone. The scary-looking Anti-Social had shoved the baby into her arms. What would he have been doing with a Clear? And what had he said?

A name ... Max.

Off in the distance, under the humming, or the buzzing, or ringing, sirens were wailing. She was in some sort of covered alley. The air was misted with thin white smoke. She turned and looked out the mouth of the alley and saw the crater the size of a jacuzzi that had opened up in the charred black asphalt, and the carpet of shards of brick and steel and glass the glare of the sun was catching that extended outward from its ragged edges. The stack of boxes beside her was scorched, and shredded, and peppered with smoldering bits of metal and melted glass and asphalt, and the storefront at the mouth of the alley was burning, and yes, those were sirens wailing, and the baby was bawling, and her ears were still ringing ... and something told her she had better get up.

She got up. She didn't appear to be injured. Except for her eardrums, which were probably punctured. She picked up the bag of bawling baby and bounced it up and down in her arms ... because that was what you did with babies, with uncorrected human babies, who were bawling inconsolably at you. She stood there, doing that, for about ten seconds, trying to figure out what to do, and what in the name of the One was happening, and other such things ... she was quite confused.

The sirens were getting louder now ... so, OK, that was Security Services, who were probably coming to retrieve this baby, and put out the fire, and survey their work. She weighed the options open to her. She could stand there bouncing the bawling baby up and down until they got there, and then give them the baby, and explain what had happened, and otherwise cooperate fully ... or she could set the baby down and run. Those were pretty much her options.

She turned and looked down into the alley. The smoke was too thick to see what was down there ... a cross street? Or was it just a dead end? It didn't matter, because what was she thinking? She was in the Zone. There was nowhere to run. Or maybe she didn't need to run. If she set the baby down on the ground, and calmly walked away from the scene, maybe they would just ignore her ... they didn't know she had the baby. The alley was covered. They couldn't see in. She could swear she had never even seen the baby, or the Anti-Social who had given her the baby. She didn't have anything to do with all this ... whatever it was that was actually happening. Whatever it was, it was definitely trouble. This was an uncorrected baby, which everyone knew wasn't allowed in the Zones. And that hole in the street had either been made by a bomb the Anti-Social had detonated or by some kind of Anti-Terrorist missile. So, yes, this was definitely her safest option, to put down the baby, who was bawling steadily, and groping for her with his little pink fingers (he had wormed his way out of the towel by now), and whose little red face was scrunched up into a Kabuki mask of extreme displeasure, and just walk away as if she didn't know anything ... even in her shell-shocked, brain-zapped state, she knew this was the thing to do.

At the same time, something, some inner voice (perhaps the voice of her intuition, or that of her maternal instincts), told her those men, those Security Specialists, speeding up the avenue towards her, sirens blaring, in their puncture-proof armor, coming to apprehend this baby, and take him away to the One knew where, and do the One only knew what with him, if possible, should not be allowed to do that ... and instead, ideally, should go fuck themselves.

She turned and peered back into the alley. The smoke was clearing. There was something down there ... a vehicle. Probably a Security vehicle. No. It was just some HVAC van. The side panel door of the van slid open. No one emerged. There was no one in there. No ... there had to be someone in there. She stood there staring down at the van, bouncing the baby up and down in her arms. He seemed to be running out of energy now. She raised him up and kissed his forehead. Her ears were still ringing. She could hear the sirens. She looked down at the face of the baby. The face looked back at her, scared and angry. This was a very angry baby. A terrified baby. Whose ears were ringing. She kissed the baby. She lied to the baby. She told the baby it would be OK. She knew that it would not be OK. She turned and looked out the entrance of the alley. No one was there. Just the sirens. She turned back and looked down the alley again. Someone was ... wait ... yes, a woman. A woman was crouched in the back of the van. She was framed in the open side panel door, looking back at her. She waved, or beckoned, or made some sort of ambiguous gesture ...

Valentina Constance Briggs, 1208.2568.709.Z23, designated Class 3 Anti-Social Person, did not hesitate ... not one second. She clutched the baby to her breast and ran. She ran into the dissolving smoke, spiraling wisps of which swirled around her. She could feel the crunch of nuggets of glass and concrete and metal through the soles of her sneakers. The sirens were drawing closer behind her, but she couldn't judge the distance as her ears were still ringing ... thoughts were racing through her mind. The thoughts in her mind were telling her a story ... a story about the woman in the van. In the story, the woman was there to help her. To help the baby. To protect the baby. To take the baby somewhere safe, some basement or secret safehouse somewhere, or maybe even somewhere outside the Zone, where everything wasn't being blown to pieces, and the sky wasn't swarming with invisible drones, and ash wasn't snowing down on everything ... and there were people out there who would help the baby, who would feed and teach and love the baby, who would love the baby as it was, and who wouldn't want to correct the baby, or medicate the baby with Zanoflaxithorinol, or some other MAO-A antagonist, or otherwise remake the baby into one more identical version of themselves (yes, it was coming back to her now, or some of it was in any event) ... or whatever.

It was just a story. She knew that it was just a story. But it was better than the other story. She ran the last few steps to the van ...

5.

Epilogue

In the 27th Century, H.C.S.T., pretty much everything that happened anywhere was documented for posterity somewhere ... somewhere meaning online, of course. The events of our story were no exception. Transparency being a guiding principle of the Age of the Renaissance of Freedom and Prosperity, if you wanted, for whatever personal reasons, which you didn't have to justify to anyone, to find out the truth or the facts of anything, like whatever was really going on in our story, you could search online on your All-in-One Viewer, and read all about it from a variety of sources, whose authors all offered their own opinions and interpretations of what it meant, none of which were censored in any way. In practice, however, when it came to accounts of historical events, or just things that had happened, the overwhelming majority of Normals turned to the Reconstruction Project, the voluminous and infinitely distensible network of interconnected online archives they unconsciously regarded as the official records, mostly because, when you searched for ... well, anything, it was always the first result that came up.

Some of what follows appears in these records. The rest is hearsay, folklore, and legend (i.e., stuff that people believe with no evidence), which doesn't mean it isn't true, but doesn't mean it is true either. So let's go ahead and start with the official stuff ...

We might as well start with Valentina, who along with Taylor and a lot of other people, disappeared in the chaos that morning, 17 April, 2610, or 02 Iyyar, 6370, or 01 Shawwal, 2049, or any of the other dates it was. According to the official transport logs, which remain accessible in the online archives of the Hadley Corporation of Menomonie, Wisconsin (which the Reconstruction Project links to), the patient, BRIGGS, Valentina Constance, 1208.2568.709.

Z23, was successfully and uneventfully transported to Gate 15, Zone 23, N. E. Region 709 at approximately 0720 that morning, processed, assigned communal housing, issued the standard hygiene kit, and was never seen or heard from again. Although presumed to have been an "enemy combatant" and thus officially "deceased without remains," no one really knows what happened to her.

There exist no records of a child named Max, or any other issue of BYRD, Taylor, 0820.2565.709.Z23, or, for that matter, of Cassandra Passwaters, who the following morning emerged from her bedroom, apologized to her annoying roommates for the drama her infectious Hepatitis had caused, and then went back to work as if nothing had happened, and so basically got away with everything ... although sometimes, early mornings, mostly, as the blistering sun broke over the rooftops, you could hear her in there, in her bedroom, crying.

Alice Williams and Rusty Braynard asked around in the Zone for a while, but they never found out what had happened to Taylor. They went on shooting up Plastomorphinol and living in squalor at 16 Mulberry with Coco Freudenheim, Coco's cat, Dexter (who lived to the age of twenty-two), Meyer Jimenez, Sylvie, Claudia, and assorted other Class 3 Anti-Social Persons who they dragged home with them throughout the years to crash there just a couple of nights.

The Day of Autonomous Decentralized Action was somewhat less historic than planned. IntraZone Waste & Security Services, with generous support from several battalions of the Hadley Corporation of Menomonie, Wisconsin's Regional and Domestic Security Divisions, neutralized most of Sector C, along with anyone who looked like anyone who had anything to do with the civil disorder (officially the "Domestic Terror Activity"), or who had ever even heard of the A.S.U., or who was still on the street after 0700. It wasn't quite the all-out purge that Meyer Jimenez had prematurely prophesied (something in the neighborhood of thirty percent of the extant A.S.P. 3s survived), but the Inner Zone and the Southeast Quadrant, and the eastern half of the Southwest Quadrant, and a number of selected Terrorist "hot-spots" scattered here and there throughout the Zone, were reduced to enormous toxic plains of melted body parts and smoldering rubble. Tens of thousands of people were slaughtered. It smelled like garlic in the Zone for weeks.

Adam was spotted in the thick of the fighting (or at least on the edge of the thick of the fighting) along with most of the Fifthian Cluster (Dorian somehow survived the carnage and made it back to tell the story) but no one actually saw Adam killed ... which didn't mean he was an agent, but didn't mean he wasn't one either. He wasn't mentioned in the official records, and no one ever saw him again.

Same kind of deal when it came to Sarah, except that she vanished before it all started. Some people say Security got her. Other people say she was Security ... people in the A.S.U., that is. Meyer Jimenez doesn't say anything. If you ask him about the A.S.U., or the D.A.D.A., or, God help you, the N.I.N., he just kind of nods and smiles knowingly, which doesn't mean anything, it being Meyer, and then launches into one of his theories.

Most of the regulars at Gillie's made it, as they were already there when all hell broke loose. By the time the Specialists sweeping for 3s stormed in with their weapons drawn and shouting at each other like they do in the movies, they were hiding in the tunnel that T.C. Johns and Young Man Henry had been digging for years, the entrance to which was through this secret trap in the floor behind the toilet, which when the Specialists got there was overflowing, thanks to the efforts of Jim MacReady, who needless to say was the last in line to crawl down through the tunnel entrance ... and into the arms of Coreen Sweeney.

Young Man Henry finally died, a few years later, of old age, probably. He died on a pallet in the back room of Gillie's. T.C. Johns was there beside him, wiping the sweat off Henry's forehead with a normally filthy piece of old bar-rag he'd especially gone and washed for that purpose. He sat there next to Henry all night, as it took him a while to finish dying, retelling old stories from when they were young, which Young Man Henry already knew, having been there in person, but he might have forgotten. People's memories get worse with age.

Billy Jensen, after going out in the semi-final round of KILL CHAIN! OUTBREAK!, resumed his routine of working diligently, sleeping soundly, eating properly, and playing KILL CHAIN! on a nightly basis. He married a Clear named Tabatha something, who raised their brood of Clarion children while Billy continued to work the night-shift, doing his best to meaningfully contribute to the profitability of Kierkegaard/Bose and the abundance level of its principals and shareholders. He enjoyed a long and contented life, throughout which he invariably slept like a baby, and was never really ecstatically happy or deeply depressed, as he had no soul.

Gregory Cramer rose through the ranks of the Interterritorial Security Division of the Hadley Corporation of Menomonie, Wisconsin's District 12 Northeast Regional Headquarters, run by Robert "Big Bob" Schirkenbeck, who Cramer artfully weaseled his way into a mentor-type relationship with, and then a few years later successfully undermined, prompting one of the Hadley Board to reach out through sub rosa channels and task him to keep him (i.e., this other Director) apprised of Schirkenbeck's every misstep, then secretly met with yet another Director who had it in for the other Director (i.e., the one who had it in for Schirkenbeck), and told him what was going on ... and otherwise meticulously boot-licked and butt-sucked and back-stabbed his way up the corporate ladder.

Following an extended and disastrously expensive stay at some celebrity Wellness compound on Baffin Bay that you could never get into, but that Cramer had allegedly wangled for him, Kyle was fired from BVCC for using the College's database crawler to search online for, and print out a list (i.e., an actual, physical paper list) of, every known instance of a Variant-Positive running amok, like Valentina, then graphing the sharply increasing frequency of such instances during the preceding decades, and then posting all this stuff online, along with his theory of the causes thereof, and repeatedly fleeping and tweaking about it, and otherwise behaving in an inappropriate and unprofessional and unstable manner. After which, he was unemployable, at least in the academic community. Once his two weeks of unemployment ran out, he secured a job as a Product Picker in Northeast Region 713, short sold the condo on Marigold Lane, and disappeared from Pewter Palisades ... as had the Fosters, mysteriously, before him.

Jimmy "Jimbo" Cartwright, III, following a period of global mourning, and the usual series of star-studded tributes reflecting back on his exalted life, and inestimable contribution to society, was buried in the earth with the other Cartwrights, on a gentle hillside overlooking the sea, and the worms and the beetles and the maggots ate him, and the pigeons ate the worms and the beetles, and Meyer Jimenez ate the pigeons.

Ashes to ashes, dust to dust.

The Normals went on with their normal lives, scanning their streams of individualized Content, taking their prescriptions, walking their Path(s), variant-correcting their kids, and so on. It wasn't like a utopia or anything. Those heat advisories remained in effect. And, all right, every now and then you had to deal with some weather event, like a super-cyclone, or mondo-tsunami, or those freakish blizzards that appeared out of nowhere and just ruined the entire season up north, and there was always the chance of some horrible accident, or a sudden and devastating Terrorist attack, probably with an improvised nuclear device, or electromagnetic pulse type gizmo, or Anthrax, or Cholera, or Encephalitis, which the Terrorists had definitely gotten their hands on (there were satellite pictures of their secret stockpiles) ... oh and let's not forget the scourge of cancer, and the scourge of dementia, and the scourge of whatever (additional information on which was available at the Scourge of Whatever website: scourgeofwhatever.ut.biz) ... hey but shares were up and trading heavily, those little green arrows were dancing along, and you could view your personal abundance level on this app that apparently would also let you virtually visit property listings that you couldn't afford at your current level, but you could sign up for free investment advice, and there were no-down weekly adjustable mortgages, and drastic reductions at Big-Buy Basement, and Brandon Westwood's stepdaughter's cousin, Kiki Brezinski, who was totally famous, although no one knew exactly what for, was hawking her new celebrity diet, or fashion line, or ... it didn't really matter, because this was the dawn of the age of something, and it was morning somewhere, and a brand new day, and the human race was marching in perfect, peaceful lockstep into the future ...

Acknowledgements

Many thanks to Julie Blumenthal, Mary Beth Wilson, Monika and Gerson Schade, Anthony Freda, Dan Zollinger, Victoria Gosling, Lorna Neuber, Michael Bartelle, Murray Miller, John Wills, Hugo Fernandez, Lanny Cotler, Jonathan Eric Miller, Paul Laup, Nathan Lemcke, Sascha Freudenheim, Steve Rinzen, Rilla Alexander, John Stauber, Martina Graichen, Maria Martinez, and everyone else who helped, or tried to help, to get this book finished and published.

C. J. Hopkins is an award-winning playwright and political satirist. His early plays and experimental stage-texts were produced during the 1990s in New York City, where he was awarded a 1994 Drama League of New York Developing Artist fellowship and a 1995 Mabou Mines Resident Artist/Jerome Foundation fellowship. Since 2001, his plays have been commissioned, produced, and have toured internationally, playing theatres and festivals including Riverside Studios (London), 59E59 Theaters (New York), Belvoir St. Theatre (Sydney), Traverse Theatre (Edinburgh), the Du Maurier World Stage Festival (Toronto), Needtheater (Los Angeles), 7 Stages (Atlanta), English Theater Berlin, the Edinburgh Festival Fringe, Adelaide Fringe, the Brighton Festival, and the Noorderzon Festival (the Netherlands). His playwriting awards include the 2002 Best of the Scotsman Fringe Firsts (*Horse Country*), the 2004 Best of the Adelaide Fringe (*Horse Country*), and a 2005 Scotsman Fringe First (*screwmachine/eyecandy*). His plays are published by Bloomsbury Publishing/Methuen Drama (UK) and Broadway Play Publishing, Inc. (US). His political satire and commentary has appeared on NPR Berlin, in *CounterPunch*, *ColdType*, *The Unz Review*, and other political journals, and has been translated into Italian, French, Spanish, Portuguese, and German.

Printed in Great Britain
by Amazon